Fantasy Masterworks

'The acknowledged mistress of the flamboyant interplanetary adventure'
　　　　　　　　　　　　　　　　　　Anthony Boucher

'Leigh Brackett's [Mars] represents the last gasp of a decadence endlessly nostalgic for the even more remote past'
　　　　　　　　　　　　　The Encyclopedia of Science Fiction

'Stories that combined suspenseful action and poetic descriptions of alien locales'
　　　　　　　　　　　　　　　　　　　　Terry Carr

'As a spinner of mood she has few equals'
　　　　　　　　　　　　　　　Fantastic Story Magazine

'One of the most influential women writers for the pulps'
　　　　　　　　　　　　　　　　　　　Mike Ashley

'Hey, this gal can *write*!'　　　　　　　Edmond Hamilton

ALSO BY LEIGH BRACKETT

Novels
No Good from a Corpse (1944)
Stranger at Home (with George Sanders, 1946)
Shadow Over Mars (or The Nemesis from Terra, 1951)
The Starmen (or Galactic Breed, The Starmen of Llyrdis, 1952)
The Sword of Rhiannon (1953)
The Big Jump (1955)
The Long Tomorrow (1955)
An Eye for an Eye (1957)
The Tiger Among Us (or Fear No Evil, 13 West Street, 1957)
Rio Bravo (1959)
Alpha Centuri … or Die! (1963)
Follow The Free Wind (1963)
People of the Talisman (1964)
Secret of Sinharat (1964)
Silent Partner (1969)
The Ginger Star (1974)
The Hounds of Skaith (1974)
The Reavers of Skaith (1976)
The Book of Skaith (1976)
Eric John Stark: Outlaw of Mars (1982)
Short Story Collections
The Coming of the Terrans (1967)
The Halfling and Other Stories (1973)
The Best of Leigh Brackett (1977)
No Good for a Corpse (1999)
Martian Quest: The Early Brackett (2002)
Stark and the Star Kings (with Edmond Hamilton, 2004)
As Editor
The Best of Planet Stories #1 (1975)
The Best of Edmond Hamilton (1977)

Fantasy Masterworks

SEA KINGS OF MARS

LEIGH BRACKETT
Edited with an Afterword by Stephen Jones

All stories © Leigh Brackett, with the exception of 'Lorelei of the Red Mist' © Leigh Brackett and Ray Bradbury
All rights reserved

This edition © The Sky Trust

The right of Leigh Brackett to be identified as the author of this work and of Stephen Jones to be identified as the editor of this work has been asserted by them in accordance with the Copyright, Designs and Patents Act 1988

The right of Stephen Jones to be identified as the author of the Afterword has been asserted by him in accordance with the Copyright, Designs and Patents Act 1988

This edition published in Great Britain in 2005 by
Gollancz
An imprint of the Orion Publishing Group
Orion House, 5 Upper St Martin's Lane, London WC2H 9EA

1 3 5 7 9 10 8 6 4 2

A CIP catalogue record for this book
is available from the British Library

ISBN 0575076895

Typeset by Deltatype Ltd, Birkenhead, Merseyside
Printed in Great Britain by Clays Ltd, St Ives plc

www.orionbooks.co.uk

ACKNOWLEDGEMENTS

With special thanks to Jo Fletcher, Malcolm Edwards, Gillian Redfearn, Hugh Lamb, Ralph Vicinanza, Ray Bradbury, Alexandra Bradbury, Randy Broecker, Jay Broecker, Val and Les Edwards, John and Kathy Pelan, Mike Ashley, Martin Trouse, Erik Arthur, Ted Ball and Bob Wardzinski.

Map of Leigh Brackett's Mars copyright © Dave Senior 2005, from a map prepared by Margaret M. Howes.

'Introduction: Letting My Imagination Go' copyright © Jonathan Bacon 1976. A version of this was originally published as part of 'Return to Wonder' by Leigh Brackett and Edmond Hamilton in *Fantasy Crossroads*, May 1976.

'The Sorcerer of Rhiannon' copyright © Street & Smith Publications, Inc. 1942. Originally published in *Astounding*, February 1942.

'The Jewel of Bas' copyright © Love Romances Publishing Company, Inc. 1944. Originally published in *Planet Stories*, Spring 1944.

'Terror out of Space' copyright © Romances Publishing Company, Inc. 1944. Originally published in *Planet Stories*, Summer 1944.

'Lorelei of the Red Mist' copyright © Romances Publishing Company, Inc. 1946. Originally published in *Planet Stories*, Summer 1946. Reprinted by permission of Ray Bradbury and his agents, Abner Stein and Son Congdon Associates, Inc.

'The Moon that Vanished' copyright © Standard Magazines, Inc. 1948. Originally published in *Thrilling Wonder Stories*, June 1949.

'Sea Kings of Mars' copyright © Standard Magazines, Inc. 1949. Originally published in *Thrilling Wonder Stories*, June 1949.

'Queen of the Martian Catacombs' copyright © Love

Romances Publishing Company, Inc. 1949. Originally published in *Planet Stories*, Summer 1949.

'Enchantress of Venus' copyright © Love Romances Publishing Company, Inc. 1949. Originally published in *Planet Stories*, Fall 1949.

'Black Amazon of Mars' copyright © Love Romances Publishing Company, Inc. 1951. Originally published in *Planet Stories*, March 1951.

'The Last Days of Shandakor' copyright © Better Publications, Inc. 1952. Originally published in *Startling Stories*, April 1951.

'The Tweener' copyright © Fantasy House, Inc. 1955. Originally published in *The Magazine of Fantasy and Science Fiction*, February 1955.

'The Road to Sinharat' copyright © Ziff-Davis Publishing Company 1963. Originally published in *Amazing Stories*, May 1963.

'Afterword: The Enchantress of Worlds' copyright © Stephen Jones 2005.

CONTENTS

Map of Mars viii

Introduction: Letting My Imagination Go by Leigh Brackett xi

The Sorcerer of Rhiannon 1

The Jewel of Bas 31

Terror out of Space 82

Lorelei of the Red Mist 113

The Moon that Vanished 176

Sea Kings of Mars 224

Queen of the Martian Catacombs 359

Enchantress of Venus 421

Black Amazon of Mars 490

The Last Days of Shandakor 558

The Tweener 590

The Road to Sinharat 608

Afterword: the Enchantress of Worlds by Stephen Jones 644

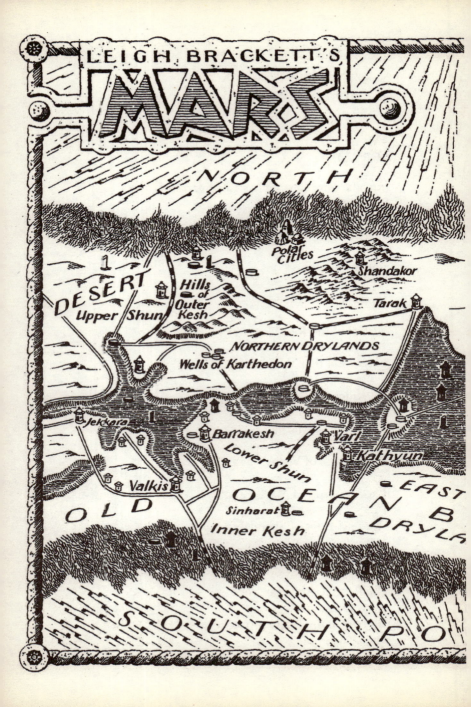

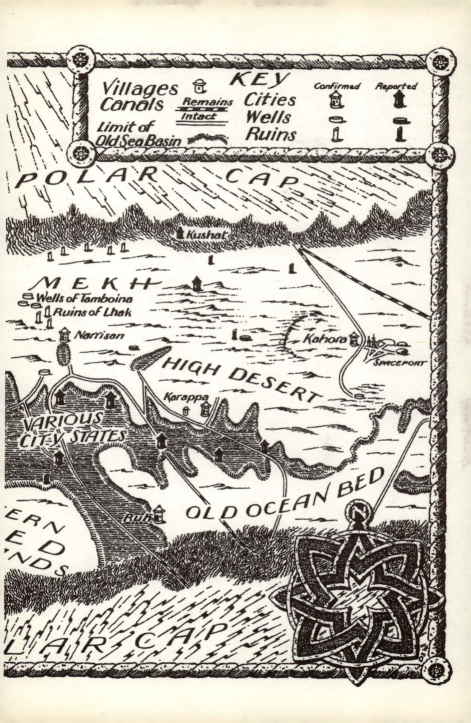

INTRODUCTION

Letting My Imagination Go

I became a writer because, I suppose, I couldn't help myself. From earliest childhood I had a compulsive desire to fill up blank pages in copybooks. When I was seven or eight, I wrote a sequel to a Douglas Fairbanks film because I wanted more and there wasn't any – infantile scribbling on odd bits of paper, but still, a beginning. At thirteen, I made a mature, reasoned decision to be a professional writer. Ten years later I sold my first story.

I got into fantasy and science fiction partly because, at a very early age, someone gave me a copy of Burroughs' *The Gods of Mars* and my entire life was changed. I watch the films of Apollo flights with my heart in my throat, and remember how long ago on a Venice beach I quarrelled furiously with my grandfather about space-flight, he saying it was impossible and could never be (*What would they push against?*), and I stamping my foot and yelling, 'But they will, they will!' And – they have. And I think this has been the single greatest thrill of my life, having dreamed of space flight and having seen it come true.

In the beginning of my writing career, I tried my hand at nearly everything and failed miserably; I hadn't enough experience of writing, or anything else, to compete in the adventure field for instance. I had been advised to try this market or that market, but not science fiction because there wasn't much money there. Finally, I decided I was going to do what I wanted to do, which was to write fantasy and science fiction, where I could really let my imagination go, even if I starved to death. I still had a lot to learn, but at least I was on the right track.

Henry Kuttner was at that time doing work for the Laurence D'Orsay Literary Agency, and he went far beyond the call of duty in criticising my manuscripts, offering help and suggestions, patiently getting me over the hurdles. I am sure that because of Hank I sold my first story much sooner that I would have done otherwise. It was also Hank who introduced me to the wonderful world of fandom, in particular the Los Angeles Science-Fiction Society. Actually, I met Edmund Hamilton and Jack Williamson through our mutual agent, Julius Schwartz, and a mutual editor, Mort Weisinger. But over the years LASFS figured as a friendly meeting place and it was there I came to know Ray Bradbury.

We used to meet every Sunday afternoon at the beach and read each other's manuscripts, sitting in the sun with the smell of frying hamburgers, dreaming furiously. I don't know who gave whom the most help, though Ray has generously given me more credit than I think I deserve; it was more or less mutual, I believe, and the wonderful thing about it was having another nut-case to talk to: we science fiction writers and readers were pretty well isolated in those days, when the average person considered the whole thing suitable only for the mentally retarded.

I began to branch out into the crime and suspense field and finally felt bold enough to do a full-length novel. This was *No Good from a Corpse*, published in '44. A friend of mine in a Beverly Hills bookstore saw to it that the book was in a stack of thrillers he sold to Howard Hawks. The first thing I knew, I was working for Mr Hawks on *The Big Sleep*, teamed with William Faulkner.

At that time I had an order for a novel (20,000 words!) from *Planet Stories*. I had written exactly 10,000 words, or one-half of the story. When this heaven-sent job in the flicks dropped out of the blue, I asked Ray Bradbury if he would like to finish the yarn because I wouldn't have time. He said yes, and forthwith did so, without any outline or a stitch of anything to go on except the first 10,000 words.

The result was 'Lorelei of the Red Mist', one-half pure Brackett, one-half pure Bradbury. I have heard all sorts of theories about how I did the action bits and he did the poetry, etc. Not so. It was not even a collaboration in the ordinary sense. Ray simply pitched in and turned out a beautiful job.

I was overawed to be working with William Faulkner (although, despite American Lit. professors and critics, I had always found him quite unreadable). In the event, we had very little contact in working, since we did alternate sections of the book with a minimum of conferring. He was punctilious, polite, unfailingly courteous, and as remote as the moon: a closed-in, closed-up, lonely man, driven by some dark inner devil. I suppose it is no secret to anyone that he would vanish sometimes for days while his loyal friends – and he had them - would front for him at the studio, seek him out, take care of him, and get him back on his feet again. Everybody pretended not to notice. Apart from these absences, he worked hard, worked long hours and proved to be remarkably good on construction.

As to his dialogue, he was famous as the writer who had never had one line of dialogue actually spoken by an actor. It was, quite simply, unreadable, and it was all changed on the set ... not by me, by Mr Hawks and Bogey, both of whom were/are pretty good at it.

I've been in and out of screenwriting ever since, and my relationship with Mr Hawks continues to this day; I am in fact at the moment awaiting his summons to discuss the current job. Then, I trust, back to Kinsman (Ohio) and my corn patch!

Leigh Brackett
May, 1969

THE SORCERER OF RHIANNON

He had been without water for three days. The last of his concentrated food, spared by the sandstorm that had caught him away from his ship and driven him beyond all hope of finding it, rattled uselessly in his belt pouch, because his throat refused to swallow.

Now Max Brandon stood on a dune of restless ochre dust, watching the coming of another storm.

It rolled crouching across the uneasy distances of the desert, touched blood-red above by the little far sun of Mars. Brandon heard the first faint keening of it above the thin whine of the eternal winds that wander across the dead sea bottoms.

Brandon's sharp-cut face, handsome with its sea-blue eyes and bronzed skin, and the thin scars of battle that enhanced rather than marred, creased into a grin.

'So the grave-robber is going to be buried instead this time,' he whispered. The skirling wind blew ochre dust in his eyes and mouth, the gold-brown stubble of beard.

'All right,' he said to the storm. 'See if you can make me stay down.' He waved a mocking hand at it and staggered down into the hollow.

To himself, he said ironically, 'There's no one here to see your act, Brandy. No pretty ladies, no interplanetary televisors. The storm doesn't care. And you're going to die, dead, just like ordinary mortals.'

His knees buckled under him, flung him headlong in the stifling dust. The simplest thing to do would be just to lie there. Drowning in these Martian sea bottoms was just like drowning in the sea. All you had to do was breathe.

He thought of all the ships that had foundered when there was water here, and how his bones would join theirs in the end. Red dust, blowing forever in the wandering wind.

His white grin flashed briefly. 'I always said, Brandy, that you knew too much to take advice.'

Everybody had advised him not to come. Jarthur, head of the Society for the Preservation of Martian Relics. Sylvia Eustace. And Dhu Kar of Venus.

Jarthur wanted to put him in the Phobos mines for looting, which was bad. Sylvia wanted to marry him, which was worse. And Dhu Kar, his best competitor and deadliest enemy, wanted to get to the Lost Islands first, which was worst of all.

'So I came,' Brandon reflected. 'Right in the middle of the stormy season. And here, apparently, I stay.'

But he couldn't stay down. Something drove him up onto his feet again, something that wouldn't listen to what his reason was saying about its being no use.

He went on, part of the time on hands and knees, to nowhere, with the Martian desert-thirst burning him like living fire, and the first red-dun veils of the storm blowing past him.

He began to see things in the clouds. Ships in full sail, the ancient high-prowed Martian galleys. He could hear the thrumming of their rigging, knowing with the last sane scrap of his mind that it was his own blood drumming in his ears.

The wind screamed over him and the red dust rolled like water. It was dark, and the galleys rushed by faster and faster. They got clearer, so that he knew that he was going, and still he wouldn't lie down.

And then, through those fleeing phantom ships, he saw a wreck tossing.

Her masts were gone, her hull canted, her high-flared bow thrust up in a last challenge to the wind. Max Brandon knew, because he could see so clearly the wide-winged bird that made her figurehead, that he was almost dead.

His dust-filled eyes lost even the phantom ships. He wondered distantly why he should imagine a wreck among them. The wind hurled him on. He fell. And, driven by some blind, dogged stubbornness, struggled up again.

The wind flung him with spiteful viciousness against something. Something solid. Something hard and unmoving, in the heart of the restless Martian desert.

It hurt. He went down and would have stayed there, but for the stubborn thing that lashed him on.

There was metal under his hands, singing with the impact of the storm. He looked up, forcing himself to see. A deck slanted down to him, bare of everything but the stumps of broken masts.

He stared at the ship, not believing his sight. But his aching body told him it was there. He thumped it with his hand, and it rang thinly.

It wasn't any use, really, because he had no water. But the thing that had driven him now kicked him up over the broken rail and along the canting deck to the broad cabin in the stern.

Feeble and distant, his heart was pounding with excitement. A ship, sunk ages ago in the Sea of Kesh, sailing through the red clouds of the storm—

It was impossible. He was delirious. But the closed door of the cabin was before him, and he tried to open it.

There was no catch.

He grew angry. He'd come this far. He wouldn't be balked. He drew himself erect, his tawny hair whipping in the storm, and roared at the door, commanding it to open.

It did. Max Brandon walked through, and it closed silently.

There was a soft light in the cabin, and a faint choking pungence. A table of Martian teak inlaid with gold stood in the centre of a room shaped to the curve of the galley's stern, furnished in sombre richness.

A man sat in a carven chair beside the table. He was fair and slight in a plain black robe, with no ornament but a curious band of grey metal about his head, bearing the figure of a wide-winged bird.

His face was gentle, grave, rather young. Only in the strong lines about his mouth and the fathomless darkness of his eyes was there any hint—

Of what? Max Brandon, dying on his feet, knew that the man wasn't there. Simply wasn't, because he couldn't be.

He looked alive, but he was too rigid, and his eyes didn't wink. Didn't wink or move, staring at the girl who sat facing him.

She was hardly more than a child, with the supple strength

of a sleeping deer in the long lines of her, and the stamp of a burning, vital pride still on her clear-cut face.

She wore a short white tunic with a jewelled girdle, and the cloth was no whiter than her skin. Her eyes looked at the man, unconquered even in death.

They were golden, those eyes, clear and rich as pure metal. Her hair grew low in a peak between them, swept back and down and hung rippling over her shoulders.

Max Brandon stared at it, swaying on his feet, feeling the blood swell and throb in his throat.

Her hair was blue.

Blue. The deep, living blue of an Earthly sea, with tints of cobalt in its ripples and the pale colour of distance where it caught the light.

He followed it down across her white arms, and then he saw the shackles on her wrists. Her hands lay on the table, slim and strong, and on the thumb of the left one was a ring with a dull-blue stone.

Brandon's brain burned with more than thirst.

'The Prira Cen!' he whispered, 'The Blue Hairs, the oldest race of Mars. Half mythical. They were almost extinct when the Sorcerers of the Lost Islands were the governing brain of the planet, and that was forty thousand years ago!'

A wave of blackness closed over him, as much from that staggering thought as from his desperate weakness. He fought it off, clinging to life for just that one instant longer—

Something sparkled dully on the table, close by the arm of the man in black. A small, transparent bottle, filled with amber liquid.

Somehow he crossed the deck. The bottle was sealed with some curious substance. He struck the neck off against the table.

A drop of the fluid splashed on his hand. It tingled as though charged with a strong current, but Brandon was beyond caring. He drank.

It was strong, burning and cooling all at once. Some of the madness died out of Brandon's eyes. He stood for a moment looking at that beautiful, incredible, impossible girl with the sea-blue hair.

A racing bolt of flame went through him suddenly, a queer shivering agony that had a perverse pleasure in it. He felt his mind rocking in its bed like an engine with a broken shaft, and then there was darkness and a great silence.

He came to sprawled in a heap of dust. For a moment he thought he was back in the desert again. Then the madness that had happened swept back and he got up, blinking into utter darkness. The light mechanism must have failed at last.

Dust rose and choked him. He blundered into a corner of the table, and something fell behind him with a dry, soft *whoosh*. He couldn't see the door at all. When he finally found it with his hands, there was no catch.

Blind panic shook him for a moment, until he remembered how he had got in. A little incredulously, he shouted at the door.

'Open!'

It didn't budge. And Brandon stood in the darkness like a trapped rat.

From somewhere, quite unbidden, a thought came.

'Set your hands on it and push. It will come open.'

He did. His palms barely touched the metal, his muscles had hardly gathered for the effort. The door broke from its hinges and fell with a thin clash on the deck.

Pale Martian daylight flooded the cabin. Brandon saw now that the cushions and hangings had crumbled to dust. The teak-wood table still stood, but its grain was splitting and softening. The man in black had vanished completely, save for the grey metal circlet that lay in a scatter of dust on the floor.

Brandon knew now what had fallen behind him. His gaze darted to the woman, and his heart contracted with a faint stab of pain.

There was only a naked skeleton, beautiful even now in its curved white perfection. The shackles, the blue stone of the thumb ring, glinted dully on fleshless bones, the jewelled girdle burned across a splintered pelvis.

That little puff of air he had let in must have done it. Whatever mechanism had controlled the door – he made a wild guess at some seleno-cell sensitive to thought currents instead of light – had gone with the rest.

Remembering the faint pungent odour, he wondered if that had had anything to do with preserving the bodies.

The cabin appeared to be hermetically sealed. The metal of the ship was some unfamiliar alloy, incredibly strong to resist the ages of immersion on the sea floor, and the further ages of dryness and wind and rubbing sand.

It was worn thin as paper under his fingers, but uncorroded.

They had had knowledge, those ancient scientists of the Lost Islands, that no one had ever found again. That was why men lost their lives in the desert, hunting for them.

Brandon looked forward along the deck. The storm had nearly buried the ship again, but the wings of the bird on the high prow still gleamed defiantly.

He grinned half derisively at the thick pulse of excitement beating in him. He was lionized as a dashing explorer, publicly cursed and secretly patronized by scientific men, the darling of wealthy collectors – all because of the archaeological treasures he stole from under the noses of planetary governments.

All this gave him money and fame and adoring fans, mostly feminine. It gave him the continual heady excitement of dancing on the edge of disaster. It gave him glamour and a gay flamboyant theatricalism, in all of which he revelled.

But underneath all that was the something that drew him to the old forgotten places and the lost and buried things. The poignant something that was real and sincere and that he didn't understand at all.

Only that he loved catching glimpses through the veil of time, finding the scraps of truth that lay solid under legends.

He went back into the cabin. The grey metal circlet he scooped out of the dust and set jauntily on his gold-brown hair. He paused over the skeleton of the woman, reluctant to touch it, but he wanted the girdle.

He reached for it. And then, oddly, he took the dull-blue ring instead.

a glamour girl, and pop about you being a bandit hunting the Eustace cash—'

'And I won't be able to rob graves in peace—'

She was suddenly pressed against him, gripping his arms with painful fingers, making choking, sounds at his shoulder.

'Oh, Brandy,' she whispered. 'I thought you were dead.'

Tobul spoke harshly in Brandon's mind. 'Hurry. Get into the flier. We'll try to find Rhiannon from the air. Hurry!'

Brandon was apprehensive about that, because of the compass suddenly going dead. If Kymra of the Blue Hair was really there ahead of them, it meant trouble for Tobul, which meant trouble for Max Brandon, and, consequently, for Sylvia.

He hesitated, and Sylvia said, 'Brandy, you'd better give up hunting for the Lost Islands. Jarthur is hopping mad, because you know what relics from there would mean to Mars, and Dhu Kar—'

'Dhu Kar?' snapped Brandon.

'He left the day after you did, as soon as he found out. And Jarthur went storming off with a bunch of policemen, to look for both of you. Of course,' she added hopefully, 'they may have got lost in a sandstorm.'

Brandon shook his head. 'It's a big desert, and they may not have been fools like me. I got too far away from my ship.'

If it was Dhu Kar who had broken into the vault at Rhiannon, that meant trouble, too. The Venusian played for keeps. Brandon had skirmished with him before, and he knew.

And yet, if he could help it, he wasn't going to let that semi-human pirate from the Venusian coal swamps steal Rhiannon from him.

He stood there, thinking these things, his profile hawk-clear with the wide-winged bird glittering above it, the red sunlight caught in his fair beard and shaggy hair, looking rather like a viking.

And Sylvia Eustace, with a curiously puzzled look in her blue eyes, took the ring from Brandon's finger and put it on her own. Then she said calmly:

'Come on, Brandy. We're going to Rhiannon.'

He followed her, not noticing the ring. Tobul, grim and silent inside him, seeing only through his eyes, knew nothing of it either.

The flier was small, fast, lovingly worked over and expertly handled. Sylvia went directly to the controls.

Brandon scowled, trying to plot the most likely course, combining his own conjectures of the position of the Lost Islands with the way shown by Tobul's compass.

Sylvia sent the ship hurtling upward. When he started to speak, she cut him short.

'I think I know the way.'

He stared at her. 'Nobody does. It's all guesswork.'

'Well,' she snapped, 'can't I guess, too?'

He shrugged and sat back in the padded seat. Sylvia's tall, boyish form, the despair of her society-loving mother, hunched over the controls. The flier shivered with the thrust of power from the rockets, and the thin, cold air screamed along the hull.

Sylvia always flew fast, but there was a tenseness about her now that was unlike her.

'We can't do much looking at this pace,' he said mildly.

'I tell you, I've studied up on it and I know the way!' There was an imperious bugle note in her voice that startled him.

Then she glanced at him. Just for an instant her eyes were puzzled and frightened, and altogether Sylvia's. But that was gone in a flash, and the ship rushed on, racing the rising moons.

In the third hour before dawn, with little Phobos rushing ahead of them and Deimos a ball of cold fire overhead, Brandon saw a shadow more solid than the shifting dunes.

Sylvia put the ship down. 'We're there,' she said. Then she laughed and shook him by the shoulders, and her blue eyes sparkled.

'Think of it, Brandy! The Lost Islands. And we'll see them together!'

'Yes,' said Brandon, and the lines of his scarred brown face were deeper. He was thinking: 'Funny she knew the way.' There came before him suddenly the picture of a reckless, vital face set with unconquerable golden eyes, and hair like a living waterfall.

Tobul said softly: 'I see what is in your mind. Kymra may have taken her, as I took you. I dare take no chances. Kill her.'

'No!'

Sylvia looked at him, startled. He gripped his seat with corded hands, and argued desperately.

'It wouldn't do any good! If Kymra is in Sylvia, she'd only go back into – wherever she was before.'

'Into some inanimate thing, Brandon. Perhaps in that state she could be forced— She would be helpless to move, as we both were in the ship. The cohesive frequencies of a disembodied intelligence undergo a violent change under solar bombardment, unless protected by some denser matter.'

'I won't!' whispered Brandon.

He clung to the seat, fighting the inexorable command of Tobul's mind. He looked at Sylvia's eager, vital face, and his heartstrings knotted in him like the straining muscles of his body.

It was futile. Slowly he drew the small needle gun he always carried and slid the clip of poisoned needles into place. He raised it and aimed, at the girl who neither moved nor spoke.

He fired.

The needles vanished in midair with little bright spurts of flame. And Sylvia laughed,

'Tobul,' she said, and the ringing bugle note that was not Sylvia's was in her voice again. 'Not that easily, Tobul! I'll fight you, just as I fought in the old days, to the last ditch!'

As though of its own volition, Brandon's voice came, gentle and strange to his ears, with a feel of barbaric iron under the velvet.

'That vault is all that is left to me of Mars, Kymra. It is mine by right of conquest and the blood my people shed.'

'Barbarian!' Sylvia tossed her head like a war horse scenting battle. 'What is in that vault is mine by right of having built it, and the blood my people shed defending it! The secret of the things you stole from us lies locked in my brain. The things of your own borrowed civilization you shall not have, either.

'This dusty shell is still Mars, and though my race is dead, its people are still mine. I'll not have them misruled by a dog of a nomad, with only four centuries of borrowed culture behind him!'

Brandon felt a blind stab of rage through Tobul's guard, and some of the velvet sloughed away from the iron ring in his voice.

'Borrowed or not, I have the knowledge. The need to rule is as strong in me as it is in you, woman of the Prira Cen!

'Your people were soft with age and culture. You conquered us, yes, because you knew more. But our blood was strong. We took what we wanted and used it against you, and we were not bound by scruples about blood-letting!

'I'm beginning to find myself again. From what I have taken from this man's mind, I see that Mars needs new rule, new strength, the knowledge that I can give it. Mars can live again. But in my way, Kymra! The way of strength and manhood.'

'The way of stupid, blundering beasts,' said Sylvia, her voice deep with some powerful emotion. 'You slaughtered the Prira Cen, the kindliest, wisest, gentlest race on Mars, because you were jealous of our knowledge. You called it "foreign domination," though we never killed a man of your people, and did you more good in ten years than you yourselves could have done in a century.

'Because we kept our race pure, you were jealous of us. Because we kept the secret of our one deadly weapon, you feared us, though we did it for our own protection.'

'We crushed you without it,' said Tobul.

'Only because we waited, not wanting to destroy you, and were betrayed. You were taking me to Rhiannon in chains Tobul, but I tell you that no torture you could devise could have forced me to tell the secret of that weapon. Nor,' she added with deliberate malice, 'another secret, which you would like now, but cannot have.'

Tobul did not answer her. Silently in Brandon's mind he said, 'Take the small tube from your right-hand pocket.'

The vice-grip of Tobul's will on his made even a pretence of resistance impossible. Brandon dropped the useless needle gun and did as he was told.

'She has nothing but the power of her mind,' murmured

He put it on his ring finger and was suddenly giddy. He gulped a food tablet and felt better. The woman's skeleton had fallen into greyish powder, broken by his slight touch.

He picked the girdle out of it and clasped it around his lean waist and turned to search the cabin.

There were chests of scrolls acid-etched on thin metal that blackened and flaked as he looked at them. The letters he did glimpse were older than any he had ever seen.

There were instruments and gadgets of utterly inexplicable design, far too many to carry. The frailer ones were ruined, anyway. He stuffed a few of the more enduring into his pockets and went out.

At the broken door he paused with a small, unpleasant shiver. To break down a door simply by touching it—

Then he grinned. 'Buck up, Brandy. This metal is so thin that a baby could knock holes in it.'

As though in mocking answer, the port rail crumpled, sending a flood of red sand across the deck. The bird on the prow trembled, and for an instant Brandon thought it was going to fly.

It fell into the dust, and was buried.

He got away from there, and watched the ship die her final death in the dry red sea. And then he said to himself:

'Now what? No water, precious little food, no idea of where I am. Speaking of water—'

That stuff in the bottle had certainly been potent. It had revived him like a shot of adrenalin. But now—

He was thirsty again.

He tried to ignore it, making his plans. He had thought he was near the Lost Islands when he landed. In fact, he'd landed because he thought he saw the outline of dry habours and stone quays.

'But I didn't. And the position of the Lost Islands is only conjecture, anyway. No two authorities agree.'

He stood there, his scarred, handsome face twisted into a defiant grin that he knew was as hollow as his stomach, the wide-winged bird on the grey circlet glittering above his forehead.

Then he forced himself to shrug jauntily and start off across the ochre sand.

Thirst grew in him with the arid touch of dust. The wind whined at him, and presently he heard a voice in it. He knew it was delirium, and refused to listen.

The spurt of strength the strange amber fluid had given him drained away. He fell in the blowing dust and cursed it in a choking whisper. And the voice said:

'Strike it with your hand.'

He did, because he thought it was his own desire speaking. He struck the side of the dune before him, weakly, with his doubled fist.

There was a flash and a small thunderclap, and water ran.

He caught it in his cupped hands and drank like an animal, splashing himself, sobbing. Then he got up and stood staring at the wet place in the dust and his wet hands.

He backed off, slowly, his blue eyes widening and paling in a stricken face. He shuddered and passed a hand across his damp beard.

'Merciful heavens!' he whispered. And gripped hard at the rising, terror in him.

'The power isn't yours,' said a gentle thoughtvoice in his brain. 'It's merely transmitted through your body.'

Brandon closed his eyes and held his clenched fists against his temples.

'No,' he said. 'I'll die decently of thirst if I have to. But I won't go mad.'

'You're not mad,' said the voice. 'Don't be frightened.'

The last was faintly condescending, which made Brandon angry. He threw his head back, so that he looked rather like the bird of prey on his circlet.

'Who are you?' he demanded. 'And where?'

'I am Tobul, Lord of the Seven Kingdoms. My body is dust. But the essential frequencies that activated that body are in you.'

'That's witchcraft,' said Brandon curtly, 'and that's madness.'

'Witchcraft to the ignorant,' murmured the voice coolly. 'Simple science to the learned. Life is essentially a matter of electrical frequencies, a consumption and emission of energy. There is nothing strange about charging metal with electrical life. Why should there be anything strange in charging any other substance with any other phase of the basic stuff of the universe?'

Brandon looked at the restless desert, tasted the dust on his tongue, listened to the wailing wind.

He pulled a hair from his tawny beard, and felt the hurt of it. He took a deep breath.

'All right,' he said. 'How did you get into me?'

But the voice whispered now, and not to him.

'Desolation,' it said. 'Death and desolation. The sea, the clouds, the strength and power of life, all gone. Is this truly Mars?'

Max Brandon felt a wrenching sadness go through him, and then a swift stab of fear, very faint, like things in a half-forgotten dream.

'I must get to Rhiannon,' said the voice of Tobul. 'At once.'

There was no emotion in it now. Brandon sensed an iron control, an almost barbarian strength.

'Rhiannon,' he repeated. 'I've never heard— You said Tobul, *Lord of the Seven Kingdoms?*'

Brandon sat down, because his knees wouldn't hold him.

'Rhiannon,' he whispered. 'That's the ancient name for the Lost Islands. And "Lord of the Seven Kingdoms" was the title of the sorcerer-scientist who ruled half of Mars, from his seat in Rhiannon.'

Ancient things. Things deeply buried, nearly forgotten, clouded by superstition and legend. Forty thousand years—

Brandon sat still, just clinging to his sanity. At length he repeated quietly:

'How did you get into me?'

'When the ship sank, so suddenly that nothing could be done, I transferred my essence to a bottle of liquid prepared for the purpose – a faintly radioactive suspension medium. Those were troubled times – one went prepared.

'The collective frequencies that form my consciousness

remained there unharmed, until you drank the liquid. Fortunately it was not poisonous, and you gave me easy entry into a satisfactory host.'

A picture of the man at whose side the bottle had been came back to Brandon – the fair, grave face and the impenetrable eyes. That man, dead forty thousand years.

Brandon ran his tongue over dry lips. 'When are you going to get out of me?'

'Probably never. I should have to build another body, and the secret of that is known only ... Brandon!'

It was as though a hand gripped his brain. The impact of that will was terrifying. Brandon felt his mind stripped naked, probed and searched and shaken, and then dropped.

'Her jewelled girdle he took,' murmured Tobul, 'and my circlet, and some instruments. The girdle is only metal and jewel – look at your hands!'

Brandon looked, raging, but unable to help himself.

'The blue ring, Brandon, that you took from her thumb, is it there?'

It glinted dully in the sun. Brandon looked at it and said simply 'I don't understand. What ring?'

Tobul whispered: 'His eyes don't see, he has no memory. Yet I can't be sure. I was faint with the effort of breaking the door, after so many centuries of quiescence. She may have blanked his mind. But it's a chance I must take.

'Brandon, we go to Rhiannon.'

Brandon got up, and there was something ominous in the set of his broad shoulders.

'Just a minute,' he said evenly. 'I want to find the Lost Islands, too. This possession business has its fascinating angles, I'll admit, so I'm trying to be tolerant of you. But I won't be ordered about.'

'Take the instrument out of your left-hand pocket and look at it.' Tobul's voice was utterly without emotion.

'Do you hear me, Tobul? I won't have the privacy of my mind invaded. I won't be ordered—'

He stopped. Again the hand of that iron will closed on his brain. The sheer calm strength of it numbed him, as though he had been an ant trying to stem an avalanche.

He fought, until sweat ran down the channels of his face and his lean body ached, fought to keep his hand from reaching into his pocket for the instrument.

But the dark iron power of Tobul's mind rolled in on him, wrapped and crushed and smothered him with a slow, patient ease.

Trudging over the ochre waste, following the mysterious, quivering needle in Tobul's instrument, Max Brandon still could grin.

'Brandy, Brandy,' he murmured. 'I always said drinking would get you into trouble!'

Two chill Martian nights passed, and two days. Brandon got used to drawing water from the dust with a blow of his fist. It pleased him, like a small boy with a firecracker.

Tobul, in a rare fit of communicativeness, said it was simply a matter of releasing mental energy which caused oxygen and hydrogen to unite from the air. The blow was only a means of directing the mental concentration.

The Lord of the Seven Kingdoms had withdrawn himself utterly. Brandon felt no discomfort, nothing different from his usual tough health. Only when he tried to disobey the pointing of the compass, he was forced back to obedience.

It galled him, but there was nothing he could do. It was terrible to think of living out his life as host for a parasitic intelligence. It outraged his pride, his individuality.

And yet, to have contact with a mind forty thousand years old; to be taken to the Lost Islands of Rhiannon, the greatest archaeological mystery of Mars—

He asked about the compass. Tobul answered absently.

'It obeys a directional impulse from the vault.' And then, even more distantly: 'The vault is still there, safe, in all this.'

For a fleeting instant, through his own excitement at the mention of a vault, Brandon caught the unguarded sorrow of Tobul, looking through an alien's eyes at the withered mummy of his world.

More and more, as he accustomed himself to his strange

condition, Brandon's mind went back to the girl with blue hair, sitting proud in her shackles across from Tobul.

'Who was she?' he asked.

The leashed fury of Tobul's answer startled him.

'The most dangerous creature on Mars. In a short time I should have destroyed her. But, somewhere, her mind lives as mine does, and defies me – Brandon! Go on!'

But Brandon stood still, with a curious chilly crinkle to his spine.

'Sorry,' he said. 'But the compass is shot.'

Tobul's armour dropped, then, for an instant. Brandon felt what a lost planet must feel, torn from its sun. He never forgot it.

'Kymra! Somehow, she has gone before me – go on, Brandon!'

Brandon shrugged and went. 'May as well die walking as sitting,' he said. 'It may not be Kymra of the Prira Cen, though. It may be just plain Dhu Kar of Venus, which is worse!'

And then, just before the swift sunset, a flier came droning low over the ochre sand, swinging in wide circles, searching.

Brandon danced like a madman on the top of a dune, obeying Tobul's command as well as his own urge. The flier came down.

A tall, slender figure in grease-stained flying togs leaped from the port and ran toward him in a cloud of dust.

'Brandy!' yelled a clear voice. 'Brandy, you idiot!'

'Good Lord!' said Brandon. 'Sylvia.'

She swept into his arms, kissed him, cursed him, and shook him all at once.

'Are you all right? What happened? I've been hunting for three days.'

He held her off and grinned into her eager gamin face, framed in a perpetually tousled mop of curly black hair, set with eyes as sea-blue and adventurous as his own, and smudged slightly with grease.

'Syl,' he said, 'for once I'm glad to see you.'

'Some day,' she grinned back, 'you'll realise my sterling worth and marry me. Then I shan't have to fight mom about being

Tobul. 'She can't fight the strength of the projector long. Fire, Brandon!'

With some foreign knowledge, he pressed a stud. A faint beam of light leaped out, splattering in blazing incandescence against the barrier of force Kymra had built around Sylvia's body.

It burned and blazed, and the force wall held stubbornly, and Sylvia's blue eyes stared at him through the fire.

'You, too, Brandy?' she said, and now the voice was her own. 'She made me understand, all in a flash. She can't hold out long. It's all so mad! Brandy, she's weakening. Brandy, can't you do something!'

He couldn't, though the sweat of agony needled his face. Out of some dim distance he sensed a growing beat and glare and thought it was from the clashing energies before him, until he realised it was in the wrong direction.

The stern plates of the cabin were glowing cherry-red.

Somehow he found his voice. 'The fuel tanks!' he yelled. 'Got to get out. Somebody's got a heat beam on us.'

Miraculously, those two warring intelligences understood. The blazing battle of force broke off. The hull plates paled—

They ran. With all their strength they leaped through the port and pelted over the desert, trailing crazy shadows from the double moons.

Light gravity and long legs took them barely out of danger. Brandon threw Sylvia flat just as the tanks let go. A thundering, howling wind swept over them with a solid wall of dust, and a vast flame pillared up into the sky.

For an incredibly long moment it painted every detail of the scene in wicked crimson – the gaunt, worn shell of a volcanic cone dead and buried for unnumbered centuries and bared capriciously now by the restless sand, a few Cyclopean blocks of Terellan marble cut to shapeless lumps by the passing years, tumbled about a gaping hole.

Directly in front of the hole was a big, fast, convertible spaceship. From it had come the heat beam.

'Dhu Kar,' said Brandon, coughing dust.

'Why does this Dhu Kar wish to kill you?' asked Tobul.

'For the same reasons I'd like to kill him,' returned Brandon grimly. 'Except that he's a vandal and a swine, and I'm a very charming fellow. Wait a bit. You'll see.'

He got up, and Sylvia, as usual, scrambled up before he could help her. Her face was pale and a little frightened, but her blue eyes danced.

'I've always wanted real adventure,' she said, with a shaky little laugh. 'I'm getting it!'

They went toward the spaceship. And up out of the black pit, looking like a misshapen demon in the light of the double moons, came a squat shape bearing a burden – a radio-controlled robot carrier.

Brandon felt the tendrils of Tobul's mind reaching out to search the mind of the man who blocked his way to the vault.

'He's looting my vault,' whispered Tobul. 'My vault, built and sealed against time forty thousand years ago. This outland dog!'

'And what he can't carry away he'll destroy, partly to cover his tracks, mostly to keep anyone else from profiting.' Brandon's tawny head came up. 'Let me handle Dhu Kar myself.'

'I can't afford to risk your body, Brandon.'

Brandon said angrily: 'Look here, Tobul—'

The iron hand of Tobul's will closed on his mind. He shrugged, and went on in silence, Sylvia's firm shoulder close to his.

Dhu Kar of Venus came out of the air lock of his ship.

He loomed hugely in the shifting light. The fish-belly white of his face and hands gleamed sharply out of the dark furs he wore against the Martian chill. He was bareheaded, according to the custom of his people, his snowy hair intricately coiled.

He held a needle gun in his hand, and his eyes were cold little chips of moonlight in his broad white face.

'Didn't know you had a woman aboard, Brandon,' he said. His voice was harsh and slurring. 'Yes, I recognise you, Miss Eustace. I'm glad you weren't harmed.'

'He'll be happy to take you home, darling, for a small consideration. Say a million credits or so.'

Brandon was advancing slowly, poised on the balls of his feet. Dhu Kar grinned.

'How right you are, Brandon. For once you're bringing me business instead of getting it away. But you can relax, Brandon. You won't have to worry about it.'

He raised his gun slightly. Sylvia cried out and made a move toward Brandon. The gun hissed softly.

The needles splattered harmlessly against a wall of force, just as Brandon's had done back in the ship. And Sylvia Eustace turned and ran.

'I'm not doing this, Brandy,' she yelled, her long legs flashing through the dust. 'Are you all right?'

'All right!' he yelled back, and rushed after her, impelled by Tobul's furious command to get to the vault tunnel first.

Dhu Kar was staring from his gun to the running man in open-mouthed amazement. Then his jaw shut hard. The girl didn't matter – he could catch her. But Brandon—

If something was wrong with his gun, he'd try something else. He fumbled in a capacious pocket, and his powerful arm flexed.

The gas capsule burst just at Brandon's feet. Tobul, concentrating every effort on catching Kymra, was caught off guard. Before he could stop himself, Brandon had breathed enough of it to drop him dazed in the sand.

He floundered away to windward, and realised that Tobul, associated as he was with Brandon's physical medium, was momentarily affected, too.

Sylvia's flying form vanished into the pit mouth. Dhu Kar laughed and ran toward Brandon, very light and swift for such a big man.

Brandon got to his feet and stood swaying, lost in a roaring mist, his hands raised blindly, waiting.

A pair of vast white hands came out of the darkness toward his throat. He caught them. He fought to hold them off, but his sinews were water.

The hands got closer. There was a face behind them now, broad and pale and contentedly smiling. Brandon's white teeth showed through his tawny beard. He gulped the clean desert air and scourged his lagging strength into his arms, to hold those hands away.

But the stuff he'd breathed sent a black tide swirling through his brain. The hands and the smiling face were drowned in it.

The wide-winged bird on his circlet gleamed in the cold light of Deimos; the lines of his scarred, handsome face were deep and strong. He dropped Dhu Kar's wrists.

The last desperate backlash of his strength went into his forward surge, the thrust of his hands to Dhu Kar's throat.

The Venusian laughed and flung him off. Brandon crumpled on the sand, and looked up at death. He was grinning, the reckless grin that women sighed at on the televisor screens.

Some little mocking imp in his blacked-out brain whispered: 'No audience, Brandy! You can quit.'

But he didn't. And death came down in two white hands.

And vanished, in a sudden coruscating puff of light.

Tobul's voice spoke, through the stifling darkness in his mind. The velvet was all gone from it now. It was clean, barbaric steel.

'I was affected only for an instant. I could have saved you this. But Kymra was gone then, and I wanted to see how men fight today.

'That circlet you wear was the crown of my fathers, when they were nomads living on raided herds and stolen grain. Keep it, Brandon. And believe me when I say I regret having to use your body. I shall try not to do it violence.'

Brandon felt a tingling fire sweep through him, and quite suddenly the effects of the gas were gone. Some vibration Tobul freed, stimulating the natural processes of his body to instantaneous reaction. He got up.

'Tobul,' he said, 'did you say that Kymra knew the secret of building a body for you?'

'Yes. But there is no way now of forcing her to do it. The girl fights well, for all she's a Blue Hair.'

'I'll find a way,' said Brandon.

Tobul's voice came deep and strong in his brain.

'I admire you, Brandon. I wish to help you all I can. But this fight is between Kymra and me. We are of opposing races, opposing creeds. The will, the actual need to rule is inherent in both of us, as the need to breathe is in you. Not the will merely for power, but for the guidance of millions of people to what we believe is a better way of life.

'We have different ways, Kymra and I. There is not room on Mars for both of them.

'We will go, Brandon. Down into the vault. Kymra is there ahead of me, but I still have some powers. One of us will not come out.'

Brandon went, down into the Stygian shadow of the tunnel. Somewhere ahead was Sylvia, and Kymra of the Prira Cen, and the powerful things in the vault he could only guess at.

Behind him, outside, was sleeping Mars, resigned to the slow advance of death, living out its little days in peace.

Behind him, too, long after the tunnel roof had killed all sound from beyond, four ships came flashing down through the moonlight, drawn by the great pyre of Sylvia's flier.

Jarthur, president of the Society for the Preservation of Martian Relics, looked out at the worn stump of the volcano – a tall, weedy man with sad Martian eyes and semimilitary authority.

'These things are all we have left,' he said to an assistant. 'These bones and shards of our history. And even these the outlanders strip from us.'

He flipped open the intership radio connection.

'Cover this area thoroughly. Issue orders that everyone found here is to be arrested. If they resist, fire. Anaesthetic needles. *No one is to be allowed to escape.*'

It was cold in the tunnel, and musty with the dead smell of time. It was dark, too, but Brandon had no trouble finding his way. The square passageway, sheathed in metal of the same forgotten alloy as Tobul's ship, ran straight ahead and down.

Tobul explained it, answering Brandon's question.

'Those were troubled times. I knew that Rhiannon might be destroyed at any time. So I built this vault, sheathed in metal that will not corrode and is harder than the finest steel. It's air-tight, and filled with a preservation gas – or was, before the Venusian broke in.

'In it I had placed the sum of our knowledge, science and arts and pleasures, and with them the two secrets we took from the Prira Cen but could not use – the machine of regeneration and the weapon.

'They're still here, waiting. They mean the rule of Mars.'

Presently Brandon came to massive metal doors that barred his way. The controls were locked from the inside. Tobul said:

'The projector, Brandon. The same one.'

He pressed the stud. The faint beam of light focused on the door. The metal glowed, wavered, and crumbled away into fine powder.

'It upsets molecular cohesion, reducing the metal to fine particles of its original elements,' Tobul explained.

Brandon shuddered, thinking what would have happened to Sylvia. The beam ate and ate into the door, crumbling a hole around the massive controls.

It went through nearly a solid foot of metal, and went dead.

'Age,' snarled Tobul. 'And all this time, Kymra—' He broke off. 'Put your hands in the hole, Brandon.'

He obeyed, remembering the cabin door on the ship and wondering if he'd be destroyed by Kymra's secret weapon as soon as he entered, or whether he'd live long enough to say goodbye to Sylvia.

The weakened metal went through, under the power impulse from Tobul's brain. The massive valves swung back—

Brandon stood frozen on the threshold.

The vault stretched away into gleaming distances filled with machines, with racks of metal scrolls and objects of a million shapes and sizes. All the life and learning of ancient Mars, the scientific powers of the Sorcerers of Rhiannon, preserved by the foresight of one man.

But it wasn't that sight, tremendous as it was, that set the blood hammering into Brandon's throat and wrists.

Directly across from the door, as though brought in just before it was closed, was a huge glass cabinet set in an intricate web of coils. These shimmered in a halo of light, at once subdued and fierce.

Beneath the cabinet were several self-sealing metal containers. On the floor of it, inside, were trays and bowls of chemicals.

Above these, in the very centre of the soft, deep glow, a shimmering thing stood, already vaguely formulated.

Witch fires danced over the chemicals, whirling upward in a spiral of incandescence. As though painted by a rapid brush, line and colour took shape—

The fires died down, the glass door opened, and a girl stepped out.

A tall, long-limbed girl, naked as the moon and as white. She moved with a vital grace, and her eyes were like bits of living gold, proud, unconquerable, meeting Brandon's own.

And her hair was blue, rippling down over her shoulders like the curl of a living wave over foamwhite coral.

Brandon heard a long, quivering sigh through his mind, and Tobul said:

'Kymra.'

The girl nodded and turned to a curious thing raised on a metal tripod. It seemed to be mainly a crystal prism forming the core of a helix, which was of some material midway between crystal and metal – partially transparent, and made up of countless intricate facets.

The helix broke at its lower end into a score of shining strands which fanned out into a circle.

Sylvia Eustace spoke suddenly from where she stood, at one side of Kymra and a little behind her.

'What are you going to do?'

Kymra's voice was very grave when she answered. Her golden eyes watched Brandon with sombre regret.

'I am going to kill,' she said quietly.

Her clear, muted voice rang softly from the metal vault, heavy with regret.

'For the first time one of the Prira Cen is going to take life wilfully. I'm sorry, Max Brandon, that you must be the innocent victim – doubly sorry because of what I have read in this girl's mind.

'But you – and I – are less important than Mars.'

Tobul, speaking aloud through Brandon's throat, said harshly: 'So you have had to come to my way at last.'

She shook her head, that glorious shining hair like the forgotten sea that had lapped this island.

'No, Tobul. Because I take no pride in it, only sorrow. If my people had seen in time that they must deal with your barbarians as they would with a horde of wild beasts, humanely but firmly—' Her white shoulders shimmered through the shadowy blue.

'But they didn't,' said Tobul, and his voice held a bitter satisfaction. 'You'll be all alone, Kymra, in an alien world.'

'No. You're not the only one who looked ahead, Tobul! My seven wisest councillors took refuge in sensitized stones, which you brought here to this vault. They knew that I would live, as they do. It was the thought-impulses of their minds that led me here, after Dhu Kar broke your sending mechanism by moving it.

'Their atomic patterns are inherent in the frequencies of their consciousness. That's the secret of building bodies, Tobul. Given the consciousness and the necessary chemicals, that machine can create an identical replica, as you see in me.

'Sylvia, my dear,' she added gently, 'it will be quite painless. If I had any other sure weapon to use against Tobul's strength, I would, and then rebuild Brandon's body. But this force projects the consciousness into some unknown dimension, just as solar rays will. It cannot be recalled.'

Her hands dropped out of sight below the prism. Brandon could see the ripple of firm muscles along her arms as she went through some complicated operation.

'Goodbye, Tobul,' she said softly. 'Strange that we must end like this, in a world so different from the one we knew.'

The prism began to glow with some queer perversion of light that seemed rather luminous darkness. It ran along the facets of the helix, faster and faster, stranger, darker, more dazzling.

Brandon felt every drop of blood in him stop for a second, and then race on again, with the swirl of that mad, black luminosity. A cold terror caught him, a thing that hadn't come at all when Dhu Kar's hands were at his throat.

He felt Tobul's being surge within him, fierce and rebellious and bitter. Not afraid, much. Only ragingly sad at his defeat, and the thought of his people being ruled by Kymra of the Prira Cen.

'Negative energy,' said Kymra's voice, ringing through the great vaulted rooms like a muted bugle. 'It taps the power of the galactic wheel itself, turning against the cohesive force of space. Energy so close to the primal warp of creation that it needs only the slightest charge to push it over into the negative – the opposite balance that everything possesses.'

The grave, sad voice beat against Brandon's ears.

'There is no defence against it, Tobul. All your force screens and projectors are worse than useless. They attract now, instead of repelling. Do you wonder we kept this weapon secret?'

The little threads of blackness spiralled out into a cone, and grew.

Brandon's heart thundered in his throat. The mocking devil in his brain laughed because the reckless grin was on his lips, playing to the audience – Sylvia's stricken eyes.

He was sorry for Sylvia. She'd be alone now, in an alien world of wealth and decorum, that only he could have taken her out of.

Alone, in an alien world—

Brandon swallowed his heart. A sudden, desperate hope flared in him. Useless, but he had to try. The thing that had driven him through the desert made him try.

He started to cry out, 'Kymra!' and Tobul's will clamped his tongue to silence.

'I will not beg for life,' he said.

Things happened then, all at once. Sylvia made a long-legged leap forward, into the path of that blackness that ribboned and twisted out from the helix. In a second it would have touched her. But Brandon, moving instinctively, so that Tobul had no time to catch his conscious thought and block it, flung himself against her.

She went sprawling over out of harm's way. Kymra caught her breath sharply and started to move the projector to a new focus. And Brandon, looking up, cried suddenly:

'Jarthur!'

He stood there, the tall, thin Martian with the sad eyes. He had a needle gun in his hand, and six or seven black-clad policemen just behind him.

He stared, momentarily stunned, at the vault and Kymra, with the blue hair cascading over her naked shoulders.

Kymra made a sharp movement. The dark light in the prism changed. The black cone unravelled itself, back into the helix. Brandon's heart gave a wild shudder of relief. Kymra was reluctant to take innocent lives.

He scrambled up, sensing Tobul's dangerous alertness. Jarthur, forcing himself to steadiness in spite of his amazement, said:

'Max Brandon, you're under arrest.'

Tobul acted with the swiftness of his barbarian ancestors. With anaesthetic needles splattering in flames from his force shield, he charged into the middle of Jarthur's group.

The shock of Brandon's immunity demoralized them. Tobul's mind put forth tendrils of iron force.

'Surround me,' he said. 'Walk forward.'

Brandon saw the look in Jarthur's eyes, midway between nightmare and reluctant acceptance of insanity. Then he obeyed. Tobul moved forward, surrounded by a living shield.

Kymra stood irresolute behind the projector, reluctant even then to destroy more of her people. And then Sylvia moved.

She uncoiled from the floor with every ounce of her lithe strength, hurtling into Kymra. Kymra's mental force shield must have been momentarily dispersed by the shock of Jarthur's entrance, and Tobul's sudden manoeuvre.

Sylvia crashed into her, knocking her away from the projector. She yelled, 'Brandy! Do something!' but it was Tobul who flung away his unwilling protectors and gained the control board behind the projector.

Kymra rose, dignified and beautiful even then, standing beside the regenerator.

'It's no use, Tobul,' she said. 'You can't use it.'

Brandon heard his voice say softly:

'You forgot the girl. She was where she could see your hands – and *she* didn't blank her mind to what she saw.'

Tobul's hands moved over the intricate controls. Almost as an afterthought, he said to Jarthur, through Brandon's mouth:

'You are no longer needed. Go.'

Jarthur's sad eyes became furious.

'See here, Brandon! I don't know what kind of madness this is – probably some secret you've stolen from this place. But you're through looting. I'm going to send you to Phobos if I die doing it!'

'You will,' said Tobul calmly, and shrugged. 'Please yourself.'

Kymra said steadily: 'You don't know how to control the force. Every living thing beyond its focus will be destroyed, and part of the inanimate substance, before you can stop it even by smashing the projector.'

'You said yourself, Kymra, that Mars is more important than any of us.'

The prism began to glow with its queer, black light.

And Brandon said desperately: 'Tobul!'

'I'm sorry to cheat you of your body, Brandon. But this must be done.'

Black rage suddenly took Brandon's mind, drowning out even the flashes of Jarthur's needles dying against the force screen.

'You fool!' he snarled. 'Can't you see that the world has changed? The things you're fighting over don't exist any more!'

'Silence, Brandon!'

The black threads were weaving themselves again around the focus of the projector, twisting out toward Kymra of the Prira Cen. In a few seconds they'd blast her out of existence, and the regenerator with her – and Brandon's only chance to get rid of Tobul and be a normal man again.

He could foresee Tobul's mind moving to silence his own. His hands were free from the projector now.

With a characteristic flourish, he ripped the circlet from his head and held it up.

'By this crown, Tobul, I've earned the right to speak!'

The mocking imp in Brandon's brain whispered: 'Every inch the hero!' And behind it he could feel the struggle in Tobul's mind.

It seemed an eternity before the quiet, curt answer came. 'Speak, then.'

Brandon spoke, aloud, to Kymra as much as to Tobul.

'You say that Mars is your first consideration, and I believe you. But you still live in the past. Can't you see that the war between Tobul's people and the Prira Cen is as dead as the dust of your bodies?

'What right has either of you to rob Mars of the other? The two of you, working together as balancing forces instead of enemies, could make Mars the greatest planet in the System. You could give her water again, and the air she's losing, the courage and will to live that she's lost.

'You could bring her the knowledge of the Lost Islands and the Prira Cen – complete, not in half-forgotten fragments. Kymra's councillors are invaluable to all humanity. What right have you, Tobul, to destroy them?

'The world has changed. With each of you, the other is the only link to the world you knew. There can be no real companionship for you with anyone else.

'What human would mate with someone forty thousand years old? Yet you're both young. Think of that, for a minute. To live for well-nigh endless years with no one to speak to, no understanding, only awe and fear and perhaps hate?

'For Heaven's sake, Tobul, if you're the brave man, the great man you believe yourself to be, face this out and see the truth in it!'

The little black threads wove out and out, and Kymra's eyes were burning gold, proud and steady.

Sylvia spoke up furiously. 'He's right, you know. You're just fooling yourselves. You don't care who you hurt as long as you don't have to share your power!'

'That's not true,' said Kymra gently. And Tobul echoed: 'No—'

Brandon felt Tobul's mind gather into itself, thinking. For an instant his body was free from compulsion. He raised his foot and sent the projector crashing to the floor.

It shattered, became meaningless, shining fragments. But the fragments lay about a gaping hole, where the little black worms had gnawed.

Jarthur had stopped the useless firing. His eyes were dazed, bewildered, but his back was stubbornly straight.

'I don't understand,' he said. 'I may be only playing into your hands, Brandon. But if there are really beings from the past who can help Mars to live again – I beg them both to do it.'

Tobul whispered in Brandon's mind: 'What is all this to you, Brandon? You, an Earthman.'

He shrugged. 'I'm a human being, too. And I think I'm seeing what I've always wanted to see. The thing that, subconsciously, has drawn me to hunt up the old, forgotten places. I'm seeing the past – the past that is as real as the future or the present – come into its own.'

'You're a looter, Brandon,' said Jarthur harshly.

'But I've never destroyed anything. Oh, I'm not excusing myself. And I'm beginning to see the error of my ways.'

'Perhaps,' said Tobul shrewdly, 'because this looks more exciting?'

Kymra said softly: 'Your barbarian ancestors, Tobul, prided themselves on being honest with themselves. Let us be.'

Brandon could feel the struggle that went on in Tobul's mind. It seemed to him that the whole universe had stopped breathing, waiting. And at last, reluctantly, Tobul said:

'Brandon speaks the truth. Much as I hate it, it is the truth. Blast you, Brandon, why did I give you my crown to wear?'

'You may have it back.' Brandon was suddenly weak, almost hysterical with relief. 'I don't want much—'

'Much?'

'Well, my body has served as your draught animal. I'm giving up a profitable career of grave robbing in order to act as your ambassador, your link between the past and the present—'

'Ambassador!' said Kymra, turning her imperious, golden gaze on him. 'Who has asked you?'

'Hm-m-m,' said Brandon. 'You'll need a personal diplomat, too. Can't expect love and kisses all in one minute, after forty thousand years – know anybody who could do it better?'

Kymra looked at Brandon's handsome head cocked back, with the wide-winged bird glittering above it and his white teeth gleaming. She laughed.

'You're mad, as well as insolent. But – Tobul?'

'Why not? Kymra, you will restore my body, of course. But before I leave this Brandon, there is something I want to do – to tame him.'

Brandon's heart gave a swift little jerk of apprehension. He stammered: 'What—' But the iron grip of Tobul's will was on his mind.

He found himself walking over to Sylvia. He found himself taking her in his arms, and whispering something, and then—

'So that,' said Tobul, 'is how it's done now. The world hasn't changed so much!'

THE JEWEL OF BAS

1

Mouse stirred the stew in the small iron pot. There wasn't much of it. She sniffed and said:

'You could have stolen a bigger joint. We'll go hungry before the next town.'

'Uh huh,' Ciaran grunted lazily.

Anger began to curl in Mouse's eyes.

'I suppose it's all right with you if we run out of food,' she said sullenly.

Ciaran leaned back comfortably against a moss-grown boulder and watched her with lazy grey eyes. He liked watching Mouse. She was a head shorter than he, which made her very short indeed, and as thin as a young girl. Her hair was black and wild, as though only wind ever combed it. Her eyes were black, too, and very bright. There was a small red thief's brand between them. She wore a ragged crimson tunic, and her bare arms and legs were as brown as his own.

Ciaran grinned. His lip was scarred, and there was a tooth missing behind it. He said, 'It's just as well. I don't want you getting fat and lazy.'

Mouse, who was sensitive about her thinness, said something pungent and threw the wooden plate at him. Ciaran drew his shaggy head aside enough to let it by and then relaxed, stroking the harp on his bare brown knees. It began to purr softly.

Ciaran felt good. The heat of the sunballs that floated always, lazy in a reddish sky, made him pleasantly sleepy. And after the clamour and crush of the market squares in the border towns, the huge high silence of the place was wonderful.

He and Mouse were camped on a tongue of land that licked out from the Phrygian hills down into the coastal plains of Atlantea. A short cut, but only gypsies like themselves ever took it. To Ciaran's left, far below, the sea spread sullen and burning cloaked in a reddish fog.

To his right, also far below, were the Forbidden Plains. Flat, desolate, and barren, reaching away and away to the up-curving rim of the world, where Ciaran's sharp eyes could just make out a glint of gold; a mammoth peak reaching for the sky.

Mouse said suddenly, 'Is that it, Kiri? Ben Beatha, the Mountain of Life?'

Ciaran struck a shivering chord from the harp. 'That's it.'

'Let's eat,' said Mouse.

'Scared?'

'Maybe you want me to go back! Maybe you think a branded thief isn't good enough for you! Well I can't help where I was born or what my parents were – and you'd have a brand on your ugly face too, if you hadn't just been lucky!'

She threw the ladle.

This time her aim was better and Ciaran didn't duck quite in time. It clipped his ear. He sprang up, looking murderous, and started to heave it back at her. And then, suddenly, Mouse was crying, stamping up and down and blinking tears out of her eyes.

'All right, I'm scared! I've never been out of a city before, and besides ...' She looked out over the silent plain, to the distant glint of Ben Beatha. 'Besides,' she whispered, 'I keep thinking of the stories they used to tell – about Bas the Immortal, and his androids, and the grey beasts that served them. And about the Stone of Destiny.'

Ciaran made a contemptuous mouth. 'Legends. Old wives' tales. Songs to give babies a pleasant shiver.' A small glint of avarice came into his grey eyes. 'But the Stone of Destiny – it's a nice story, that one. A jewel of such power that owning it gives a man rule over the whole world ...'

He squinted out across the barren plain. 'Some day,' he said softly, 'maybe I'll see if that one's true.'

'Oh, Kiri.' Mouse came and caught his wrists in her small strong hands. 'You wouldn't. It's forbidden – and no one that's gone into the Forbidden Plains has ever come back.'

'There's always a first time.' He grinned. 'But I'm not going now, Mousie. I'm too hungry.'

She picked up the plate silently and ladled stew into it and set it down. Ciaran laid his harp down and stretched – a tough, wiry little man with legs slightly bandy and a good-natured hard face. He wore a yellow tunic even more ragged than Mouse's.

They sat down. Ciaran ate noisily with his fingers. Mouse fished out a hunk of meat and nibbled it moodily. A breeze came up, pushing the sunballs around a little and bringing tatters of red fog in off the sea. After a while Mouse said:

'Did you hear any of the talk in the market squares, Kiri?'

He shrugged. 'They gabble. I don't waste my time with it.'

'All along the border countries they were saying the same thing. People who live or work along the edge of the Forbidden Plains have disappeared. Whole towns of them, sometimes.'

'One man falls into a beast-pit,' said Ciaran impatiently, 'and in two weeks of gossip the whole country has vanished. Forget it.'

'But it's happened before, Kiri. A long time ago ...'

'A long time ago some wild tribe living on the Plains came in and got tough, and that's that!' Ciaran wiped his hands on the grass and said angrily, 'If you're going to nag all the time about being scared ...'

He caught the plate out of her hands just in time. She was breathing hard, glaring at him. She looked like her name, and cute as hell. Ciaran laughed.

'Come here, you.'

She came, sulkily. He pulled her down beside him and kissed her and took the harp on his knees. Mouse put her head on his shoulder. Ciaran was suddenly very happy.

He began to draw music out of the harp. There was a lot of distance around him, and he tried to fill it up with music, a fine free spate of it out of the thrumming strings. Then he sang. He had a beautiful voice, clear and true as a new blade, but soft. It was a simple tune, about two people in love. Ciaran liked it.

After a while Mouse reached up and drew his head around, stroking the scar on his lip so he had to stop singing. She wasn't glaring any longer. Ciaran bent his head.

His eyes were closed. But he felt her body stiffen against him, and her lips broke away from his with a little gasping cry.

'Kiri – Kiri, look!'

He jerked his head back, angry and startled. Then the anger faded.

There was a different quality to the light. The warm, friendly, reddish sunlight that never dimmed or faded.

There was a shadow spreading out in the sky over Ben Beatha. It grew and widened, and the sunballs went out, one by one, and darkness came toward them over the Forbidden Plains.

They crouched, clinging together, not speaking, not breathing. An uneasy breeze sighed over them, moving out. Then, after a long time, the sunballs sparked and burned again, and the shadow was gone.

Ciaran dragged down an unsteady breath. He was sweating, but where his hands and Mouse's touched, locked together, they were cold as death.

'What is it, Kiri?'

'I don't know.' He got up, slinging the harp across his back without thinking about it. He felt naked suddenly, up there on the high ridge. Stripped and unsafe. He pulled Mouse to her feet. Neither of them spoke again. Their eyes had a queer stunned look.

This time it was Ciaran that stopped, with the stewpot in his hands, looking at something behind Mouse. He dropped it and jumped in front of her, pulling the wicked knife he carried from his girdle. The last thing he heard was her wild scream.

But he had time enough to see. To see the creatures climbing up over the crest of the ridge beside them, fast and silent and grinning, to ring them in with wands tipped at the point with opals like tiny sunballs.

They were no taller than Mouse, but thick and muscular, built like men. Grey animal fur grew on them like the body-hair of a hairy man, lengthening into a coarse mane over the skull. Where the skin showed it was grey and wrinkled and tough.

Their faces were flat, with black animal nose-buttons. They had sharp teeth, grey with a bright, healthy greyness. Their eyes were blood-pink, without whites or visible pupils.

The eyes were the worst.

Ciaran yelled and slashed out with his knife. One of the grey brutes danced in on lithe, quick feet and touched him on the neck with its jewelled wand.

Fire exploded in Ciaran's head, and then there was darkness, pierced by Mouse's scream. As he slid down into it he thought:

'They're Kalds. The beasts of legend that served Bas the Immortal and his androids. Kalds, that guarded the Forbidden Plains from man!'

Ciaran came to, on his feet and walking. From the way he felt, he'd been walking a long time, but his memory was vague and confused. He had been relieved of his knife, but his harp was still with him.

Mouse walked beside him. Her black hair hung over her face and her eyes looked out from behind it, sullen and defiant.

The grey beasts walked in a rough circle around them, holding their wands ready. From the way they grinned, Ciaran had an idea they hoped they'd have an excuse for using them.

With a definitely uneasy shock, Ciaran realised that they were far out in the barren waste of the Forbidden Plains.

He got a little closer to Mouse. 'Hello.'

She looked at him. 'You and your short cuts! So all that talk in the border towns was just gabble, huh?'

'So it's my fault! If that isn't just like a woman...' Ciaran made an impatient gesture. 'All right, all right! That doesn't matter now. What does matter is where are we going and why?'

'How should I— Wait a minute. We're stopping.'

The Kalds warned them with their wands to stand. One of the grey brutes seemed to be listening to something that Ciaran couldn't hear. Presently it gestured and the party started off again in a slightly different direction.

After a minute or two a gully appeared out of nowhere at their feet. From up on the ridge the Forbidden Plains had looked perfectly flat, but the gully was fairly wide and cut in clean like a sword gash, hidden by a slight roll of the land. They scrambled down the steep bank and went along the bottom.

Again with an uneasy qualm, Ciaran realised they were headed in the general direction of Ben Beatha.

The old legends had been gradually lost in the stream of time, except to people who cared for such things, or made a living from singing about them, like Ciaran. But in spite of that Ben Beatha was taboo.

The chief reason was physical. The Plains, still called Forbidden, ringed the mountain like a protective wall, and it was an indisputable fact whether you liked it or not that people who went out onto them didn't come back. Hunger, thirst, wild beasts, or devils – they didn't come back. That discouraged a lot of travelling.

Besides, the only reason for attempting to reach Ben Beatha was the legend of the Stone of Destiny, and people had long ago lost faith in that. Nobody had seen it. Nobody had seen Bas the Immortal who was its god and guardian, nor the androids that were his servants, nor the Kalds that were slaves to both of them.

Long, long ago people were supposed to have seen them. In the beginning, according to the legends, Bas the Immortal had lived in a distant place – a green world where there was only one huge sunball that rose and set regularly, where the sky was sometimes blue and sometimes black and silver, and where the horizon curved down. The manifest idiocy of all that still tickled people so they liked to hear songs about it.

Somewhere on that green world, somehow, Bas had acquired the flaming stone that gave him the power of life and death and destiny. There were a lot of conflicting and confused stories about trouble between Bas and the inhabitants of the funny world with the sky that changed like a woman's fancy. Eventually he was supposed to have gathered up a lot of these inhabitants through the power of the Stone and transported them somehow across a great distance to the world where they now lived.

Ciaran had found that children loved these yarns particularly. Their imaginations were still elastic enough not to see the ridiculous side. He always gave the Distance Cycle a lot of schmaltz.

So after Bas the Immortal and his Stone of Destiny had got all these people settled in a new world, Bas created his androids. Khafre and Steud, and brought the Kalds from somewhere out in that vague Distance; another world, perhaps. And there were wars and revolts and raiding parties, and bitter struggles between

Bas and the androids and the humans for power, with Bas always winning because of the Stone. There was a bottomless well of material there for ballads. Ciaran used it frequently.

But the one legend that had always maintained its original shape under the battering of generations was the one about Ben Beatha, the Mountain of Life, being the dwelling place of Bas the Immortal and his androids and the Kalds. And somewhere under Ben Beatha was the Stone, whose possession could give a man life eternal and the powers of whatever god you chose to believe in.

Ciaran had toyed with that one in spite of his scepticism. Now it looked as though he was going to see for himself.

He looked at the Kalds, the creatures who didn't exist, and found his scepticism shaken. Shaken so hard he felt sick with it, like a man waking up to find a nightmare beside him in the flesh, booting his guts in.

If the Kalds were real, the androids were real. From the androids you went to Bas, and from Bas to the Stone of Destiny.

Ciaran began to sweat with sheer excitement.

Mouse jerked her head up suddenly. 'Kiri – listen!'

From somewhere up ahead and to the right there began to come a rhythmic, swinging clank of metal. Underneath it Ciaran made out the shuffle of bare or sandalled feet.

The Kalds urged them on faster with the jewel-tipped wands. The hot opalescence of the tips struck Ciaran all at once. A jewel-fire that could shock a man to unconsciousness like the blow of a fist, just by touching.

The power of the Stone, perhaps. The Stone of Destiny, sleeping under Ben Beatha.

The shuffle and clank got louder. Quite suddenly they came to a place where the gully met another one almost at right angles, and stopped. The ears of the Kalds twitched nervously.

Mouse shrank in closer against Ciaran. She was looking off down the new cut. Ciaran looked, too.

There were Kalds coming toward them. About forty of them, with wands. Walking between their watchful lines were some ninety or a hundred humans, men and women, shackled together by chains run through loops in iron collars. They were so close together they had to lock-step, and any attempt at attacking their guards would have meant the whole column falling flat.

Mouse said, with vicious clarity, 'One man falls into a beast-pit, and in two weeks of gossip a whole town is gone. Hah!'

Ciaran's scarred mouth got ugly. 'Keep going, Mousie. Just keep it up.' He scowled at the slave gang and added, 'But what the hell is it all about? What do they want us for?'

'You'll find out,' said Mouse. 'You and your short cuts.'

Ciaran raised his hand. Mouse ducked and started to swing on him. A couple of Kalds moved in and touched them apart, very delicately, with the wands. They didn't want knockouts this time. Just local numbness.

Ciaran was feeling murderous enough to start something anyway, but a second flick of the wand on the back of his neck took the starch out of him. By that time the slave party had come up and stopped.

Ciaran stumbled over into line and let the Kalds lock the collar around his neck. The man in front of him was huge, with a mane of red hair and cords of muscle on his back the size of Ciaran's arm. He hadn't a stitch on but a leather G-string. His freckled, red-haired skin was slippery with sweat. Ciaran, pressed up against him, shut his mouth tight and began to breathe very hard with his face turned as far away as he could get it.

They shackled Mouse right at the back of him. She put her arms around his waist, tighter than she really had to. Ciaran squeezed her hands.

2

The Kalds started the line moving again, using the wands like ox-goads. They shuffled off down the gully, going deeper and deeper into the Forbidden Plains.

Very softly, so that nobody but Ciaran could hear her, Mouse whispered, 'These locks are nothing. I can pick them any time.'

Ciaran squeezed her hand again. It occurred to him that Mouse was a handy girl to have around.

After a while she said, 'Kiri – that shadow. We did see it?'

'We did.' He shivered in spite of himself.

'What was it?'

'How should I know? And you better save your breath. Looks like a long walk ahead of us.'

It was. They threaded their way through a growing maze of cracks in the plain, cracks that got deeper and deeper, so you had to look straight up to see the red sky and the little floating suns. Ciaran found himself watching furtively to make sure they were still shining. He wished Mousie hadn't reminded him of the shadow. He'd never been closer to cold, clawing panic than in those moments on the ridge.

The rest of the slave gang had obviously come a long way already. They were tired. But the Kalds goaded them on, and it wasn't until about a third of the line was being held up bodily by those in front or behind that a halt was called.

They came to a fairly wide place where three of the gullies came together. The Kalds formed the line into a circle, squeezed in on itself so they were practically sitting in each other's laps, and then stood by watchfully, lolling pink tongues over their bright grey teeth and letting the wands flash in the dimmed light.

Ciaran let his head and shoulders roll over onto Mousie. For some time he had felt her hands working around her own collar, covered by her hair and the harp slung across his back. She wore a rather remarkable metal pin that had other functions than holding her tunic on, and she knew how to use it.

Her collar was still in place, but he knew she could slide out of it now any time she wanted. She bent forward over him as though she was exhausted. Her black hair fell over his face and neck. Under it her small quick hands got busy.

The lock snapped quietly, and the huge red-haired man collapsed slowly on top of Ciaran. His voice whispered, but there was nothing weak about it.

He said, 'Now me.'

Ciaran squirmed and cursed. The vast weight crushed him to silence.

'I'm a hunter. I can hear a rabbit breathing in its warren. I heard the woman speak. Free me or I'll make trouble.'

Ciaran sighed resignedly, and Mouse went to work.

Ciaran looked around the circle of exhausted humans. Charcoal burners, trappers, hoop-shavers – the lean, tough, hard-bitten riff-raff of the border wilderness. Even the women were tough. Ciaran began to get ideas.

There was a man crushed up against them on the other side – the man who had hitherto been at the head of the column. He was tall and stringy like a hungry cat, and just as mean looking, hunched over his knees with his face buried in his forearms and a shag of iron-grey hair falling over his shoulders.

Ciaran nudged him. 'You – don't make any sign. Game to take a chance?'

The shaggy head turned slightly, just enough to unveil an eye. Ciaran wished suddenly he'd kept his mouth shut. The eye was pale, almost white, with a queer unhuman look as though it saw only gods or devils, and nothing in between.

Ciaran had met hermits before in his wanderings. He knew the signs. Normally he rather liked hermits, but this one gave him unpleasant qualms in the stomach.

The man dragged a rusty voice up from somewhere. 'We are enslaved by devils. Only the pure can overcome devils. Are you pure?'

Ciaran managed not to choke. 'As a bird in its nest,' he said. 'A newly fledged bird. In fact, a bird still in the shell.'

The cold, pale eye looked at him without blinking.

Ciaran resisted an impulse to punch it and said, 'We have a means of freeing ourselves. If enough could be free, when the time came we might rush the Kalds.'

'Only the pure can prevail against devils.'

Ciaran gave him a smile of beatific innocence. The scar and the missing tooth rather spoiled the effect, but his eyes made up for it in bland sweetness.

'You shall lead us, Father,' he cooed. 'With such purity as yours, we can't fail.'

The hermit thought about that for a moment and then said, 'I will pass the word. Give me the feke.'

Ciaran's jaw dropped. His eyes got glassy.

'The feke,' said the hermit patiently. 'The jiggler.'

Ciaran closed his eyes. 'Mouse,' he said weakly, 'give the gentleman the picklock.'

Mouse slid it to him, a distance of about two inches. The red-haired giant took some of his weight off Ciaran. Mouse was looking slightly dazed herself.

'Hadn't I better do it for you?' she asked, rather pompously.

The hermit gave her a cold glance. He bent his head and brought his hands up between his knees. His collar-mate on the other side never noticed a thing, and the hermit beat Mouse's time by a good third.

Ciaran laughed. He lay in Mouse's lap and had mild hysterics. Mouse cuffed him furiously across the back of his neck, and even that didn't stop him.

He pulled himself up, looked through streaming eyes at Mouse's murderous small face, and bit his knuckles to keep from screaming.

The hermit was already quietly at work on the man next him.

Ciaran unslung his harp. The grey Kalds hadn't noticed anything yet. Both Mouse and the hermit were very smooth workers. Ciaran plucked out a few sonorous minor chords, and the Kalds flicked their blood-pink eyes at him, but didn't seem to think the harp called for any action.

Ciaran relaxed and played louder.

Under cover of the music he explained his plan to the big red hunter, who nodded and began whispering to his other collar-mate. Ciaran began to sing.

He gave them a lament, one of the wild dark things the Cimmerians sing at the bier of a chief and very appropriate to the occasion. The Kalds lounged, enjoying the rest. They weren't watching for it, so they didn't see, as Ciaran did, the breathing of the word of hope around the circle.

Civilised people would have given the show away. But these were bordermen, as wary and self-contained as animals. It was only in their eyes that you could see anything. They got busy, under cover of their huddled bodies and long-haired, bowed-over heads, with every buckle and pin they could muster.

Mouse and the hermit passed instructions along the line, and since they were people who were used to using their hands with skill, it seemed as though a fair number of locks might get picked. The collars were left carefully in place.

Ciaran finished his lament and was halfway through another when the Kalds decided it was time to go.

They moved in to goad the line back into position. Ciaran's harp crashed out suddenly in angry challenge, and the close-packed circle split into a furious confusion.

Ciaran slung his harp over his shoulder and sprang up, shaking off the collar. All around him was the clash of chain metal on rock, the scuffle of feet, the yells and heavy breathing of angry men. The Kalds came leaping in, their wands flashing. Somebody screamed. Ciaran got a fistful of Mouse's tunic in his left hand and started to butt through the mêlée. He had lost track of the hermit and the hunter.

Then, quite suddenly, it was dark.

Silence closed down on the gully. A black, frozen silence with not even a sound of breathing in it. Ciaran stood still, looking up at the dark sky. He didn't even tremble. He was beyond that.

Black darkness, in a land of eternal light.

Somewhere then, a woman screamed with a terrible mad strength, and hell broke loose.

Ciaran ran. He didn't think about where he was going, only that he had to get away. He was still gripping Mouse. Bodies thrashed and blundered and shrieked in the darkness. Twice he and Mouse were knocked kicking. It didn't stop them.

They broke through finally into a clear space. There began to be light again, pale and feeble at first but flickering back toward normal. They were in a broad gully kicked smooth on the bottom by the passing of many feet. They ran down it.

After a while Mouse fell and Ciaran dropped beside her. He lay there, fighting for breath, twitching and jerking like an animal with sheer panic. He was crying a little because it was light again.

Mouse clung to him, pressing tight as though she wanted to merge her body with his and hide it. She had begun to shake.

'Kiri,' she whispered, over and over again. 'Kiri, what was it?'

Ciaran held her head against his shoulder and stroked it. 'I don't know, honey. But it's all right now. It's gone.'

Gone. But it could come back. It had once. Maybe next time it would stay.

Darkness, and the sudden cold.

The legends began crawling through Ciaran's mind. If Bas the Immortal was true, and the Stone of Destiny was true, and the Stone gave Bas power over the life and death of a world ... then ... ?

Maybe Bas was getting tired of the world and wanted to throw it away.

The rational stubbornness in man that says a thing is not because it's never been before helped Ciaran steady down. But he couldn't kid himself that there hadn't been darkness where no darkness had even been dreamed of before.

He shook his head and started to pull Mouse to her feet, and then his quick ears caught the sound of someone coming toward them, running. Several someones.

There was no place to hide. Ciaran got Mouse behind him and waited, half crouching.

It was the hunter, with the hermit loping like a stringy cat at his heels and a third man behind them both. They all looked a little crazy, and they didn't seem to be going to stop.

Ciaran said, 'Hey!'

They slowed down, looking at him with queer, blank eyes. Ciaran blew up, because he had to relax somehow.

'It's all over now. What are you scared of? It's gone.' He cursed them, with more feeling than fairness. 'What about the Kalds? What happened back there?'

The hunter wiped a huge hand across his red-bearded face. 'Everybody went crazy,' he said thickly. 'Some got killed or hurt. Some got away, like us. The rest were caught again.' He jerked his head back. 'They're coming this way. They're hunting us. They hunt by scent, the grey beasts do.'

'Then we've got to get going.' Ciaran turned around. 'Mouse. You, Mousie! Snap out of it, honey. It's all right now.'

She shivered and choked over her breath, and the hermit fixed them both with pale, mad eyes.

'It was a warning,' he said. 'A portent of judgement when only the pure shall be saved.' He pointed a bony finger at Ciaran. 'I told you that evil could not prevail against devils!'

That got through to Mouse. Sense came back into her black eyes. She took a step toward the hermit and let go.

'Don't you call him evil – or me either! We've never hurt anybody yet, beyond lifting a little food or a trinket. And besides, who the hell are you to talk! Anybody as handy with a picklock as you are has had plenty of practice...'

Mouse paused for breath, and Ciaran got a look at the hermit's face. His stomach quivered. He tried to shut Mouse up, but she was feeling better and beginning to enjoy herself. She plunged into a detailed analysis of the hermit's physique and heredity. She had a vivid and inventive mind.

Ciaran finally got his hand over her mouth, taking care not to get bitten. 'Nice going,' he said, 'but we've got to get out of here. You can finish later.'

She started to heel his shins, and then quite suddenly she stopped and stiffened up under his hands. She was looking at the hermit. Ciaran looked, too. His insides knotted, froze, and began to do tricks.

The hermit said quietly, 'You are finished now.' His pale eyes held them, and there was nothing human about his gaze, or the cold calm of his voice.

'You are evil. You are thieves – and I know, for I was a thief myself. You have the filth of the world on you, and no wish to clean it off.'

He moved toward them. It was hardly a step, hardly more than an inclination of the body, but Ciaran gave back before it.

'I killed a man. I took a life in sin and anger, and now I have made my peace. You have not. You will not. And if need comes, I can kill again – without remorse.'

He could, too. There was nothing ludicrous about him now. He was stating simple fact, and the dignity of him was awesome. Ciaran scowled down at the dust.

'Hell,' he said, 'we're sorry, Father. Mouse has a quick tongue, and we've both had a bad scare. She didn't mean it. We respect any man's conscience.'

There was a cold, hard silence, and then the third man cried out with a sort of subdued fury:

'Let's go! Do you want to get caught again?'

He was a gnarled, knotty, powerful little man, beginning to grizzle but not to slow down. He wore a kilt of skins. His hide was dark and tough as leather, his hazel eyes set in nests of wrinkles.

The hunter, who had been hearing nothing but noises going back and forth over his head, turned and led off down the gully. The others followed, still not speaking.

Ciaran was thinking, He's crazy. He's clear off his head – and of all the things we didn't need, a crazy hermit heads the list!

There was a cold spot between his shoulders that wouldn't go away even when he started sweating with exertion.

The gully was evidently a main trail to Somewhere. There were many signs of recent passage by a lot of people, including an occasional body kicked off to the side and left to dry.

The little knotty man, who was a trapper named Ram, examined the bodies with a terrible stony look in his eyes.

'My wife and my first son,' he said briefly. 'The grey beasts took them while I was gone.'

He turned grimly away.

Ciaran was glad when the bodies proved to be the wrong ones.

Ram and the big red hunter took turns scaling the cleft walls for a look. Mouse said something about taking to the face of the Plains where they wouldn't be hemmed in. They looked at her grimly.

'The grey beasts are up there,' they said. 'Flanking us. If we go up, they'll only take us and chain us again.'

Ciaran's heart took a big, staggering jump. 'In other words, they're herding us. We're going the way they want us to, so they don't bother to round us up.'

The hunter nodded professionally. 'Is a good plan.'

'Oh, fine!' snarled Ciaran. 'What I want to know is, is there any way out?'

The hunter shrugged.

'I'm going on anyway,' said Ram. 'My wife and son...'

Ciaran thought about the Stone of Destiny, and was rather glad there was no decision to make.

They went on, at an easy jog trot. By bits and pieces Ciaran built up the picture – raiding gangs of Kalds coming quietly onto isolated border villages, combing the brush and the forest for stragglers. Where they took the humans, or why, nobody could guess.

The red hunter froze to a dead stop. The others crouched behind him, instinctively holding their breath.

The hunter whispered, 'People. Many of them.' His flat palm made an emphatic move for quiet.

Small cold prickles flared across Ciaran's skin. He found Mouse's hand in his and squeezed it. Suddenly, with no more voice than the sigh of a breeze through bracken, the hermit laughed.

'Judgement,' he whispered. 'Great things moving.' His pale eyes were fey. 'Doom and destruction, a shadow across the world, a darkness and a dying.'

He looked at them one by one, and threw his head back, laughing without sound, the stringy cords working in his throat.

'And of all of you, I *alone* have no fear!'

They went on, slowly, moving without sound in small shapeless puddles of shadow thrown by the floating sunballs. Ciaran found himself almost in the lead, beside the hunter.

They edged around a jog in the cleft wall. About ten feet ahead of them the cleft floor plunged underground, through a low opening shored with heavy timbers.

There were two Kalds lounging in front of it, watching their wands flash in the light.

The five humans stopped. The Kalds came toward them, almost lazily, running rough grey tongues over their shiny teeth. Their blood-pink eyes were bright with pleasure.

Ciaran groaned. 'This is it. Shall we be brave, or just smart?'

The hunter cocked his huge fists. And then Ram let go a queer animal moan. He shoved past Ciaran and went to his knees beside something Ciaran hadn't noticed before.

A woman lay awkwardly against the base of the cliff. She was brown and stringy and not very young, with a plain, good face.

A squat, thick-shouldered boy sprawled almost on top of her. There was a livid burn on the back of his neck. They were both dead.

Ciaran thought probably the woman had dropped from exhaustion, and the kid had died fighting to save her. He felt sick.

Ram put a hand on each of their faces. His own was stony and quite blank. After the first cry he didn't make a sound.

He got up and went for the Kald nearest to him.

3

He did it like an animal, quick and without thinking. The Kald was quick, too. It jabbed the wand at Ram, but the little brown man was coming so fast that it didn't stop him. He must have died in mid-leap, but his body knocked the Kald over and bore him down.

Ciaran followed him in a swift cat leap.

He heard the hunter grunting and snarling somewhere behind him, and the thudding of bare feet being very busy. He lost sight of the other Kald. He lost sight of everything but a muscular grey arm that was trying to pull a jewel-tipped wand from under Ram's corpse. There was a terrible stink of burned flesh.

Ciaran grabbed the grey wrist. He didn't bother with it, or the arm. He slid his grip up to the fingers, got his other hand beside it, and started wrenching.

Bone cracked and split. Ciaran worked desperately, from the thumb and the little finger. Flesh tore. Splinters of grey bone came through. Ciaran's hands slipped in the blood. The grey beast opened its mouth, but no sound came. Ciaran decided then the things were dumb. It was human enough to sweat.

Ciaran grabbed the wand.

A grey paw, the other one, came clawing for his throat around the bulk of Ram's shoulders. He flicked it with the wand. It went away, and Ciaran speared the jewel tip down hard against the Kald's throat.

After a while Mouse's voice came to him from somewhere. 'It's done, Kiri. No use overcooking it.'

It smelled done, all right. Ciaran got up. He looked at the wand in his hand, holding it away off. He whistled.

Mouse said, 'Stop admiring yourself and get going. The hunter says he can hear chains.'

Ciaran looked around. The other Kald lay on the ground. Its neck seemed to be broken. The body of the squat, dark boy lay on top of it. The hunter said:

'He didn't feel the wand. I think he'd be glad to be a club for killing one of them, if he knew it.'

Ciaran said, 'Yeah.' He looked at Mouse. She seemed perfectly healthy. 'Aren't women supposed to faint at things like this?'

She snorted. 'I was born in the Thieves' Quarter. We used to roll skulls instead of pennies. They weren't so scarce.'

'I think,' said Ciaran, 'the next time I get married I'll ask more questions. Let's go.'

They went down the ramp leading under the Forbidden Plains. The hunter led, like a wary beast. Ciaran brought up the rear. They both carried the stolen wands.

The hermit hadn't spoken a word, or moved a hand to help.

It was fairly dark there underground, but not cold. In fact, it was hotter than outside, and got worse as they went down. Ciaran could hear a sound like a hundred armourers beating on shields. Only louder. There was a feeling of a lot of people moving around but not talking much, and an occasional crash or metallic screaming that Ciaran didn't have any explanation for. He found himself not liking it.

They went a fairish way on an easy down-slope, and then the light got brighter. The hunter whispered, 'Careful!' and slowed down. They drifted like four ghosts through an archway into a glow of clear bluish light.

They stood on a narrow ledge. Just here it was hand-smoothed, but on both sides it ran in nature-eroded roughness into a jumble of stalactites and wind-galleries. Above the ledge, in near darkness, was the high roof arch, and straight ahead, there was just space. Eventually, a long way off, Ciaran made out a wall of rock.

Below there was a pit. It was roughly barrel-shaped. It was deep. It was so deep that Ciaran had to crane over the edge to see bottom. Brilliant blue-white flares made it brighter than daylight about two-thirds of the way up the barrel.

There were human beings labouring in the glare. They were tiny things no bigger than ants from this height. They wore no chains, and Ciaran couldn't see any guards. But after the first look he quit worrying about any of that. The Thing growing up in the pit took all his attention.

It was built of metal. It rose and spread in intricate swooping curves of shining whiteness, filling the whole lower part of the cavern. Ciaran stared at it with a curious numb feeling of awe.

The thing wasn't finished. He had not the faintest idea what it was for. But he was suddenly terrified of it.

It was more than just the sheer crushing size of it, or the unfamiliar metallic construction that was like nothing he had seen or even dreamed of before. It was the thing itself.

It was Power. It was Strength. It was a Titan growing there in the belly of the world, getting ready to reach out and grip it and play with it, like Mouse gambling with an empty skull.

He knew, looking at it, that no human brain in his own scale and time of existence had conceived that shining monster, nor shaped of itself one smallest part of it.

The red hunter said simply, 'I'm scared. And this smells like a trap.'

Ciaran swallowed something that might have been his heart. 'We're in it, pal, like it or don't. And we'd better get out of sight before that chain-gang runs into us.'

Off to the side, along the rough part of the ledge where there were shadows and holes and pillars of rock, seemed the best bet. There was a way down to the cavern floor – a dizzy zig-zag of ledges, ladders, and steps. But once on it you were stuck, and without cover.

They edged off, going as fast as they dared. Mouse was breathing rather heavily and her face was white enough to make the brand show like a blood-drop between her brows.

The hermit seemed to be moving in a private world of his own. The sight of the shining giant had brought a queer blaze to his eyes, something Ciaran couldn't read and didn't like. Otherwise, he might as well have been dead. He hadn't spoken since he cursed them, back in the gully.

They crouched down out of sight among a forest of stalactites. Ciaran watched the ledge. He whispered, 'They hunt by scent?'

The hunter nodded. 'I think the other humans will cover us. Too many scents in this place. But how did they have those two waiting for us at the cave mouth?'

Ciaran shrugged. 'Telepathy. Thought transference. Lots of the backwater people have it. Why not the Kalds?'

'You don't,' said the hunter, 'think of them as having human minds.'

'Don't kid yourself. They think, all right. They're not human, but they're not true animals either.'

'Did they think *that*?' The hunter pointed at the pit.

'No,' said Ciaran slowly. 'They didn't.'

'Then who—' He broke off. 'Quiet! Here they come.'

Ciaran held his breath, peering one-eyed around a stalactite. The slave gang, with the grey guards, began to file out of the tunnel and down the steep descent to the bottom. There was no trouble. There was no trouble left in any of those people. There were several empty collars. There were also fewer Kalds. Some had stayed outside to track down the four murderous fugitives, which meant no escape at that end.

Ciaran got an idea. When the last of the line and the guards were safely over the edge he whispered, 'Come on. We'll go down right on their tails.'

Mouse gave him a startled look. He said impatiently, 'They won't be looking back and up – I hope. And there won't be anybody else coming up while they're going down. You've got a better idea about getting down off this bloody perch, spill it!'

She didn't have, and the hunter nodded. 'Is good. Let's go.'

They went, like the very devil. Since all were professionals in their own line they didn't make any more fuss than so many leaves falling. The hermit followed silently. His pale eyes went to the shining monster in the pit at every opportunity.

He was fermenting some idea in his shaggy head. Ciaran had a hunch the safest thing would be to quietly trip him off into space. He resisted it, simply because knifing a man in a brawl was one thing and murdering an unsuspecting elderly man in cold blood was another.

Later, he swore a solemn oath to drop humanitarianism, but hard.

Nobody saw them. The Kalds and the people below were all too busy not breaking their necks to have eyes for anything else. Nobody came down behind them – a risk they had had to run. They were careful to keep a whole section of the descent between them and the slave gang.

It was a hell of a long way down. The metal monster grew and grew and slid up beside them, and then above them, towering against the vault. It was beautiful. Ciaran loved its beauty even while he hated and feared its strength.

Then he realised there were people working on it, clinging like flies to its white beams and arches. Some worked with wands not very different from the one he carried, fusing metal joints in a sparkle of hot light. Others guided the huge metal pieces into place, bringing them up from the floor of the cavern on long ropes and fitting them delicately.

With a peculiar dizzy sensation, Ciaran realised there was no more weight to the metal than if it were feathers.

He prayed they could get past those workers without being seen, or at least without having an alarm spread. The four of them crawled down past two or three groups of them safely, and then one man, working fairly close to the cliff, raised his head and stared straight at them.

Ciaran began to make frantic signs. The man paid no attention to them. Ciaran got a good look at his eyes. He let his hands drop.

'He doesn't see us,' whispered Mouse slowly. 'Is he blind?'

The man turned back to his work. It was an intricate fitting of small parts into a pierced frame. Work that in all his wanderings Ciaran had never seen done anywhere, in any fashion.

He shivered. 'No. He just – doesn't see us.'

The big hunter licked his lips nervously, like a beast in a deadfall. His eyes glittered. The hermit laughed without any sound. They went on.

It was the same all the way down. Men and women looked at them, but didn't see.

In one place they paused to let the slave gang get farther ahead. There was a woman working not far out. She looked like a starved cat, gaunt ribs showing through torn rags. Her face was twisted with the sheer effort of breathing, but there was no expression in her eyes.

Quite suddenly, in the middle of an unfinished gesture, she collapsed like wet leather and fell. Ciaran knew she was dead before her feet cleared the beam she was sitting on.

That happened twice more on the way down. Nobody paid any attention.

Mouse wiped moisture off her forehead and glared at Ciaran. 'A fine place to spend a honeymoon. You and your lousy short cuts!'

For once Ciaran had no impulse to cuff her.

The last portion of the descent was covered by the backs of metal lean-tos full of heat and clamour. The four slipped away into dense shadow between two of them, crouched behind a mound of scrap. They had a good view of what happened to the slave gang.

The Kalds guided it out between massive pillars of white metal that held up the giant web overhead. Fires flared around the cliff foot. A hot blue-white glare beat down, partly from some unfamiliar light-sources fastened in the girders, partly from the mouths of furnaces hot beyond any heat Ciaran had ever dreamed of.

Men and women toiled sweating in the smoke and glare, and never looked at the newcomers in their chains. There were no guards.

The Kalds stopped the line in a clear space beyond the shacks and waited. They were all facing the same way, expectant, showing their bright grey teeth and rolling their blood-pink eyes.

Ciaran's gaze followed theirs. He got rigid suddenly, and the sweat on him turned cold as dew on a toad's back.

He thought at first it was a man, walking down between the pillars. It was man-shaped, tall and slender and strong, and sheathed from crown to heels in white mesh metal that shimmered like bright water.

But when it came closer he knew he was wrong. Some animal instinct in him knew even before his mind did. He wanted to snarl and put up his hackles, and tuck in his tail and run.

The creature was sexless. The flesh of its hands and face had a strange unreal texture, and a dusky yellow tinge that never came in living flesh.

Its face was human enough in space – thin, with light angular bones. Only it was regular and perfect like something done carefully in marble, with no human softness or irregularity. The lips were bloodless. There was no hair, not even any eyelashes.

The eyes in that face were what set Ciaran's guts to knotting like a nest of cold snakes. They were not even remotely human. They were like pools of oil under the lashless lids – black, deep, impenetrable, without heart or soul or warmth.

But wise. Wise with a knowledge beyond humanity, and strong with a cold, terrible strength. And old. There were none of the usual signs of age. It was more than that. It was a psychic, unhuman feel of antiquity; a time that ran back and back and still back to an origin as unnatural as the body it spawned.

Ciaran knew what it was. He had made songs about the creature and sung them in crowded market-places and smoky wine-shops. He'd scared children with it, and made grown people shiver while they laughed.

He wasn't singing now. He wasn't laughing. He was looking at one of the androids of Bas the Immortal – a creature born of the mysterious power of the Stone, with no faintest link to humanity in its body or its brain.

Ciaran knew then whose mind had created the shining monster towering above them. And he knew more than ever that it was evil.

The android walked out onto a platform facing the slave gang, so that it was above them, where they could all see. In its right hand it carried a staff of white metal with a round ball on top. The staff and the mesh-metal sheath it wore blazed bright silver in the glare.

The chained humans raised their heads. Ciaran saw the white

scared glint of their eyeballs, heard the hard suck of breath and the uneasy clashing of link metal.

The Kalds made warning gestures with their wands, but they were watching the android.

It raised the staff suddenly, high over its head. The gesture put the ball top out of Ciaran's sight behind a girder. And then the lights dimmed and went out.

For a moment there was total darkness, except for the dull marginal glow of the forges and furnaces. Then, from behind the girder that hid the top of the staff, a glorious opaline light burst out, filling the space between the giant pillars, reaching out and up into the dim air with banners of shimmering flame.

The Kalds crouched down in attitudes of worship, their blood-pink eyes like sentient coals. A trembling ran through the line of slaves, as though a wind had passed across them and shaken them like wheat. A few cried out, but the sounds were muffled quickly to silence. They stood still, staring up at the light.

The android neither moved nor spoke, standing like a silver lance.

Ciaran got up. He didn't know that he did it. He was distantly aware of Mouse beside him, breathing hard through an open mouth and catching opaline sparks in her black eyes. There was other movement, but he paid no attention.

He wanted to get closer to the light. He wanted to see what made it. He wanted to bathe in it. He could feel it pulsing in him, sparkling in his blood. He also wanted to run away, but the desire was stronger than the fear. It even made the fear rather pleasurable.

He was starting to climb over the pile of scrap when the android spoke. Its voice was light, clear, and carrying. There was nothing menacing about it. But it stopped Ciaran like a blow in the face, penetrating even through his semi-drugged yearning for the light.

He knew sound. He knew mood. He was as sensitive to them as his own harp in the way he made his living. He felt what was in that voice; or rather, what wasn't in it. And he stopped, dead still.

It was a voice speaking out of a place where no emotion, as

humanity knew the word, had ever existed. It came from a brain as alien and incomprehensible as darkness in a world of eternal light; a brain no human could ever touch or understand, except to feel the cold weight of its strength and cower as a beast cowers before the terrible mystery of fire.

'Sleep,' said the android. 'Sleep, and listen to my voice. Open your minds, and listen.'

4

Through a swimming rainbow haze Ciaran saw the relaxed, dull faces of the slaves.

'You are nothing. You are no one. You exist only to serve; to work; to obey. Do you hear and understand?'

The line of humans swayed and made a small moaning sigh. It held nothing but amazement and desire. They repeated the litany through thick animal mouths.

'Your minds are open to mine. You will hear my thoughts. Once told, you will not forget. You will feel hunger and thirst, but not weariness. You will have no need to stop and rest, or sleep.'

Again the litany. Ciaran passed a hand over his face. He was sweating. In spite of himself the light and the soulless, mesmeric voice were getting him. He hit his own jaw with his knuckles, thanking whatever gods there were that the source of the light had been hidden from him. He knew he could never have bucked it.

More, perhaps, of the power of the Stone of Destiny?

A sudden sharp rattle of fragments brought his attention to the scrap heap. The hermit was already half way over it.

And Mouse was right at his heels.

Ciaran went after her. The rubble slipped and slid, and she was already out of reach. He called her name in desperation. She didn't hear him. She was hungry for the light.

Ciaran flung himself bodily over the rubbish. Out on the

floor, the nearest Kalds were shaking off their daze of worship. The hermit was scrambling on all fours, like a huge grey cat.

Mouse's crimson tunic stayed just out of reach. Ciaran threw a handful of metal fragments at her back. She turned her head and snarled at him. She didn't see him. Almost as an automatic reflex she hurled some stuff at his face, but she didn't even slow down. The hermit cried out, a high, eerie scream.

A huge hand closed on Ciaran's ankle and hauled him back. He fought it, jabbing with the wand he still carried. A second remorseless hand prisoned his wrist.

The red hunter said dispassionately, 'They come. We go.'

'Mouse! Let me go, damn you! *Mouse!*'

'You can't help her. We go, quick.'

Ciaran went on kicking and thrashing.

The hunter banged him over the ear with exquisite judgement, took the wand out of his limp hand and tossed him over one vast shoulder. The light hadn't affected the hunter much. He'd been in deeper shadow than the others, and his half-animal nerves had warned him quicker even than Ciaran's. Being a wise wild thing, he had shut his eyes at once.

He doubled behind the metal sheds and began to run in dense shadow.

Ciaran heard and felt things from a great misty distance. He heard the hermit yell again, a crazy votive cry of worship. He felt the painful jarring of his body and smelled the animal rankness of the hunter.

He heard Mouse scream, just once.

He tried to move; to get up and do something. The hunter slammed him hard across the kidneys. Ciaran was aware briefly that the lights were coming on again. After that it got very dark and very quiet.

The hunter breathed in his ear, 'Quiet! Don't move.'

There wasn't much chance of Ciaran doing anything. The hunter lay on top of him with one freckled paw covering most of his face. Ciaran gasped and rolled his eyes.

They lay in a troughed niche of rough stone. There was black shadow on them from an overhang, but the blue glare burned beyond it. Even as he watched it dimmed and flickered and then steadied again.

High up over his head the shining metal monster reached for the roof of the cavern. It had grown. It had grown enormously, and a mechanism was taking shape inside it; a maze of delicate rods and crystal prisms, of wheels and balances and things Ciaran hadn't any name for.

Then he remembered about Mouse, and nothing else mattered.

The hunter lay on him, crushing him to silence. Ciaran's blue eyes blazed. He'd have killed the hunter then, if there had been any way to do it. There wasn't. Presently he stopped fighting.

Again the red giant breathed in his ear: 'Look over the edge.'

He took his hand away. Very, very quietly, Ciaran raised his head a few inches and looked over.

Their niche was some fifteen feet above the floor of the pit. Below and to the right was the mouth of a square tunnel. The crowded, sweating confusion of the forges and workshops spread out before them, with people swarming like ants after a rain.

Standing at the tunnel mouth were two creatures in shining metal sheaths – the androids of Bas the Immortal.

Their clear, light voices rose up to where Ciaran and the hunter lay.

'Did you find out?'

'Failing – as we judged. Otherwise, no change.'

'No change.' One of the slim unhumans turned and looked with its depthless black eyes at the soaring metal giant. 'If we can only finish it in time!'

The other said, 'We can, Khafre. We must.'

Khafre made a quick, impatient gesture. 'We need more slaves! These human cattle are frail. You drive them, and they die.'

'The Kalds...'

'Are doing what they can. Two more chains have just come. But it's still not enough to be safe! I've told the beasts to raid farther in, even to the border cities if they have to.'

'It won't help if the humans attack us before we're done.'

Khafre laughed. There was nothing pleasant or remotely humorous about it.

'*If* they could track the Kalds this far, we could handle them easily. After we're finished, of course, they'll be subjugated anyway.'

The other nodded. Faintly uneasy, it said, 'If we finish in time. If we don't ...'

'If we don't,' said Khafre, 'none of it matters, to them or us or the Immortal Bas.' Something that might have been a shudder passed over its shining body. Then it threw back its head and laughed again, high and clear.

'But we will finish it, Steud! We're unique in the universe, and nothing can stop us. This means the end of boredom, of servitude and imprisonment. With this world in our hands, nothing can stop us!'

Steud whispered, 'Nothing!' Then they moved away, disappearing into the seething clamour of the floor.

The red hunter said, 'What were they talking about?'

Ciaran shook his head. His eyes were hard and curiously remote. 'I don't know.'

'I don't like the smell of it, little man. It's bad.'

'Yeah.' Ciaran's voice was very steady. 'What happened to Mouse?'

'She was taken with the others. Believe me, little man – I had to do what I did or they'd have taken you, too. There was nothing you could do to help her.'

'She – followed the light.'

'I think so. But I had to run fast.'

There was a mist over Ciaran's sight. His heart was slugging him. Not because he particularly cared, he asked, 'How did we get away? I thought I saw the big lights come on ...'

'They did. And then they went off again, all of a sudden. They weren't expecting it. I had a head start. The grey beasts hunt by scent, but in that stewpot there are too many scents. They lost us, and when the lights came on again I saw this niche and managed to climb to it without being seen.'

He looked out over the floor, scratching his red beard. 'I think they're too busy to bother about two people. No, three.' He chuckled. 'The hermit got away, too. He ran past me in the dark, screaming like an ape about revelations and The Light. Maybe they've got him again by now.'

Ciaran wasn't worrying about the hermit. 'Subjugation,' he said slowly. 'With this world in their hands, nothing can stop them.' He looked out across the floor of the pit. No guards. You didn't need any guards when you had a weapon like that light. Frail human cattle driven till they died, and not knowing about it nor caring.

The world in their hands. An empty shell for them to play with, to use as they wanted. No more market places, no more taverns, no more songs. No more little people living their little lives the way they wanted to. Just slaves with blank faces, herded by grey beasts with shining wands and held by the androids' light.

He didn't know why the androids wanted the world or what they were going to do with it. He only knew that the whole thing made him sick – sick all through, in a way he'd never felt before.

The fact that what he was going to do was hopeless and crazy never occurred to him. Nothing occurred to him, except that somewhere in that seething slave-pen Mouse was labouring, with eyes that didn't see and a brain that was only an open channel for orders. Pretty soon, like the woman up on the girder, she was going to hit her limit and die.

Ciaran said abruptly, 'If you want to kill a snake, what do you do?'

'Cut off its head, of course.'

Ciaran got his feet under him. 'The Stone of Destiny,' he whispered. 'The power of life and death. Do you believe in legends?'

The hunter shrugged. 'I believe in my hands. They're all I know.'

'I'm going to need your hands, to help me break one legend and built another!'

'They're yours, little man. Where do we go?'

'Down that tunnel. Because, if I'm not clear off, that leads to Ben Beatha, and Bas the Immortal – and the Stone.'

Almost as though it were a signal, the blue glare dimmed and flickered. In the semi-darkness Ciaran and the hunter dropped down from the niche and went into the tunnel.

It was dark, with only tiny spots of blue radiance at wide intervals along the walls. They had gone quite a distance before these strengthened to their normal brightness, and even then it was fairly dark. It seemed to be deserted.

The hunter kept stopping to listen. When Ciaran asked irritably what was wrong, he said:

'I think there's someone behind us. I'm not sure.'

'Well, give him a jab with the wand if he gets too close. Hurry up!'

The tunnel led straight toward Ben Beatha, judging from its position in the pit. Ciaran was almost running when the hunter caught his shoulder urgently.

'Wait! There's movement up ahead ...'

He motioned Ciaran down. On their hands and knees they crawled forward, holding their wands ready.

A slight bend in the tunnel revealed a fork. One arm ran straight ahead. The other bent sharply upward, toward the surface.

There were four Kalds crouched on the rock between them, playing some obscure game with human finger bones.

Ciaran got his weight over his toes and moved fast. The hunter went beside him. Neither of them made a sound. The Kalds were intent on their game and not expecting trouble.

The two men might have got away with it, only that suddenly from behind them, someone screamed like an angry cat.

Ciaran's head jerked around, just long enough to let him see the hermit standing in the tunnel, with his stringy arms lifted and his grey hair flying, and a light of pure insanity blazing in his pale eyes.

'Evil!' he shrieked. 'You are evil to defy The Light, and the servants of The Light!'

He seemed to have forgotten all about calling the Kalds demons a little while before.

The grey beasts leaped up, moving in quickly with their wands ready. Ciaran yelled with sheer fury. He went for them, the rags of his yellow tunic streaming.

He wasn't quite clear about what happened after that. There was a lot of motion, grey bodies leaping and twisting and jewel-tips flashing. Something flicked him stunningly across the temple. He fought in a sort of detached fog where everything was blurred and distant. The hermit went on screaming about Evil and The Light. The hunter bellowed a couple of times, things thudded and crashed, and once Ciaran poked his wand straight into a blood-pink eye.

Sometime right after that there was a confused rush of running feet back in the tunnel. The hunter was down. And Ciaran found himself running up the incline, because the other way was suddenly choked with Kalds.

He got away. He was never sure how. Probably instinct warned him to go in time so that, in the confusion, he was out of sight before the reinforcements saw him. Three of the original four Kalds were down and the fourth was busy with the hermit. Anyway, for the moment, he made it.

When he staggered finally from the mouth of the ramp, drenched with sweat and gasping, he was back on the Forbidden Plains and Ben Beatha towered above him – a great golden Titan reaching for the red sky.

The tumbled yellow rock of its steep slopes was barren of any growing thing. There were no signs of buildings, or anything built by hands, human or otherwise. High up, almost in the apex of the triangular peak, was a square, balconied opening that might have been only a wind-eroded niche in the cliff-face.

Ciaran stood on widespread legs, studying the mountain with sullen stubborn eyes. He believed in legend, now. It was all he believed in. Somewhere under the golden peak was the Stone of Destiny and the demigod who was its master.

Behind him were the creatures of that demigod, and the monster they were building – and a little black-haired Mouse who was going to die unless something was done about it.

A lot of other people, too. A whole sane comfortable world. But Mouse was about all he could handle, just then.

He wasn't Ciaran the bard any longer. He wasn't a human, attached to a normal human world. He moved in a strange land of gods and demons, where everything was as mad as a drunkard's nightmare, and Mouse was the only thing that held him at all to the memory of a life wherein men and women fought and laughed and loved.

His scarred mouth twitched and tightened. He started off across the rolling, barren rise to Ben Beatha – a tough, bandy-legged little man in yellow rags, with a brown, expressionless face and a forgotten harp slung between his shoulders, moving at a steady gypsy lope.

A wind sighed over the Forbidden Plains, rolling the sunballs in the red sky. And then, from the crest of Ben Beatha, the darkness came.

This time Ciaran didn't stop to be afraid. There was nothing left inside him to be afraid with. He remembered the hermit's words: *Judgement. Great things moving. Doom and destruction, a shadow across the world, a darkness and a dying*. Something of the same feeling came to him, but he wasn't human any longer. He was beyond fear. Fate moved, and he was part of it.

Stones and shade tricked his feet in the darkness. All across the Forbidden Plains there was night and a wailing wind and a sharp chill of cold. Far, far away there was a faint red glow on the sky where the sea burned with its own fire.

Ciaran went on.

Overhead, then, the sunballs began to flicker. Little striving ripples of light went out across them, lighting the barrens with an eerie witch-glow. The flickering was worse than the darkness. It was like the last struggling pulse of a dying man's heart. Ciaran was aware of a coldness in him beyond the chill of the wind.

A shadow across the world, a darkness and a dying...

He began to climb Ben Beatha.

5

The stone was rough and fairly broken, and Ciaran had climbed mountains before. He crawled upward, through the sick light and the cold wind that screamed and fought him harder the higher he got. He retained no very clear memory of the climb. Only after a long, long time he fell inward over the wall of a balcony and lay still.

He was bleeding from rock-tears and his heart kicked him like the heel of a vicious horse. But he didn't care. The balcony was man-made, the passage at the back of it led somewhere – and the light had come back in the sky.

It wasn't quite the same, though. It was weaker, and less warm.

When he could stand up he went in along the passage, square-hewn in the living rock of Ben Beatha, the Mountain of Life.

It led straight in, lit by a soft opaline glow from hidden light-sources. Presently it turned at right angles and became a spiral ramp, leading down.

Corridors led back from it at various levels, but Ciaran didn't bother about them. They were dark, and the dust of ages lay unmarked on their floors.

Down and down, a long, long way. Silence. The deep uncaring silence of death and the eternal rock – dark titans who watched the small furious ant-scurryings of man and never, never for one moment, gave a damn.

And then the ramp flattened into a broad high passage cut deep in the belly of the mountain. And the passage led to a door of gold, twelve feet high and intricately graved and pierced, set with symbols that Ciaran had heard of only in legend: the *Hun-Lahun-Mehen*, the Snake, the Circle, and the Cross, blazing in hot jewel-fires.

But above them, crushing and dominant on both valves of the great door, was the *crux ansata*, the symbol of eternal life, cut from some lustreless stone so black it was like a pattern of blindness on the eyeball.

Ciaran shivered and drew a deep, unsteady breath. One brief moment of human terror came to him. Then he set his two hands on the door and pushed it open.

He came into a small room hung with tapestries and lit dimly by the same opaline glow as the hallway. The half-seen pictures showed men and beasts and battles against a background at once tantalisingly familiar and frighteningly alien.

There was a rug on the floor. It was made from the head and hide of a creature Ciaran had never even dreamed of before – a thing like a huge tawny cat with a dark mane and great, shining fangs.

Ciaran padded softly across it and pushed aside the heavy curtains at the other end.

At first there was only darkness. It seemed to fill a large space; Ciaran had an instinctive feeling of size. He went out into it, very cautiously, and then his eyes found a pale glow ahead in the blackness, as though someone had crushed a pearl with his thumb and smeared it across the dark.

He was a thief and a gypsy. He made no more sound than a wisp of cloud, drifting toward it. His feet touched a broad, shallow step, and then another. He climbed, and the pearly glow grew stronger and became a curving wall of radiance.

He stopped just short of touching it, on a level platform high above the floor. He squinted against its curdled, milky thickness, trying to see through.

Wrapped in the light, cradled and protected by it like a bird in the heart of a shining cloud, a boy slept on a couch made soft with furs and coloured silks. He was quite naked, his limbs flung out carelessly with the slim angular grace of his youth. His skin was white as milk, catching a pale warmth from the light.

He slept deeply. He might almost have been dead, except for the slight rise and fall of his breathing. His head was rolled over so that he faced Ciaran, his cheek pillowed on his upflung arm.

His hair, thick, curly, and black almost to blueness, had grown out long across his forearm, across the white fur beneath it, and down onto his wide slim shoulders. The nails of his lax hand, palm up above his head, stood up through the hair. They were inches long.

His face was just a boy's face. A good face, even rather handsome, with strong bone just beginning to show under the roundness. His cheek was still soft as a girl's, the lashes of his closed lids dark and heavy.

He looked peaceful, even happy. His mouth was curved in a vague smile, as though his dreams were pleasant. And yet there was something there ...

A shadow. Something unseen and untouchable, something as fragile as the note of a shepherd's pipe brought from far off on a vagrant breeze. Something as indescribable as death – and as broodingly powerful. Ciaran sensed it, and his nerves throbbed suddenly like the strings of his own harp.

He saw then that the couch the boy slept on was a huge *crux ansata*, cut from the dead-black stone, with the arms stretching from under his shoulders and the loop like a monstrous halo above his head.

The legends whispered through Ciaran's head. The songs, the tales, the folklore. The symbolism, and the image-patterns.

Bas the Immortal was always described as a giant, like the mountain he lived in, and old, because Immortal suggests age. Awe, fear, and unbelief spoke through those legends, and the child-desire to build tall. But there was an older legend ...

Ciaran, because he was a gypsy and a thief and had music in him like a drunkard has wine, had heard it, deep in the black forests of Hyperborea where even gypsies seldom go. The oldest legend of all – the tale of the Shining Youth from Beyond, who walked in beauty and power, who never grew old, and who carried in his heart a bitter darkness that no one could understand.

The Shining Youth from Beyond. A boy sleeping with a smile on his face, walled in living light.

Ciaran stood still, staring. His face was loose and quite blank. His heartbeats shook him slightly, and his breath had a rusty sound in his open mouth.

After a long time he started forward, into the light.

It struck him, hurled him back numbed and dazed. Thinking of Mouse, he tried it twice more before he was convinced. Then he tried yelling. His voice crashed back at him from the unseen walls, but the sleeping boy never stirred, never altered even the rhythm of his breathing.

After that Ciaran crouched in the awful laxness of impotency, and thought about Mouse, and cried.

Then, quite suddenly, without any warning at all, the wall of light vanished.

He didn't believe it. But he put his hand out again, and nothing stopped it, so he rushed forward in the pitch blackness until he hit the stone arm of the cross. And behind him, and all around him, the light began to glow again.

Only now it was different. It flickered and dimmed and struggled, like something fighting not to die. Like something else ...

Like the sunballs. Like the light in the sky that meant life to a world. Flickering and feeble like an old man's heart, the last frightened wing-beats of a dying bird ...

A terror took Ciaran by the throat and stopped the breath in it, and turned his body colder than a corpse. He watched ...

The light glowed and pulsed, and grew stronger. Presently he was walled in by it, but it seemed fainter than before.

A terrible feeling of urgency came over Ciaran, a need for haste. The words of the androids came back to him: *Failing, as we judged. If we finish in time. If we don't, none of it matters.*

A shadow across the world, a darkness and a dying. Mouse slaving with empty eyes to build a shining monster that would harness the world to the wills of nonhuman brains.

It didn't make sense, but it meant something. Something deadly important. And the key to the whole mad jumble was here – a dark-haired boy dreaming on a stone cross.

Ciaran moved closer. He saw then that the boy had stirred, very slightly, and that his face was troubled. It was as though the dimming of the light had disturbed him. Then he sighed and smiled again, nestling his head deeper into the bend of his arm.

'Bas,' said Ciaran. 'Lord Bas!'

His voice sounded hoarse and queer. The boy didn't hear him. He called again, louder. Then he put his hand on one slim white shoulder and shook it hesitantly at first, and then hard, and harder.

The boy Bas didn't even flicker his eyelids.

Ciaran beat his fists against the empty air and cursed without any voice. Then, almost instinctively, he crouched on the stone platform and took his harp in his hands.

It wasn't because he expected to do anything with it. It was simply that harping was as natural to him as breathing, and what was inside him had to come out some way. He wasn't thinking about music. He was thinking about Mouse, and it just added up to the same thing.

Random chords at first, rippling up against the wall of milky light. Then the agony in him began to run out through his fingertips onto the strings, and he sent it thrumming strong across the still air. It sang wild and savage, but underneath it there was the sound of his own heart breaking, and the fall of tears.

There was no time. There wasn't even any Ciaran. There was only the harp crying a dirge for a black-haired Mouse and the world she lived in. Nothing mattered but that. Nothing would ever matter.

Then finally there wasn't anything left for the harp to cry about. The last quiver of the strings went throbbing off into a dull emptiness, and there was only an ugly little man in yellow rags crouched silent by a stone cross, hiding his face in his hands.

Then, faint and distant, like the echo of words spoken in another world, another time:

Don't draw the veil. Marsali – don't . . . !

Ciaran looked up, stiffening. The boy's lips moved. His face, the eyes still closed, was twisted in an agony of pleading. His hands were raised, reaching, trying to hold something that slipped through his fingers like mist.

Dark mist. The mist of dreams. It was still in his eyes when he opened them. Grey eyes, clouded and veiled, and then with the dream-mist thickening into tears . . .

He cried out, '*Marsali!*' as though his heart was ripped out of him with the breath that said it. Then he lay still on the couch, his eyes staring unfocused at the milky light, with the tears running out of them.

Ciaran said softly, 'Lord Bas . . .'

'Awake,' whispered the boy. 'I'm awake again. Music – a harp crying out . . . I didn't want to wake! Oh, God, I didn't want to!'

He sat up suddenly. The rage, the sheer blind fury in his young face rocked Ciaran like a blow of a fist.

'Who waked me? Who dared to wake me?'

There was no place to run. The light held him. And there was Mouse. Ciaran said:

'I did, Lord Bas. There was need to.'

The boy's grey eyes came slowly to focus on his face. Ciaran's heart kicked once and stopped beating. A great cold stillness breathed from somewhere beyond the world and walled him in, closer and tighter than the milky light. Close and tight, like the packed earth of a grave.

A boy's face, round and smooth and soft. No shadow even of down on the cheeks, the lips still pink and girlish. Long dark lashes, and under them ...

Grey eyes. Old with suffering, old with pain, old with an age beyond human understanding. Eyes that had seen birth and life and death in an endless stream, flowing by just out of reach, just beyond hearing. Eyes looking out between the bars of a private hell that was never built for any man before.

One strong young hand reached down among the furs and silks and felt for something, and Ciaran knew the thing was death.

Ciaran, suddenly, was furious himself.

He struck a harsh, snarling chord on the harpstrings, thinking of Mouse. He poured his fury out in bitter, pungent words, the gypsy argot of the Quarters, and all the time Bas fumbled to get the hidden weapon in his hands.

It was the long nails that saved Ciaran's life. They kept Bas from closing his fingers, and in the meantime some of Ciaran's vibrant rage had penetrated. Bas whispered:

'You love a woman.'

'Yeah,' said Ciaran. 'Yeah.'

'So do I. A woman I created, and made to live in my dreams. Do you know what you did when you waked me?'

'Maybe I saved the world. If the legends are right, you built it. You haven't any right to let it die so you can sleep.'

'I built another world, little man. Marsali's world. I don't want to leave it.' He bent forward, toward Ciaran. 'I was happy in that world. I built it to suit me. I belong in it. Do you know why? Because it's made from my own dreams, as I want it. Even the people. Even Marsali. Even myself.

'They drove me away from one world. I built another, but it was no different. I'm not human. I don't belong with humans, nor in any world they live in. So I learned to sleep, and dream.'

He lay back on the couch. He looked pitifully young, with the long lashes hiding his eyes.

'Go away. Let your little world crumble. It's doomed anyway. What difference do a few life-spans make in eternity? Let me sleep.'

Ciaran struck the harp again. '*No!* Listen ...'

He told Bas about the slave gangs, the androids, the shining monster in the pit – and the darkness that swept over the world. It was the last that caught the boy's attention.

He sat up slowly. 'Darkness? You! How did you get to me, past the light?'

Ciaran told him.

'The Stone of Destiny,' whispered the Immortal. Suddenly he laughed. He laughed to fill the whole dark space beyond the light; terrible laughter, full of hate and a queer perverted triumph.

He stopped, as suddenly as he had begun, and spread his hands flat on the coloured silks, the long nails gleaming like knives. His eyes widened, grey windows into a deep hell, and his voice was no more than a breath.

'Could that mean that I will die, too?'

Ciaran's scarred mouth twitched. 'The Stone of Destiny ...'

The boy leaped up from his couch. His hand swept over some hidden control in the arm of the stone cross, and the milky light died out. At the same time, an opaline glow suffused the darkness beyond.

Bas the Immortal ran down the steps – a dark-haired, graceful boy running naked in the heart of an opal.

Ciaran followed.

They came to the hollow core of Ben Beatha – a vast pyramidal space cut in the yellow rock. Bas stopped, and Ciaran stopped behind him.

The whole space was laced and twined and webbed with crystal. Rods of it, screens of it, meshes of it. A shining helix ran straight up overhead, into a shaft that seemed to go clear through to open air.

In the crystal, pulsing along it like the life-blood in a man's veins, there was light.

It was like no light Ciaran had ever seen before. It was no colour, and every colour. It seared the eye with heat, and yet it was cold and pure like still water. It throbbed and beat. It was alive.

Ciaran followed the crystal maze down and down, to the base of it. There, in the very heart of it, lying at the hub of a shining web, lay *something*.

Like a black hand slammed across the eyeballs, darkness fell.

For a moment he was blind, and through the blindness came a soft whisper of movement. Then there was light again; a vague smeared spot of it on the pitch black.

It glowed and faded and glowed again. The rusty gleam slid across the half-crouched body of Bas the Immortal, pressed close against the crystal web. It caught in his eyes, turning them hot and lambent like beast-eyes in the dark of a cave-mouth.

Little sparks of hell-fire in a boy's face, staring at the Stone of Destiny.

A stone no bigger than a man's heart, with power in it. Even dying, it had power. Power to build a world, or smash it. Power never born of Ciaran's planet, or any planet, but something naked and perfect – an egg from the womb of space itself.

It fought to live, lying in its crystal web. It was like watching somebody's heart stripped clean and struggling to beat. The fire in it flickered and flared, sending pale witch-lights dancing up along the crystal maze.

Outside, Ciaran knew, all across the world, the sunballs were pulsing and flickering to the dying beat of the Stone.

Bas whispered, 'It's over. Over and done.'

Without knowing it, Ciaran touched the harpstrings and made them shudder. 'The legends were right, then. The Stone of Destiny kept the world alive.'

'Alive. It gave light and warmth, and before that it powered the ship that brought me here across space, from the third planet of our sun to the tenth. It sealed the gaps in the planet's crust and drove the machinery that filled the hollow core inside with air. It was my strength. It built my world; *my* world, where I would be loved and respected – all right, and worshipped!'

He laughed, a small bitter sob.

'A child I was. After all those centuries, still a child playing with a toy.'

His voice rang out louder across the flickering dimness. A boy's voice, clear and sweet. he wasn't talking to Ciaran. He wasn't even talking to himself. He was talking to Fate, and cursing it.

'I took a walk one morning. That was all I did. I was just a fisherman's son walking on the green hills of Atlantis above the sea. That was all I wanted to be – a fisherman's son, someday to be a fisherman myself, with sons of my own. And then from nowhere, out of the sky, the meteorite fell. There was thunder, and a great light, and then darkness. And when I woke again I was a god.

'I took the Stone of Destiny out of its broken shell. The light from it burned in me, and I was a god. And I was happy. *I didn't know.*

'I was too young to be a god. A boy who never grew older. A boy who wanted to play with other boys, and couldn't. A boy who wanted to age, to grow a beard and a man's voice, and find a woman to love. It was hell, after the thrill wore off. It was worse, when my mind and heart grew up, and my body didn't.

'And they said I was no god, but a blasphemy, a freak.

'The priests of Dagon, of all the temples of Atlantis, spoke against me. I had to run away. I roamed the whole earth before the Flood, carrying the Stone. Sometimes I ruled for centuries, a god-king, but always the people tired of me and rose against me. They hated me, because I lived forever and never grew old.

'A man they might have accepted. But a boy! A brain with all the wisdom it could borrow from time, grown so far from theirs that it was hard to talk to them – and a body too young even for the games of manhood!'

Ciaran stood frozen, shrinking from the hell in the boy-god's agonised voice.

'So I grew to hate them, and when they drove me out I turned on them, and used the power of the Stone to destroy. I know what happened to the cities of the Gobi, to Angkor, and the temples of Mayapan! So the people hated me more because they feared me more, and I was alone. No one has ever been alone as I was.

'So I built my own world, here in the heart of a dead planet.

And in the end it was the same, because the people were human and I was not. I created the androids, freaks like myself, to stand between me and my people – my own creatures, that I could trust. And I built a third world, in my dreams.

'And now the Stone of Destiny has come to the end of its strength. Its atoms are eaten away by its own fire. The world it powered will die. And what will happen to me? Will I go on living, even after my body is frozen in the cold dark?'

Silence, then. The pulsing beat of light in the crystal rods. The heart of a world on its deathbed.

Ciaran's harp crashed out. It made the crystal sing. His voice came with it:

'Bas! The monster in the pit, that the androids are building – I know now what it is! They knew the Stone was dying. They're going to have power of their own, and take the world. You can't let them, Bas! You brought us here. We're your people. You can't let the androids have us!'

The boy laughed, a low, bitter sound. 'What do I care for your world or your people? I only want to sleep.' He caught his breath in and turned around, as though he was going back to the place of the stone cross.

6

Ciaran stroked the harpstrings. 'Wait ...' It was all humanity crying out of the harp. Little people, lost and frightened and pleading for help. No voice could have said what it said. It was Ciaran himself, a channel for the unthinking pain inside him.

'Wait. You were human once. You were young. You laughed and quarrelled and ate and slept, and you were free. That's all we ask. Just those things. Remember Bas the fisherman's son, and help us.'

Grey eyes looking at him. Grey eyes looking from a boy's face. 'How could I help you even if I wanted to?'

'There's some power left in the Stone. And the androids are

your creatures. You made them. You can destroy them. If you could do it before they finish this thing – from the way they spoke, they mean to destroy you with it.'

Bas laughed.

Ciaran's hand struck a terrible chord from the harp, and fell away.

Bas said heavily, 'They'll draw power from the gravitic force of the planet and broadcast it the same way. It will never stop as long as the planet spins. If they finish it in time, the world will live. If they don't ...' He shrugged. 'What difference does it make?'

'So,' whispered Ciaran, 'we have a choice of a quick death, or a lingering one. We can die free, on our own feet, or we can die slaves.' His voice rose to a full-throated shout. '*God! You're no god!* You're a selfish brat sulking in a corner. All right, go back to your Marsali! And I'll play god for a minute.'

He raised the harp.

'I'll play god, and give 'em the clean way out!'

He drew his arm back to throw – to smash the crystal web. And then, with blinding suddenness, there was light again.

They stood frozen, the two of them, blinking in the hot opalescence. Then their eyes were drawn to the crystal web.

The Stone of Destiny still fluttered like a dying heart, and the crystal rods were dim.

Ciaran whispered, 'It's too late. They're finished.'

Silence again. They stood almost as though they were waiting for something, hardly breathing, with Ciaran still holding the silent harp in his hand.

Very, very faintly, under his fingers, the strings began to thrum.

Vibration. In a minute Ciaran could hear it in the crystal. It was like the buzz and strum of insects just out of earshot. He said:

'What's that?'

The boy's ears were duller than his. But presently he smiled and said, 'So that's how they're going to do it. Vibration, that will shake Ben Beatha into a cloud of dust, and me with it. They must believe I'm still asleep.' He shrugged. 'What matter? It's death.'

Ciaran slung the harp across his back. There was a curious finality in the action.

'There's a way from here into the pit. Where is it?'

Bas pointed across the open space. Ciaran started walking. He didn't say anything.

Bas said, 'Where are you going?'

'Back to Mouse,' said Ciaran simply.

'To die with her.' The crystal maze hummed eerily. 'I wish I could see Marsali again.'

Ciaran stopped. He spoke over his shoulder, without expression. 'The death of the Stone doesn't mean your death, does it?'

'No. The first exposure to its light when it landed, blazing with the heat of friction, made permanent changes in the cell structure of my body. I'm independent of it – as the androids are of the culture vats they grew in.'

'And the new power source will take up where the Stone left off?'

'Yes. Even the wall of rays that protected me and fed my body while I slept will go on. The power of the Stone was broadcast to it, and to the sunballs. There were no mechanical leads.'

Ciaran said softly, 'And you love this Marsali? You're happy in this dream world you created? You could go back there?'

'Yes,' whispered Bas. 'Yes. Yes!'

Ciaran turned. 'Then help us destroy the androids. Give us our world, and we'll give you yours. If we fail – well, we have nothing to lose.'

Silence. The crystal web hummed and sang – death whispering across the world. The Stone of Destiny throbbed like the breast of a dying bird. The boy's grey eyes were veiled and remote. It seemed almost that he was asleep.

Then he smiled – the drowsy smile of pleasure he had worn when Ciaran found him, dreaming on the stone cross.

'Marsali,' he whispered. 'Marsali.'

He moved forward then, reaching out across the crystal web. The long nails on his fingers scooped up the Stone of Destiny, cradled it, caged it in.

Bas the Immortal said, 'Let's go, little man.'

Ciaran didn't say anything. He looked at Bas. His eyes were wet. Then he got the harp in his hands again and struck it, and the thundering chords shook the crystal maze to answering music.

It drowned the faint death-whisper. And then, caught between two vibrations, the shining rods split and fell, with a shiver of sound like the ringing of distant bells.

Ciaran turned and went down the passage to the pit. Behind him came the dark-haired boy with the Stone of Destiny in his hands.

They came along the lower arm of the fork where Ciaran and the hunter had fought the Kalds. There were four of the grey beasts still on guard.

Ciaran had pulled the wand from his girdle. The Kalds started up, and Ciaran got ready to fight them. But Bas said, 'Wait.'

He stepped forward. The Kalds watched him with their blood-pink eyes, yawning and whimpering with animal nervousness. The boy's dark gaze burned. The grey brutes cringed and shivered and then dropped flat, hiding their faces against the stone.

'Telepaths,' said Bas to Ciaran, 'and obedient to the strongest mind. The androids know that. The Kalds weren't put there to stop me physically, but to send the androids warning if I came.'

Ciaran shivered. 'So they'll be waiting.'

'Yes, little man. They'll be waiting.'

They went down the long tunnel and stepped out on the floor of the pit.

It was curiously silent. The fires had died in the forges. There was no sound of hammering, no motion. Only blazing lights and a great stillness, like someone holding his breath. There was no one in sight.

The metal monster climbed up the pit. It was finished now. The intricate maze of grids and balances in its belly murmured with the strength that spun up through it from the core of the planet. It was like a vast spider, making an invisible thread of power to wrap around the world and hold it, to be sucked dry.

An army of Kalds began to move on silent feet, out from the screening tangle of sheds and machinery.

The androids weren't serious about that. It was just a skirmish, a test to see whether Bas had been weakened by his age-long sleep. He hadn't been. The Kalds looked at the Stone of Destiny and from there to Bas's grey eyes, cringed, whimpered, and lay flat.

Bas whispered, 'Their minds are closed to me, but I can feel – the androids are working, preparing some trap ...'

His eyes were closed now, his young face set with concentration. 'They don't want me to see, but my mind is older than theirs, and better trained, and I have the power of the Stone. I can see a control panel. It directs the force of their machine ...'

He began to move, then, rapidly, out across the floor. His eyes were still closed. It seemed he didn't need them for seeing.

People began to come out from behind the sheds and the cooling forges. Blank-faced people with empty eyes. Many of them, making a wall of themselves against Bas.

Ciaran cried out, '*Mouse* ... !'

She was there. Her body was there, thin and erect in the crimson tunic. Her black hair was still wild around her small brown face. But Mouse, the Mouse that Ciaran knew, was dead behind her dull black eyes. Ciaran whispered, '*Mouse* ...'

The slaves flowed in and held the two of them, clogged in a mass of unresponsive bodies.

'Can't you free them, Bas?'

'Not yet. Not now. There isn't time.'

'Can't you do with them what you did with the Kalds?'

'The androids control their minds through hypnosis. If I fought that control, the struggle would blast their minds to death or idiocy. And there isn't time ...' There was sweat on his smooth young forehead. 'I've got to get through. I don't want to kill them ...'

Ciaran looked at Mouse. 'No,' he said hoarsely.

'But I may have to, unless ... Wait! I can channel the power of the Stone through my own brain, because there's an affinity between us. Vibration, cell to cell. The androids won't have made a definite command against music. Perhaps I can jar their minds open, just enough, that you can call them with your harp, as you called me.'

A tremor almost of pain ran through the boy's body.

'Lead them away, Ciaran. Lead them as far as you can. Otherwise many of them will die. And hurry!'

Bas raised the Stone of Destiny in his clasped hands and pressed it to his forehead. And Ciaran took his harp.

He was looking at Mouse when he set the strings to singing. That was why it wasn't hard to play as he did. It was something from him to Mouse. A prayer. A promise. His heart held out on a song.

The music rippled out across the packed mass of humanity. At first they didn't hear it. Then there was a stirring and a sigh, a dumb, blind reaching. Somewhere the message was getting through the darkness clouding their minds. A message of hope. A memory of red sunlight on green hills, of laughter and home and love.

Ciaran let the music die to a whisper under his fingers, and the people moved forward, toward him, wanting to hear.

He began to walk away, slowly, trailing the harp-song over his shoulder – and they followed. Haltingly, in twos and threes, until the whole mass broke and flowed like water in his wake.

Bas was gone, his slim young body slipping fast through the broken ranks of the crowd.

Ciaran caught one more glimpse of Mouse before he lost her among the others. She was crying, without knowing or remembering why.

If Bas died, if Bas was defeated, she would never know nor remember.

Ciaran led them as far as he could, clear to the wall of the pit. He stopped playing. They stopped, too, standing like cattle, looking at nothing, with eyes turned inward to their clouded dreams.

Ciaran left them there, running out alone across the empty floor.

He followed the direction Bas had taken. He ran, fast, but it was like a nightmare where you run and run and never get anywhere. The lights glared down and the metal monster sighed and churned high up over his head, and there was no other sound, no other movement but his own.

Then, abruptly, the lights went out.

He stumbled on, hitting brutally against unseen pillars, falling and scrambling in scrap heaps. And after an eternity he saw light again, up ahead.

The Light he had seen before, here in the pit. The glorious opalescent light that drew a man's mind and held it fast to be chained.

Ciaran crept in closer.

There was a control panel on a stone dais – a meaningless jumbled mass of dials and wires. The androids stood before it. One of them was bent over, its yellowish hands working delicately with the controls. The other stood erect beside it, holding a staff. The metal ball at the top was open, spilling the opalescent blaze into the darkness.

Ciaran crouched in the shelter of a pillar, shielding his eyes. Even now he wanted to walk into that light and be its slave.

The android with the staff said harshly, 'Can't you find the wavelength? He should have been dead by now.'

The bending one tensed and then straightened, the burning light sparkling across its metal sheath. Its eyes were black and limitless, like evil itself, and no more human.

'Yes,' it said. 'I have it.'

The light began to burst stronger from the staff, a swirling dangerous fury of it.

Ciaran was hardly breathing. The light-source, whatever it was, was part of the power of the Stone of Destiny. Wavelengths meant nothing to him, but it seemed the danger was to the Stone – and Bas carried it.

The android touched the staff. The light died, clipped off as the metal ball closed.

'If there's any power left in the Stone,' it whispered, 'our power-wave will blast its subatomic reserve – and Bas the Immortal with it!'

Silence. And then in the pitch darkness a coal began to glow.

It came closer. It grew brighter, and a smudged reflection behind and above it became the head and shoulders of Bas the Immortal.

The android whispered, 'Stronger! *Hurry!*'

A yellowish hand made a quick adjustment. The Stone of Destiny burned brighter. It burst with light. It was like a sunball, stabbing its hot fury into the darkness.

The android whispered, '*More!*'

The Stone filled all the pit with a deadly blaze of glory.

Bas stopped, looking up at the dais. He grinned. A naked boy, beautiful with youth, his grey eyes veiled and sleepy under dark lashes.

He threw the Stone of Destiny up on the dais. An idle boy tossing stones at a treetop.

Light. An explosion of it, without sound, without physical force. Ciaran dropped flat on his face behind the pillar. After a long time he raised his head again. The overhead lights were on, and Bas stood on the dais beside two twisted, shining lumps of mad-made soulless men.

The android flesh had taken the radiation as leather takes heat, warping, twisting, turning black.

'Poor freaks,' said Bas softly. 'They were like me, with no place in the universe that belonged to them. So they dreamed, too – only their dreams were evil.'

He stooped and picked up something – a dull, dark stone, a thing with no more life nor light than a waterworn pebble.

He sighed and rolled it once between his palms, and let it drop.

'If they had had time to learn their new machine a little better, I would never have lived to reach them in time.' He glanced down at Ciaran, standing uncertainly below. 'Thanks to you, little man, they didn't have quite time enough.'

He gestured to a staff. 'Bring it, and I'll free your Mouse.'

7

A long time afterward Mouse and Ciaran and Bas the Immortal stood in the opal-tinted glow of the great room of the *crux ansata*. Outside the world was normal again, and safe. Bas had left full instructions about controlling and tending the centrifugal power plant.

The slaves were freed, going home across the Forbidden Plains – forbidden no longer. The Kalds were sleeping, mercifully; the big sleep from which they would never wake. The world was free, for humanity to make or mar on its own responsibility.

Mouse stood very close to Ciaran, her arm around his waist, his around her shoulders. Crimson rags mingling with yellow; fair shaggy hair mixing with black. Bas smiled at them.

'Now,' he said, 'I can be happy, until the planet itself is dead.'

'You won't stay with us? Our gratitude, our love...'

'Will be gone with the coming generations. No, little man. I built myself a world where I belong – the only world where I can ever belong. And I'll be happier in it than any of you, because it *is* my world – free of strife and ugliness and suffering. A beautiful world, for me and Marsali.'

There was a radiance about him that Ciaran would put into a song some day, only half understanding.

'I don't envy you,' whispered Bas, and smiled. Youth smiling in a spring dawn. 'Think of us sometimes, and be jealous.'

He turned and walked away, going lightly over the wide stone floor and up the steps to the dais. Ciaran struck the harpstrings. He sent the music flooding up against the high vault, filling all the rocky space with a thrumming melody.

He sang. The tune he had sung for Mouse, on the ridge above the burning sea. A simple tune, about two people in love.

Bas lay down on the couch of furs and coloured silks, soft on the shaft of the stone cross. He looked back at them once, smiling. One slim white arm raised in a brief salute and swept down across the black stone.

The milky light rose on the platform. It wavered, curdled, and thickened to a wall of warm pearl. Through it, for a moment, they could see him, his dark head pillowed on his forearm, his body sprawled in careless, angular grace. Then there was only the warm, soft shell of light.

Ciaran's harp whispered to silence. The tunnel into the pit was sealed. Mouse and Ciaran went out through the golden doors and closed them, very quietly – doors that would never be opened again as long as the world lived.

Then they came into each other's arms, and kissed.

Rough, tight arms on living flesh, lips that bruised and breaths that mingled, hot with life. Temper and passion, empty bellies, a harp that sang in crowded market squares, and no roof to fight under but the open sky.

And Ciaran didn't envy the dark-haired boy, dreaming on the stone cross.

TERROR OUT OF SPACE

1

Lundy was flying the aero-space convertible by himself. He'd been doing it for a long time. So long that the bottom half of him was dead to the toes and the top half even deader, except for two separate aches like ulcerated teeth; one in his back, one in his head.

Thick pearly-grey Venusian sky went past the speeding flier in streamers of torn cloud. The rockets throbbed and pounded. Instruments jerked erratically under the swirl of magnetic currents that makes the Venusian atmosphere such a swell place for pilots to go nuts in.

Jackie Smith was still out cold in the copilot's seat. From in back, beyond the closed door to the tiny inner cabin, Lundy could hear Farrell screaming and fighting.

He'd been screaming a long time. Ever since the shot of *avertin* Lundy had given him after he was taken had begun to wear thin. Fighting the straps and screaming, a hoarse jarring sound with no sense in it.

Screaming to be free, because of *It*.

Somewhere inside of Lundy, inside the tumpled, sweat-soaked black uniform of the Tri-World Police, Special Branch, and the five-foot-six of thick springy muscle under it, there was a knot. It was a large knot, and it was very, very cold in spite of the sweltering heat in the cabin, and it had a nasty habit of yanking itself tight every few minutes, causing Lundy to jerk and sweat as though he'd been spiked.

Lundy didn't like that cold tight knot in his belly. It meant he was afraid. He'd been afraid before, plenty of times, and he wasn't ashamed of it. But right now he needed all the brains and guts he had to get *It* back to Special headquarters at Vhia, and he didn't want to have to fight himself, too.

Fear can screw things for you. It can make you weak when you need to be strong, if you're going to go on living. You, and the two other guys depending on you.

Lundy hoped he could keep from getting too much afraid, and too tired – because It was sitting back there in its little strongbox in the safe, waiting for somebody to crack.

Farrell was cracked wide open, of course, but he was tied down. Jackie Smith had begun to show signs before he passed out, so that Lundy had kept one hand over the anaesthetic needle gun holstered on the side of his chair. And Lundy thought,

The hell of it is, you don't know when It *starts to work on you. There's no set pattern, or if there is we don't know it. Maybe right now the readings I see on those dials aren't there at all ...*

Down below the torn grey clouds he could see occasional small patches of ocean. The black, still, tideless water of Venus, that covers so many secrets of the planet's past.

It didn't help Lundy any. It could be right or wrong, depending on what part of the ocean it was – and there was no way to tell. He hoped nothing would happen to the motors. A guy could get awfully wet, out in the middle of that still black water.

Farrell went on screaming. His throat seemed to be lined with impervium. Screaming and fighting the straps, because *It* was locked up and calling for help.

'I'm cold,' he said. 'Hi, Midget.'

Lundy turned his head. Normally he had a round, fresh, merry face, with bright dark eyes and a white, small-boyish grin. Now he looked like something the waiter had swept out from under a table at four AM on New Year's Day.

'You're cold,' he said sourly. He licked sweat off his lips. 'Oh, fine! That was all I needed.'

Jackie Smith stirred slightly, groaned, to joggle himself. His black tunic was open over his chest, showing the white strapping of bandages, and his left hand was thrust in over the locked top of the tunic's zipper. He was a big man, not any older than Lundy, with big, ugly, pleasant features, a shock of coarse pale hair, and skin like old leather.

'On Mercury, where I was born,' he said, 'the climate is suitable for human beings. You Old-World pantywaists ...' He broke off, turned white under the leathery burn, and said

83

through set teeth, 'Oi! Farrell sure did a good job on me.'

'You'll live,' said Lundy. He tried not to think about how close both he and Smith had come to not living. Farrell had put up one hell of a fight, when they caught up with him in a native village high up in the Mountains of White Cloud.

Lundy still felt sick about that. The bull-meat, the hard boys, you didn't mind kicking around. But Farrell wasn't that kind. He was just a nice guy that got trapped by something too big for him.

A nice guy, crazy blind in love with somebody that didn't exist. A decent hardworking guy with a wife and two kids who'd lost his mind, heart, and soul to a Thing from outer space, so that he was willing to kill to protect *It*.

Oh, hell! thought Lundy wearily, *won't he ever stop screaming?*

The rockets beat and thundered. The torn grey sky whipped past. Jackie Smith sat rigid, with closed eyes, white around the lips and breathing in shallow, careful gasps. And Vhia still a long way off.

Maybe farther off than he knew. Maybe he wasn't heading toward Vhia at all. Maybe *It* was working on him, and he'd never know it till he crashed.

The cold knot tightened in his belly like a cold blade stabbing.

Lundy cursed. Thinking things like that was a sure way to punch your ticket right straight to blazes.

But you couldn't help thinking, about *It*. The Thing you had caught in a special net of tight-woven metal mesh, aiming at something Farrell could see but you couldn't. The Thing you had forced into the glassite box and covered up with a black cloth, because you had been warned not to look at *It*.

Lundy's hands tingled and burned, not unpleasantly. He could still feel the small savage Thing fighting him, hidden in the net. It had felt vaguely cylindrical, and terribly alive.

Life. Life from outer space, swept out of a cloud of cosmic dust by the gravitic pull of Venus. Since Venus had hit the cloud there had been a wave of strange madnesses on the planet. Madnesses like Farrell's that had led to murder, and some things even worse.

Scientists had some ideas about that life from Out There. They'd had a lucky break and found one of The Things, dead, and there were vague stories going around of a crystalline-appearing substance that wasn't really crystal, about three inches long and magnificently etched and fluted, and supplied with some odd little gadgets nobody would venture an opinion about.

But the Thing didn't do them much good, dead. They had to have one alive, if they were going to find out what made it tick and learn how to put a stop to what the telecommentators had chosen to call The Madness from Beyond, or The Vampire Lure.

One thing about it everybody knew. The guys who suddenly went sluggy and charged off the rails all made it clear that they had met the ultimate Dream Woman of all women and all dreams. Nobody else could see her, but that didn't bother them any. They saw her, and she was – *She*. And her eyes were always veiled.

And *She* was a whiz at hypnosis and mind-control. That's why *She*, or *It*, hadn't been caught alive before. Not before Lundy and Smith, with every scientific aid Special could give them, had tracked down Farrell and managed to get the breaks.

The breaks. Plain fool luck. Lundy moved his throbbing head stiffly on his aching neck, blinked sweat out of his bloodshot eyes, and wished to hell he was home in bed.

Jackie Smith said suddenly, 'Midget, I'm cold. Get me a blanket.'

Lundy looked at him. His pale green eyes were half open, but not as though they saw anything. He was shivering.

'I can't leave the controls, Jackie.'

'Nuts. I've got one hand. I can hang onto this lousy tin fish that long.'

Lundy scowled. He knew Smith wasn't kidding about the cold. The temperatures on Mercury made the first-generation colonists sensitive to anything below the range of an electric furnace. With the wound and all, Smith might wind up with pneumonia if he wasn't covered.

'Okay.' Lundy reached out and closed the switch marked A. 'But I'll let Mike do the flying. He can probably last five minutes before he blows his guts out.'

Iron Mike was just a pattycake when it came to Venusian atmosphere flying. The constant magnetic compensation heated the robot coils to the fusing point in practically no time at all.

Lundy thought fleetingly that it was nice to know there were still a couple of things men could do better than machinery.

He got up, feeling like something that had stood outside rusting for four hundred years or so. Smith didn't turn his head. Lundy growled at him.

'Next time, sonny, you wear your long woollen undies and let me alone!'

Then he stopped. The knot jerked tight in his stomach. Cold sweat needled him, and his nerves stung in a swift rush of fire.

Farrell had quit screaming.

There was silence in the ship. Nothing touched it. The rockets were outside it and didn't matter. Even Jackie Smith's careful breathing had stopped. Lundy went forward slowly, toward the door. Two steps.

It opened. Lundy stopped again, quite still.

Farrell was standing in the opening. A nice guy with a wife and two kids. His face still looked like that, but the eyes in it were not sane, nor even human.

Lundy had tied him down to the bunk with four heavy straps. Breast, belly, thighs, and feet. The marks of them were on Farrell. They were cut into his shirt and pants, into his flesh and sinew, deep enough to show his bare white ribs. There was blood. A lot of blood. Farrell didn't mind.

'I broke the straps,' he said. He smiled at Lundy. 'She called me and I broke the straps.'

He started to walk to the safe in the corner of the cabin. Lundy gagged and pulled himself up out of a cold black cloud and got his feet to moving.

Jackie Smith said quietly, 'Hold it, Midget. She doesn't like it there in the safe. She's cold and wants to come out.'

Lundy looked over his shoulder. Smith was hunched around in his seat, holding the needle-gun from Lundy's holster on the pilot's chair. His pale green eyes had a distant, dreamy glow, but Lundy knew better than to trust it.

He said, without inflection, 'You've seen *Her*.'

'No. No, but – I've heard her.' Smith's heavy lips twitched and parted. The breath sucked through between them, hoarse and slow.

Farrell went down on his knees beside the safe. He put his hands on its blank and gleaming face and turned to Lundy. He was crying.

'Open it. You've got to open it. She wants to come out. She's frightened.'

Jackie Smith raised the gun, a fraction of an inch. 'Open it, Midget,' he whispered. 'She's cold in there.'

Lundy stood still. The sweat ran on him and he was colder than a frog's belly in the rain; and for no reason at all he said thickly,

'No. *She*'s hot. *She* can't breathe in there. *She*'s hot.'

Then he jerked his head up and yelled. He came around to face Smith, unsteady but fast, and started for him.

Smith's ugly face twisted as though he might be going to cry. 'Midget! I don't want to shoot you. Open the safe!'

Lundy said, 'You damned fool,' with no voice at all, and went on.

Smith hit the firing stud.

The anaesthetic needles hit Lundy across the chest. They didn't hurt much. Just a stinging prick. He kept going. No reason. It was just something he seemed to be doing at the time.

Behind him Farrell whimpered once like a puppy and lay down across the little safe. He didn't move again. Lundy got down on his hands and knees and reached in a vague sort of way for the controls. Jackie Smith watched him with dazed green eyes.

Quite suddenly, Iron Mike blew his guts out.

The control panel let go a burst of blue flame. The glare and heat of it knocked Lundy backward. Things hissed and snarled and ran together, and the convertible began to dance like a leaf in a gale. The automatic safety cut the rockets dead.

The ship began to fall.

Smith said something that sounded like *She* and folded up his chair. Lundy rubbed his hands across his face. The lines of it were blurred and stupid. His dark eyes had no sense in them.

He began to crawl over the lurching floor toward the safe.

The clouds outside ripped and tore across the ship's nose, and presently only water showed. Black, still, tideless water dotted with little islands of floating weed that stirred and slithered with a life of their own.

Black water, rushing up.

Lundy didn't care. He crawled through Farrell's blood, and he didn't care about that, either. He pushed Farrell's body back against the cabin wall and began to scratch at the shiny door, making noises like a hound shut out and not happy about it.

The ship hit the water with a terrific smack. Spray geysered up, dead white against the black sea, fell back, and closed in. Presently even the ripples went away.

Dark green weed-islands twined sinuously upon themselves, a flock of small seadragons flapped their jewelled wings down and began to fish, and none of them cared at all about the ship sinking away under them.

Not even Lundy cared, out cold in the space-tight cabin, with his body wedged up against the safe and tears drying with the sweat on his stubbled cheeks.

2

The first thing Lundy knew about was the stillness. A dead feeling, as though everything in creation had stopped breathing.

The second thing was his body. It hurt, like hell, and it was hot, and it didn't like the thick, foul air it was getting. Lundy pushed himself into a sitting position and tried to boot his brain into action. It was hard work, because someone had split his head open four ways with an axe.

It wasn't really dark in the cabin. A wavering silver glow almost like moonlight came in through the ports. Lundy could see pretty well. He could see Farrell's body sprawled out on the floor, and a mess of junk that had once been equipment.

He could see the safe.

He looked at it a long time. There wasn't much to look at.

Just an open safe with nothing in it, and a piece of black cloth dropped on the floor.

'Oh, Lord,' whispered Lundy. 'Oh, my Lord!'

Everything hit him at once then. There wasn't much in him but his stomach, and that was tied down. But it tried hard to come up. Presently the spasms stopped, and then Lundy heard the knocking.

It wasn't very loud. It had a slow, easy rhythm, as though the knocker had a lot of time and didn't care when he got in. It came from the airlock panel.

Lundy got up. Slowly, cold as a toad's belly and as white. His lips drew back from his teeth and stayed there, frozen.

The knocking kept on. A sleepy kind of sound. The guy outside could afford to wait. Sometime that locked door was going to open, and he could wait. He wasn't in a hurry. He would never be in a hurry.

Lundy looked all around the cabin. He didn't speak. He looked sideways out of the port. There was water out there. The black sea-water of Venus; clear and black, like deep night.

There was level sand spreading away from the ship. The silver light came up out of it. Some kind of phosphorescence, as bright as moonlight and faintly tinged with green.

Black sea-water. Silver sand. The guy kept on knocking at the door. Slow and easy. Patient. One – two. One – two. Just off beat with Lundy's heart.

Lundy went to the inner cabin, walking steadily. He looked around carefully and then went back. He stopped by the lock panel.

'Okay, Jackie,' he said. 'In a minute. In a minute, boy.'

Then he turned and went very fast to the port locker and got a quart bottle out of its shock cradle, and raised it. It took both hands.

After a while he dropped the bottle and stood still, not looking at anything, until he stopped shaking. Then he pulled his vac-suit down off its hook and climbed into it. His face was grey and quite blank.

He took all the oxygen cylinders he could carry, emergency rations, and all the benzedrine in the medicine kit. He put the limit dose of the stimulant down on top of the brandy before he locked his helmet. He didn't bother with the needle gun. He took the two Service blasters – his own, and Smith's. The gentle knocking didn't stop.

He stood for a moment looking at the open safe and the black cloth dropped beside it. Something cruel came into his face. A tightness, a twitching and setting of muscles, and a terrible look of patience.

Being under water wouldn't bother a Thing from outer space. He reached up and lifted the net of tight-woven metal-mesh down off its hook and fastened it on his belt. Then he walked over and opened the airlock door.

Black water swirled in around his weighted boots, and then the door opened wide and Jackie Smith came in.

He'd been waiting in the flooded lock-chamber. Kicking his boots against the inner door, easy, with the slow breathing of the sea. Now the water pushed his feet down and held him upright from behind, so he could walk in and stand looking at Lundy. A big blond man with green eyes, and white bandages strapped under his open black tunic, looking at Lundy. Not long. Only for a second. But long enough.

Lundy stopped himself after the third scream. He had to, because he knew if he screamed again he'd never stop. By that time the black water had pushed Jackie Smith away, over to the opposite wall, and covered his face.

'Oh, Lord,' whispered Lundy. 'Oh, Lord, *what did he see before he drowned?*'

No one answered. The black water pushed at Lundy, rising high around him, trying to take him over to Jackie Smith. Lundy's mouth began to twitch.

He shut his teeth on his lower lip, holding it, holding his throat. He began to run, clumsily, fighting the water, and then he stopped that, too. He walked, not looking behind him, cut into the flooded lock. The door slid shut behind him, automatically.

He walked out across the firm green-silver sand, swallowing the blood that ran in his mouth and choked him.

He didn't hurry. He was going to be walking for a long, long time. From the position of the ship when it fell he ought to be able to make it to the coast – unless *It* had been working on him so the figures on the dials hadn't been there at all.

He checked his direction, adjusted the pressure-control in his vac-suit, and plodded on in the eerie undersea moonlight. It wasn't hard going. If he didn't hit a deep somewhere, or meet something too big to handle, or furnish a meal for some species of hungry Venus-weed, he ought to live to face up to the Old Man at H.Q. and tell him two men were dead, the ship lost, and the job messed to hell and gone.

It was beautiful down there. Like the dream-worlds you see when you're doped or delirious. The phosphorescence rose up into the black water and danced there in wavering whorls of cold fire. Fish, queer gaudy little things with jewelled eyes, flicked past Lundy in darts of sudden colour, and there were great stands of weed like young forests, spangling the dark water and the phosphorescent glow with huge burning spots of blue and purple and green and silver.

Flowers. Lundy got too close to some of them once. They reached out and opened round mouths full of spines and sucked at him hungrily. The fish gave them a wide berth. After that, so did Lundy.

He hadn't been walking more than half an hour when he hit the road.

It was a perfectly good road, running straight across the sand. Here and there it was cracked, with some of the huge square blocks pushed up or tipped aside, but it was still a good road, going somewhere.

Lundy stood looking at it with cold prickles running up and down his spine. He'd heard about things like this. Nobody knew an awful lot about Venus yet. It was a young, tough, be-damned-to-you planet, and it was apt to give the snoopy scientific guys a good swift boot in their store teeth.

But even a young planet has a long past and stories get around. Legends, songs, folk tales. It was pretty well accepted that a lot of Venus that was under water now hadn't been once, and vice versa. The old girl had her little whimsies while doing the preliminary mock-up of her permanent face.

So once upon a time this road had crossed a plain under a hot pearl-grey sky, going somewhere. Taking caravans from the seacoast, probably. Bales of spices and spider-silk and casks of *vakhi* from the Nahali canebrakes, and silver-haired slavegirls from the high lands of the Cloud People, going along under sultry green *liha*-trees to be sold.

Now it crossed a plain of glowing sand under still black water. The only trees that shadowed it were tall weeds with brilliant, hungry flowers, and the only creatures that followed it were little fish with jewelled eyes. But it was still there, still ready, still going somewhere.

It was headed the same way Lundy was. It must have made a bend somewhere and turned to meet him. Lundy licked cold sweat off his lips and stepped out on it.

He stepped slow and careful, like a man coming alone down the aisle of an empty church.

He walked on the road for a long time. The weeds crowded in thicker along its edges. It seemed to run right through a dense forest of them that spread away as far as Lundy could see on either side. He was glad of the road. It was wide, and if he stayed in the middle of it the flowers couldn't reach him.

It got darker outside, because of the weeds covering the sand. Whatever made the phosphorescence didn't like being crowded that way, and pretty soon it was so dark that Lundy had to switch on the light in the top of his helmet. In the edges of the beam he could see the weed fronds moving lazily with the slow breathing of the sea.

The flowers were brighter here. They hung like lamps in the black water, burning with a light that seemed to come out of themselves. Sullen reds and angry yellows, and coldly vicious blues.

Lundy didn't like them.

The weeds grew in thicker and closer. They bulged out their roots, in over the stone edges. The flowers opened their bright hungry mouths and yearned at Lundy, reaching.

Reaching. Not quite touching. Not yet.

He was tired. The brandy and the benzedrine began to die in him. He changed his oxygen cylinder. That helped, but not much. He took more dope, but he was afraid to go heavy on it lest he drive his heart too hard. His legs turned numb.

He hadn't slept for a long time. Tracking Farrell hadn't been any breeze, and taking him – and *It* – had been plain and fancy hell. Lundy was only human. He was tired. Bushed. Cooked. Beat to the socks.

He sat down and rested a while, turning off his light to save the battery. The flowers watched him, glowing in the dark. He closed his eyes, but he could still feel them, watching and waiting.

After a minute or two he got up and went on.

The weeds grew thicker, and taller, and heavier with flowers.

More benzedrine, and damn the heart. The helmet light cut a cold white tunnel through the blackness. He followed it, walking faster. Weed fronts met and interlaced high above him, closing him in. Flowers bent inward, downward. Their petals almost brushed him. Fleshy petals, hungry and alive.

He started to run, over the wheel-ruts and the worn hollows of the road that still went somewhere, under the black sea.

Lundy ran clumsily for a long time between the dark and pressing walls. The flowers got closer. They got close enough to catch his vac-suit, like hands grasping and slipping and grasping again. He began using the blaster.

He burned off a lot of them that way. They didn't like it. They began swaying in from their roots and down from the laced ceiling over his head. They hurt. They were angry. Lundy ran, sobbing without tears.

The road did him in. It crossed him up, suddenly, without warning. It ran along smoothly under the tunnel of weeds, and then it was a broken, jumbled mass of huge stone blocks, tipped up and thrown around like something a giant's kid got tired of playing with.

And the weeds had found places to stand in between them.

Lundy tripped and fell, cracking his head against the back of his helmet. For a moment all he could see was bright light flashing. Then that stopped, and he realised he must have jarred a connection loose somewhere because his own light was out.

He began to crawl over a great tilted block. The flowers burned bright in the darkness. Bright and close. Very close.

Lundy opened his mouth. Nothing came out but a hoarse animal whimper. He was still holding a blaster. He fired it off a couple of times, and then he was on top of the block, lying flat on his belly.

He knew it was the end of the line, because he couldn't move any more.

The bright flowers came down through the dark. Lundy lay watching them. His face was quite blank. His dark eyes held a stubborn hatred, but nothing else.

He watched the flowers fasten on his vac-suit and start working. Then, from up ahead, through the dark close tunnel of the weeds, he saw the light.

It flared out suddenly, like lightning. A sheet of hot, bright gold cracking out like a whipped banner, lighting the end of the road.

Lighting the city, and the little procession coming out of it.

Lundy didn't believe any of it. He was half dead already, with his mind floating free of his body and beginning to be wrapped up in dark clouds. He watched what he saw incuriously.

The golden light died down, and then flared out twice more, rhythmically. The road ran smooth again beyond the end of the tunnel, straight across a narrow plain. Beyond that, the city rose.

Lundy couldn't see much of it, because of the weeds. But it seemed to be a big city. There was a wall around it, of green marble veined with dusky rose, the edges worn round by centuries of water. There were broad gates of pure untarnished gold, standing open on golden pintles. Beyond them was a vast square paved in cloud-grey quartz, and the buildings rose around it like the castles Lundy remembered from Earth and his childhood, when there were clouds of a certain kind at sunset.

That's what the whole place looked like, under the flaring golden light. Cloud-cuckoo land at sunset. Remote, dreaming in beauty, with the black water drawn across it like a veil – something never destroyed because it never existed.

The creatures who came from between the golden gates and down the road were like tiny wisps of those clouds, torn free by some cold wandering breeze and driven away from the light.

They came drifting toward Lundy. They didn't seem to be moving fast, but they must have been because quite suddenly they were among the weeds. There were a lot of them; maybe forty or fifty. They seemed to be between three and four feet tall, and they were all the same sad, blue-grey, twilight colour.

Lundy couldn't see what they were. They were vaguely man-shaped, and vaguely finny, and something that was more than vaguely something else, only he couldn't place it.

He was suddenly beyond caring. The dull black curtain around his mind got a hole in it, and fear came shrieking through it. He could feel the working and pulling of his vac-suit where the flowers were chewing on it as though it were his own skin.

He could feel sweat running cold on his body. In a minute that would be sea water running, and then ...

Lundy began to fight. His lips peeled back off his teeth, but he didn't make any noise except his heavy breathing. He fought the flowers, partly with the blaster, partly with brute strength. No science, no thought. Just the last blind struggle of an animal that didn't want to die.

The flowers held him. They smothered him, crushed him down, wrapped him in lovely burning petals of destruction. He seared a lot of them, but there were always more. Lundy didn't fight long.

He lay on his back, knees drawn up a little toward a rigid, knotted belly, blind with sweat, his heart kicking him like a logger's boot. Cold, tense – waiting.

And then the flowers went away.

They didn't want to. They let go reluctantly, drawing back and snarling like cats robbed of a fat mouse, making small hungry feints at him. But they went.

Lundy came nearer fanning off for keeps then than he ever had. Reaction wrung him out like a wet bar-rag. His heart quit beating; his body jerked like something on a string. Then, through a mist that might have been sweat, or tears, on the edge of the Hereafter, he saw the little blue-grey people looking down at him.

They hovered in a cloud above him, holding place with membranes as fluttering and delicate as bird-calls on a windy day.

The membranes ran between arm- and leg-members, both of which had thin flat swimming-webs. There were suckers on the legs, about where the heels would have been if they'd had feet.

Their bodies were slender and supple, and definitely feminine without having any of the usual human characteristics. They were beautiful. They weren't like anything Lundy had even seen before, or even dreamed about, but they were beautiful.

They had faces. Queer little pixie things. Their noses were round and tiny and rather sweet, but their eyes were their dominant feature.

Huge round golden eyes with pupils of deep brown. Soft eyes, gentle, inquiring, it made Lundy feel like crying, and so scared it made him mad.

The flowers kept weaving around, hopefully. When one got too close to Lundy, one of the little people would slap it gently, the way you would a pet dog, and shoo it away.

'Do you live?'

3

Lundy wasn't surprised by the telepathic voice. Thought-communication was commoner than speech and a lot simpler in many places on the inhabited worlds. Special gave its men a thorough training in it.

'I live, thanks to you.'

There was something in the quality of the brain he touched that puzzled him. It was like nothing he'd ever met before.

He got to his feet, not very steadily. 'You came just in time. How did you know I was here?'

'Your fear-thoughts carried to us. We know what it is to be afraid. So we came.'

'There's nothing I can say but "Thank you."'

'But of course we helped! Why not? You needn't thank us.'

Lundy looked at the flowers burning sullenly in the gloom. 'How is it you can boss them around? Why don't they ...'

'But they're not cannibals! Not like – *The Others*.' There was pure cold dread in that last thought.

'Cannibals.' Lundy looked up at the cloud of dainty blue-grey woman-things. His skin got cold and a size too small for him.

Their soft golden eyes smiled down at him. 'We're different from you, yes. Just as we're different from the fish. What is your thought? Bright things growing – weed – yes, they're kin to us.'

Kin, thought Lundy. Yeah. About like we are to the animals. Plants. Living plants were no novelty on Venus. Why not plants with thinking minds? Plants that carried their roots along with them, and watched you with sad soft eyes.

'Let's get out of here,' said Lundy.

They went down along the dark tunnel and out onto the road, and the flowers yearned like hungry dogs after Lundy but didn't touch him. He started out across the narrow plain, with the plant-women drifting cloudlike around him.

Seaweed. Little bits of kelp that could talk to you. It made Lundy feel queer.

The city made him feel queer, too. It was dark when he first saw it from the plain, with only the moonlight glow of the sand to touch it. It was a big city, stretching away behind its barrier wall. Big and silent and very old, waiting there at the end of its road.

It was curiously more real in the dim light. Lundy lost trace of the water for a moment. It was like walking toward a sleeping city in the moonlight, feeling the secretive, faintly hostile strength of it laired and leashed, until dawn ...

Only there would never be a dawn for this city. Never, any more.

Lundy wanted suddenly to run away.

'Don't be afraid. We live there. It's safe.'

Lundy shook his head irritably. Quite suddenly the brilliant light flared out again, three regular flashes. It seemed to come from somewhere to the right, out of a range of undersea mountains. Lundy felt a faint trembling of the sand. A volcanic fissure, probably, opened when the sand sank.

The golden light changed the city again. Cloud-cuckoo land

at sunset – a place where you could set your boots down on a dream.

When he went in through the gates he was awed, but not afraid. And then, while he stood in the square looking up at the great dim buildings, the thought came drifting down to him out of the cloud of little woman-things.

'It *was* safe. It was happy – before *She* came.'

After a long moment Lundy said, 'She?'

'We haven't seen her. But our mates have. She came a little while ago and walked through the streets, and all our mates left us to follow her. They say she's beautiful beyond any of us, and...'

'And her eyes are hidden, and they have to see them. They have to look into her eyes or go crazy, so they follow her.'

The sad little blue-grey cloud stirred in the dark water. Golden eyes looked down at him.

'How did you know? Do you follow her, too?'

Lundy took a deep, slow breath. The palms of his hands were wet. 'Yes. Yes, I followed her, too.'

'We feel your thought ...' They came down close around him. Their delicate membranes fluttered like fairy wings. Their golden eyes were huge and soft and pleading.

'Can you help us? Can you bring our mates back safe? They've forgotten everything. If The Others should come ...'

'The Others?'

Lundy's brain was drowned in stark and terrible fear. Pictures came through it. Vague gigantic dreams of nightmare ...

'They come, riding the currents that go between the hot cracks in the mountains and the cold deeps. They eat. They destroy.' The little woman-things were shaken suddenly like leaves in a gust of wind.

'We hide from them in the buildings. We can keep them out, away from our seed and the little new ones. But our mates have forgotten. If The Others come while they follow *Her*, outside and away from safety, they'll all be killed. We'll be left alone, and there'll be no more seed for us, and no more little new ones.'

They pressed in close around him, touching him with their small blue-grey forefins.

'Can you help us? Oh, can you help us?'

Lundy closed his eyes. His mouth twitched and set. When he opened his eyes again they were hard as agates.

'I'll help you,' he said, 'or die trying.'

It was dark in the great square, with only the pale sand-glow seeping through the gates. For a moment the little blue-grey woman-creatures clung around him, not moving, except as the whole mass of them swayed slightly with the slow rhythm of the sea.

Then they burst away from him, outward, in a wild surge of hope – and Lundy stood with his mouth open, staring.

They weren't blue-grey any longer. They glowed suddenly, their wings and their dainty, supple bodies, a warm soft green that had a vibrant pulse of life behind it. And they blossomed.

The long, slender, living petals must have been retracted, like the fronds of a touch-me-not, while they wore the sad blue-grey. Now they broke out like coronals of flame around their small heads.

Blue and scarlet and gold, poppy-red and violet and flame, silver-white and warm pink like a morning cloud, streaming in the black water. Streaming from small green bodies that rolled and tumbled high up against the dark, dreaming buildings like the butterflies that had danced there before the sunlight was lost forever.

Quite suddenly, then, they stopped. They drifted motionless in the water, and their colours dimmed. Lundy said,

'Where are they?'

'Deep in the city, beyond our buildings here – in the streets where only the curious young ones ever go. Oh, bring them back! Please bring them back!'

He left them hovering in the great dark square and went on into the city.

He walked down broad paved streets channelled with wheel-ruts and hollowed by generations of sandalled feet. The great water-worn buildings lifted up on either side, lit by the erratic glare of the distant fissure.

The window-openings, typical of most Venusian architecture, were covered by grilles of marble and semi-precious stone, intricately hand-pierced like bits of jewellery. The great golden doors stood open on their uncorroded hinges. Through them Lundy could watch the life of the little plant-people being lived.

In some of the buildings the lower floor had been covered with sand. Plant-women hovered protectively over them, brushing the sand smooth where the water disturbed it. Lundy guessed that these were seed beds.

In other places there were whole colonies of tiny flower-things still rooted in the sand; a pale spring haze of green in the dimness. They sat in placid rows, nodding their pastel baby coronals and playing solemnly with bits of bright weed and coloured stones. Here, too, the plant-women watched and guarded lovingly.

Several times Lundy saw groups of young plantlings, grown free of the sand, being taught to swim by the woman-creatures, tumbling in the black water like bright petals on a spring wind.

All the women were the same sad blue-grey, with their blossoms hidden.

They'd stay that way, unless he, Lundy, could finish the job Special had sent him to do. The job he hadn't been quite big enough to handle up to now.

Farrell, with the flesh flayed off his bones, and not feeling it because *She* was all he could think of. Jackie Smith, drowned in a flooded lock because *She* wanted to be free and he had helped her.

Was this Lundy guy so much bigger than Farrell and Smith, and all the other men who had gone crazy over *Her*? Big enough to catch The Vampire Lure in a net and keep it there, and not go nuts himself?

Lundy didn't feel that big. Not anywhere near that big.

He was remembering things. The first time he'd had *It* in a net. The last few minutes before the wreck, when he'd heard *Her* crying for freedom from inside the safe. Jackie Smith's face when he walked in with the water from the flooded lock, and his, Lundy's, own question – *Oh Lord, what did he see before he drowned?*

The tight cold knot was back in Lundy's belly again, and this time it had spurs on.

He left the colony behind him, walking down empty streets lit by the rhythmic flaring of the volcanic fissure. There was damage here. Pavements cracked and twisted with the settling, towers shaken down, the carved stone jalousies split out of the windows. Whole walls had fallen in, in some places, and most of the golden doors were wrecked, jammed wide open or gone entirely.

A dead city. So dead and silent that you couldn't breathe with it, and so old it made you crawl inside.

A swell place to go mad in, following a dream.

After a long time Lundy saw them – the mates of the little seaweed women. A long, long trail of them like a flight of homing birds, winding between the dark and broken towers.

They looked like their women. A little bigger, a little coarser, with strong tough dark-green bodies and brilliant coronals. Their golden eyes were fixed on something Lundy couldn't see, and they looked like the eyes of Lucifer yearning at the gates of Heaven.

Lundy began to run against the water, cutting across a wide plaza to get under the head of the procession. He unhooked the net from his belt with hands that felt like a couple of dead fish.

Then he staggered suddenly, lost his footing, and went sprawling. It was as though somebody had pushed him with a strong hand. When he tried to get up it pushed him again, hard. The golden glare from the fissure was steadier now, and very bright.

The trail of little man-things bent suddenly in a long whipping bow, and Lundy knew what was the matter.

There was a current rising in the city. Rising like the hot white winds that used to howl in from the sea, carrying the rains.

'They ride the currents that go between the hot cracks in the mountains and the cold deeps. They eat. They destroy.'

The Others. The Others, who were cannibals ...

She led the bright trail of plant-men between the towers, and there was a current rising in the streets.

Lundy got up. He balanced himself against the thrust of the current and ran, following the procession. It was clumsy work, with the water and his leaded boots. He tried to gauge where *It* – or *She* – was from the focus of the plant-men's eyes.

The hot light flared up brighter. The water pulled and shoved at him. He looked back once, but he couldn't see anything in the shadows between the towers. He was scared.

He shook the net out, and he was scared.

Funny that *It* – or *She* – didn't see him. Funny *It* didn't sense his mind, even though he tried to keep it closed. But he wasn't a very big object down there in the shadows under the walls, and creating an illusion for that many minds would be a strain on anything, even a creature from outer space.

He'd had the breaks once before, when he caught up with Farrell. He prayed to have the again.

He got them, for what good it did him.

The current caught the procession and pulled it down close to Lundy. He watched their eyes. She was still leading them. She had a physical body even if you couldn't see it, and the current would pull it, no matter how tiny it was.

He cast his net out, fast.

It bellied out in the black water and came swooping back to his pull, and there was something in it. Something tiny and cylindrical and vicious. Something alive.

He drew the net tight, shivering and sweating with nervous excitement. And the plant-men attacked.

They swooped on him in a brilliant cloud. Their golden eyes burned. There was no sense in them. Their minds shrieked and clamoured at him, a formless howl of rage – and fear, for *Her*.

They beat at him with their little green fins. Their coronals blazed, hot angry splashes of coloured flame against the dark water. They wrenched at the net, tore at it, beating their membranes like wings against the rising current.

Lundy was a solid, muscular little guy. He snarled and fought for the net like a wolf over a yearling lamb. He lost it anyway. He fell on his face under a small mountain of churning man-things and lay gasping for the breath they knocked out of him, thankful for the vac-suit that saved him from being crushed flat.

He watched them take the net. They clustered around it in a globe like a swarm of bees, rolling around in the moving water. Their golden eyes had a terrible stricken look.

They couldn't open the net. Lundy had drawn it tight and fastened it, and they didn't have fingers. They stroked and pawed it with their fins, but they couldn't let *Her* out.

Lundy got up on his hands and knees. The current quickened. It roared down between the broken towers like a black wind and took the swarm of man-things with it, still clutching the net.

And then The Others came.

4

Lundy saw them a long way off. For a moment he didn't believe it. He thought they must be shadows cast by the fitful glare of the fissure. He braced himself against a building and stood watching.

Stood watching, and then seeing as the rushing current brought them closer. He didn't move, except to lift his jaw a little trying to breathe. He simply stood, cold as a dead man's feet and just as numb.

They looked something like the giant rays he'd seen back on Earth, only they were plants. Great sleek bulbs of kelp with their leaves spread like wings to the current. Their long teardrop bodies ended in a flange like a fishtail that served as a rudder, and they had tentacles for arms.

They were coloured a deep red-brown like dried blood. The golden flare of the fissure made their cold eyes gleam. It showed their round mouth-holes full of sharp hairspines, and the stinging deadly cups on the undersides of their huge tentacles.

Those arms were long enough and tough enough to pierce even the fabric of a vac-suit. Lundy didn't know whether they ate flesh or not, but it didn't matter. He wouldn't care, after he'd been slapped with one of those tentacles.

The net with *Her* in it was getting away from him, and The Others were coming down on top of him. Even if he'd wanted to quit his job right then there wasn't any place to hide in these ruined, doorless buildings.

Lundy shot his suit full of precious oxygen and added himself to the creatures riding that black current to hell.

It swept him like a bubble between the dead towers, but not fast enough. He wasn't very far ahead of the kelp-things. He tried to swim, to make himself go faster, but it was like racing an oared dinghy against a fleet of sixteen-metre sloops with everything set.

He could see the cluster of plant-men ahead of him. They hadn't changed position. They rolled and tumbled in the water, using a lot of the forward push to go around with, so that Lundy was able to overhaul them.

But not fast enough. Not nearly fast enough.

The hell of it was he couldn't see anything to do if he got there. The net was way inside the globe. They weren't going to let him take it away. And if he did, what would it get anybody? They'd still follow *Her*, without sense enough to run away from the kelp-beasts.

Unless …

It hit Lundy all of a sudden. A hope, a solution. Hit him neatly as the leading kelp-thing climbed up on his heels and brought its leaf-wings in around him, hard.

Lundy let go an animal howl of fear and kicked wildly, shooting more air into his suit. He went up fast, and the wings grazed his boots but didn't quite catch him. Lundy rolled over and fed the thing a full charge out of his blaster, right through the eye.

It began to thrash and flounder like a shot bird. The ones coming right behind it got tangled up with it and then stopped to eat. Pretty soon there were a lot of them tumbling around it and fighting like a flock of gulls over a fish. Lundy swam furiously, cursing the clumsy suit.

There were a lot of the things that hadn't stopped, and the ones that had wouldn't stay long. Lundy kicked and strained and sweated. He was scared. He had the wind up so hard it was blowing his guts out, and it was like swimming in a nightmare, when you're tied to the spot.

The current seemed to move faster up where he was now. He gathered his thoughts into a tight beam and threw them into the heart of the cluster of plant-men, at the creature in the net.

I can free you. I'm the only one that can.

A voice answered him, inside his mind. The voice he had heard once before, back in the cabin of the wrecked flier. A voice as sweet and small as Pan-pipes calling on the Hills of Fay.

I know. My thought crossed yours ... The elfin voice broke suddenly, almost on a gasp of pain. Very faintly, Lundy heard:

Heavy! Heavy! I am slow ...

A longing for something beyond his experience stabbed Lundy like the cry of a frightened child. And then the globe of man-things burst apart as though a giant wind had struck them.

Lundy watched them wake up, out of their dream.

She had vanished, and now they didn't know why they were here or what they were doing. They had a heart-shaking memory of some beauty they couldn't touch, and that was all. They were lost, and frightened.

Then they saw The Others.

It was as though someone had hit them a stunning blow with his fist. They hung motionless, swept along by the current, staring back with dazed golden eyes. Their brilliant petals curled inward and vanished, and the green of their bodies dulled almost to black.

The kelp-beasts spread their wings wide and rushed toward them like great dark birds. And up ahead, under the sullen golden glare, Lundy saw the distant buildings of the colony. Some of the doors were still open, with knots of tiny figures waiting beside them.

Lundy was still a little ahead of the kelp-things. He grabbed up the floating net and hooked it to his belt, and then steered himself clumsily toward a broken tower jutting up to his right.

He hurled a wild telepathic shout at the plant-men, trying to make them turn and run, telling them that he'd hold off The Others. They were too scared to hear him. He cursed them, almost crying. On the third try he got through and they came to life in a hurry, rushing away with all the speed they had.

By that time Lundy was braced on his pinnacle of stone, and the kelp-beasts were right on top of him.

He got busy with both blasters. He burned down a lot of the things. Pretty soon the water all around him was full of thrashing bodies where the living had stopped to fight over the dead. But he couldn't get them all, and a few got by him.

Almost without turning his head he could see the huge red bird-shapes overhauling stragglers, wrapping them in broad wings, and then lying quiet in the rush of the current, feeding.

They kept the doors open, those little woman-things. They waited until the last of their mates came home, and then slammed the golden panels on the blunt noses of the kelp-things. Not many of the little men were lost. Only a few small wives would hide their petals and wear their sad blue-grey. Lundy felt good about that.

It was nice he felt good about something, because Old Mr Grim was climbing right up on Lundy's shoulders, showing his teeth. The kelp-beasts had finally found out who was hurting them. Also, now, Lundy was the only food in sight.

They were ganging up for a rush, wheeling and side-slipping in the spate of black water. Lundy got two more, and then one blaster charge fizzled out, and right after it the other one became dull.

Lundy stood alone on his broken tower and watched death sweep in around him. And the sweet elfin voice spoke out of the net:

Let me free. Let me free!

Lundy set his jaw tight and did the only thing he could think of. He deflated his vac-suit and jumped, plunging down into the black depths of the ruined building.

The kelp-things folded their leaves back like the wings of a diving bird and came down after him, using their tails for power.

Fitful flares of light came through broken walls and window openings. Lundy went down a long way. He didn't have to bother about stairs. The quakes had knocked most of the floors out.

The kelp-things followed him. Their long sinuous bodies were manoeuvrable as a shark's, and they were fast.

And all the time the little voice cried in his mind, asking for freedom.

Lundy hit bottom.

The walls were fairly solid down here, and it was dark, and

the place was choked with rubble. Things got a little confused. Lundy's helmet light was shot, and he wouldn't have used it anyway because it would have guided the hunters.

He felt them, swirling and darting around him. He ran, to no place in particular. The broken stones tripped him. Three times great sinewy bodies brushed him, knocking him spinning, but they couldn't quite find him in the darkness, chiefly because they got in each other's way.

Lundy fell through suddenly into a great hall, lying beside whatever room he had been in and a little below it. It was hardly damaged. Golden doors stood open to the water, and there was plenty of light.

Plenty of light for Lundy to see some more of the kelp-beasts poking hopeful faces in, and plenty of light for them to see Lundy.

The elfin voice called, *Let me out! Let me out!*

Lundy didn't have breath enough left to curse. He turned and ran, and the kelp-beasts gave a lazy flirt of their tails and caught up with him in the first thirty feet. They almost laughed in his face.

The only thing that saved Lundy was that when they opened their leaf-wings to take him they interfered with each other. It slowed them, just for a moment. Just long enough for Lundy to see the door.

A little door of black stone with no carving on it, standing half-open on a golden pivot, about ten feet away.

Lundy made for it. He dodged out from under one huge swooping wing, made a wild leap that almost tore him apart, and grabbed the edge of the door with his hands, doubling up and pulling.

A tentacle tip struck his feet. His lead boots hit the floor, and for a minute he thought his legs were broken. But the surge of water the blow made helped to carry him in through the narrow opening.

Half a dozen blunt red-brown heads tried to come through after him, and were stopped. Lundy was down on his hands and knees. He was trying to breathe, but somebody had put a heavy building on his chest. Also, it was getting hard to see anything.

He crawled over and put his shoulder against the door and pushed. It wouldn't budge. The building had settled and jammed the pivot for keeps. Even the butting kelp-things couldn't jar it.

But they kept on trying. Lundy crawled away. After a while some of the weight went off his chest and he could see better.

A shaft of fitful golden light shot in through a crack about ten feet above him. A small crack, not even big enough to let a baby in and out. It was the only opening other than the door.

The room was small, too. The stone walls were dead black, without ornament or carving, except on the rear wall.

There was a square block of jet there, about eight feet long by four wide, hollowed in a peculiar and unpleasantly suggestive fashion. Above it there was a single huge ruby set in the stone, burning red like a foretaste of hell fire.

Lundy had seen similar small chambers in old cities still on dry land. They were where men had gone to die for crimes against society and the gods.

Lundy looked at the hungry monsters pushing at the immovable door and laughed. There was no particular humour in it. He fired his last shot, and sat down.

The brutes might go away sometime, maybe. But unless they went within a very few minutes, it wasn't going to matter. Lundy's oxygen was getting low, and it was still a long way to the coast.

The voice from the net cried out, *Let me free!*

'The hell with you,' said Lundy. He was tired. He was so tired he didn't care much whether he lived or died.

He made sure the net was fast to his belt, and tightly closed.

'If I live, you go back to Vhia with me. If I die – well, you won't be able to hurt anybody again. There'll be one less devil loose on Venus.'

Free! Free! Free! I must be free! This heavy weight...

'Sure. Free to lead guys like Farrell into going crazy, and leaving their wives and kids. Free to kill...' He looked with sultry eyes at the net. 'Jackie Smith was my pal. You think I'd let you go? You think anything you could do would make me let you go?'

Then he saw her.

Right through the net, as though the metal mesh was cellophane. She crouched there in his lap, a tiny thing less than two feet high, doubled over her knees. The curve of her back was something an angel had carved out of a whisp of warm, pearl-pink cloud.

5

Lundy broke into a trembling sweat. He shut his eyes. It didn't matter. He saw her. He couldn't help seeing her. He tried to fight his mind, but he was tired ...

Her hair hid most of her. It had black night in it, and moonbeams, and glints of fire like a humming-bird's breast. Hair you dream about. Hair you could smother yourself in, and die happy.

She raised her head slowly, letting the veil of warm darkness fall away from her. Her eyes were shadowed, hidden under thick lashes. She raised her hands to Lundy, like a child praying.

But she wasn't a child. She was a woman, naked as a pearl, and so lovely that Lundy sobbed with it, in shivering ecstasy.

'No,' he said hoarsely. 'No. No!'

She held her arms up to be free, and didn't move.

Lundy tore the net loose from his belt and flung it on the altar block. He got up and went lurching to the door, but the kelp-things were still there, still hungry. He sat down again, in a corner as far away from both places as he could get, and took some benzedrine.

It was the wrong thing to do. He'd about reached his limit. It made him lightheaded. He couldn't fight her, couldn't shut her out. She knelt on the altar with her hands stretched out to him, and a shaft of golden light falling on her like something in a church.

'Open your eyes,' she said. 'Open your eyes and look at me.'

Let me free. Let me free!

Freedom Lundy didn't know anything about. The freedom of outer space, with the whole Milky Way to play in and nothing to hold you back. And with the longing, fear. A blind, stricken terror...

'No!' Lundy said.

Things got dark for Lundy. Presently he found himself at the altar block, fumbling at the net.

He wrenched away and went stumbling back to his corner. He was twitching all over like a frightened dog.

'Why do you want to do it? Why do you have to torture me – drive them crazy for something they can't have – kill them?'

Torture? Crazy? Kill? I don't understand. They worship me. It is pleasant to be worshipped.

'Pleasant!' Lundy was yelling aloud, and didn't know it. 'Pleasant, damn you! So you kill a good guy like Farrell, and drown Jackie Smith ...'

Kill? Wait – give me the thought again ...

Something inside Lundy turned cold and still, holding its breath. He sent the thought again. Death. Cessation. Silence, and the dark.

The tiny glowing figure on the black stone bent over its knees again, and it was sadder than a seabird's cry at sunset.

So will I be soon. So will all of us. Why did this planet take us out of space? The weight, the pressure breaks and crushes us, and we can't get free. In space there was no death, but now we die ...

Lundy stood quite still. The blood beat like drums in his temples.

'You mean that all you creatures out of space are dying? That the – the madness will stop of itself?'

Soon. Very soon. There was no death in space! There was no pain! We didn't know about them. Everything here was new, to be tasted and played with. We didn't know ...

'Hell!' said Lundy, and looked at the creatures beating at the crack of the stone door. He sat down.

You, too, will die.

Lundy raised his head slowly. His eyes had a terrible brightness.

'You like to be worshipped,' he whispered. 'Would you like to be worshipped after you die? Would you like to be remembered always as something good and beautiful – a goddess?'

That would be better than to be forgotten.

'Will you do what I ask of you, then? You can save my life, if you will. You can save the lives of a lot of those little flower-people. I'll see to it that everyone knows your true story. Now you're hated and feared, but after that you'll be loved.'

Will you let me free of this net?

'If you promise to do what I ask?'

I would rather die at least free of this net. The tiny figure trembled and shook back the veil of dark hair. *Hurry. Tell me ...*

'Lead these creatures away from the door. Lead all of them in the city away, to the fire in the mountain where they'll be destroyed.'

They will worship me. It is better than dying in a net. I promise.

Lundy got up and went to the altar. His feet were not steady. His hands were not steady, either, untying the net. Sweat ran in his eyes. She didn't have to keep her promise. She didn't have to ...

The net fell away. She stood up on her tiny pink feet. Slowly, like a swirl of mist straightening in a little breeze. She threw her head back and smiled. Her mouth was red and sulky, her teeth whiter than new snow. Her lowered lids had faint blue shadows traced on them.

She began to grow, in the golden shaft of light, like a pillar of cloud rising toward the sun. Lundy's heart stood still. The clear gleam of her skin, the line of her throat and her young breasts, the supple turn of her flank and thigh ...

You worship me, too.

Lundy stepped back, two lurching steps. 'I worship you,' he whispered. 'Let me see your eyes.'

She smiled and turned her head away. She stepped off the altar block, floating past him through the black water. A dream-thing, without weight or substance, and more desirable than all the women Lundy had seen in his life or his dreams.

He followed her, staggering. He tried to catch her. 'Open your eyes! Please open your eyes!'

She floated on, through the crack of the stone door. The kelp-things didn't see her. All they saw was Lundy coming toward them.

'Open your eyes!'

She turned, then, just before Lundy had stepped out to death in the hall beyond. He stopped, and watched her raise her shadowed lids.

He screamed, just once, and fell forward onto the black floor.

He never knew how long he lay there. It couldn't have been long in time, because he still had, barely, enough oxygen to make it to the coast when he came to. The kelp-beasts were gone.

But the time to Lundy was an eternity – an eternity he came out of with whitened hair and bitter lines around his mouth, and a sadness that never left his eyes.

He'd only had his dream a little while. A few brief moments, already shadowed by death. His mind was drugged and tired, and didn't feel things as deeply and clearly as it might. That was all that saved him.

But he knew what Jackie Smith saw before he drowned. He knew why men had died or gone mad forever, when they looked into the eyes of their dream, and by looking, destroyed it.

Because, behind those shadowed, perfect lids, there was – *Nothing*.

LORELEI OF THE RED MIST

Leigh Brackett and Ray Bradbury

The Company dicks were good. They were plenty good. Hugh Starke began to think maybe this time he wasn't going to get away with it.

His small stringy body hunched over the control bank, nursing the last ounce of power out of the Kallman. The hot night sky of Venus fled past the ports in tattered veils of indigo. Starke wasn't sure where he was any more. Venus was a frontier planet, and still mostly a big X, except to the Venusians – who weren't sending out any maps. He did know that he was getting dangerously close to the Mountains of White Cloud. The backbone of the planet, towering far into the stratosphere, magnetic trap, with God knew what beyond. Maybe even God wasn't sure.

But it looked like over the mountains or out. Death under the guns of the Terro-Venus Mines, Incorporated, Special Police, or back to the Luna cell blocks for life as an habitual felon.

Starke decided he would go over.

Whatever happened, he'd pulled off the biggest lone-wolf caper in history. The T-V Mines payroll ship, for close to a million credits. He cuddled the metal strongbox between his feet and grinned. It would be a long time before anybody equalled that.

His mass indicators began to jitter. Vaguely, a dim purple shadow in the sky ahead, the Mountains of White Cloud, stood like a wall against him. Starke checked the positions of the pursuing ships. There was no way through them. He said flatly, 'All right, damn you,' and sent the Kallman angling up into the thick blue sky.

He had no very clear memories after that. Crazy magnetic vagaries, always a hazard on Venus, made his instruments useless. He flew by the seat of his pants and he got over, and the T-V men didn't. He was free, with a million credits in his kick.

Far below in the virgin darkness he saw a sullen crimson smear on the night, as though someone had rubbed it with a bloody thumb. The Kallman dipped toward it. The control bank flickered with blue flame, the jet timers blew, and then there was just the screaming of air against the falling hull.

Hugh Starke sat still and waited ...

He knew, before he opened his eyes, that he was dying. He didn't feel any pain, he didn't feel anything, but he knew just the same. Part of him was cut loose. He was still there, but not attached anymore.

He raised his eyelids. There was a ceiling. It was a long way off. It was black stone veined with smoky reds and ambers. He had never seen it before.

His head was tilted toward the right. He let his gaze move down that way. There were dim tapestries, more of the black stone, and three tall archways giving onto a balcony. Beyond the balcony was a sky veiled and clouded with red mist. Under the mist, spreading away from a murky line of cliffs, was an ocean. It wasn't water and it didn't have any waves on it, but there was nothing else to call it. It burned, deep down inside itself, breathing up the red fog. Little angry bursts of flame coiled up under the flat surface, sending circles of sparks flaring out like ripples from a dropped stone.

He closed his eyes and frowned and moved his head restively. There was the texture of fur against his skin. Through the cracks of his eyelids he saw that he lay on a high bed piled with silks and soft tanned pelts. His body was covered. He was rather glad he couldn't see it. It didn't matter because he wouldn't be using it any more anyway, and it hadn't been such a hell of a body to begin with. But he was used to it, and he didn't want to see it now, the way he knew it would have to look.

He looked along over the foot of the bed, and he saw the woman.

She sat watching him from a massive carved chair softened with a single huge white pelt like a drift of snow. She smiled, and let him look. A pulse began to beat under his jaw, very feebly.

She was tall and sleek and insolently curved. She wore a sort of tabard of pale grey spider-silk, held to her body by a jewelled girdle, but it was just a nice piece of ornamentation. Her face was narrow, finely cut, secret, faintly amused. Her lips, her eyes, and her flowing silken hair were all the same pale cool shade of aquamarine.

Her skin was white, with no hint of rose. Her shoulders, her forearms, the long flat curve of her thighs, the pale-green tips of her breasts, were dusted with tiny particles that glistened like powdered diamond. She sparkled softly like a fairy thing against the snowy fur, a creature of foam and moonlight and clear shallow water. Her eyes never left his, and they were not human, but he knew that they would have done things to him if he had had any feeling below the neck.

He started to speak. He had no strength to move his tongue. The woman leaned forward, and as though her movement were a signal four men rose from the tapestried shadows by the wall. They were like her. Their eyes were pale and strange like hers.

She said, in liquid High Venusian, 'You're dying, in this body. But *you* will not die. You will sleep now, and wake in a strange body, in a strange place. Don't be afraid. My mind will be with yours, I'll guide you, don't be afraid. I can't explain now, there isn't time, but don't be afraid.'

He drew back his thin lips baring his teeth in what might have been a smile. If it was, it was wolfish and bitter, like his face.

The woman's eyes began to pour coolness into his skull. They were like two little rivers running through the channels of his own eyes, spreading in silver-green quiet across the tortured surface of his brain. His brain relaxed. It lay floating on the water, and then the twin streams became one broad, flowing stream, and his mind, or ego, the thing that was intimately himself, vanished along it.

It took him a long, long time to regain consciousness. He felt as though he'd been shaken until pieces of him were scattered all over inside. Also, he had an instinctive premonition that the minute he woke up he would be sorry he had. He took it easy, putting himself together.

He remembered his name, Hugh Starke. He remembered the mining asteroid where he was born. He remembered the Luna cell blocks where he had once come near dying. There wasn't much to choose between them. He remembered his face decorating half the bulletin boards between Mercury and The Belt. He remembered hearing about himself over the telecasts, stuff to frighten babies with, and he thought of himself committing his first crime – a stunted scrawny kid of eighteen swinging a spanner on a grown man who was trying to steal his food.

The rest of it came fast, then. The T-V Mines job, the getaway that didn't get, the Mountains of White Cloud. The crash ...

The woman.

That did it. His brain leaped shatteringly. Light, feeling, a naked sense of reality swept over him. He lay perfectly still with his eyes shut, and his mind clawed at the picture of the shining woman with sea-green hair and the sound of her voice saying, *You will not die, you will wake in a strange body, don't be afraid ...*

He was afraid. His skin pricked and ran cold with it. His stomach knotted with it. His skin, his stomach, and yet somehow they didn't feel just right, like a new coat that hasn't shaped to you ...

He opened his eyes, a cautious crack.

He saw a body sprawled on its side in dirty straw. The body belonged to him, because he could feel the straw pricking it, and the itch of little things that crawled and ate and crawled again.

It was a powerful body, rangy and flat-muscled, much bigger than his old one. It had obviously not been starved the first twenty-some years of its life. It was stark naked. Weather and violence had written history on it, wealed white marks on leathery bronze skin, but nothing seemed to be missing. There was black hair on its chest and thighs and forearms, and its hands were lean and sinewy for killing.

It was a human body. That was something. There were so many other things it might have been that his racial snobbery wouldn't call human. Like the nameless shimmering creature who smiled with strange pale lips.

Starke shut his eyes again.

He lay, the intangible self that was Hugh Starke, bellied down in the darkness of the alien shell, quiet, indrawn, waiting. Panic crept up on its soft black paws. It walked around the crouching ego and sniffed and patted and nuzzled, whining, and then struck with its raking claws. After a while it went away, empty.

The lips that were now Starke's lips twitched in a thin, cruel smile. He had done six months once in the Luna solitary crypts. If a man could do that, and come out sane and on his two feet, he could stand anything. Even this.

It came to him then, rather deflatingly, that the woman and her four companions had probably softened the shock by hypnotic suggestion. His subconscious understood and accepted the change. It was only his conscious mind that was superficially scared to death.

Hugh Starke cursed the woman with great thoroughness, in seven languages and some odd dialects. He became healthily enraged that any dame should play around with him like that. Then he thought, What the hell, I'm alive. And it looks like I got the best of the trade-in!

He opened his eyes again, secretly, on his new world.

He lay at one end of a square stone hall, good sized, with two straight lines of pillars cut from some dark Venusian wood. There were long crude benches and tables. Fires had been burning on round brick hearths spaced between the pillars. They were embers now. The smoke climbed up, tarnishing the gold and bronze of shields hung on the walls and pediments, dulling the blades of longswords, the spears, the tapestries and hides and trophies.

It was very quiet in the hall. Somewhere outside of it there was fighting going on. Heavy, vicious fighting. The noise of it didn't touch the silence, except to make it deeper.

There were two men besides Starke in the hall.

They were close to him, on a low dais. One of them sat in a carved high seat, not moving, his big scarred hands flat on the table in front of him. The other crouched on the floor by his feet. His head was bent forward so that his mop of lint-white hair hid his face and the harp between his thighs. He was a little man, a swamp-edger from his albino colouring. Starke looked back at the man in the chair.

The man spoke harshly. 'Why doesn't she send word?'

The harp gave out a sudden bitter chord. That was all.

Starke hardly noticed. His whole attention was drawn to the speaker. His heart began to pound. His muscles coiled and lay ready. There was a bitter taste in his mouth. He recognised it. It was hate.

He had never seen the man before, but his hands twitched with the urge to kill.

He was big, nearly seven feet, and muscled like a draught horse. But his body, naked above a gold-bossed leather kilt, was lithe and quick as a greyhound in spite of its weight. His face was square, strong-boned, weathered, and still young. It was a face that had laughed a lot once, and liked wine and pretty girls. It had forgotten those things now, except maybe the wine. It was drawn and cruel with pain, a look as of something in a cage. Starke had seen that look before, in the Luna blocks. There was a thick white scar across the man's forehead. Under it his blue eyes were sunken and dark behind half-closed lids. The man was blind.

Outside, in the distance, men screamed and died.

Starke had been increasingly aware of a soreness and stricture around his neck. He raised a hand, careful not to rustle the straw. His fingers found a long tangled beard, felt under it, and touched a band of metal.

Starke's new body wore a collar, like a vicious dog.

There was a chain attached to the collar. Starke couldn't find any fastening. The business had been welded on for keeps. His body didn't seem to have liked it much. The neck was galled and chafed.

The blood began to crawl up hot into Starke's head. He'd worn chains before. He didn't like them. Especially around the neck.

A door opened suddenly at the far end of the hall. Fog and red daylight spilled in across the black stone floor. A man came in. He was big, half naked, blond, and bloody. His long blade trailed harshly on the flags. His chest was laid open to the bone and he held the wound together with his free hand.

'Word from Beudag,' he said. 'They've driven us back into the city, but so far we're holding the Gate.'

No one spoke. The little man nodded his white head. The

man with the slashed chest turned and went out again, closing the door.

A peculiar change came over Starke at the mention of the name Beudag. He had never heard it before, but it hung in his mind like a spear point, barbed with strange emotion. He couldn't identify the feeling, but it brushed the blind man aside. The hot simple hatred cooled. Starke relaxed in a sort of icy quiet, deceptively calm as a sleeping cobra. He didn't question this. He waited, for Beudag.

The blind man struck his hands down suddenly on the table and stood up. 'Romna,' he said, 'give me my sword.'

The little man looked at him. He had milk-blue eyes and a face like a friendly bulldog. He said, 'Don't be a fool, Faolan.'

Faolan said softly, 'Damn you. Give me my sword.'

Men were dying outside the hall, and not dying silently. Faolan's skin was greasy with sweat. He made a sudden, darting grab towards Romna.

Romna dodged him. There were tears in his pale eyes. He said brutally, 'You'd only be in the way. Sit down.'

'I can find the point,' Faolan said, 'to fall on it.'

Romna's voice went up to a harsh scream. 'Shut up. Shut up and sit down.'

Faolan caught the edge of the table and bent over it. He shivered and closed his eyes, and the tears ran out hot under the lids. The bard turned away, and his harp cried out like a woman.

Faolan drew a long sighing breath. He straightened slowly, came round the carved high seat, and walked steadily toward Starke.

'You're very quiet, Conan,' he said. 'What's the matter? You ought to be happy, Conan. You ought to laugh and rattle your chain. You're going to get what you wanted. Are you sad because you haven't a mind any more, to understand that with?'

He stopped and felt with one sandalled foot across the straw until he touched Starke's thigh. Starke lay motionless.

'Conan,' said the blind man gently, pressing Starke's belly with his foot. 'Conan the dog, the betrayer, the butcher, the knife in the back. Remember what you did at Falga, Conan? No, you don't remember now. I've been a little rough with you, and you don't remember any more. But I remember, Conan. As long as I live in darkness, I'll remember.'

Romna stroked the harp strings and they wept savage tears for strong men dead of treachery. Low music, distant but not soft. Faolan began to tremble, a shallow animal twitching of the muscles. The flesh of his face was drawn, iron shaping under the hammer. Quite suddenly he went down on his knees. His hands struck Starke's shoulders, slid inward to the throat, and locked there.

Outside, the sound of fighting had died away.

Starke moved, very quickly. As though he had seen it and knew it was there, his hand swept out and gathered in the slack of the heavy chain and swung it.

It started out to be a killing blow. Starke wanted with all his heart to beat Faolan's brains out. But at the last second he pulled it, slapping the big man with exquisite judgement across the back of the head. Faolan grunted and fell sideways, and by that time Romna had come up. He had dropped his harp and drawn a knife. His eyes were startled.

Starke sprang up. He backed off, swinging the slack of the chain warningly. His new body moved magnificently. Outside everything was fine, but inside his psycho-neural setup had exploded into civil war. He was furious with himself for not having killed Faolan. He was furious with himself for losing control enough to want to kill a man without reason. He hated Faolan. He did not hate Faolan because he didn't know him well enough. Starke's trained, calculating unemotional brain was at grips with a tidal wave of baseless emotion.

He hadn't realised it was baseless until his mental monitor, conditioned through years of bitter control, had stopped him from killing. Now he remembered the woman's voice saying, *My mind will be with yours, I'll guide you ...*

Catspaw, huh? Just a hired hand, paid off with a new body in return for two lives. Yeah, two. This Beudag, whoever he was. Starke knew now what that cold alien emotion had been leading up to.

'Hold it,' said Starke hoarsely. 'Hold everything. *Catspaw! You green-eyed she-devil! You picked the wrong guy this time.*'

Just for a fleeting instant he saw her again, leaning forward with her hair like running water cross the soft foam-sparkle of her shoulders. Her sea-pale eyes were full of mocking laughter, and a direct, provocative admiration. Starke heard her quite plainly:

'You may not have any choice, Hugh Starke. They know Conan, even if you don't. Besides, it's of no great importance. The end will be the same for them – it's just a matter of time. You can save your new body or not, as you wish.' She smiled. 'I'd like it if you did. It's a good body. I knew it, before Conan's mind broke and left it empty.'

A sudden thought came to Starke. 'My box, the million credits.'

'Come and get them.' She was gone. Starke's mind was clear, with no alien will tramping around in it. Faolan crouched on the floor, holding his head. He said:

'Who spoke?'

Romna the bard stood staring. His lips moved, but no sound came out.

Starke said, 'I spoke. Me, Hugh Starke. I'm not Conan, and I never heard of Falga, and I'll brain the first guy that comes near me.'

Faolan stayed motionless, his face blank, his breath sobbing in his throat. Romna began to curse, very softly, not as though he were thinking about it. Starke watched them.

Down the hall the doors burst open. The heavy reddish mist coiled in with the daylight across the flags, and with them a press of bodies hot from battle, bringing a smell of blood.

Starke felt the heart contract in the hairy breast of the body named Conan, watching the single figure that led the pack.

Romna called out, 'Beudag!'

She was tall. She was built and muscled like a lioness, and she walked with a flat-hipped arrogance, and her hair was like coiled flame. Her eyes were blue, hot and bright, as Faolan's might have been once. She looked like Faolan. She was dressed like him, in a leather kilt and sandals, her magnificent body bare above the waist. She carried a longsword slung across her back, the hilt standing above the left shoulder. She had been using it. Her skin was smeared with blood and grime. There was a long cut on her thigh and another across her flat belly, and bitter weariness lay on her like a burden in spite of her denial of it.

'We've stopped them, Faolan,' she said. 'They can't breach the Gate, and we can hold Crom Dhu as long as we have food. And the sea feeds us.' She laughed, but there was a hollow sound to it. 'Gods, I'm tired!'

She halted then, below the dais. Her flame-blue gaze swept across Faolan, across Romna, and rose to meet Hugh Starke's, and stayed there.

The pulse began to beat under Starke's jaw again, and this time his body was strong, and the pulse was like a drum throbbing.

Romna said, 'His mind has come back.'

There was a long, hard silence. No one in the hall moved. Then the men behind Beudag, big brawny kilted warriors, began to close in on the dais, talking in low snarling undertones that rose toward a mob howl. Faolan rose up and faced them, and bellowed them to quiet.

'He's mine to take! Let him alone.'

Beudag sprang up onto the dais, one beautiful flowing movement. 'It isn't possible,' she said. 'His mind broke under torture. He's been a drooling idiot with barely the sense to feed himself. And now, suddenly, you say he's normal again?'

Starke said, 'You know I'm normal. You can see it in my eyes.'

'Yes.'

He didn't like the way she said that. 'Listen, my name is Hugh Starke. I'm an Earthman. This isn't Conan's brain come back. This is a new deal. I got shoved into his body. What it did before I got it I don't know, and I'm not responsible.'

Faolan said, 'He doesn't remember Falga. He doesn't remember the longships at the bottom of the sea,' Faolan laughed.

Romna said quietly, 'He didn't kill you, though. He could have, easily. Would Conan have spared you?'

Beudag said, 'Yes, if he had a better plan. Conan's mind was like a snake. It crawled in the dark, and you never knew where it was going to strike.'

Starke began to tell them how it happened, the chain swinging idly in his hand. While he was talking he saw a face reflected in a polished shield hung on a pillar. Mostly it was just a tangled black mass of hair, mounted on a frame of long, harsh, jutting bone. The mouth was sensuous, with a dark sort of laughter on it. The eyes were yellow. The cruel, brilliant yellow of a killer hawk.

Starke realised with a shock that the face belonged to him.

'A woman with pale green hair,' said Beudag softly. 'Rann,' said Faolan, and Romna's harp made a sound like a high-priest's curse.

'Her people have that power,' Romna said. 'They can think a man's soul into a spider, and step on it.'

'They have many powers. Maybe Rann followed Conan's mind, wherever it went, and told it what to say, and brought it back again.'

'Listen,' said Starke angrily. 'I didn't ask ...'

Suddenly, without warning, Romna drew Beudag's sword and threw it at Starke.

Starke dodged it. He looked at Romna with ugly yellow eyes. 'That's fine. Chain me up so I can't fight and kill me from a distance.' He did not pick up the sword. He'd never used one. The chain felt better, not being too different from a heavy belt or a length of cable, or other chains he's swung on occasion.

Romna said, 'Is that Conan?'

Faolan snarled, 'What happened?'

'Romna threw my sword at Conan. He dodged it, and left it on the ground.' Beudag's eyes were narrowed. 'Conan could catch a flying sword by the hilt, and he was the best fighter on the Red Sea, barring you, Faolan.'

'He's trying to trick us. Rann guides him.'

'The hell with Rann!' Starke clashed his chain. 'She wants me to kill the both of you, I still don't know why. All right. I could have killed Faolan, easy. But I'm not a killer. I never put down anyone except to save my own neck. So I didn't kill him in spite of Rann. And I don't want any part of you, or Rann either. All I want is to get the hell out of here!'

Beudag said, 'His accent isn't Conan's. And the look in his

eyes is different, too.' Her voice had an odd note in it. Romna glanced at her. He fingered a few rippling chords on his harp, and said:

'There's one way you could tell for sure.'

A sullen flush began to burn on Beudag's cheekbones. Romna slid unobtrusively out of reach. His eyes danced with malicious laughter.

Beudag smiled, the smile of an angry cat, all teeth and no humour. Suddenly she walked toward Starke, her head erect, her hands swinging loose and empty at her sides. Starke tensed warily, but the blood leaped pleasantly in his borrowed veins.

Beudag kissed him.

Starke dropped the chain. He had something better to do with his hands.

After a while he raised his head for breath, and she stepped back, and whispered wonderingly.

'It isn't Conan.'

The hall had been cleared. Starke had washed and shaved himself. His new face wasn't bad. Not bad at all. In fact, it was pretty damn good. And it wasn't known around the System. It was a face that could own a million credits and no questions asked. It was a face that could have a lot of fun on a million credits.

All he had to figure out now was a way to save the neck the face was mounted on, and get his million credits back from that beautiful she-devil named Rann.

He was still chained, but the straw had been cleaned up and he wore a leather kilt and a pair of sandals. Faolan sat in his high seat nursing a flagon of wine. Beudag sprawled wearily on a fur rug beside him. Romna sat cross-legged, his eyes veiled sleepily, stroking soft wandering music out of his harp. He looked fey. Starke knew his swamp-edgers. He wasn't surprised.

'This man is telling the truth,' Romna said. 'But there's another mind touching his. Rann's, I think. Don't trust him.'

Faolan growled, 'I couldn't trust a god in Conan's body.'

Starke said, 'What's the setup? All the fighting out there, and this Rann dame trying to plant a killer on the inside. And what happened at Falga? I never heard of this whole damn ocean, let alone a place called Falga.'

The bard swept his hand across the strings. 'I'll tell you, Hugh Starke. And maybe you won't want to stay in that body any longer.'

Starke grinned. He glanced at Beudag. She was watching him with a queer intensity from under lowered lids. Starke's grin changed. He began to sweat. Get rid of this body, hell! It was really a body. His own stringy little carcass had never felt like this.

The bard said, 'In the beginning, in the Red Sea, was a race of people having still their fins and scales. They were amphibious, but after a while part of this race wanted to remain entirely on land. There was a quarrel, and a battle, and some of the people left the sea forever. They settled along the shore. They lost their fins and most of their scales. They had great mental powers and they loved ruling. They subjugated the human peoples and kept them almost in slavery. They hated their brothers who still lived in the sea, and their brothers hated them.

'After a time a third people came to the Red Sea. They were rovers from the North. They raided and reaved and wore no man's collar. They made a settlement on Crom Dhu, the Black Rock, and built longships, and took toll of the coastal towns.

'But the slave people didn't want to fight against the rovers. They wanted to fight with them and destroy the sea-folk. The rovers were human, and blood calls to blood. And the rovers liked to rule, too, and this is a rich country. Also, the time had come in their tribal development when they were ready to change from nomadic warriors to builders in their own country.

'So the rovers, and the sea-folk, and the slave-people who were caught between the two of them, began their struggle for the land.'

The bard's fingers thrummed against the strings so that they beat like angry hearts. Starke saw that Beudag was still watching him, weighing every change of expression on his face. Romna went on:

'There was a woman named Rann, who had green hair and great beauty, and ruled the sea-folk. There was a man called

Faolan of the Ships, and his sister Beudag, which means Dagger-in-the-Sheath, and they two ruled the outland rovers. And there was the man called Conan.'

The harp crashed out like a sword-blade striking.

'Conan was a great fighter and a great lover. He was next under Faolan of the Ships, and Beudag loved him, and they were plighted. Then Conan was taken prisoner by the sea-folk during a skirmish, and Rann saw him – and Conan saw Rann.'

Hugh Starke had a fleeting memory of Rann's face smiling, and her low voice saying, *It's a good body. I knew it, before* ...

Beudag's eyes were two stones of blue vitriol under her narrow lids.

'Conan stayed a long time at Falga with Rann of the Red Sea. Then he came back to Crom Dhu, and said that he had escaped, and had discovered a way to take the longships into the harbour of Falga, at the back of Rann's fleet; and from there it would be easy to take the city, and Rann with it. And Conan and Beudag were married.'

Starke's yellow hawk eyes slid over Beudag, sprawled like a long lioness in power and beauty. A muscle began to twitch under his cheekbone. Beudag flushed, a slow deep colour. Her gaze did not waver.

'So the longships went out from Crom Dhu, across the Red Sea. And Conan led them into a trap at Falga, and more than half of them were sunk. Conan thought his ship was free, that he had Rann and all she'd promised him, but Faolan saw what had happened and went after him. They fought, and Conan laid his sword across Faolan's brow and blinded him; but Conan lost the fight. Beudag brought them home.

'Conan was chained naked in the market place. The people were careful not to kill him. From time to time other things were done to him. After a while his mind broke, and Faolan had him chained here in the hall, where he could hear him babble and play with his chain. It made darkness easier to bear.

'But since Falga, things have gone badly for Crom Dhu. Too many men were lost, too many ships. Now Rann's people have us bottled up here. They can't break in, we can't break out. And so we stay, until ...' The harp cried out a bitter question, and was still.

After a minute or two Starke said slowly, 'Yeah, I get it. Stalemate for both of you. And Rann figured if I could kill off the leaders, your people might give up.' He began to curse. 'What a lousy, dirty, sneaking trick! And who told her she could use me...' He paused. After all, he'd be dead now. After all, a new body, and a cool million credits. Ah, the hell with Rann. He hadn't asked her to do it. And he was nobody's hired killer. Where did she get off, sneaking around his mind, trying to make him do things he didn't even know about? Especially to someone like Beudag.

Still, Rann herself was nobody's crud.

And just where was Hugh Starke supposed to cut in on this deal? Cut was right. Probably with a longsword, right through the belly. Swell spot he was in, and a good three strikes on him already.

He was beginning to wish he'd never seen the T V Mines payroll ship, because then he might never have seen the Mountains of White Cloud.

He said, because everybody seemed to be waiting for him to say something. 'Usually when there's a deadlock like this, somebody calls in a third party. Isn't there somebody you can yell for?'

Faolan shook his rough red head. 'The slave people might rise, but they haven't arms and they're not used to fighting. They'd only get massacred, and it wouldn't help us any.'

'What about those other – uh – people that live in the sea? And just what is that sea, anyhow? Some radiation from it wrecked my ship and got me into this bloody mess.'

Beudag said lazily, 'I don't know what it is. The seas our forefathers sailed on were water, but this is different. It will float a ship, if you know how to build the hull – very thin, of a white metal we mine from the foothills. But when you swim in it, it's like being in a cloud of bubbles. It tingles, and the farther down you go in it the stranger it gets, dark and full of fire. I stay down for hours sometimes, hunting the beasts that live there.'

Starke said, 'For hours? You have diving suits, then. What are they?'

127

She shook her head, laughing. 'Why weigh yourself down that way? There's no trouble to breathe in this ocean.'

'For cripesake,' said Starke. 'Well I'll be damned. Must be a heavy gas, then, radioactive, surface tension under atmospheric pressure, enough to float a light hull, and high oxygen content without any dangerous mixture. Well, well. Okay, why doesn't somebody go down and see if the sea-people will help? They don't like Rann's branch of the family, you said.'

'They don't like us, either,' said Faolan. 'We stay out of the southern part of the sea. They wreck our ships, sometimes.' His bitter mouth twisted in a smile. 'Did you want to go to them for help?'

Starke didn't quite like the way Faolan sounded. 'It was just a suggestion,' he said.

Beudag rose, stretching, wincing as the stiffened wounds pulled her flesh. 'Come on, Faolan. Let's sleep.'

He rose and laid his hand on her shoulder. Romna's harpstrings breathed a subtle little mockery of sound. The bard's eyes were veiled and sleepy. Beudag did not look at Starke, called Conan.

Starke said, 'What about me?'

'You stay chained,' said Faolan. 'There's plenty of time to think. As long as we have food – and the sea feeds us.'

He followed Beudag, through a curtained entrance to the left. Romna got up, slowly, slinging the harp over one white shoulder. He stood looking steadily into Starke's eyes in the dying light of the fires.

'I don't know,' he murmured.

Starke waited, not speaking. His face was without expression.

'Conan we knew. Starke we don't know. Perhaps it would have been better if Conan had come back.' He ran his thumb absently over the hilt of the knife in his girdle. 'I don't know. Perhaps it would have been better for all of us if I'd cut your throat before Beudag came in.'

Starke's mouth twitched. It was not exactly a smile.

'You see,' said the bard seriously, 'to you, from Outside, none of this is important, except as it touches you. But we live in this little world. We die in it. To us, it's important.'

The knife was in his hand now. It leaped up glittering into the dregs of the firelight, and fell, and leaped again.

'You fight for yourself, Hugh Starke. Rann also fights through you. I don't know.'

Starke's gaze did not waver.

Romna shrugged and put away the knife. 'It is written of the gods,' he said, sighing. 'I hope they haven't done a bad job of the writing.'

He went out. Starke began to shiver slightly. It was completely quiet in the hall. He examined his collar, the rivets, every separate link of the chain, the staple to which it was fixed. Then he sat down on the fur rug provided for him in place of the straw. He put his face in his hands and cursed, steadily, for several minutes, and then struck his fists down hard on the floor. After that he lay down and was quiet. He thought Rann would speak to him. She did not.

The silent black hours that walked across his heart were worse than any he had spent in the Luna crypts.

She came soft-shod, bearing a candle. Beudag, the Dagger-in-the-Sheath. Starke was not asleep. He rose and stood waiting. She set the candle on the table and came, not quite to him, and stopped. She wore a length of thin white cloth twisted loosely at the waist and dropping to her ankles. Her body rose out of it straight and lovely, touched mystically with shadows in the little wavering light.

'Who are you?' she whispered. 'What are you?'

'A man. Not Conan. Maybe not Hugh Starke any more. Just a man.'

'I loved the man called Conan, until...' She caught her breath, and moved closer. She put her hand on Starke's arm. The touch went through him like white fire. The warm clean healthy fragrance of her tasted sweet in his throat. Her eyes searched his.

'If Rann has such great powers, couldn't it be that Conan was forced to do what he did? Couldn't it be that Rann took his mind and moulded it her way, perhaps without his knowing it?'

'It could be.'

'Conan was hot-tempered and quarrelsome, but he...'

Starke said slowly, 'I don't think you could have loved him if he hadn't been straight.'

Her hand lay still on his forearm. She stood looking at him, and then her hand began to tremble, and in a moment she was crying, making no noise about it. Starke drew her gently to him. His eyes blazed yellowly in the candlelight.

'Woman's tears,' she said impatiently, after a bit. She tried to draw away. 'I've been fighting too long, and losing, and I'm tired.'

He let her step back, not far. 'Do all the women of Crom Dhu fight like men?'

'If they want to. There have always been shield-maidens. And since Falga, I would have had to fight anyway, to keep from thinking.' She touched the collar on Starke's neck. 'And from seeing.'

He thought of Conan in the market square, and Conan shaking his chain and gibbering in Faolan's hall, and Beudag watching it. Starke's fingers tightened. He slid his palms upward along the smooth muscles of her arms, across the straight, broad planes of her shoulders, onto her neck, the proud strength of it pulsing under his hands. Her hair fell loose. He could feel the redness of it burning him.

She whispered, 'You don't love me.'

'No.'

'You're an honest man, Hugh Starke.'

'You want me to kiss you.'

'Yes.'

'You're an honest woman, Beudag.'

Her lips were hungry, passionate, touched with the bitterness of tears. After a while Starke blew out the candle...

'I could love you, Beudag.'

'Not the way I mean.'

'The way you mean. I've never said that to any woman before. But you're not like any woman before. And – I'm a different man.'

'Strange – so strange. Conan, and yet not Conan.'

'I could love you, Beudag – if I lived.'

Harpstrings gave a thrumming sigh in the darkness, the

faintest whisper of sound. Beudag started, sighed, and rose from the fur rug. In a minute she had found flint and steel and got the candle lighted. Romna the bard stood in the curtained doorway, watching them.

Presently he said, 'You're going to let him go.'

Beudag said, 'Yes.'

Romna nodded. He did not seem surprised. He walked across the dais, laying his harp on the table, and went into another room. He came back almost at once with a hacksaw.

'Bend your neck,' he said to Starke.

The metal of the collar was soft. When it was cut through Starke got his fingers under it and bent the ends outward, without trouble. His old body could never have done that. His old body could never have done a lot of things. He figured Rann hadn't cheated him. Not much.

He got up, looking at Beudag. Beudag's head was dropped forward, her face veiled behind shining hair.

'There's only one possible way out of Crom Dhu,' she said. There was no emotion in her voice. 'There's a passage leading down through the rock to a secret harbour, just large enough to moor a skiff or two. Perhaps, with the night and the fog, you can slip through Rann's blockade. Or you can go aboard one of her ships, for Falga.' She picked up the candle. 'I'll take you down.'

'Wait,' Starke said. 'What about you?'

She glanced at him, surprised. 'I'll stay, of course.'

He looked into her eyes. 'It's going to be hard to know each other that way.'

'You can't stay here, Hugh Starke. The people would tear you to pieces the moment you went into the street. They may even storm the hall, to take you. Look here.' She set the candle down and led him to a narrow window, drawing back the hide that covered it.

Starke saw narrow twisting streets dropping steeply toward the sullen sea. The longships were broken and sunk in the harbour. Out beyond, riding lights flickering in the red fog, were other ships. Rann's ships.

'Over there,' said Beudag, 'is the mainland. Crom Dhu is connected to it by a tongue of rock. The sea-folk hold the land beyond it, but we can hold the rock bridge as long as we live. We have enough water, enough food from the sea. But there's no soil nor game on Crom Dhu. We'll be naked after a while, without leather or flax, and we'll have scurvy without grain and fruit. We're beaten, unless the gods send us a miracle. And we're beaten because of what was done at Falga. You can see how the people feel.'

Starke looked at the dark streets and the silent houses leaning on each other's shoulders, and the mocking lights out in the fog. 'Yeah,' he said. 'I can see.'

'Besides, there's Faolan. I don't know whether he believes your story. I don't know whether it would matter.'

Starke nodded. 'But you won't come with me?'

She turned away sharply and picked up the candle again. 'Are you coming, Romna?'

The bard nodded. He slung his harp over his shoulder. Beudag held back the curtain of a small doorway far to the side. Starke went through it and Romna followed, and Beudag went ahead with the candle. No one spoke.

They went along a narrow passage, past store rooms and armouries. They paused once while Starke chose a knife, and Romna whispered: 'Wait!' He listened intently. Starke and Beudag strained their ears along with him. There was no sound. Romna shrugged. 'I thought I heard sandals scraping stone,' he said. They went on.

The passage lay behind a wooden door. It led downward steeply through the rock, a single narrow way without side galleries or branches. In some places there were winding steps. It ended, finally, in a flat ledge low to the surface of the cove, which was a small cavern closed in with the black rock. Beudag set the candle down.

There were two little skiffs built of some light metal moored to rings in the ledge. Two long sweeps leaned against the cave wall. They were of a different metal, oddly vaned. Beudag laid one across the thwarts of the nearest boat. Then she turned to Starke. Romna hung back in the shadows by the tunnel mouth.

Beudag said quietly, 'Goodbye, man without a name.'

'It has to be goodbye?'

'I'm leader now, in Faolan's place. Besides, these are my people.' Her fingers tightened on his wrists. 'If you could ...' Her eyes held a brief blaze of hope. Then she dropped her head and said, 'I keep forgetting you're not one of us. Goodbye.'

'Goodbye, Beudag.'

Starke put his arms around her. He found her mouth, almost cruelly. Her arms were tight about him, her eyes half closed and dreaming. Starke's hands slipped upward, toward her throat, and locked on it.

She bent back, her body like a steel bow. Her eyes got fire in them, looking into Starke's, but only for a moment. His fingers pressed expertly on the nerve centres. Beudag's head fell forward limply, and then Romna was on Starke's back and his knife was pricking Starke's throat.

Starke caught his wrist and turned the blade away. Blood ran onto his chest, but the cut was not into the artery. He threw himself backward onto the stone. Romna couldn't get clear in time. The breath went out of him in a rushing gasp. He didn't let go of the knife. Starke rolled over. The little man didn't have a chance with him. He was tough and quick, but Starke's sheer size smothered him. Starke could remember when Romna would not have seemed small to him. He hit the bard's jaw with his fist. Romna's head cracked hard against the stone. He let go of the knife. He seemed to be through fighting. Starke got up. He was sweating, breathing heavily, not because of his exertion. His mouth was glistening and eager, like a dog's. His muscles twitched, his belly was hot and knotted with excitement. His yellow eyes had a strange look.

He went back to Beudag.

She lay on the black rock, on her back. Candlelight ran pale gold across her brown skin, skirting the sharp strong hollows between her breasts and under the arching rim of her rib-case. Starke knelt, across her body, his weight pressed down against her harsh breathing. He stared at her. Sweat stood out on his face. He took her throat between his hands again.

He watched the blood grow dark in her cheeks. He watched the veins coil on her forehead. He watched the redness blacken in her lips. She fought a little, very vaguely, like someone moving in a dream. Starke breathed hoarsely, animal-like through an open mouth.

Then, gradually his body became rigid. His hands froze, not releasing pressure, but not adding any. His yellow eyes widened. It was as though he were trying to see Beudag's face and it was hidden in dense clouds.

Behind him, back in the tunnel, was the soft, faint whisper of sandals on uneven rock. Sandals, walking slowly. Starke did not hear. Beudag's face glimmered deep in a heavy mist below him, a blasphemy of a face, distorted, blackened.

Starke's hands began to open.

They opened slowly. Muscles stood like coiled ropes in his arms and shoulders, as though he moved them against heavy weights. His lips peeled back from his teeth. He bent his neck, and sweat dropped from his face and glittered on Beudag's breast.

Starke was now barely touching Beudag's neck. She began to breathe again, painfully.

Starke began to laugh. It was not nice laughter. 'Rann,' he whispered. 'Rann, you she-devil.' He half fell away from Beudag and stood up, holding himself against the wall. He was shaking violently. 'I wouldn't use your hate for killing, so you tried to use my passion.' He cursed her in a flat sibilant whisper. He had never in his profane life really cursed anyone before.

He heard an echo of laughter dancing in his brain.

Starke turned. Faolan of the Ships stood in the tunnel mouth. His head was bent, listening, his blind dark eyes fixed on Starke as though he saw him.

Faolan said softly 'I hear you, Starke. I hear the others breathing, but they don't speak.'

'They're all right. I didn't mean to do …'

Faolan smiled. He stepped out on the narrow ledge. He knew where he was going, and his smile was not pleasant.

'I heard your steps in the passage beyond my room. I knew Beudag was leading you, and where, and why. I would have been here sooner, but it's a slow way in the dark.'

The candle lay in his path. He felt the heat of it close to his leg, and stopped and felt for it, and ground it out. It was dark, then. Very dark, except for a faint smudgy glow from the scrap of ocean that lay along the cave floor.

'It doesn't matter,' Faolan said, 'as long as I came in time.'

Starke shifted his weight warily. 'Faolan ...'

'I wanted you alone. On this night of all nights I wanted you alone. Beudag fights in my place now, Conan. My manhood needs proving.'

Starke strained his eyes in the gloom, measuring the ledge, measuring the place where the skiff was moored. He didn't want to fight Faolan. In Faolan's place he would have felt the same. Starke understood perfectly. He didn't hate Faolan, he didn't want to kill him, and he was afraid of Rann's power over him when his emotions got control. You couldn't keep a determined man from killing you and still be uninvolved emotionally. Starke would be damned if he'd kill anyone to suit Rann.

He moved, silently, trying to slip past Faolan on the outside and get into the skiff. Faolan gave no sign of hearing him. Starke did not breathe. His sandals came down lighter than snowflakes. Faolan did not swerve. He would pass Starke with a foot to spare. They came abreast.

Faolan's hand shot out and caught in Starke's long black hair. The blind man laughed softly and closed in.

Starke swung one fist from the floor. Do it the quickest way and get clear. But Faolan was fast. He came in so swiftly that Starke's fist jarred harmlessly along his ribs. He was bigger than Starke, and heavier, and the darkness didn't bother him.

Starke bared his teeth. Do it quick, brother, and clear out! Or that green-eyed she-cat ... Faolan's brute bulk weighed him down. Faolan's arm crushed his neck. Faolan's fist was knocking his guts loose. Starke got moving.

He'd fought in a lot of places. He'd learned from stokers and tramps, Martian Low-Canallers, red-eyed Nahali in the running gutters of Lhi. He didn't use his knife. He used his knees and feet and elbows and his hands, fist and flat. It was a good fight. Faolan was a good fighter, but Starke knew more tricks.

One more, Starke thought. One more and he's out. He drew back for it, and his heel struck Romna, lying on the rock. He staggered, and Faolan caught him with a clean swinging blow.

Starke fell backward against the cave wall. His head cracked the rock. Light flooded crimson across his brain and then paled and grew cooler, a wash of clear silver-green like water. He sank under it...

He was tired, desperately tired. His head ached. He wanted to rest, but he could feel that he was sitting up, doing something that had to be done. He opened his eyes.

He sat in the stern of a skiff. The long sweep was laid into its crutch, held like a tiller bar against his body. The blade of the sweep trailed astern in the red sea, and where the metal touched there was a spurt of silver fire and a swirling of brilliant motes. The skiff moved rapidly through the sullen fog, through a mist of blood in the hot Venusian night.

Beudag crouched in the bow, facing Starke. She was bound securely with strips of the white cloth she had worn. Bruises showed dark on her throat. She was watching Starke with the intent, unwinking, perfectly expressionless gaze of a tigress.

Starke looked away, down at himself. There was blood on his kilt, a brown smear of it across his chest. It was not his blood. He drew the knife slowly out of its sheath. The blade was dull and crusted, still a little wet.

Starke looked at Beudag. His lips were stiff, swollen. He moistened them and said hoarsely, 'What happened?'

She shook her head, slowly, not speaking. Her eyes did not waver.

A black, cold rage took hold of Starke and shook him. Rann! He rose and went forward, letting the sweep go where it would. He began to untie Beudag's wrists.

A shape swam toward them out of the red mist. A longship with two heavy sweeps bursting fire astern and a slender figurehead shaped like a woman. A woman with hair and eyes of aquamarine. It came alongside the skiff.

A rope ladder snaked down. Men lined the low rail. Slender men with skin that glistened white like powdered snow, and hair the colour of distant shallows.

One of them said, 'Come aboard, Hugh Starke.'

Starke went back to the sweep. It bit into the sea, sending the skiff in a swift arc away from Rann's ship.

Grappels flew, hooking the skiff at thwart and gunwale. Bows appeared in the hands of the men, wicked curving things with barbed metal shafts on the string. The man said again, politely, 'Come aboard.'

Hugh Starke finished untying Beudag. He didn't speak. There seemed to be nothing to say. He stood back while she climbed the ladder and then followed. The skiff was cast loose. The longship veered away, gathering speed.

Starke said, 'Where are we going?'

The man smiled. 'To Falga.'

Starke nodded. He went below with Beudag into a cabin with soft couches covered with spider-silk and panels of dark wood beautifully painted, dim fantastic scenes from the past of Rann's people. They sat opposite each other. They still did not speak.

They reached Falga in the opal dawn – a citadel of basalt cliffs rising sheer from the burning sea, with a long arm holding a harbour full of ships. There were green fields inland, and beyond, cloaked in the eternal mists of Venus, the Mountains of White Clouds lifted spaceward. Starke wished that he had never seen the Mountains of White Cloud. Then, looking at his hands, lean and strong on his long thighs, he wasn't so sure. He thought of Rann waiting for him. Anger, excitement, a confused violence of emotion set him pacing nervously.

Beudag sat quietly, withdrawn, waiting.

The longship threaded the crowded moorings and slid into place alongside a stone quay. Men rushed to make fast. They were human men, as Starke judged humans, like Beudag and himself. They had the shimmering silver hair and fair skin of the plateau peoples, the fine-cut faces and straight bodies. They wore leather collars with metal tags and they went naked like beasts, and they were gaunt and bowed with labour. Here and there a man with pale blue-green hair and resplendent harness stood godlike above the swarming masses.

Starke and Beudag went ashore. They might have been prisoners or honoured guests, surrounded by their escort from the ship. Streets ran back from the harbour, twisting and climbing crazily up the cliffs. Houses climbed on each other's backs.

It had begun to rain, the heavy steaming downpour of Venus, and the moist heat brought out the choking stench of people, too many people.

They climbed, ankle deep in water sweeping down the streets that were half stairway. Thin naked children peered out of the houses, out of narrow alleys. Twice they passed through market squares where women with the blank faces of defeat drew back from stalls of coarse food to let the party through.

There was something wrong. After a while Starke realised it was the silence. In all that horde of humanity no one laughed, or sang, or shouted. Even the children never spoke above a whisper. Starke began to feel a little sick. Their eyes had a look in them ...

He glanced at Beudag, and away again.

The waterfront streets ended in a sheer basalt face honeycombed with galleries. Starke's party entered them, still climbing. They passed level after level of huge caverns, open to the sea. There was the same crowding, the same stench, the same silence. Eyes glinted in the half-light, bare feet moved furtively on stone. Somewhere a baby cried thinly, and was hushed at once.

They came out on the cliff top, into the clean high air. There was a city here. Broad streets, lined with trees, low rambling villas of the black rock set in walled gardens, drowned in brilliant vines and giant ferns and flowers. Naked men and women worked in the gardens, or hauled carts of rubbish through the alleys, or hurried on errands, slipping furtively across the main streets where they intersected the mews.

The party turned away from the sea, heading toward an ebon palace that sat like a crown above the city. The steaming rain beat on Starke's bare body, and up here you could get the smell of the rain, even through the heavy perfume of the flowers. You could smell Venus in the rain – musky and primitive and savagely alive, a fecund giantess with passion flowers in her outstretched hands. Starke set his feet down like a panther and his eyes burned a smoky amber.

They entered the palace of Rann ...

She received them in the same apartment where Starke had

come to after the crash. Through a broad archway he could see the high bed where his old body had lain before the life went out of it. The red sea steamed under the rain outside, the rusty fog coiling languidly through the open arches of the gallery. Rann watched them lazily from a raised couch set massively into the wall. Her long sparkling legs sprawled arrogantly across the black spider-silk draperies. This time her tabard was a pale yellow. Her eyes were still the colour of shoal-water, still amused, still secret, still dangerous.

Starke said, 'So you made me do it after all.'

'And you're angry.' She laughed, her teeth showing white and pointed as bone needles. Her gaze held Starke's. There was nothing casual about it. Starke's hawk eyes turned molten yellow, like hot gold, and did not waver.

Beudag stood like a bronze spear, her forearms crossed beneath her bare sharp breasts. Two of Rann's palace guards stood behind her.

Starke began to walk toward Rann.

She watched him come. She let him get close enough to reach out and touch her, and then she said slyly, 'It's a good body, isn't it?'

Starke looked at her for a moment. Then he laughed. He threw back his head and roared, and struck the great corded muscles of his belly with his fist. Presently he looked straight into Rann's eyes and said:

'I know you.'

She nodded. 'We know each other. Sit down, Hugh Starke.' She swung her long legs over to make room, half erect now, looking at Beudag. Starke sat down. He did not look at Beudag.

Rann said, 'Will your people surrender now?'

Beudag did not move, not even her eyelids. 'If Faolan is dead – yes.'

'And if he's not?'

Beudag stiffened. Starke did too.

'Then,' said Beudag quietly, 'They'll wait.'

'Until he is?'

'Or until they must surrender.'

Rann nodded. To the guards she said, 'See that this woman is well fed and well treated.'

Beudag and her escort had turned to go when Starke said, 'Wait.' The guards looked at Rann, who nodded, and glanced quizzically at Starke. Starke said:

'Is Faolan dead?'

Rann hesitated. Then she smiled. 'No. You have the most damnably tough mind, Starke. You struck deep, but not deep enough. He may still die, but ... No, he's not dead.' She turned to Beudag and said with easy mockery, 'You needn't hold anger against Starke. I'm the one who should be angry.' Her eyes came back to Starke. They didn't look angry.

Starke said, 'There's something else. Conan – the Conan that used to be, before Falga.'

'Beudag's Conan.'

'Yeah. Why did he betray his people?'

Rann studied him. Her strange pale lips curved, her sharp white teeth glistened wickedly with barbed humour. Then she turned to Beudag. Beudag was still standing like a carved image, but her smooth muscles were ridged with tension, and her eyes were not the eyes of an image.

'Conan or Starke,' said Rann, 'she's still Beudag, isn't she? All right, I'll tell you. Conan betrayed his people because I put it into his mind to do it. He fought me. He made a good fight of it. But he wasn't quite as tough as you are, Starke.'

There was a silence. For the first time since entering the room, Hugh Starke looked at Beudag. After a moment she sighed and lifted her chin and smiled, a deep, faint smile. The guards walked out beside her, but she was more erect and lighter of step than either of them.

'Well,' said Rann, when they were gone, 'and what about you, Hugh-Starke-Called-Conan.'

'Have I any choice?'

'I always keep my bargains.'

'Then give me my dough and let me clear the hell out of here.'

'Sure that's what you want?'

'That's what I want.'

'You could stay a while, you know.'

'With you?'

Rann lifted her frosty-white shoulders. 'I'm not promising half my kingdom, or even part of it. But you might be amused.'

'I got no sense of humour.'

'Don't you even want to see what happens to Crom Dhu?'

'And Beudag.' He stopped, then fixed Rann with uncompromising yellow eyes. 'No. Not Beudag. What are you going to do to her?'

'Nothing.'

'Don't give me that.'

'I say again, nothing. Whatever is done, her own people will do.'

'What do you mean?'

'I mean that little Dagger-in-the-Sheath will be rested, cared for, and fattened, for a few days. Then I shall take her aboard my own ship and join the fleet before Crom Dhu. Beudag will be made quite comfortable at the masthead, where her people can see her plainly. She will stay there until the Rock surrenders. It depends on her own people how long she stays. She'll be given water. Not much, but enough.'

Starke stared at her. He stared at her a long time. Then he spat deliberately on the floor and said in a perfectly flat voice: 'How soon can I get out of here?'

Rann laughed, a small casual chuckle. 'Humans,' she said, 'are so damned queer. I don't think I'll ever understand them.' She reached out and struck a gong that stood in a carved frame beside the couch. The soft deep shimmering note had a sad quality of nostalgia. Rann lay back against the silken cushions and sighed.

'Goodbye, Hugh Starke.'

A pause. Then, regretfully:

'Goodbye – Conan!'

They had made good time along the rim of the Red Sea. One of Rann's galleys had taken them to the edge of the Southern Ocean and left them on a narrow shingle beach under the cliffs. From there they had climbed to the rimrock and gone on foot – Hugh-Starke-Called-Conan and four of Rann's arrogant shining men. They were supposed to be guide and escort. They were courteous, and they kept pace uncomplainingly though Starke marched as though the devil were pricking his heels. But they were armed, and Starke was not.

Sometimes, very faintly, Starke was aware of Rann's mind touching his with the velvet delicacy of a cat's paw. Sometimes he started out of his sleep with her image sharp in his mind, her lips touched with the mocking, secret smile. He didn't like that. He didn't like it at all.

But he liked even less the picture that stayed with him waking or sleeping. The picture he wouldn't look at. The picture of a tall woman with hair like loose fire on her neck, walking on light proud feet between her guards.

She'll be given water, Rann said. Not much, but enough.

Starke gripped the solid squareness of the box that held his million credits and set the miles reeling backward from under his sandals.

On the fifth night one of Rann's men spoke quietly across the campfire. 'Tomorrow,' he said, 'we'll reach the pass.'

Starke got up and went away by himself, to the edge of the rimrock that fell sheer to the burning sea. He sat down. The red fog wrapped him like a mist of blood. He thought of the blood on Beudag's breast the first time he saw her. He thought of the blood on his knife, crusted and dried. He thought of the blood poured rank and smoking into the gutters of Crom Dhu. The fog has to be red, he thought. Of all the goddamn colours in the universe, it has to be red. Red like Beudag's hair.

He held out his hands and looked at them, because he could still feel the silken warmth of that hair against his skin. There was nothing there now but the old white scars of another man's battles.

He set his fists against his temples and wished for his old body back again – the little stunted abortion that had clawed and scratched its way to survival through sheer force of mind. A most damnably tough mind, Rann had said. Yeah. It had had to be tough. But a mind was a mind. It didn't have emotions. It just figured out something coldly and then went ahead and never questioned, and it controlled the body utterly, because the body was only the worthless machinery that carried the mind around. Worthless. Yeah. The few women he'd ever looked at had told him that – and he hadn't even minded much. The old body hadn't given him any trouble.

He was having trouble now.

Starke got up and walked.

Tomorrow we reach the pass.

Tomorrow we go away from the Red Sea. There are nine planets and the whole damn Belt. There are women on all of them. All shapes, colours, and sizes, human, semi-human, and God knows what. With a million credits a guy could buy half of them, and with Conan's body he could buy the rest. What's a woman, anyway? Only a ...

Water. She'll be given water. Not much, but enough.

Conan reached out and took hold of a spire of rock, and his muscles stood out like knotted ropes. 'Oh God,' he whispered, 'what's the matter with me?'

'*Love.*'

It wasn't God who answered. It was Rann. He saw her plainly in his mind, heard her voice like a silver bell.

'Conan was a man, Hugh Starke. He was whole, body and heart and brain. He knew how to love, and with him it wasn't women, but one woman – and her name was Beudag. I broke him, but it wasn't easy. I can't break you.'

Starke stood for a long, long time. He did not move, except that he trembled. Then he took from his belt the box containing his million credits and threw it out as far as he could over the cliff edge. The red mist swallowed it up. He did not hear it strike the surface of the sea. Perhaps in that sea there was no splashing. He did not wait to find out.

He turned back along the rimrock, toward a place where he remembered a cleft, or chimney, leading down. And the four shining men who wore Rann's harness came silently out of the heavy luminous night and ringed him in. Their sword-points caught sharp red glimmers from the sky.

Starke had nothing on him but a kilt and sandals, and a cloak of tight-woven spider-silk that shed the rain.

'Rann sent you?' he said.

The men nodded.

'To kill me?'

Again they nodded. The blood drained out of Starke's face, leaving it grey and stony under the bronze. His hand went to his throat, over the gold fastening of his cloak.

The four men closed in like dancers.

Starke loosed his cloak and swung it like a whip across their faces. It confused them for a second, for a heartbeat – no more, but long enough. Starke left two of them to tangle their blades in the heavy fabric and leaped aside. A sharp edge slipped and turned along his ribs, and then he had reached in low and caught a man around the ankles, and used the thrashing body for a flail.

The body was strangely light, as though the bones in it were no more than rigid membrane, like a fish.

If he had stayed to fight, they would have finished him in seconds. They were fighting men, and quick. But Starke didn't stay. He gained his moment's grace and used it. They were hard on his heels, their points all but pricking his back as he ran, but he made it. Along the rimrock, out along a narrow tongue that jutted over the sea, and then outward, far outward, into red fog and dim fire that rolled around his plummeting body.

Oh God, he thought, if I guessed wrong and there *is* a beach...

The breath tore out of his lungs. His ears cracked, went dead. He held his arms out beyond his head, the thumbs locked together, his neck braced forward against the terrific upward push. He struck the surface of the sea.

There was no splash.

Dim coiling fire that drifted with infinite laziness around him, caressing his body with slow, tingling sparks. A feeling of lightness, as though his flesh had become one with the drifting fire. A sense of suffocation that had no basis in fact and gave way gradually to a strange exhilaration. There was no shock of impact, no crushing pressure. Merely a cushioning softness, like dropping into a bed of compressed air. Starke felt himself turning end over end, pinwheel fashion, and then that stopped, so that he sank quietly and without haste to the bottom.

Or rather, into the crystalline upper reaches of what seemed to be a forest.

He could see it spreading away along the downward-sloping floor of the ocean, into the vague red shadows of distance. Slender fantastic trunks upholding a maze of delicate shining branches, without leaves or fruit. They were like trees exquisitely moulded from ice, transparent, holding the lambent shifting fire of the strange sea. Starke didn't think they were, or ever had been, alive. More like coral, he thought, or some vagary of mineral deposit. Beautiful, though. Like something you'd see in a dream. Beautiful, silent, and somehow deadly.

He couldn't explain that feeling of deadliness. Nothing moved in the red drifts between the trunks. It was nothing about the trees themselves. It was just something he sensed.

He began to move among the upper branches, following the downward drop of the slope.

He found that he could swim quite easily. Or perhaps it was more like flying. The dense gas buoyed him up, almost balancing the weight of his body, so that it was easy to swoop along, catching a crystal branch and using it as a lever to throw himself forward to the next one.

He went deeper and deeper into the heart of the forbidden Southern Ocean. Nothing stirred. The fairy forest stretched limitless ahead. And Starke was afraid.

Rann came into his mind abruptly. Her face, clearly outlined, was full of mockery.

'I'm going to watch you die, Hugh-Starke-Called-Conan. But before you die, I'll show you something. Look.'

Her face dimmed, and in its place was Crom Dhu rising bleak into the red fog, the longships broken and sunk in the harbour, and Rann's fleet around it in a shining circle.

One ship in particular. The flagship. The vision in Starke's mind rushed toward it, narrowed down to the masthead platform. To the woman who stood there, naked, erect, her body lashed tight with thin cruel cords.

A woman with red hair blowing in the slow wind, and blue eyes that looked straight ahead like a falcon's, at Crom Dhu.

Beudag.

Rann's laughter ran across the picture and blurred it like a ripple of ice-cold water.

'You'd have done better,' she said, 'to take the clean steel when I offered it to you.'

She was gone, and Starke's mind was as empty and cold as the mind of a corpse. He found that he was standing still, clinging to a branch, his face upturned as though by some blind instinct, his sight blurred.

He had never cried before in all his life, nor prayed.

There was no such thing as time, down there in the smoky shadows of the sea bottom. It might have been minutes or hours later that Hugh Starke discovered he was being hunted.

There were three of them, slipping easily among the shining branches. They were pale golden, almost phosphorescent, about the size of large hounds. Their eyes were huge, jewel-like in their slim sharp faces. They possessed four members that might have been legs and arms, retracted now against their arrowing bodies. Golden membranes spread wing-like from head to flank, and they moved like wings, balancing expertly the thrust of the flat, powerful tails.

They could have closed in on him easily, but they didn't seem to be in any hurry. Starke had sense enough not to wear himself out trying to get away. He kept on going, watching them. He discovered that the crystal branches could be broken, and he selected himself one with a sharp forked tip, shoving it sword-wise under his belt. He didn't suppose it would do much good, but it made him feel better.

He wondered why the things didn't jump him and get it over with. They looked hungry enough, the way they were showing him their teeth. But they kept about the same distance away, in a sort of crescent formation, and every so often the ones on the outside would make a tentative dart at him, then fall back as he swerved away. It wasn't like being hunted so much as ...

Starke's eyes narrowed. He began suddenly to feel much more afraid than he had before, and he wouldn't have believed that possible.

The things weren't hunting him at all. They were herding him.

There was nothing he could do about it. He tried stopping, and they swooped in and snapped at him, working expertly together so that while he was trying to stab one of them with his clumsy weapon, the others were worrying his heels like sheep-dogs at a recalcitrant wether.

Starke, like the wether, bowed to the inevitable and went where he was driven. The golden hounds showed their teeth in animal laughter and sniffed hungrily at the thread of blood he left behind him in the slow red coils of fire.

After a while he heard the music.

It seemed to be some sort of a harp, with a strange quality of vibration in the notes. It wasn't like anything he'd ever heard before. Perhaps the gas of which the sea was composed was an extraordinarily good conductor of sound, with a property of diffusion that made the music seem to come from everywhere at once – softly at first, like something touched upon in a dream, and then, as he drew closer to the source, swelling into a racing, rippling flood of melody that wrapped itself around his nerves with a demoniac shiver of ecstasy.

The golden hounds began to fret with excitement, spreading their shining wings, driving him impatiently faster through the crystal branches.

Starke could feel the vibration growing in him – the very fibres of his muscles shuddering in sympathy with the unearthly harp. He guessed there was a lot of the music he couldn't hear. Too high, too low for his ears to register. But he could feel it.

He began to go faster, not because of the hounds, but because he wanted to. The deep quivering in his flesh excited him. He began to breathe harder, partly because of increased exertion, and some chemical quality of the mixture he breathed made him slightly drunk.

The thrumming harp-song stroked and stung him, waking a deeper, darker music, and suddenly he saw Beudag clearly – half-veiled and mystic in the candlelight at Faolan's dun; smooth curving bronze, her hair loose fire about her throat. A great stab of agony went through him. He called her name, once, and the harp-song swept it up and away, and then suddenly there was no music any more, and no forest, and nothing but cold embers in Starke's heart.

He could see everything quite clearly in the time it took him to float from the top of the last tree to the floor of the plain. He had no idea how long a time that was. It didn't matter. It was one of those moments when time doesn't have any meaning.

The rim of the forest fell away in a long curve that melted glistening into the spark-shot sea. From it the plain stretched out, a level glassy floor of black obsidian, the spew of some long-dead volcano. Or was it dead? It seemed to Starke that the light here was redder, more vital, as though he were close to the source from which it sprang.

As he looked farther over the plain, the light seemed to coalesce into a shimmering curtain that wavered like the heat veils that dance along the Mercurian Twilight Belt at high noon. For one brief instant he glimpsed a picture on the curtain – a city, black, shining, fantastically turreted, the gigantic reflection of a Titan's dream. Then it was gone, and the immediate menace of the foreground took all of Starke's attention.

He saw the flock, herded by more of the golden hounds. And he saw the shepherd, with the harp held silent between his hands.

The flock moved slightly, phosphorescently.

One hundred, two hundred silent, limply floating warriors drifting down the red dimness. In pairs, singly, or in pallid clusters they came. The golden hounds winged silently, leisurely around them, channelling them in tides that sluiced toward the fantastic ebon city.

The shepherd stood, a crop of obsidian, turning his shark-pale face. His sharp, aquamarine eyes found Starke. His silvery hand leapt beckoning over hard-threads, striking them a blow. Reverberations ran out, seized Starke, shook him. He dropped his crystal dagger.

Hot screens of fire exploded in his eyes, bubbles whirled and danced in his eardrums. He lost all muscular control. His dark head fell forward against the thick blackness of hair on his chest; his golden eyes dissolved into weak, inane yellow, and his mouth loosened. He wanted to fight, but it was useless. This shepherd was one of the sea-people he had come to see, and one way or another he would see him.

Dark blood filled his aching eyes. He felt himself led, nudged, forced first this way, then that. A golden hound slipped by, gave him a pressure which rolled him over into a current of sea-blood. It ran down past where the shepherd stood with only a harp for a weapon.

Starke wondered dimly whether these other warriors in the flock, drifting, were dead or alive like himself. He had another surprise coming.

They were all Rann's men. Men of Falga. Silver men with burning green hair. Rann's men. One of them, a huge warrior coloured like powdered salt, wandered aimlessly by on another tide, his green eyes dull. He looked dead.

What business had the sea-people with the dead warriors of Falga? Why the hounds and the shepherd's harp? Questions eddied like lifted silt in Starke's tired, hanging head. Eddied and settled flat.

Starke joined the pilgrimage.

The hounds with deft flickerings of wings ushered him into the midst of the flock. Bodies brushed against him. *Cold* bodies. He wanted to cry out. the cords of his neck constricted. In his mind the cry went forward:

'Are you alive, men of Falga?'

No answer; but the drift of scarred, pale bodies. The eyes in them knew nothing. They had forgotten Falga. They had forgotten Rann for whom they had lifted blade. Their tongues lolling in mouths asked nothing but sleep. They were getting it.

A hundred, two hundred strong they made a strange human river slipping toward the gigantic city wall. Starke-called-Conan and his bitter enemies going together. From the corners of his eyes, Starke saw the shepherd move. The shepherd was like Rann and her people who had years ago abandoned the sea to live on land. The shepherd seemed colder, more fish-like, though. There were small translucent webs between the thin fingers and spanning the long-toed feet. Thin, scar-like gills in the shadow of his tapered chin, lifted and sealed in the current, eating, taking sustenance from the blood-coloured sea.

The harp spoke and the golden hounds obeyed. The harp spoke and the bodies twisted uneasily, as in a troubled sleep. A triple chord of it came straight at Starke. His fingers clenched.

'—and the dead shall walk again—'

Another ironic ripple of music.

'—and Rann's men will rise again, this time against her—'

Starke had time to feel a brief, bewildered shivering, before the current hurled him forward. Clamouring drunkenly, witlessly, all about him, the dead, muscle-less warriors of Falga tried to crush past him, all of them at once...

Long ago some vast sea Titan had dreamed of avenues struck from black stone. Each stone the size of three men tall. There had been a dream of walls going up and up until they dissolved into scarlet mist. There had been another dream of sea-gardens in which fish hung like exotic flowers, on tendrils of sensitive film-tissue. Whole beds of fish clung to a garden base, like colonies of flowers aglow with sunlight. And on occasion a black amoebic presence filtered by, playing the gardener, weeding out an amber flower here, an amythystine bloom there.

And the sea Titan had dreamed of endless balustrades and battlements, of windowless turrets where creatures swayed like radium-skinned phantoms, carrying their green plumes of hair in their lifted palms, and looked down with curious, insolent eyes from on high. Women with shimmering bodies like some incredible coral harvested and kept high over these black stone streets, each in its archway.

Starke was alone. Falga's warriors had gone off along a dim subterranean vent, vanished. Now the faint beckoning of harp and the golden hounds behind him turned him down a passage that opened out into a large circular stone room, one end of which opened out into a hall. Around the ebon ceiling, slender schools of fish swam. It was their bright effulgence that gave light to the room. They had been there, breeding, eating, dying, a thousand years, giving light to the place, and they would be there breeding and dying, a thousand more.

The harp faded until it was only a murmur.

Starke found his feet. Strength returned to him. He was able to see the man in the centre of the room well. Too well.

The man hung in the fire tide. Chains of wrought bronze held his thin fleshless ankles so he couldn't escape. His body desired it. It floated up.

It had been dead a long time. It was gaseous with decomposition and it wanted to rise to the surface of the Red Sea. The chains prevented this. Its arms weaved like white scarves before a sunken white face. Black hair trembled on end.

He was one of Faolan's men. One of the Rovers. One of those who had gone down at Falga because of Conan.

His name was Geil.

Starke remembered.

The part of him that was Conan remembered the name.

The dead lips moved.

'Conan. What luck is this! Conan. I make you welcome.'

The words were cruel, the lips around them loose and dead. It seemed to Starke an anger and embittered wrath lay deep in those hollow eyes. The lips twitched again.

'I went down at Falga for you and Rann, Conan. Remember?'

Part of Starke remembered and twisted in agony.

'We're all here, Conan. All of us. Clev and Mannt and Bron and Aesur. Remember Aesur, who could shape metal over his spine, prying it with his fingers? Aesur is here, big as a sea-monster, waiting in a niche, cold and loose as string. The sea-shepherds collected us. Collected us for a purpose of irony. Look!'

The boneless fingers hung out, as in a wind, pointing.

Starke turned slowly, and his heart pounded an uneven, shattering drum beat. His jaw clinched and his eyes blurred. That part of him that was Conan cried out. Conan was so much of him and he so much of Conan it was impossible for a cleavage. They'd grown together like pearl material around sand-specule, layer on layer. Starke cried out.

In the hall which this circular room overlooked, stood a thousand men.

In lines of fifty across, shoulder to shoulder, the men of Crom Dhu stared unseeingly up at Starke. Here and there a face became shockingly familiar. Old memory cried their names.

'Bron! Clev! Mannt! Aesur!'

The collected decomposition of their bodily fluids raised them, drifted them above the flaggings. Each of them was chained, like Geil.

Geil whispered. 'We have made a union with the men of Falga!'

Starke pulled back.

'Falga!'

'In death, all men are equals.' He took his time with it. He was in no hurry. Dead bodies under-sea are never in a hurry. They sort of bump and drift and bide their time. 'The dead serve those who give them a semblance of life. Tomorrow we march against Crom Dhu.'

'You're crazy! Crom Dhu is *your* home! It's the place of Beudag and Faolan—'

'And—' interrupted the hanging corpse, quietly, 'Conan? Eh?' He laughed. A crystal dribble of bubbles ran up from the slack mouth. 'Especially Conan. Conan who sank us at Falga ...'

Starke moved swiftly. Nobody stopped him. He had the corpse's short blade in an instant. Geil's chest made a cold, silent sheath for it. The blade went like a fork through butter.

Coldly, without noticing this, Geil's voice spoke out:

'Stab me, cut me. You can't kill me any deader. Make sections of me. Play butcher. A flank, a hand, a heart! And while you're at it, I'll tell you the plan.'

Snarling, Starke seized the blade out again. With blind violence he gave sharp blow after blow at the body, cursing bitterly, and the body took each blow, rocking in the red tide a little, and said with a matter-of-fact-tone:

'We'll march out of the sea to Crom Dhu's gates. Romna and the others, looking down, recognising us, will have the gates thrown wide to welcome us.' The head tilted lazily, the lips peeled wide and folded down languidly over the words. 'Think of the elation, Conan! The moment when Bron and Mannt and Aesur and I and yourself, yes, even yourself, Conan, return to Crom Dhu!'

Starke saw it, vividly. Saw it like a tapestry woven for him. He stood back, gasping for breath, his nostrils flaring, seeing what his blade had done to Geil's body, and seeing the great stone gates of Crom Dhu crashing open. The deliberation. The happiness, the elation of Faolan and Romna to see old friends returned. Old Rovers, long thought dead. Alive again, come to help! It made a picture!

With great deliberation, Starke struck flat across before him.

Geil's head, severed from its lazy body, began, with infinite tiredness, to float toward the ceiling. As it travelled upward, now facing, now bobbling the back of its skull toward Starke, it finished its nightmare speaking:

'And then, once inside the gates, what then, Conan? Can you guess? Can you guess what we'll do, Conan?'

Starke stared at nothingness, the sword trembling in his fist. From far away he heard Geil's voice:

'—we will kill Faolan in his hall. He will die with surprised lips. Romna's harp will lie in his disembowelled stomach. His heart with its last pulsings will sound the strings. And as for Beudag—'

Starke tried to push the thoughts away, raging and helpless. Geil's body was no longer anything to look at. He had done all he could to it. Starke's face was bleached white and scraped down to the insane bone of it. 'You'd kill your own people!'

Geil's separated head lingered at the ceiling, light-fish illuminating its ghastly features. 'Our people? But we have no people! We're another race now. The dead. We do the bidding of the sea-shepherds.'

Starke looked out into the hall, then he looked at the circular wall.

'Okay,' he said, without tone in his voice. 'Come out. Wherever you're hiding and using this voice-throwing act. Come on out and talk straight.'

In answer, an entire section of ebon stones fell back on silent hingework. Starke saw a long slender black marble table. Six people sat behind it in carven midnight thrones.

They were all men. Naked except for film-like garments about their loins. They looked at Starke with no particular hatred or curiosity. One of them cradled a harp. It was the shepherd who'd drawn Starke through the gate. Amusedly, his webbed fingers

153

lay on the strings, now and then bringing out a clear sound from one of the two hundred strands.

The shepherd stopped Starke's rush forward with a cry of that harp!

The blade in his hand was red hot. He dropped it.

The shepherd put the head on the story. 'And then? And then we will march Rann's dead warriors all the way to Falga. There, Rann's people, seeing the warriors, will be overjoyed, hysterical to find their friends and relatives returned. They, too, will fling wide Falga's defences. And death will walk in, disguised as resurrection.'

Starke nodded, slowly, wiping his hand across his cheek. 'Back on Earth we call that psychology. *Good* psychology. But will it fool Rann?'

'Rann will be with her ships at Crom Dhu. While she's gone, the innocent population will let in their lost warriors gladly.' The shepherd had amused green eyes. He looked like a youth of some seventeen years. Deceptively young. If Starke guessed right, the youth was nearer to two centuries old. That's how you lived and looked when you were under the Red Sea. Something about the emanations of it kept part of you young.

Starke lidded his yellow hawk's eyes thoughtfully. 'You've got all aces. You'll win. But what's Crom Dhu to you? Why not just Rann? She's one of you; you hate her more than you do the Rovers. Her ancestors came up on land; you never got over hating them for that—'

The shepherd shrugged. 'Toward Crom Dhu we have little actual hatred. Except that they are by nature land-men, even if they do rove by boat, and pillagers. One day they might try their luck on the sunken devices of this city.'

Starke put a hand out. 'We're fighting Rann, too. Don't forget, we're on your side!'

'Whereas we are on no one's,' retorted the green-haired youth, 'except our own. Welcome to the army which will attack Crom Dhu.'

'Me! By the gods, over my dead body!'

'That,' said the youth, amusedly, 'is what we intend. We've worked many years, you see, to perfect the plan. We're not much good out on land. We needed bodies that could do the work for us. So, every time Faolan lost a ship or Rann lost a ship, we were there, with our golden hounds, waiting. Collecting. Saving. Waiting until we had enough of each side's warriors. They'll do the fighting for us. Oh, not for long, of course. The Source energy will give them a semblance of life, a momentary electrical ability to walk and combat, but once out of water they'll last only half an hour. But that should be time enough once the gates of Crom Dhu and Falga are open.'

Starke said, 'Rann will find some way around you. Get her first. Attack Crom Dhu the following day.'

The youth deliberated. 'You're stalling. But there's sense in it. Rann is most important. We'll get Falga first, then. You'll have a bit of time in which to raise false hopes.'

Starke began to get sick again. The room swam.

Very quietly, very easily, Rann came into his mind again. He felt her glide in like the merest touch of a sea fern weaving in a tide pool.

He closed his mind down, but not before she snatched at a shred of thought. Her aquamarine eyes reflected desire and inquiry.

'Hugh Starke, you're with the sea people?'

Her voice was soft. He shook his head.

'Tell me, Hugh Starke. How are you plotting against Falga?'

He said nothing. He thought nothing. He shut his eyes.

Her fingernails glittered, raking at his mind. 'Tell me!'

His thoughts rolled tightly into a metal sphere which nothing could dent.

Rann laughed unpleasantly and leaned forward until she filled every dark horizon of his skull with her shimmering body. 'All right. I *gave* you Conan's body. Now I'll take it away.'

She struck him a combined blow of her eyes, her writhing lips, her bone-sharp teeth. 'Go back to your old body, go back to your old body, Hugh Starke,' she hissed. 'Go back! Leave Conan to his idiocy. Go back to your old body!'

Fear had him. He fell down upon his face, quivering and jerking. You could fight a man with a sword. But how could you fight this thing in your brain? He began to suck sobbing breaths through his lips. He was screaming. He could not hear himself. Her voice rushed in from the dim outer red universe, destroying him.

'Hugh Starke! Go back to your old body!'

His old body was – dead!

And she was sending him back into it.

Part of him shot endwise through red fog.

He lay on a mountain plateau overlooking the harbour of Falga.

Red fog coiled and snaked around him. Flame birds dived eerily down at his staring, blind eyes.

His old body held him.

Putrefaction stuffed his nostrils. The flesh sagged and slipped greasily on his loosened structure. He felt small again and ugly. Flame birds nibbled, picking, choosing between his ribs. Pain gorged him. Cold, blackness, nothingness filled him. Back in his old body. Forever.

He didn't want that.

The plateau, the red fog vanished. The flame birds, too.

He lay once more on the floor of the sea shepherds, struggling.

'That was just a start,' Rann told him. 'Next time, I'll leave you up there on the plateau in that body. *Now*, will you tell the plans of the sea people? And go on living in Conan? He's yours, if you tell.' She smirked. 'You don't want to be dead.'

Starke tried to reason it out. Any way he turned was the wrong way. He grunted out a breath. 'If I tell, you'll still kill Beudag.'

'Her life in exchange for what you know, Hugh Starke.'

Her answer was too swift. It had the sound of treachery. Starke did not believe. He would die. That would solve it. Then, at least, Rann would die when the sea people carried out their strategy. That much revenge, at least, damn it.

Then he got the idea.

He coughed out a laugh, raised his weak head to look at the startled sea shepherd. His little dialogue with Rann had taken about ten seconds, actually, but it had seemed a century. The sea shepherd stepped forward.

Starke tried to get to his feet. 'Got – got a proposition for you.

You with the harp. Rann's inside me. *Now*. Unless you guarantee Crom Dhu and Beudag's safety, I'll tell her some things she might want to be in on!'

The sea shepherd drew a knife.

Starke shook his head, coldly. 'Put it away. Even if you get me I'll give the whole damned strategy to Rann.'

The shepherd dropped his hand. He was no fool.

Rann tore at Starke's brain. 'Tell me! Tell me their plan!'

He felt like a guy in a revolving door. Starke got the sea men in focus. He saw that they were afraid now, doubtful and nervous. 'I'll be dead in a minute,' said Starke. 'Promise me the safety of Crom Dhu and I'll die without telling Rann a thing.'

The sea shepherd hesitated, then raised his palm upward. 'I promise,' he said. 'Crom Dhu will go untouched.'

Starke sighed. He let his head fall forward until it hit the floor. Then he rolled over, put his hands over his eyes. 'It's a deal. Go give Rann hell for me, will you, boys? Give her hell!'

As he drifted into mind darkness, Rann waited for him. Feebly, he told her, 'Okay, duchess. You'd kill me even if I'd told you the idea. I'm ready. Try your god-awfullest to shove me back into that stinking body of mine. I'll fight you all the way there!'

Rann screamed. It was a pretty frustrated scream. Then the pains began. She did a lot of work on his mind in the next minute.

That part of him that was Conan held on like a clam holding to its precious contents.

The odour of putrid flesh returned. The blood mist returned. The flame birds fell down at him in spirals of sparks and blistering smoke, to winnow his naked ribs.

Starke spoke one last word before the blackness took him. 'Beudag.'

He never expected to awaken again.

He awoke just the same.

There was red sea all around him. He lay on a kind of stone bed, and the young sea shepherd sat beside him, looking down at him, smiling delicately.

Starke did not dare move for a while. He was afraid his head might fall off and whirl away like a big fish, using its ears as propellers. 'Lord,' he muttered, barely turning his head.

The sea creature stirred. 'You won. You fought Rann, and won.'

Starke groaned. 'I feel like something passed through a wild-cat's intestines. She's gone. Rann's gone.' He laughed. 'That makes me sad. Somebody cheer me up. Rann's gone.' He felt of his big, flat-muscled body. 'She was bluffing. Trying to decide to drive me batty. She knew she couldn't really tuck me back into that carcass, but she didn't want me to know. It was like a baby's nightmare before it's born. Or maybe you haven't got a memory like me.' He rolled over, stretching. 'She won't ever get in my head again. I've locked the gate and swallowed the key.' His eyes dilated. 'What's *your* name?'

'Linnl,' said the man with the harp. 'You didn't tell Rann our strategy?'

'What do *you* think?'

Linnl smiled sincerely. 'I think I like you, man of Crom Dhu. I think I like your hatred for Rann. I think I like the way you handled the entire matter, wanted to kill Rann and save Crom Dhu, and being so willing to die to accomplish either.'

'That's a lot of thinking. Yeah, and what about that promise you made?'

'It will be kept.'

Starke gave him a hand. 'Linnl, you're okay. If I ever get back to Earth, so help me, I'll never bait a hook again and drop it in the sea.' It was lost to Linnl. Starke forgot it, and went on, laughing. There was an edge of hysteria to it. Relief. You got booted around for days, people milled in and out of your mind like it was a bargain basement counter, pawing over the treads and convolutions, yelling and fighting; the woman you loved was starved on a ship masthead, and as a climax a lady with green eyes tried to make you a filling for an accident-mangled body. And now you had an ally.

And you couldn't believe it.

He laughed in little starts and stops, his eyes shut.

'Will you let me take care of Rann when the time comes?'

His fingers groped hungrily upward, closed on an imaginary figure of her, pressed, tightened, choked.

Linnl said, 'She's yours. I'd like the pleasure, but you have as much if not more of a revenge to take. Come along. We start now. You've been asleep for one entire period.'

Starke let himself down gingerly. He didn't want to break a leg off. He felt if someone touched him he might disintegrate.

He managed to let the tide handle him, do all the work. He swam carefully after Linnl down three passageways where an occasional silver inhabitant of the city slid by.

Drifting below them in a vast square hall, each gravitating but imprisoned by leg-shackles, the warriors of Falga looked up with pale cold eyes at Starke and Linnl. Occasional discharges of light-fish from interstices in the walls passed luminous, fleeting glows over the warriors. The light-fish flirted briefly in a long shining rope that tied knots around the dead faces and as quickly untied them. Then the light-fish pulsed away and the red colour of the sea took over.

Bathed in wine, thought Starke, without humour. He leaned forward.

'Men of Falga!'

Linnl plucked a series of harp-threads.

'Aye.' A deep suggestion of sound issued from a thousand dead lips.

'We go to sack Rann's citadel!'

'Rann!' came the muffled thunder of voices.

At the sound of another tune, the golden hounds appeared. They touched the chains. The men of Falga, released, danced through the red sea substance.

Siphoned into a valve mouth, they were drawn out into a great volcanic courtyard. Starke went close after. He stared down into a black ravine, at the bottom of which was a blazing caldera.

This was the Source Life of the Red Sea. Here it had begun a millennium ago. Here the savage cyclones of sparks and fire energy belched up, shaking titanic black garden walls, causing currents and whirlpools that threatened to suck you forward and shoot you violently up to the surface, in cannulas of force, thrust, in capillaries of ignited mist, in chutes of colour that threatened to cremate but only exhilarated you, gave you a seething rebirth!

He braced his legs and fought the suction. An unbelievable sinew of fire sprang up from out the ravine, crackling and roaring.

The men of Falga did not fight the attraction.

They moved forward in their silence and hung over the incandescence.

The vitality of the Source grew upward in them. It seemed to touch their sandalled toes first, and then by a process of shining osmosis, climb up the limbs, into the loins, into the vitals, delineating their strong bone structure as mercury delineates the glass thermometer with a rise of temperature. The bones flickered like carved polished ivory through the momentarily film-like flesh. The ribs of a thousand men expanded like silvered spider legs, clenched, then expanded again. Their spines straightened, their shoulders flattened back. Their eyes, the last to take the fire, now were ignited and glowed like candles in refurbished sepulchres. The chins snapped up, the entire outer skins of their bodies broke into silver brilliance.

Swimming through the storm of energy like nightmare figments, entering cold, they reached the far side of the ravine, resembling smelted metal from blast furnaces. When they brushed into one another, purple sparks sizzled, jumped from head to head, from hand to hand.

Linnl touched Starke's arm. 'You're next.'

'No thank you.'

'Afraid?' laughed the harp-shepherd. 'You're tired. It will give you new life. You're next.'

Starke hesitated only a moment. Then he let the tide drift him rapidly out. He was afraid. Damned afraid. A belch of fire caught him as he arrived in the core of the ravine. He was wrapped in layers of ecstasy. Beudag pressed against him. It was her consuming hair that netted him and branded him. It was her warmth that crept up his body into his chest and into his head. Somebody yelled somewhere in animal delight and unbearable passion. Somebody danced and threw out his hands and crushed that solar warmth deeper into his huge body. Somebody felt all tiredness, oldness flumed away, a whole new feeling of warmth and strength inserted.

That somebody was Starke.

Waiting on the other side of the ravine were a thousand men of Falga. What sounded like a thousand harps began playing now, and as Starke reached the other side, the harps began marching, and the warriors marched with them. They were still dead, but you would never know it. There were no minds inside those bodies. The bodies were being activated from outside. But you would never know it.

They left the city behind. In embering ranks, the soldier-fighters were led by golden hounds and distant harps to a place where a huge intra-coastal tide swept by.

They got on the tide for a free ride. Linnl beside him, using his harp, Starke felt himself sucked down through a deep where strange monsters sprawled. They looked at Starke with hungry eyes. But the harp wall swept them back.

Starke glanced about at the men. They don't know what they're doing, he thought. Going home to kill their parents and their children, to set the flame to Falga, and they don't know it. Their alive-but-dead faces tilted up, always upward, as though visions of Rann's citadel were there.

Rann. Starke let the wrath simmer in him. He let it cool. Then it was cold. Rann hadn't bothered him now for hours. Was there a chance she'd read his thought in the midst of that fighting nightmare? Did she know this plan for Falga? Was that an explanation for her silence now?

He sent his mind ahead, subtly. *Rann. Rann.* The only answer was the move of silver bodies through the fiery deeps.

Just before dawn they broke surface of the sea.

Falga drowsed in the red-smeared fog silence. Its slave streets were empty and dew-covered. High up, the first light was bathing Rann's gardens and setting her citadel aglow.

Linnl lay in the shallows beside Starke. They both were smiling half-cruel smiles. They had waited long for this.

Linnl nodded. 'This is the day of the carnival. Fruit, wine and love will be offered the returned soldiers of Rann. In the streets there'll be dancing.'

Far over to the right lay a rise of mountain. At its blunt peak – Starke stared at it intently – rested a body of a little, scrawny Earthman, with flame-birds clustered on it. He'd climb that mountain later. When it was over and there was time.

'What are you searching for?' asked Linnl.

Starke's voice was distant. 'Someone I used to know.'

Filing out on the stone quays, their rusling sandals eroded by time, the men stood clean and bright. Starke paced, a caged animal, at their centre, so his dark body would pass unnoticed.

They were seen.

The cliff guard looked down over the dirty slave dwellings, from their arrow galleries, and set up a cry. Hands waved, pointed frosty white in the dawn. More guards loped down the ramps and galleries, meeting, joining others and coming on.

Linnl, in the sea by the quay, suggested a theme on the harp. The other harps took it up. The shuddering music lifted from the water and, with a gentle firmness, set the dead feet marching down the quays, upward through the narrow, stifling alleys of the slaves, to meet the guard.

Slave people peered out at them tiredly from their choked quarters. The passing of warriors was old to them, of no significance.

These warriors carried no weapons. Starke didn't like that part of it. A length of chain even, he wanted. But this emptiness of the hands. His teeth ached from too long a time of clenching his jaws tight. The muscles of his arms were feverish and nervous.

At the edge of the slave community, at the cliff base, the guard confronted them. Running down off the galleries, swords naked, they ran to intercept what they took to be an enemy.

The guards stopped in blank confusion.

A little laugh escaped Starke's lips. It was a dream. With fog over, under and in between its parts. It wasn't real to the guard, who couldn't believe it. It wasn't real to these dead men either, who were walking around. He felt alone. He was the only live one. He didn't like walking with dead men.

The captain of the guard came down warily, his green eyes suspicious. The suspicion faded. His face fell apart. He had lain on his fur pelts for months thinking of his son who had died to defend Falga.

Now his son stood before him. Alive.

The captain forgot he was captain. He forgot everything. His sandals scraped over stones. You could hear the air go out of his lungs and come back in as a numbed prayer.

'My son! In Rann's name. They said you were slain by Faolan's men one hundred darknesses ago. My son!'

A harp tinkled somewhere.

The son stepped forward, smiling.

They embraced. The son said nothing. He couldn't speak.

This was the signal for the others. The whole guard, shocked and surprised, put away their swords and sought out old friends, brothers, fathers, uncles, sons!

They moved up the galleries, the guard and the returned warriors, Starke in their midst. Threading up the cliff, through passage after passage, all talking at once. Or so it seemed. The guards did the talking. None of the dead warriors replied. They only *seemed* to. Starke heard the music strong and clear everywhere.

They reached the green gardens atop the cliff. By this time the entire city was awake. Women came running, bare-breasted and sobbing, and throwing themselves forward into the ranks of their lovers. Flowers showered over them.

'So this is war,' muttered Starke, uneasily.

They stopped in the centre of the great gardens. The crowd milled happily, not yet aware of the strange silence from their men. They were too happy to notice.

'Now,' cried Starke to himself. 'Now's the time. Now!'

As if in answer, a wild skirling of harps out of the sky.

The crowd stopped laughing only when the returned warriors of Falga swept forward, their hands lifted and groping before them ...

The crying in the streets was like a far siren wailing. Metal made a harsh clangour that was sheathed in silence at the same moment metal found flesh to lie in. A vicious pantomime was concluded in the green moist gardens.

Starke watched from Rann's empty citadel. Fog plumes

strolled by the archways and a thick rain fell. It came like a blood squall and washed the garden below until you could not tell rain from blood.

The returned warriors had gotten their swords by now. First they killed those nearest them in the celebration. Then they took the weapons from the victims. It was very simple and very unpleasant.

The slaves had joined the battle now. Swarming up from the slave town, plucking up fallen daggers and short swords, they circled the gardens, happening upon the arrogant shining warriors of Rann, who had so far escaped the quiet, deadly killing of the alive-but-dead men.

Dead father killed startled, alive son. Dead brother garroted unbelieving brother. Carnival indeed in Falga.

An old man waited alone. Starke saw him. The old man had a weapon, but refused to use it. A young warrior of Falga, harped on by Linnl's harp, walked quietly up to the old man. The old man cried out. His mouth formed words. 'Son! What *is* this?' He flung down his blade and made to plead with his boy.

The son stabbed him with silent efficiency, and without a glance at the body, walked onward to find another.

Starke turned away, sick and cold.

A thousand such scenes were being finished.

He set fire to the black spider-silk tapestries. They whispered and talked with flame. The stone echoed his feet as he searched room after room. Rann had gone, probably last night. That meant that Crom Dhu was on the verge of falling. Was Faolan dead? Had the people of Crom Dhu, seeing Beudag's suffering, given in? Falga's harbour was completely devoid of ships, except for small fishing skiffs.

The fog waited for him when he returned to the garden. Rain found his face.

The citadel of Rann was fire-encrusted and smoke-shrouded as he looked up at it.

A silence lay in the garden. The fight was over.

The men of Falga, still shining with Source-Life, hung their blades from uncomprehending fingers, the light beginning to leave their green eyes. Their skin looked dirty and dull.

Starke wasted no time getting down the galleries, through the slave quarter and to the quays again.

Linnl awaited him, gently petting the obedient harp.

'It's over. The slaves will own what's left. They'll be our allies, since we've freed them.'

Starke didn't hear. He was squinting off over the Red Sea.

Linnl understood. He plucked two tones from the harp, which pronounced the two words uppermost in Starke's thought.

'Crom Dhu.'

'If we're not too late.' Starke leaned forward. 'If Faolan lives. If Beudag still stands at the masthead.'

Like a blind man he walked straight ahead, until he fell into the sea.

It was not quite a million miles to Crom Dhu. It only seemed that far.

A sweep of tide picked them up just off shore from Falga and siphoned them rapidly, through deeps along coastal latitudes, through crystal forests. He cursed every mile of the way.

He cursed the time it took to pause at the Titan's city to gather fresh men. To gather Clev and Mannt and Aesur and Bron. Impatiently, Starke watched the whole drama of the Source-Fire and the bodies again. This time it was the bodies of Crom Dhu men, hung like beasts on slow-turned spits, their limbs and vitals soaking through and through, their skins taking bronze colour, their eyes holding flint-sparks. And then the harps wove a garment around each, and the garment moved the men instead of the men the garment.

In the tidal basilic now, Starke twisted. Coursing behind him were the new bodies of Clev and Aesur! The current elevated them, poked them through obsidian needle-eyes like spider-silk threads.

There was good irony in this. Crom Dhu's men, fallen at Falga under Conan's treachery, returned now under Conan to exonerate that treachery.

Suddenly they were in Crom Dhu's outer basin. Shadows swept over them. The long dark falling shadows of Falga's longboats lying in that harbour. Shadows like black culling-nets let down. The school of men cleaved the shadow nets. The tide ceased here, eddied and distilled them.

Starke glared up at the immense silver bottom of a Falgian ship. He felt his face stiffen and his throat tighten. Then, flexing knees, he rammed upward; night air broke dark red around his head.

The harbour held flare torches on the rims of long ships. On the neck of land that led from Crom Dhu to the mainland the continuing battle sounded. Faint cries and clashing made their way through the fog veils. They sounded like echoes of past dreams.

Linnl let Starke have the leash. Starke felt something pressed into his fist. A coil of slender green woven reeds, a rope with hooked weights on the end of it. He knew how to use it without asking. But he wished for a knife now, even though he realised carrying a knife in the sea was all but impossible if you wanted to move fast.

He saw the sleek naked figurehead of Rann's best ship a hundred yards away, a floating silhouette, its torches hanging fire like Beudag's hair.

He swam toward it, breathing quietly. When at last the silvered figurehead with the mocking green eyes and the flag of shoal-shallow hair hung over him, he felt the cool white ship metal kiss his fingers.

The smell of torch-smoke lingered. A rise of faint shouts from the land told of another rush upon the Gate. Behind him – a ripple. Then – a thousand ripples.

The resurrected men of Crom Dhu rose in dents and stirrings of sparkling wine. They stared at Crom Dhu and maybe they knew what it was and maybe they didn't. For one moment, Starke felt apprehension. Suppose Linnl was playing a game. Suppose, once these men had won the battle, they went on into Crom Dhu to rupture Romna's harp and make Faolan the blinder? He shook the thought away. That would have to be handled in time. On either side of him Clev and Mannt appeared. They looked at Crom Dhu, their lips shut. Maybe they saw Faolan's eyrie and heard a harp that was more than these harps that sang them to black and plunder – Romna's instrument telling bard-tales of the rovers and the coastal wars and the old, living days. Their eyes looked and looked at Crom Dhu, but saw nothing.

The sea shepherds appeared now, the followers of Linnl, each with his harp; and the harp music began, high. So high you couldn't hear it. It wove a tension on the air.

Silently, with a grim certainty, the dead-but-not-dead gathered in a bronze circle about Rann's ship. The very silence of their encirclement made your skin crawl and sweat break cold on your cheeks.

A dozen ropes went ravelling, looping over the ship side. They caught, held, grapnelled, hooked.

Starke had thrown his, felt it bite and hold. Now he scrambled swiftly, cursing, up its length, kicking and slipping at the silver hull.

He reached the top.

Beudag was there.

Half over the low rail he hesitated, just looking at her.

Torchlight limned her, shadowed her. She was still erect; her head was tired and her eyes closed, her face thinned and less brown, but she was still alive. She was coming out of a deep stupor now, at the whistle of ropes and the grate of metal hooks on the deck.

She saw Starke and her lips parted. She did not look away from him. His breath came out of him, choking.

It almost cost him his life, his standing there, looking at her.

A guard, with flesh like new snow, shafted his bow from the turret and let it loose. A chain lay on deck. Thankfully, Starke took it.

Clev came over the rail beside Starke. His chest took the arrow. The shaft burst half through and stopped, held. Clev kept going after the man who had shot it. He caught up with him.

Beudag cried out. 'Behind you, Conan!'

Conan! In her excitement, she gave the old name.

Conan he *was*. Whirling, he confronted a wiry little fellow, chained him brutally across the face, seized the man's falling sword, used it on him. Then he walked in, got the man's jaw, unbalanced him over into the sea.

The ship was awake now. Most of the men had been down

below, resting from the battles. Now they came pouring up, in a silver spate. Their yelling was in strange contrast to the calm silence of Crom Dhu's men. Starke found himself busy.

Conan had been a healthy animal, with great recuperative powers. Now his muscles responded to every trick asked of them. Starke leaped cleanly across the deck, watching for Rann, but she was nowhere to be seen. He engaged two blades, dispatched one of them. More ropes ravelled high and snaked him. Every ship in the harbour was exploding with violence. More men swarmed over the rail behind Starke, silently.

Above the shouting, Beudag's voice came, at sight of the fighting men. 'Clev! Mannt! Ausur!'

Starke was a god; anything he wanted he could have. A man's head? He could have it. It meant acting the guillotine with knife and wrist and lunged body. Like – *this!* His eyes were smoking amber and there were deep lines of grim pleasure tugging at his lips. An enemy cannot fight without hands. One man, facing Starke, suddenly displayed violent stumps before his face, not believing them.

Are you watching, Faolan? cried Starke inside himself, delivering blows. Look here, Faolan! God, no, you're blind. *Listen* then! Hear the ring of steel on steel. Does the smell of hot blood and hot bodies reach you? Oh, if you could see this tonight, Faolan, Falga would be forgotten. This is Conan, out of idiocy, with a guy named Starke wearing him and telling him where to go!

It was not safe on deck. Starke hadn't particularly noticed before, but the warriors of Crom Dhu didn't care whom they attacked now. They were beginning to do surgery to one another. They excised one another's shoulders, severed limbs in blind instantaneous obedience. This was no place for Beudag and himself.

He cut her free of the masthead, drew her quickly to the rail.

Beudag was laughing. She could do nothing but laugh. Her eyes were shocked. She saw dead men alive again, lashing out with weapons; she had been starved and made to stand night and day, and now she could only laugh.

Starke shook her.

She did not stop laughing.

'Beudag! You're all right. You're free.'

She stared at nothing. 'I'll – I'll be all right in a minute.'

He had to ward off a blow from one of his own men. He parried the thrust, then got in and pushed the man off the deck, over into the sea. That was the only thing to do. You couldn't kill them.

Beudag stared down at the tumbling body.

'Where's Rann?' Starke's yellow eyes narrowed, searching.

'She *was* here.' Beudag trembled.

Rann looked out of her eyes. Out of the tired numbness of Beudag, an echo of Rann. Rann was nearby, and this was her doing.

Instinctively, Starke raised his eyes.

Rann appeared at the masthead, like a flurry of snow. Her green-tipped breasts were rising and falling with emotion. Pure hatred lay in her eyes. Starke licked his lips and readied his sword.

Rann snapped a glance at Beudag. Stooping, as in a dream, Beudag picked up a dagger and held it to her own breast.

Starke froze.

Rann nodded, with satisfaction. 'Well, Starke? How will it be? Will you come at me and have Beudag die. Or will you let me go free?'

Starke's palms felt sweaty and greasy. 'There's no place for you to go. Falga's taken. I can't guarantee your freedom. If you want to go over the side, into the sea, that's your chance. You might reach the shore and your own men.'

'Swimming? With the *sea-beasts* waiting?' She accented the *beasts* heavily. She was one of the sea-*people*. They, Linnl and his men, were sea-*beasts*. 'No, Hugh Starke. I'll take a skiff. Put Beudag at the rail where I can watch her all the way. Guarantee my passage to shore and my own men there, and Beudag lives.'

Starke waved his sword. 'Get going.'

He didn't want to let her go. He had other plans, good plans for her. He shouted the deal down to Linnl. Linnl nodded back, with much reluctance.

Rann, in a small silver skiff, headed toward land. She handled the boat and looked back at Beudag all the while. She passed through the sea-beasts and touched the shore. She lifted her hand and brought it smashing down.

Whirling, Starke swung his fist against Beudag's jaw. Her hand was already striking the blade into her breast. Her head flopped back. His fist carried through. She fell. The blade clattered. He kicked it overboard. Then he lifted Beudag. She was warm and good to hold. The blade had only pricked her breast. A small rivulet of blood ran.

On the shore, Rann vanished upward on the rocks, hurrying to find her men.

In the harbour the harp music paused. The ships were taken. Their crews lay filling the decks. Crom Dhu's men stopped fighting as quickly as they'd started. Some of the bright shining had culled from the bronze of their arms and bare torsos. The ships began to sink.

Linnl swam below, looking up at Starke. Starke looked back at him and nodded at the beach. 'Swell. Now, let's go get that she-devil,' he said.

Faolan waited on his great stone balcony, overlooking Crom Dhu. Behind him the fires blazed high and their eating sound of flame on wood filled the pillared gloom with sound and furious light.

Faolan leaned against the rim, his chest swathed in bandage and healing ointment, his blind eyes flickering, looking down again and again with a fixed intensity, his head tilted to listen.

Romna stood beside him, filled and refilled the cup that Faolan emptied into his thirsty mouth, and told him what happened. Told of the men pouring out of the sea, and Rann appearing on the rocky shore. Sometimes Faolan leaned to one side, weakly, toward Romna's words. Sometimes he twisted to hear the thing itself, the thing that happened down beyond the Gate of besieged Crom Dhu.

Romna's harp lay untouched. He didn't play it. He didn't need to. From below, a great echoing of harps, more liquid than his, like a waterfall drenched the city, making the fog sob down red tears.

'Are those harps?' cried Faolan.

'Yes, harps!'

'What was that?' Faolan listened, breathing harshly, clutching for support.

'A skirmish,' said Romna.

'Who won?'

'*We* won.'

'And *that?*' Faolan's blind eyes tried to see until they watered.

'The enemy falling back from the Gate!'

'And that sound, and that sound?' Faolan went on and on, feverishly, turning this way and that, the lines of his face agonised and attentive to each eddy and current and change of tide. The rhythm of swords through fog and body was a complicated music whose themes he must recognise. 'Another fell! I heard him cry. And another of Rann's men!'

'Yes,' said Romna.

'But why do our warriors fight so quietly? I've heard nothing from their lips. So quiet.'

Romna scowled. 'Quiet. Yes – quiet.'

'And where did they come from? All our men are in the city?'

'Aye.' Romna shifted. He hesitated, squinting. He rubbed his bulldog jaw. 'Except those that died at – Falga.'

Faolan stood there a moment. Then he rapped his empty cup.

'More wine, bard. More wine.'

He turned to the battle again.

'Oh, gods, if I could see it, if I could only see it!'

Below, a ringing crash. A silence. A shouting, a pouring of noise.

'The Gate!' Faolan was stricken with fear. 'We've lost! My sword!'

'Stay, Faolan!' Romna laughed. Then he sighed. It was a sigh that did not believe. 'In the name of ten thousand mighty gods, would that I were blind now, or could see better.'

Faolan's hand caught, held him. 'What *is* it? Tell!'

'Clev! And Tlan! And Conan! And Bron! And Mannt! Standing in the gate, like wine visions! Swords in their hands!'

Faolan's hand relaxed, then tightened. 'Speak their names again, and speak them slowly. And tell the truth.' His skin shivered like that of a nervous animal. 'You said – Clev? Mannt? Bron?'

'And Tlan! And Conan! Back from Falga. They've opened the Gate and the battle's won. It's over, Faolan, Crom Dhu will sleep tonight.'

Faolan let him go. A sob broke from his lips. 'I will get drunk. Drunker than ever in my life. Gloriously drunk. Gods, but if I could have seen it. Been in it. Tell me again of it, Romna ...'

Faolan sat in the great hall, on his carved high-seat, waiting.

The pad of sandals on stone outside, the jangle of chains.

A door flung wide, red fog sluiced in, and in the sluice, people walking. Faolan started up. 'Clev? Mannt? Aesur?'

Starke came forward into the firelight. He pressed his right hand to the open mouth of a wound on his thigh. 'No, Faolan. Myself and two others.'

'Beudag?'

'Yes.' And Beudag came wearily to him.

Faolan stared. 'Who's the other? It walks light. It's a woman.'

Starke nodded. 'Rann.'

Faolan rose carefully from his seat. He thought the name over. He took a short sword from a place beside the high seat. He stepped down. He walked toward Starke. 'You brought Rann alive to me?'

Starke pulled the chain that bound Rann. She ran forward in little steps, her white face down, her eyes slitted with animal fury.

'Faolan's blind,' said Starke. 'I let you live for one damned good reason, Rann. Okay, go ahead.'

Faolan stopped walking, curious. He waited.

Rann did nothing.

Starke took her hand and wrenched it behind her back. 'I said "go ahead." Maybe you didn't hear me.'

'I will,' she gasped, in pain.

Starke released her. 'Tell me what happens, Faolan.'

Rann gazed steadily at Faolan's tall figure there in the light.

Faolan suddenly threw his hands to his eyes and choked.

Beudag cried out, seized his arm.

'I can see!' Faolan staggered, as if jolted. 'I can see!' First he shouted it, then he whispered it. '*I can see.*'

Starke's eyes blurred. He whispered to Rann, tightly. 'Make him see it, Rann, or you die now. Make him see it!' To Faolan: 'What do you see?'

Faolan was bewildered; he swayed. He put out his hands to shape the vision. 'I – I see Crom Dhu. It's a good sight. I see the ships of Rann. Sinking!' He laughed a broken laugh. 'I – see the fight beyond the Gate!'

Silence swam in the room, over their heads.

Faolan's voice went alone, and hypnotized, into that silence.

He put out his big fists, shook them, opened them. 'I see Mannt, and Aesur and Clev! Fighting as they always fought. I see Conan as he was. I see Beudag wielding steel again, on the shore! I see the enemy killed! I see men pouring out of the sea with brown skins and dark hair. Men I knew a long darkness ago. Men that roved the sea with me. *I see Rann captured!*' He began to sob with it, his lungs filling and releasing it, sucking on it, blowing it out. Tears ran down from his vacant, blazing eyes. 'I see Crom Dhu as it was and is and shall be! *I see, I see, I see!*'

Starke felt the chill on the back of his neck.

'I see Rann captured and held, and her men dead around her on the land before the Gate. I see the Gate thrown open—' Faolan halted. He looked at Starke. 'Where are Clev and Mannt? Where is Bron and Aesur?'

Starke let the fires burn on the hearths a long moment. Then he replied.

'They went back into the sea, Faolan.'

Faolan's fingers fell emptily. 'Yes,' he said, heavily. 'They had to go back, didn't they? They couldn't stay, could they? Not even for one night of food on the table, and wine in the mouth, and women in the deep warm furs before the hearth. Not even for one toast.' He turned. 'A drink, Romna. A drink for everyone.'

Romna gave him a full cup. He dropped it, fell down to his knees, clawed at his breast. 'My heart!'

'Rann, you sea-devil!'

Starke held her instantly by the throat. He put pressure on

the small raging pulses on either side of her snow-white neck. 'Let him go, Rann!' More pressure. '*Let him go!*' Faolan grunted. Starke held her until her white face was dirty and strange with death.

It seemed like an hour later when he released her. She fell softly and did not move. She wouldn't move again.

Starke turned slowly to look at Faolan.

'You saw, didn't you, Faolan?' he said.

Faolan nodded blindly, weakly. He roused himself from the floor, groping. 'I saw. For a moment, I saw everything. And Gods! but it made good seeing! Here, Hugh-Starke-Called-Conan, gave this other side of me something to lean on.'

Beudag and Starke climbed the mountain above Falga the next day. Starke went ahead a little way, and with his coming the flame birds scattered, glittering away.

He dug the shallow grave and did what had to be done with the body he found there, and then when the grave was covered with thick grey stones he went back for Beudag. They stood together over it. He had never expected to stand over a part of himself, but here he was, and Beudag's hand gripped his.

He looked suddenly a million years old standing there. He thought of Earth and the Belt and Jupiter, of the joy streets in the Jekkara Low Canals of Mars. He thought of space and the ships going through it, and himself inside them. He thought of the million credits he had taken in that last job. He laughed ironically.

'Tomorrow, I'll have the sea creatures hunt for a little metal box full of credits.' He nodded solemnly at the grave. 'He wanted that. Or at least he thought he did. He killed himself getting it. So if the sea-people find it, I'll send it up here to the mountain and bury it down under the rocks in his fingers. I guess that's the best place.'

Beudag drew him away. They walked down the mountain toward Falga's harbour where a ship waited them. Walking, Starke lifted his face. Beudag was with him, and the sails of the ship were rising to take the wind, and the Red Sea waited for them to travel it. What lay on its far side was something for

Beudag and Faolan-of-the-Ships and Romna and Hugh-Starke-Called-Conan to discover. He felt damned good about it. He walked on steadily, holding Beudag near.

And on the mountain, as the ship sailed, the flame bird soared down fitfully and frustratedly to beat at the stone mound, ceased, and mourning shrilly, flew away.

THE MOON THAT VANISHED

1
DOWN TO THE DARKLING SEA

The stranger was talking about him – the tall stranger who was a long way from his native uplands, who wore plain leather and did not belong in this swamp-coast village. He was asking questions, talking, watching.

David Heath knew that, in the same detached way in which he realised that he was in Kalruna's dingy Palace of All Possible Delights, that he was very drunk but not nearly drunk enough, that he would never be drunk enough and that presently, when he passed out, he would be tossed over the back railing into the mud, where he might drown or sleep it off as he pleased.

Heath did not care. The dead and the mad do not care. He lay without moving on the native hide-frame cot, the leather mask covering the lower part of his face, and breathed the warm golden vapour that bubbled in a narghile-like bowl beside him. Breathed, and tried to sleep, and could not. He did not close his eyes. Only when he became unconscious would he do that.

There would be a moment he could not avoid, just before his drugged brain slipped over the edge into oblivion, when he would no longer be able to see anything but the haunted darkness of his own mind, and that moment would seem like all eternity. But afterward, for a few hours, he would find peace.

Until then he would watch, from his dark corner, the life that went on in the Palace of All Possible Delights.

Heath rolled his head slightly. By his shoulder, clinging with its hooked claws to the cot frame, a little bright-scaled dragon crouched and met his glance with jewel-red eyes in which there were peculiar sympathy and intelligence. Heath smiled and settled back. A nervous spasm shook him but the drug had relaxed him so that it was not severe and passed off quickly.

No one came near him except the emerald-skinned girl from the deep swamps who replenished his bowl. She was not human and therefore did not mind that he was David Heath. It was as though there were a wall around him beyond which no man stepped or looked.

Except, of course, the stranger.

Heath let his gaze wander. Past the long low bar where the common seamen lay on cushions of moss and skins, drinking the cheap fiery *thul*. Past the tables, where the captains and the mates sat, playing their endless and complicated dice games. Past the Nahali girl who danced naked in the torchlight, her body glimmering with tiny scales and as sinuous and silent in motion as the body of a snake.

The single huge room was open on three sides to the steaming night. It was there that Heath's gaze went at last. Outside, to the darkness and the sea, because they had been his life and he loved them.

Darkness on Venus is not like the darkness of Earth or Mars. The planet is hungry for light and will not let it go. The face of Venus never sees the sun but even at night the hope and the memory of it are there, trapped in the eternal clouds.

The air is the colour of indigo and it carries its own pale glow. Heath lay watching how the slow hot wind made drifts of light among the *liha*-trees, touched the muddy harbour beaches with a wavering gleam and blended into the restless phosphorescence of the Sea of Morning Opals. Half a mile south the river Omaz flowed silently down, still tainted with the reek of the Deep Swamps.

Sea and sky – the life of David Heath and his destruction.

The heavy vapour swirled in Heath's brain. His breathing slowed and deepened. His lids grew heavy.

Heath closed his eyes.

An expression of excitement, of yearning, crossed his face, mingled with a vague unease. His muscles tensed. He began to whimper, very softly, the sound muffled by the leather mask.

The little dragon cocked its head and watched, still as a carven image.

Heath's body, half naked in a native kilt, began to twitch, then to move in spasmodic jerks. The expression of unease deepened, changed gradually to one of pure horror. The cords in his throat stood out like wires as he tried to cry out and could not. Sweat gathered in great beads on his skin.

Suddenly the little dragon raised its wings and voiced a hissing scream.

Heath's nightmare world rocked around him, riven with loud sounds. He was mad with fear, he was dying, vast striding shapes thronged toward him out of a shining mist. His body was shaken, cracking, frail bones bursting into powder, his heart tearing out of him, his brain a part of the mist, shining, burning. He tore the mask from his face and cried out a name, *Ethne!*, and sat up – and his eyes were wide open, blind and deep.

Somewhere, far off, he heard thunder. The thunder spoke. It called his name. A new face pushed in past the phantoms of his dream. It swelled and blotted out the others. The face of the stranger from the High Plateaus. He saw every line of it, painted in fire upon his brain.

The square jaw, hard mouth, nose curved like a falcon's beak, the scars wealed, white against white skin, eyes like moonstones, only hot, bright – the long silver hair piled high in the intricate tribal knot and secured with a warrior's golden chains.

Hands shook him, slapped his face. The little dragon went on screaming and flapping, tethered by a short thong to the head of Heath's cot so that it could not tear out the eyes of the stranger.

Heath caught his breath in a long shuddering sob and sprang.

He would have killed the man who had robbed him of his little time of peace. He tried, in deadly silence, while the seamen and the masters and the mates and the dancing girls watched, not moving, sidelong out of their frightened, hateful eyes. But the Uplander was a big man, bigger than Heath in his best days had ever been. And presently Heath lay panting on the cot, a sick man, a man who was slowly dying and had no strength left.

The stranger spoke. 'It is said that you found the Moonfire.'

Heath stared at him with his dazed, drugged eyes and did not answer.

'It is said that you are David Heath the Earthman, captain of the *Ethne*.'

Still Heath did not answer. The rusty torchlight flickered over him, painting highlight and shadow. He had always been a lean, wiry man. Now he was emaciated, the bones of his face showing terribly ridged and curved under the drawn skin. His black hair and unkempt beard were shot through with white.

The Uplander studied Heath deliberately, contemptuously. He said, 'I think they lie.'

Heath laughed. It was not a nice laugh.

'Few men have ever reached the Moonfire,' the Venusian said. 'They were the strong ones, the men without fear.'

After a long while Heath whispered, 'They were fools.'

He was not speaking to the Uplander. He had forgotten him. His dark mad gaze was fixed on something only he could see.

'Their ships are rotting in the weed beds of the Upper Seas. The little dragons have picked their bones.' Heath's voice was slow, harsh and toneless, wandering. 'Beyond the Sea of Morning Opals, beyond the weeds and the Guardians, through the Dragon's Throat and still beyond – I've seen it, rising out of the mists, out of the Ocean-That-Is-Not-Water.'

A tremor shook him, twisting the gaunt bones of his body. He lifted his head, like a man straining to breathe, and the running torchlight brought his face clear of the shadows. In all the huge room there was not a sound, not a rustle, except for a small sharp gasp that ran through every mouth and then was silent.

'The gods know where they are now, the strong brave men who went through the Moonfire. The gods know what they are now. Not human if they live at all.'

He stopped. A deep slow shudder went through him. He dropped his head. 'I was only in the fringe of it. Only a little way.'

In the utter quiet the Uplander laughed. He said, 'I think you lie.'

Heath did not raise his head nor move.

The Venusian leaned over him, speaking loudly, so that even

across the distance of drugs and madness the Earthman should hear.

'You're like the others, the few who have come back. But they never lived a season out. They died or killed themselves. How long have you lived?'

Presently he grasped the Earthman's shoulder and shook it roughly. 'How long have you lived?' he shouted and the little dragon screamed, struggling against its thong.

Heath moaned. 'Through all hell,' he whispered. 'Forever.'

'Three seasons,' said the Venusian. 'Three seasons, and part of a fourth.' He took his hand away from Heath and stepped back. 'You never saw the Moonfire. You knew the custom, how the men who break the taboo must be treated until the punishment of the gods is finished.'

He kicked the bowl, breaking it, and the bubbling golden fluid spilled out across the floor in a pool of heady fragrance. 'You wanted *that*, and you knew how to get it, for the rest of your sodden life.'

A low growl of anger rose in the Palace of All Possible Delights.

Heath's blurred vision made out the squat fat bulk of Kalruna approaching. Even in the depths of his agony he laughed, weakly. For more than three seasons Kalruna had obeyed the traditional law. He had fed and made drunk the pariah who was sacred to the anger of the gods – the gods who guarded so jealously the secret of the Moonfire. Now Kalruna was full of doubt and very angry.

Heath began to laugh aloud. The effects of his uncompleted jag were making him reckless and hysterical. He sat up on the cot and laughed in their faces.

'I was only in the fringe,' he said. 'I'm not a god. I'm not even a man any more. But I can show you if you want to be shown.'

He pulled himself to his feet, and as he did so, in a motion as automatic as breathing, he loosed the little dragon and set it on his naked shoulder. He stood swaying a moment and then began to walk out across the room, slowly, uncertainly, but with his head stubbornly erect. The crowd drew apart to make a path for him and he walked along it in the silence, clothed in his few sad rags of dignity, until he came to the railing and stopped.

'Put out the torches,' he said. 'All but one.'

Kalruna said hesitantly, 'There's no need. I believe you.'

There was fear in the place now – fear, and fascination. Every man glanced sideways, looking for escape, but no one went away.

Heath said again, 'Put out the torches.'

The tall stranger reached out and doused the nearest one in its bucket, and presently in all that vast room there was darkness, except for one torch far in the back.

Heath stood braced against the rail, staring out into the hot indigo night.

The mists rose thick from the Sea of Morning Opals. They crept up out of the mud, and breathed in clouds from the swamps. The slow wind pushed them in long rolling drifts, blue-white and glimmering against the darker night.

Heath looked hungrily into the mists. His head was thrown back, his whole body strained upward and presently he raised his arms in a gesture of terrible longing.

'Ethne,' he whispered. 'Ethne.'

Almost imperceptibly, a change came over him. The weakness, the look of the sodden wreck, left him. He stood firm and straight, and the muscles rose coiled and beautiful on the long lean frame of his bones, alive with the tension of strength.

His face had altered even more. There was a look of power on it. The dark eyes burned with deep fires, glowing with a light that was more than human, until it seemed that his whole head was crowned with a strange nimbus.

For one short moment, the face of David Heath was the face of a god.

'Ethne,' he said.

And she came.

Out of the blue darkness, out of the mist, drifting tenuous and lovely toward the Earthman. Her body was made from the glowing air, the soft drops of the mist, shaped and coloured by the force that was in Heath. She was young, not more than nineteen, with the rosy tint of Earth's sun still in her cheeks, her eyes wide and bright as a child's, her body slim with the sweet angularity of youth.

The first time I saw her, when she stepped down the loading ramp for her first look at Venus and the wind took her hair and played with it and she walked light and eager as a colt on a spring morning. Light and merry always, even walking to her death.

The shadowy figure smiled and held out her arms. Her face was the face of a woman who has found love and all the world along with it.

Closer and closer she drifted to Heath and the Earthman stretched out his hands to touch her.

And in one swift instant, she was gone.

Heath fell forward against the rail. He stayed there a long time. There was no god in him now, no strength. He was like a flame suddenly burned out and dead, the ashes collapsing upon themselves. His eyes were closed and tears ran out from under the lashes.

In the steaming darkness of the room no one moved.

Heath spoke once. 'I couldn't go far enough,' he said, 'into the Moonfire.'

He dragged himself upright after a while and went toward the steps, supporting himself against the rail, feeling his way like a blind man. He went down the four steps of hewn logs and the mud of the path rose warm around his ankles. He passed between the rows of mud-and-wattle huts, a broken scarecrow of a man plodding through the night of an alien world.

He turned down the side path that led to the anchorage. His feet slipped into the deeper mud at the side and he fell, face down. He tried once to get up, then lay still, already sinking into the black, rich ooze. The little dragon rode on his shoulder, pecking at him, screaming, but he did not hear.

He did not know it when the tall stranger from the High Plateaus picked him out of the mud a few seconds later, dragon and all, and carried him away, down to the darkling sea.

2
THE EMERALD SAIL

A woman's voice said, 'Give me the cup.'

Heath felt his head being lifted, and then the black, stinging taste of Venusian coffee slid like liquid fire down his throat. He made his usual waking fight against fear and reality, gasped and opened his eyes.

He lay in his own bunk, in his own cabin, aboard the *Ethne*. Across from him, crouched on a carven chest, the tall Venusian sat, his head bowed under the low scarlet arch of the deck above. Beside Heath, looking down at him, was a woman.

It was still night. The mud that clung to Heath's body was still wet. They must have worked hard, he thought, to bring him to.

The little dragon flopped down to its perch on Heath's shoulder. He stroked its scaly neck and lay watching his visitors.

The man said, 'Can you talk now?'

Heath shrugged. His eyes were on the woman. She was tall but not too tall, young but not too young. Her body was everything a woman's body ought to be, of its type, which was wide-shouldered and leggy, and she had a fine free way of moving it. She wore a short tunic of undyed spider silk, which exactly matched the soft curling hair that fell down her back – a bright, true silver with little peacock glints of colour in it.

Her face was one that no man would forget in a hurry. It was a face shaped warmly and generously for all the womanly things – passion and laughter and tenderness. But something had happened to it. Something had given it a bitter sulky look. There were resentment in it and deep anger and hardness – and yet, with all that, it was somehow a pathetically eager face with lost and frightened eyes.

Heath remembered vaguely a day when he would have liked to solve the riddle of that contradictory face. A day long ago, before Ethne came.

He said, speaking to both of them, 'Who are you and what do you want with me?'

He looked now directly at the man and it was a look of sheer black hatred. 'Didn't you have enough fun with me at Kalruna's?'

'I had to be sure of you,' the stranger said. 'Sure that you had not lied about the Moonfire.'

He leaned forward, his eyes narrowed and piercing. He did not sit easily. His body was curved like a bent bow. In the light of the hanging lantern his scarred, handsome face showed a ripple of little muscles under the skin. A man in a hurry, Heath thought, a man with a sharp goad pricking his flanks.

'And what was that to you?' said Heath.

It was a foolish question. Already Heath knew what was coming. His whole being drew in upon itself, retreated.

The stranger did not answer directly. Instead he said, 'You know the cult that calls itself guardian of the Mysteries of the Moon.'

'The oldest cult on Venus and one of the strongest. One of the strangest, too, on a moonless planet,' Heath said slowly to no one in particular. 'The Moonfire is their symbol of godhead.'

The woman laughed without mirth. 'Although,' she said, 'they've never seen it.'

The stranger went on, 'All Venus knows about you, David Heath. The word travels. The priests know too – the Children of the Moon. They have a special interest in you.'

Heath waited. He did not speak.

'You belong to the gods for their own vengeance,' the stranger said. 'But the vengeance hasn't come. Perhaps because you're an Earthman and therefore less obedient to the gods of Venus. Anyway, the Children of the Moon are tired of waiting. The longer you live the more men may be tempted to blasphemy, the less faith there will be in the ability of the gods to punish men for their sins.' His voice had a biting edge of sarcasm. 'So,' he finished, 'the Children of the Moon are coming to see to it that you die.'

Heath smiled. 'Do the priests tell you their secrets?'

The man turned his head and said, 'Alor.'

The woman stepped in front of Heath and loosed her tunic at the shoulder. 'There,' she said furiously. 'Look!'

Her anger was not with Heath. It was with what he saw. The tattoo branded between her white breasts – the round rayed symbol of the Moon.

Heath caught his breath and let it out in a long sigh. 'A handmaiden of the temple,' he said and looked again at her face. Her eyes met his, silvery-cold, level, daring him to say more.

'We are sold out of our cradles,' she said. 'We have no choice. And our families are very proud to have a daughter chosen for the temple.'

Bitterness and pride and the smouldering anger of the slave.

She said, 'Broca tells the truth.'

Heath's body seemed to tighten in upon itself. He glanced from one to the other and back again, not saying anything, and his heart beat fast and hard, knocking against his ribs.

Alor said, 'They will kill you and it won't be easy dying. I know. I've heard men screaming sometimes for many nights and their sin was less than yours.'

Heath said out of a dry mouth, 'A runaway girl from the temple gardens and a thrower of spears. Their sin is great too. They didn't come halfway across Venus just to warn me. I think they lie. I think the priests are after them.'

'We're all three proscribed,' said Broca, 'but Alor and I could get away. You they'll hunt down no matter where you go – except one place.'

And Heath said, 'Where is that?'

'The Moonfire.'

After a long while Heath uttered a harsh grating sound that might have been a laugh.

'Get out,' he said. 'Get away from me.'

He got to his feet, shaking with weakness and fury. 'You lie, both of you – because I'm the only living man who has seen the Moonfire and you want me to take you there. You believe the legends. You think the Moonfire will change you into gods. You're mad, like all the other fools, for the power and the glory you think you'll have. Well, I can tell you this – the Moonfire will give you nothing but suffering and death.'

His voice rose. 'Go lie to someone else. Frighten the Guardians of the Upper Seas. Bribe the gods themselves to take you there. But get away from me!'

The Venusian rose slowly. The cabin was small for him, the deck beams riding his shoulders. He swept the little dragon aside. He took Heath in his two hands and he said, 'I will reach the Moonfire, and you will take me there.'

Heath struck him across the face.

Sheer astonishment held Broca still for a moment and Heath said, 'You're not a god yet.'

The Venusian opened his mouth in a snarling grin. His hands shifted and tightened.

The woman said sharply, 'Broca!' She stepped in close, wrenching at Broca's wrists. 'Don't kill him, you fool!'

Broca let his breath out hard between his teeth. Gradually his hands relaxed. Heath's face was suffused with dark blood. He would have fallen if the woman had not caught him.

She said to Broca, 'Strike him – but not too hard.'

Broca raised his fist and struck Heath carefully on the point of the jaw.

It could not have been more than two of the long Venusian hours before Heath came to. He did that slowly as always – progressing from a vast vague wretchedness to an acute awareness of everything that was the matter with him. His head felt as though it had been cleft in two with an axe from the jaw upward.

He could not understand why he should have wakened. The drug alone should have been good for hours of heavy sleep. The sky beyond the cabin port had changed. The night was almost over. He lay for a moment, wondering whether or not he was going to be sick, and then suddenly he realised what had wakened him in spite of everything.

The *Ethne* was under way.

His anger choked him so that he could not even swear. He dragged himself to his feet and crossed the cabin, feeling even then that she was not going right, that the dawn wind was strong and she was rolling to it, yawing.

He kicked open the door and came out on deck.

The great lateen sail of golden spider silk, ghostly in the blue air, slatted and spilled wind, shaking against loose yards. Heath turned and made for the raised poop, finding strength in his fear for the ship. Broca was up there, braced against the loom of the stern sweep. The wake lay white on the black water, twisting like a snake.

The woman Alor stood at the rail, staring at the low land that lay behind them.

Broca made no protest as Heath knocked him aside and took the sweep. Alor turned and watched but did not speak.

The *Ethne* was small and the simple rig was such that one man could handle it. Heath trimmed the sail and in a few seconds she was stepping light and dainty as her namesake, her wake straight as a ruled line.

When that was done Heath turned upon them and cursed them in a fury greater than that of a woman whose child has been stolen.

Broca ignored him. He stood watching the land and the lightening sky. When Heath was all through the woman said, 'We had to go. It may already be too late. And you weren't going to help.'

Heath didn't say anything more. There weren't any words. He swung the helm hard over.

Broca was beside him in one step, his hand raised and then suddenly Alor cried out, '*Wait!*'

Something in her voice brought both men around to look at her. She stood at the rail, facing into the wind, her hair flying, the short skirt of her tunic whipped back against her thighs. Her arm was raised in a pointing gesture.

It was dawn now.

For a moment Heath lost all sense of time. The deck lifting lightly under his feet, the low mist and dawn over the Sea of Morning Opals, the dawn that gave the sea its name. It seemed that there had never been a Moonfire, never been a past or a future, but only David Heath and his ship and the light coming over the water.

It came slowly, sifting down like a rain of jewels through the miles of pearl-grey cloud. Cool and slow at first, then warming and spreading, turning the misty air to drops of rosy fire, opaline, glowing, low to the water, so that the little ship seemed to be drifting through the heart of a fire-opal as vast as the universe.

The sea turned colour, from black to indigo streaked with milky bands. Flights of the small bright dragons rose flashing from the weed-beds that lay scattered on the surface in careless patterns of purple and ochre and cinnabar and the weed itself stirred with dim sentient life, lifting its tendrils to the light.

For one short moment David Heath was completely happy.

Then he saw that Broca had caught up a bow from under the taffrail. Heath realised that they must have fetched all their traps coolly aboard while he was in Kalruna's. It was one of the great longbows of the Upland barbarians and Broca bent its massive arc as though it had been a twig and laid across it a bone-barbed shaft.

A ship was coming toward them, a slender shape of pearl flying through the softly burning veils of mist. Her sail was emerald green. She was a long way off but she had the wind behind her and she was coming down with it like a swooping dragon.

'That's the *Lahal*,' said Heath. 'What does Johor think he's doing?'

Then he saw, with a start of incredulous horror, that on the prow of the oncoming ship the great spiked ram had been lowered into place.

During the moment when Heath's brain struggled to understand why Johor, ordinary trading skipper of an ordinary ship, should wish to sink him, Alor said five words.

'The Children of the Moon.'

Now, on the *Lahal*'s foredeck, Heath could distinguish four tiny figures dressed in black.

The long shining ram dipped and glittered in the dawn.

Heath flung himself against the stern sweep. The *Ethne*'s golden sail cracked taut. She headed up into the wind. Heath measured his distance grimly and settled down.

Broca turned on him furiously. 'Are you mad? They'll run us down! Go the other way.'

Heath said, 'There is no other way. They've got me pinned on a lee shore.' He was suddenly full of a blind rage against Johor and the four black-clad priests.

There was nothing to do but wait – wait and sail the heart out of his ship and hope that enough of David Heath still lived to get them through. *And if not*, Heath thought, *I'll take the* Lahal *down with me!*

Broca and Alor stood by the rail together, watching the racing green sail. They did not speak. There was nothing to say. Heath saw that now and again the woman turned to study him.

The wakes of the two ships lay white on the water, two legs of a triangle rushing toward their apex.

Heath could see Johor now, manning the sweep. He could see the crew crouching in the waist, frightened sailors rounded up to do the bidding of the priests. They were armed and standing by with grapnels.

Now, on the foredeck, he could see the Children of the Moon.

They were tall men. They wore tunics of black link mail with the rayed symbol of the Moon blazed in jewels on their breasts. They rode the pitching deck, their silver hair flying loose in the wind, and their bodies were as the bodies of wolves that run down their prey and devour it.

Heath fought the stern sweep, fought the straining ship, fought with wind and distance to cheat them of their will.

And the woman Alor kept watching David Heath with her bitter challenging eyes and Heath hated her as he did the priests, with a deadly hatred, because he knew what he must look like with his beaked bony face and wasted body, swaying and shivering over the loom of the sweep.

Closer and closer swept the emerald sail, rounded and gleaming like a peacock's breast in the light. Pearl white and emerald, purple and gold, on a dark blue sea, the spiked ram glittering – two bright dragons racing toward marriage, toward death.

Close, very close. The rayed symbols blazed fire on the breasts of the Children of the Moon.

The woman Alor lifted her head high into the wind and cried out – a long harsh ringing cry like the scream of an eagle. It ended in a name, and she spoke it like a curse.

'*Vakor!*'

One of the priests wore the jewelled fillet that marked him

leader. He flung up his arms, and the words of his malediction came hot and bitter down the wind.

Broca's bowstring thrummed like a great harp. The shaft fell short and Vakor laughed.

The priests went aft to be safe from buckling timbers and the faces of the seamen were full of fear.

Heath cried out a warning. He saw Alor and Broca drop flat to the deck. He saw their faces. They were the faces of a man and a woman who were on the point of death and did not like it but were not afraid. Broca reached out and braced the woman's body with his own.

Heath shoved *Ethne*'s nose fair into the wind and let her jibe.

The *Lahal* went thundering by not three yards away, helpless to do anything about it.

The kicking sweep had knocked Heath into the scuppers, half dazed. He heard the booming sail slat over, felt the wrenching shudder that shook the *Ethne* down to her last spike and prayed that the mast would stay in her. As he dragged himself back he saw that the priest Vakor had leaped onto the *Lahal*'s high stern. He was close enough for Heath to see his face.

They looked into each other's eyes and the eyes of Vakor were brilliant and wild, the eyes of a fanatic. He was not old. His body was virile and strong, his face cut in fine sweeping lines, the mouth full and sensuous and proud. He was tense with cheated fury and his voice rang against the wind like the howling of a beast.

'We will follow! We will follow, and the gods will slay!'

As the rush of the *Lahal* carried him away, Heath heard the last echo of his cry.

'*Alor!*'

With all the strength he had left Heath quieted his outraged ship and let her fill away on the starboard tack. Broca and Alor got slowly to their feet. Broca said, 'I thought you'd wrecked her.'

'They had the wind of me,' Heath said. 'I couldn't come about like a Christian.'

Alor walked to the stern and watched where the *Lahal*

wallowed and staggered as she tried to stop her headlong rush. 'Vakor!' she whispered, and spat into the sea.

Broca said, 'They will follow us. Alor told me – they have a chart, the only one, that shows the way to the Moonfire.'

Heath shrugged. He was too weary now to care. He pointed off to the right.

'There's a strong ocean current runs there, like a river in the sea. Most skippers are afraid of it but their ships aren't like the *Ethne*. We'll ride it. After that we'll have to trust to luck.'

Alor swung around sharply. 'Then you will go to the Moonfire.'

'I didn't say that. Broca, get me the bottle out of my cabin locker.'

But it was the woman who fetched it to him and watched him drink, then said, 'Are you all right?'

'I'm dying, and she asks me that,' said Heath.

She looked a moment steadily into his eyes and oddly enough there was no mockery in her voice when she spoke, only respect.

'You won't die,' she said and went away.

In a few moments the current took the *Ethne* and swept her away northward. The *Lahal* vanished into the mists behind them. She was cranky in close handling and Heath knew that Johor would not dare the swirling current.

For nearly three hours he stayed at his post and took the ship through. When the ocean stream curved east he rode out of it into still water. Then he fell down the deck and slept.

Once again the tall barbarian lifted him like a child and laid him in his bunk.

All through the rest of that day and the long Venusian night, while Broca steered, Heath lay in bitter sleep. Alor sat beside him, watching the nightmare shadows that crossed his face, listening as he moaned and talked, soothing his worst tremors.

He repeated the name of Ethne over and over again and a puzzled strangely wistful look came in the eyes of Alor.

When it was dawn again Heath awoke and went on deck. Broca said with barbarian bluntness, 'Have you decided?'

Heath did not answer and Alor said, 'Vakor will hunt you

down. The word has gone out all over Venus, wherever there are men. There'll be no refuge for you – except one.'

Heath smiled, a mirthless baring of the teeth. 'And that's the Moonfire. You make it all so simple.'

And yet he knew she spoke the truth. The Children of the Moon would never leave his track. He was a rat in a maze and every passage led to death.

But there were different deaths. If he had to die it would not be as Vakor willed but with Ethne – an Ethne more real than a shadow – in his arms again.

He realised now that deep in his mind he had always known, all these three seasons and more that he had clung to a life not worth the living. He had known that someday he must go back again.

'We'll go to the Moonfire,' he said, 'and perhaps we shall all be gods.'

Broca said, 'You are weak, Earthman. You didn't have the courage.'

Heath said one word.

'Wait.'

3
OVER THE BAR

The days and the nights went by, and the *Ethne* fled north across the Sea of Morning Opals, north toward the equator. They were far out of the trade lanes. All these vast upper reaches were wilderness. There were not even fishing villages along the coast. The great cliffs rose sheer from the water and nothing could find a foothold there. And beyond, past the Dragon's Throat, lay only the barren death-trap of the Upper Seas.

The *Ethne* ran as sweetly as though she joyed to be free again, free of the muddy harbour and the chains. And a change came over Heath. He was a man again. He stood shaved and clean and erect on his own deck and there was no decision to be made anymore, no doubt. The long dread, the long delay, were over and he too, in his own bitter way, was happy.

They had seen nothing more of the *Lahal* but Heath knew quite well that she was there somewhere, following. She was not as fleet as the *Ethne* but she was sound and Johor was a good sailor. Moreover, the priest Vakor was there and he would drive the *Lahal* over the Mountains of White Cloud if he had to – to catch them.

He said once to Alor, 'Vakor seems to have a special hatred for you.'

Her face twisted with revulsion and remembered shame. 'He is a beast,' she said. 'He is a serpent, a lizard that walks like a king.' She added, 'We've made it easy for him, the three of us together like this.'

From where he sat steering Heath looked at her with a remote curiosity. She stood, long legged, bold-mouthed, looking back with sombre smoky eyes at the white wake unrolling behind them.

He said, 'You must have loved Broca to break your vows for him. Considering what it means if they catch you.'

Alor looked at him, then laughed, a brief sound that had no humour in it.

'I'd have gone with any man strong enough to take me out of the temple,' she said. 'And Broca is strong and he worships me.'

Heath was genuinely astonished. 'You don't love him?'

She shrugged. 'He is good to look at. He is a chief of warriors and he is a man and not a priest. But love—'

She asked suddenly, 'What is it like – to love as you loved your Ethne?'

Heath started. 'What do you know about Ethne?' he asked harshly.

'You have talked of her in sleep. And Broca told me how you called her shadow in Kalruna's place. You dared the Moonfire to gain her back.'

She glanced at the ivory figurehead on the high curving bow, the image of a woman, young and slim and smiling.

'I think you are a fool,' she said abruptly. 'I think only a fool would love a shadow.'

She had left him and gone down into the cabin before he could gather words, before he could take her white neck between his hands and break it.

Ethne – Ethne!

He cursed the woman of the temple gardens.

He was still in a brooding fury when Broca came up out of the cabin to relieve him at the sweep.

'I'll steer a while yet,' Heath told him curtly. 'I think the weather's going to break.'

Clouds were boiling up in the south as the night closed down. The sea was running in long easy swells as it had done for all these days but there was a difference, a pulse and a stir that quivered all through the ship's keel.

Broca, stretching huge shoulders, looked away to the south and then down at Heath.

'I think you talk too much to my woman,' he said.

Before Heath could answer the other laid his hand lightly on the Earthman's shoulder. A light grip but with strength enough behind it to crack Heath's bones.

He said, 'Do not talk so much to Alor.'

'I haven't sought her out,' Heath snapped savagely. 'She's your woman – you worry about her.'

'I am not worried about her,' Broca answered calmly. 'Not about her and you.'

He was looking down at Heath as he spoke and Heath knew the contrast they made – his own lean body and gaunt face against the big barbarian's magnificent strength.

'But she is always with you on the deck, listening to your stories of the sea,' said Broca. 'Do not talk to her so much,' he repeated and this time there was an edge to his voice.

'For heaven's sake!' said Heath jeeringly. 'If I'm a fool what are you? A man mad enough to look for power in the Moonfire and faithfulness in a temple wench! And now you're jealous.'

He hated both Broca and Alor bitterly in this moment and out of his hate he spoke.

'Wait until the Moonfire touches you. It will break your strength and your pride. After that you won't care who your woman talks to or where.'

Broca gave him a stare of unmoved contempt. Then he turned his back and settled down to look out across the darkening sea.

After a while, the amusing side of the whole thing struck Heath, and he began to laugh.

They were, all three of them, going to die. Somewhere out there to the south, Vakor came like a black shepherd, driving them toward death. Dreams of empire, dreams of glory and a voyage that tempted the vengeance of the gods – and at such a time that barbarian chief could be jealous.

With sudden shock he realised just how much time Alor had spent with him. Out of habit and custom as old as the sea he had helped to while away the long hard hours with a sailor's yarns. Looking back he could see Alor's face, strangely young and eager as she listened, could remember how she asked questions and wanted to learn the ways and the working of the ship.

He could remember now how beautiful she looked with the wind in her hair, her firm strong body holding the *Ethne* steady in a quartering sea.

The storm brewed over the hours and at last it broke.

Heath had known that the Sea of Morning Opals would not let him go without a struggle. It had tried him with shallows, with shifting reefs, with dead calms and booming solar tides and all the devices of current, fog and drifting weed. He had beaten all of them. Now he was almost within sight of the Dragon's Throat, the gateway to the Upper Seas, and it was a murderous moment for a storm out of the south.

The night had turned black. The sea burned with white phosphorescence, a boiling cauldron of witch-fire. The wind was frightening. The *Ethne* plunged and staggered, driving under a bare pole, and for once Heath was glad of Broca's strength as they fought the sweep together.

He became aware that someone was beside him and knew that it was Alor.

'Go below!' he yelled and caught only the echo of her answer. She did not go but threw her weight too against the sweep.

Lightning bolts as broad as comets' tails came streaking down with a rush and a fury as though they had started their run from another star and gathered speed across half the galaxy. They lit the Sea of Morning Opals with a purple glare until the thunder brought the darkness crashing down again. Then the rain fell like a river rolling down the belts of cloud.

Heath groaned inwardly. The wind and the following sea had taken the little ship between them and were hurling her forward. At the speed she was making now she would hit the Dragon's Throat at dawn. She would hit it full tilt and helpless as a drifting chip.

The lightning showed him the barbarian's great straining body, gleaming wet, his long hair torn loose from its knots and chains, streaming with wind and water. It showed him Alor too. Their hands and their shoulders touched, straining together.

It seemed that they struggled on that way for centuries and then, abruptly, the rain stopped, the wind slackened, and there was a period of eerie silence. Alor's voice sounded loud in Heath's ears, crying, 'Is it over?'

'No,' he answered. 'Listen!'

They heard a deep and steady booming, distant in the north – the boom of surf.

The storm began again.

Dawn came, hardly lighter than the night. Through the flying wrack Heath could see cliffs on either side where the mountain ranges narrowed in, funnelling the Sea of Morning Opals into the strait of the Dragon's Throat. The driven sea ran high between them, bursting white against the black rock.

The *Ethne* was carried headlong, a leaf in a millrace.

The cliffs drew in and in until there was a gap of no more than a mile between them. Black brooding titans and the space below a fury of white water, torn and shredded by fang-like rocks.

The Dragon's Throat.

When he had made the passage before Heath had had fair weather and men for the oars. Even then it had not been easy. Now he tried to remember where the channel lay, tried to force the ship toward what seemed to be an open lane among the rocks.

The *Ethne* gathered speed and shot forward into the Dragon's Throat.

She fled through a blind insanity of spray and wind and sound.

Time and again Heath saw the loom of a towering rock before him and wrenched the ship aside or fought to keep away from death that was hidden just under the boiling surface. Twice, three times, the *Ethne* gave a grating shudder and he thought she was gone.

Once, toward the last, when it seemed that there was no hope, he felt Alor's hand close over his.

The high water saved them, catching them in its own rush down the channel, carrying them over the rocks and finally over the bar at the end of the gut. The *Ethne* came staggering out into the relative quiet of the Upper Seas, where the pounding waves seemed gentle and it was all done so quickly, over so soon. For a long time the three of them stood sagging over the sweep, not able to realise that it was over and they still lived.

The storm spent itself. The wind settled to a steady blow. Heath got a rag of sail up. Then he sat down by the tiller and bowed his head over his knees and thought about how Alor had caught his hand when she believed she was going to die.

4
'I WILL WAIT!'

Even this early it was hot. The Upper Seas sprawled along the equator, shallow landlocked waters choked with weed and fouled with shifting reefs of mud, cut into a maze of lakes and blind channels by the jutting headlands of the mountains.

The wind dropped to a flat calm. They left the open water behind them, where it was swept clean by the tides from the Sea of Morning Opals. The floating weed thickened around them, a blotched ochre plain that stirred with its own dim mindless life. The air smelled rotten.

Under Heath's direction they swung the weed-knife into place, the great braced blade that fitted over the prow. Then, using the heavy sweep as a sculling oar, they began to push the *Ethne* forward by the strength of their sweating backs.

Clouds of the little bright-scaled dragons rose with hissing screams, disturbed by the ship. This was their breeding ground. They fought and nested in the weed and the steaming air was full of the sound of their wings. They perched on the rail and in the rigging, watching with their red eyes. The creature that rode Heath's shoulder emitted harsh cries of excitement. Heath tossed him into the air and he flew away to join his mates.

There was life under the weed, spawning in the hot stagnant waters, multiform and formless, swarming, endlessly hungry. Small reptilian creatures flopped and slithered through the weed, eating the dragon's eggs, and here and there a flat dark head would break through with a snap and a crunch, and it would watch the *Ethne* with incurious eyes while it chewed and swallowed.

Constantly Heath kept watch.

The sun rose high above the eternal clouds. The heat seeped down and gathered. The scull moved back and forth, the knife bit, the weed dragged against the hull and behind them the cut closed slowly as the stuff wrapped and coiled upon itself.

Heath's eyes kept turning to Alor.

He did not want to look at her. He did not wish to remember the touch of her hand on his. He wished only to remember Ethne, to remember the agony of the Moonfire and to think of the reward that lay beyond it if he could endure. What could a temple wench mean to him beside that?

But he kept looking at her covertly. Her white limbs glistened with sweat and her red mouth was sullen with weariness and even so there was a strange wild beauty about her. Time and again her gaze would meet his, a quick hungry glance from under her lashes, and her eyes were not the eyes of a temple wench. Heath cursed Broca in his heart for making him think of Alor and he cursed himself because now he could not stop thinking of her.

They toiled until they could not stand. Then they sprawled on the deck in the breathless heat to rest. Broca pulled Alor to him.

'Soon this will all be over,' he said. 'Soon we will reach the Moonfire. You will like that, Alor – to be mated to a god!'

She lay unresponsive in the circle of his arm, her head turned away. She did not answer.

Broca laughed. 'God and goddess. Two of a kind as we are now. We'll build our thrones so high the sun can see them.' He rolled her head on his shoulder, looking down intently into her face. 'Power, Alor. Strength. We will have them together.' He covered her mouth with his, and his free hand caressed her, deliberate, possessive.

She thrust him away. 'Don't,' she said angrily. 'It's too hot and I'm too tired.' She got up and walked to the side, standing with her back to Broca.

Broca looked at her. Then he turned and looked at Heath. A dark flash reddened his skin. He said slowly, 'Too hot and too tired – and besides, the Earthman is watching.'

He sprang up and caught Alor and swung her around, one huge hand tangled in her hair, holding her. As soon as he touched her Heath also sprang up and said harshly, 'Let her alone!'

Broca said, 'She is my mate but I may not touch her.' He glared down into Alor's blazing eyes and said, 'She is my mate – or isn't she?'

He flung her away. He turned his head from side to side, half blind with rage.

'Do you think I didn't see you?' he asked thickly. 'All day, looking at each other.'

Heath said, 'You're crazy.'

'Yes,' answered Broca, 'I am.' He took two steps toward Heath and added, 'Crazy enough to kill you.'

Alor said, 'If you do you'll never reach the Moonfire.'

Broca paused, trapped for one moment between his passion and his dream. He was facing the stern. Something caused his gaze to waver from Heath and then, gradually, his expression changed. Heath swung around and Alor gave a smothered cry.

Far behind them, vague in the steaming air, was an emerald sail.

The *Lahal* must have come through the Dragon's Throat as soon as the storm was over. With men to man the rowing benches she had gained on the *Ethne* during the calm. Now she too was in the weed, and the oars were useless but there were men to scull her. She would move faster than the *Ethne* and without pause.

There would be little rest for Heath and Broca and the woman.

They swayed at the sculling oar all the stifling afternoon and all the breathless night, falling into the dull, half-hypnotized rhythm of beasts who walk forever around a water-wheel. Two of them working always, while the third slept, and Broca never took his eyes from Alor. With his tremendous vitality it seemed that he never slept and during the periods when Heath and Alor were alone at the oar together they exchanged neither words nor glances.

At dawn they saw that the *Lahal* was closer.

Broca crouched on the deck. He lifted his head and looked at the green sail. Heath saw that his eyes were very bright and that he shivered in spite of the brooding heat.

Heath's heart sank. The Upper Seas were rank with fever, and it looked as though the big barbarian was in for a bad go of it. Heath himself was pretty well immune to it but Broca was used to the clean air of the High Plateaus and the poison was working in his blood.

He measured the speed of the two ships and said, 'It's no use. We must stand and fight.'

Heath said savagely, 'I thought you wanted to find the Moonfire. I thought you were the strong man who could win through it where everybody else has failed. I thought you were going to be a god.'

Broca got to his feet. 'With fever or without it I'm a better man than you.'

'Then work! If we can just keep ahead of them until we clear the weed—'

Broca said, 'The Moonfire?'

'Yes.'

'We will keep ahead.'

He bent his back to the scull and the *Ethne* crept forward through the weed. Her golden sail hung from the yard with a terrible stillness. The heat pressed down upon the Upper Seas as though the sun itself were falling through the haze. Astern the *Lahal* moved steadily on.

Broca's fever mounted. He turned from time to time to curse Vakor, shouting at the emerald sail.

'You'll never catch us, priest!' He would cry. 'I am Broca of the tribe of Sarn and I will beat you – and I will beat the Moonfire. You will lie on your belly, priest, and lick my sandals before you die.'

Then he would turn to Alor, his eyes shining. 'You know the legends, Alor! The man who can bathe in the heart of the Moonfire has the power of the High Ones. He can build a world to suit himself, he can be king and lord and master. He can give his woman-god a palace of diamonds with a floor of gold. That is true, Alor. You have heard the priests say it in the temple.'

Alor answered, 'It is true.'

'A new world, Alor. A world of our own.'

He made the great sweep swing in a frenzy of strength and once again the mystery of the Moonfire swept over Heath. Why, since the priests knew the way there, did they not themselves become gods. Why had no man ever come out of it with godhead – only a few, a handful like himself, who had not had the valour to go all the way in.

And yet there was godhead there. He knew because within himself there was the shadow of it.

The endless day wore on. The emerald sail came closer.

Toward mid-afternoon there was a sudden clattering flight of the little dragons and all life stopped still in the weed. The reptilian creatures lay motionless with dragon's eggs unbroken in their jaws. No head broke the surface to feed. The dragons flew away in a hissing cloud. There was utter silence.

Heath flung himself against the sweep and stopped it.

'Be quiet,' he said. 'Look. Out there.'

They followed his gesture. Far away over the port bow, flowing toward them, was a ripple in the weed. A ripple as though the very bed of the Upper Seas was in motion.

'What is it?' whispered Alor, and saw Heath's face, and was silent.

Sluggishly, yet with frightening speed, the ripple came toward them. Heath got a harpoon out of the stern locker. He watched the motion of the weed, saw it gradually slow and stop in a puzzled way. Then he threw the harpoon as far away from the ship as he could with all his strength and more.

The ripple began again. It swerved and sped toward where the harpoon had fallen.

'They'll attack anything that moves,' said Heath. 'It lost us because we stopped. Watch.'

The weed heaved and burst open, its meshes snapping across a scaled and titanic back. There seemed to be no shape to the creature, no distinguishable head. It was simply a vast and hungry blackness that spread upward and outward and the luckless brutes that cowered near it hissed and thrashed in their efforts to escape, and were engulfed and vanished.

Again Alor whispered, 'What is it?'

'One of the Guardians,' Heath answered. 'The Guardians of the Upper Seas. They will crush a moving ship to splinters and eat the crew.'

He glanced back at the *Lahal*. She, too, had come to a dead stop. The canny Vakor had scented the danger also.

'We'll have to wait,' said Heath, 'until it goes away.'

They waited. The huge shape of darkness sucked and floundered in the weed and was in no hurry to go.

Broca sat staring at Heath. He was deep in fever and his eyes were not sane. He began to mutter to himself, incoherent ramblings in which only the name Alor and the word Moonfire were distinguishable.

Suddenly, with startling clarity, he said, 'The Moonfire is nothing without Alor.'

He repeated 'Nothing!' several times, beating his huge fists on his knees each time he said it. Then he turned his head blindly from side to side as though looking for something. 'She's gone. Alor's gone. She's gone to the Earthman.'

Alor spoke to him, touched him, but he shook her off. In his fever-mad brain there was only one truth. He rose and went toward David Heath.

Heath got up. 'Broca!' he said. 'Alor is there beside you. She hasn't gone!'

Broca did not hear. He did not stop.

Alor cried out, '*Broca!*'

'No,' said Broca. 'You love him. You're not mine anymore. When you look at me I am nothing. Your lips have no warmth in them.' He reached out toward David Heath and he was blind and deaf to everything but the life that was in him to be torn out and trampled upon and destroyed.

In the cramped space of the afterdeck there was not much room to move. Heath did not want to fight. He tried to dodge the sick giant but Broca pinned him against the rail. Fever or no fever, Heath had to fight him and it was not much use. Broca was beyond feeling pain.

His sheer weight crushed Heath against the rail, bent his spine almost to breaking and his hands found Heath's throat. Heath struck and struck again and wondered if he had come all this way to die in a senseless quarrel over a woman.

Abruptly he realised that Broca was letting go, was sliding down against him to the deck. Through a swimming haze he saw Alor standing there with a belaying pin in her hand. He began to tremble, partly with reaction but mostly with fury that he should have needed a woman's help to save his life. Broca lay still, breathing heavily.

'Thanks,' said Heath curtly. 'Too bad you had to hit him. He didn't know what he was doing.'

Alor said levelly, 'Didn't he?'

Heath did not answer. He started to turn away and she caught him, forcing him to look at her.

'Very likely I will die in the Moonfire,' she said. 'I haven't the faith in my strength that Broca has. So I'm going to say this now – I love you, David Heath. I don't care what you think or what you do about it but I love you.'

Her eyes searched his face, as though she wanted to remember every line and plane of it. Then she kissed him and her mouth was tender and very sweet.

She stepped back and said quietly, 'I think the Guardian has gone. The *Lahal* is under way again.'

Heath followed her without a word to the sweep. Her kiss

burned in him like sweet fire. He was shaken and utterly confused.

They toiled together while Broca slept. They dared not pause. Heath could distinguish the men now aboard the *Lahal*, little bent figures sculling, sculling and there were always fresh ones. He could see the black tunics of the Children of the Moon who stood upon the foredeck and waited.

The *Ethne* moved more and more slowly as the hours passed and the gap between the two ships grew steadily smaller. Night came and through the darkness they could hear the voice of Vakor howling after them.

Toward midnight Broca roused. The fever had left him but he was morose and silent. He thrust Alor roughly aside and took the sweep and the *Ethne* gathered speed.

'How much farther?' he asked. And Heath panted, 'Not far now.'

Dawn came and still they were not clear of the weed. The *Lahal* was so near them now that Heath could see the jewelled fillet on Vakor's brow. He stood alone, high on the upper brace of the weed-knife, and he watched them, laughing.

'Work!' he shouted at them. 'Toil and sweat! You, Alor – woman of the gardens! This is better than the Temple. Broca – thief and breaker of the Law – strain your muscles there! And you, Earthman. For the second time you defy the gods!' He leaned out over the weed as though he would reach ahead and grasp the *Ethne* in his bare hands and drag her back.

'Sweat and strain, you dogs! You can't escape!'

And they did sweat and strain and fresh relays of men worked at the sweep of the *Lahal*, breaking their hearts to go faster and ever faster. Vakor laughed from his high perch and it seemed futile for the *Ethne* to go on any longer with this lost race.

But Heath looked ahead with burning sunken eyes. He saw how the mists rose and gathered to the north, how the colour of the weed changed, and he urged the others on. There was a fury in him now. It blazed brighter and harder than Broca's, this iron fury that would not, by the gods themselves, be balked of the Moonfire.

They kept ahead – so little ahead that the *Lahal* was almost within arrow-shot of them. Then the weed thinned and the *Ethne* began to gain a little and suddenly, before they realised it, they were in open water.

Like mad creatures they worked the scull and Heath steered the *Ethne* where he remembered the northern current ran, drawn by the Ocean-That-Is-Not-Water. After the terrible labour of the weed it seemed that they were flying. But as the mists began to wreathe about them the *Lahal* too had freed herself and was racing toward them with every man on the rowing benches.

The mists thickened around them. The black water began to have a rare occasional hint of gold, like shooting sparks beneath the surface. There began to be islands, low and small, rank with queer vegetation. The flying dragons did not come here nor the Guardians nor the little reptiles. It was very hot and very still.

Through the stillness the voice of Vakor rose on a harsh wild screaming as he cursed the rowers on.

The current grew more swift and the dancing flecks of gold brightened in the water. Heath's face bore a strange unhuman look. The oars of the *Lahal* beat and churned and bowmen stood now on the foredeck, ready to shoot when they came within range.

Then, incredibly, Vakor gave one long high scream and flung up his hand and the oars stopped. Vakor stretched both arms above his head, his fists clenched, and he hurled after them one terrible word of malediction.

'I will wait, blasphemers! If so be you live I will be here – waiting!'

The emerald sail dwindled in the *Ethne*'s wake, faded and was lost in the mist.

Broca said, 'They had us. Why did they stop?'

Heath pointed. Up ahead the whole misty north was touched with a breath of burning gold.

'The Moonfire!'

5
INTO THE MOONFIRE

This was the dream that had driven Heath to madness, the nightmare that had haunted him, the memory that had drawn him back in spite of terror and the certainty of destruction. Now it was reality and he could not separate it from the dream.

Once again he watched the sea change until the *Ethne* drifted not on water but on a golden liquid that lapped her hull with soft rippling fire. Once again the mist enwrapped him, shining, glowing.

The first faint tingling thrill moved in his blood and he knew how it would be – the lying pleasure that mounted through ecstasy to unendurable pain. He saw the dim islands, low and black, a maze through which a ship might wander forever without finding the source that poured out this wonder of living light.

He saw the bones of ships that had died searching. They lay on the island beaches and the mist made them a bright shroud. There were not many of them. Some were so old that the race that built them had vanished out of the memory of Venus.

The hushed unearthly beauty wrenched Heath's heart and he was afraid unto dying and yet filled with lust, with a terrible hunger.

Broca drew the air deep into his lungs as though he would suck the power out of the Moonfire.

'Can you find it again?' he asked. 'The heart of it.'

'I can find it.'

Alor stood silent and unmoving. She was all silver in this light, dusted with golden motes.

Heath said, 'Are you afraid, breaking the taboo?'

'Habit is hard to break.' She turned to him and asked, 'What is the Moonfire?'

'Haven't the priests told you?'

'They say that Venus once had a moon. It rode in the clouds like a disc of fire and the god who dwelt within it was supreme over all the other gods. He watched the surface of the planet and all that was done upon it. But the lesser gods were jealous, and one day they were able to destroy the palace of the Moon-god.

'All the sky of Venus was lighted by that destruction. Mountains fell and seas poured out of their beds and whole nations died. The Moon-god was slain and his shining body fell like a meteor through the clouds.

'But a god cannot really die. He only sleeps and waits. The golden mist is the cloud of his breathing, and the shining of his body is the Moonfire. A man may gain divinity from the heart of the sleeping god but all the gods of Venus will curse him if he tries because man has no right to steal their powers.'

'And you don't believe that story,' said Heath.

Alor shrugged. 'You have seen the Moonfire. The priests have not.'

'I didn't get to the heart of it,' Heath said. 'I only saw the edge of the crater and the light that comes up out of it, the lovely hellish light.'

He stopped, shuddering, and brooded as he had so many times before on the truth behind the mystery of the Moonfire. Presently he said slowly, 'There was a moon, of course, or there could be no conception of one in folklore. I believe it was radioactive, some element that hasn't been found yet or doesn't exist at all on Earth or Mars.'

'I don't understand,' said Alor. 'What is "radioactive"?' She used the Terran word, as Heath had, because there was no term for it in Venusian.

'It's a strange sort of fire that burns in certain elements. It eats them away, feeding on its own atoms, and the radiation from this fire is very powerful.' He was silent for a moment, his eyes half closed. 'Can't you feel it?' he asked. 'The first little fire that burns in your own blood?'

'Yes,' Alor whispered. 'I feel it.'

And Broca said, 'It is like wine.'

Heath went on, putting the old, old thoughts into words. 'The moon was destroyed. Not by jealous gods but by collision with another body, perhaps an asteroid. Or maybe it was burst apart by its own blazing energy. I think that a fragment of it survived and fell here and that its radiation permeated and changed the sea and the air around it.

'It changes men in the same way. It seems to alter the whole electrical set-up of the brain, to amplify its power far beyond anything human. It gives the mind a force of will strong enough to control the free electrons in the air – to create ...'

He paused, then finished quietly, 'In my case, only shadows. And when that mutation occurs a man doesn't need the gods of Venus to curse him. I got only a little of it but that was enough.'

Broca said, 'It is worth bearing pain to become a god. You had no strength.'

Heath smiled crookedly. 'How many gods have come out of the Moonfire?'

Broca answered, 'There will be one soon.' Then he caught Alor by the shoulders and pulled her to him, looking down into her face. 'No,' he said. 'Not one. Two.'

'Perhaps,' said Heath, 'there will be three.'

Broca turned and gave him a chill and level look. 'I do not think,' he said, 'that your strength is any greater now.'

After that, for a long while, they did not speak. The *Ethne* drifted on, gliding on the slow currents that moved between the islands. Sometimes they sculled, the great blade of the sweep hidden in a froth of flame. The golden glow brightened and grew and with it grew the singing fire in their blood.

Heath stood erect and strong at the helm, the old Heath who had sailed the Straits of Lhiva in the teeth of a summer gale and laughed about it. All weariness, all pain, all weakness, were swept away. It was the same with the others. Alor's head was high and Broca leaped up beside the figurehead and gave a great ringing shout, a challenge to all the gods there were to stop him.

Heath found himself looking into Alor's eyes. She smiled, an aching thing of tears and tenderness and farewell.

'I think none of us will live,' she whispered. 'May you find your shadow, David, before you die.'

Then Broca had turned toward them once more and the moment was gone.

Within the veil of the Moonfire there was no day nor night

nor time. Heath had no idea how long the *Ethne*'s purple hull rode the golden current. The tingling force spread through his whole body and pulsed and strengthened until he was drunk with the pleasure of it and the islands slipped by, and there was no sound or movement but their own in all that solemn sea.

And at last he saw ahead of him the supernal brightness that poured from the heart of the Moonfire, the living core of all the brightness of the mist. He saw the land, lifting dark and vague, drowned in the burning haze, and he steered toward it along the remembered way. There was no fear in him now. He was beyond fear.

Broca cried out suddenly, 'A ship!'

Heath nodded. 'It was there before. It will be there when the next man finds his way here.'

Two long arms of the island reached out to form a ragged bay. The *Ethne* entered it. They passed the derelict ship, floating patiently, untouched here by wind or tide or ocean rot. Her blue sail was furled, her rigging all neat and ready. She waited to begin the voyage home. She would wait a long, long time.

As they neared the land they sighted other ships. They had not moved nor changed since Heath had seen them last, three years ago.

A scant few they were, that had lived to find the Dragon's Throat and pass it, that had survived the Upper Seas and the island maze of the Moonfire and had found their goal at last. Some of them floated still where their crews had left them, their sad sails drooping from the yards.

Others lay on their sides on the beach, as though in sleep. There were strange old keels that had not been seen on the seas of Venus for a thousand years. The golden mist preserved them and they waited like a pack of faithful dogs for their masters to return.

Heath brought the *Ethne* in to shore at the same spot where he had beached her before. She grounded gently and he led the way over the side. He remembered the queer crumbling texture of the dark earth under his feet. He was shaken with the force that throbbed in his flesh. As before it hovered now on the edge of pain.

He led the way inland and no one spoke.

The mist thickened around them, filled with dancing sparks of light. The bay was lost behind its wreathing curtain. They walked forward and the ground began to rise under their feet slowly. They moved as in a dream and the light and the silence crushed them with great awe.

They came upon a dead man.

He lay upon his face, his arms stretched out toward the mystery that lay beyond, his hands still yearned toward the glory he had never reached. They did not disturb him.

Mist, heavier, the glow brightening, the golden motes whirling and flickering in a madder dance. Heath listened to the voice of pain that spoke within him, rising with every step he took toward a soundless scream.

I remember, I remember! The bones, the flesh, the brain, each atom of them a separate flame, bursting, tearing to be free. I cannot go on, I cannot bear it! Soon I shall waken, safe in the mud behind Kalruna's.

But he did not wake and the ground rose steadily under his feet and there was a madness on him, a passion and a suffering that were beyond man's strength to endure. Yet he endured.

The swirling motes began to shape themselves into vague figures, formless giants that towered and strode around them. Heath heard Alor's moan of terror and forced himself to say, 'They're nothing. Shadows out of our own mind. The beginning of the power.'

Farther they went and farther still, and then at last Heath stopped and flung up his arm to point, looking at Broca.

'Your godhead lies there. Go and take it!'

The eyes of the barbarian were dazed and wild, fixed on the dark dim line of the crater that showed in the distance, fixed on the incredible glory that shone there.

'It beats,' he whispered, 'like the beating of a heart.'

Alor drew back, away from him, staring at the light. 'I am afraid,' she said. 'I will not go.' Heath saw that her face was agonised, her body shaken like his own. Her voice rose in a wail. 'I can't go! I can't stand it. I'm dying!' Suddenly she caught Heath's hands. 'David, take me back. *Take me back!*'

Before he could think or speak Broca had torn Alor away from him and struck him a great swinging blow. Heath fell to the ground and the last thing he heard was Alor's voice crying his name.

6
END OF THE DREAM

Heath was not unconscious long, for when he lifted his head again he could still see the others in the distance. Broca was running like a madman up the slope of the crater, carrying Alor in his arms. Ghostly and indistinct, he stood for an instant on the edge. Then he leaped over and was gone.

Heath was alone.

He lay still, fighting to keep his mind steady, struggling against the torture of his flesh.

'Ethne, Ethne,' he whispered. 'This is the end of the dream.'

He began to crawl, inch by bitter inch, toward the heart of the Moonfire.

He was closer to it now than he had been before. The strange rough earth cut his hands and his bare knees. The blood ran but the pain of it was less than a pinprick against the cosmic agony of the Moonfire. Broca must have suffered too, yet he had gone running to his fate. Perhaps his nervous system was duller, more resistant to shock. Or perhaps it was simply that his lust for power carried him on.

Heath had no wish for power. He did not wish to be a god. He wished only to die and he knew that he was going to very soon. But before he died he would do what he had failed to do before. He would bring Ethne back. He would hear her voice again and look into her eyes and they would wait together for the final dark.

Her image would vanish with his death, for then mind and memory would be gone. But he would not see the life go out of her as he had all those years ago by the Sea of Morning Opals.

She would be with him until the end, sweet and loving and merry, as she had always been.

He said her name over and over again as he crawled. He tried to think of nothing else, so that he might forget the terrible unhuman things that were happening within him.

'Ethne, Ethne,' he whispered. His hands clawed the earth and his knees scraped it and the brilliance of the Moonfire wrapped him in golden banners of mist. Yet he would not stop, though the soul was shaken out of him.

He reached the edge of the crater and looked down upon the heart of the Moonfire.

The whole vast crater was a sea of glowing vapour, so dense that it moved in little rippling waves, tipped with a sparkling froth. There was an island in that sea, a shape like a fallen mountain that burned with a blinding intensity, so great that only the eyes of god could bear to look at it.

It rode in the clouds like a disc of fire.

Heath knew that his guess was right. It did not matter. Body of a sleeping god or scrap of a fallen moon – it would bring Ethne back to him and for that was all he cared.

He dragged himself over the edge and let himself go, down the farther slope. He screamed once when the vapour closed over him.

After that there was a period of utter strangeness.

It seemed that some force separated the atoms that composed the organism called David Heath and reshuffled them into a different pattern. There was a wrench, an agony beyond anything he had known before and then, abruptly, the pain was gone. His body felt well and whole, his mind was awake, alert and clear with a dawning awareness of new power.

He looked down at himself, ran his hands over his face. He had not changed. And yet he knew that he was different. He had taken the full force of the radiation this time and apparently it had completed the change begun three years ago. He was not the same David Heath, perhaps, but he was no longer trapped in the no-man's-land between the old and the new.

He no longer felt that he was going to die and he no longer wished to. He was filled with a great strength and a great joy. He could bring his Ethne back now and they could live on together here in the golden garden of the Moonfire.

It would have to be here. He was sure of that. He had only been into the fringe of the Moonfire before, but he did not believe that that was the whole reason why he could create nothing but shadows. There was not a sufficient concentration of the raw energy upon which the mind's telekinetic power worked.

Probably, even in the outer mists of the Moonfire, there were not enough free electrons. But here, close to the source, the air was raging with them. Raw stuff of matter, to be shaped and formed.

David Heath rose to his feet. He lifted his head and his arms reached out longingly. Straight and shining and strong he stood in the living light and his dark face was the face of a happy god.

'Ethne,' he whispered. 'Ethne. This is not the end of the dream, but the beginning!'

And she came.

By the power, the exultant strength that was in him, Heath brought her out of the Moonfire. Ethne, slim and smiling, indistinct at first, a shadow in the mist, but growing clearer, coming toward him. He could see her white limbs, the pale flame of her hair, her red mouth bold and sweet, her wistful eyes.

Heath recoiled with a cry. It was not Ethne who stood before him. It was Alor.

For a time he could not move but stared at what he had created. The apparition smiled at him and her face was the face of a woman who has found love and with it the whole world.

'No,' he said. 'It isn't you I want. It's Ethne!' He struck the thought of Alor from his mind and the image faded and once again he called Ethne to him.

And when she came it was not Ethne but Alor.

He destroyed the vision. Rage and disappointment almost too great to bear drove him to wander in the fog. Alor, Alor! Why did that wench of the temple gardens haunt him now?

He hated her, yet her name sang in his heart and would not be silenced. He could not forget how she had kissed him and how her eyes had looked then and how her last desperate cry had been for him.

He could not forget that his own heart had shaped her image while only his mind, his conscious mind, had said the name of Ethne.

He sat down and bent his head over his knees and wept, because he knew now that this was the end of the dream. He had lost the old love forever without knowing it. It was a cruel thing, but it was true. He had to make his peace with it.

And already Alor might be dead.

That thought cut short his grieving for what was gone. He leaped up, filled with dread. He stood for a moment, looking wildly about, and the vapour was like golden water so that he could see only a few feet away. Then he began to run, shouting her name.

For what might have been centuries in that timeless place he ran, searching for her. There was no answer to his cries. Sometimes he would see a dim figure crouching in the mist, and he would think that he had found her but each time it was the body of a man, dead for God knew how long. They were all alike. They were emaciated, as though they had died of starvation and they were all smiling. There seemed to be lost visions still in their open eyes.

These were the gods of the Moonfire – the handful of men through all the ages who had fought their way through to the ultimate goal.

Heath saw the cruelty of the jest. A man could find godhead in the golden lake. He could create his own world within it. But he could never leave it unless he were willing to leave also the world in which he was king. They would have learned that, these men, as they started back toward the harbour, away from the source.

Or perhaps there was more to it. Perhaps they never tried to leave.

Heath went on through the beautiful unchanging mist, calling Alor's name, and there was no answer. He realised that it was becoming more difficult for him to keep his mind on his quest. Half-formed imaged flickered vaguely around him. He grew excited and there was an urgency in him to stop and bring the visions clear, to build and create.

He fought off the temptation but there came a time when he had to stop because he was too tired to go on. He sank down and the hopelessness of his search came over him. Alor was gone and he could never find her. In utter dejection he crouched there, his face buried in his hands, thinking of her, and all at once he heard her voice speaking his name. He stared up and she was there, holding out her hands to him.

He caught her to him and stroked her hair and kissed her, half sobbing with joy at having found her. Then a sudden thought came to him. He drew back and said, 'Are you really Alor or only the shadow of my mind?'

She did not answer but only held up her mouth to be kissed again.

Heath turned away, too weary and hopeless even to destroy the vision. And then he thought, 'Why should I destroy it? If the woman is lost to me why shouldn't I keep the dream?'

He looked at her again and she was Alor, clothed in warm flesh, eager-eyed.

The temptation swept over him again and this time he did not fight it. He was a god, whether he wished it or not. He would create.

He threw the whole force of his mind against the golden mist, and the intoxication of sheer power made him drunk and mad with joy.

The glowing cloud drew back to become a horizon and a sky. Under Heath's feet an island grew, warm sweet earth, rich with grass and rioting with flowers, a paradise lost in a dreaming sea. Wavelets whispered on the wide beaches, the drooping fronds of the *liha*-trees stirred lazily in the wind and bright birds darted, singing. Snug in the little cove a ship floated, a lovely thing that angels might have built.

Perfection, the unattainable wish of the soul. And Alor was with him to share it.

He knew now why no one had ever come out of the Moonfire.

He took the vision of Alor by the hand. He wandered with it along the beaches and presently he was aware of something missing. He smiled, and once again the little dragon rode his shoulder and he stroked it and there was no least flaw in this Elysium. David Heath had found his godhead.

But some stubborn corner of his heart betrayed him. It said, *This is all a lie and Alor waits for you. If you tarry you and she will be as those others, who are dead and smiling in the Moonfire.*

He did not want to listen. He was happy. But something made him listen and he knew that as long as the real Alor lived he could not really be content with a dream. He knew that he must destroy this paradise before it destroyed him. He knew that the Moonfire was a deadly thing and that men could not be given the power of gods and continue sane.

And yet he could not destroy the island. He could not!

Horror overcame him that he had so far succumbed, that he could no longer control his own will. And he destroyed the island and the sea and the lovely ship and it was harder than if he had torn his own flesh from the bones.

And he destroyed the vision of Alor.

He knew that if he wished to escape the madness and the death of the Moonfire he must not again create so much as a blade of grass. Nothing. Because he would never again have the strength to resist the unholy joy of creation.

7
TO WALK DIVINE

Once more he ran shouting through the golden fog. And it might have been a year or only a moment later that he heard Alor's voice very faintly in the distance, calling his name.

He followed the sound, crying out more loudly, but he did not hear her again. Then, looming in shadowy grandeur through the mist, he saw a castle. It was a typical Upland stronghold but it was larger than the castle of any barbarian king and it was built out of one huge crimson jewel of the sort called Dragon's Blood.

Heath knew that he was seeing part of Broca's dream.

Steps of beaten gold led up to a greater door. Two tall warriors, harnesses blazing with gems, stood guard. Heath went between them and they caught and held him fast. Broca's hatred for the Earthman was implicit in the beings his mind created.

Heath tried to tear himself free but their strength was more than human. They took him down fantastic corridors, over floors of pearl and crystal and precious metals. The walls were lined with open chests, full of every sort of treasure the barbarian mind could conceive. Slaves went silent footed on their errands and the air was heavy with perfume and spices. Heath thought how strange it was to walk through the halls of another man's dream.

He was brought into a vast room where many people feasted. There were harpists and singers and dancing girls and throngs of slaves, men who wrestled and men who fought and danced with swords. The men and women at the long tables looked like chieftains and their wives but they wore plain leather and tunics without decoration, so that Broca's guardsmen and even his slaves were more resplendent than they.

Above the shouting and the revelry Broca sat, high on a throne-chair that was made like a silver dragon with its jewelled wings spread wide. He wore magnificent harness and a carved diamond that only a high king may wear hung between his eyebrows. He drank wine out of a golden cup and watched the feasting with eyes that had in them no smallest flicker of humanity. God or demon, Broca was no longer a man.

Alor sat beside him. She wore the robes of a queen but her face was hidden in her hands and her body was still as death.

Heath's cry carried across all the noise of the feast. Broca leaped to his feet and an abrupt silence fell. Everyone, guards, chieftains and slaves, turned to watch as Heath was led toward the throne – and they all hated him as Broca hated.

Alor raised her head and looked into his eyes. And she asked, in his own words, 'Are you really David or only the shadow of my mind?'

'I am David,' he told her and was glad he had destroyed his paradise.

Broca's mad gaze fixed on Heath. 'I didn't think you had the strength,' he said, and then he laughed. 'But you're not a god! You stand there captive and you have no power.'

Heath knew that he could fight Broca on his own grounds but he did not dare. One taste of that ecstasy had almost destroyed him. If he tried it again he knew that he and the barbarian would hurl their shadow-armies against each other as long as they lived and he would be as mad as Broca.

He looked about him at the hostile creatures who were solid and real enough to kill him at Broca's word. Then he said to Alor, 'Do you wish to stay here now?'

'I wish to go out of the Moonfire with you, David, if I can. If not I wish to die.'

The poison had not touched her yet. She had come without desire. Though she had bathed in the Moonfire she was still sane.

Heath turned to Broca. 'You see, she isn't worthy of you.'

Broca's face was dark with fury. He took Alor between his great hands and said, 'You will stay with me. You're part of me. Listen, Alor. There's nothing I can't give you. I'll build other castles, other tribes, and I'll subdue them and put them in your lap. God and goddess together, Alor! We'll reign in glory.'

'I'm no goddess,' Alor said. 'Let me go.'

And Broca said, 'I'll kill you, first.' His gaze lowered on Heath. 'I'll kill you both.'

Heath said, 'Do the high gods stoop to tread on ants and worms? We don't deserve such honour, she and I. We're weak and even the Moonfire can't give us strength.'

He saw the flicker of thought in Broca's face and went on. 'You're all-powerful, there's nothing you can't do. Why burden yourself with a mate too weak to worship you? Create another Alor, Broca! Create a goddess worthy of you!'

After a moment Alor said, 'Create a woman who can love you, Broca, and let us go.'

For a time there was silence in the place. The feasters and the dancers and the slaves stood without moving and their eyes glittered in the eerie light. And then Broca nodded.

'It is well,' he said. 'Stand up, Alor.'

She stood. The look of power came into the face of the tall

barbarian, the wild joy of moulding heart's desire out of nothingness. Out of the golden air he shaped another Alor. She was not a woman but a thing of snow and flame and wonder, so that beside her the reality appeared drab and beautiless. She mounted the throne and sat beside her creator and put her hand in his and smiled.

Broca willed the guardsmen to let Heath free. He went to Alor and Broca said contemptuously, 'Get out of my sight.'

They went together across the crowded place, toward the archway through which Heath had entered. Still there was silence and no one moved.

As they reached the archway it vanished, becoming solid wall. Behind them Broca laughed and suddenly the company burst also into wild jeering laughter.

Heath caught Alor tighter by the hand and led her toward another door. It, too, disappeared and the mocking laughter screamed and echoed from the vault.

Broca shouted, 'Did you think that I would let you go – you two who betrayed me when I was a man? Even a god can remember!'

Heath saw that the guardsmen and the others were closing in, and he saw how their eyes gleamed. He was filled with a black fear and he put Alor behind him.

Broca cried, 'Weakling! Even to save your life, you can't create!'

It was true. He dared not. The shadow-people drew in upon him with their soulless eyes and their faces that were mirrors of the urge to kill.

And then, suddenly, the answer came. Heath's answer rang back. 'I will not create – *but I will destroy!*'

Once again he threw the strength of his mind against the Moonfire but this time there was no unhealthy lure to what he did. There was no desire in him but his love for Alor and the need to keep her safe.

The hands of the shadow-people reached out and dragged him away from Alor. He heard her scream and he knew that if he failed they would both be torn to pieces. He summoned all the force that was in him, all the love.

He saw the faces of the shadow-people grow distorted and blurred. He felt their grip weaken and suddenly they were only shadows, a dim multitude in a crumbling castle of dreams.

Broca's goddess faded with the dragon throne and Broca's kingly harness was only a web of memories half seen above the plain leather.

Broca leaped to his feet with a wild, hoarse cry.

Heath could feel how their two minds locked and swayed on that strange battleground. And as Broca fought to hold his vision, willing the particles of energy into the semblance of matter, so Heath fought to tear them down, to disperse them. For a time the shadows held in that half-world between existence and nothingness.

Then the walls of the castle wavered and ran like red water and were gone. The goddess Alor, the dancers and the slaves and the chieftains, all were gone, and there were only the golden fog and a tall barbarian, stripped of his dreams, and the man Heath and the woman Alor.

Heath looked at Broca and said, 'I am stronger than you, because I threw away my godhead.'

Broca panted. 'I will build again!'

Heath said, 'Build.'

And he did, his eyes blazing, his massive body shaken with the force of his will.

It was all there again, the castle and the multitude of feasters and the jewels.

Broca screamed to his shadow-people. '*Kill!*'

But again, as their hands reached out to destroy, they began to weaken and fade.

Heath cried, 'If you want your kingdom, Broca, let us go!'

The castle was now no more than a ghostly outline. Broca's face was beaded with sweat. His hands clawed the air. He swayed with his terrible effort but Heath's dark eyes were bleak and stern. If he had now the look of a god it was a god as ruthless and unshakeable as fate.

The vision crumbled and vanished.

Broca's head dropped. He would not look at them from the

bitterness of his defeat. 'Get out,' he whispered. 'Go and let Vakor greet you.'

Heath said, 'It will be a cleaner death than this.'

Alor took his hand and they walked away together through the golden mist. They turned once to look back and already the castle walls were built again, towering magnificent.

'He'll be happy,' Heath said, 'until he dies.'

Alor shuddered. 'Let us go.'

They went together, away from the pulsing heart of the Moonfire, past the slopes of the crater and down the long way to the harbour. Finally they were aboard the *Ethne* once again.

As they found their slow way out through the island maze Heath held Alor in his arms. They did not speak. Their lips met often with the poignancy of kisses that will not be for long. The golden mists thinned and the fire faded in their blood and the heady sense of power was gone but they did not know nor care.

They came at last out of the veil of the Moonfire and saw ahead the green sail of the *Lahal*, where Vakor waited.

Alor whispered, 'Goodbye, my love, my David!' and left the bitterness of her tears upon his mouth.

The two ships lay side by side in the still water. Vakor was waiting as Heath and Alor came aboard with the other Children of the Moon beside him. He motioned to the seamen who stood there also and said, 'Seize them.'

But the men were afraid and would not touch them.

Heath saw their faces and wondered. Then, as he looked at Alor, he realised that she was not as she had been before. There was something clean and shining about her now, a new depth and a new calm strength, and in her eyes a strange new beauty. He knew that he himself had changed. They were no longer gods, he and Alor, but they had bathed in the Moonfire and they would never again be quite the same.

He met Vakor's gaze and was not afraid.

The cruel, wolfish face of the priest lost some of its assurance. A queer look of doubt crossed over it.

He said, 'Where is Broca?'

'We left him there, building empires in the mist.'

'At the heart of the Moonfire?'

'Yes.'

'You lie!' cried Vakor. 'You could not have come back yourselves, from the heart of the sleeping god. No one ever has.' But still the doubt was there.

Heath shrugged. 'It doesn't really matter,' he said, 'whether you believe or not.'

There was a long, strange silence. Then the four tall priests in their black tunics said to Vakor, 'We must believe. Look into their eyes.'

With a solemn ritual gesture they stepped back and left Vakor alone.

Vakor whispered, 'It can't be true. The law, the taboo is built on that rock. Men will come out of the fringe as you did, Heath, wrecked and cursed by their blasphemy. But not from the Moonfire itself. Never! That is why the law was made, lest all of Venus die in dreams.'

Alor said quietly, 'All those others wanted power. We wanted only love. We needed nothing else.'

Again there was silence while Vakor stared at them and struggled with himself. Then, very slowly, he said, 'You are beyond my power. The sleeping god received you and has chosen to let you go unscathed. I am only a Child of the Moon. I may not judge.'

He covered his face and turned away.

One of the lesser priests spoke to Johor. 'Let them be given men for their oars.'

And Heath and Alor understood that they were free.

Weeks later, Heath and Alor stood at dawn on the shore of the Sea of Morning Opals. The breeze was strong off the land. It filled the golden sail of the *Ethne*, so that she strained at her mooring lines, eager to be free.

Heath bent and cast them off.

They stood together silently and watched as the little ship gathered speed, going lightly, sweetly and alone into the glory of the morning. The ivory image that was her figurehead lifted its arms to the dawn and smiled and Heath waited there until the last bright gleam of the sail was lost and with it the last of his old life, his memories and his dreams.

Alor touched him gently. He turned and took her in his arms, and they walked away under the *liha*-trees, while the young day brightened in the sky. And they thought how the light of the sun they never saw was more beautiful and full of promise than all the naked wonder of the Moonfire that they had held within their hands.

SEA-KINGS OF MARS

1
THE DOOR TO INFINITY

Matt Carse knew he was being followed almost as soon as he left Madam Kan's. The laughter of the little dark women was still in his ears and the fumes of *thil* lay like a hot sweet haze across his vision – but they did not obscure from him the whisper of sandalled feet close behind him in the chill Martian night.

Carse quietly loosened his proton-gun in its holster but he did not attempt to lose his pursuer. He did not slow nor quicken his pace as he went through Jekkara.

'The Old Town,' he thought. 'That will be the best place. Too many people about here.'

Jekkara was not sleeping despite the lateness of the hour. The Low Canal towns never sleep, for they lie outside the law and time means nothing to them. In Jekkara and Valkis and Barrakesh night is only a darker day.

Carse walked beside the still black waters in their ancient channel, cut in the dead sea-bottom. He watched the dry wind shake the torches that never went out and listened to the broken music of the harps that were never stilled. Lean lithe men and women passed him in the shadowy streets, silent as cats except for the chime and whisper of the tiny bells the women wear, a sound as delicate as rain, distillate of all the sweet wickedness of the world.

They paid no attention to Carse, though despite his Martian dress he was obviously an Earthman and though an Earthman's life is usually less than the light of a snuffed candle along the Low Canals. Carse was one of them. The men of Jekkara and Valkis and Barrakesh, are the aristocracy of thieves and they admire skill and respect knowledge and know a gentleman when they meet one.

That was why Matthew Carse, ex-Fellow of the Interplanetary Society of Archaeologists, ex-assistant to the chair of Martian Antiquities at Kahora, dweller on Mars for thirty of his thirty-five years, had been admitted to their far more exclusive society of thieves and had sworn with them the oath of friendship that may not be broken.

Yet now, through the streets of Jekkara, one of Carse's 'friends' was stalking him with all the cunning of a sandcat. He wondered momentarily whether the Earth Police Control might have sent an agent here looking for him and immediately discarded that possibility. Agents of anybody's police did not live in Jekkara. No, it was some Low-Canaller on business of his own.

Carse left the canal, turning his back on the dead sea-bottom and facing what had once been inland. The ground rose sharply to the upper cliffs, much gnawed and worn by time and the eternal wind. The old city brooded there, the ancient stronghold of the Sea Kings of Jekkara, its glory long stripped from it by the dropping of the sea.

The New Town of Jekkara, the living town down by the canal, had been old when Ur of the Chaldees was a raw young village. Old Jekkara, with its docks of stone and marble still standing in the dry and dust-choked harbour, was old beyond any Earth conception of the world. Even Carse, who knew as much about it as any living man, was always awed by it.

He chose now to go this way because it was utterly dead and deserted and a man might be alone to talk to his friend.

The empty houses lay open to the night. Time and the scouring wind had worn away their corners and the angles of their doorways, smoothed them into the blurred and weary land. The little low moons made a tangle of conflicting shadows among them. With no effort at all the tall Earthman in his long dark cloak bended into the shadows and disappeared.

Crouched in the shelter of a wall he listened to the footsteps of the man who followed him. They grew louder, quickened, slowed indecisively, then quickened again. They drew abreast, passed and suddenly Carse had moved in a great catlike spring out into the street and a small wiry body was writhing in his grasp, mewing with fright as it shrank from the icy jabbing of the proton-gun in its side.

'No!' it squealed. 'Don't! I have no weapon. I mean no harm. I want only to talk to you.' Even through the fear a note of cunning crept into the voice. 'I have a gift.'

Carse assured himself that the man was unarmed and then relaxed his grip. He could see the Martian quite clearly in the moonlight – a ratlike small thief and an unsuccessful one from the worn kilt and harness and the lack of ornaments.

The dregs and sweepings of the Low Canals produced such men as this and they were brothers to the stinging worms that kill furtively out of the dust. Carse did not put his gun away.

'Go ahead,' he said. 'Talk.'

'First,' said the Martian, 'I am Pankawr of Barrakesh. You may have heard of me.' He strutted at the sound of his own name like a shabby bantam rooster.

'No,' said Carse. 'I haven't.'

His tone was like a slap in the face. Penkawr gave a snarling grin.

'No matter. I have heard of you, Carse. As I said, I have a gift for you. A most rare and valuable gift.'

'Something so rare and valuable that you had to follow me in the darkness to tell me about it, even in Jekkara.' Carse frowned at Penkawr, trying to fathom his duplicity. 'Well, what is it?'

'Come and I'll show you.'

'Where is it?'

'Hidden. Well hidden up near the palace quays.'

Carse nodded. 'Something too rare and valuable to be carried or shown even in a thieves' market. You intrigue me, Penkawr. We will go and look at your gift.'

Penkawr showed his pointed teeth in the moonlight and set off. Carse followed. He moved lightly, poised for instant action. His gun hand swung loose and ready at his side. He was wondering what sort of price Penkawr of Barrakesh planned to ask for his 'gift'.

As they climbed upward toward the palace, scrambling over

worn reefs and along cliff-faces that still showed the erosion of the sea, Carse had as always the feeling that he was climbing a sort of ladder into the past. It turned him cold with a queer shivering thrill to see the great docks still standing, marked with the mooring of ships. In the eerie moonlight one could almost imagine ...

'In here,' said Penkawr.

Carse followed him into a dark huddle of crumbling stone. He took a little krypton-lamp from his belt-pouch and touched it to a glow. Penkawr knelt and scrabbled among the broken stones of the floor until he brought forth a long thin bundle wrapped in rags.

With a strange reverence, almost with fear, he began to unwrap it. Carse knelt beside him. He realised that he was holding his breath, watching the Martian's lean dark hands, waiting. Something in the man's attitude had caught him into the same taut mood.

The lamplight struck a spark of deep fire from a half-covered jewel, and then a clean brilliance of metal. Carse leaned forward. Penkawr's eyes, slanted wolf-eyes yellow as topaz, glanced up and caught the Earthman's hard blue gaze, held it for a moment, then shifted away. Swiftly he drew the last covering from the object on the floor.

Carse did not move. The thing lay bright and burning between them and neither man stirred nor seemed even to breathe. The red glow of the lamp painted their faces, lean bone above iron shadows, and the eyes of Matthew Carse were the eyes of a man who looks upon a miracle.

After a long while he reached out and took the thing into his hands. The beautiful and deadly slimness of it, the length and perfect balance, the black hilt and guard that fitted perfectly his large hand, the single smoky jewel that seemed to watch him with a living wisdom, the name etched in most rare and most ancient symbols upon the blade. He spoke, and his voice was no more than a whisper.

'The sword of Rhiannon!'

Penkawr let out his breath in a sharp sigh. 'I found it,' he said. '*I* found it.'

Carse said, 'Where?'

'It does not matter where. I found it. It is yours – for a small price.'

'A small price.' Carse smiled. 'A small price for the sword of a god.'

'An evil god,' muttered Penkawr. 'For more than a million years, Mars has called him the Cursed One.'

'I know,' Carse nodded. 'Rhiannon, the Cursed One, the Fallen One, the rebel one of the gods of long ago. I know the legend, yes. The legend of how the old gods conquered Rhiannon and thrust him into a hidden tomb.'

Penkawr looked away. He said, 'I know nothing of any tomb.'

'You lie,' Carse told him softly. 'You found the Tomb of Rhiannon or you could not have found his sword. You found, somehow, the key to the oldest sacred legend on Mars. The very stones of that place are worth their weight in gold to the right people.'

'I found no tomb,' Penkawr insisted sullenly. He went on quickly. 'But the sword itself is worth a fortune. I daren't try to sell it – these Jekkarans would snatch it away from me like wolves, if they saw it.

'But you can sell it, Carse.' The little thief was shivering in the urgency of his greed. 'You can smuggle it to Kahora and sell it to some Earthman for a fortune.'

'And I will,' Carse nodded. 'But first we will get the other things in that tomb.'

Penkawr had a sweat of agony upon his face. After a long time he whispered, 'Leave it at the sword, Carse. That's enough.'

It came to Carse that Penkawr's agony was blended of greed and fear. And it was not fear of the Jekkarans but of something else, something that would have to be awesome indeed to daunt the greed of Penkawr.

Carse swore contemptuously. 'Are you afraid of the Cursed One? Afraid of a mere legend that time has woven around some old king who's been a ghost for a million years?'

He laughed and made the sword flash in the lamplight. 'Don't worry, little one. I'll keep the ghosts away. Think of the money.

You can have your own palace with a hundred lovely slaves to keep you happy.'

He watched fear struggle again with greed in the Martian's face.

'I saw something there, Carse. Something that scared me, I don't know why.'

Greed won out. Penkawr licked dry lips. 'But perhaps, as you say, it is all only legend. And there are treasures there – even my half-share of them would make me wealthy beyond dreams.'

'Half?' Carse repeated blandly. 'You're mistaken, Penkawr. Your share will be one-third.'

Penkawr's face distorted with fury, and he leaped up. 'But I found the Tomb! It's my discovery!'

Carse shrugged. 'If you'd rather not share that way, then keep your secret to yourself. Keep it – till your "brothers" of Jekkara tear it from you with hot pincers when I tell them what you've found.'

'You'd do that?' choked Penkawr. 'You'd tell them and get me killed?'

The little thief stared in impotent rage at Carse, standing tall in the lampglow with the sword in his hands, his cloak falling back from his naked shoulders, his collar and belt of jewels looted from a dead king flaring. There was no softness in Carse, no relenting. The deserts and the suns of Mars, the cold and the heat and the hunger of them, had flayed away all but the bone and the iron sinew.

Penkawr shivered. 'Very well, Carse. I'll take you there – for one-third share.'

Carse nodded and smiled. 'I thought you would.'

Two hours later, they were riding up into the dark time-worn hills that loomed behind Jekkara and the dead sea-bottom.

It was very late now, an hour that Carse loved because it seemed then that Mars was most perfectly itself. It reminded him of a very old warrior, wrapped in a black cloak and holding a broken sword, dreaming the dreams of age which are so close to reality, remembering the sound of trumpets and the laughter and the strength.

The dust of the ancient hills whispered under the eternal

wind. Phobos had set, and the stars were coldly brilliant. The lights of Jekkara and the great black blankness of the dead sea-bottom lay far behind and below them now. Penkawr led the way up ascending gorges, their ungainly mounts picking their way with astonishing agility over the treacherous ground.

'This is how I stumbled on the place,' Penkawr said. 'On a ledge my beast broke its leg in a hole – and the sand widened the hole as it flowed inward, and there was the tomb, cut right into the rock of the cliff. But the entrance was choked when I found it.'

He turned and fixed Carse with a sulky yellow stare. '*I* found it,' he repeated. 'I still don't see why I should give you the lion's share.'

'Because I'm the lion,' said Carse cheerfully.

He made passes with the sword, feeling it blend with his flexing wrist, watching the starlight slide down the blade. His heart was beating high with excitement and it was the excitement of the archaeologist as well as of the looter.

He knew better than Penkawr the importance of this find. Martian history is so vagely long that it fades back into a dimness from which only vague legends have come down – legends of human and half-human races, of forgotten wars, of vanished gods.

Greatest of those gods had been the Quiru, hero-gods who were human yet superhuman, who had had all wisdom and power. But there had been a rebel among them – dark Rhiannon, the Cursed One, whose sinful pride had caused some mysterious catastrophe.

The Quiru, said the myths, had for that sin crushed Rhiannon and locked him into a hidden tomb. And for more than a million years men had hunted the Tomb of Rhiannon because they believed it held the secrets of Rhiannon's power.

Carse knew too much archaeology to take old legends too seriously. But he did believe that there was an incredibly ancient tomb that had engendered all these myths. And as the oldest relic on Mars it and the things in it would make Matthew Carse the richest man on three worlds – if he lived.

'This way,' said Penkawr abruptly. He had ridden in silence for a long time, brooding.

They were far up in the highest hills behind Jekkara. Carse followed the little thief along a narrow ledge on the face of a steep cliff.

Penkawr dismounted and rolled aside a large stone, disclosing a hole in the cliff that was big enough for a man to wriggle through.

'You first,' said Carse. 'Take the lamp.'

Reluctantly Penkawr obeyed, and Carse followed him into the foxhole.

At first there was only an utter darkness beyond the glow of the krypton-lamp. Penkawr slunk, cringing now like a frightened jackal.

Carse snatched the lamp away from him and held it high. They had scrambled through the narrow foxhole into a corridor that led straight back into the cliff. It was square and without ornament, the stone beautifully polished. He started off along it, Penkawr following.

The corridor ended in a vast chamber. It too was square and magnificently plain from what Carse could see of it. There was a dais at one end with an altar of marble, upon which was carved the same symbol that appeared on the hilt of the sword – the *ouroboros* in the shape of a winged serpent. But the circle was broken, the head of the serpent lifted as though looking into some new infinity.

Penkawr's voice came in a reedy whisper from behind his shoulder. 'It was here that I found the sword. There are other things around the room but I did not touch them.'

Carse had already glimpsed objects ranged around the walls of the great chamber, glittering vaguely through the gloom. He hooked the lamp to his belt and started to examine them.

Here was treasure, indeed! There were suits of mail of the finest workmanship, blazoned with patterns of unfamiliar jewels. There were strangely shaped helmets of unfamiliar glistening metals. A heavy throne-like chair of gold, subtly inlaid in dark metal, had a big tawny gem burning in each arm-post.

All these things, Carse knew, were incredibly ancient. They must come from the farthest past of Mars.

'Let us hurry!' Penkawr pleaded.

Carse relaxed and grinned at his own forgetfulness. The scholar in him had for the moment superseded the looter.

'We'll take all we can carry of the smaller jewelled things,' he said. 'This first haul alone will make us rich.'

'But you'll be twice as rich as I,' Penkawr said sourly. 'I could have got an Earthman in Barrakesh to sell these things for me for a half share only.'

Carse laughed. 'You should have done so, Penkawr. When you ask help from a noted specialist you have to pay high fees.'

His circuit of the chamber had brought him back to the altar. Now he saw that behind the altar lay a door. He went through it, Penkawr following reluctantly at his heels.

Beyond the doorway was a short passage and at the end of it a door of metal, small and heavily barred. The bars had been lifted, and the door stood open an inch or two. Above it was an inscription in the ancient changeless High Martian characters, which Carse read with practised ease.

The doom of Rhiannon, dealt unto him forever by the Quiru who are lords of space and time!

Carse pushed the metal door aside and stepped through. And then he stood quite still, looking.

Beyond the door was a great stone chamber as large as the one behind him.

But in this room there was only one thing.

It was a great bubble of darkness. A big, brooding sphere of quivering blackness, through which shot little coruscating particles of brilliance like falling stars seen from another world. And from this weird bubble of throbbing darkness the lamplight recoiled, afraid.

Something – awe, superstition or some purely physical force – sent a cold tingling shock racing through Carse's body. He felt his hair rising and his flesh seemed to draw away from his bones. He tried to speak and could not, his throat knotted with anxiety and tension.

'This is the thing I told you of,' whispered Penkawr. 'This is the thing I told you I saw.'

Carse hardly heard him. A conjecture so vast that he could not grasp it shook his brain. The scholar's ecstasy was upon him, the ecstasy of discovery that is akin to madness.

This brooding bubble of darkness – it was strangely like the darkness of those blank black spots far out in the galaxy which some scientists have dreamed are holes in the continuum itself, windows into the infinite outside our universe!

Incredible, surely, and yet that cryptic Quiru inscription – fascinated by the thing, despite its aura of danger, Carse took two steps toward it.

He heard the swift scrape of sandals on the stone floor behind him as Penkawr moved fast. Carse knew instantly that he had blundered in turning his back on the disgruntled little thief. He started to whirl and raise the sword.

Penkawr's thrusting hands jabbed his back before he could complete the movement. Carse felt himself pitched into the brooding blackness.

He felt a terrible rending shock through each atom of his body, and then the world seemed to fall away from him.

'*Go share Rhiannon's doom, Earthman! I told you I could get another partner!*'

Penkawr's snarling shout came to him from a great distance as he tumbled into a black, bottomless infinity.

2
ALIEN WORLD

Carse seemed to plunge through a nighted abyss, buffeted by all the shrieking winds of space. An endless, endless fall with the timelessness and the choking horror of a nightmare.

He struggled with the fierce revulsion of an animal trapped by the unknown. His struggle was not physical, for in that blind and screaming nothingness his body was useless. It was a mental fight, the man's inner core of courage reasserting itself, willing itself to stop this nightmare fall through darkness.

And then as he fell, a more terrifying sensation shook him. A feeling that he was *not alone* in this nightmare plunge through infinity, that a dark strong pulsating presence was close beside him, grasping for him, groping with eager fingers for his brain.

Carse made a supreme desperate mental effort. His sensation of falling seemed to lessen and then he felt solid rock slipping under his hands and feet. He scrambled frantically forward in physical effort this time.

He found himself quite suddenly outside the dark bubble again on the floor of the inner chamber of the Tomb.

'What in the Nine Hells...' he began shakily and then stopped because the oath seemed so pitifully inadequate for what had happened.

The little krypton-lamp hooked to his belt still cast its reddish glow, the sword of Rhiannon still glittered in his hand.

And the bubble of darkness still gloomed and brooded a foot away from him, flickering with its whirl of diamond motes.

Carse realised that all his nightmare plunging through space had been during the moment he was inside the bubble. What devil's trick of ancient science *was* the thing anyway? Some queer perpetual vortex of force that the mysterious Quiru of long ago had set up, he supposed.

But why had he seemed to fall through infinities inside the thing? And whence had come that terrifying sensation of strong fingers groping eagerly at his brain as he fell?

'A trick of old Quiru science,' he muttered shakenly. 'And Penkawr's superstitions made him think he could kill me by pushing me into it.'

Penkawr? Carse leaped to his feet, the sword of Rhiannon glittering wickedly in his hand.

'Black his thieving little soul!'

Penkawr was not here now. But he wouldn't have had time to go far. The smile on Carse's face was not pleasant as he went through the doorway.

In the outer chamber he suddenly stopped dead. There were

things here now – big stranger glittering objects – that had not been here before.

Where had they come from? Had he been longer in that bubble of darkness than he thought? Had Penkawr found these things in hidden crypts and ranged them here to await his return?

Carse's wonder increased as he examined the objects that now loomed amid the mail and other relics he had seen before. These objects did not look like mere art-relics – they looked like carefully fashioned, complicated instruments of unguessable purpose.

The biggest of them was a crystal wheel, the size of a small table, mounted horizontally atop a dull metal sphere. The wheel's rim glistened with jewels cut in precise polyhedrons. And there were other smaller devices of linked crystal prisms and tubes and things built of concentric metal rings and squat looped tubes of massive metal.

Could these glittering objects be the incomprehensible devices of an ancient alien Martian science? That supposition seemed incredible. The Mars of the far past, scholars knew, had been a world of sword-fighting sea-warriors whose galleys and kingdoms had clashed on long-lost oceans.

Yet, perhaps, in the Mars of the even farther past, there had been a science whose techniques were unfamiliar and un-recognisable.

'But where could Penkawr have found them when we didn't see them before? And why didn't he take any of them with him?'

Memory of Penkawr reminded him that the little thief would be getting farther away every moment. Grimly gripping the sword, Carse turned and hurried down the square stone corridor toward the outer world.

As he strode on Carse became aware that the air in the tomb was now strangely damp. Moisture glistened on the walls. He had not noticed that most un-Martian dampness before and it startled him.

'Probably seepage from underground springs, like those that feed the canals,' he thought. 'But it wasn't there before.'

His glance fell on the floor of the corridor. The drifted dust lay over it thickly as when they had entered. But there were no footprints in it now. No prints at all except those he was now making.

A horrible doubt, a feeling of unreality, clawed at Carse. The un-Martian dampness, the vanishing of their footprints – what had happened to everything in the moment he'd been inside the dark bubble?

He came to the end of the square stone corridor. And it was closed. It was closed by a massive slab of monolithic stone.

Carse stopped, staring at the slab. He fought down his increasing sense of weird unreality and made explanations for himself.

'There must have been a stone door I didn't see – and Penkawr has closed it to lock me in.'

He tried to move the slab. It would not budge nor was there any sign of key, knob or hinge.

Finally Carse stepped back and levelled his proton-pistol. Its hissing streak of atomic flame crackled into the rock slab, searing and splitting it.

The slab was thick. He kept the trigger of his gun depressed for minutes. Then, with a hollowly reverberating crash, the fragments of the split slab fell back in toward him.

But beyond, instead of the open air, there lay a solid mass of dark red soil.

'The whole Tomb of Rhiannon – buried, now! Penkawr must have started a cave-in.'

Carse didn't believe that. He didn't believe it at all but he tried to make himself believe, for he was becoming more and more afraid. And the thing of which he was afraid was impossible.

With blind anger he used the flaming beam of the pistol to undercut the mass of soil that blocked his way. He worked outward until the beam suddenly died as the charge of the gun ran out. He flung away the useless pistol and attacked the hot smoking mass of soil with the sword.

Panting, dripping, his mind a whirl of confused speculations, he dug outward through the soft soil till a small hole of brilliant daylight opened in front of him.

Daylight? Then he'd been in that weird bubble of darkness longer than he had imagined.

The wind blew in through the little opening, upon his face. And it was a warm wind. A warm wind and a *damp* wind, such as never blows on desert Mars.

Carse squeezed through and stood in the bright day looking outward.

There are times when a man has no emotion, no reaction. Times when all the centres are numbed and the eyes see and the ears hear but nothing communicates itself to the brain, which is protected in this way from madness.

He tried finally to laugh at what he saw though he heard his own laughter as a dry choking cry.

'Mirage, of course,' he whispered. 'A big mirage. Big as all Mars.'

The warm breeze lifted Carse's tawny hair, blew his cloak against him. A cloud drifted over the sun and somewhere a bird screamed harshly. He did not move.

He was looking at an ocean.

It stretched out to the horizon ahead, a vast restlessness of water, milky-white and pale with a shimmering phosphorescence even in daylight.

'Mirage,' he said again stubbornly, his reeling mind clinging with the desperation of fear to that one shred of explanation. 'It has to be. Because this is still Mars.'

Still Mars, still the same planet. The same high hills up into which Penkawr had led him by night.

Or were they the same? Before, the foxhole entrance to the Tomb of Rhiannon had been in a steep cliff-face. Now he stood on the grassy slope of a great hill.

And there were rolling green hills and dark forest down there below him, where before had been only desert. Green hills, green woods and a bright brawling river that ran down a gorge to what had been dead sea-bottom but was now – sea.

Carse's numbed gaze swept along the great coast of the distant shoreline. And down on that far sunlit coast he saw the glitter of a white city and knew that it was Jekkara.

Jekkara, bright and strong between the verdant hills and the mighty ocean, that ocean that had not been seen upon Mars for nearly a million years.

Matthew Carse knew then that it was no mirage. He sat and hid his face in his hands. His body was shaken by deep tremors and his nails bit into his own flesh until blood trickled down his cheeks.

He knew now what had happened to him in that vortex of darkness, and it seemed to him that a cold voice repeated a certain warning inscription in tones of distant thunder.

'The Quiru are lords of space and time – *of time* – OF TIME!'

Carse, staring out over the green hills and the milky ocean, made a terrible effort to grapple with the incredible.

'*I have come into the past of Mars. All my life I have studied and dreamed of that past. Now I am in it. I, Matthew Carse, archaeologist, renegate, looter of tombs.*

'*The Quiru for their own reasons built a way and I came through it. Time is to us the unknown dimension but the Quiru knew it!*'

Carse had studied science. You had to know the elements of a half-dozen sciences to be a planetary archaeologist. He frantically ransacked memory now for an explanation.

Had his first guess about that bubble of darkness been right? Was it really a hole in the continuun of the universe? If that were so he could dimly understand what had happened to him.

For the space-time continuum of the universe was finite, limited. Einstein and Riemann had proved that long ago. And he had fallen clear out of that continuum and then back into it again – but into a different timeframe from his own.

What was it that Kaufman had once written? 'The Past is the Present-that-exists-at-a-distance.' He had come back into that other distant Present, that was all. There was no reason to be afraid.

But he *was* afraid. The horror of that nightmare transition to this green and smiling Mars of long ago wrenched a gusty cry from his lips.

Blindly, still gripping the jewelled sword, he leaped up and turned to re-enter the buried Tomb of Rhiannon.

'I can go back the way I came, back through that hole in the continuum.'

He stopped a convulsive shudder running through his frame. He could not make himself face again that bubble of glittering gloom, that dreadful plunge through inter-dimensional infinity.

He dared not. He had not the Quiru's wisdom. In that perilous plunge across time mere chance had flung him into this past age. He could not count on chance to return him to his own far-future age.

'I'm here,' he said. 'I'm here in the distant past of Mars and I'm here to stay.'

He turned back around and gazed out again upon that incredible vista. He stayed there a long time, unmoving. The sea-birds came and looked at him and flashed away on their sharp white wings. The shadows lengthened.

His eyes swung again to the white towers of Jekkara down in the distance, queenly in the sunlight above the harbour. It was not the Jekkara he knew, the thieves' city of the Low Canals, rotting away into dust, but it was a link to the familiar and Carse desperately needed such a link.

He would go to Jekkara. And he would try not to think. He must not think at all or surely his mind would crack.

Carse gripped the haft of the jewelled sword and started down the grassy slope of the hill.

3
CITY OF THE PAST

It was a long way to the city. Carse moved at a steady plodding pace. He did not try to find the easiest path but rammed his way through and over all obstacles, never deviating from the straight line that led to Jekkara. His cloak hampered him and he tore it off. His face was empty of all expression but sweat ran down his cheeks and mingled with the salt of tears.

He walked between two worlds. He went through valleys drowsing in the heat of the summer day, where leafy branches of strange trees raked his face and the juice of crushed grasses stained his sandals. Life, winged and furred and soft of foot, fled from him with a stir and a rustle. And yet he knew that he walked in a desert, where even the wind had forgotten the names of the dead for whom it mourned.

He crossed high ridges, where the sea lay before him and he could hear the boom of the surf on the beaches. And yet he saw only a vast dead plain, where the dust ran in little wavelets among the dry reefs. The truths of thirty years living are not easily forgotten.

The sun sank slowly toward the horizon. As Carse topped the last ridge above the city and started down he walked under a vault of flame. The sea burned as the white phosphorescence took colour from the clouds. With dazed wonder Carse saw the gold and crimson and purple splash down the long curve of the sky and run out over the water.

He could look down upon the harbour. The docks of marble that he had known so well, worn and cracked by ages and whelmed by desert sand, lying lonely beneath the moons. The same docks, and yet now, mirage-like, the sea filled the basin of the harbour.

Round-hulled trading ships lay against the quays and the shouts of stevedores and sweating slaves rose up to him on the evening air. Shallops came and went amid the ships and out beyond the breakwater he saw the fishing fleet of Jekkara coming home with sails of cinnabar dark against the west.

By the palace quays, near the very spot where he had gone with Penkawr to see the sword of Rhiannon, a long lean dark war-gallery with a brazen ram crouched like a sullen black panther. Beyond it were other galleys. And above them, tall and proud, the white towers of the palace rose.

'*I have come far back into the past of Mars indeed! For this is the Mars of a million years ago that archaeology has always pictured!*'

A planet of conflicting civilizations which had developed little science yet but which cherished a legend of the super-science of the great Quiru who had been before even this time.

'*A planet of the lost past that God's law intended no man of my own time ever to see!*'

Matthew Carse shivered as though it were very cold. Slowly, slowly, he went down into the streets of Jekkara and it seemed to him, in the sunset, that the whole city was stained with blood.

The walls closed him in. There was a mist before his eyes and a roaring in his ears but he was aware of people. Lean lithe men and woman who passed him in the narrow ways, who jostled against him and went on, then stopped and turned to stare. The dark and catlike people of Jekkara. Jekkara of the Low Canals and of this other age.

He heard the music of the harps and the chiming whisper of the little bells the women wore. The wind touched his face but it was a moist wind and warm, heavy with the breath of the sea, and it was more than a man could bear.

Carse went on but he had no idea where he was going or what he had to do. He went on only because he was already moving and had not the wit to stop.

One foot before the other, stolid, blind, like a man bewitched, he walked through the streets among the dark Jekkarans, a tall blond man trailing a naked sword.

The people of the city watched him. People of the harbour-side, of the wine-shops and the twisting alleys. They drew away before and closed in behind, following and staring at him.

The gap of ages lay between them. His kilt was of a strange cloth, an unknown dye. His ornaments were of a time and country they would never see. And his face was alien.

This very alienage held them back for a time. Some breath of the incredible truth clung to him and made them afraid. Then someone said a name and someone else repeated it and in the space of a few seconds there was no more mystery, no more fear – only hate.

Carse heard the name. Dimly, from a great distance, he heard it as it grew from a whisper into a howling cry that ran wolf-like through the streets.

'Khond! Khond! A spy from Khondor!' And then another word. '*Slay!*'

The name of 'Khond' meant nothing to Carse, but he recognised it for what it was, an epithet and a curse. The voice of the mob carried to him the warning of death and he tried to rouse himself, for the instinct of survival is strong, but his brain was numbed and would not wake.

A stone struck him on the cheek. The physical shock brought him to a little. Blood ran into his mouth. The salt-sweet taste of it told him of destruction already begun. He tried to shake the dark veils aside, far enough at least to see the enemy that threatened him.

He had come out into an open space by the docks. Now, in the twilight, the sea flamed with cold white fire. Masts of the moored ships stood black against it. Phobos was rising, and in the mingled light Carse saw that there were creatures climbing into the rigging of the ships and that they were furred and chained and not wholly human.

And he saw on the wharfside two slender white-skinned men with wings. They wore the loin-cloth of the slave and their wings were broken.

The square was filled with people. More of them poured in from the narrow alley-mouths, drawn by the shout of *Spy!* It echoed from the buildings and the name of 'Khondor' hammered at him.

From the wharfside, from the winged slaves and the chained creatures of the ships, a fervent cry reached him.

'Hail, Khondor! Fight, man!'

Women screamed like harpies. Another stone whistled past his ear. The mob surged and jostled but those nearest Carse held back, wary of the great jewelled sword with its shining blade.

Carse shouted. He swung the sword in a humming arc around him and the Jekkarans, who had shorter blades, melted back.

Again from the wharfside he heard, 'Hail, Khondor! Down with the Serpent, down with Sark! Fight, Khond!'

He knew that the slaves would have helped him if they could.

One part of his mind was beginning to function now – the part that had to do with a long experience in saving his own neck. He was only a few paces away from the buildings at his back. He whirled and leaped suddenly, the bright steel swinging.

It bit twice into flesh and then he had gained the doorway of a ship's chandler, so that they could only come at him from the front. A small advantage but every second a man could stay alive was a second gained.

He made a flickering barrier of steel before him and then bellowed, in their own High Martian, 'Wait! I am no Khond!'

The crowd broke into jeering laughter.

'He says he is not of Khondor!'

'Your own friends hail you, Khond! Hark to the Swimmers and the Skyfolk!'

Carse cried. 'No! I am not of Khondor. I am not—' He stopped short. He had almost said he was not of Mars.

A green-eyed girl, hardly more than a child, darted almost into the circle of death he wove before him. Her teeth showed white as a rat's.

'Coward!' She screamed. 'Fool! Where but in Khondor do they breed men like you, with pale hair and sickly skin? Where else could you be from, oh clumsy thing with the barbarous speech?'

Something of the strange look returned to Carse's face and he said, 'I am from Jekkara.'

They laughed. They shrieked with laughter until the square rocked with it. Now they had lost all awe of him. His every word stamped him as what the girl had called him, a coward and a fool. Almost contemptuously, they attacked.

This was real enough to Carse, this mass of hate-filled faces and wicked short-swords coming at him. He struck out ragingly with the long sword of Rhiannon, his rage less against this murderous rabble than against the fate that had pitchforked him into their world.

Several of them died on the jewelled sword and the rest drew back. They stood glaring at him like jackals who have trapped a wolf. Then through their hissing came an exultant cry.

'The Sark soldiers are coming! They'll cut down this Khond spy for us!'

Carse, backed against a locked door and panting, saw a little phalanx of black-mailed black-helmed warriors pushing through the rabble like a ship through waves.

They were coming straight toward him and the Jekkarans were already yelling in eager anticipation of the kill.

4
PERILOUS SECRET

The door against which Carse's back was braced suddenly gave way, opening inward. He reeled backward into the black interior.

As he staggered for balance the door suddenly slammed shut again. He heard a bar fall and then a low, throaty chuckle from beside him.

'That will hold them for a while. But we'd better get out of here quickly, Khond. Those Sark soldiers will cut the door open.'

Carse swung around, his sword raised, but was blind in the darkness of the room. He could smell rope and tar and dust but could see nothing.

A frantic hammering began outside the door. Then Carse's eyes, becoming accustomed to the obscurity, made out a ponderous corpulent figure close beside him.

The man was big, fleshy and soft-looking, a Martian who wore a kilt that looked ridiculously scanty on his fat figure. His face was moonlike, creased and crinkled in a reassuring grin as his small eyes looked unfearingly at Carse's raised sword.

'I'm not Jekkara or Sark either,' he said reassuringly. 'I'm Boghaz Hoi of Valkis and I've my own reasons for helping any man of Khond. But we'll have to go quickly.'

'Go where?'

Carse had to drag the words out, he was still breathing so painfully.

'To a place of safety.' The other paused as new louder hammering began upon the door. 'That's the Sarks. I'm leaving. Come or stay as you like, Khond.'

He turned toward the back of the dark room, moving with astonishing lightness and ease for one so corpulent. He did not look back to see if Carse was following.

But there was really no choice for Carse. Half-dazed as he still was he was of no mind to face the eruption of those mailed soldiers and the Jekkaran rabble. He followed Boghaz Hoi.

The Valkisian chuckled as he squeezed his bulk through a small open window at the rear of the room.

'I know every rathole in this harbour quarter. That's why, when I saw you backed against old Taras Thur's door, I simply went around through and let you in. Snatched you from under their noses.'

'But why?' Carse asked again.

'I told you – I have a sympathy for Jekkaras. They're men enough to snap their fingers at Sark and the damned Serpent. I help one when I can.'

It didn't make sense to Carse. But how could it? How could he know anything of the hates and passions of this Mars of the remote past?

He was trapped in this strange Mars of long ago and he had to grope his way in it like an ignorant child. It was certain that the mob out there had tried to kill him.

They had taken him for a Khond. Not the Jekkaran rabble alone but those strange slaves the semi-humans with the broken wings, the furred sleek chained creatures who had cheered him from the galleys.

Carse shivered. Until now, he had been too dazed to think of the strangeness of those not-quite-human slaves.

And who were the Khonds?

'This way,' Boghaz Hoi interrupted his thoughts.

They had threaded a shadowy little labyrinth of stinking alleys and the fat Valkisian was squeezing through a narrow door into the dark interior of a little hut.

Carse followed him inside. He heard the whistle of the blow in the dark and tried to dodge but there was no time.

The concussion exploded a bomb of stars inside his head and he felt the rough floor grinding his face.

He awoke with flickering light in his eyes. There was a small bronze lamp burning on a stool close to him. He was lying on the dirt floor of the hut. When he tried to move he found that his wrists and ankles were bound to pegs driven into the packed earth.

Sickening pain racked his head and he sank back. There was a rustle of movement and Boghaz Hoi crouched down beside him. The Valkisian's moonface was expressive of sympathy as he held a clay cup of water to Carse's lips.

'I struck too hard I'm afraid. But then, in the dark with an armed man, one has to be careful. Do you feel like talking now?'

Carse looked up at him and old habit made him control the rage that shook him. 'About what?' he said.

Boghaz said, 'I am a frank and truthful man. When I saved you from the mob out there my only idea was to rob you.'

Carse saw that his jewelled belt and collar had been transferred to Boghaz, who wore them both around his neck. The Valkisian now raised a plump hand and fingered them lovingly.

'Then,' he continued, 'I got a closer look – at that.' He nodded toward the jewelled sword that leaned against the stool, shimmering in the lamplight. 'Now, many men would examine it and see only a handsome sword. But I, Boghaz, am a man of education. I recognised the symbols on that blade.'

He leaned forward. 'Where did you get it?'

A warning instinct made Carse lie readily. 'I bought it from a trader.'

Boghaz shook his head. 'No you didn't. There are spots of corrosion on the blade, scales of dust in the carvings. The hilt has not been polished. No trader would sell it in that condition.

'No, my friend, that sword has lain a long time in the dark, in the tomb of him who owned it – the tomb of Rhiannon.'

Carse lay without moving, looking at Boghaz. He did not like what he saw.

The Valkisian had a kind and merry face. He would be excellent company over a bottle of wine. He would love a man like a brother and regret exceedingly the necessity of cutting out his heart.

Carse schooled his expression into sullen blankness. 'It may be Rhiannon's sword for all I know. Nevertheless, I bought it from a trader.'

The mouth of Boghaz, which was small and pink, puckered and he shook his head. He reached out and patted Carse's cheek.

'Please don't lie to me, friend. It upsets me to be lied to.'

'I'm not lying,' Carse said. 'Listen – you have the sword. You have my ornaments. You have all you can get out of me. Just be satisfied.'

Boghaz sighed. He looked down appealingly at Carse. 'Have you no gratitude? Didn't I save your life?'

Carse said sardonically, 'It was a noble gesture.'

'It was. It was indeed. If I'm caught for it my life won't be worth *that*.' He snapped his fingers. 'I cheated the mob of a moment's pleasure and it wouldn't do a bit of good now to tell them that you really aren't a Khond at all.'

He let that fall very casually but he watched Carse shrewdly from under his fat eyelids.

Carse looked back at him, hard-eyed, and his face showed nothing.

'What gave you that idea?'

Boghaz laughed. 'No Khond would be ass enough to show his face in Jekkara to begin with. And especially if he'd found the lost secret all Mars has hunted for an age – the secret of the Tomb of Rhiannon.'

Carse's face moved no muscle but he was thinking swiftly. So the Tomb was a lost mystery in *this* time as in his own future time?

He shrugged. 'I know nothing of Rhiannon or his Tomb.'

Boghaz squatted down on the floor beside Carse and smiled down at him like one humouring a child who wishes to play.

'My friend, you are not being honest with me. There's no man on Mars who doesn't know that the Quiru long, long ago left our world because of what Rhiannon, the Cursed One among them, had done. And all men know they built a secret tomb before they left, in which they locked Rhiannon and his powers.

'Is it wonderful that men should covet the powers of the gods? Is it strange that ever since men have hunted that lost Tomb? And now that you have found it do I, Boghaz, blame you for wanting to keep the secret to yourself?'

He patted Carse's shoulder and beamed.

'It is but natural on your part. But the secret of the Tomb is too big for you to handle. You need my brains to help you. Together, with that secret, we can take what we want of Mars.'

Carse said without emotion, 'You're crazy. I have no secret. I bought the sword from a trader.'

Boghaz stared at him for a long moment. He stared very sadly. Then he sighed heavily.

'Think, my friend. Wouldn't it be better to tell me than to make me force it out of you?'

'There's nothing to tell,' Carse said harshly.

He did not wish to be tortured. But that odd warning instinct had returned more strongly. Something deep within him warned him not to tell the secret of the Tomb!

And anyway, even if he told the fat Valkisian was likely to kill him then to prevent him from telling anyone else the secret.

Boghaz sorrowfully shrugged fat shoulders. 'You force me to extreme measures. And I hate that. I'm too chicken-hearted for this work. But if it's necessary—'

He was reaching into his belt-pouch for something when suddenly both men heard a sound of voices in the alleyway outside and the tramp of heavily-shod feet.

Outside, a voice cried, '*There!* That is the sty of the Boghaz hog!'

A fist began to hammer on the door with such force that the small room rang like the inside of a drum.

'Open up, there, fat scum of Valkis!'

Heavy shoulders began to heave against the door.

'Gods of Mars!' groaned Boghaz. 'That Sark press-gang has tracked us down!'

He grabbed up the sword of Rhiannon and was in the act of

hiding it in his bed when the warped planks of the door gave under the tremendous beating, and a spate of armed men burst into the room.

5
SLAVE OF SARK

Boghaz recovered himself with magnificent aplomb. He bowed deeply to the leader of the press-gang, a huge black-bearded, hawk-nosed man wearing the same black mail that Carse had seen on the Sark soldiers in the square.

'My lord Scyld!' said Boghaz. 'I regret that I am corpulent, and therefore slow of motion. I would not for worlds have given your lordship the trouble of breaking my poor door, especially' – his face beamed with the light of pure innocence – 'especially as I was about to set out in search of you.'

He gestured toward Carse.

'I have him for you, you see,' he said. 'I have him safe.'

Scyld set his fists on his hips, thrust his spade beard up into the air and laughed. Behind him the soldiers of the press-gang took it up and, behind them, the rabble of Jekkarans who had come to see the fun.

'He has him safe,' said Scyld, 'for us.'

More laughter.

Scyld stepped closer to Boghaz. 'I suppose,' he said, 'that it was your loyalty that prompted you to spirit this Khond dog away from my men in the first place.'

'My lord,' protested Boghaz, 'the mob would have killed him.'

'That's why my men went in – we wanted him alive. A dead Khond is of no use to us. But you had to be helpful, Boghaz. Fortunately you were seen.' He reached out and fingered the stolen ornaments that Boghaz wore around his neck. 'Yes,' said Scyld, 'very fortunately.'

He wrenched the collar and the belt away, admired the play

of light on the jewels and dropped them into his belt-pouch. Then he moved to the bed, where the sword lay half-concealed among the blankets. He picked it up, felt the weight and balance of the blade, examined casually the chasing on the steel and smiled.

'A real weapon,' he said. 'Beautiful as the Lady herself – and just as deadly.'

He used the point to cut Carse free of his bonds.

'Up, Khond,' he said, and helped him with the toe of his heavy sandal.

Carse staggered to his feet and shook his head once to clear it. Then, before the men of the press-gang could grasp him, he smashed his hard fist savagely into the expansive belly of Boghaz.

Scyld laughed. He had a deep, hearty seaman's laugh. He kept guffawing as his soldiers pulled Carse away from the doubled-up gasping Valkisian.

'No need for that now,' Scyld told him. 'There's plenty of time. You two are going to see a lot of each other.'

Carse watched a horrible realisation break over the fat face of Boghaz.

'My lord,' quavered the Valkisian, still gasping. 'I am a loyal man. I wish only to serve the interests of Sark and her Highness, the Lady Ywain.' He bowed.

'Naturally,' said Scyld. 'And how could you better serve both Sark and the Lady Ywain than by pulling an oar in her war-galley?'

Boghaz was losing colour by the second. 'But, my lord—'

'What?' cried Scyld fiercely. 'You protest? Where is your loyalty, Boghaz?' He raised the sword. 'You know what the penalty is for treason.'

The men of the press-gang were near to bursting with suppressed laughter.

'Nay,' said Boghaz hoarsely. 'I am loyal. No one can accuse me of treason. I wish only to serve—' He stopped short, apparently realising that his own tongue had trapped him neatly.

Scyld brought the flat of the blade down in a tremendous thwack across Boghaz' enormous buttocks.

'Go then and serve!' he shouted.

Boghaz leaped forward, howling. The press-gang grabbed him. In a few seconds they had shackled him and Carse securely together.

Scyld complacently thrust the sword of Rhiannon into his own sheath after tossing his own blade to a soldier to carry. He led the way swaggeringly out of the hut.

Once again, Carse made a pilgrimage through the streets of Jekkara but this time by night and in chains, stripped of his jewels and his sword.

It was to the palace quays they went, and the cold shivering thrill of unreality came again upon Carse as he looked at the high towers ablaze with light and the soft white fires of the sea that glowed far out in the darkness.

The whole palace quarter swarmed with slaves, with men-at-arms in the sable mail of Sark, with courtiers and women and jongleurs. Music and the sounds of revelry came from the palace itself as they passed beneath it.

Boghaz spoke to Carse in a rapid undertone. 'The blockheads didn't recognise that sword. Keep quiet about your secret – or they'd take us both to Caer Dhu for questioning and you know what *that* means!' He shuddered over all his great body.

Carse was too numbed to answer. Reaction from this incredible world and from sheer physical fatigue was sweeping over him like a wave.

Boghaz continued loudly for the benefit of their guards. 'All this splendour is in honour of the Lady Ywain of Sark! A princess as great as her father, King Garach! To serve in *her* galley will be a privilege.'

Scyld laughed mockingly. 'Well said, Valkisian! And your fervent loyalty shall be rewarded. That privilege will be yours a long time.'

The black war-galley loomed up before them, their destination. Carse saw that it was long, rakish, with a rowers' pit splitting its deck down the middle and a low stern-castle aft.

Flamboys were blazing on the low poop-deck back there and

ruddy light spilled from the windows of the cabins beneath it. Sark soldiers clustered back there, chaffing each other loudly.

But in the long dark rowers' pit there was only a bitter silence.

Scyld raised his bull voice in a shout. 'Ho, there, Callus!'

A large man came grunting out of the shadowy pit, negotiating the catwalk with practised skill. His right hand clutched a leathern bottle and his left a black whip – a longlashed thing, supple from much use.

He saluted Scyld with the bottle, not troubling to speak.

'Fodder for the benches,' Scyld said. 'Take them,' He chuckled. 'And see that they're chained to the same oar.'

Callus looked at Carse and Boghaz, then smiled lazily and gestured with the bottle. 'Get aft, carrion,' he grunted and let the lash run out.

Carse glared at him out of red eyes and snarled. Boghaz gripped the Earthman by the shoulder and shook him.

'Come on, fool!' he said. 'We'll get enough beatings without you asking for them.'

He pulled Carse with him, down into the rowers' pit and forward along the catwalk between the benches.

The Earthman, numbed by shock and exhaustion, was only dimly aware of faces turned to watch them, of the mutter of chains and the smell of the bilges. He only half saw the round curious heads of the two furry creatures who slept on the catwalk and who moved to let them pass.

The last starboard bench facing the stern-castle had only one sleeping man chained to is oar, its other two places being empty. The press-gang stood by until Carse and Boghaz were safely chained.

Then they went off with Scyld. Callus cracked his whip with a sound like a gunshot, apparently as a reminder to all hands, and went forward.

Boghaz nudged Carse in his ribs. Then he leaned over and shook him. But Carse was beyond caring what Boghaz had to say. He was sound asleep, doubled over the loom of the oar.

Carse dreamed. He dreamed that he was again taking that

nightmare plunge through the shrieking infinities of the dark bubble in Rhiannon's tomb. He was falling, falling—

And again he had that sensation of a strong, living presence close beside him in the awful plunge, of something grasping at his brain with a dark and dreadful eagerness.

'No!' Carse whispered in his dream. '*No!*'

He husked that refusal again – a refusal of something that the dark presence was asking him to do, something veiled and frightful.

But the pleading became more urgent, more insistent, and whatever it was that pleaded seemed now far stronger than in the Tomb of Rhiannon. Carse uttered a shuddering cry.

'*No. Rhiannon!*'

He found himself suddenly awake, looking dazedly along the moonlit oar-bank.

Callus and the overseer were striding along the catwalk, lashing the slaves to wakefulness. Boghaz was looking at Carse with a strange expression.

'You cried out to the Cursed One!' he said.

The other slave at their oar was staring at him too and so were the luminous eyes of the two furry shadows chained to the catwalk.

'A bad dream,' Carse muttered. 'That was all.'

He was interrupted by a whistle and crack and a searing pain along his back.

'Stand to your oar, carrion!' roared Callus' voice from above him.

Carse voiced a tigerish cry but Boghaz instantly stopped his mouth with one big paw. Steady!' he warned. 'Steady!'

Carse got hold of himself but not in time to avoid another stroke of the whip. Callus stood grinning down at him.

'You'll want care,' he said. 'Care, and watching.'

Then he lifted his head and yelled along the oar-bank. 'All right, you scum, you carrion! Sit up to it! We're starting on the tide for Sark and I'll flay alive the first man who loses stroke!'

Overhead seamen were busy in the rigging. The sails fell wide from the yards, dark in the moonlight.

There was a sudden pregnant silence along the ship, a drawing of breath and tightening of sinews. On a platform at the end of the catwalk a slave crouched ready over a great hide drum.

An order was given. The fist of the drummer clenched and fell.

All along the oar-bank the great sweeps shot out, found water, bit and settled to a steady rhythm. The drum-beat gave the time and the lash enforced it. Somehow Carse and Boghaz managed to do what they had to do.

The rowers' pit was too deep for sight, except what one could glimpse through the oar-ports. But Carse heard the full-throated cheer of the crowd on the quays as the war-galley of Ywain of Sark cleared the slip, standing out into the open harbour.

The night breeze was light and the sails drew little. The drum picked up the beat, drove it faster, sent the long sweeps swinging and set the scarred and sweating backs of the slaves to their full stretch and strain.

Carse felt the lift of the hull to the first swell of the open sea. Through the oarport, he glimpsed a heaving ocean of milky flame. He was bound for Sark across the White Sea of Mars.

6
ON THE MARTIAN SEA

The galley raised a fair breeze at last and the slaves were allowed to rest. Again Carse slept. When he awoke for the second time it was dawn.

Through the oar-port he watched the sea change colour with the sunrise. He had never seen anything so ironically beautiful. The water caught the pale tints of the first light and warmed them with its own phosphorescent fire – amethyst and pearl and rose and saffron. Then, as the sun rose higher, the sea changed to one sheet of burning gold.

Carse watched until the last colour had faded, leaving the water white again. He was sorry when it was all gone. It was all unreal and he could pretend that he was still asleep, in Madam

Kan's on the Low Canal, dreaming the dreams that come with too much *thil*.

Boghaz snored untroubled by his side. The drummer slept beside his drum. The slaves drooped over the oars, resting.

Carse looked at them. They were a vicious, hard-bitten lot – mostly convicted criminals, he supposed. He thought he could recognize Jekkaran, Valiskian and Keshi types.

But a few of them, like the third man at his own oar, were of a different breed. Khonds, he supposed, and he could see why he had been mistaken for one of them. They were big raw-boned men with light eyes and fair or ruddy hair and a barbarian look that Carse liked.

His gaze dropped to the catwalk and he saw clearly now the two creatures who lay shackled there. The same breed as those who had cheered him in the square last night, from the wharfside ships.

They were not human. Not quite. They were kin to the seal and the dolphin, to the strong perfect loveliness of a cresting wave. Their bodies were covered with short dark fur, thinning to a fine down on the face. Their features were delicately cut, handsome. They rested but did not sleep and their eyes were open, large and dark and full of intelligence.

These, he guessed, were what the Jekkarans had referred to as Swimmers. He wondered what their function was, aboard ship. One was a man, the other a woman. He could not, somehow, think of them as merely male and female like beasts.

He realised that they were studying him with fixed curiosity. A small shiver ran over him. There was something uncanny about their eyes, as though they could see beyond ordinary horizons.

The woman spoke in a soft voice, 'Welcome to the brotherhood of the lash.'

Her tone was friendly. Yet he sensed in it a certain reserve, a note of puzzlement.

Carse smiled at her. 'Thanks.'

Again, he was conscious that he spoke the old High Martian with an accent. It was going to be a problem to explain his race, for he knew that the Khonds themselves would not make the same mistake the Jekkarans had.

The next words of the Swimmer convinced him of that. 'You are not of Khondor,' she said, 'though you resemble its people. What is your country?'

A man's rough voice joined in. 'Yes, what is it, stranger?'

Carse turned to see that the big Khond slave, who was third man on his oar, eyeing him with hostile suspicion.

The man went on, 'Word went round that you were a captured Khond spy but that's a lie. More likely you're a Jekkaran masquerading as a Khond, set here among us by the Sarks.'

A low growl ran through the oar bank.

Carse had known he would have to account for himself somehow and had been thinking quickly. Now he spoke up.

'I'm not Jekkaran but a tribesman from far beyond Shun. From so far that all this is like a new world to me.'

'You might be,' the big Khond conceded grudgingly. 'You've got a queer look and way of talking. What brought you and this hog of Valkis aboard?'

Boghaz was awake now and the fat Valkisian answered hastily. 'My friend and I were wrongfully accused of theft by the Sarks! The shame of it – I, Boghaz of Valkis, convicted of pilfering! An outrage against justice!'

The Khond spat disgustedly and turned away. 'I thought so.'

Presently Boghaz found an opportunity to whisper to Carse. 'They think now we're a pair of condemned thieves. Best let them think so, my friend.'

'What are you but that?' Carse retorted brutally.

Boghaz studied him with shrewd little eyes. 'What are *you*, friend?'

'You heard me – I come from far beyond Shun.'

From beyond Shun and from beyond this whole world, Carse thought grimly. But he couldn't tell these people the incredible truth about himself.

The fat Valkisian shrugged. 'If you wish to stick to that it's all right with me. I trust you implicitly. Are we not partners?'

Carse smiled sourly at that ingenuous question. There was something about the impudence of this fat thief which he found amusing.

Boghaz detected his smile. 'Ah, you are thinking of my unfortunate violence toward you last night. It was mere impulsiveness. We shall forget it. I, Boghaz, have already forgotten it,' he added magnanimously.

'The fact remains that you, my friend, possess the secret of' – he lowered his voice to a murmur – 'of the Tomb of Rhiannon. It's lucky that Scyld was too ignorant to recognise the sword! For that secret, rightly exploited, can make us the biggest men on Mars!'

Carse asked him, 'Why is the Tomb of Rhiannon so important?'

The question took Boghaz off guard. He looked startled.

'Do you pretend that you don't even know that?'

Carse reminded, 'I told you I come from so far that this is all a new world to me.'

Boghaz' fat face showed mixed incredulity and puzzlement. Finally he said, 'I can decide whether you're really what you say or whether you're pretending childish ignorance for your own reasons.'

He shrugged. 'Whichever is the case you could soon get the story from the others. I might as well be truthful.'

He spoke in a rapid undertone, watching Carse shrewdly. 'Even a remote barbarian will have heard of the superhuman Quiru, who long ago possessed all power and scientific wisdom. And of how the Cursed One among them, Rhiannon, sinned by teaching too much wisdom to the Dhuvians.

'Because of what that led to the Quiru left our world, going no man knows whither. But before they left they seized the sinner Rhiannon and locked him in a hidden tomb and locked in with him his instruments of awful power.

'Is it wonderful that all Mars has hunted that Tomb for an age? Is it strange that either the Empire of Sark or the Sea-Kings would do anything to possess the Cursed One's lost powers? And now that you have found the Tomb do I, Boghaz, blame you for being cautious with your secret?'

Carse ignored the last. He was remembering now – remembering those strange instruments of jewels and prisms and metal in Rhiannon's Tomb.

Were those really the secrets of an ancient, great science – a science that had long been lost to the half-barbaric Mars of this age?

He asked, 'Who are these Sea-Kings? I take it that they're enemies of the Sarks?'

Boghaz nodded. 'Sark rules the lands east, north and south of the White Sea. But in the west are small free kingdoms of hardy sea-rovers like the Khonds and their Sea-Kings defy the power of Sark.'

He added, 'Aye and there are many even in my own subject lands of Valkis and elsewhere who secretly hate Sark because of the Dhuvians.'

'The Dhuvians?' Carse repeated. 'You mentioned them before. Who are they?'

Boghaz snorted. 'Look, friend, it's all very well to pretend ignorance but that's carrying it too far! There's no tribesman from so far away that he doesn't know and fear the accursed Serpent!'

So the Serpent was a generic name from the mysterious Dhuvians? Why were they called so, Carse wondered?

Carse became suddenly aware that the woman Swimmer was looking at him fixedly. For a startled moment he had the eery sensation that she was looking into his thoughts.

'Shallah is watching us – best be quiet now,' Boghaz whispered hastily. 'Everyone knows that the Halflings can read the mind a little.'

If that were so, Carse thought grimly, Shallah the Swimmer must have found profoundly astonishing matter in his own thoughts.

He had been pitchforked into a wholly unfamiliar Mars, most of which was still a mystery to him.

But if Boghaz spoke truth, if those strange objects in the Tomb of Rhiannon were instruments of a great lost scientific power, then even though he was a slave he held the key to a secret coveted by all this world.

That secret could be his death. He must guard it jealously till he won free of this brutal bondage. For a resolve to regain his freedom and a grim growing hatred of the swaggering Sarks were all that he was sure of now.

The sun rose high, blazing down into the unprotected oar-pit. The wind that hummed through the taut cordage aloft did nothing to relieve the heat down here. The men broiled like fish on a griddle, and so far neither food nor water had been forthcoming.

Carse watched with sullen eyes the Sark soldiers lounging arrogantly on the deck above the sunken oar-pit. On the after part of that deck rose the low main cabin, the door to which remained closed. Atop the flat roof stood the steersman, a husky Sark sailor who held the massive tiller and who took his orders from Scyld.

Scyld himself stood up there, his spade beard thrust up as he looked unseeingly over the misery in the oar-pit toward the distant horizon. Occasionally he rapped out curt commands to the steersman.

Rations came at last – black bread and a pannikin of water, served out by one of the strange winged slaves Carse had glimpsed before in Jekkara. The Sky Folk, the mob had called them.

Carse studied this one with interest. He looked like a crippled angel, with his shining wings cruelly broken and his beautiful suffering face. He moved slowly along the catwalk in his task as though walking were a burden to him. He did not smile or speak and his eyes were veiled.

Shallah thanked him for her food. He did not look at her but went away, dragging his empty basket. She turned to Carse.

'Most of them,' she said, 'die when their wings are broken.'

He knew she meant a death of the spirit. And sight of that broken-winged Halfling somehow gave Carse a bitterer hatred of the Sarks than his own enslavement had aroused. 'Curse the brutes who would do a thing like that!' he muttered.

'Aye, cursed be they who foregather in evil with the Serpent!' growled Jaxart, the big Khond at their oar. 'Cursed be their king and his she-devil daughter Ywain! Had I the chance I'd sink us all beneath the waves to thwart whatever deviltry she's been hatching at Jekkara.'

'Why hasn't she shown herself?' Carse asked. 'Is she so delicate that she'll keep her cabin all the way to Sark?'

'That hellcat delicate?' Jaxart spat in loathing and said, 'She's wantoning with the lover hidden in her cabin. He crept aboard at Sark, all hooded and cloaked, and hasn't come out since. But we saw him.'

Shallah looked aft with fixed gaze and murmured, 'It is no lover she is hiding but accursed evil. I sensed it when it came aboard.'

She turned her disturbing luminous gaze on Carse. 'I think there is a curse on you too, stranger. I can feel it but I cannot understand you.'

Carse again felt a little chill. These Halflings with their extrasensory powers could just vaguely sense his incredible alienage. He was glad when Shallah and Naram, her mate, turned away from him.

Often in the hours that followed Carse found his gaze going up to the afterdeck. He had a grim desire to see this Ywain of Sark whose slave he now was.

In mid-afternoon, after blowing steadily for hours, the wind began to fail and dropped finally to a flat calm.

The drum thundered. The sweeps went out and once again Carse was sweating at the unfamiliar labour, snarling at the kiss of the lash on his back.

Only Boghaz seemed happy.

'I am no seafaring man,' he said, shaking his head. 'For a Khond like you Jaxart, sea-roving is natural. But I was delicate in my youth and forced to quieter pursuits. Ah blessed calm! Even the drudgery of the oars is preferable to bounding like a wild thing over the waters.'

Carse was touched by this pathetic speech until he discovered that Boghaz had good reason not to mind the rowing inasmuch as he was only bending back and forth while Carse and Jaxart pulled. Carse dealt him a blow that nearly knocked him off the bench and after that he pulled his weight, groaning.

The afternoon wore on, hot and endless, to the ceaseless beat of the oars.

The palms of Carse's hands blistered, then broke and bled.

He was a powerful man, but even so the strength ran out of him like water and his body felt as though it had been stretched on the rack. He envied Jaxart, who behaved as though he had been born in the oar banks.

Gradually sheer exhaustion dulled his agony somewhat. He fell into a sort of drugged stupor, wherein his body performed its task mechanically.

Then, in the last golden blaze of daylight, he lifted his head to gasp for breath and saw, through the wavering haze that obscured his vision, a woman standing on the deck above him, looking at the sea.

7
THE SWORD

She might be both Sark and devil as the others had said. But whatever she was, she stopped Carse's breath and held him staring.

She stood like a dark flame in a nimbus of sunset light. Her habit was that of a young warrior, a hauberk of black mail over a short purple tunic, with a jewelled dragon coiling on the curve of her mailed breast and a short sword at her side.

Her head was bare. She wore her black hair short, cut square above the eyes and falling to her shoulders. Under dark brows her eyes had smouldering fires in them. She stood with straight long legs braced slightly apart, peering out over the sea.

Carse felt the surge of a bitter admiration. This woman owned him and he hated her and all her race but he could not deny her burning beauty and her strength.

'*Row*, you carrion!'

The oath and the lash brought him back from his staring. He had lost stroke, fouling the whole starboard bank, and Jaxart was cursing and Callus was using the whip.

He beat them all impartially and fat Boghaz wailed at the top of his lungs, 'Mercy, oh Lady Ywain! Mercy, mercy!'

'Shut up, scum!' snarled Callus and lashed them until blood ran.

Ywain glanced gown into the pit. She rapped out a name. 'Callus!'

The oar-bank captain bowed. 'Yes, Highness.'

'Pick up the beat,' she said. 'Faster. I want to raise the Black Banks at dawn.' She looked directly at Carse and Boghaz and added, 'Flog every man who loses stroke.'

She turned away. The drum beat quickened. Carse looked with bitter eyes at Ywain's back. It would be good to tame this woman. It would be good to break her utterly, to tear her pride out by the roots and stamp on it.

The lash rapped out the time on his unwilling back and there was nothing for it but to row.

Jaxart grinned a wolf's grin. Between strokes he panted, 'Sark rules the White Sea to hear them tell it. But the Sea Kings still come out! Even Ywain won't dawdle on the way!'

'If their enemies may be out why don't they have escort ships for this galley?' Carse asked, gasping.

Jaxart shook his head. 'That I can't understand myself. I heard that Garach sent his daughter to overawe the subject king of Jekkara, who's been getting too ambitious. But why she came without escort ships—'

Boghaz suggested, 'Perhaps the Dhuvians furnished her with some of their mysterious weapons for protection?'

The big Khond snorted. 'The Dhuvians are too crafty to do that. They'll use their strange weapons sometimes in behalf of their Sark allies, yes. That's why the alliance exists. But *give* those weapons to Sark, teach Sarks how to use them? They're not *that* foolish!'

Carse was getting a clearer idea of this ancient Mars. These peoples were all half-barbaric – all but the mysterious Dhuvians. *They* apparently possessed at least some of the lost ancient science of this world and jealously guarded it and used it for their own and their Sark allies' purposes.

Night fell. Ywain remained on deck and the watches were doubled. Naram and Shallah, the two Swimmers, stirred restlessly in their shackles. In the torchlit gloom their eyes were luminous with some secret excitement.

Carse had neither the strength nor the inclination to appreciate the wonder of the glowing sea by moonlight. To make matters worse a headwind sprang up and roughened the waves to an ugly cross-chop that made the oars doubly difficult to handle. The drum beat inexorably.

A dull fury burned in Carse. He ached intolerably. He bled and his back was striped with fiery weals. The oar was heavy. It was heavier than all Mars and it bucked and fought him like a live thing.

Something happened to his face. A strange stony look came over it and all the colour went out of his eyes, leaving them bleak as ice and not quite sane. The drumbeat merged into the pounding of his own heart, roaring louder with every painful stroke.

A wave sprang up, the long sweep crabbed, the handle took Carse across the chest and knocked the wind out of him. Jaxart, who was experienced, and Boghaz, who was heavy, regained control almost at once though not before the overseer was on hand to curse them for lazy carrion – his favourite word – and to lay on the whip.

Carse let go of the oar. He moved so fast, in spite of his hampering chains, that the overseer had no idea what was happening until suddenly he was lying across the Earthman's knees and trying to protect his head from the blows of the Earthman's wrist-cuffs.

Instantly the oar-bank went mad. The stroke was hopelessly lost. Men shouted for the kill. Callus rushed up and hit Carse over the head with the loaded butt of his whip, knocking him half senseless. The overseer scrambled back to safety, eluding Jaxart's clutching arms. Boghaz made himself as small as possible and did nothing.

Ywain's voice came down from the deck. 'Callus!'

The oar-bank captain knelt, trembling. 'Yes, Highness?'

'Flog them all until they remember that they're no longer

men but slaves.' Her angry, impersonal gaze rested on Carse. 'As for that one – he's new, isn't he?'

'Yes. Highness.'

'Teach him,' she said.

They taught him. Callus and the overseer together taught him. Carse bowed his head over his arms and took it. Now and again Boghaz screamed as the lash flicked too far over and caught him instead. Between his feet Carse saw dimly the red streams that trickled down into the bilges and stained the water. The rage that had burned in him chilled and altered as iron tempers under the hammer.

At last they stopped. Carse raised his head. It was the greatest effort he had ever made but stiffly, stubbornly, he raised it. He looked directly at Ywain.

'Have you learned your lesson, slave?' she asked.

It was a long time before he could form the words to answer. He was beyond caring now whether he lived or died. His whole universe was centred on the woman who stood arrogant and untouchable above him.

'Come down yourself and teach me if you can,' he answered hoarsely and called her a name in the lowest vernacular of the streets – a name that said there was nothing she could teach a man.

For a moment no one moved or spoke. Carse saw her face go white and he laughed, a hoarse terrible sound in the silence. Then Scyld drew his sword and vaulted over the rail into the oar pit.

The blade flashed high and bright in the torchlight. It occurred to Carse that he had travelled a long way to die. He waited for the stroke but it did not come and then he realised that Ywain had cried out to Scyld to stop.

Scyld faltered, then turned, puzzled, looking up. 'But, Highness—'

'Come here,' she said, and Carse saw that she was staring at the sword in Scyld's hand, the sword of Rhiannon.

Scyld climbed the ladder back up to the deck, his black-browed face a little frightened. Ywain met him.

'Give me that,' she said. And when he hesitated, 'The sword, fool!'

He laid it in her hands and she looked at it, turning it over in the torchlight, studying the workmanship, the hilt with its single smoky jewel, the etched symbols on the blade.

'Where did you get this, Scyld?'

'I—' He stammered, not liking to make the admission, his hand going instinctively to his stolen collar.

Ywain snapped, 'Your thieving doesn't interest me. Where did you get it?'

He pointed to Carse and Boghaz. 'From them, Highness, when I picked them up.'

She nodded. 'Fetch them aft to my quarters.'

She disappeared inside the cabin. Scyld, unhappy and completely bewildered, turned to obey her order and Boghaz moaned.

'Oh, merciful gods!' He whispered. 'That's done it!' He leaned closer to Carse and said rapidly while he still had the chance, 'Lie, as you never lied before! If she thinks you know the secret of the Tomb she or the Dhuvians will force it out of you!'

Carse said nothing. He was having all he could do to retain consciousness. Scyld called profanely for wine, which was brought. He forced some of it down Carse's throat then had him and Boghaz released from the oar and marched up to the afterdeck.

The wine and the sea wind up on deck revived Carse enough so that he could keep his feet under him. Scyld ushered them ungently into Ywain's torchlit cabin, where she sat with the sword of Rhiannon laid on the carven table before her.

In the opposite bulkhead was a low door leading into an inner cabin. Carse saw that it was open the merest crack. No light showed but he got the feeling that someone – something – was crouching behind it, listening. It made him remember Jaxart's word and Shallah's.

There was a taint in the air – a faint musky odour, dry and sickly. It seemed to come from that inner cabin. It had a strange effect on Carse. Without knowing what it was he hated it.

He thought that if it was a lover Ywain was hiding in there it must be a strange sort of lover.

Ywain took his mind off that. Her gaze stabbed at him, and once again he thought that he had never seen such eyes. Then she said to Scyld, 'Tell me – the full story.'

Uncomfortably, in halting sentences, he told her. Ywain lookd at Boghaz.

'And you, fat one. How did you come by the sword?'

Boghaz sighed, nodding at Carse. 'From him, Highness. It's a handsome weapon and I'm a thief by trade.'

'Is that the only reason you wanted it?'

Boghaz's face was a model of innocent surprise. 'What other reason could there be? I'm not fighting man. Besides, there were the belt and collar. You can see for yourself, Highness, that all are valuable.'

Her face did not show whether she believed him or not. She turned to Carse.

'The sword belonged to you, then?'

'Yes.'

'Where did you get it?'

'I bought it from a trader.'

'Where?'

'In the northern country, beyond Shun.'

Ywain smiled. 'You lie.'

Carse said wearily, 'I came by the weapon honestly' – he had, in a sense – 'and I don't care whether you believe it or not.'

The crack of that inner door mocked Carse. He wanted to break it open, to see what crouched there, listening, watching out of the darkness. He wanted to see what made that hateful smell.

Almost, it seemed, there was no need for that. Almost, it seemed, he knew.

Unable to contain himself any longer, Scyld burst out, 'Your pardon, Highness! But why all this fuss about a sword?'

'You're a good soldier, Scyld,' she answered thoughtfully, 'but in many ways a blockhead. Did you clean this blade?'

'Of course. And bad condition it was in, too.' He glanced

disgustedly at Carse. 'It looked as though he hadn't touched it for years.'

Ywain reached out and laid her hand upon the jewelled hilt. Carse saw that it trembled. She said softly, 'You were right, Scyld. It hadn't been touched, for years. Not since Rhiannon, who made it, was walled away in his tomb to suffer for his sins.'

Scyld's face went completely blank. His jaw dropped. After a long while he said one word, '*Rhiannon!*'

8
THE THING IN THE DARK

Ywain's level gaze fastened on Carse. 'He knows the secret of the Tomb, Scyld. He must know it if he had the sword.'

She paused and when she spoke again her words were almost inaudible, like the voicing of an inner thought.

'A dangerous secret. So dangerous that I almost wish ...'

She broke off short, as though she had already said too much. Did she glance quickly at the inner door?

In her old imperious tone she said to Carse, 'One more chance, slave. Where is the Tomb of Rhiannon?'

Carse shook his head. 'I know nothing,' he said and gripped Boghaz' shoulder to steady himself. Little crimson droplets had trickled down to dye the rug under his feet. Ywain's face seemed far away.

Scyld said hoarsely, 'Give him to me, Highness.'

'No. He's too far gone for your methods now. I don't want him killed yet. I must – take thought to this.'

She frowned, looking from Carse to Boghaz and back again.

'They object to rowing, I believe. Very well. Take the third man off their oar. Let these two work it without help all night. And tell Callus to lay the lash on the fat one twice in every glass, five strokes.'

Boghaz wailed. 'Highness, I implore you! I would tell if I could but I know nothing. I swear it!'

She shrugged. 'Perhaps not. In that case you will wish to persuade your comrade to talk.'

She turned again to Scyld. 'Tell Callus also to douse the tall one with seawater, as often as he needs it.' Her white teeth glinted. 'It has a healing property.'

Scyld laughed.

Ywain motioned him to go. 'See that they're kept at it but on no account is either one to die. When they're ready to talk bring them to me.'

Scyld saluted and marched his prisoners back again to the rowers' pit. Jaxart was taken off the oar and the endless nightmare of the dark hours continued for Carse.

Boghaz was crushed and trembling. He screamed mightily as he took his five strokes and then moaned in Carse's ear, 'I wish I'd never seen your bloody sword! She'll take us to Caer Dhu – and the gods have mercy on us.'

Carse bared his teeth in what might have been a grin. 'You talked differently in Jekkara.'

'I was a free man then and the Dhuvians were far away.'

Carse felt some deep and buried nerve contract at the mention of that name. He said in an odd voice, 'Boghaz, what was that smell in the cabin?'

'Smell? I noticed none.'

'Strange,' Carse thought, *'when it drove me nearly mad. Or perhaps I'm mad already.'*

'Jaxart was right, Boghaz. There is someone hidden there, in the inner cabin.'

With some irritation Boghaz said, 'Ywain's wantoning is nothing to me.'

They laboured in silence for a while. Then Carse asked abruptly, 'Who are the Dhuvians?'

Boghaz stared at him. 'Where do you really come from man?'

'As I told you – from far beyond Shun.'

'It must have been from far indeed if you haven't heard of Caer Dhu and the Serpent!'

Then Boghaz shrugged fat shoulders as he laboured. 'You're playing some deep game of your own, I suppose. All this pretended ignorance – but I don't mind playing that game with you.'

He went on, 'You know at least that since long ago there have been human peoples on our world and also the not-quite-human peoples, the Halflings. Of the humans the great Quiru, who are gone, were the greatest. They had so much science and wisdom that they're still revered as superhuman.

'But there were also the Halflings – the races who are man-like but not descended of the same blood. The Swimmers, who sprang from the sea-creatures, and the Sky Folk, who came from the winged things – and the Dhuvians, who are from the serpent.'

A cold breath swept through Carse. Why was it that all this which he heard for the first time seemed so familiar to him?

Certainly he had never heard before this story of ancient Martian evolution, of intrinsically alien stocks evolving into superficially similar pseudo-human peoples. He had not heard it before – *or had he?*

'Crafty and wise as the snake that fathered them were the Dhuvians always,' Boghaz was continuing. 'So crafty that they prevailed on Rhiannon of the Quiru to teach them some of his science.

'Some but not all! Yet what they learned was enough that they could make their black city of Caer Dhu impregnable and could occasionally intervene with their scientific weapons so as to make their Sark allies the dominant human nation.'

'And *that* was Rhiannon's sin?' Carse said.

'Aye, that was the Cursed One's sin for in his pride he had defied the other Quiru who counselled him not to teach the Dhuvians such powers. For that sin the other Quiru condemned Rhiannon and entombed him in a hidden place before they left our world. At least so says the legend.'

'But the Dhuvians themselves are no mere legends?'

'They are not, damn them,' Boghaz muttered. 'They are the reason all free men hate the Sarks, who hold evil alliance with the Serpent.'

They were interrupted by the broken winged slave, Lorn. He

had been sent to dip up a bucket of seawater and now appeared with it.

The winged man spoke and even now his voice had music on it. 'This will be painful, stranger. Bear it if you can – it will help you.' He raised the bucket. Glowing water spilled out, covering Carse's body with a bright sheath.

Carse knew why Ywain had smiled. Whatever chemical gave the sea its phosphorescence might be healing but the cure was worse than the wounds. The corrosive agony seemed to eat the flesh from his bones.

The night wore on and after a while Carse felt the pain grow less. His weals no longer bled and the water began to refresh him. To his own surprise he saw the second dawn break over the White Sea.

Soon after sunrise a cry came down from the masthead. The Black Banks lay ahead.

Through the oar port Carse saw a welter of broken water that stretched for miles. Reefs and shoals, with here and there black jagged fangs of rock showing through the foam. 'They're not going to try to run that mess?' he exclaimed.

'It's the shortest route to Sark,' Boghaz said. 'As for running the Banks – why do you suppose every Sark galley carries captive Swimmers?'

'I've wondered.'

'You'll soon see.'

Ywain came on deck and Scyld joined her. They did not look down at the two haggard scarecrows sweating at the oar.

Boghaz instantly wailed piteously. 'Mercy, Highness!'

Ywain paid no attention. She ordered Scyld, 'Slow the beat and send the Swimmers out.'

Naram and Shallah were unshackled and ran forward. Metal harnesses were locked to their bodies. Long wire lines ran from these harnesses to ringbolts in the forecastle deck.

The two Swimmers dived fearlessly into the foaming waters. The wire lines tautened and Carse glimpsed the heads of the two bobbing like corks as they swam smoothly ahead of the galley into the roaring Banks.

'You see?' said Boghaz. 'They feel out the channel. They can guide a ship through anything.'

To the slow beat of the drum the black galley forged into the broken water.

Ywain stood, hair flying in the breeze and hauberk shining, by the man at the tiller. She and Scyld peered closely ahead. The rough water shook along the keel with a hiss and a snarl and once an oar splintered on a rock but they crept on safely.

It was a long slow weary passage. The sun rose toward the zenith. There was an aching tension aboard the galley.

Carse only dimly heard the roar of breakers as he and Boghaz laboured at their oar.

The fat Valkisian was groaning ceaselessly now. Carse's arms felt like lead, his brain seemed clamped in steel.

At last the galley found smooth water, shot clear of the Banks. Their dull thunder came now from astern. The Swimmers were hauled back in.

Ywain glanced down into the oarpit for the first time, at the staggering slaves.

'Give them a brief rest,' she rapped. 'The wind should rise soon.'

Her eyes swung to Carse and Boghaz. 'And, Scyld, I'll see those two again now.'

Carse watched Scyld cross the deck and came down the ladder. He felt a sick apprehension.

He did not want to go up to that cabin again. He did not want to see again that door with its mocking crack nor smell that sickly evil smell.

But he and Boghaz were again unshackled and herded aft, and there was nothing he could do.

The door swung shut behind them. Scyld, Ywain behind the carved table, the sword of Rhiannon gleaming before her. The tainted air and the low door in the bulkhead, not quite closed – not quite.

Ywain spoke. 'You've had the first taste of what I can do to you. Do you want the second? Or will you tell me the location of Rhiannon's Tomb and what you found there?'

Carse answered tonelessly. 'I told you before that I don't know.'

He was not looking at Ywain. That inner door fascinated him, held his gaze. Somewhere, far at the back of his mind, something stirred and woke. A prescience, a hate, a horror that he could not understand.

But he understood well enough that this was the climax, the end. A deep shudder ran through him, an involuntary tightening of nerves.

'What is it that I do not know but can somehow almost remember?'

Ywain leaned forward. 'You're strong. You pride yourself on that. You feel that you can stand physical punishment, perhaps more than I would dare to give you. I think you could. But there are other ways. Quicker, surer ways and even a strong man has no defence against them.'

She followed the line of his gaze to the inner door. 'Perhaps,' she said softly, 'you can guess what I mean.'

Carse's face was empty now of all expression. The musky smell was heavy as smoke in his throat. He felt it coil and writhe inside him, filling his lungs, stealing into his blood. Poisonously subtle, cruel, cold with a primal coldness. He swayed on his feet but his fixed stare did not waver.

He said hoarsely, 'I can guess.'

'Good. Speak now and that door need not open.'

Carse laughed, a low, harsh sound. His eyes were clouded and strange.

'Why should I speak? You would only destroy me later to keep the secret safe.'

He stepped forward. He knew that he moved. He knew that he spoke though the sound of his own voice was vague in his ears.

But there was a dark confusion in him. The veins of his temples stood out like knotted cords, and the blood throbbed in his brain. Pressure, as of something bursting, breaking its bonds, tearing itself free.

He did not know why he stepped forward, toward that door. He did not know why he cried out in a tone that was not his, '*Open then, Child of the Snake!*'

Boghaz let out a wailing shriek and crouched down in a corner, hiding his face. Ywain started up, astonished and suddenly pale. The door swung slowly back.

There was nothing behind it but darkness and a shadow. A shadow cloaked and hooded and so crouched in the lightless cabin that it was no more than the ghost of a shadow.

But it was there. And the man Carse, caught fast in the trap of his strange fate, recognised it for what it was.

It was fear, the ancient evil thing that crept among the grasses in the beginning, apart from life but watching it with eyes of cold wisdom, laughing its silent laughter, giving nothing but the bitter death.

It was the Serpent.

The primal ape in Carse wanted to run, to hide away. Every cell of his flesh recoiled, every instinct warned him.

But he did not run and there was an anger in him that grew until it blotted out the fear, blotted out Ywain and the others, everything but the wish to destroy utterly the creature crouching beyond the light.

His own anger – or something greater? Something born of a shame and an agony that he could never know?

A voice spoke to him out of the darkness, soft and sibilant.

'You have willed it. Let it be so.'

There was utter silence in the cabin. Scyld had recoiled. Even Ywain had drawn back to the end of the table. The cowering Boghaz hardly breathed.

The shadow had stirred with a slight, dry rustle. A spot of subdued brilliance had appeared, held by unseen hands – a brilliance that shed no glow around it. It seemed to Carse like a ring of little stars, incredibly distant.

The stars began to move, to circle their hidden orbit, to spin faster and faster until they became a wheel, peculiarly blurred. From them now came a thin high note, a crystal song that was like infinity, without beginning and end.

A song, a call, attuned to his hearing alone? Or was it his hearing? He could not tell. Perhaps he heard it with his flesh instead, with every quivering nerve. The others, Ywain and Scyld and Boghaz, seemed unaffected.

Carse felt a coldness stealing over him. It was as though those tiny singing stars called to him across the universe, charming him out into the deeps of space where the empty cosmos sucked him dry of warmth and life.

His muscles loosened. He felt his sinews melt and flow away on the icy tide. He felt his brain dissolving.

He went slowly to his knees. The little stars sang on and on. He understood them now. They were asking him a question. He knew that when he answered he could sleep. He would not wake again but that did not matter. He was afraid now but if he slept he would forget his fear.

Fear – fear! The old, old racial terror that haunts the soul, the dread that slides in the quiet dark—

In sleep and death he could forget that fear. He need only answer that hypnotic whispered question.

'Where is the Tomb?

Answer. Speak. But something still chained his tongue. The red flame of anger still flickered in him, fighting the brilliance of the singing stars.

He struggled but the star-song was too strong. He heard his dry lips slowly speaking. 'The Tomb, the place of Rhiannon ...'

'Rhiannon! Dark Father who taught you power, thou spawn of the serpent's egg!'

The name rang in him like a battle cry. His rage soared up. The smoky jewel in the hilt of the sword on the table seemed suddenly to call to his hand. He leaped and grasped its hilt.

Ywain sprang forward with a startled cry but it was too late.

The great jewel seemed to blaze, to catch up the power of the singing, shining stars and hurl it back.

The crystal song keened and broke. The brilliance faded. He had shattered the strange hypnosis.

Blood flowed again into Carse's veins. The sword felt alive in his hands. He shouted the name Rhiannon and plunged forward into the dark.

He heard a hissing scream as his long blade went home to the heart of the shadow.

9
GALLEY OF DEATH

Carse straightened slowly and turned in the doorway, his back to the thing he had slain but had not seen. He had no wish to see it. He was utterly shaken and in a strange mood, full of a vaulting strength that verged on madness.

The hysteria, he thought, that comes when you've taken too much, when the walls close in and there's nothing to do but fight before you die.

The cabin was full of a stunned silence. Scyld had the staring look of an idiot, his mouth fallen open. Ywain had put one hand to the edge of the table and it was strange to see in her that one small sign of weakness. She had not taken her eyes from Carse.

She said huskily, 'Are you man or demon that you can stand against Caer Dhu?'

Carse did not answer. He was beyond speech. Her face floated before him like a silver mask. He remembered the pain, the shameful labour at the sweep, the scars of the lash that he carried. He remembered the voice that had said to Callus, 'Teach him!'

He had slain the Serpent. After that it seemed an easy thing to kill a queen.

He began to move, covering the few short steps that lay between them, and there was something terrible about the slow purposefulness of it, the galled and shackled slave carrying the great sword, its blade dark with alien blood.

Ywain gave back one step. Her hand faltered to her own hilt. She was not afraid of death. She was afraid of the thing that she saw in Carse, the light that blazed in his eyes. A fear of the soul and not the body.

Scyld gave a hoarse cry. He drew his sword and lunged.

They had all forgotten Boghaz, crouching quiet in his corner. Now the Valkisian rose to his feet, handling his great bulk with unbelievable speed. As Scyld passed him he raised both hands and brought the full weight of his gyves down with tremendous strength on the Sark's head.

Scyld dropped like a stone.

And now Ywain had found her pride again. The sword of Rhiannon rose high for the death stroke and quick, quick as lightning, she drew her own short blade and parried it as it fell.

The force of the blow drove her weapon out of her hands. Carse had only to strike again. But it seemed that with that effort something had gone out of him. He saw her mouth open to voice an angry shout for aid and he struck her across the face with his hilt reversed, so that she slid stunned to the deck, her cheek laid open.

And then Boghaz was thrusting him back, saying, 'Don't kill her! We may buy our lives with hers!'

Carse watched as Boghaz bound and gagged her and took the dagger from her belt-sheath.

It occurred to him that they were two slaves who had overpowered Ywain of Sark and struck down her captain and that the lives of Matt Carse and Boghaz of Valkis were worth less than a puff of wind as soon as it was discovered.

So far, they were safe. There had been little noise and there were no sounds of alarm outside.

Boghaz shut the inner door as though to block off even the memory of what lay within. Then he took a closer look at Scyld, who was quite dead. He picked up the man's sword and stood still for a minute, catching his breath.

He was staring at Carse with a new respect that had in it both awe and fear. Glancing at the closed door, he muttered, 'I would not have believed it possible. And yet I saw it.' He turned back to Carse. 'You cried out upon Rhiannon before you struck. Why?'

Carse said impatiently, 'How can a man know what he's saying, at a time like that?'

The truth was that he didn't know himself why he had spoken the Cursed One's name, except that it had been thrust at him so often that he supposed it had become a sort of obsession. The Dhuvian's little hypnosis gadget had thrown his whole mind off balance for a while. He remembered only a towering anger – the gods knew he had had enough to make any man angry.

It was probably not so strange that the Dhuvian's hypnotic science hadn't been able to put him completely under. After all he was an Earthman and a product of another age. Even so it had been a near thing – horribly near. He didn't want to think about it any more.

'That's over now. Forget it. We've got to think how to get ourselves out of this mess.'

Boghaz's courage seemed to have drained away. He said glumly, 'We'd better kill ourselves at once and have done with it.'

He meant it. Carse said, 'If you feel that way why did you strike out to save my life?'

'I don't know. Instinct, I suppose.'

'All right. My instinct is to go on living as long as possible.'

It didn't look as though that would be very long. But he was not going to take Boghaz's advice and fall upon the sword of Rhiannon. He weighted it in his hands, scowling, and then looked from it to his fetters.

He said suddenly, 'If we could free the rowers they'd fight. They're all condemned for life – nothing to lose. We might take the ship.'

Boghaz's eyes widened, then narrowed shrewdly. He thought it over. Then he shrugged. 'I suppose one can always die. It's worth trying. Anything's worth trying.'

He tested the point of Ywain's dagger. It was thin and strong. With infinite skill, he began to pick the lock of the Earthman's gyves.

'Have you a plan?' he asked.

Carse grunted. 'I'm no magician. I can only try.' He glanced at Ywain. 'You stay here, Boghaz. Barricade the door. Guard her. If things go wrong she's our last and only hope.'

The cuffs hung loose now on his wrist and ankles. Reluctantly he laid down the sword. Boghaz would need the dagger to free himself but there was another one on Scyld's body. Carse took it and hid it under his kilt. As he did so he gave Boghaz a few brief instructions.

A moment later Carse opened the cabin door just widely enough to step outside. From behind him came a good enough imitation of Scyld's gruff voice, calling for a guard. A soldier came.

'Take this slave back to the oar-bank,' ordered the voice that aped Scyld's. 'And see that the lady Ywain is not disturbed.'

The man saluted and began to herd the shuffling Carse away. The cabin door banged shut and Carse heard the sound of the bar dropping into place.

Across the deck, and down the ladder. *Count the soldiers, think how it must be done!*

No. Don't think. Don't, or you'll never try it.

The drummer, who was a slave himself. The two Swimmers. The overseer, up at the forward end of the catwalk, lashing a rower. Rows of shoulders, bending over the oars, back and forth. Rows of faces above them. The faces of rats, of jackals, of wolves. The creak and groan of the looms, the reek of sweat and bilgewater, and incessant beat, beat, beat of the drum.

The soldier turned Carse over to Callus and went away. Jaxart was back on the oar and with him a lean Sark convict with a brand on his face. They glanced up at Carse and then away again.

Callus thrust the Earthman roughly onto the bench, where he bent low over the oar. Callus stooped to fix the master chain to his leg-irons, growling as he did so.

'I hope that Ywain lets me have you when she's all through with you, carrion! I'll have fun while you last—'

Callus stopped very suddenly and said no more, then or ever. Carse had stabbed his heart with such swift neatness that not even Callus was aware of the stroke until he ceased to breathe.

'Keep stroke!' snarled Carse to Jaxart under his breath. The big Khond obeyed. A smouldering light came into his eyes. The branded man laughed once, silently, with a terrible eagerness.

Carse cut the key to the master locks free from its thong on Callus' girdle and let the corpse down gently into the bilges.

The man across the catwalk on the port car had seen as had the drummer. 'Keep stroke!' said Carse again and Jaxart glared and the stroke was kept. But the drum beat faltered and died.

Carse shook off his manacles. His eyes met the drummer's

and the rhythm started again but already the overseer was on his way off, shouting.

'What's the matter there, you pig?'

'My arms are weary,' the man quavered.

'Weary are they? I'll weary your back for you too if it happens again!'

The man on the port oar, a Khond, said deliberately, 'Much is going to happen, you Sark scum.' He took his hands off the oar.

The overseer advanced upon him. 'Is it now? Why, the filth is a very prophet!'

His lash rose and fell once and then Carse was on him. One hand clamped the man's mouth shut and the other plunged the dagger in. Swiftly, silently, a second body rolled into the bilges.

A deep animal cry broke out along the oar-bank and was choked down as Carse raised his arms in a warning gesture, looking upwards at the deck. No one had noticed, yet. There had been nothing to draw notice.

Inevitably, the rhythm of the oars had broken but that was not unusual and, in any case, it was the concern of the overseer. Unless it stopped altogether no one would wander. If luck would only hold ...

The drummer had the sense or the habit to keep on. Carse passed the word along – 'Keep stroke, until we're all free!' The beat picked up again, slowly. Crouching low, Carse opened the master locks. The men needed no warning to be easy with their chains as they freed themselves, one by one.

Even so, less than half of them were loose when an idle soldier chose to lean on the deck rail and look down.

Carse had just finished releasing the Swimmers. He saw the man's expression change from boredom to incredulous awareness and he caught up the overseer's whip and sent the long lash singing upward. The soldier bellowed the alarm as the lash coiled around his neck and brought him crashing down into the pit.

Carse leaped to the ladder. 'Come on, you scum, you rabble!' he shouted. 'Here's your chance!'

And they were after him like one man, roaring the beast roar of creatures hungry for vengeance and blood. Up the ladder they poured, swinging their chains, and those that were still held to the benches worked like madmen to be free.

They had the brief advantage of surprise, for the attack had come so quickly on the heels of the alarm that swords were still half drawn, bows still unstrung. But it wouldn't last long. Carse knew well how short a time it would last.

'Strike! Strike hard while you can!'

With belaying pins, with their shackles, with their fists, the galley slaves charge in and the soldiers met them. Carse with his whip and his knife, Jaxart howling the word *Khondor* like a battle-cry, naked bodies against mail, desperation against discipline. The Swimmers slipped like brown shadows through the fray and the slave with the broken wings had somehow possessed himself of a sword. Seamen reinforced the soldiers but still the wolves came up out of the pit.

From the forecastle and the steersman's platform bowmen began to take their toll but the fight became so closely locked that they had to stop for fear of killing their own men. The salt-sweet smell of blood rose on the air. The decks were slippery with it. And gradually the superior force of the soldiery began to tell. Carse saw that the slaves were being driven back and the number of the dead was growing.

In a furious surge he broke through to the cabin. The Sarks must have thought it strange that Ywain and Scyld had not appeared but they had had little time to do anything about it. Carse pounded on the cabin door, shouting Boghaz's name.

The Valkisian drew the bar, and Carse burst in.

'Carry the wench up to the steersman's platform,' he panted. 'I'll cut your way.'

He snatched up the sword of Rhiannon and went out again with Boghaz behind him, bearing Ywain in his arms.

The ladder was only a short two paces from the door. The bowmen had come down to fight and there was no one up on the platform but the frightened Sark sailor who clung to the tiller bar. Carse, swinging the great sword, cleared the way and held the ladder foot while Boghaz climbed up and set Ywain on her feet where all could see her.

'Look you!' he bellowed. 'We have Ywain!'

He did not need to tell them. The sight of her, bound and gagged in the hands of a slave, was like a blow to the soldiers and like a magic potion to the rebels. Two mingled sounds went up, a groan and a cheer.

Someone found Scyld's body and dragged it out on deck. Doubly leaderless now, the Sarks lost heart. The tide of battle turned then and the slaves took their advantage in both hands.

The sword of Rhiannon led them. It slashed the halliards that brought the dragon flag of Sark plunging down from the masthead. And under its blade the last Sark soldier died.

There was an abrupt cessation of sound and movement. The black galley drifted with the freshening wind. The sun was low on the horizon. Carse climbed wearily to the steersman's platform.

Ywain, still fast in Boghaz's grip, followed him, eyes full of hell-fire.

Carse went to the forward edge of the platform and stood leaning on the sword. The slaves, exhausted with fighting and drunk with victory, gathered on the deck below like a ring of panting wolves.

Jaxart came out from searching the cabins. He shook his dripping blade up at Ywain and shouted, 'A fine lover she kept in her cabin! The spawn of Caer Dhu, the stinking Serpent!'

There was an instant reaction from the slaves. They were tense and bristling again at that name, afraid even in their numbers. Carse made his voice heard with difficulty.

'The thing is dead. Jaxart – will you cleanse the ship?'

Jaxart paused before he turned to obey. 'How did you know it was dead?'

Carse said, 'I killed it.'

The men stared up at him as though he were something more than human. The awed muttering went around – 'He slew the Serpent!'

With another man Jaxart returned to the cabin and brought

the body out. No word was spoken. A wide lane was cleared to the lee rail and the black, shrouded thing was carried along it, faceless, formless, hidden in its robe and cowl, symbol even in death of infinite evil.

Again Carse fought down that cold repellent fear and the touch of strange anger. He forced himself to watch.

The splash it made as it fell was shockingly loud in the stillness. Ripples spread in little lines of fire and died away.

Then men began to talk again. They began to shout up to Ywain, taunting her. Someone yelled for her blood and there would have been a stampede up the ladder but that Carse threatened them with his long blade.

'No! She's our hostage and worth her weight in gold.'

He did not specify how but he knew the argument would satisfy them for a while. And much as he hated Ywain he somehow did not want to see her torn to pieces by this pack of wild beasts.

He steered their thoughts to another subject.

'We have to have a leader now. Whom will you choose?'

There was only one answer to that. They roared his name until it deafened him, and Carse felt a savage pleasure at the sound of it. After days of torment it was good to know he was a man again, even in an alien world.

When he could make himself heard he said, 'All right. Now listen well. The Sarks will kill us by slow death for what we've done – *if* they catch us. So here's my plan. We'll join the free rovers, the Sea-Kings who lair at Khondor!'

To the last man they agreed and the name *Khondor* rang up into the sunset sky.

The Khonds among the slaves were like wild men. One of them stripped a length of yellow cloth from the tunic of a dead soldier, fashioned a banner out of it and ran it up in place of the dragon flag of Sark.

At Carse's request, Jaxart took over the handling of the galley and Boghaz carried Ywain down again and locked her in the cabin.

The men dispersed, eager to be rid of their shackles, eager to loot the bodies of clothes and weapons and to dip into the wine-casks. Only Naram and Shallah remained, looking up at Carse in the afterglow.

'Do you agree?' he asked them.

Shallah's eyes glowed with the same eerie light that he had seen in them before.

'You are a stranger,' she said softly. 'Stranger to us, stranger to our world. And I say again that I can sense a black shadow in you that makes me afraid, for you will cast it wherever you go.'

She turned from him then and Naram said, 'We go homeward now.'

The two Swimmers poised for a moment on the rail. They were free now, free of their chains, and their bodies ached with the joy of it, stretching upward, supple, sure. Then they vanished overside.

After a moment Carse saw them again, rolling and plunging like dolphins, racing each other, calling to each other in their soft clear voices as they made the waves foam flame.

Demos was already high. The afterglow was gone and Phobos came up swiftly out of the east. The sea turned glowing silver. The Swimmers went away toward the west, trailing their wakes of fire, a tracery of sparkling light that grew fainter and vanished altogether.

The black galley stood on for Khondor, its taut sails dark against the sky. And Carse remained as he was, standing on the platform, holding the sword of Rhiannon between his hands.

10
THE SEA KINGS

Carse was leaning on the rail, watching the sea, when the Sky Folk came. Time and distance had dropped behind the galley. Carse had rested. He wore a clean kilt, he was washed and shaven, his wounds were healing. He had regained his ornaments and the hilt of the long sword gleamed above his left shoulder.

Boghaz was beside him. Boghaz was always beside him. He pointed now to the western sky and said, 'Look there.'

Carse saw what he took to be a flight of birds in the distance. But they grew rapidly larger and presently he realised that they were men, or half-men, like the slave with the broken wing.

They were not slaves and their wings stretched wide, flashing in the sun. Their slim bodies, completely naked, gleamed like ivory. They were incredibly beautiful, arrowing down out of the blue.

They had a kinship with the Swimmers. The Swimmers were the perfect children of the sea and these were brother to wind and cloud and the clean immensity of the sky. It was as though some master hand had shaped them both out of their separate elements, moulding them in strength and grace that was freed from all the earth-bound clumsiness of men, dreams made into joyous flesh.

Jaxart, who was at the helm, called down to them. 'Scouts from Khondor!'

Carse mounted to the platform. The men gathered on the deck to watch as the four Sky Folk came down in a soaring rush.

Carse glanced forward to the sheer of the prow. Lorn, the winged slave, had taken to brooding there by himself, speaking to no one. Now he stood erect and one of the four went to him.

The others came to rest on the platform, folding their bright wings with a whispering rustle.

They greeted Jaxart by name, looking curiously at the long black galley and the hard-bitten mongrel crew that sailed her and, above all, at Carse. There was something in their searching gaze that reminded the Earthman uncomfortably of Shallah.

'Our chief,' Jaxart told them. 'A barbarian from the back door of Mars but a man of his hands and no fool, either. The Swimmers will have told the tale, how he took the ship and Ywain of Sark together.'

'Aye.' They acknowledged Carse with grave courtesy.

The Earthman said, 'Jaxart has told me that all who fight Sark may have freedom of Khondor. I claim that right.'

'We will carry word to Rold, who heads the council of the Sea Kings.'

The Khonds on deck began to shout their own messages then, the eager words of men who have been a long time away from home. The Sky Men answered in their clear sweat voices and presently darted away, their pinions beating up into the blue air, higher and higher, growing tiny in the distance.

Lorn remained standing in the bow, watching until there was nothing left but empty sky.

'We'll raise Khondor soon,' said Jaxart and Carse turned to speak to him. Then some instinct made him look back, and he saw that Lorn was gone.

There was no sign of him in the water. He had gone overside without a word and he must have sunk like a drowning bird, pulled down by the weight of his useless wings.

Jaxart growled, 'It was his will and better so.' He cursed the Sarks and Carse smiled an ugly smile.

'Take heart,' he said, 'we may thrash them yet. How is it that Khondor has held out when Jekkara and Valkis fell?'

'Because not even the scientific weapons of the Sarks' evil allies, the Dhuvians, can touch us there. You'll understand why when you see Khondor.'

Before noon they sighted land, a rocky and forbidding coast. The cliffs rose sheer out of the sea and behind them forested mountains towered like a giant's wall. Here and there a narrow fiord sheltered a fishing village and an occasional lonely steading clung to the high pasture-land. Millions of sea birds nested on the rocks and the surf made a collar of white flame along the cliffs.

Carse sent Boghaz to the cabin for Ywain. She had remained there under guard and he had not seen her since the mutiny – except once.

It had been the first night after the mutiny. He had with Boghaz and Jaxart been examining the strange instruments that they had found in the inner cabin of the Dhuvian.

'These are Dhuvian weapons that only they know how to use,' Boghaz had declared. 'Now we know why Ywain had no escort ship. She needed none with a Dhuvian and his weapons aboard her galley.'

Jaxart looked at the things with loathing and fear. 'Science of the accursed Serpent! We should throw them after his body.'

'No,' Carse said, examining the things. 'If it were possible to discover the way in which these devices operate—'

He had soon found that it would not be possible without prolonged study. He knew science fairly well, yes. But it was the science of his own different world.

These instruments had been built out of a scientific knowledge alien in nearly every way to his own. The science of Rhiannon, of which these Dhuvian weapons represented but a small part!

Carse could recognise the little hypnosis machine that the Dhuvian had used upon him in the dark. A little metal wheel set with crystal stars, that revolved by a slight pressure of the fingers. And when he set it turning it whispered a singing note that so chilled his blood with memory that he hastily set the thing down.

The other Dhuvian instruments were even more incomprehensible. One consisted of a large lens surrounded by oddly asymmetrical crystal prisms. Another had a heavy metal base in which flat metal vibrators were mounted. He could only guess that these weapons exploited the laws of alien and subtle optical and sonic sciences.

'No man can understand the Dhuvian science,' muttered Jaxart. 'Not even the Sarks, who have alliance with the Serpent.'

He stared at the instruments with the half-superstitious hatred of a non-scientific folk for mechanical weapons.

'But perhaps Ywain, who is daughter of Sark's king, might know,' Carse speculated. 'It's worth trying.'

He went to the cabin where she was being guarded with that purpose in mind. Ywain sat there and she wore now the shackles he had worn.

He came in upon her suddenly, catching her as she sat with her head bowed and her shoulders bent in utter weariness. But at the sound of the door she straightened and watched him, level-eyed. He saw how white her face was and how the shadows lay in the hollows of the bones.

He did not speak for a long time. He had no pity for her. He looked at her, liking the taste of victory, liking the thought that he could do what he wanted with her.

When he asked her about the Dhuvian scientific weapons they had found Ywain laughed mirthlessly.

'You must be an ignorant barbarian indeed if you think the Dhuvians would instruct even me in their science. One of them came with me to overawe with those things the Jekkaran ruler, who was waxing rebellious. But S'San would not let me even touch those things.'

Carse believed her. It accorded with what Jaxart had said, that the Dhuvians jealously guarded their scientific weapons from even their allies, the Sarks.

'Besides,' Ywain said mockingly, 'why should Dhuvian science interest you if you hold the key to the far greater science locked in Rhiannon's tomb?'

'I do hold the key and that secret,' Carse told her and his answer took the mockery out of her face.

'What are you going to do with it?' she asked.

'On that,' Carse said grimly, 'my mind is clear. Whatever power that tomb gives me I'll use against Sark and Caer Dhu – and I hope it's enough to destroy you down to the last stone in your city!'

Ywain nodded. 'Well answered. And now what about me? Will you have me flogged and chained to an oar? Or will you kill me here?'

He shook his head slowly, answering her last question. 'I could have let my wolves tear you if I had wished you killed now.'

Her teeth showed briefly in what might have been a smile. 'Small satisfaction in that. Not like doing it with one's own hands.'

'I might have done that too, here in the cabin.'

'And you tried, yet did not. Well then – what?'

Carse did not answer. It came to him that, whatever he might do to her, she would still mock him to the very end. There was the steel of pride in this woman.

He had marked her though. The gash on her cheek would heal and fade but never vanish. She would never forget him as long as she lived. He was glad he had marked her.

'No answer?' she mocked. 'You're full of indecision for a conqeror.'

Carse went around the table to her with a pantherish step. He still did not answer her because he did not know. He only knew that he hated her as he had never hated anything in his life before. He bent over her, his face dead white, his hands open and hungry.

She reached up swiftly and found his throat. Her fingers were as strong as steel and the nails bit deep.

He caught her wrists and bent them away, the muscles of his arms standing out like ropes against her strength. She strove against him in silent fury and then suddenly she broke. Her lips parted as she strained for breath and Carse suddenly set his own lips against them.

There was no love, no tenderness in that kiss. It was a gesture of male contempt, brutal and full of hate. Yet for one strange moment— then her sharp teeth had met in his lower lip and his mouth was full of blood and she was laughing.

'You barbarian swine,' she whispered. 'Now my brand is on you.'

He stood looking at her. Then he reached out and caught her by the shoulders and the chair went over with a crash.

'Go ahead,' she said, 'if it pleases you.'

He wanted to break her between his two hands. He wanted...

He thrust her from him and went out and he had not passed the door since.

Now he fingered the new scar on his lip and watched her come onto the deck with Boghaz. She stood very straight in her jewelled hauberk but the lines around her mouth were deeper and her eyes, for all their bitter pride, were sombre.

He did not go to her. She was left alone with her guard, and

Carse could glance at her covertly. It was easy to guess what was in her mind. She was thinking how it felt to stand on the deck of her own ship, a prisoner. She was thinking that the brooding coast ahead was the end of all her voyaging. She was thinking that she was going to die.

The cry came down from the masthead – '*Khondor!*'

Carse saw at first only a great craggy rock that towered high above the surf, a sort of blunt cape between two fiords. Then, from that seemingly barren and uninhabitable place, Sky Folk came flying until the air throbbed with the beating of their wings. Swimmers came also, like a swarm of little comets that left trails of fire in the sea. And from the fiord-mouths came longships, smaller than the galley, swift as hornets, with shields along their sides.

The voyage was over. The black galley was escorted with cheers and shouting into Khondor.

Carse understood now what Jaxart had meant. Nature had made a virtually impregnable fortress out of the rock itself, walled in by impassable mountains from land attack, protected by unscalable cliffs from the sea, its only gateway the narrow twisting fiord on the north side. That too was guarded by ballistas which could make the fiord a death trap for any ship that entered it.

The tortuous channel widened at the end into a landlocked harbour that not even the winds could attack. Khond longships, fishing boats and a scattering of foreign craft filled the basin and the black galley glided like a queen among them.

The quays and the dizzy flight of steps that led up to the summit of the rock, connecting on the upper levels with tunnelled galleries, were thronged with the people of Khondor and the allied clans that had taken refuge with them. They were a hardy lot with a raffish sturdy look that Carse liked. The cliffs and the mountain peaks flung back their cheering in deafening echoes.

Under cover of the noise Boghaz said urgently to Carse for the hundredth time, 'Let me bargain with them for the secret! I can get us each a kingdom – more, if you will!'

And for the hundredth time, Carse answered, 'I have not said that I know the secret. If I do it is my own.'

Boghaz swore in an ecstasy of frustration and demanded of the gods what he had done to be thus hardly used.

Ywain's eyes turned upon the Earthman once and then away.

Swimmers in their gleaming hundreds, Sky Folk with their proud wings folded – for the first time Carse saw their women, creatures so exquisitely lovely that it hurt to look at them – the tall fair Khonds and the foreign stocks, a kaleidoscope of colours and glinting steel. Mooring lines snaked out, were caught and snubbed around the bollards. The galley came to rest.

Carse led his crew ashore and Ywain walked erect beside him, wearing her shackles as though they were golden ornaments she had chosen to become her.

There was a group standing apart on the quay, waiting. A handful of hard-bitten men who looked as though seawater ran in their veins instead of blood, tough veterans of many battles, some fierce and dark-visaged, some with ruddy laughing faces, one with cheek and sword-arm hideously burned and scarred.

Among them was a tall Khond with a look of harnessed lightning about him and hair the colour of new copper and by his side stood a girl dressed in a blue robe.

Her straight fair hair was bound back by a fillet of plain gold and between her breasts, left bare by the loose outer garment, a single black pearl glowed with lustrous darkness. Her left hand rested on the shoulder of Shallah the Swimmer.

Like all the rest the girl was paying more attention to Ywain than she was to Carse. He realised somewhat bitterly that the whole crowd had gathered less to see the unknown barbarian who had done it all than to see the daughter of Garach of Sark walking in chains.

The red-haired Khond remembered his manners enough to make the sign of peace and say, 'I am Rold of Khondor. We, the Sea Kings, make you welcome.' Carse responded but saw that already he was half forgotten in the man's savage pleasure at the plight of his arch-enemy.

They had much to say to each other, Ywain and the Sea Kings.

Carse looked again at the girl. He had heard Jaxart's eager greeting to her and knew now that she was Emer, Rold's sister.

He had never seen anyone like her before. There was a touch of the fey, of the elfin, about her, as though she lived in the human world by courtesy and could leave it any time she chose.

Her eyes were grey and sad, but her mouth was gentle and shaped for laughter. Her body had the same quick grace he had noticed in the Halflings and yet it was a very humanly lovely body.

She had pride, too – pride to match Ywain's own though they were so different. Ywain was all brilliance and fire and passion, a rose with blood-red petals. Carse understood her. He could play her own game and beat her at it.

But he knew that he would never understand Emer. She was part of all the things he had left behind him long ago. She was the lost music and the forgotten dreams, the pity and the tenderness, the whole shadowy world he had glimpsed in childhood but never since.

All at once she looked up and saw him. Her eyes met his – met and held, and would not go away. He saw their expression change. He saw every drop of colour drain from her face until it was like a mask of snow. He heard her say,

'*Who are you?*'

He bent his head. 'Lady Emer, I am Carse the barbarian.'

He saw how her fingers dug into Shallah's fur and he saw how the Swimmer watched him with her soft hostile gaze. Emer's voice answered, almost below the threshold of hearing.

'You have no name. You are as Shallah said – a stranger.'

Something about the way she said the word made it seem full of an eerie menace. And it was so uncannily close to the truth. He sensed suddenly that this girl had the same extra-sensory power as the Halflings, developed in her human brain to even greater strength.

But he forced a laugh. 'You must have many strangers in Khondor these days.' He glanced at the Swimmer. 'Shallah distrusts me, I don't know why. Did she tell you also that I carry a dark shadow with me wherever I go?'

'She did not need to tell me,' Emer whispered. 'Your face is only a mask and behind it is a darkness and a wish – and they are not of our world.'

She came to him with slow steps, as though drawn against her will. He could see the dew of sweat on her forehead, and abruptly he began to tremble himself, a shivering deep within him that was not of the flesh.

'I can see ... I can almost see ...'

He did not want her to say any more. He did not want to hear it.

'No!' he cried out. '*No!*'

She suddenly fell forward, her body heavy against him. He caught her and eased her down to the grey rock, where she lay in a dead faint.

He knelt helplessly beside her but Shallah said quietly, 'I will care for her.' He stood up and then Rold and the Sea Kings were around them like a ring of startled eagles.

'The seeing was upon her,' Shallah told them.

'But it has never taken her like this before,' Rold said worriedly. 'What happened? My thought was all on Ywain.'

'What happened is between the lady Emer and the stranger,' said Shallah. She picked up the girl in her strong arms and bore her away.

Carse felt that strange inner fear still chilling him. The 'seeing' they had called it. Seeing indeed, not of any supernatural kind, but of strong extra-sensory powers that had looked deep into his mind.

In sudden reaction of anger Carse said, 'A fine welcome! All of us brushed aside for a look at Ywain and then your sister faints at sight of me!'

'By the gods!' Rold groaned. 'Your pardon – we had not meant it so. As for my sister, she is too much with the Halflings and given as they are to dreams of the mind.'

He raised his voice. 'Ho, there, Ironbeard! Let us redeem our manners!'

The largest of the Sea Kings, a grizzled giant with a laugh like the north wind, came forward and before Carse realised their intention they had tossed him onto their shoulders and marched with him up the quays where everyone could see him.

'Hark, you!' Rold bellowed. '*Hark!*'

The crowd quieted at his voice.

'Here is Carse, the barbarian. He took the galley – he captured Ywain – he slew the Serpent! How do you greet him?'

Their greeting nearly brought down the cliffs. The two big men bore Carse up the steps and would not put him down. The people of Khondor streamed after them, accepting the men of his crew as their brothers. Carse caught a glimpse of Boghaz, his face one vast porcine smile, holding a giggling girl in each arm.

Ywain walked alone in the centre of a guard of the Sea Kings. The scarred man watched her with a brooding madness in his unwinking eyes.

Rold and Ironbeard dumped Carse to his feet at the summit, panting.

'You're a heavyweight, my friend,' gasped Rold, grinning. 'Now – does our penance satisfy you?'

Carse swore, feeling shamefaced. Then he stared in wonder at the city of Khondor.

A monolithic city, hewn in the rock itself. The crest had been split, apparently by diastrophic convulsions in the remoter ages of Mars. All along the inner cliffs of the split were doorways and the openings of galleries, a perfect honeycomb of dwellings and giddy flights of steps.

Those who had been too old or disabled to climb the long way down to the harbour cheered them now from the galleries or from the narrow streets and squares.

The sea wind blew keen and cold at this height, so that there was always a throb and a wail in the streets of Khond, mingling with the booming voices of the waves below. From the upper crags there was a coming and going of the Sky Folk, who seemed to like the high places as though the streets cramped them. Their fledglings tossed on the wind, swooping and tumbling in their private games, with bursts of elfin laughter.

Landward Carse looked down upon green fields and pasture land, locked tight in the arms of the mountains. It seemed as though this place could withstand a siege forever.

They went along the rocky ways with the people of Khondor pouring after them, filling the eyrie-city with shouts and laughter. There was a large square, with two squat strong porticoes facing each other across it. One had carven pillars before it, dedicated to the God of Waters and the God of the Four Winds. Before the other a golden banner whipped, broidered with the eagle badge of Khondor.

At the threshold of the palace Ironbeard clapped the Earthman on the shoulder, a staggering buffet.

'There'll be heavy talk along with the feasting of the Council tonight. But we have plenty of time to get decently drunk before that. How say you?'

And Carse said, 'Lead on!'

11
DREAD ACCUSATION

That night torches lighted the banquet hall with a smoky glare. Fires burned on round hearths between the pillars, which were hung with shields and the ensigns of many ships. The whole vast room was hollowed out of the living rock with galleries that gave upon the sea.

Long tables were set out. Servants ran among them with flagons of wine and smoking joints fresh from the fires. Carse had nobly followed the lead of Ironbeard all afternoon and to his somewhat unsteady sight it seemed that all of Khondor was feasting there to the wild music of harps and the singing of the skalds.

He sat with the Sea Kings and the leaders of the Swimmers and the Sky Folk on the raised dais at the north end of the hall. Ywain was there also. They had made her stand and she had remained motionless for hours, giving no sign of weakness, her head still high. Carse admired her. He liked it in her that she was still the proud Ywain.

Around the curving wall had been set the figureheads of ships taken in war so that Carse felt surrounded by shadowy looming monsters that quivered on the brink of life with the torchlight picking glints from a jewelled eye or a gilded talon, momentarily lighting a carven face half ripped away by a ram.

Emer was nowhere in the hall.

Carse's head rang with the wine and the talking and there was a mounting excitement in him. He fondled the hilt of the sword of Rhiannon where it lay between his knees. Presently, presently, it would be time.

Rold set his drinking-horn down with a bang.

'Now,' he said, 'let's get to business.' He was a trifle thick-tongued, as they all were, but fully in command of himself. 'And the business, my lords? Why, a very pleasant one.' He laughed. 'One we've thought on for a long time, all of us – the death of Ywain of Sark!'

Carse stiffened. He hadn't been expecting that. 'Wait! She's my captive.'

They all cheered him at that and drank his health again, all except Thorn of Tarak, the man with the useless arm and the twisted cheek, who had sat silent all evening, drinking steadily but not getting drunk.

'Of course,' said Rold. 'Therefore the choice is yours.' He turned to look at Ywain with pleasant speculation. 'How shall she die?'

'Die?' Carse got to his feet. 'What is this talk of Ywain dying?'

They stared at him rather stupidly, too astonished for the moment to believe that they had heard him right. Ywain smiled grimly.

'But why else did you bring her here?' demanded Ironbeard. 'The sword is too clean a death or you would have slain her on the galley. Surely you gave her to us for our vengeance?'

'I have not given her to anyone!' Carse shouted. 'I say she is mine and I say she is not to be killed!'

There was a stunned pause. Ywain's eyes met the Earthman's, bright with mockery. Then Thorn of Tarak said one word, '*Why?*'

He was looking straight at Carse now with his dark mad eyes and the Earthman found his question hard to answer.

'Because her life is worth too much, as a hostage. Are you

babes, that you can't see that? Why, you could buy the release of every Khond slave – perhaps even bring Sark to terms!'

Thorn laughed. It was not pleasant laughter.

The leader of the Swimmers said, 'My people would not have it so.'

'Nor mine,' said the winged man.

'Nor mine!' Rold was on his feet now, flushed with anger. 'You're an outlander, Carse. Perhaps you don't understand how things are with us!'

'No,' said thorn of Tarak softly. 'Give her back. She, that learned kindness at Garach's knee, and drank wisdom from the teachers of Caer Dhu. Set her free again to mark others with her blessing as she marked me when she burned my longship.' His eyes burned into the Earthman. 'Let her live – because the barbarian loves her.'

Carse stared at him. He knew vaguely that the Sea Kings tensed forward, watching him – the nine chiefs of war with the eyes of tigers, their hands already on their sword-hilts. He knew that Ywain's lips curved as though at some private jest. And he burst out laughing.

He roared with it. 'Look you!' he cried, and turned his back so that they might see the scars of the lash. 'Is that a love-note Ywain has written on my hide? And if it were – it was no song of passion the Dhuvian was singing me when I slew him!'

He swung round again, hot with wine, flushed with the power he knew he had over them.

'Let any man of you say that again and I'll take the head from his shoulders. Look at you. Great nidderings, quarrelling over a wench's life! Why don't you gather, all of you, and make an assault on Sark!'

There was a great clatter and scraping of feet as they rose, howling at him in their rage at his impudence, bearded chins thrust forward, knotty fists hammering on the boat.

'What do you take yourself for, you pup of the sandhills?' Rold shouted. 'Have you never heard of the Dhuvians and their weapons, who are Sark's allies? How many Khonds do you think have died these long years past, trying to face those weapons?'

'But suppose,' asked Carse, 'you had weapons of your own?'

Something in his voice penetrated even to Rold, who scowled at him. 'If you have a meaning, speak it plainly!'

'Sark could not stand against you,' Carse said, 'if you had the weapons of Rhiannon.'

Ironbeard snorted. 'Oh, aye, the Cursed One! Find his Tomb and the powers in its and we'll follow you to Sark, fast enough.'

'Then you have pledged yourselves,' Carse said and held the sword aloft. 'Look there! Look well – does any man among you know enough to recognise this blade?'

Thorn of Tarak reached out his one good hand and drew the sword closer that he might study it. Then his hand began to tremble. He looked up at the others and said in a strange awed voice, 'It is the sword of Rhiannon.'

A harsh sibilance of indrawn breath and then Carse spoke.

'There is my proof. I hold the secret of the Tomb.'

Silence. Then a guttural sound from Ironbeard and after that, mounting, wild excitement that burst and spread like flame.

'He knows the secret! By the gods *he knows!*'

'Would you face the Dhuvian weapons if you had the greater powers of Rhiannon?' Carse asked.

There was such a crazy clamour of excitement that it took moments for Rold's voice to be heard. The tall Khond's face was half doubtful.

'Could we use Rhiannon's weapons of power if we had them? We can't even understand the Dhuvian weapons you captured in the galley.'

'Give me time to study and test them and I'll solve the way of using Rhiannon's instruments of power,' Carse replied confidently.

He was sure that he could. It would take time but he was sure that his own knowledge of science was sufficient to decipher the operation of at least some of those weapons of an alien science.

He swung the great sword high, glittering in the red light of the torches, and his voice rang out, 'And if I arm you thus will you make good your word? Will you follow me to Sark?'

All doubts were swept away by the challenge, by the heaven-sent opportunity to strike at last at Sark on at least even terms.

The answer of the Sea Kings roared out. 'We'll follow!'

It was then that Carse saw Emer. She had come onto the dais by some inner passage, standing now between two brooding giant figureheads crusted with the memory of the sea, and her eyes were fixed on Carse, wide and full of horror.

Something about her compelled them, even in that moment, to turn and stare. She stepped out into the open space above the table. She wore only a loose white robe and her hair was unbound. It was as though she had just risen from sleep and was walking still in the midst of a dream.

But it was an evil dream. The weight of it crushed her, so that her steps were slow and her breathing laboured and even these fighting men felt the touch of it on their own hearts.

Emer spoke and her words were very clear and measured.

'I saw this before when the stranger first came before me, but my strength failed me and I could not speak. Now I shall tell you. You must destroy this man. He is danger, he is darkness, he is death for us all!'

Ywain stiffened, her eyes narrowing. Carse felt her glance on him, intense with interest. But his attention was all on Emer. As on the quay he was filled with a strange terror that had nothing to do with ordinary fear, an unexplainable dread of this girl's strong extra-sensory powers.

Rold broke in and Carse got a grip on himself. Fool, he thought, to be upset by woman's talk, woman's imaginings …

'—the secret of the Tomb!' Rold was saying. 'Did you not hear? He can give us the power of Rhiannon!'

'Aye,' said Emer sombrely. 'I heard and I believe. He knows well the hidden place of the Tomb and he knows the weapons that are there.'

She moved closer, looking up at Carse where he stood in the torchlight, the sword in his hands. She spoke now directly to him.

'Why should you not know, who have brooded there so long in the darkness? Why should you not know, who made those powers of evil with your own hands?'

Was it the heat and the wine that made the rock walls reel and put the cold sickness in his belly? He tried to speak and only a hoarse sound came, without words. Emer's voice went on, relentless, terrible.

'*Why should you not know – you who are the Cursed One, Rhiannon!*'

The rock walls gave back the word like a whispered curse, until the hall was filled with the ghostly name *Rhiannon!* It seemed to Carse that the very shields rang with it and the banners trembled. And still the girl stood unmoving, challenging him to speak, and his tongue was dead and dry in his mouth.

They stared at him, all of them – Ywain and the Sea Kings and the feasters silent amid the spilled wine and the forgotten banquet.

It was as though he were Lucifer fallen, crowned with all the wickedness of the world.

Then Ywain laughed, a sound with an odd note of triumph in it. 'So that is why! I see it now – why you called upon the Cursed One in the cabin there, when you stood against the power of Caer Dhu that no man can resist, and slew S'San.'

Her voice rang out mockingly. 'Hail, Lord Rhiannon!'

That broke the spell. Carse said, 'You lying vixen. You salve your pride with that. No mere man could down Ywain of Sark but a god – that's different.'

He shouted at them all. 'Are you fools or children that you listen to such madness? You, there, Jaxart – you toiled beside me at the oar. Does a god bleed under the lash like a common slave?'

Jaxart said slowly, 'That first night in the galley I heard you cry Rhiannon's name.'

Carse swore. He rounded on the Sea Kings. 'You're warriors, not serving-maids. Use your wits. Has my body mouldered in a tomb for ages? Am I a dead thing walking?'

Out of the tail of his eyes he saw Boghaz moving toward the dais and here and there the drunken devils of the galley's crew were rising also, loosening their swords, to rally to him.

Rold put his hands on Emer's shoulders and said sternly, 'What say you to this, my sister?'

'I have not spoken of the body,' Emer answered, 'only of the mind. The mind of the mighty Cursed One could live on and on. It did live and now it has somehow entered into this barbarian, dwelling here as a snail lies curled within its shell.'

She turned again to Carse. 'In yourself you are alien and strange and for that alone I would fear you because I do not understand. But for that alone I would not wish you dead. But I say that Rhiannon watches through your eyes and speaks with your tongue, that in your hands are his sword and sceptre. And therefore I ask your death.'

Carse said harshly, 'Will you listen to this crazy child?'

But he saw the deep doubt in their faces. The superstitious fools! There was real danger here.

Carse looked at his gathering men, figuring his chances of fighting clear if he had to. he mentally cursed the yellow-haired witch who had spoken this incredible, impossible madness.

Madness, yes. And yet the quivering fear in his own heart had crystalized into a single stabbing shaft.

'If I were possessed,' he snarled, 'would I not be the first to know?'

'*Would I not?*' echoed the question in Carse's brain. And memories came rushing back – the nightmare darkness of the Tomb, where he had seemed to feel an eager alien presence, and the dreams and the half-remembered knowledge that was not his own. It was not true. It could not be true. He would not let it be true.

Boghaz came up onto the dais. He gave Carse one queer shrewd glance but when he spoke to the Sea Kings his manner was smoothly diplomatic.

'No doubt the Lady Emer has wisdom far beyond mine and I mean her no disrespect. However, the barbarian is my friend and I speak from my own knowledge. He is what he says, no more and no less.'

The men of the galley crew growled a warning assent to that.

Boghaz continued. 'Consider, my lords. Would Rhiannon slay a Dhuvian and make war on the Sark? Would he offer victory to Khondor?'

'No!' said Ironbeard. 'By the gods, he wouldn't. He was all for the Serpent's spawn.'

Emer spoke, demanding their attention. 'My lords, have I ever lied or advised you wrongly?'

They shook their heads and Rold said, 'No. But your word is not enough in this.'

'Very well, forget my word. There is a way to prove whether or not he is Rhiannon. Let him pass the testing before the Wise Ones.'

Rold pulled at his beard, scowling. Then he nodded. 'Wisely said,' he agreed and the others joined in.

'Aye – let it be proved.'

Rold turned to Carse. 'You will submit?'

'No,' Carse answered furiously. 'I will not. To the devil with all such superstitious flummery! If my offer of the Tomb isn't enough to convince you of where I stand – why, you can do without it and without me.'

Rold's face hardened. 'No harm will come to you. If you're not Rhiannon you have nothing to fear. Again, will you submit?'

'*No!*'

He began to stride back along the table toward his men, who were already bunched together like wolves snarling for a fight. But Thorn of Tarak caught his ankle as he passed and brought him down and the men of Khondor swarmed over the galley's crew, disarming them before any blood was shed.

Carse struggled like a wildcat among the Sea Kings, in a brief passion of fury that lasted until Ironbeard struck him regretfully on the head with a brass-bound drinking horn.

12
THE CURSED ONE

The darkness lifted slowly. Carse was conscious first of sounds – the suck and sigh of water close at hand, the muffled roaring of surf beyond a wall of rock. Otherwise it was still and heavy.

Light came next, a suffused soft glow. When he opened his eyes he saw high above him a rift of stars and below that was arching rock, crusted with crystalline deposits that gave back a gentle gleaming.

He was in a sea cave, a grotto floored with a pool of milky flame. As his sight cleared he saw that there was a ledge on the opposite side of the pool, with steps leading down from above. The Sea Kings stood there with shackled Ywain and Boghaz and the chief men of the Swimmers and the Sky Folk. All watched him and none spoke.

Carse found that he was bound upright to a thin spire of rock, quite alone.

Emer stood before him, waist deep in the pool. The black pearl gleamed between her breasts, and the bright water ran like a spilling of diamonds from her hair. In her hands she held a great rough jewel, dull grey in colour and cloudy as though it slept.

When she saw that his eyes were open she said clearly, 'Come, oh my masters! It is time.'

A regretful sigh murmured through the grotto. The surface of the pool was disturbed with a trembling of phosphorescence and the waters parted smoothly as three shapes swam slowly to Emer's side. They were the heads of three Swimmers, white with age.

Their eyes were the most awful things that Carse had ever seen. For they were young with an alien sort of youth that was not of the body and in them was a wisdom and a strength that frightened him.

He strained against his bonds, still half dazed from Ironbeard's blow, and he heard above him a rustling as of great birds roused from slumber.

Looking up he saw on the shadowy ledges three brooding figures, the old, old eagles of the Sky Folk with tired wings, and in their faces too was the light of wisdom divorced from flesh.

He found his tongue, then. He raged and struggled to be free and his voice had a hollow empty sound in the quiet vault and they did not answer and his bonds were tight.

He realized at last that it was no use. He leaned, breathless and shaken, against the spire of rock.

A harsh cracked whisper came then from the ledge above. 'Little sister – lift up the stone of thought.'

Emer raised the cloudy jewel in her hands.

It was an eerie thing to watch. Carse did not understand at first. Then he saw that as the eyes of Emer and the Wise Ones grew dim and veiled the cloudy grey of the jewel cleared and brightened.

It seemed that all the power of their minds was pouring into the focal point of the crystal, blending through it into one strong beam. And he felt the pressure of those gathered minds upon his own mind!

Carse sensed dimly what they were doing. The thoughts of the conscious mind were a tiny electric pulsation through the neurones. That electric pulse could be dampened, neutralised, by a stronger counter-impulse such as they were focusing on him through that electro-sensitive crystal.

They themselves could not know the basic science behind their attack upon his mind! These Halflings, strong in extra-sensory powers, had perhaps long ago discovered that the crystals could focus their minds together and had used the discovery without ever knowing its scientific basis.

'But I can hold them off,' Carse whispered thickly to himself. 'I can hold them all off!'

It enraged him, that calm impersonal beating down of his mind. He fought it with all the force within him, but it was not enough.

And then, as before when he had faced the singing stars of the Dhuvian, some force in him that did not seem his own came to aid him.

It built a barrier against the Wise Ones and held it, held it until Carse moaned in agony. Sweat ran down his face and his body writhed and he knew dimly that he was going to die, that he couldn't stand any more.

His mind was like a closed room that is suddenly burst open by contending winds that turn over the piled-up memories and shake the dusty dreams and reveal everything, even in the darkest corners.

All except one. One place where the shadow was solid and impenetrable, and would not be dispersed.

The jewel blazed between Emer's hands. And there was a stillness like the silence in the spaces between the stars.

Emer's voice rang clear across it.

'Rhiannon, *speak!*'

The dark shadow that Carse felt laired in his mind quivered, stirred but gave no other sign. He felt that it waited and watched.

The silence pulsed. Across the pool, the watchers on the ledge moved uneasily.

Boghaz's voice came querulously, 'It is madness! How can this barbarian be the Cursed One of long ago?'

But Emer paid no heed and the jewel in her hands blazed higher and higher.

'The Wise Ones have strength, Rhiannon! They can break this man's mind. They *will* break it unless you speak!'

And, savagely triumphant now, 'What will you do then? Creep into another man's brain and body? You cannot, Rhiannon. For you would have so ere now if you could!'

Across the pool Ironbeard said hoarsely, 'I do not like this!'

But Emer went mercilessly on and now her voice seemed the only thing in Carse's universe – relentless, terrible.

'The man's mind is cracking, Rhiannon. A minute more – a minute more, and your only instrument becomes a helpless idiot. Speak now, if you would save him!'

Her voice rang and echoed from the vaulting rock of the cavern and the jewel in her hands was a living flame of force.

Carse felt the agony that convulsed that crouching shadow in his mind – agony of doubt, of fear—

And then suddenly that dark shadow seemed to explode through all Carse's brain and body, to possess him utterly in every atom. And he heard his own voice, alien in tone and timbre, shouting, '*Let the man's mind live! I will speak!*'

The thunderous echoes of that terrible cry died slowly and in the pregnant hush that followed Emer gave back one step and then another, as though her very flesh recoiled.

The jewel in her hands dimmed suddenly. Fiery ripples broke and fled as the Swimmers shrank away and the wings of the Sky Folk clashed against the rock. In the eyes of all of them was the light of realization and of fear.

From the rigid figures that watched across the water, from Rold and the Sea Kings, came a shivering sigh that was a name.

'Rhiannon! The Cursed One!'

It came to Carse that even Emer, who had dared to force into the open the hidden thing she had sensed in his mind, was afraid of the thing now that she had evoked it.

And he, Matthew Carse, was afraid. He had known fear before. But even the terror he had felt when he faced the Dhuvian was as nothing to this blind shuddering agony. Dreams, illusions, the figments of an obsessed mind – he had tried to believe that that was what these hints of strangeness were. But not now. Not now! He knew the truth and it was a terrible thing to know.

'It proves nothing!' Boghaz was wailing insistently. 'You have hypnotized him, made him admit the impossible.'

'It is Rhiannon,' whispered one of the Swimmers. She raised her white-furred shoulders from the water, her ancient hands lifted. 'It is Rhiannon in the stranger's body.'

And then, in a chilling cry, 'Kill the man before the Cursed One uses him to destroy us all!'

A hellish clamour broke instantly from the echoing walls as an ancient dread screamed from human and Halfling throats.

'*Kill him! Kill!*'

Carse, helpless himself but one in feeling with the dark thing within him, felt that dark one's wild anxiety. He heard the ringing voice that was not his own shouting out above the clamour.

'*Wait!* You are afraid because I am Rhiannon! But I have not come back to harm you!'

'Why have you come back then?' whispered Emer.

She was looking into Carse's face. And by her dilated eyes Carse knew that his face must be strange and awful to look upon.

Through Carse's lips, Rhiannon answered, 'I have come to redeem my sin – I swear it!'

Emer's white, shaken face flashed burning hate. 'Oh, father

of lies! Rhiannon, who brought evil on our world by giving the Serpent power, who was condemned and punished for his crime – Rhiannon, the Cursed One, turned saint!'

She laughed, a bitter laughter born of hate and fear, that was picked up by the Swimmers and the Sky Folk.

'For your own sake you must believe me!' raged the voice of Rhiannon. 'Will you not even listen?'

Carse felt the passion of the dark being who had used him in this unholy fashion. He was one with that alien heart that was violent and bitter and yet lonely – lonely as no other could understand the word.

'Listen to Rhiannon?' cried Emer. 'Did the Quiru listen long ago? They judged you for your sin!'

'Will you deny me the chance to redeem myself?' The Cursed One's tone was almost pleading. 'Can you not understand that this man Carse is my only chance to undo what I did?'

His voice rushed on, urgent, eager. 'For an age, I lay fixed and frozen in an imprisonment that not even the pride of Rhiannon could withstand. I realised my sin. I wished only to undo it but could not.

'Then into my tomb and prison from outside came this man Carse. I fitted the immaterial electric web of my mind into his brain. I could not dominate him, for his brain was alien and different. But I could influence him a little and I thought that I could act through him.

'For *his* body was not bound in that place. In him my mind at least could leave it. And in him I left it, not daring to let even him know that I was within his brain.

'I thought that through him I might find a way to crush the Serpent whom I raised from the dust to my sorrow long ago.'

Rold's shaking voice cut across the passionate pleading that came from Carse's lips. There was a wild look on the Khond's face.

'Emer, let the Cursed One speak no longer! Lift the spell of your minds from the man!'

'Lift the spell!' echoed Ironbeard hoarsely.

'Yes,' whispered Emer. 'Yes.'

*

Once again the jewel was raised and now the Wise Ones gathered all their strength, spurred by the terror that was on them. The electro-sensitive crystal blazed and it seemed to Carse like bale-fire searing his mind. For Rhiannon fought against it, fought with the desperation of madness.

'You must listen! You must believe!'

'No!' said Emer. 'Be silent! Release the man or he will die!'

One last wild protest, broken short by the iron purpose of the Wise Ones. A moment of hesitation – a stab of pain too deep for human understanding – and then the barrier was gone.

The alien presence, the unholy sharing of the flesh, were gone and the mind of Matthew Carse closed over the shadow and hid it. The voice of Rhiannon was stilled.

Like a dead man Carse sagged against his bonds. The light went out of the crystal. Emer let her hands fall. her head bent forward so that her bright hair veiled her face and the Wise Ones covered their faces also and remained motionless. The Sea Kings, Ywain, even Boghaz, were held speechless, like men who have narrowly escaped destruction and only realise later how close death has come.

Carse moaned once. For a long time that and his harsh gasping breathing were the only sounds.

Then Emer said, 'The man must die.'

There was nothing in her now but weariness and a grim truth. Carse heard dimly Rold's heavy answer.

'Aye. There is no other way.'

Boghaz would have spoken but they silenced him.

Carse said thickly, 'It isn't true. Such things can't be.'

Emer raised her head and looked at him. Her attitude had changed. She seemed now to have no fear of Carse himself, only pity for him.

'Yet you know that it is true.'

Carse was silent. He knew.

'You have done no wrong, stranger,' she said. 'In your mind I saw many things that are strange to me, much that I cannot understand, but there was no evil there. Yet Rhiannon lives in you and we dare not let him live.'

'But he can't control me!' Carse made an effort to stand,

lifting his head so that he should be heard, for his voice was drained of strength like his body.

'You heard him admit that himself. He cannot dominate me. My will is my own.'

Ywain said slowly, 'What of S'San, and the sword? It is not the mind of Carse the barbarian that controlled you then.'

'He cannot master you,' said Emer, 'except when the barriers of your own mind weaken under stress. Great fear or pain or weariness – perhaps even the unconsciousness of sleep or wine – might give the Cursed One his chance and then it would be too late.'

Rold said, 'We dare not take the risk.'

'But I can give you the secret of Rhiannon's Tomb!' cried Carse.

He saw that thought begin to work in their minds and he went on, the ghastly unfairness of the whole thing acting as a spur.

'Do you call this justice, you men of Khondor who cry out against the Sarks. Will you condemn me when you know I'm innocent? Are you such cowards that you'll doom your people to live forever under the dragon's claw because of a shadow out of the past?

'Let me lead you to the Tomb. Let me give you victory. That will prove I have no part with Rhiannon!'

Boghaz's mouth fell open in horror. 'No, Carse, no! Don't *give* it to them!'

Rold shouted, 'Silence!'

Ironbeard laughed grimly. 'Let the Cursed One lay hands upon his weapons?' That would be madness indeed!'

'Very well,' said Carse. 'Let Rold go. I'll map the way for him. Keep me here. Guard me. That should be safe enough. You can kill me swiftly if Rhiannon takes control of me.'

He caught them with that. The only thing greater than their hate and dread of the Cursed One was their burning desire for the legendary weapons of power that might in time mean victory and freedom for Khondor.

They pondered, doubtful, hesitating. But he knew their decision even before Rold turned and said, 'We accept, Carse.

It would be safer to slay you out of hand but – we need those weapons.'

Carse felt the cold presence of imminent death withdraw a little. He warned, 'It won't be easy. The Tomb is near Jekkara.'

Ironbeard asked, 'What of Ywain?'

'Death and at once!' said Thorn of Tarak harshly.

Ywain stood silent, looking at them all with cool, careless unconcern.

But Emer interposed. 'Rold goes into danger. Until he returns safely let Ywain be kept in case we need a hostage for him.'

It was only now that Carse saw Boghaz in the shadows, shaking his head in misery, tears running down his fat cheeks.

'He *gives* them a secret worth a kingdom!' wailed Boghaz. 'I have been robbed!'

13
CATASTROPHE

The days that followed after that were long strange days for Matthew Carse. He drew a map from memory of the hills above Jekkara and the place of the Tomb and Rold studied it until he knew it as he knew his own courtyard. Then the parchment was burned.

Rold took one longship and a picked crew, and left Khondor by night. Jaxart went with him. Everyone knew the dangers of that voyage. But one swift ship, with Swimmers to scout the way, might elude the Sark patrols. They would beach in a hidden cove Jaxart knew of, west of Jekkara, and go the rest of the way overland.

'If aught goes wrong on the return,' Rold said grimly, 'we'll sink our ship at once.'

After the longship sailed there was nothing to do but wait.

Carse was never alone. He was given three small rooms in a disused part of the palace and guards were with him always.

A corroding fear crept in his mind, no matter how he fought

it down. He caught himself listening for an inner voice to speak, watching for some small sign or gesture that was not his own. The horror of the ordeal in the place of the Wise Ones had left its mark. He knew now. And, knowing, he could never for one moment forget.

It was not fear of death that oppressed him, though he was human and did not want to die. It was dread of living again through that moment when he had ceased to be himself, when his mind and body were possessed in every cell by the invader. Worse than the dread of madness was the uncanny fear of Rhiannon's domination.

Emer came again and again to talk with him and study him. He knew she was watching him for signs of Rhiannon's resurgence. But as long as she smiled he knew that he was safe.

She would not look into his mind again. But she referred once to what she had seen there.

'You come from another world,' she said with quiet sureness. 'I think I knew that when first I saw you. The memories of it were in your mind – a desolate, desert place, very strange and sad.'

They were on his tiny balcony, high under the crest of the rock, and the wind blew clean and strong down from the green forests.

Carse nodded. 'A bitter world. But it had its own beauty.'

'There is beauty even in death,' said Emer, 'but I am glad to be alive.'

'Let's forget that other place, then. Tell me of this one that lives so strongly. Rold said you were much with the Halflings.'

She laughed. 'He chides me sometimes, saying that I am a changeling and not human at all.'

'You don't look human now,' Carse told her, 'with the moonlight on your face and your hair all tangled with it.'

'Sometimes I wish it were true. You have never been to the Isles of the Sky Folk?'

'No.'

'They're like castles rising from the sea, almost as tall as Khondor. When the Sky Folk take me there I feel the lack of wings, for I must be carried or remain on the ground while they soar and swoop around me. It seems to me then that flying is the most beautiful thing in the world and I weep because I can never know it.

'But when I go with the Swimmers I am happier. My body is much like theirs though never quite so fleet. And it is wonderful – oh, wonderful – to plunge down into the glowing water and see the gardens that they keep, with the strange sea-flowers bowing to the tide and the little bright fish darting like birds among them.

'And their cities, silver bubbles in the shallow ocean. The heavens there are all glowing fire, bright gold when the sun shines, silver at night. It is always warm and the air is still and there are little ponds where the babies play, learning to be strong for the open sea.

'I have learned much from the Halflings,' she finished.

'But the Dhuvians are Halflings too?' Carse said.

Emer shivered. 'The Dhuvians are the oldest of the Halfling races. There are but few of them now and those all dwell at Caer Dhu.'

Carse asked suddenly, 'You have Halfling wisdom – is there no way to be rid of the monstrous thing within me?'

She answered sombrely, 'Not even the Wise Ones have learned that much.'

The Earthman's fists closed savagely on the rock of the gallery.

'It would have been better if you'd killed me there in the cave!'

Emer put her gentle hand on his and said, 'There is always time for death.'

After she left him Carse paced the floor for hours, wanting the release of wine and not daring to take it, afraid to sleep. When exhaustion took him at last, his guards strapped him to his bed and one stood by with a drawn sword and watched, ready to wake him instantly if he should seem to dream.

And he did dream. Sometimes they were nothing more than nightmares born of his own anguish, and sometimes the dark whisper of an alien voice came gliding into his mind, saying, '*Do not be afraid. Let me speak, for I must tell you.*'

Many times Carse awoke with the echo of his screaming in his ears, and the sword's point at his throat.

'*I mean no harm or evil. I can stop your fears if you will only listen!*'

Carse wondered which he would do first – go mad or fling himself from the balcony into the sea.

Boghaz clung closer to him than ever. He seemed fascinated by the thing that lurked in Carse. He was awed too but not too much awed to be furious over the disposal of the Tomb.

'I told you to let me bargain for it!' he would say. 'The greatest source of power on Mars and you give it away! *Give* it without even exacting a promise that they won't kill you when they get it.'

His fat hands made a gesture of finality. 'I repeat, you have robbed me, Carse. Robbed me of my kingdom.'

And Carse, for once, was glad of the Valkisian's effrontery because it kept him from being alone. Boghaz would sit, drinking enormous quantities of wine, and every so often he would look at Carse and chuckle.

'People always said that I had a devil in me. But you, Carse – you have *the* devil in you!'

'*Let me speak, Carse, and I will make you understand!*'

Carse grew gaunt and hollow-eyed. His face twitched and his hands were unsteady.

Then the news came, brought by a winged man who flew exhausted into Khondor.

It was Emer who told Carse what had happened. She did not really need to. The moment he saw her face, white as death, he knew.

'Rold never reached the Tomb,' she said. 'A Sark patrol caught them on the outward voyage. They say Rold tried to slay himself to keep the secret safe but he was prevented. They have taken him to Sark.'

'But the Sarks don't even know that he has the secret,' Carse protested, clutching at that straw, and Emer shook her head.

'They're not fools. They'll want to know the plans of

Khondor and why he was bound toward Jekkara with a single ship. They'll have the Dhuvians question him.'

Carse realised sickly what that meant. The Dhuvians' hypnotic science had almost conquered his own stubbornly alien brain. It would soon suck all Rold's secrets out of him.

'Then there is no hope?'

'No hope,' said Emer. 'Not now nor ever again.'

They were silent for a while. The wind moaned in the gallery, and the waved rolled in solemn thunder against the cliffs below.

Carse said, 'What will be done now?'

'The Sea Kings have sent word through all the free coasts and isles. Every ship and every man is gathering here now and Ironbeard will lead them on to Sark.

'There is a little time. Even when the Dhuvians have the secret it will take them time to go to the Tomb and bring the weapons back and learn their use. If we can crush Sark before then...'

'*Can* you crush Sark?' asked Carse.

She answered honestly. 'No. The Dhuvians will intervene and even the weapons they already have will turn the scale against us.

'But we must try and die trying, for it will be a better death than the one that will come after when Sark and the Serpent level Khondor into the sea.'

He stood looking down at her and it seemed to him that no moment of his life had been more bitter than this.

'Will the Sea Kings take me with them?' Stupid question. He knew the answer before she gave it to him.

'They are saying now that this was all a trick of Rhiannon's, misleading Rold to get the secret into Caer Dhu. I have told them it was not so but—'

She made a small gesture and turned her head away. 'Ironbeard, I think, believes me. He will see that your death is swift and clean.'

After a while Carse said, 'And Ywain?'

Thorn of Tarak has arranged that. Her they will take with them to Sark, lashed to the bow of the leader's ship.'

There was another silence. It seemed to Carse that the very air was heavy, so that it weighed upon his heart.

He found that Emer had left silently. He turned and went out onto the little gallery, where he stood staring down at the sea.

'Rhiannon,' he whispered, 'I curse you. I curse the day I came to Khondor with the promise of your tomb.'

The light was fading. The sea was like a bath of blood in the sunset. The wind brought him broken shouts and cries from the city and far below longships raced into the fiord.

Carse laughed mirthlessly. 'You've got what you wanted,' he told the Presence within him, 'but you won't enjoy it long!' Small triumph.

The strain of the past few days and this final shock were too much for any man to take. Carse sat down on the carven bench and put his head between his hands and stayed that way, too weary even for emotion. The voice of the dark invader whispered in his brain and for the first time Carse was too numb to fight it down.

'*I might have saved you this if you had listened. Fools and children, all of you, that you would not listen!*'

'Very well then – speak,' Carse muttered heavily. 'The evil is done now and Ironbeard will be here soon. I give you leave, Rhiannon. Speak.'

And he did, flooding Carse's mind with the voice of thought, raging like a storm wind trapped in a narrow vault, desperate, pleading.

'*If you'll trust me, Carse, I could still save Khondor. Lend me your body, let me use it—*'

'I'm not far gone enough for that, even now.'

'*Gods above!*' Rhiannon's thought raged. '*And there's so little time—*'

Carse could sense how he fought to master his fury and when the thought-voice came again it was controlled and quiet with a terrible sincerity.

'*I told the truth in the grotto. You were in my tomb, Carse. How long do you think I could lie there alone in the dreadful darkness outside space and time and not be changed? I'm no god! Whatever you may call us now we Quiru were never gods – only a race of men who came before the other men.*

'*They call me evil, the Cursed One – but I was not! Vain and proud, yes, and a fool, but not wicked in intent. I taught the Serpent Folk because they were clever and flattered me – and when they used my teaching to work evil I tried to stop them and failed because they had learned defences from me and even my power could not reach them in Caer Dhu.*

'*Therefore my brother Quiru judged me. They condemned me to remain imprisoned beyond space and time, in the place which they prepared, as long as the fruits of my sin endured in this world. Then they left me.*

'*We were the last of our race. There was nothing to hold them here, nothing they could do. They wanted only peace and learning. So they went away along the path they had chosen. And I waited. Can you think what that waiting must have been?*'

'I think you deserved it,' Carse said thickly. He was suddenly tense. The shadow, the beginning of a hope ...

Rhiannon went on. '*I did. But you gave me the chance to undo my sin, to be free to follow my brothers.*'

The thought-voice rose with a passion that was strong, dangerously strong.

'*Lend me your body, Carse! Lend me your body, that I may do it!*'

'No!' cried Carse. '*No!*'

He sprang up, conscious now of his peril, fighting with all his strength against that wild demanding force. He thrust it back, closing his mind against it.

'You cannot master me,' he whispered. 'You cannot!'

'*No,*' sighed Rhiannon, '*I cannot.*'

And the inner voice was gone.

Carse leaned against the rock, sweating and shaken but fired by a last, desperate hope. No more than an idea, really, but enough to spur him on. Better anything than this witing for death like a mouse in a trap.

If the gods of chance would only give him a little time ...

From inside he heard the opening of the door and the challenge of the guards, and his heart sank. He stood breathless, listening for the voice of Ironbeard.

14
DARING DECEPTION

But it was not Ironbeard who spoke. It was Boghaz, it was Boghaz alone who came out onto the balcony, very downcast and sad.

'Emer sent me,' he said. 'She told me the tragic news and I had to come to say goodbye.'

He took Carse's hand. 'The Sea Kings are holding their last council of war before starting for Sark but it will not be long. Old friend, we have been through much together. You have grown to be like my own brother and this parting wrings my heart.'

The fat Valkisian seemed genuinely affected. There were tears in his eyes as he looked at Carse.

'Yes, like my own brother,' he repeated unsteadily. 'Like brothers, we have quarrelled but we have shed blood together too. A man does not forget.'

He drew a long sigh. 'I should like to have something of yours to keep by me, friend. Some small trinket for memory's sake. Your jewelled collar, perhaps, your belt – you will not miss them now and I should cherish them all the days of my life.'

He wiped a tear away and Carse took him not too gently by the throat.

'You hypocritical scoundrel!' he snarled into the Valkisian's startled ear. 'A small trinket, eh? By the gods, for a moment you had me fooled!'

'But, my friend—' squeaked Boghaz.

Carse shook him once and let him to. In a rapid undertone he said, 'I'm not going to break your heart yet if I can help it. Listen, Boghaz. How would you like to gain back the power of the Tomb?'

Boghaz's mouth fell open. 'Mad,' he whispered. 'The poor fellow's lost his wits from shock.'

Carse glanced inside. The guards were lounging out of earshot. They had no reason to care what went on on the balcony.

There were three of them, mailed and armed. Boghaz was weaponless as a matter of course and Carse could not possibly escape unless he grew wings.

Swiftly the Earthman spoke.

'This venture of the Sea Kings is hopeless. The Dhuvians will help Sark and Khondor will be doomed. And that means you too, Boghaz. The Sarks will come and if you survive their attack, which is doubtful, they'll flay you alive and give what's left of you to the Dhuvians.'

Boghaz thought about that and it was not a pleasant thought.

'But,' he stammered, 'to regain Rhiannon's weapons now – it's impossible! Even if you could escape from here no man alive could get into Sark and snatch them from under Garach's nose!'

'No man,' said Carse. 'But I'm not just a man, remember? And whose weapons were they to begin with?'

Realisation began to dawn in the Valkisian's eyes. A great light broke over his moon face. He almost shouted and caught himself with Carse's hand already over his mouth.

'I salute you, Carse!' he whispered. 'The Father of Lies himself could not do better.' He was beside himself with ecstasy. 'It is sublime. It is worthy of – of Boghaz!'

Then he sobered and shook his head. 'But it is also sheer insanity.'

Carse took him by the shoulders. 'As it was before on the galley – nothing to lose, all to gain. Will you stand by me?'

The Valkisian closed his eyes. 'I am tempted,' he murmured. 'As a craftsman, as an artist, I would like to see the flowering of this beautiful deceit.'

He shivered all over. 'Flayed alive, you say. And then the Dhuvians. I suppose you're right. We're dead men anyway.' His eyes popped open. 'Hold on there! For Rhiannon all might be well in Sark but I'm only Boghaz, who mutinied against Ywain. Oh, no! I'm better off in Khondor.'

'Stay, then, if you think so.' Carse shook him. 'You fat fool! I'll protect you. As Rhiannon I can do that. And as the saviours of Khondor, with those weapons in our hands, there's no end to what we can do. How would you like to be King of Valkis?'

'Well—' Boghaz sighed. 'You would tempt the devil himself. And speaking of devils—' He looked narrowly at Carse. 'Can you keep yours down? It's an unchancy thing to have a demon for a bunkmate.'

Carse said, 'I can keep him down. You heard Rhiannon himself admit it.'

'Then,' said Boghaz, 'we'd best move quickly before the Sea Kings end their council.' He chuckled. 'Old Ironbeard has helped us, ironically enough. Every man is ordered to duty and our crew is aboard the galley, waiting – and not very happy about it either!'

'Help! Come quickly – Carse has thrown himself into the sea!'

They rushed onto the balcony, where Boghaz was leaning out, pointing down to the churning waves below.

'I tried to hold him,' he wailed, 'but I could not.'

One of the guards grunted. 'Small loss,' he said and then Carse stepped out of the shadows against the wall and struck him a sledgehammer blow that felled him and Boghaz whirled around to lay a second man on his back.

The third one they knocked down between them before he could get his sword clear of the scabbard. The other two were climbing to their feet again with some idea of going on with the fight but Carse and the Valkisian had no time to waste and knew it. Fists hammered stunning blows with brutal accuracy and within a few minutes the three unconscious men were safely bound and gagged.

Carse started to take the sword from one of them and Boghaz coughed with some embarrassment.

'Perhaps you'll want your own blade back,' he said.

'Where is it?'

'Fortunately, just outside, where they made me leave it.'

Carse nodded. It would be good to have the sword of Rhiannon in his hands again.

Crossing the room Carse stopped long enough to pick up a cloak belonging to one of the guards. He looked sidelong at

Boghaz. How did you so fortunately chance to have my sword?' he asked.

'Why, being your best friend and second in command, I claimed it.' The Valkisian smiled tenderly. 'You were about to die – and I knew you would want me to have it.'

'Boghaz,' said Carse, 'your love for me is a beautiful thing.'

'I have always been sentimental by nature.' The Valkisian motioned him aside, at the door. 'Let me go first.'

He stepped out in the corridor, then nodded and Carse followed him. The long blade stood against the wall. He picked it up and smiled.

'From now on,' he said, 'remember. I am Rhiannon!'

There was little traffic in this part of the palace. The halls were dark, lighted at infrequent intervals by torches. Boghaz chuckled.

'I know my way around this place,' he said. 'In fact I have found ways in and out that even the Khonds have forgotten.'

'Good,' said Carse. 'You lead then. We go first to find Ywain.'

'*Ywain!*' Boghaz stared at him. 'Are you crazy, Carse? This is no time to be toying with that vixen!'

Carse snarled. 'She must be with us to bear witness in Sark that I am Rhiannon. Otherwise the whole scheme will fail. Now will you go?'

He had realised that Ywain was the keystone of his whole desperate gamble. His trump card was the fact that she had *seen* Rhiannon possess him.

'There is truth in what you say,' Boghaz admitted, then added dismally, 'But I like it not. First a devil, then a hellcat with poison on her claws – this is surely a voyage for madmen!'

Ywain was imprisoned on the same upper level. Boghaz led the way swiftly and they met no one. Presently, around the bend where two corridors met, Carse saw a single torch burning by a barred door that had one small opening in its upper half. A sleepy guard drowsed there over his spear.

Boghaz drew a long breath. 'Ywain can convince the Sarks,' he whispered, 'but can you convince her?'

'I must,' Carse answered grimly.

'Well then – I wish us luck!'

According to the plan they had made on the way Boghaz sauntered ahead to talk to the guard, who was glad to have news of what was going on. Then, in the middle of a sentence, Boghaz allowed his voice to trail off. Open-mouthed, he stared over the guard's shoulder.

The startled man swung around.

Carse came down the corridor. He strode as though he owned the world, the cloak thrown back from his shoulders, his tawny head erect, his eyes flashing. The wavering torchlight struck fire from his jewels and the sword of Rhiannon was a shaft of wicked silver in his hand.

He spoke in the ringing tones he remembered from the grotto.

'Down on your face, you scum of Khondor – unless you wish to die!'

The man stood transfixed, his spear half raised. Behind him Boghaz uttered a frightened whimper.

'By the gods,' he moaned, 'the devil has possessed him again. It is Rhiannon, broken free!'

Very godlike in the brazen light, Carse raised the sword, not as a weapon but as a talisman of power. He allowed himself to smile.

'So you know me. It is well.' He bent his gaze on the white-faced guard. 'Do *you* doubt, that I must teach you?'

'No,' the guard answered hoarsely. 'No, Lord!'

He went to his knees. The spear-point clashed on rock as he dropped it. Then he bellied down and hid his face in his hands.

Boghaz whimpered again, 'Lord Rhiannon.'

'Bind him,' said Carse, 'and open me this door.'

It was done. Boghaz lifted the three heavy bars from their sockets. The door swung inward and Carse stood upon the threshold.

She was waiting, standing tensely erect in the gloom. They had not given her so much as a candle and the tiny cell was closed except for the barred slot in the door. The air was stale and drank with a taint of mouldy straw from the pallet that was the only furniture. And she wore her fetters still.

Carse steeled himself. He wondered whether in the

hidden depths of his mind the Cursed One watched. Almost, he thought, he heard the echo of dark laughter mocking the man who played at being a god.

Ywain said, 'Are you indeed Rhiannon?'

Marshal the deep proud voice, the look of brooding fire in the glance.

'You have known me before,' said Carse. 'How say you now?'

He waited, while her eyes searched him in the half light. And then slowly her head bent, stiffly as became Ywain of Sark even before Rhiannon.

'Lord,' she said.

Carse laughed shortly and turned to the cringing Boghaz.

'Wrap her in the cloths from the pallet. You must carry her – and bear her gently, swine!'

Boghaz scurried to obey. Ywain was obviously furious at the indignity but she held her tongue on that score.

'We are escaping then?' she asked.

'We are leaving Khondor to its fate.' Carse gripped the sword. 'I would be in Sark when the Sea Kings come that I may blast them myself, with my own weapons!'

Boghaz covered her face with the rags. Her hauberk and the hampering chains were hidden. The Valkisian lifted what might have been only a dirty bundle to his massive shoulder. And over the bundle he gave Carse a beaming wink.

Carse himself was not so sure. In this moment, grasping at the chance for freedom, Ywain would not be too critical. But it was a long way to Sark.

Had he detected in her manner just the faintest note of mockery when she bent her head?

15
UNDER THE TWO MOONS

Boghaz, with the true instinct of his breed, had learned every rathole in Khondor. He took them out of the palace by a way so long disused that the dust lay inches thick and the postern door had almost rotted away. Then, by crumbling stairways and steep alleys that were no more than cracks in the rock, he led the way around the city.

Khondor seethed. The night wind carried echoes of hastening feet and taut voices. The upper air was full of beating wings where the Sky Folk went, dark against the stars. There was no panic. But Carse could feel the anger of the city, and the hard grim tension of a people about to stride back against certain doom. From the distant temple he could hear the voices of women chanting to the gods.

The hurrying people they met paid them little heed. It was only a fat sailor with a bundle and a tall man muffled in a cloak, going down toward the harbour. What matter for notice in that?

They climbed the long, long steps downward to the basin and there was much coming and going on the dizzy way, but still they passed unchallenged. Each Khond was too full of his own worries this fateful night to pay attention to his neighbour.

Nevertheless Carse's heart was pounding and his ears ached from listening for the alarm which would surely come as soon as Ironbeard went up to slay his captive.

They gained the quays. Carse saw the tall mast of the galley towering above the longships and made for it with Boghaz panting at his heels.

Torches burned here by the hundreds. By their light fighting men and supplies were pouring aboard the longships. The rock walls rang with the tumult. Small craft darted between the outer moorings.

Carse kept his head lowered, shouldering his way through the crowd. The water was alive with Swimmers and there were women with set white faces who had come to bid their men farewell.

As they neared the galley Carse let Boghaz get ahead of him. He paused in the shelter of a pile of casks, pretending to bind up his sandal thong while the Valkisian went aboard with his burden. He heard the crew, sullen-faced and nervous, hailing Boghaz and asking for news.

Boghaz disposed of Ywain by dumping her casually in the cabin, and then called all hands forward for a conference by the wine-butt, which was locked in the lazarette there. The Valkisian had his speech by heart.

'News?' Carse heard him say. 'I'll give you news! Since Rold was taken there's an ugly temper in the city. We were their brothers yesterday. Today we're outlaws and enemies again. I've heard them talking in the wine-shops and I tell you our lives aren't worth *that!*'

While the crew was muttering uneasily over that Carse darted over the side unseen. Before he gained the cabin he heard Boghaz finish.

'There was a mob already gathering when I left. If we want to save our hides we'd better cast off now while we have the chance!'

Carse had been pretty sure what the reaction of the crew would be to that story and he was not sure at all that Boghaz was stretching it too much. He had seen mobs turn before and his crew of convict Sarks, Jekkarans and others might soon be in a nasty spot.

Now, with the cabin door closed and barred, he leaned against the panel, listening. He heard the padding of bare feet on the deck, the quick shouting of orders, the rattle of the blocks as the sails came down from the yards. The mooring lines were cast off. The sweeps came out with a ragged rumble. The galley rode free.

'Ironbeard's orders!' Boghaz shouted to someone on shore. 'A mission for Khondor!'

The galley quivered, then began to gather way with the measured booming of the drum. And then, over all the near confusion of sound, Carse heard what his ears had been straining to hear – the distant roar from the crest of the rock, the alarm sweeping through the city, rushing toward the harbour stair.

He stood in an agony of fear lest everyone else should hear it too and know its meaning without being told. But the din of the harbour covered it long enough and by the time word had been brought down from the crest the black galley was already in the roadstead, speeding down into the mouth of the fiord.

In the darkness of the cabin Ywain spoke quietly. 'Lord Rhiannon – may I be allowed to breathe?'

He knelt and stripped the cloths from her and she sat up.

'My thanks. Well, we are free of the palace and the harbour but there still remains the fiord. I heard the outcry.'

'Aye,' said Carse. 'And the Sky Folk will carry word ahead.' He laughed. 'Let us see if they can stop Rhiannon by flinging pebbles from the cliffs!'

He left her then, ordering her to remain where she was, and went out on deck.

They were well along the channel now, racing under a fast stroke. The sails were beginning to catch the wind that blew between the cliffs. He tried to remember how the ballista defences were set, counting on the fact that they were meant to bear on ships coming into the fiord, not going out.

Speed would be the main thing. If they could drive the galley fast enough they'd have a chance.

In the faint light of Demos no one saw him. Not until Phobos topped the cliffs and sent a shaft of greenish light. Then the men saw him there, his cloak whipping in the wind, the long sword in his hands.

A strange sort of cry went up – half welcome for the Carse they remembered, half fear because of what they had heard about him in Khondor.

He didn't give them time to think. Swinging the sword high, he roared at them, 'Pull, there, you apes! Pull, or they'll sink us!'

Man or devil, they knew he spoke the truth. They pulled.

Carse leaped up to the steersman's platform. Boghaz was already there. He cowered convincingly against the rail as Carse approached but the man at the tiller regarded him with wolfish eyes in which there was an ugly spark. It was the man with the branded cheek, who had been at the oar with Jaxart on the day of the mutiny.

'I'm captain now,' he said to Carse. 'I'll not have you on my ship to curse it!'

Carse said with terrible slowness, 'I see you do not know me. Tell him, man of Valkis!'

But there was no need for Boghaz to speak. There came a whistling of pinions down the wind and a winged man stooped low in the moonlight over the ship.

'Turn back! Turn back!' he cried. 'You bear – !'

'Aye!' Carse shouted back. 'Rhiannon's wrath, Rhiannon's power!'

He lifted the sword hilt high so that the dark jewel blazed evilly in Phobos' light.

'Will you stand against me? Will you dare?'

The Skyman swerved away and rose wailing in the wind. Carse turned upon the steersman.

'And you,' he said. 'How say you now?'

He saw the wolf-eyed flicker from the blazing jewel to his own face and back again. The look of terror he was beginning to know too well came into them and they dropped.

'I dare not stand against Rhiannon,' the man said hoarsely.

'Give me the helm,' said Carse and the other stood aside, the brand showing livid on his whitened cheek.

'Make speed,' Carse ordered, 'if you would live.'

And speed they made, so that the galley went with a frightening rush between the cliffs, a black and ghostly ship between the white fire of the fiord and the cold grey moonlight. Carse saw the open sea ahead and steeled himself, praying.

A whining snarl echoed from the rock as the first of the great ballistas crashed. A spout of water rose by the galley's bow and she shuddered and raced on.

Crouched over the tiller bar, his cloak streaming, his face intense and strange in the eerie glow, Carse ran the gauntlet in the throat of the fiord.

Ballistas twanged and thundered. Great stoned rained into the water, so that they sailed through a burning cloud of mist and spray. But it was as Carse had hoped. The defences, invincible to frontal attack, were weak when taken in reverse. The bracketing of the channel was imperfect, the aim poor against a fleeing target. Those things and the headlong speed of the galley saved them.

They came out into open water. The last stone fell far astern and they were free. There would be quick pursuit – that he knew. But for the moment they were safe.

Carse realised then the difficulties of being a god. He wanted to sit down on the deck and take a long pull of the wine cask to get over his shakes. But instead he had to force a ringing laugh, as though it amused him to see these childish humans try to prevail against the invincible.

'Here, you who call yourself captain! Take the helm – and set a course for Sark.'

'Sark!' The unlucky man had much to contend with that night. 'My Lord Rhiannon, have pity! We are proscribed convicts in Sark!'

'Rhiannon will protect you,' Boghaz said.

'*Silence!*' roared Carse. 'Who are you to speak for Rhiannon?' Boghaz cringed abjectly and Carse said, 'Fetch the Lady Ywain to me – but first strike off her chains.'

He descended the ladder to stand upon the deck, waiting. Behind him he heard the branded man groan and mutter, '*Ywain! Gods above, the Khonds would have been a better death!*'

Carse stood unmoving and the men watched him, not daring to speak, wanting to rise and kill him, but afraid. Afraid of the Cursed One that could blast them all.

Ywain came to him, free of her chains now, and bowed. He turned and called out to the crew.

'You rose against her once, following the barbarian. Now the barbarian is no more as you knew him. And you will serve Ywain again. Serve her well and she will forget your crime.'

He saw her eyes blaze at that. She started to protest and he gave her a look that stopped the words in her throat.

'Pledge them,' he commanded. 'On the honour of Sark.'

She obeyed. But it seemed to Carse again that she was still not quite convinced that he was actually Rhiannon.

She followed him to the cabin and asked if she might enter. He gave her leave and sent Boghaz after wine and then for a time there was silence. Carse sat brooding in Ywain's chair, trying to still the nervous pounding of his heart and she watched him from under lowered lids.

The wine was brought. Boghaz hesitated and then perforce left them alone.

'Sit down,' said Carse, 'and drink.'

Ywain pulled up a low stool and sat with her long legs thrust out before her, slender as a boy in her black mail. She drank and said nothing.

Carse said abruptly, 'You doubt me still.'

She started. 'No, Lord!'

Carse laughed. 'Don't think to lie to me. A stiff-necked, haughty wench you are, Ywain, and clever. An excellent prince for Sark despite your sex.'

Her mouth twisted rather bitterly. 'My father Garach fashioned me as I am. A weakling with no son — someone had to carry the sword while he toyed with the sceptre.'

'I think,' said Carse, 'that you have not altogether hated it.'

She smiled. 'No. I was never bred for silken cushions.' She continued suddenly, 'But let us have no more talk of my doubting, Lord Rhiannon. I have known you before — once in this cabin when you faced S'San and again in the place of the Wise Ones. I know you now.'

'It does not greatly matter whether you doubt or not, Ywain. The barbarian alone overcame you and I think Rhiannon would have no trouble.'

She flushed an angry red. Her lingering suspicion of him was plain now — her anger with him betrayed it.

'The barbarian did not overcome me! He kissed me and I let him enjoy that kiss so that I could leave the mark of it on his face forever!'

Carse nodded, goading her. 'And for a moment you enjoyed it also. You're a woman, Ywain, for all your short tunic and your mail. And a woman always knows the one man who can master her.'

'You think so?' she whispered.

She had come close to him now, her red lips parted as they had been before — tempting, deliberately provocative.

'I know it,' he said.

'If you were merely the barbarian and nothing else,' she murmured, 'I might know it also.'

The trap was almost undisguised. Carse waited until the tense silence had gone flat. Then he said coldly, 'Very likely you would. However I am not the barbarian now, but Rhiannon. And it is time you slept.'

He watched her with grim amusement as she drew away, disconcerted and perhaps for the first time in her life completely at a loss. He knew that he had dispelled her lingering doubt about him for the time being at least.

He said, 'You may have the inner cabin.'

'Yes, Lord,' she answered and now there was no mockery in her tone.

She turned and crossed the cabin slowly. She pushed open the inner door and then halted, her hand on the doorpost, and he saw an expression of loathing come into her face.

'Why do you hesitate?' he asked.

'The place still reeks of the serpent taint,' she said. 'I had rather sleep on deck.'

'Those are strange words, Ywain. S'San was your counsellor, your friend. I was forced to slay him to save the barbarian's life – but surely Ywain of Sark has no dislike of her allies!'

'Not my allies – Garach's.' She turned and faced him and he saw that her anger over her discomfiture had made her forget caution.

'Rhiannon or no Rhiannon,' she cried, 'I will say what has been in my mind to say all these years. I hate your crawling pupils of Caer Dhu! I loathe them utterly – and now you may slay me if you will!'

And she strode out onto the deck, letting the door slam shut behind her.

Carse sat still behind the table. He was trembling all over with nervous strain and presently he would pour wine to aid him. But just now he was amazed to find how happy it could make him to know that Ywain too hated Caer Dhu.

The wind had dropped by midnight and for hours the galley forged on under oars, moving at far less than her normal speed because they were short-handed in the rowers' pit, having lost the Khonds that made up the full number.

And at dawn the lookout sighted four tiny specks on the horizon that were the hulls of longships, coming on from Khondor.

16
VOICE OF THE SERPENT

Carse stood on the afterdeck with Boghaz. It was mid-morning. The calm still held and now the longships were close enough to be seen from the deck.

Boghaz said, 'At this rate they'll overhaul us by nightfall.'

'Yes.' Carse was worried. Undermanned as she was the galley could not hope to outdistance the Khonds under oars alone. And the last thing Carse wanted was to be forced into the position of fighting Ironbeard's men. He knew he couldn't do it.

'They'll break their hearts to catch us,' he said. 'And these are only the van. The whole of the Sea Kings' fleet will be coming on behind them.'

Boghaz looked at the following ships. 'Do you think we'll ever reach Sark?'

'Not unless we raise a fair wind,' Carse said grimly, 'and even then not by much of margin. Do you know any prayers?'

'I was well instructed in my youth,' answered Boghaz piously.

'Then pray!'

But all that long hot day there was no more than a breath of air to ripple the galley's sails. The men wearied at the sweeps. They had not much heart for the business at best, being trapped between two evils with a demon for captain, and they had only so much strength.

The longships doggedly, steadily, grew closer.

In the late afternoon, when the setting sun made a magnifying glass of the lower air the lookout reported other ships far back in the distance. Many ships – the armada of the Sea Kings.

Carse looked up into the empty sky, bitter of heart.

The breeze began to strengthen. As the sails filled the rowers roused themselves and pulled with renewed vigour. Presently Carse ordered the sweeps in. The wind blew strongly. The galley picked up speed and the longships could no more than hold their own.

Carse knew the galley's speed. She was a fast sailer and with her greater spread of canvas might hope to keep well ahead of the pursuers if the wind held.

If the wind held...

The next few days were enough to drive a man mad. Carse drove the men in the pit without mercy and each time the sweeps had to be run out the beat grew slower as they reached the point of exhaustion.

By the narrowest margin Carse kept the galley ahead. Once, when it seemed they were surely caught, a sudden storm saved them by scattering the lighter ships, but they came on again. And now a man could see the horizon dotted with a host of sails where the armada irresistibly advanced.

The immediate pursuers grew from four to five, and then to seven. Carse remembered the old adage that a stern chase is a long one but it seemed that this one could not go on much longer.

There came another time of flat hot calm. The rowers drooped and sweated at the oars, driven only by their fear of the Khonds and try as they would there was no bite in the stroke.

Carse stood by the after rail, watching his face lined and grim. The game was up. The lean longships were putting on a burst of speed, closing in for the kill.

Suddenly, sharply, there came a hail from the masthead.

'Sail ho!'

Carse whirled, following the line of the lookout's pointing arm.

'Sark ships!'

He saw them ahead, racing up under fast beat, three tall war-galleys of the patrol.

Leaping to the edge of the rowers' pit, he shouted to the men.

'Pull, you dogs! Lay into it! There's help on the way!'

They found their last reserves of energy. The galley made a desperate lurching run. Ywain came to Carse's side.

'We're close to Sark now, Lord Rhiannon. If we can keep ahead a little longer ...'

The Khonds rushed down on them, pushing furiously in a last attempt to ram and sink the galley before the Sarks could reach them. But they were too late.

The patrol ships swept by. They charged in among the Khonds and scattered them and the air was filled with shouts and the twanging of bowstrings, and the terrible ripping sound of splintering oars as a whole bank was crushed into matchwood.

There began a running fight that lasted all afternoon. The desperate Khonds hung on and would not be driven off. The Sark ships closed in around the galley, a mobile wall of defence. Time and again the Khonds attacked, their light swift craft darting in hornet-like, and were driven off. The Sarks carried ballistas, and Carse saw two of the Khond ships holed and sunk by the hurtling stones.

A light breeze began to blow. The galley picked up speed. And now blazing arrows flew, searching out the bellying sails. Two of the escort ships fell back with their canvas ablaze but the Khonds suffered also. There were only three of them left in the fight and the galley was by now well ahead of them.

They came in sight of the Sark coast, a low dark line above the water. And then, to Carse's great relief, other ships came out to meet them, drawn by the fighting, and the three remaining Khond longships put about and drew off.

It was all easy after that. Ywain was in her own place again. Fresh rowers were put aboard from other ships and one swift craft went ahead of them to carry warning of the attack and news of Ywain's coming.

But the smoke of the burning longships astern was a painful thing to Carse. He looked at the massed sails of the Sea Kings in the far distance and felt the huge and crushing weight of the battle that was to come. It seemed to him in that moment that there was no hope.

They came in late afternoon into the harbour of Sark. A broad estuary offered anchorage for countless ships and on both sides of the channel the city sprawled in careless strength.

It was a city whose massive arrogance suited the men who had built it. Carse saw great temples and the squat magnificence of the palace, crowning the highest hill. The buildings were almost ugly in their solid strength, their buttressed shoulders jutting against the sky, brilliant with harsh colours and strong designs.

Already this whole harbour area was in a feverish sweat of activity. Word of the Sea Kings' coming had started a swift manning of ships and readying of defences, the uproar and tumult of a city preparing for war.

Boghaz, beside him, muttered, 'We're mad to walk like this into the dragon's throat. If you can't carry it off as Rhiannon, if you make one slip ...'

Carse said, 'I can do it. I've had considerable practice by now in playing the Cursed One.'

But inwardly he was shaken. Confronted by the massive might of Sark it seemed a mad insolence to attempt to play the god here.

Crowds along the waterfront cheered Ywain wildly as she disembarked. And they stared in some amazement at the tall man with her, who looked like a Khond and wore a great sword.

Soldiers formed a guard around them and forced a way through the excited mob. The cheering followed them as they went up through the crowded city streets toward the brooding palace.

They passed at length into the cool dimness of the palace halls. Carse strode down huge echoing rooms with inlaid floors and massive pillars that supported giant beams covered with gold. He noticed that the serpent motif was strong in the decorations.

He wished he had Boghaz with him. He had been forced, for appearance sake, to leave the fat thief behind and he felt terribly alone.

At the silvery doors of the throne room the guard halted. A chamberlain wearing mail under his velvet gown came forward to greet Ywain.

'Your father, the Sovereign King Garach, is overjoyed at your safe return and wishes to welcome you. But he begs you to wait as he is closeted with the Lord Hishah, the emissary from Caer Dhu.'

Ywain's lips twisted. 'So already he asks aid of the Serpent.' She nodded imperiously at the closed door. 'Tell the king I will see him now.'

The chamberlain protested. 'But, Highness—'

'Tell him,' said Ywain, 'or I will enter without permission. Say that there is one with me who demands admittance and whom not Garach nor all Caer Dhu may deny.'

The chamberlain looked in frank puzzlement at Carse. He hesitated, then bowed and went in through the silver doors.

Carse had caught the note of bitterness in Ywain's voice when she spoke of the Serpent. He taxed her with it.

'No, Lord,' she said. 'I spoke once and you were lenient. It is not my place to speak again. Besides' – she shrugged – 'you see how my father bars me from his confidence in this, even though I must fight his battles for him.'

'You do not wish aid from Caer Dhu even now?'

She remained silent, and Carse said, 'I bid you to speak!'

'Very well then. It is natural for two strong peoples to fight for mastery when their interests clash on every short of the same sea. It is natural for men to want power. I could have gloried in this coming battle, gloried in a victory over Khondor. But—'

'Go on.'

She cried out then with controlled passion. 'But I have wished that Sark had grown great by fair force of arms, man against man, as it was in the old days before Garach made alliance with Caer Dhu! And now there is no glory in a victory won before even the hosts have met.'

'And your people,' asked Carse. 'Do they share your feelings in this?'

'They do, Lord. But enough are tempted by power and spoils—'

She broke off, looking Carse straight in the face.

'I have already said enough to bring your wrath upon me. Therefore I will finish, for I think now that Sark is truly doomed,

333

even in victory. The Serpent gives us aid not for our sakes, but as part of its own design. We have become no more than tools by which Caer Dhu gains its ends. And now that you have come back to lead the Dhuvians—'

She stopped and there was no need for her to finish. The opening of the door saved Carse from the necessity of an answer.

The chamberlain said apologetically, 'Highness, your father sends answer that he does not understand your bold words and again begs you to wait his pleasure.'

Ywain thrust him angrily aside and strode to the tall doors, flinging them open. She stood back and said to Carse, 'Lord, will you enter?'

He drew a deep breath and entered, striding down the long dim length of the throne room like a very god with Ywain following behind.

The place seemed empty except for Garach, who had sprung to his feet on the dais at the far end. He wore a robe of black velvet worked in gold and he had Ywain's graceful height and handsomeness of feature. But her honest strength was not in him, nor her pride, nor her level glance. For all his greying beard he had the mouth of a petulant, greedy child.

Beside him, withdrawn in the shadows by the high seat, another stood also. A dark figure, hooded and cloaked, its face concealed, its hands hidden in the wide sleeves of its robe.

'What means this?' cried Garach angrily. 'Daughter or not, Ywain, I'll not stand for such insolence!'

Ywain bent her knee. 'My father,' she said clearly, 'I bring you the Lord Rhiannon of the Quiru, returned from the dead.'

Garach's face paled by degrees to the colour of ash. His mouth opened, but words came. He stared at Carse and then at Ywain and finally at the cowled, hooded Dhuvian.

'This is madness,' he stammered at last.

'Nevertheless,' said Ywain, 'I bear witness to its truth. Rhiannon's mind lives in the body of this barbarian. He spoke to the Wise Ones at Khondor and he has spoken since to me. It is Rhiannon who stands before you.'

Again there was silence as Garach stared and stared and

trembled. Carse stood tall and lordly, outwardly contemptuous of doubt and waiting for acknowledgement.

But the old chilling fear was in him. He knew that ophidian eyes watched him from the shadow under the Dhuvian's cowl and it seemed that he could feel their cold gaze sliding through his imposture as a knife blade slips through paper.

The mind-knowledge of the Halflings. The strong extra-sensory perception that could see beyond the appearances of the flesh. And the Dhuvians, for all their evil, were Halflings too.

Carse wanted nothing more at that moment than to break and run. But he forced himself to play the god, arrogant and self-assured, smiling at Garach's fear.

Deep within his brain, in the corner that was no longer his own, he felt a strange and utter stillness. It was as though the invader, the Cursed One, had gone.

Carse forced himself to speak, making his voice ring back from the walls in stern echoes.

'The memories of children are indeed short when even the favourite pupil has forgotten the master.'

And he bent his gaze upon Hishah the Dhuvian.

'Do you also doubt me, child of the snake? Must I teach you again, as I taught S'San?'

He lifted the great sword and Garach's eyes flickered to Ywain.

She said, 'The Lord Rhiannon slew S'San, aboard the galley.'

Garach dropped to his knees.

'Lord,' he said submissively, 'what is your will?'

Carse ignored him, looking still at the Dhuvian. And the cowled figure moved forward with a peculiar gliding step and spoke in its soft hateful voice.

'Lord, I also ask – what is your will?'

The dark robe rippled as the creature seemed to kneel.

'It is well.' Carse crossed his hands over the hilt of the sword, dimming the lustre of the jewel.

'The fleet of the Sea Kings stands in to attack soon. I would have my ancient weapons brought to me that I may crush the enemies of Sark and Caer Dhu, who are also my enemies.'

A great hope sprang into Garach's eyes. It was obvious that

fear gnawed his vitals – fear of many things, Carse thought, but just now, above all, fear of the Sea Kings. He glanced aside at Hishah and the cowled creature said,

'Lord, your weapons have been taken to Caer Dhu.'

The Earthman's heart sank. Then he remembered Rold of Khondor, and how they must have broken him to get the secret of the Tomb and a blind rage came over him. The snarl of fury in his voice was not feigned, only the sense of his words.

'You dared to tamper with the power of Rhiannon?' He advanced toward the Dhuvian. 'Can it be that the pupil now hopes to outrival the master?'

'No, Lord!' The veiled head bowed. 'We have but kept your weapons safe for you.'

Carse permitted his features to relax somewhat.

'Very well, then. See that they are returned to me here and at once!'

Hishah rose. 'Yes, Lord. I will go now to Caer Dhu to do your bidding.'

The Dhuvian glided toward an inner door and was gone, leaving Carse in a secret sweat of mingled relief and apprehension.

17
CAER DHU

The next few hours were an eternity of unbearable tension for Carse.

He demanded an apartment for himself, on the ground that he must have privacy to draw his plans. And there he paced up and down in a fine state of nerves, looking most ungodlike.

It seemed that he had succeeded. The Dhuvian had accepted him. Perhaps, he thought, the Serpent folk after all lacked the astoundingly developed extra-sensory powers of the Swimmers and the winged men.

It appeared that all he had to do now was to wait for the Dhuvian to return with the weapons, load them aboard his ship and go away. He could do that, for no one would dare to question the plans of Rhiannon and he had time also. The Sea Kings' fleet was standing off, waiting for all its force to come up. There would be no attack before dawn, none at all if he succeeded.

But some raw primitive nerve twitched to the sense of danger and Carse was oppressed by a foreboding fear.

He sent for Boghaz on the pretext of giving orders concerning the galley. His real reason was that he could not bear to be alone. The fat thief was jubilant when he heard the news.

'You have brought it off,' he chuckled, rubbing his hands together in delight. 'I have always said, Carse, that sheer gall would carry a man through anything. I, Boghaz, could not have done better.'

Carse said dourly, 'I hope you're right.'

Boghaz gave him a sidelong glance. 'Carse—'

'Yes?'

'What of the Cursed One himself?'

'Nothing. Not a sign. It worries me, Boghaz. I have the feeling that he's waiting.'

'When you get the weapons in your hands,' Boghaz said meaningly, 'I'll stand by you with a belaying pin.'

The soft-footed chamberlain brought word at last that Hishah had returned from Caer Dhu and awaited audience with him.

'It is well,' said Carse and then nodded curtly toward Boghaz. 'This man will come with me to supervise the handling of the weapons.'

The Valkisian's ruddy cheeks lost several shades of colour but he came perforce at Carse's heels.

Garach and Ywain were in the throne room and the black-cowled creature from Caer Dhu. All bowed as Carse entered.

'Well,' he demanded of the Dhuvian, 'have you obeyed my command?'

'Lord,' said Hishah softly, 'I took counsel with the Elders, who send you this word. Had they known that the Lord Rhiannon had returned they would not have presumed to touch those things which are his. And now they fear to touch them again lest in their ignorance they do damage or cause destruction.

'Therefore, Lord, they beg you to arrange this matter

yourself. Also they have not forgotten their love for Rhiannon, whose teachings raised them from the dust. They wish to welcome you to your old kingdom in Caer Dhu, for your children have been long in darkness and would once again know the light of Rhiannon's wisdom, and his strength.'

Hishah made a now obeisance. 'Lord, will you grant them this?'

Carse stood silent for a moment, trying desperately to conceal his dread. He could not go to Caer Dhu. He dared not go! How long could he hope to conceal his deception from the children of the Serpent, the oldest deceiver of all?

If, indeed, he had concealed it at all. Hishah's soft words reeked of a subtle trap.

And trapped he was and knew it. He dared not go – but even more he dared not refuse.

He said, 'I am pleased to grant them their request.'

Hishah bowed his head in thanks. 'All preparations are made. The King Garach and his daughter will accompany you that you may be suitably attended. Your children realise the need for haste – the barge is waiting.'

'Good.' Carse turned on his heel, fixing Boghaz as he did so with a steely look.

'You will attend me also, man of Valkis. I may have need of you with regard to the weapons.'

Boghaz got his meaning. If he had paled before he turned now a living white with pure horror but there was not a word he could say. Like a man led to execution he followed Carse out of the throne room.

Night brooded black and heavy as they embarked at the palace stair in a low black craft without sail or oar. Creatures hooded and robed like Hishah thrust long poles into the water and the barge moved out into the estuary, heading up away from the sea.

Garach crouched amid the sable cushion of a divan, an unkingly figure with shaking hands and cheeks the colour of bone. His eyes kept furtively seeking the muffled form of Hishah.

It was plain that he did not relish this visit to the court of his allies.

Ywain had withdrawn herself to the side of the barge, where she sat looking out into the sombre darkness of the marshy shore. Carse thought she seemed more depressed than she ever had when she was a prisoner in chains.

He too sat by himself, outwardly lordly and magnificent, inwardly shaken to the soul. Boghaz crouched nearby. His eyes were the eyes of a sick man.

And the Cursed One, the real Rhiannon was still. Too still. In that buried corner of Carse's mind there was not a stir, not a flicker. It seemed that the dark outcast of the Quiru was like all the others aboard withdrawn and waiting.

It seemed a long way up the estuary. The water slid past the barge with a whisper of sibilant mirth. The black-robed figures bent and swayed at the poles. Now and again a bird cried from the marshland and the night air was heavy and brooding.

Then, in the light of the little low moons, Carse saw ahead the ragged walls and ramparts of a city rising from the mists, an old, old city walled like a castle. It sprawled away into ruin on all sides and only the great central keep was whole.

There was a flickering radiance in the air around the place. Carse thought that it was his imagination, a visual illusion caused by the moonlight and the glowing water and the pale mist.

The barge drew in toward a crumbling quay. It came to rest and Hishah stepped ashore, bowing as he waited for Rhiannon to pass.

Carse strode up along the quay with Garach and Ywain and the shivering Boghaz following. Hishah remained deferentially at the Earthman's heels.

A causeway of black stone, much cracked by the weight of years, led up toward the citadel. Carse set his feet resolutely upon it. Now he was sure that he could see a faint, pulsing web of light around Caer Dhu. It lay over the whole city, glimmering with a steely luminescence, like starlight on a frosty night.

He did not like the look of it. And he approached it, where it crossed the causeway like a veil before the great gate, he liked it less and less.

Yet no one spoke, no one faltered. He seemed to be expected to lead the way, and he did not dare to betray his ignorance of the nature of the thing. So he forced his steps to go on, strong and sure.

He was close enough to the gleaming web to feel a strange prickling of force. One more stride would have taken him into it. And then Hishah said sharply in his ear, 'Lord! Have you forgotten the Veil, whose touch is death?'

Carse recoiled. A shock of fear went through him and at the same time he realised that he had blundered badly.

He said quickly, 'Of course I have not forgotten!'

'No, Lord,' Hishah murmured. 'How indeed could you forget when it was you who taught us the secret of the Veil which warps space and shields Caer Dhu from any force?'

Carse knew now that that gleaming web was a defensive barrier of energy, of such potent energy that it somehow set up a space-strain which nothing could penetrate.

It seemed incredible. Yet Quiru science had been great and Rhiannon had taught some of it to the forefathers of these Dhuvians.

'How, indeed, could *you* forget?' Hishah repeated.

There was no hint of mockery in his words and yet Carse felt that it was there.

The Dhuvian stepped forward, raising his sleeved arms in a signal to some watcher within the gate. The luminescence of the Veil died out above the causeway, leaving a path open through it.

And as Carse turned to go on he saw that Ywain was staring at him with a look of startled wonder in which a doubt was already beginning to grow. The great gate swung open and the Lord Rhiannon of the Quiru was received into Caer Dhu.

The ancient halls were dimly lighted by what seemed to be globes of prisoned fire that stood on tripods at long intervals, shedding a cool greenish glow. The air was warm and the taint of the Serpent lay heavy in it, closing Carse's throat with its hateful sickliness.

Hishah went before them now and that in itself was a sign

of danger, since Rhiannon should have known the way. But Hishah said that he wished the honour of announcing his lord and Carse could do nothing but choke down his growing terror and follow.

They came into a vast central place, closed in by towering walls of the black rock that rose to a high vault, lost in darkness overhead. Below, a single large globe lightened the heavy shadows.

Little light for human eyes. But even that was too much!

For here the children of the serpent were gathered to greet their lord. And here in their own place they were not shrouded in the cowled robes they wore when they went among men.

The Swimmers belonged to the sea, the Sky Folk to the high air, and they were perfect and beautiful in accordance with their elements. Now Carse saw the third pseudo-human race of the Halflings – the children of the hidden places, the perfect, dreadfully perfect offspring of another great order of life.

In that first overwhelming shock of revulsion Carse was hardly aware of Hishah's voice saying the name of Rhiannon and the soft, sibilant cry of greeting that followed was only the tongue of nightmare speaking.

From the edges of the wide floor they hailed him and from the open galleries above, their depthless eyes glittering, their narrow ophidian heads bowed in homage.

Sinuous bodies that moved with effortless ease, seeming to flow rather than step. Hands with supple jointless fingers and feet that made no sound and lipless mouths that seemed to open always on silent laughter, infinitely cruel. And all through that vast place whispered a dry harsh rustling, the light friction of skin that had lost its primary scales but not its serpentine roughness.

Carse raised the sword of Rhiannon in acknowledgement of that welcome and forced himself to speak.

'Rhiannon is pleased by the greeting of his children.'

It seemed to him that a little hissing ripple of mirth ran through the great hall. But he could not be sure, and Hishah said,

'My Lord, here are your ancient weapons.'

They were in the centre of the cleared space. All the cryptic mechanisms he had seen in the Tomb were here, the great flat crystal wheel, the squat looped metal rods, the others, all glittering in the dim light.

Carse's heart leaped and settled to a heavy pounding. 'Good,' he said. 'The time is short – take them aboard the barge, that I may return to Sark at once.'

'Certainly, Lord,' said Hishah. 'But will you not inspect them first to make sure that all is well. Our ignorant handling ...'

Carse strode to the weapons and made a show of examining them. Then he nodded.

'No damage has been done. And now—'

Hishah broke in, unctuously courteous. 'Before you go, will you not explain the workings of these instruments? Your children were always hungry for knowledge.'

'There is no time for that,' Carse said angrily. 'Also, you are as you say – children. You could not comprehend.'

'Can it be, Lord,' asked Hishah very softly, 'that you yourself do not comprehend?'

There was a moment of utter stillness. The icy certainty of doom took Carse in its grip. He saw now that the ranks of the Dhuvians had closed in behind them, barring all hope of escape.

Within the circle Garach and Ywain and Boghaz stood with him. There was shocked amazement on Garach's face and the Valkisian sagged with the weight of horror that had come as no surprise to him. Ywain alone was not amazed, or horrified. She looked at Carse with the eyes of a woman who fears but in a different way. It came to Carse that she feared for him, that she did not want him to die.

In a last desperate attempt to save himself Carse cried out furiously,

'What means this insolence? Would you have me take up my weapons and use them against you?'

'Do so, if you can,' Hishah said softly. 'Do so, oh false Rhiannon, for assuredly by no other means will you ever leave Caer Dhu!'

18
THE WRATH OF RHIANNON

Carse stood where he was, surrounded by the crystal and metal mechanisms that had no meaning for him, and knew with terrible finality that he was beaten. And now the hissing laughter broke forth on all sides, infinitely cruel and jeering.

Garach put out a trembling hand toward Hishah. 'Then,' he stammered, 'this is not Rhiannon?'

'Even your human mind should tell you that much now,' answered Hishah contemptuously. He had thrown back his cowl and now he moved toward Carse, his ophidian eyes full of mockery.

'By the touching of minds alone I would have known you false but even that I did not need. You, Rhiannon! Rhiannon of the Quiru, who came in peace and brotherhood to greet his children in Caer Dhu!'

The stealthy evil laughter hissed from every Dhuvian throat and Hishah threw his head back, the skin of his throat pulsing with his mirth.

'Look at him, my brothers! Hail Rhiannon, who did not know of the Veil nor why it guards Caer Dhu!'

And they hailed him, bowing low.

Carse stood very still. For the moment he had even forgotten to be afraid.

'You fool,' said Hishah. 'Rhiannon hated us at the end. For at the end he learned his folly, learned that the pupils to whom he gave the crumbs of knowledge had grown too clever. With the Veil, whose secret he had taught us, we made our city impregnable even to his mighty weapons, so that when he turned finally against us it was too late.'

Carse said slowly, 'Why did he turn against you?'

Hishah laughed. 'He learned the use we had for the knowledge he had given us.'

Ywain came forward, one step, and said, 'What was that use?'

'I think you know already,' Hishah answered. 'That is why

you and Garach were summoned here – not only to see this impostor unmasked but to learn once and for all your place in our world.'

His soft voice had in it now the bite of the conqueror.

'Since Rhiannon was locked in his tomb we have gained subtle dominance on every shore of the White Sea. We are few in number and averse to open warfare. Therefore we have worked through the human kingdoms, using your greedy people as our tools.

'Now we have the weapons of Rhiannon. Soon we will master their use and then we will no longer need human tools. The Children of the Serpent will rule in every palace – and we will require only obedience and respect from our subjects.

'How think you of that, Ywain of the proud head, who has always loathed and scorned us?'

'I think,' said Ywain, 'that I will fall upon my own sword first.'

Hishah shrugged. 'Fall then.' He turned to Garach. 'And you?'

But Garach had already crumpled to the stones in a dead faint.

Hishah turned again to Carse. 'And now,' he said, 'you shall see how we welcome our lord!'

Boghaz moaned and covered his face with his hands. Carse gripped the futile sword tighter and asked in a strange, low voice, 'And no one ever knew that Rhiannon had finally turned against you Dhuvians?'

Hishah answered softly, 'The Quiru knew but nevertheless they condemned Rhiannon because his repentance came too late. Other than they only we knew. And why should we tell the world when it pleased our humour to see Rhiannon, who hated us, cursed as our friend?'

Carse closed his eyes. The world rocked under him, and there was a roaring in his ears, as the revelation burst upon him.

Rhiannon had spoken the truth in the place of the Wise Ones. Had spoken truth when he voiced his hatred of the Dhuvians!

The hall was filled with a sound like the rustling of dry leaves as the ranks of the Dhuvians closed gently in toward Carse.

With an effort of will almost beyond human strength Carse threw open all the channels of his mind, trying desperately now in this last minute to reach inward to that strangely silent, hidden corner.

He cried aloud, '*Rhiannon!*'

That hoarse cry made the Dhuvians pause. Not because of fear but because of laughter. This, indeed, was the climax of the jest!

Hishah cried, 'Aye, call upon Rhiannon! Perhaps he will come from his Tomb to aid you!'

And they watched Carse out of their depthless jeering eyes as he swayed in torment.

But Ywain knew. Swiftly she moved to Carse's side and her sword came rasping out of the sheath, to protect him as long as it could.

Hishah laughed. 'A fitting pair – the princess without an empire and the would-be-god!'

Carse said again, in a broken whisper, '*Rhiannon!*'

And Rhiannon answered.

From the depths of Carse's mind where he had lain hidden the Cursed One came, surging in terrible strength through every cell and atom of the Earthman's brain, possessing him utterly now that Carse had opened the way.

As it had been before in the place of the Wise One the consciousness of Matthew Carse stood aside in his own body and watched and listened.

He heard the voice of Rhiannon – the real and godlike voice that he had only copied – ring forth from his own lips in anger that was beyond human power to know.

'*Behold your Lord, oh crawling children of the Serpent! Behold – and die!*'

The mocking laughter died away into silence. Hishah gave back and into his eyes came the beginning of fear.

Rhiannon's voice rolled out, thundering against the walls. The strength and fury of Rhiannon blazed in the Earthman's face and now his body seemed to tower over the Dhuvians and the sword was a thing of lightning in his hands.

'*What now of the touching of minds, Hishah? Probe deeply – more deeply than you did before when your feeble powers could not penetrate the mental barrier I set against you!*'

Hishah voiced a high and hissing scream. He recoiled in horror and the circle of the Dhuvians broke as they turned to seek their weapons, their lipless mouths stretched wide in fear.

Rhiannon laughed, the terrible laughter of one who has waited through an age for vengeance and finds it at last.

'*Run! Run and strive – for in your great wisdom you have let Rhiannon through your guarding Veil and death is in Caer Dhu!*'

And the Dhuvians ran, writhing in the shadows as they caught up the weapons they had not thought to need. The green light glinted on the shining tubes and prisms.

But the hand of Carse, guided now by the sure knowledge of Rhiannon, had darted toward the biggest of the ancient weapons – toward the rim of the great flat crystal wheel. He set the wheel to spinning.

There must have been some intricate triggering of power within the metal globe, some hidden control that his fingers touched. Carse never knew. He only knew that a strange dark halo appeared in the dim air, enclosing himself and Ywain and the shuddering Boghaz and Garach, who had risen doglike to his hands and knees and was watching with eyes that held no shred of sanity. The ancient weapons were also enclosed in that ring of dark force, and a faint singing rose from the crystal rods.

The dark ring began to expand, like a circular wave sweeping outward.

The weapons of the Dhuvians strove against it. Lances of lightning, of cold flame and searing brilliance, leaped toward it, struck – and splintered and died. Powerful electric discharges that broke themselves on the invisible dielectric that shielded Rhiannon's circle.

Rhiannon's ring of dark force expanded relentlessly, out and out, and where it touched the Dhuvians the cold ophidian bodies withered and shrivelled and lay like cast-off skins upon the stones.

Rhiannon spoke no more. Carse felt the deadly throb of power in his hand as the shining wheel spun faster and faster on its mount and his mind shuddered away from what he could sense in Rhiannon's mind.

For he could sense dimly the nature of the Cursed One's terrible weapon. It was akin to that deadly ultra-violet radiation of the Sun which would destroy all life were it not for the shielding ozone in the atmosphere.

But where the ultra-violet radiation known to Carse's Earth science was easily absorbed, that of Rhiannon's ancient alien science lay in uncharted octaves below the four-hundred angstrom limit and could be produced as an expanding halo that no known mater could absorb. And where it touched living tissue, it killed.

Carse hated the Dhuvians but never in the world had there been such hatred in a human heart as he felt now in Rhiannon.

Garach began to whimper. Whimpering he recoiled from the blazing eyes of the man who towered above him. Half scrambling, half running, he darted away with a sound like laughter in his throat.

Straight out into the dark ring he ran and death received him and silently withered him.

Spreading, spreading, the silent force pulsed outward. Through metal and flesh and stone it went, withering, killing, hunting down the last child of the Serpent who fled through the dark corridors of Caer Dhu. No more weapons flamed against it. No more supple arms were raised to fend it off.

It struck the enclosing Veil at last. Carse felt the subtle shock of its checking and then Rhiannon stopped the wheel.

There was a time of utter silence as those three who were left alive in the city stood motionless, too stunned almost to breathe.

At last the voice of Rhiannon spoke. '*The Serpent is dead. Let his city and my weapons that have wrought such evil in this world – pass with the Dhuvians*'

He turned from the crystal wheel and sought another instrument, one of the squat looped metal rods.

He raised the small black thing and pressed a secret spring

and from the leaden tube that formed its muzzle came a little spark, too bright for the eye to look upon.

Only a tiny fleck of light that settled on the stones. But it began to grow. It seemed to feed on the atoms of the rocks as flame feeds on wood. Like wildfire it leaped across the flags. It touched the crystal wheel and the weapon that had destroyed the Serpent was itself consumed.

A chain-reaction such as no nuclear scientist of Earth had conceived, one that could make the atoms of metal and crystal and stone as unstable as the high-number radioactive elements.

Rhiannon said, '*Come*.'

They walked through the empty corridors in silence and behind them the strange witchfire fed and fattened and the vast central hall was enveloped in its swift destruction.

The knowledge of Rhiannon guided Carse to the nerve-centre of the Veil, to a chamber by the great gate, there to set the controls so that the glimmering web was forever darkened.

They passed out of the citadel and went back down the broken causeway to the quay where the black barge floated.

Then they turned, and looked back, upon the destruction of a city.

They shielded their eyes, for the strange and awful blaze had something in it of the fire of the Sun. It had raced hungrily outward through the sprawling ruins, and made of the central keep a torch that lighted all the sky, blotting out the stars, paling the low moons.

The causeway began to burn, a lengthening tongue of flame between the reeds of the marshland.

Rhiannon raised the squat looped tube again. From it, now, a dim little globule of light not a spark, flew toward the nearing blaze.

And the blaze hesitated, wavered, then began to dull and die.

The witchfire of strange atomic reaction the Rhiannon had triggered he had now damped and killed by some limiting counter-factor whose nature Carse could not dream. They poled the barge out onto the water as the quivering radiance behind them sank and died. And then the night was dark again and of Caer Dhu there was nothing to be seen but steam.

The voice of Rhiannon spoke, once more. '*It is done,*' he said. '*I have redeemed my sin.*'

The Earthman felt the utter weariness of the being within him as the possession was withdrawn from his brain and body.

And then, again, he was only Matthew Carse.

19
JUDGEMENT OF THE QUIRU

The whole world seemed hushed and still in the dawn as their barge went down to Sark. None of them spoke and none of them looked back at the vast white steam that still rolled solemnly up across the sky.

Carse felt numbed, drained of all emotion. He had let the wrath of Rhiannon use him and he could not yet feel quite the same. He knew that there was something of it still in his face, or the other two would not quite meet his eyes nor did they break the silence.

The great crowd gathered on the waterfront of Sark was silent too. It seemed that they had stood there for long looking toward Caer Dhu, and even now, after the glare of its destruction had died out of the sky, they stared with white, frightened faces.

Carse looked out at the Khond longships riding with their sails slack against the yards and knew that that terrible blaze had awed the Sea Kings into waiting.

The black barge glided in to the palace stair. The crowd surged forward as Ywain stepped ashore, their voices rising in a strange hushed clamour. And Ywain spoke to them.

'Caer Dhu and the Serpent both are gone – destroyed by the Lord Rhiannon.'

She turned instinctively toward Carse. And the eyes of all that vast throng dwelt upon him as the word spread, growing at last to an overwhelming cry of thankfulness.

'Rhiannon! Rhiannon the Deliverer!'

He was the Cursed One no longer, at least not to these Sarks.

And for the first time, Carse realised the loathing they had had for the allies Garach had forced upon them.

He walked toward the palace with Ywain and Boghaz and knew with a sense of awe how it felt to be a god. They entered the dim cool halls and it seemed already as though a shadow had gone out of them. Ywain paused at the doors of the throne room as though she had just remembered that she was ruler now in Garach's place.

She turned to Carse and said, 'If the Sea Kings still attack ...'

'They won't – not until they know what happened. And now we must find Rold if he still lives.'

'He lives,' said Ywain. 'After the Dhuvians emptied Rold of his knowledge my father held him as hostage for me.'

They found the Lord of Khondor at last, chained in the dungeons deep under the palace walls. He was wasted and drawn with suffering but he still had the spirit left to raise his red head and snarl at Carse and Ywain.

'Demon,' he said. 'Traitor. Have you and your hellcat come at last to kill me?'

Carse told him the story of Caer Dhu and Rhiannon, watching Rold's expression change slowly from savage despair to a stunned and unbelieving joy.

'Your fleet stands off Sark under Ironbeard,' he finished. 'Will you take this word to the Sea Kings and bring them in to parley?'

'Aye,' said Rold. 'By the gods I will!' He stared at Carse, shaking his head. 'A strange dream of madness these last days have been! And now – to think that I would have slain you gladly in the place of the Wise Ones with my own hand!'

That was shortly after dawn. By noon the council of the Sea Kings was assembled in the throne room with Rold at their head and Emer, who had refused to stay behind in Khondor.

They sat around a long table. Ywain occupied the throne and Carse stood apart from all of them. His face was stern and very weary and there was in it still a hint of strangeness.

He said with finality, 'There need be no war now. The Serpent is gone and without its power Sark can no longer oppress her neighbours. The subject cities, like Jekkara and Valkis, will be freed. The empire of Sark is no more.'

Ironbeard leaped to his feet, crying fiercely, 'Then now is our chance to destroy Sark forever!'

Others of the Sea Kings rose. Thorn of Tarak loud among them, shouting their assent. Ywain's hand tightened upon her sword.

Carse stepped forward, his eyes blazing. 'I say there will be peace! Must I call upon Rhiannon to enforce my word?'

They quieted, awed by that threat, and Rold bade them sit and hold their tongues.

'There has been enough of fighting and bloodshed,' he told them sternly. 'And for the future we can meet Sark on equal terms. I am Lord of Khondor and I say that Khondor will make peace!'

Caught between Carse's threat and Rold's decision the Sea Kings one by one agreed. Then Emer spoke. 'The slaves must all be freed – human and Halfling alike.'

Carse nodded. 'It will be done.'

'And,' said Rold, 'there is another condition.' He faced Carse with unalterable determination. 'I have said we will make peace with Sark – but not, though you bring fifty Rhiannons against us, with a Sark that is ruled by Ywain!'

'Aye,' roared the Sea Kings, looking wolf-eyed at Ywain. 'That is our word also!'

There was a silence then and Ywain rose from the high sea, her face proud and sombre.

'The condition is met,' she said. 'I have no wish to rule over a Sark tamed and stripped of empire. I hated the Serpent as you did – but it is too late for me to be queen of a petty village of fishermen. The people may choose another ruler.'

She stepped down from the dais and went from them to stand erect by a window at the far end of the room, looking out over the harbour.

Carse turned to the Sea Kings. 'It is agreed, then.'

And they answered, 'It is agreed.'

Emer, whose fey gaze had not wavered from Carse since the

beginning of the parley, came to his side now, laying her hand on his. 'And where is your place in this?' she asked softly.

Carse looked down at her, rather dazedly. 'I have not had time to think.'

But it must be thought of, now. And he did not know.

As long as he bore within him the shadow of Rhiannon this world would never accept him as a man. Honour he might have but never anything more and the lurking fear of the Cursed One would remain. Too many centuries of hate had grown around that name.

Rhiannon had redeemed his crime but even so, as long as Mars lived, he would be remembered as the Cursed One.

As though in answer, for the first time since Caer Dhu the dark invader stirred and his thought-voice whispered in Carse's mind.

'*Go back to the Tomb and I will leave you, for I would follow my brothers. After that you are free. I can guide you back along that pathway to your own time if you wish. Or you can remain here.*'

And still Carse did not know.

He liked this green and smiling Mars. But as he looked at the Sea Kings, who were waiting for his answer, and then beyond them through the windows to the White Sea and the marshes, it came to him that this was not his world, that he could never truly belong to it.

He spoke at last and as he did so he saw Ywain's face turned toward him in the shadows.

'Emer knew and the Halflings also that I was not of your world. I came from out of space and time, along the pathway which is hidden in the Tomb of Rhiannon.'

He paused to let them grasp that and they did not seem greatly astonished. Because of what had happened they could believe anything of him, even though it be beyond their comprehension.

Carse said heavily, 'A man is born into one world and there he belongs. I am going back to my own place.'

He could see that even though they protested courteously, the Sea Kings were relieved.

'The blessings of the gods attend you, stranger,' Emer whispered and kissed him gently on the lips.

Then she went and the jubilant Sea Kings went with her. Boghaz had slipped out and Carse and Ywain were alone in the great empty room.

He went to her, looking into her eyes that had not lost their old fire even now. 'And where will you go now?' he asked her.

She answered quietly, 'If you will let me I go with you.'

He shook his head. 'No. You could not live in my world, Ywain. It's a cruel and bitter place, very old and near to death.'

'It does not matter. My own world also is dead.'

He put his hands on her shoulders, strong beneath the mailed shirt. 'You don't understand. I came a long way across time – a million years.' He paused, not quite knowing how to tell her.

'Look out there. Think how it will be when the White Sea is only a desert of blowing dust – when the green is gone from the hills and the white cities are crumbled and the river beds are dry.'

Ywain understood and sighed. 'Age and death come at last to everything. And death will come very swiftly to me if I remain here. I am outcast and my name is hated even as Rhiannon's was.'

He knew that she was not afraid of death but was merely using that argument to sway him.

And yet the argument was true.

'Could you be happy,' he asked, 'with the memory of your own world haunting you at every step?'

'I have never been happy,' she answered, 'and therefore I shall not miss it.' She looked at him fairly. 'I will take the risk. Will you?'

His fingers tightened. 'Yes,' he said huskily. 'Yes, I will.'

He took her in his arms and kissed her and when she drew back she whispered, with a shyness utterly new in her, 'The "Lord Rhiannon" spoke truly when he taunted me concerning the barbarian.' She was silent a moment, then added, 'I think which world we dwell in will not matter much, as long as we are together in it.'

Days later the black galley pulled into Jekkara harbour, finishing her last voyage under the ensign of Ywain of Sark.

It was a strange greeting she and Carse received there, where the whole city had gathered to see the stranger, who was also the Cursed One, and the Sovereign Lady of Sark, who was no more a sovereign. The crowd kept back at a respectful distance and they cheered the destruction of Caer Dhu and the death of the Serpent. But for Ywain they had no welcome.

Only one man stood on the quay to meet them. It was Boghaz – a very splendid Boghaz, robed in velvet and loaded down with jewels, wearing a golden circlet on his head.

He had vanished out of Sark on the day of the parley on some mission of his own and it seemed that he had succeeded.

He bowed to Carse and Ywain with grandiloquent politeness.

'I have been to Valkis,' he said. 'It's a free city again – and because of my unparalleled heroism in helping to destroy Caer Dhu I have been chosen king.'

He beamed, then added with a confidential grin, 'I always did dream of looting a royal treasury!'

'But,' Carse reminded him, 'it's *your* treasury now.'

Boghaz started. 'By the gods it is so!' He drew himself up, waxing suddenly stern. 'I see that I shall have to be severe with thieves in Valkis. There will be heavy punishment for any crime against property – especially royal property!'

'And fortunately,' said Carse gravely, 'you are acquainted with all the knavish tricks of thieves.'

'That is true,' said Boghaz sententiously. 'I have always said that knowledge is a valuable thing. Behold now, how my purely academic studies of the lawless elements will help me to keep my people safe!'

He accompanied them through Jekkara, until they reached the open country beyond, and then he bade them farewell, plucking off a ring which he thrust into Carse's hand. Tears ran down his fat cheeks.

'Wear this, old friend, that you may remember Boghaz, who guided your steps wisely through a strange world.'

He turned and stumbled away and Carse watched his fat figure vanish into the streets of the city, where they had first met.

All alone Carse and Ywain made their way into the hills above Jekkara and came at last to the Tomb. They stood together on the rocky ledge, looking out across the wooded hills and the glowing sea, and the distant towers of the city white in the sunlight.

'Are you still sure,' Carse asked her, 'that you wish to leave all this?'

'I have no place here now,' she answered sadly. 'I would be rid of this world as it would be rid of me.'

She turned and strode without hesitation into the dark tunnel. Ywain the Proud, that not even the gods themselves could break! Carse went with her, holding a lighted torch.

Through the echoing vault and beyond the door marked with the curse of Rhiannon, into the inner chamber, where the torchlight struck against darkness – the utter darkness of that strange aperture in the space-time continuum of the universe.

At that last moment Ywain's face showed fear and she caught the Earthman's hand. The tiny motes swarmed and flickered before them in the gloom of time itself. The voice of Rhiannon spoke to Carse and he stepped forward into the darkness, holding tightly to Ywain's hand.

This time, at first, there was no headlong plunge into nothingness. The wisdom of Rhiannon guided and steadied them. The torch went out. Carse dropped it. His heart pounded and he was blind and deaf in the soundless vortex of force.

Again Rhiannon spoke. '*See now with my mind what your human eyes could not see before!*'

The pulsing darkness cleared in some strange way that had nothing to do with light or sight. Carse looked upon Rhiannon.

His body lay in a coffin of dark crystal whose inner facets glowed with the subtle force that prisoned him forever as though frozen in the heart of a jewel.

Through the cloudy substance, Carse could make out dimly a naked form of more than human strength and beauty, so vital and instinct with life that it seemed a terrible thing to prison it in that narrow space. The face also was beautiful, dark and imperious and stormy even now, with the eyes closed as though in death.

But there could be no death in this place. It was beyond time and without time there is no decay and Rhiannon would have all eternity to lie there, remembering his sin.

While he stared, Carse realised that the alien being had withdrawn from him so gently and carefully that there had been no shock. His mind was still in touch with the mind of Rhiannon but the strange dualism was ended. The Cursed One had released him.

Yet, through that sympathy that still existed between these two minds that had been one for so long, Carse heard Rhiannon's passionate call – a mental cry that pulsed far out along the pathway through space and time.

'My brothers of the Quiru, hear me! I have undone my ancient crime.'

Again he called with all the wild strength of his will. There was a period of silence, of nothingness and then, gradually, Carse sensed the approach of other minds, grave and powerful and stern.

He would never know from what far world they had come. Long ago the Quiru had gone out by this road that led beyond the universe, to cosmic regions forever outside his ken. And now they had come back briefly in answer to Rhiannon's call.

Dim and shadowy, Carse saw godlike forms come slowly into being, tenuous as shining smoke in the gloom.

'Let me go with you, my brothers! For I have destroyed the Serpent and my sin is redeemed.'

It seemed that the Quiru pondered, searching Rhiannon's heart for truth. Then at last one stepped forward and laid his hand upon the coffin. The subtle fires died within it. 'It is our judgement that Rhiannon may go free.'

A giddiness came over Carse. The scene began to fade. he saw Rhiannon rise and go to join his brothers of the Quiru, his body growing shadowy as he passed.

He turned once to look at Carse, and his eyes were open now, full of a joy beyond human understanding.

'Keep my sword, Earthman – bear it proudly, for without you I could never have destroyed Caer Dhu.'

Dizzy, half fainting, Carse received the last mental command.

And as he staggered with Ywain through the dark vortex, falling now with nightmare swiftness through the eerie gloom, he heard the last ringing echo of Rhiannon's farewell.

20
THE RETURN

There was solid rock under their feet at last. They crept trembling away from the vortex, white-faced and shaken, saying nothing, wanting only to be free of that dark vault.

Carse found the tunnel. But when he reached the end he was oppressed by a dread that he might be once again lost in time, and dared not look out.

He need not have feared. Rhiannon had guided them surely. He stood again among the barren hills of his own Mars. It was sunset, and the vast reaches of the dead sea-bottom were flooded with the dull red light. The wind came cold and dry out of the desert, blowing the dust, and there was Jekkara in the distance – his own Jekkara of the Low Canals.

He turned anxiously to Ywain, watching her face as she looked for the first time upon his world. He saw her lips tighten as though over a deep pain.

Then she threw her shoulders back and smiled and settled the hilt of her sword in its sheath.

'Let us go,' she said and placed her hand again in his.

They walked the long weary way across the desolate land and the ghosts of the past were all around them. Now, over the bones of Mars, Carse could see the living flesh that had clothed it once in splendour, the tall trees and the rich earth, and he would never forget.

He looked out across the dead sea-bottom and knew that all the years of his life he would hear the booming roll of surf on the shores of a spectral ocean.

Darkness came. The little low moons rose in the cloudless

sky. Ywain's hand was firm and strong in his. Carse was aware of a great happiness rising within him. His steps quickened.

They came into the streets of Jekkara, the crumbling streets beside the Low-Canal. The dry wind shook the torches and the sound of the harps was as he remembered and the little dark women made tinkling music as they walked.

Ywain smiled. 'It is still Mars,' she said.

They walked together through the twisting ways – the man who still bore in his face the dark shadow of a god and the woman who had been a queen. The people drew apart to let them pass, staring after them in wonder, and the sword of Rhiannon was like a sceptre in Carse's hand.

QUEEN OF THE MARTIAN CATACOMBS

1

For hours the hard-pressed beast had fled across the Martian desert with its dark rider. Now it was spent. It faltered and broke stride, and when the rider cursed and dug his heels into the scaly sides, the brute only turned its head and hissed at him. It stumbled on a few more paces into the lee of a sandhill, and there it stopped, crouching down in the dust.

The man dismounted. The creature's eyes burned like green lamps in the light of the little moons, and he knew that it was no use trying to urge it on. He looked back, the way he had come.

In the distance there were four black shadows grouped together in the barren emptiness. They were running fast. In a few minutes they would be upon him.

He stood still, thinking what he should do next. Ahead, far ahead, was a low ridge, and beyond the ridge lay Valkis and safety, but he could never make it now. Off to his right, a lonely tor stood up out of the blowing sand. There were tumbled rocks at its foot.

'They tried to run me down in the open,' he thought. 'But here, by the Nine Hells, they'll have to work for it!'

He moved then, running toward the tor with a lightness and speed incredible in anything but an animal or a savage. He was of Earth stock, built tall, and more massive than he looked by reason of his leanness. The desert wind was bitter cold, but he did not seem to notice it, though he wore only a ragged shirt of Venusian spider silk, open to the waist. His skin was almost as dark as his black hair, burned indelibly by years of exposure to some terrible sun. His eyes were startlingly light in colour, reflecting back the pale glow of the moons.

With the practised ease of a lizard he slid in among the loose and treacherous rocks. Finding a vantage point, where his back was protected by the tor itself, he crouched down.

After that he did not move, except to draw his gun. There was something eerie about his utter stillness, a quality of patience as unhuman as the patience of the rock that sheltered him.

The four black shadows came closer, resolved themselves into mounted men.

They found the beast, where it lay panting, and stopped. The line of the man's footprints, already blurred by the wind but still plain enough, showed where he had gone.

The leader motioned. The others dismounted. Working with the swift precision of soldiers, they removed equipment from their saddle-packs and began to assemble it.

The man crouching under the tor saw the thing that took shape. It was a Banning shocker, and he knew that he was not going to fight his way out of this trap. His pursuers were out of range of his own weapon. They would remain so. The Banning, with its powerful electric beam, would take him – dead or senseless, as they wished.

He thrust the useless gun back into his belt. He knew who these men were, and what they wanted with him. They were officers of the Earth Police Control, bringing him a gift – twenty years in the Luna cell-blocks.

Twenty years in the grey catacombs, buried in the silence and the eternal dark.

He recognised the inevitable. He was used to inevitables – hunger, pain, loneliness, the emptiness of dreams. He had accepted a lot of them in his time. Yet he made no move to surrender. He looked out at the desert and the night sky, and his eyes blazed, the desperate, strangely beautiful eyes of a creature very close to the roots of life, something less and more than man. His hands found a shard of rock and broke it.

The leader of the four men rode slowly toward the tor, his right arm raised.

His voice carried clearly on the wind. 'Eric John Stark!' he called, and the dark man tensed in the shadows.

The rider stopped. He spoke again, but this time in a different tongue. It was no dialect of Earth, Mars or Venus, but a strange speech, as harsh and vital as the blazing Mercurian valleys that bred it.

'*Oh N'Chaka, oh Man-without-a-tribe, I call you!*'

There was a long silence. The rider and his mount were motionless under the low moons, waiting.

Eric John Stark stepped slowly out from the pool of blackness under the tor.

'Who calls me N'Chaka?'

The rider relaxed somewhat. He answered in English, 'You know perfectly well who I am, Eric. May we meet in peace?'

Stark shrugged. 'Of course.'

He walked on to meet the rider, who had dismounted, leaving his beast behind. He was a slight, wiry man, this EPC officer, with the rawhide look of the frontiers still on him. His hair was grizzled and his sun-blackened skin was deeply lined, but there was nothing in the least aged about his hard good-humoured face nor his remarkably keen dark eyes.

'It's been a long time, Eric,' he said.

Stark nodded. 'Sixteen years.' The two men studied each other for a moment, and then Stark said, 'I thought you were still on Mercury, Ashton.'

'They've called all us experienced hands in to Mars.' He held out cigarettes. 'Smoke?'

Stark took one. They bent over Ashton's lighter, and then stood there smoking while the wind blew red dust over their feet and the three men of the patrol waited quietly beside the Banning. Ashton was taking no chances. The electro-beam could stun without injury.

Presently Ashton said, 'I'm going to be crude, Eric. I'm going to remind you of some things.'

'Save it,' Stark retorted. 'You've got me. There's no need to talk about it.'

'Yes,' said Ashton, 'I've got you, and a damned hard time I've had doing it. That's why I'm going to talk about it.'

His dark eyes met Stark's cold stare and held it.

'Remember who I am – Simon Ashton. Remember who came along when the miners in that valley on Mercury had a wild boy in a cage, and were going to finish him off like they had the tribe that raised him. Remember all the years after that, when I brought that boy up to be a civilised human being.'

Stark laughed, not without a certain humour. 'You should have left me in the cage. I was caught a little old for civilising.'

'Maybe. I don't think so. Anyway, I'm reminding you,' Ashton said.

Stark said, with no particular bitterness, 'You don't have to get sentimental. I know it's your job to take me in.'

Ashton said deliberately, 'I won't take you in, Eric, unless you make me.' He went on then, rapidly, before Stark could answer. 'You've got a twenty-year sentence hanging over you, for running guns to the Middle-Swamp tribes when they revolted against Terro-Venusian Metals, and a couple of similar jobs.

'All right. So I know why you did it, and I won't say I don't agree with you. But you put yourself outside the law, and that's that. Now you're on your way to Valkis. You're headed into a mess that'll put you on Luna for life, the next time you're caught.'

'And this time you don't agree with me.'

'No. Why do you think I near broke my neck to catch you before you got there?' Ashton bent closer, his face very intent. 'Have you made any deal with Delgaun of Valkis? Did he send for you?'

'He sent for me, but there's no deal yet. I'm on the beach. Broke. I got a message from this Delgaun, whoever he is, that there was going to be a private war back in the Drylands, and he'd pay me to help fight it. After all, that's my business.'

Ashton shook his head.

'This isn't a private war, Eric. It's something a lot bigger and nastier than that. The Martian Council of City-States and the Earth Commission are both in a cold sweat, and no one can find out exactly what's going on. You know what the Low-Canal towns are – Valkis, Jekkara, Barakesh. No law-abiding Martian, let alone an Earthman, can last five minutes in them. And the back-blocks are absolutely *verboten*. So all we get is rumours.

'Fantastic rumours about a barbarian chief named Kynon, who seems to be promising heaven and earth to the tribes of Kesh and Shun – some wild stuff about the ancient cult of the Ramas that everybody thought was dead a thousand years ago. We know that Kynon is tied up somehow with Delgaun, who is a most efficient bandit, and we know that some of the top criminals of the whole System are filtering in to join up. Knighton and Walsh of Terra, Themis of Mercury, Arrod of Callisto Colony – and, I believe, your old comrade in arms, Luthar the Venusian.'

Stark gave a slight start, and Ashton smiled briefly.

'Oh, yes,' he said. 'I heard about that.' Then he sobered. 'You can figure that set-up for yourself, Eric. The barbarians are going to go out and fight some kind of a holy war, to suit the entirely unholy purposes of men like Delgaun and the others.

'Half a world is going to be raped, blood is going to run deep in the Drylands – and it will all be barbarian blood spilled for a lying promise, and the carrion crows of Valkis will get fat on it. Unless, somehow, we can stop it.'

He paused, then said flatly, 'I want you to go on to Valkis, Eric – but as my agent. I won't put it on the grounds that you'd be doing civilisation a service. You don't owe anything to civilisation, Lord knows. But you might save a lot of your own kind of people from getting slaughtered to say nothing of the border-state Martians who'll be the first to get Kynon's axe.

'Also, you could wipe that twenty-year hitch on Luna off the slate, maybe even work up a desire to make a man of yourself, instead of a sort of tiger wandering from one kill to the next.' He added, 'If you live.'

Stark said slowly, 'You're clever, Ashton. You know I've got a feeling for all planetary primitives like those who raised me, and you appeal to that.'

'Yes,' said Ashton, 'I'm clever. But I'm not a liar. What I've told you is true.'

Stark carefully ground out the cigarette beneath his heel. Then he looked up. 'Suppose I agree to become your agent in this, and go off to Valkis. What's to prevent me from forgetting all about you, then?'

Ashton said softly, 'Your word, Eric. You get to know a man pretty well when you know him from boyhood on up. Your word is enough.'

There was a silence, and then Stark held out his hand. 'All right, Simon – but only for this one deal. After that, no promises.'

'Fair enough.' They shook hands.

'I can't give you any suggestions,' Ashton said. 'You're on your own, completely. You can get in touch with me through the Earth Commission office in Tarak. You know where that is?'

Stark nodded. 'On the Dryland Border.'

'Good luck to you, Eric.'

He turned, and they walked back together to where the three men waited. Ashton nodded, and they began to dismantle the Banning. Neither they nor Ashton looked back, as they rode away.

Stark watched them go. He filled his lungs with the cold air, and stretched. Then he roused the beast out of the sand. It had rested, and was willing to carry him again as long as he did not press it. He set off again, across the desert.

The ridge grew as he approached it, looming into a low mountain chain much worn by the ages. A pass opened before him, twisting between the hills of barren rock.

He traversed it, coming out at the farther end above the basin of a dead sea. The lifeless land stretched away into darkness, a vast waste of desolation more lonely even than the desert. And between the sea-bottom and the foothills, Stark saw the lights of Valkis.

2

There were many lights, far below. Tiny pinpricks of flame where torches burned in the streets beside the Low-Canal – the thread of black water that was all that remained of a forgotten ocean.

Stark had never been here before. Now he looked at the city that sprawled down the slope under the low moons, and shivered, the primitive twitching of the nerves that an animal feels in the presence of death.

For the streets where the torches flared were only a tiny part of Valkis. The life of the city had flowed downward from the cliff-tops, following the dropping level of the sea. Five cities, the oldest scarcely recognisable as a place of human habitation. Five harbours, the docks and quays still standing, half buried in the dust.

Five ages of Martian history, crowned on the topmost level with the ruined palace of the old pirate kings of Valkis. The towers still stood, broken but indomitable, and in the moonlight they had a sleeping look, as though they dreamed of blue water and the sound of waves, and of tall ships coming in heavy with treasure.

Stark picked his way slowly down the steep descent. There was something fascinating to him in the stone houses, roofless and silent in the night. The paving blocks still showed the rutting of wheels where carters had driven to the marketplace, and princes had gone by in gilded chariots. The quays were scarred where ships had lain against them, rising and falling with the tides.

Stark's senses had developed in a strange school, and the thin veneer of civilisation he affected had not dulled them. Now it seemed to him that the wind had the echoes of voices in it, and the smell of spices and fresh-spilled blood.

He was not surprised when, in the last level above the living town, armed men came out of the shadows and stopped him.

They were lean, dark men, very wiry and light of foot, and their faces were the faces of wolves – not primitive wolves at all, but beasts of prey that had been civilised for so many thousands of years that they could afford to forget it.

They were most courteous, and Stark would not have cared to disobey their request.

He gave his name. 'Delgaun sent for me.'

The leader of the Valkisians nodded his narrow head. 'You're expected.' His sharp eyes had taken in every feature of the Earthman, and Stark knew that his description had been memorised down to the last detail. Valkis guarded its doors with care.

'Ask in the city,' said the sentry. 'Anyone can direct you to the palace.'

Stark nodded and went on, down through the long-dead streets in the moonlight and the silence.

With shocking suddenness, he was plunged into the streets of the living.

It was very late now, but Valkis was awake and stirring. Seething, rather. The narrow twisting ways were crowded. The laughter of women came down from the flat roofs. Torchlight flared, gold and scarlet, lighting the wineshops, making blacker the shadows of the alley-mouths.

Stark left his beast at a *serai* on the edge of the canal. The paddocks were already jammed. Stark recognized the long-legged brutes of the Dryland breed, and as he left a caravan passed him, coming in, with a jangling of bronze bangles and a great hissing and stamping in the dust.

The riders were tall barbarians – Keshi, Stark thought, from the way they braided their tawny hair. They wore plain leather, and their blue-eyed women rode like queens.

Valkis was full of them. For days, it seemed, they must have poured in across the dead sea bottom, from the distant oases and the barren deserts of the back-blocks. Brawny warriors of Kesh and Shun, making holiday beside the Low-Canal, where there was more water than any of them had seen in their lives.

They were in Valkis, these barbarians, but they were not part of it. Shouldering his way through the streets, Stark got the peculiar flavour of the town, that he guessed could never be touched or changed by anything.

In a square, a girl danced to the music of harp and drum. The air was heavy with the smell of wine and burning pitch and incense. A lithe, swart Valkisian in his bright kilt and jewelled girdle leaped out and danced with the girl, his teeth flashing as he whirled and postured. In the end he bore her off, laughing, her black hair hanging down his back.

Women looked at Stark. Women graceful as cats, bare to the waist, their skirts slit at the sides above the thigh, wearing no ornaments but the tiny golden bells that are the peculiar property of the Low-Canal towns, so that the air is always filled with their delicate, wanton chiming.

Valkis had a laughing, wicked soul. Stark had been in many

places in his life, but never one before that beat with such a pulse of evil, incredibly ancient, but strong and gay.

He found the palace at last – a great rambling structure of quarried stone, with doors and shutters of beaten bronze closed against the dust and the incessant wind. He gave his name to the guard and was taken inside, through halls hung with antique tapestries, the flagged floors worn hollow by countless generations of sandalled feet.

Again, Stark's half-wild senses told him that life within these walls had not been placid. The very stones whispered of age-old violence, the shadows were heavy with the lingering ghosts of passion.

He was brought before Delgaun, the lord of Valkis, in the big central room that served as his headquarters.

Delgaun was lean and catlike, after the fashion of his race. His black hair showed a stippling of silver, and the hard beauty of his face was strongly marked, the lined drawn deep and all the softness of youth long gone away. He wore a magnificent harness, and his eyes, under fine dark brows, were like drops of hot gold.

He looked up as the Earthman came in, one swift penetrating glance. Then he said, 'You're Stark.'

There was something odd about those yellow eyes, bright and keen as a killer hawk's yet somehow secret, as though the true thoughts behind them would never show through. Instinctively, Stark disliked the man.

But he nodded and came up to the council table, turning his attention to the others in the room. A handful of Martians – Low-Canallers, chiefs and fighting men from their ornaments and their proud looks – and several outlanders, their conventional garments incongruous in this place.

Stark knew them all. Knighton and Walsh of Terra, Themis of Mercury, Arrod of Callisto Colony – and Luhar of Venus. Pirates, thieves, renegades, and each one an expert in his line.

Ashton was right. There was something big, something very big and very ugly, shaping between Valkis and the Drylands.

But that was only a quick, passing thought in Stark's mind.

It was on Luhar that his attention centred. Bitter memory and hatred had come to savage life within him as soon as he saw the Venusian.

The man was handsome. A cashiered officer of the crack Venusian Guards, very slim, very elegant, his pale hair cropped short and curling, his dark tunic fitting him like a second skin.

He said, 'The aborigine! I thought we had enough barbarians here without sending for more.'

Stark said nothing. He began to walk toward Luhar.

Luhar said sharply, 'There's no use in getting nasty, Stark. Past scores are past. We're on the same side now.'

The Earthman spoke, then, with a peculiar gentleness.

'We were on the same side once before. Against Terror-Venus Metals. Remember?'

'I remember very well!' Luhar was speaking now not to Stark alone, but to everyone in the room. 'I remember that your innocent barbarian friends had me tied to the block there in the swamps, and that you were watching the whole thing with honest pleasure. If the Company men hadn't come along, I'd be screaming there yet.'

'You sold us out,' Stark said. 'You had it coming.'

He continued to walk toward Luhar.

Delgaun spoke. He did not raise his voice, yet Stark felt the impact of his command.

'There will be no fighting here,' Delgaun said. 'You are both hired mercenaries, and while you take my pay you will forget your private quarrels. Do you understand?'

Luhar nodded and sat down, smiling out of the corner of his mouth at Stark, who stood looking with narrowed eyes at Delgaun.

He was still half blind with his anger against Luhar. His hands ached for the kill. But even so, he recognised the power in Delgaun.

A sound shockingly akin to the growl of a beast echoed in his throat. Then, gradually, he relaxed. The man Delgaun he would have challenged. But to do so would wreck the mission that he had promised to carry out here for Ashton.

He shrugged, and joined the others at the table.

Walsh of Terra rose abruptly and began to prowl back and forth.

'How much longer do we have to wait?' he demanded.

Delgaun poured wine into a bronze goblet. 'Don't expect me to know,' he snapped. He shoved the flagon along the table toward Stark.

Stark helped himself. The wine was warm and sweet on his tongue. He drank slowly, sitting relaxed and patient while the others smoked nervously or rose to pace up and down.

Stark wondered what, or who, they were waiting for. But he did not ask.

Time went by.

Stark raised his head, listening. 'What's that?'

Their duller ears had heard nothing, but Delgaun rose and flung open the shutters of the window near him.

The Martian dawn, brilliant and clear, flooded the dead sea bottom with harsh light. Beyond the black line of the canal a caravan was coming toward Valkis through the blowing dust.

It was no ordinary caravan. Warriors rode before and behind, their spearheads blazing in the sunrise. Jewelled trappings on the beasts, a litter with curtains of crimson silk, barbaric splendour. Clear and thin on the air came the wild music of pipes and the deep-throated throbbing of drums.

Stark guessed without being told who it was that rode out of the desert like a king.

Delgaun made a harsh sound in his throat. 'It's Kynon, at last!' he said, and swung around from the window. His eyes sparkled with some private amusement. 'Let us go and welcome the Giver of Life!'

Stark went with them, out into the crowded streets. A silence had fallen on the town. Valkisian and barbarian alike were caught now in a breathless excitement, pressing through the narrow ways, flowing toward the canal.

Stark found himself beside Delgaun in the great square of the slave market, standing on the auction block, above the heads of the throng. The stillness, the expectancy of the crowd were uncanny...

To the measured thunder of drums and the wild skirling of desert pipes, Kynon of Shun came into Valkis.

3

Straight into the square of the slave market the caravan came, and the people pressed back against the walls to make way for them. Stamping of padded hooves on the stones, ring and clash of harness, brave glitter of spears and the great two-handed broadswords of the Drylands, with drumbeats to shake the heart and the savage cry of the pipes to set the blood leaping. Stark could not restrain an appreciative thrill in himself.

The advance guard reached the slave block. Then, with deafening abruptness, the drummers crossed their sticks and the pipers ceased, and there was utter silence in the square.

It lasted for almost a minute, and then from every barbarian throat the name of Kynon roared out until the stones of the city echoed with it.

A man leaped from the back of his mount to the block, standing at its outer edge where all could see, his hands flung up.

'I greet you, my brothers!'

And the cheering went on.

Stark studied Kynon, surprised that he was so young. He had expected a grey-bearded prophet, and instead, here was a brawny-shouldered man of war standing as tall as himself.

Kynon's eyes were a bright, compelling blue, and his face was the face of a young eagle. His voice had deep music in it – the kind of voice that can sway crowds to madness.

Stark looked from him to the rapt faces of the people – even the Valkisians had caught the mood – and thought that Kynon was the most dangerous man he had ever seen. This tawny-haired barbarian in his kilt of bronze-bossed leather was already half a god.

Kynon shouted to the captain of his warriors, 'Bring the captive and the old man!' Then he turned again to the crowd, urging them to silence. When at last the square was still, his voice rang challengingly across it.

'There are still those who doubt me. Therefore I have come to Valkis, and this day – now! – I will show proof that I have not lied!'

A roar and a mutter from the crowd. Kynon's men were lifting to the block a tottering ancient so bowed with years that he could barely stand, and a youth of Terran stock. The boy was in chains. The old man's eyes burned, and he looked at the boy beside him with a terrible joy.

Stark settled down to watch. The litter with the curtains of crimson silk was now beside the block. A girl, a Valkisian, stood beside it, looking up. It seemed to Stark that her green eyes rested on Kynon with a smouldering anger.

He glanced away from the serving girl, and saw that the curtains were partly open. A woman lay on the cushions within. He could not see much of her, except that her hair was like dark flame and she was smiling, looking at the old man and the naked boy. Then her glance, very dark in the shadows of the litter, shifted away and Stark followed it and saw Delgaun. Every muscle of Delgaun's body was drawn taut, and he seemed unable to look away from the woman in the litter.

Stark smiled very slightly. The outlanders were cynically absorbed in what was going on. The crowd had settled again to that silent, breathless tension. The sun blazed down out of the empty sky. The dust blew, and the wind was sharp with the smell of living flesh.

The old man reached out and touched the boy's smooth shoulder, and his gums showed bluish as he laughed.

Kynon was speaking again.

'There are still those who doubt me, I say! Those who scoffed when I said that I possessed the ancient secret of the Ramas of long ago – the secret by which one man's mind may be transferred into another's body. But none of you after today will doubt that I hold that secret!

'I, myself, am not a Rama.' He glanced down along his powerful frame, half-consciously flexing his muscles, and laughed.

'Why should I be a Rama? I have no need, as yet, for the Sending-on of Minds!'

Answering laughter, half ribald, from the crowd.

'No,' said Kynon, 'I am not a Rama. I am a man like you. Like you, I have no wish to grow old, and in the end, to die.'

He swung abruptly to the old man.

'You, Grandfather! Would you not wish to be young again – to ride out to battle, to take the woman of your choice?'

The old man wailed, 'Yes! Yes!' and his gaze dwelt hungrily upon the boy.

'And you shall be!' The strength of a god rang in Kynon's voice. He turned again to the crowd and cried out.

'For years I suffered in the desert alone, searching for the lost secret of the Ramas. And I found it, my brothers! I hold their ancient power. I alone – in these two hands I hold it, and with it I shall begin a new era for our Dryland races!

'There will be fighting, yes. There will be bloodshed. But when that is over and the men of Kesh and Shun are free from their ancient bondage of thirst and the men of the Low-Canals have regained their own – then I shall give new life, unending life, to all who have followed me. The aged and lamed and wounded can choose new bodies from among the captives. There will be no more age, no more sickness, no more death!'

A rippling, shivering sigh from the crowd. Eyeballs gleaming in the bitter light, mouths open on the hunger that is nearest to the human soul.

'Lest anyone still doubt my promise,' said Kynon, 'watch. Watch – and I will show you!'

They watched. Not stirring, hardly breathing, they watched.

The drums struck up a slow and solemn beat. The captain of the warriors, with an escort of six men, marched to the litter and took from the woman's hands a bundle wrapped in silks. Bearing it as though it were precious beyond belief, he came to the block and lifted it up, and Kynon took it from him.

The silken wrappings fluttered loose, fell away. And in Kynon's hands gleamed two crystal crowns and a shining rod.

He held them high, the sunlight glancing in cold fire from the crystal.

'Behold!' he said. 'The Crowns of the Ramas!'

The crowd drew breath then, one long rasping *Ah!*

The solemn drumbeat never faltered. It was as though the pulse of the whole world throbbed within it. Kynon turned. The old man began to tremble. Kynon placed one crown on his wrinkled scalp, and the tottering creature winced as though in pain, but his face was ecstatic.

Relentlessly, Kynon crowned with the second circlet the head of the frightened boy.

'Kneel,' he said.

They knelt. Standing tall above them, Kynon held the rod in his two hands, between the crystal crowns.

Light was born in the rod. It was no reflection of the sun. Blue and brilliant, it flashed along the rod and leaped from it to wake an answering brilliance in the crowns, so that the old man and the youth were haloed with a chill, supernal fire.

The drumbeat ceased. The old man cried out. His hands plucked feebly at his head, then went to his breast and clenched there. Quite suddenly he fell forward over his knees. A convulsive tremor shook him. Then he lay still.

The boy swayed and then fell forward also, with a clashing of chains.

The light died out of the crowns. Kynon stood a moment longer, rigid as a statue, holding the rod which still flickered with blue lightning. Then that also died.

Kynon lowered the rod. In a ringing voice he cried, 'Arise, Grandfather!'

The boy stirred. Slowly, very slowly, he rose to his feet. Holding out his hands, he stared at them, and then touched his thighs, and his flat belly, and the deep curve of his chest.

Up the firm young throat the wondering fingers went, to the smooth cheeks, to the thick fair hair above the crown. A cry broke from him.

With the perfect accent of the Drylands, the Earth boy cried in Martian, 'I am in the youth's body! I am young again!'

A scream, a wail of ecstasy, burst from the crowd. It swayed like a great beast, white faces turned upward. The boy fell down and embraced Kynon's knees.

Eric John Stark found that he himself was trembling slightly. The Valkisian wore a look of intense satisfaction under his mask of awe. The others were almost as rapt and open-mouthed as the crowd.

Stark turned his head slightly and looked down at the litter. One white hand was already drawing the curtains, so that the scarlet silk appeared to shake with silent laughter.

The serving girl beside it had not moved. Still she looked up at Kynon, and there was nothing in her eyes but hate.

After that there was bedlam, the rush and trample of the crowd, the beating of drums, the screaming of pipes, deafening uproar. The crowns and the crystal rod were wrapped again and taken away. Kynon raised up the boy and struck off the chains of captivity. He mounted, with the boy beside him. Delgaun walked before him through the streets, and so did the outlanders.

The body of the old man was disregarded, except by some of Kynon's barbarians who wrapped it in a white cloth and took it away.

Kynon of Shun came in triumph to Delgaun's palace. Standing beside the litter, he gave his hand to the woman, who stepped out and walked beside him through the bronze door.

The women of Shun are tall and strong, bred to stand beside their men in war as well as love, and this red-haired daughter of the Drylands was enough to stop a man's heart with her proud step and her white shoulders, and her eyes that were the colour of smoke. Stark's gaze followed her from a distance.

Presently in the council room were gathered Delgaun and the outlanders, Kynon and his bright-haired queen – and no other Martians but those three.

Kynon sprawled out in the high seat at the head of the table. His face was beaming. He wiped the sweat off it, and then filled a goblet with wine, looking around the room with his bright blue eyes.

'Fill up, gentlemen. I'll give you a toast.' He lifted the goblet. 'Here's to the secret of the Ramas, and the gift of life!'

Stark put down his goblet, still empty. He stared directly at Kynon.

'You have no secret,' said Stark deliberately.

Kynon sat perfectly still, except that, very slowly, he put his own goblet down. Nobody else moved.

Stark's voice sounded loud in the stillness.

'Furthermore,' he said, 'that demonstration in the square was a lie from beginning to end.'

4

Stark's words had the effect of an electric shock on the listeners. Delgaun's black brows went up, and the woman came forward a little to stare at the Earthman with profound interest.

Kynon asked a question, of nobody in particular. 'Who,' he demanded, 'is this great black ape?'

Delgaun told him.

'Ah, yes,' said Kynon. 'Eric John Stark, the wild man from Mercury.' He scowled threateningly. 'Very well – explain how I lied in the square!'

'Certainly. First of all, the Earth boy was a prisoner. He was told what he had to do to save his neck, and then was carefully coached in his part. Secondly, the crystal rod and the crowns are a fake. You used a simple Purcell unit in the rod to produce an electronic brush discharge. That made the blue light. Thirdly, you gave the old man poison, probably by means of a sharp point on the crown. I saw him wince when you put it on him.'

Stark paused. 'The old man died. The boy went through his sham. And that was that.'

Again there was a flat silence. Luhar crouched over the table, his face avid with hope. The woman's eyes dwelt on Stark and did not turn away.

Then, suddenly, Kynon laughed. He roared with it until the tears ran.

'It was a good show, though,' he said at last. 'Damned good.

You'll have to admit that. The crowd swallowed it, horns, hoof and hide.'

He got up and came round to Stark, clapping him on the shoulder, a blow that would have laid a lesser man flat.

'I like you, wild man. Nobody else here had the guts to speak out, but I'll give you odds they were all thinking the same thing.'

Stark said, 'Just where were you, Kynon, during those years you were supposed to be suffering alone in the desert?'

'Curious, aren't you? Well, I'll let you in on a secret.' Kynon lapsed abruptly into perfectly good colloquial English. 'I was on Terra, learning about things like the Purcell electronic discharge.'

Reaching over, he poured wine for Stark and held it out to him. 'Now you know. Now we all know. So let's wash the dust out of our throats and get down to business.'

Stark said, 'No.'

Kynon looked at him. 'What now?'

'You're lying to your people,' Stark said flatly. 'You're making false promises, to lead them into war.'

Kynon was genuinely puzzled by Stark's anger. 'But of course!' he said. 'Is there anything new or strange in that?'

Luhar spoke up, his voice acid with hate. 'Watch out for him, Kynon. He'll sell you out, he'll cut your throat, if he thinks it best for the barbarians.'

Delgaun said, 'Stark's reputation is known all over the system. There's no need to tell us that again.'

'No.' Kynon shook his head, looking very candidly at Stark. 'We sent for you, didn't we, knowing that? All right.'

He stepped back a little, so that the others were included in what he was going to say.

'My people have a just cause for war. They go hungry and thirsty, while the City-States along the Dryland Border hog all the water sources and grow fat. Do you know what it means to watch your children die crying for water on a long march, to come at last to the oasis and find the well sanded in by a storm, and go on again, trying to save your people and your herd? Well,

I do! I was born and bred in the Drylands, and many a time I've cursed the border states with a tongue like a dry stick.

'Stark, you should know the workings of the barbarian mind as well as I do. The men of Kesh and Shun are traditional enemies. Raiding and thieving, open warfare over water and grass. I had to give them a rallying point – a faith strong enough to unite them. Resurrecting the Rama legend was the only hope I had.

'And it has worked. The tribes are one people now. They can go on and take what belongs to them – the right to live. I'm not really so far out in my promises, at all. Now do you understand?'

Stark studied him, with his cold cat-eyes. 'Where do the men of Valkis come in – the men of Jekkara and Barakesh? Where do *we* come in, the hired bravoes?'

Kynon smiled. It was a perfectly sincere smile, and it had no humour in it, only a great pride and a cheerful cruelty.

'We're going to build an empire,' he said softly. 'The City-States are disorganised, too starved or too fat to fight. And Earth is taking us over. Before long, Mars will be hardly more than another Luna.

'We're going to fight that. Drylander and Low-Canaller together, we're going to build a power out of dust and blood – and there will be loot in plenty to go round.'

'That's where my men come in,' said Delgaun, and laughed. 'We low-Canallers live by rapine.'

'And you,' said Kynon, "the hired bravoes", are in it to help. I need you and the Venusian, Stark, to train my men, to plan campaigns, to give me all you know of guerrilla fighting. Knighton has a fast cruiser. He'll bring us supplies from outside. Walsh is a genius, they tell me, at fashioning weapons. Themis is a mechanic, and also the cleverest thief this side of hell – saving your presence, Delgaun! Arrod organised and bossed the Brotherhood of the Little Worlds, which had the Space Patrol going mad for years. He can do the same for us. So there you have it. Now, Stark, what do you say?'

The Earthman answered slowly, 'I'll go along with you – as long as no harm comes to the tribes.'

Kynon laughed. 'No need to worry about that.'

'Just one more question,' Stark said. 'What's going to happen when the people find out that this Rama stuff is just a myth?'

'They won't,' said Kynon. 'The crowns will be destroyed in battle, and it will be very tragic, but very final. No one knows how to make more of them. Oh, I can handle the people! They'll be happy enough, with good land and water.'

He looked around then and said plaintively, 'And now can we sit down and drink like civilised men?'

They sat. The wine went round, and the vultures of Valkis drank to each other's luck and loot, and Stark learned that the woman's name was Berild.

Kynon was happy. He had made his point with the people, and he was celebrating. But Stark noticed that though his tongue grew thick, it did not loosen.

Luhar grew steadily more morose and silent, glancing covertly across the table at Stark. Delgaun toyed with his goblet, and his yellow gaze which gave nothing away moved restlessly between Berild and Stark.

Berild drank not at all. She sat a little apart, with her face in shadow, and her red mouth smiled. Her thoughts, too, were her own secret. But Stark knew that she was still watching him, and he knew that Delgaun was aware of it.

Presently Kynon said, 'Delgaun and I have some talking to do, so I'll bid you gentlemen farewell for the present. You, Stark, and Luhar – I'm going back into the desert at midnight, and you're going with me, so you'd better get some sleep.'

Stark nodded. He rose and went out, with the others.

An attendant showed him to his quarters, in the north wing. Stark had not rested for twenty-four hours, and he was glad of the chance to sleep.

He lay down. The wine spun in his head, and Berild's smile mocked him. Then his thoughts turned to Ashton, and his promise. Presently he slept, and dreamed.

He was a boy on Mercury again, running down a path that led from a cave mouth to the floor of a valley. Above him the mountains rose into the sky and were lost beyond the shallow atmosphere. The rocks danced in the terrible heat, but the soles of his feet were like iron, and trod them lightly. He was quite naked.

The blaze of the sun between the valley walls was like the shining heart of Hell. It did not seem to the boy N'Chaka that it could ever be cold again, yet he knew that when darkness came there would be ice on the shallows of the river. The gods were constantly at war.

He passed a place, ruined by earthquake. It was a mine, and N'Chaka remembered dimly that he had once lived there, with several white-skinned creatures shaped like himself. He went on without a second glance.

He was searching for Tika. When he was old enough, he would mate with her. He wanted to hunt with her now, for she was fleet and as keen as he at scenting out the great lizards.

He heard her voice calling his name. There was terror in it, and N'Chaka began to run. He saw her, crouched between two huge boulders, her light fur stained with blood.

A vast black-winged shadow swooped down upon him. It glared at him with its yellow eyes, and its long beak tore at him. He thrust his spear at it, but talons hooked into his shoulder, and the golden eyes were close to him, bright and full of death.

He knew those eyes. Tika screamed, but the sound faded, everything faded but those eyes. He sprang up, grappling with the thing ...

A man's voice yelling, a man's hands thrusting him away. The dream receded. Stark came back to reality, dropping the scared attendant who had come to waken him.

The man cringed away from him. 'Delgaun sent me. He wants you – in the council room.' Then he turned and fled.

Stark shook himself. The dream had been terribly real. He went down to the council room. It was dusk now, and the torches were lighted.

Delgaun was waiting, and Berild sat beside him at the table. They were alone there. Delgaun looked up, with his golden eyes.

'I have a job for you, Stark,' he said. 'You remember the captain of Kynon's men, in the square today?'

'I do.'

'His name is Freka, and he's a good man, but he's addicted to a certain vice. He'll be up to his ears in it by now, and somebody has to get him back by the time Kynon leaves. Will you see to it?'

Stark glanced at Berild. It seemed to him that she was amused, whether at him or at Delgaun he could not tell. He asked,

'Where will I find him?'

'There's only one place where he can get his particular poison – Kala's, out on the edge of Valkis. It's in the old city, beyond the lower quays.' Delgaun smiled. 'You may have to be ready with your fists, Stark. Freka may not want to come.'

Stark hesitated. Then, 'I'll do my best,' he said, and went out into the dusky streets of Valkis.

He crossed a square, heading away from the palace. A twisting lane swallowed him up. And quite suddenly, someone took his arm and said rapidly.

'Smile at me, and then turn aside into the alley.'

The hand on his arm was small and brown, the voice very pretty with its accompaniment of little chiming bells. He smiled, as she had bade him, and turned aside into the alley, which was barely more than a crack between two rows of houses.

Swiftly, he put his hands against the wall, so that the girl was prisoned between them. A green-eyed girl, with golden bells braided in her black hair, and impudent breasts bare above a jewelled girdle. A handsome girl, with a proud look to her.

The serving girl who had stood beside the litter in the square, and had watched Kynon with such bleak hatred.

'Well,' said Stark. 'And what do you want with me, little one?'

She answered, 'My name is Fianna. And I do not intend to kill you, neither will I run away.'

Stark let his hands drop. 'Did you follow me, Fianna?'

'I did. Delgaun's palace is full of hidden ways, and I know them all. I was listening behind the panel in the council room. I heard you speak out against Kynon, and I heard Delgaun's order, just now.'

'So?'

'So, if you meant what you said about the tribes, you had better get away now, while you have the chance. Kynon lied to you. He will use you, and then kill you, as he will use and then destroy his own people.' Her voice was hot with bitter fury.

Stark gave her a slow smile that might have meant anything, or nothing.

'You're a Valkisian, Fianna. What do you care what happens to the barbarians?'

Her slightly tilted green eyes looked scornfully into his.

'I'm not trying to trap you, Earthman. I hate Kynon. And my mother was a woman of the desert.'

She paused, then went on sombrely, 'Also, I serve the lady Berild, and I have learned many things. There is trouble coming, greater trouble than Kynon knows.' She asked, suddenly, 'What do you know of the Ramas?'

'Nothing,' he answered, 'except that they don't exist now, if they ever did.'

Fianna gave him an odd look. 'Perhaps they don't. Will you listen to me, Earthman from Mercury? Will you get away, now that you know you're marked for death?'

Stark said, 'No.'

'Even if I tell you that Delgaun has set a trap for you at Kala's?'

'No. But I will thank you for your warning, Fianna.'

He bent and kissed her, because she was very young and honest. Then he turned and went on his way.

5

Night came swiftly. Stark left behind him the torches and the laughter and the sounding harps, coming into the streets of the old city where there was nothing but silence and the light of the low moons.

He saw the lower quays, great looming shapes of marble

rounded and worn by time, and went toward them. Presently he found that he was following a faint but definite path, threaded between the ancient houses. It was very still, so that the dry whisper of the drifting dust was audible.

He passed under the shadow of the quays, and turned into a broad way that had once led up from the harbour. A little way ahead, on the other side, he saw a tall building, half fallen in ruin. Its windows were shattered, barred with light, and from it came the sound of voices and a thin thread of music, very reedy and evil.

Stark approached it, slipping through the ragged shadows as though he had no more weight to him than a drift of smoke. Once a door banged and a man came out of Kala's and passed by, going down to Valkis. Stark saw his face in the moonlight. It was the face of a beast, rather than a man. He muttered to himself as he went, and once he laughed, and Stark felt a loathing in him.

He waited until the sound of footsteps had died away. The ruined houses gave no sign of danger. A lizard rustled between the stones, and that was all. The moonlight lay bright and still on Kala's door.

Stark found a little shard of rock and tossed it, so that it make a sharp snicking sound against the shadowed wall beyond him. Then he held his breath, listening.

No one, nothing, stirred. Only the dry wind sighed in the empty houses.

Stark went out, across the open space, and nothing happened. He flung open the door of Kala's dive.

Yellow light spilled out, and a choking wave of hot and stuffy air. Inside, there were tall lamps with quartz lenses, each of which poured down a beam of throbbing, gold-orange light. And in the little pools of radiance, on filthy furs and cushions on the floor, lay men and women whose faces were slack and bestial.

Stark realized now what secret vice Kala sold here. Shanga – the going back – the radiation that caused temporary artificial atavism and let men wallow for a time in beasthood. It was supposed to have been stamped out when the Lady Fand's dark Shanga ring had been destroyed. But it still persisted, in places like this outside the law.

He looked for Freka, and recognized the tall barbarian. He was sprawled under one of the Shanga lamps, eyes closed, face brutish, growling and twitching in sleep like the beast he had temporarily become.

A voice spoke from behind Stark's shoulder. 'I am Kala. What do you wish, Outlander?'

He turned. Kala might have been beautiful once, a thousand years ago as you reckon sin. She wore still the sweet chiming bells in her hair, and Stark thought of Fianna. The woman's ravaged face turned him sick. It was like the reedy, piping music, woven out of the very heart of evil.

Yet her eyes were shrewd, and he knew that she had not missed his searching look around the room, nor his interest in Freka. There was a note of warning in her voice.

He did not want trouble, yet. Not until he found some hint of the trap Fianna had told him of.

He said, 'Bring me wine.'

'Will you try the lamp of Going-back, Outlander? It brings much joy.'

'Perhaps later. Now, I wish wine.'

She went away, clapping her hands for a slatternly wench who came between the sprawled figures with an earthern mug. Stark sat down beside a table, where his back was to the wall and he could see both the door and the whole room.

Kala had returned to her own heap of furs by the door, but her basilisk eyes were alert.

Stark made a pretence of drinking, but his mind was very busy, very cold.

Perhaps this, in itself, was the trap. Freka was temporarily a beast. He would fight, and Kala would shriek, and the other dull-eyed brutes would rise and fight also.

But he would have needed no warning about that – and Delgaun himself had said there would be trouble.

No. There was something more.

He let his gaze wander over the room. It was large, and there were other rooms off it, the openings hung with ragged curtains. Through the rents, Stark could see others of Kala's customers sprawled under Shanga-lamps, and some of these had gone so far back from humanity that they were hideous to behold. But still there was no sign of danger to himself.

There was only one odd thing. The room nearest to where Freka sat was empty, and its curtains were only partly drawn.

Stark began to brood on the emptiness of that room.

He beckoned Kala to him. 'I will try the lamp,' he said. 'But I wish privacy. Have it brought to that room, there.'

Kala said, 'That room is taken.'

'But I see no one!'

'It is taken, it is paid for, and no one may enter. I will have your lamp brought here.'

'No,' said Stark. 'The hell with it. I'm going.'

He flung down a coin and went out. Moving swiftly outside, he placed his eye to a crack in the nearest shutter, and waited.

Luhar of Venus came out of the empty room. His face was worried, and Stark smiled. He went back and stood flat against the wall beside the door.

In a moment it opened and the Venusian came out, drawing his gun as he did so.

Stark jumped him.

Luhar let out one angry cry. His gun went off a vicious streak of flame across the moonlight, and then Stark's great hand crushed the bones of his wrist together so that he dropped it clashing on the stones. He whirled around, raking Stark's face with his nails as he clawed for the Earthman's eyes, and Stark hit him. Luhar fell, rolling over, and before he could scramble up again Stark had picked up the gun and thrown it away into the ruins across the street.

Luhar came up from the pavement in one catlike spring. Stark fell with him, back through Kala's door, and they rolled together among the foul furs and cushions. Luhar was built of spring steel, with no softness in him anywhere, and his long fingers were locked around Stark's throat.

Kala screamed with fury. She caught a whip from among her cushions – a traditional weapon along the Low Canals – and began to lash the two men impartially, her hair flying in tangled locks across her face. The bestial figures under the lamps shambled to their feet, and growled.

The long lash ripped Stark's shirt and the flesh of his back beneath it. He snarled and staggered to his feet, with Luhar still clinging to the death grip on his throat. He pushed Luhar's face away from him with both hands and threw himself forward, over a table, so that Luhar was crushed beneath him.

The Venusian's breath left him with a whistling grunt. His fingers relaxed. Stark struck his hands away. He rose and bent over Luhar and picked him up, gripping him cruelly so that he turned white with the pain, and raised him high and flung him bodily into the growling, beast-faced men who were shambling toward him.

Kala leaped at Stark, cursing, striking him with the coiling lash. He turned. The thin veneer of civilisation was gone from Stark now, erased in a second by the first hint of battle. His eyes blazed with a cold light. He took the whip out of Kala's hand and laid his palm across her evil face, and she fell and lay still.

He faced the ring of bestial, Shanga-sodden men who walled him off from what he had been sent to do. There was a reddish tinge to his vision, partly blood, partly sheer rage. He could see Freka standing erect in the corner, his head weaving from side to side brutishly.

Stark raised the whip and strode into the ring of men who were no longer quite men.

Hands struck and clawed him. Bodies reeled and fell away. Blank eyes glittered, and red mouths squealed, and there was a mingling of snarls and bestial laughter in his ears. The blood-lust had spread to these creatures now. They swarmed upon Stark and bore him down with the weight of their writhing bodies.

They bit him and savaged him in a blind way, and he fought his way up again, shaking them off with his great shoulders, trampling them under his boots. The lash hissed and sang, and the smell of blood rose on the choking air.

Freka's dazed, brutish face swam before Stark. The Martian growled and flung himself forward. Stark swung the loaded butt of the whip. It cracked solidly on the Shunni's temple, and he sagged into Stark's arms.

Out of the corner of his eyes, Stark saw Luhar. He had risen and crept around the edge of the fight. He was behind Stark now, and there was a knife in his hand.

Hampered by Freka's weight, Stark could not leap aside. As Luhar rushed in, he crouched and went backward, his head and shoulders taking the Venusian low in the belly. He felt the hot kiss of the blade in his flesh, but the wound was glancing, and before Luhar could strike again, Stark twisted like a great cat and struck down. Luhar's skull rang on the flagging. The Earthman's fist rose and fell twice. After that, Luhar did not move.

Stark got to his feet. He stood with his knees bent and his shoulders flexed, looking from side to side, and the sound that came out of his throat was one of pure savagery.

He moved forward a step or two, half naked, bleeding, towering like a dark colossus over the lean Martians, and the brutish throng gave back from him. They had taken more mauling than they liked, and there was something about the Outlander's simple desire to rend them apart that penetrated even their Shanga-clouded minds.

Kala sat up on the floor, and snarled, 'Get out.'

Stark stood a moment or two longer, looking at them. Then he lifted Freka to his feet and laid him over his shoulder like a sack of meal and went out, moving neither fast nor slow, but in a straight line, and way was made for him.

He carried the Shunni down through the silent streets, and into the twisting, crowded ways of Valkis. There, too, the people stared at him and drew back, out of his path. He came to Delgaun's palace. The guards closed in behind him, but they did not ask that he stop.

Delgaun was in the council room, and Berild was still with him. It seemed that they had been waiting, over their wine and their private talk. Delgaun rose to his feet as Stark came in, so sharply that his goblet fell and spilled a red pool of wine at his feet.

Stark let the Shunni drop to the floor.

'I have brought Freka,' he said. 'Luhar is still at Kala's.'

He looked into Delgaun's eyes, golden and cruel, the eyes of his dream. It was hard not to kill.

Suddenly the woman laughed, very clear and ringing, and her laughter was all for Delgaun.

'Well done, wild man,' she said to Stark. 'Kynon is lucky to have such a captain. One word for the future, though – watch out for Freka. He won't forgive you this.'

Stark said thickly, looking at Delgaun, 'This hasn't been a night for forgiveness.' Then he added, 'I can handle Freka.'

Berild said, 'I like you, wild man.' Her eyes dwelt on Stark's face, curious, compelling. 'Ride beside me when we go. I would know more about you.'

And she smiled.

A dark flush crept over Delgaun's face. In a voice tight with fury he said, 'Perhaps you've forgotten something, Berild. There is nothing for you in this barbarian, this creature of an hour!'

He would have said more in his anger, but Berild said sharply,

'We will not speak of time. Go now, Stark. Be ready at midnight.'

Stark went. And as he went, his brow was furrowed deep by a strange doubt.

6

At midnight, in the great square of the slave market, Kynon's caravan formed again and went out of Valkis with thundering drums and skirling pipes. Delgaun was there to see them go, and the cheering of the people rang after them on the desert wind.

Stark rode alone. He was in a brooding mood and wanted no company, least of all that of the Lady Berild. She was beautiful, she was dangerous, and she belonged to Kynon, or to Delgaun, or perhaps to both of them. In Stark's experience, women like that were sudden death, and he wanted no part of her. At any rate, not yet.

Luhar rode ahead with Kynon. He had come dragging into the square at the mounting, his face battered and swollen, an ugly look in his eyes. Kynon gave one quick look from him to Stark, who had his own scars, and said harshly,

'Delgaun tells me there's a blood feud between you two. I want no more of it, understand? After you're paid off you can kill each other and welcome, but not until then. Is that clear?'

Stark nodded, keeping his mouth shut. Luhar muttered assent, and they had not looked at each other since.

Freka rode in his customary place by Kynon, which put him near to Luhar. It seemed to Stark that their beasts swung close together more often than was necessary from the roughness of the track.

The big barbarian captain sat rigidly erect in his saddle, but Stark had seen his face in the torchlight, sick and sweating, with the brute look still clouding his eyes. There was a purple mark on his temple, but Stark was quite sure that Berild had spoken the truth – Freka would not forgive him either the indignity or the hangover of his unfinished wallow under the lamps of Shanga.

The dead sea bottom widened away under the black sky. As they left the lights of Valkis behind, winding their way over the sand and the ribs of coral, dropping lower with every mile into the vast basin, it was hard to believe that there could be life anywhere on a world that could produce such cosmic desolation.

The little moons fled away, trailing their eerie shadows over rock formations tortured into impossible shapes by wind and water, peering into clefts that seemed to have no bottom, turning the sand white as bone. The iron stars blazed, so close that the wind seemed edged with their frosty light. And in all that endless space nothing moved, and the silence was so deep that the coughing howl of a sand-cat far away to the east made Stark jump with its loudness.

Yet Stark was not oppressed by the wilderness. Born and bred to the wild and barren places, this desert was more kin to him than the cities of men.

After a while there was a jangling of brazen bangles behind

him and Fianna came up. He smiled at her, and she said rather sullenly,

'The Lady Berild sent me, to remind you of her wish.'

Stark glanced to where the scarlet-curtained litter rocked along, and his eyes glinted.

'She's not one to let go of a thing, is she?'

'No.' Fianna saw that no one was within earshot, and then said quietly, 'Was it as I said, at Kala's?'

Stark nodded. 'I think, little one, that I owe you my life. Luhar would have killed me as soon as I tackled Freka.'

He reached over and touched her hand where it lay on the bridle. She smiled, a young girl's smile that seemed very sweet in the moonlight, honest and comradely.

It was odd to be talking of death with a pretty girl in the moonlight.

Stark said, 'Why does Delgaun want to kill me?'

'He gave no reason, when he spoke to the man from Venus. But perhaps I can guess. He knows that you're as strong as he is, and so he fears you. Also, the Lady Berild looked at you in a certain way.'

'I thought Berild was Kynon's woman.'

'Perhaps she is – for the time,' answered Fianna enigmatically. Then she shook her head, glancing around with what was almost fear. 'I have risked much already. Please – don't let it be known that I've spoken to you, beyond what I was sent to say.'

Her eyes pleaded with him, and Stark realised with a shock that Fianna, too, stood on the edge of a quicksand.

'Don't be afraid,' he said, and meant it. 'We'd better go.'

She swung her beast around, and as she did so she whispered, 'Be careful, Eric John Stark!'

Stark nodded. He rode behind her, thinking that he liked the sound of his name on her lips.

The Lady Berild lay among her furs and cushions, and even then there was no indolence about her. She was relaxed as a cat is, perfectly at ease and yet vibrant with life. In the shadows of the litter her skin showed silver-white and her loosened hair was a sweet darkness.

'Are you stubborn, wild man?' she asked. 'Or do you find me distasteful?'

He had not realised before how rich and soft her voice was. He looked down at the magnificent supple length of her, and said,

'I find you most damnably attractive – and that's why I'm stubborn.'

'Afraid?'

'I'm taking Kynon's pay. Should I take his woman also?'

She laughed, half scornfully. 'Kynon's ambitions leave no room for me. We have an agreement, because a king must have a queen – and he finds my counsel useful. You see, I am ambitious, too! Apart from that, there is nothing.'

Stark looked at her, trying to read her smoke-grey eyes in the gloom. 'And Delgaun?'

'He wants me, but …' She hesitated, and then went on, in a tone quite different from before, her voice low and throbbing with a secret pleasure as vast and elemental as the star-shot sky.

'I belong to no one,' she said. 'I am my own.'

Stark knew that for the moment she had forgotten him.

He rode for a time in silence, and then he said slowly, repeating Delgaun's words,

'Perhaps you have forgotten something, Berild. There is nothing for you in me, the creature of an hour.'

He saw her start, and for a moment her eyes blazed and her breath was sharply drawn. Then she laughed, and said,

'The wild man is also a parrot. And an hour can be a long time – as long as eternity, if one wills it so.'

'Yes,' said Stark, 'I have often thought so, waiting for death to come at me out of a crevice in the rocks. The great lizard stings, and his bite is fatal.'

He leaned over in the saddle, his shoulders looming above hers, naked in the biting wind.

'My hours with women are short ones,' he said. 'They come after the battle, when there is time for such things. Perhaps then I'll come and see you.'

He spurred away and left her without a backward look, and the skin of his back tingled with the expectancy of a flying knife.

But the only thing that followed him was a disturbing echo of laughter down the wind.

Dawn came. Kynon beckoned Stark to his side, and pointed out at the cruel waste of sand, with here and there a reef of bassalt black against the burning white.

'This is the country you will lead your men over. Learn it.' He was speaking to Luhar as well. 'Learn every water hole, every vantage point, every trail that leads toward the Border. There are no better fighters than the Dryland men when they're well led, and you must prove to them that you can lead. You'll work with their own chieftains – Freka, and the others you'll meet when we reach Sinharat.'

Luhar said, 'Sinharat?'

'My headquarters. It's about seven days' march – an island city, old as the moons. The Rama cult was strong there, legend has it, and it's a sort of holy place to the tribesmen. That's why I picked it.'

He took a deep breath and smiled, looking out over the dead sea bottom toward the Border, and his eyes held the same pitiless light as the sun that baked the desert.

'Very soon, now,' he said, more to himself than the others. 'Only a handful of days before we drown the Border states in their own blood. And after that...'

He laughed, very softly, and said no more. Stark could believe that what Berild said of him was true. There was a flame of ambition in Kynon that would let nothing stand in its way.

He measured the size and the strength of the tall barbarian, the eagle look of his face and the iron that lay beneath his joviality. Then Stark, too, stared off toward the Border and wondered if he would ever see Tarak or hear Simon Ashton's voice again.

For three days they marched without incident. At noon they made a dry camp and slept away the blazing hours, and then went on again under a darkening sky, a long line of tall men and rangy beasts, with the scarlet litter blooming like a strange flower in the midst of it. Jingling bridles and dust, and padded hoofs trampling the bones of the sea, toward the island city of Sinharat.

Stark did not speak again to Berild, nor did she send for him.

Fianna would pass him in the camp, and smile sidelong, and go on. For her sake, he did not stop her.

Neither Luhar nor Freka came near him. They avoided him pointedly, except when Kynon called them all together to discuss some point of strategy. But the two seemed to have become friends, and drank together from the same bottle of wine.

Stark slept always beside his mount, his back guarded and his gun loose. The hard lessons learned in his childhood had stayed with him, and if there was a footfall near him in the dust he woke often before the beast did.

Toward morning of the fourth night the wind, that never seemed to falter from its steady blowing, began to drop. At dawn it was dead still, and the rising sun had a tinge of blood. The dust rose under the feet of the beasts and fell again where it had risen.

Stark began to sniff the air. More and more often he looked toward the north, where there was a long slope as flat as his palm that stretched away farther than he could see.

A restless unease grew within him. Presently he spurred ahead to join Kynon.

'There is a storm coming,' he said, and turned his head northward again.

Kynon looked at him curiously.

'You even have the right direction,' he said. 'One might think you were a native.' He, too, gazed with brooding anger at the long sweep of emptiness.

'I wish we were closer to the city. But one place is as bad as another when the khamsin blows, and the only thing to do is keep moving. You're a dead dog if you stop – dead and buried.'

He swore, with a curious admixture of blunt Anglo-Saxon in his Martian profanity, as though the storm were a personal enemy.

'Pass the word along to force it – dump whatever they have to to lighten the loads. And get Berild out of that damned litter. Stick by her, will you, Stark? I've got to stay here, at the head of the line. And don't get separated. Above all, *don't get separated*!'

Stark nodded and dropped back. He got Berild mounted, and

they left the litter there, a bright patch of crimson on the sand, its curtains limp in the utter stillness.

Nobody talked much. The beasts were urged on to the top of their speed. They were nervous and fidgety, inclined to break out of line and run for it. The sun rose higher.

One hour.

The windless air shimmered. The silence lay upon the caravan with a crushing hand. Stark went up and down the line, lending a hand to the sweating drovers with the pack animals that now carried only water skins and a bare supply of food. Fianna rode close beside Berild.

Two hours.

For the first time that day there was a sound in the desert.

It came from far off, a moaning wail like the cry of a giantess in travail. It rushed closer, rising as it did so to a dry and bitter shriek that filled the whole sky, shook it, and tore it open, letting in all the winds of hell.

It struck swiftly. One moment the air was clear and motionless. The next, it was blind with dust and screaming as it fled, tearing with demoniac fury at everything in its path.

Stark spurred toward the women, who were only a few feet away but already hidden by the veil of mingled dust and sand.

Someone blundered into him in the murk. Long hair whipped across his face and he reached out, crying 'Fianna! Fianna!' A woman's hand caught his, and a voice answered, but he could not hear the words.

Then, suddenly, his beast was crowded by other scaly bodies. The woman's grip had broken. Hard masculine hands clawed at him. He could make out, dimly, the features of two men, close to his.

Luhar, and Freka.

His beast gave a great lurch, and sprang forward. Stark was dragged from the saddle, to fall backward into the raging sand.

7

He lay half-stunned for a moment, his breath knocked out of him. There was a terrible reptilian screaming sounding thin through the roar of the wind. Vague shapes bolted past him, and twice he was nearly crushed by their trampling hooves.

Luhar and Freka must have waited their chance. It was so beautifully easy. Leave Stark alone and afoot, and the storm and the desert between them would do the work, with no blame attaching to any man.

Stark got to his feet, and a human body struck him at the knees so that he went down again. He grappled with it, snarling, before he realised that the flesh between his hands was soft and draped in silken cloth. Then he saw that he was holding Berild.

'It was I,' she gasped, 'and not Fianna.'

Her words reached him very faintly, though he knew she was yelling at the top of her lungs. She must have been knocked from her own mount when Luhar thrust between them.

Gripping her tightly, so that she should not be blown away, Stark struggled up again. With all his strength, it was almost impossible to stand.

Blinded, deafened, half strangled, he fought his way forward a few paces, and suddenly one of the pack beasts loomed shadow-like beside him, going by with a rush and a squeal.

By the grace of Providence and his own swift reflexes, he caught its pack lashings, clinging with the tenacity of a man determined not to die. It floundered about, dragging them, until Berild managed to grasp its trailing halter rope. Between them, they fought the creature down.

Stark clung to its head while the woman clambered to its back, twisting her arm through the straps of the pad. A silken scarf whipped toward him. He took it and tied it over the head of the beast so it could breathe, and after that it was quieter.

There was no direction, no sight of anything, in that howling inferno. The caravan seemed to have been scattered like a drift of autumn leaves. Already, in the few brief moments he had stood still, Stark's legs were buried to the knees in a substratum of sand that rolled like water. He pulled himself free and started on, going nowhere, remembering Kynon's words.

Berild ripped her thin robe apart and gave him another strip of silk for himself. He bound it over his nose and eyes, and some of the choking and the blindness abated.

Stumbling, staggering, beaten by the wind as a child is beaten by a strong man, Stark went on, hoping desperately to find the main body of the caravan, and knowing somehow that the hope was futile.

The hours that followed were nightmare. He shut his mind to them, in a way that a civilised man would have found impossible. In his childhood there had been days, and nights, and the problems had been simple ones – how to survive one span of light that one might then struggle to survive the span of darkness that came after. One thing, one danger, at a time.

Now there was a single necessity. Keep moving. Forget tomorrow, or what happened to the caravan, or where the little Fianna with her bright eyes may be. Forget thirst, and the pain of breathing, and the fiery lash of sand on naked skin. Only don't stand still.

It was growing dark when the beast fell against a half-buried boulder and snapped its foreleg. Stark gave it a quick and merciful death. They took the straps from the pad and linked themselves together. Each took as much food as they could carry, and Stark shouldered the single skin of water that fortune had vouchsafed them.

They staggered on, and Berild did not whimper.

Night came, and still the khamsin blew. Stark wondered at the woman's strength, for he had to help her only when she fell. He had lost all feeling himself. His body was merely a thing that continued to move only because it had been ordered not to stop.

The haze in his own mind had grown as thick as the black obscurity of the night. Berild had ridden all day, but he had walked, and there was an end even to his strength. He was approaching it now, and was too weary even to be afraid.

He became aware at some indeterminate time that Berild

had fallen and was dragging her weight against the straps. He turned blindly to help her up. She was saying something, crying his name, striking at him so that he should hear her words and understand.

At last he did. He pulled the wrappings from his face and breathed clean air. The wind had fallen. The sky was growing clear.

He dropped in his tracks and slept, with the exhausted woman half dead beside him.

Thirst brought them both awake in the early dawn. They drank from the skin, and then sat for a time looking at the desert, and at each other, thinking of what lay ahead.

'Do you know where we are?' Stark asked.

'Not exactly.' Berild's face was shadowed with weariness. It had changed, and somehow, to Stark, it had grown more beautiful, because there was no weakness in it.

She thought a minute, looking at the sun. 'The wind blew from the north,' she said. 'Therefore we have come south from the track. Sinharat lies that way, across the waste they call the Belly of Stones.' She pointed to the north and east.

'How far?'

'Seven, eight days, afoot.'

Stark measured their supply of water and shook his head. 'It'll be dry walking.'

He rose and took up the skin, and Berild came beside him without a word. Her red hair hung loose over her shoulders. The rags of her silken robe had been torn away by the wind, leaving her only the loose skirt of the desert women, and her belt and collar of jewels.

She walked erect with a steady, swinging stride, and it was almost impossible for Stark to remember her as she had been, riding like a lazy queen in her scarlet litter.

There was no way to shelter themselves from the midday sun. The sun of Mars at its worst, however, was only a pale candle beside the sun of Mercury, and it did not bother Stark. He made Berild lie in the shadow of his own body, and he watched her face, relaxed and unfamiliar in sleep.

For the first time, then, he was conscious of a strangeness in her. He had seen so little of her before, in Valkis, and almost nothing on the trail. Now, there was little of her mind or heart that she could conceal from him.

Or was there? There were moments, while she slept, when the shadows of strange dreams crossed her face. Sometimes, in the unguarded moment of waking, he would see in her eyes a look he could not read, and his primitive senses quivered with a vague ripple of warning.

Yet all through those blazing days and frosty nights, tortured with thirst and weary to exhaustion, Berild was magnificent. Her white skin was darkened by the sun and her hair became a wild red mane, but she smiled and set her feet resolutely by his, and Stark thought she was the most beautiful creature he had ever seen.

On the fourth day they climbed a scarp of limestone worn in ages past by the sea, and looked out over the place called the Belly of Stones.

The sea-bottom curved downward below them into a sort of gigantic basin, the farther rim of which was lost in shimmering waves of heat. Stark thought that never, even on Mercury, had he seen a place more cruel and utterly forsaken of gods or men.

It seemed as though some primal glacier must have met its death here in the dim dawn of Mars, hollowing out its own grave. The body of the glacier had melted away, but its bones were left.

Bones of basalt, of granite and marble and porphyry, of every conceivable colour and shape and size, picked up by the ice as it marched southward from the pole and dropped here as a cairn to mark its passing.

The Belly of Stones. Stark thought that its other name was Death.

For the first time, Berild faltered. She sat down and bent her head over her hands.

'I am tired,' she said. 'Also, I am afraid.'

Stark asked, 'Has it ever been crossed?'

'Once. But they were a war party, mounted and well supplied.'

Stark looked out across the stones. 'We will cross it,' he said.

Berild raised her head. 'Somehow I believe you.' She rose slowly and put her hands on his breast, over the strong beating of his heart.

'Give me your strength, wild man,' she whispered. 'I shall need it.'

He drew her to him and kissed her, and it was a strange and painful kiss, for their lips were cracked and bleeding from their terrible thirst. Then they went down together into the place called the Belly of Stones.

8

The desert had been a pleasant and kindly place. Stark looked back upon it with longing. And yet this inferno of blazing rock was so like the valleys of his boyhood that it did not occur to him to lie down and die.

They rested for a time in the sheltered crevice under a great leaning slab of blood-red stone, moistening their swollen tongues with a few drops of stinking water from the skin. At nightfall they drank the last of it, but Berild would not let him throw the skin away.

Darkness, and a lunar silence. The chill air sucked the day's heat out of the rocks and the iron frost came down, so that Stark and the red-haired woman must keep moving or freeze.

Stark's mind grew clouded. He spoke from time to time, in a croaking whisper, dropping back into the harsh mother-tongue of the Twilight Belt. It seemed to him that he was hunting, as he had so many times before, in the waterless places – for the blood of the great lizard would save him from thirst.

But nothing lived in the Belly of Stones. Nothing, but the two who crept and staggered across it under the low moons.

Berild fell, and could not rise again. Stark crouched beside her. Her face stared up at him, while in the moonlight, her eyes burning and strange.

'I will not die!' she whispered, not to him, but to the gods. '*I will not die!*'

And she clawed the sand and the bitter rocks, dragging herself onward. It was uncanny, the madness that she had for life.

Stark raised her up and carried her. His breath came in deep sobbing gasps. After a while he, too, fell. He went on like a beast on all fours, dragging the woman.

He knew dimly that he was climbing. There was a glimmering of dawn in the sky. His hands slipped on a lip of sand and he went rolling down a smooth slope. At length he stopped and lay on his back like a dead thing.

The sun was high when consciousness returned to him. He saw Berild lying near him and crawled to her, shaking her until her eyes opened. Her hands moved feebly and her lips formed the same four words. *I will not die.*

Stark strained his eyes to the horizon, praying for a glimpse of Sinharat, but there was nothing, only emptiness and sand. With great difficulty he got the woman to her feet, supporting her.

He tried to tell her that they must go on, but he could no longer form the words. He could only gesture and urge her forward, in the direction of the city.

But she refused to go. 'Too far ... die ... without water ...'

He knew that she was right, but still he was not ready to give up.

She began to move away from him, toward the south, and he thought that she had gone mad and was wandering. Then he saw that she was peering with awful intensity at the line of the scarp that formed this wall of the Belly of Stones. It rose into a great ridge, serrated like the backbone of a whale, and some three miles away a long dorsal fin of reddish rock curved out into the desert.

Berild made a little sobbing noise in her throat. She began to plod toward the distant promontory.

Stark caught up with her. He tried to stop her, but she would not be stopped, turning a feral glare upon him.

She croaked, 'Water!' and pointed.

He was sure now that she was mad. He told her so, forcing the painful words out of his throat, reminding her of Sinharat and that she was going away from any possible help.

She said again, quite sanely, 'Too far. Two – three days without water,' She pointed. 'Monastery – old well – a chance ...'

Stark decided that he had little to lose by trusting her. He nodded and went with her toward the curve of rock.

The three miles might have been three hundred. At last they came up under the ragged cliffs – and there was nothing there but sand.

Stark looked at the woman. A great rage and a deep sense of futility came over him. They were indeed lost.

But Berild had gone a few steps farther. With a hoarse cry, she bent over what had seemed merely a slab of stone fallen from the cliff, and Stark saw that it was a carven pillar, half buried. Now he was able to make out the mounded shape of a ruin, of which only the foundations and a few broken columns were left.

For a long while Berild stood by the pillar, her eyes closed. Stark got the uncanny feeling that she was visualising the place as it had been, though the wall must have been dust a thousand years ago. Presently she moved. He followed her, and it was strange to see her, on the naked sand, treading the arbitrary patterns of vanished corridors.

She came to a halt, in a broad flat space that might once have been a central courtyard. There she fell on her knees and began to dig.

Stark got down beside her. They scrabbled like a pair of dogs in the yielding sand. Stark's nails slipped across something hard, and there was a yellow glint through the dusty ochre. Within a few minutes they had bared a golden cover six feet across, very massive and wonderfully carved with the symbols of some lost god of the sea.

Stark struggled to lift the thing away. He could not move it. Then Berild pressed a hidden spring and the cover slid back of itself. Beneath it, sweet and cold, protected through all these ages, water stirred gently against mossy stones.

An hour later, Stark and Berild lay sleeping soaked to the skin, their very hair dripping with the blessed dampness.

That night, when the low moons roved over the desert, they sat by the well, drowsy with an animal sense of rest and repletion. And Stark looked at the woman and said,

'I know you now.'

'What do you know, wild man?'

Stark said quietly, 'You are a Rama.'

She did not answer at once. Then she said, 'I was bred in these deserts. Is it so strange that I should know of this well?'

'Strange that you didn't mention it before. You were afraid, weren't you, that if you led me here your secret would come out? But it was that, or die.'

He leaned forward, studying her.

'If you had led me straight to the well, I might not have wondered. But you had to stop and remember, how the halls were built and where the doorways were that led to the inner court. You lived in this place when it was whole. And no one, not even Kynon himself, knows of it but you.'

'You dream, wild man. The moon is in your eyes.'

Stark shook his head slowly. 'I know.'

She laughed, and stretched her arms wide on the sand.

'But I am young,' she said. 'And men have told me I am beautiful. It is good to be young, for youth has nothing to do with ashes and empty skulls.'

She touched his arm, and little darts of fire went through his flesh, warm from his fingertips.

'Forget your dreams, wild man. They're madness, gone with the morning.'

He looked down at her in the clear pale light, and she was young, and beautifully made, and her lips were smiling.

He bent his head. Her arms went round him. Her hair blew soft against his cheek. Then, suddenly, she set her teeth cruelly into his lip. He cried out and thrust her away, and she sat back on her heels, mocking him.

'That,' she said, 'is because you called Fianna's name instead of mine, when the storm broke.'

Stark cursed her. There was a taste of blood in his mouth. He reached out and caught her, and again she laughed, a peculiarly sweet, wicked sound.

The wind blew over them, sighing, and the desert was very still.

For two days they remained among the ruins. At evening of the second day Stark filled the water skin, and Berild replaced the golden cover on the well. They began the last long march toward Sinharat.

9

Stark saw it rising against the morning sky – a city of gold and marble, high on an island of rose-red coral laid bare by the vanished sea. Sinharat, the Ever Living.

Yet it had died. As he came closer to it, plodding slowly through the sand, he saw that the place was no more than a beautiful corpse, the lovely towers broken, the roofless palaces open to the sky. Whatever life Kynon and his armies might have foisted upon Sinharat was no more than the fleeting passage of ants across the perfect bones of the dead.

'What was it like before?' he asked, 'with the blue water around it, and the banners flying?'

Berild turned a dark, calculating look upon him.

'I told you before to forget that madness. If you talk it, no one will believe you.'

'No one?'

'You had best not anger me, wild man,' she said quietly. 'I may be your only hope of life, before this is over.'

They did not speak again, going with slow weary steps toward the city.

In the desert below the coral cliffs the armies of Kynon were encamped. The tall warriors of Kesh and Shun waiting, with their women and their beasts and their shining spears, for the pipers to cry them over the Border. The skin tents and the long picket lines were too many to count. In the distance, a convertible Kallman spacer that Stark recognised as Knighton's made an ugly, jarring incongruity.

Lookouts sighted the two toiling figures in the distance. Men and women and children began to stream out across the sand, and presently a great cheering arose. Where he had looked on emptiness for days, Stark was smothered now by the press of thousands. Berild was picked up and carried on the shoulders of two chiefs, and men would have carried Stark also, but he fought them off.

Broad flights of steps were cut in the coral. The throng flowed upward along them. Ahead of them all went Eric John Stark, and he was smiling. From time to time he asked a question, and men drew back from that question, and his smile.

Up the steps and into the streets of Sinharat he went, with a slow, restless stride, asking,

'Where is Luhar of Venus?'

Every man there read death in his face, but they did not try to stop him.

People came out of the graceful ruins, drawn by the clamour, and the tide rolled down the broad ways, the rose-red streets of coral, until it spread out in the square before a great palace of gold and ivory and white marble blinding in the sun.

Luhar of Venus came down the terraced steps, fresh from sleep, his pale hair tumbled, his eyes still drowsy.

Others came through the door behind him. Stark did not see them. They did not matter. Berild didn't matter, calling his name from where she sat on the shoulders of the chiefs. Nothing, no one mattered, but himself and Luhar.

He crossed the square, not hurrying, a dark ravaged giant in rags. He saw Luhar pause on the bottom step. He saw the sleep and the vagueness go out of the Venusian's eyes as they rested first on the red-haired woman, then on himself. He saw the fear come into them, and the undying hate.

Someone got between him and Luhar. Stark lifted the man and flung him aside without breaking his stride, and went on. Luhar half turned. He would have run away, back into the palace, but there were too many now between him and the door. He crouched and drew his gun.

Stark sprang.

He came like a great black panther leaping, and he struck

low. Luhar's shot went over his back. After that there was no more shooting. There was a moment, terribly short and silent, in which the two men lay entangled, straining against each other in a sort of stasis. Then Luhar screamed.

Stark knew dimly that there were hands, many of them, trying to drag him away. He clung growling to the Venusian until he was torn loose by main force. He struggled against his captors, and through a red haze he saw Kynon's face, close to his and very angry. Luhar was not yet dead.

'I warned you, Stark!' said Kynon furiously. 'I warned you.'

Men were bending over Luhar. Knighton, Walsh, Themis, Arrod. Stark saw that Delgaun was among them. He did not question at the time how word had gone back to Valkis and sent Delgaun racing across the dead sea bottom with his hired bravos to search for the red-haired woman. It was right that Delgaun should be there.

In short ragged sentences, Stark told how Luhar and Freka had tried to kill him, and how Berild had been lost with him.

Kynon turned to the Venusian. Death was already glazing the cloud-grey eyes, but it had not quenched the hatred and venom.

'He lies,' whispered Luhar. 'I saw him – he tried to run away and take the woman with him.'

Luhar of Venus, taking vengeance with his last breath.

Freka pushed forward, transparently eager to pick up his cue. 'It is so,' he said. 'I was with Luhar. I saw it also.'

Delgaun laughed. Cruel, silent laughter. He stood up, and looked at Berild.

Berild's eyes were blazing. She ignored Delgaun and spoke to Kynon.

'You fool. Can't you see that they hate him? What Stark says is true. And I would have died in the desert because of them, if Stark hadn't been a better man than all of you.'

'Strange words,' said Delgaun, 'coming from a man's own mate. Perhaps Luhar did lie, after all. Perhaps it was not Stark who tried to run away, but you.'

She cursed him, with an ancient curse, and Kynon looked at

her sullenly. He said to the men who held Stark, 'Chain him below, in the dungeons.' Then he took Berild's arm and went with her into the palace.

Stark fought until someone behind him knocked him on the head with the butt of a spear. The last thing he saw was the face of Fianna, standing out from the crowd, wide-eyed with pity and love.

He came to in a place of cold, dry stone. There was an iron collar around his neck, and a five-foot chain ran from it to a ring in the wall. The cell was small. A gate of iron bars closed the single entrance. Beyond was an open well, with other cell doors around it, and above were thick stone gratings open to the sky. He guessed that the place was built beneath some inner court of the palace.

There were no other prisoners. But there was a guard, a thick-shouldered barbarian who sat on the execution block in the centre of the well, with a sword and a jug of wine. A guard who watched the captive Stark, and smiled.

Freka.

When he saw that Stark was awake, Freka lifted up the jug and laughed. 'Here's to Death,' he said. 'For no one else comes here!'

He drank, and after that he did not speak, only sat and smiled.

Stark said nothing either. He waited, with the same unhuman patience he had shown when he waited for his captors under the tor.

The dim daylight faded from the gratings. Darkness came, and the pale glimmer of the moons. Freka became a silvered statue of a man, sitting on the block. Stark's eyes glowed.

The empty jug dropped and broke. Freka rose. He took the naked sword in his hand and crossed the open space to the cell. He lifted the outer bar away. It fell with a great echoing clang, and Freka entered.

'Stand up, Outlander,' he said. 'Stand up and face the steel. After that you'll sleep in a coral pit, and not even the worms will find you.'

'Beast of Shanga!' Stark said contemptuously, and set his back against the wall, to give himself all the slack of the chain.

He saw the bright steel glimmer in the air, up and down again, but when the blow fell he had leaped aside, and the point struck ringing against the stone. Stark darted in to grapple.

His fingers slipped on hard muscle, and Freka wrenched away. He was a fighting man, and no weakling. The iron collar dug painfully into the Earthman's throat and the heavy chain threw him backward. Freka laughed, deep in his chest. The sword glinted hungrily.

Then, as though she had taken shape suddenly from the shadows, Fianna was in the doorway. The little gun in her hand made a hissing spurt of flame. Freka screamed once, and fell. He did not move again.

'The swine,' Fianna said, without emotion. 'Delgaun ordered him to wait, until it was sure that Kynon would not come down to talk to you. Then the story was to be that you had escaped somehow, with Berild's aid.'

She stepped over the body and unlocked the iron collar with a key she took from her girdle.

Stark took her slender shoulders gently between his hands. 'Are you a witch-girl, that you know all things and always come when I need you?'

She gave him a deep, strange look. In the dusk, her proud young face was unfamiliar, touched with something fey and sad. He wished that he could see her eyes more clearly.

'I know all things because I must,' she told him wearily. 'And I think that you are my only hope – perhaps the only hope of Mars.'

He drew her to him, and kissed her, and stroked her dark head. 'You're too young to concern yourself with the destinies of worlds.'

He felt her tremble. 'The youth of the body is only illusion, when the mind is old.'

'And is yours old, little one?'

'Old,' she whispered. 'As old as Berild's.'

He felt her tears warm against his skin, and she was like a child in his arms.

'Then you know about her,' said Stark.

'Yes.'

He paused. 'And Delgaun?'

'Delgaun also.'

'I thought so,' Stark said. He nodded, scowling at the barred moonlight in the well. 'There are things I must know, myself – but we'd best get out of here. Did Berild send you?'

'Yes – as soon as she could get the key from Kynon. She is waiting for you.' She stirred Freka's body with her foot. 'Bring that. We'll hide it in the pit he meant for you.'

Stark heaved the body over his shoulder and followed the girl through a twisting maze of corridors, some pitch dark, some feebly lighted by the moons. Fianna moved as surely as though she were in the main square at high noon. There was the silence of death in these cold tunnels, and the dry faint smell of eternity.

At length Fianna whispered. 'Here. Be careful.'

She put out a hand to guide him, but Stark's eyes were like a cat's in the dark. He made out a space where the rock with which the ancient builders had faced these subterranean ways gave place to the original coral.

Ragged black mouths opened in the coral, entrances to some unguessed catacombs beneath. Stark consigned Freka to the nearest pit, and then reluctantly threw his sword in after him.

'You won't need it,' Fianna told him, 'and besides, it would be recognised. This will be a bitter night enough, without rousing the men of Shun over Freka's death.'

Stark listened to the distant sliding echoes from the pit, and shivered. He had so nearly finished there himself. He was glad to follow Fianna away from that place of darkness and silent death.

He stopped her in a place where a bar of moonlight came splashing through a great crack in the tunnel roof.

'Now,' he said, 'we will talk.'

She nodded. 'Yes. The time has come for that.'

'There are lies everywhere,' said Stark. 'I am tangled up in lies. You know the truth that is behind this war of Kynon's. Tell me.'

'Kynon's truth is simple,' she answered, speaking slowly, choosing her words. 'He wants land and power, conquest. He will pour out the blood of his people for that, and after that he plans to use the men of the Low-Canals under Delgaun to keep the tribesmen in line. It may be true, as he said, that they would be satisfied with grazing land and water – but they would lose their freedom, and their pride, and I think he has judged them wrongly. I think they would revolt.'

She looked up at Stark. 'He planned to use your knowledge, and then destroy you if you became troublesome.'

'I guessed that. What about the others?'

'The outlanders? Use them, keep them as subordinates, or pay them off. Kill them, if necessary.'

'Now,' said Stark. 'What of Delgaun and Berild?'

Fianna said softly. 'Their truth, too, is simple. They took Kynon's idea of empire, and stretched it further. It was Delgaun's idea to bring the strangers in. They would use Kynon and the tribes until the victory was won. Then they would do away with Kynon and rule themselves – with the outlanders and their ships and their powerful weapons to oppress Low-Canaler and Drylander alike.

'That way, they could rape a world. More outland vultures would come, drawn by the smell of loot. The Martian men would fight as long as there was the hope of plunder – after that, they would be slaves to hold the empire. Their masters would grow fat on tribute from the City-States and from the men of Earth who have built here, or who wish to build. An evil plan – but profitable.'

Stark thought about Knighton and Walsh of Terra, Themis of Mercury, Arrod of Callisto Colony. He thought of others like them, and what they would do, with their talons hooked in the heart of Mars. He thought of Delgaun's yellow eyes.

He thought of Berild, and he was sick with loathing.

Fianna came close to him, speaking in a different tone that had care and anxiety only for him.

'I have told you this, because I know what Berild plans.

Tonight – oh, tonight is a black and evil time, and death waits in Sinharat! It is very close to me, I know. And you must follow your own heart, Eric John Stark. I cannot tell you more.'

He kissed her again, because she was sweet and very brave. Then she led him on through the dark labyrinth, to where Berild was waiting, with her dangerous beauty and all the evil of the ages in her soul.

10

They came out of the darkness so suddenly that Stark blinked in the unaccustomed light of torches set in great silver sconces on the walls.

The floor had been artificially smoothed, but otherwise the crypt was as the eroding action of the sea had shaped it out of the coral reef. It was not large, and it was like a cavern in a fairy tale, walled and roofed with the fantastic wreathing shapes of the rose-red coral. At one end there was a golden coffer set with flaming jewels.

Berild was there. Her wonderful hair was dressed and shining, and her body was clothed all in white, her arms and shoulders warm bronze from the kiss of the desert sun.

Kynon was there, also. He stood motionless and silent, and he did not so much as turn his head when Fianna and Stark came in. His eyes were wide open and blank as a blind man's.

'I have been waiting,' said Berild, 'and the time is short.'

She seemed angry and impatient, and Stark said, 'Freka is dead. It was necessary to hide his body.'

She nodded and turned to the girl. 'Go now, Fianna.'

Fianna bent her head and went away. She did not look at Stark. It was as though she had no interest in anything that happened.

Stark looked at Kynon, who had not moved or spoken.

'He is safe enough,' said Berild, answering Stark's unspoken question. 'I drugged his wine so that his mind was opened to mine, and he is my creature as long as I will it.'

Hypnosis, Stark thought. His nerves were beginning to do strange things. He wished desperately that he were back in the cell facing Freka's sword, which at least would deal with him openly and without guile or subterfuge.

Berild set her hands on Stark's shoulders, and smiled as she had done that night by the ancient well.

'I offer you three things tonight, wild man,' she said. Her eyes challenged him, and the scent of her hair was sweet and maddening.

'Your life – and power – and myself.'

Stark let his hands slip lightly down from her shoulders to her waist. 'And how will you do this thing?' he asked.

'Easily,' she said, and laughed. She was very proud, and sure of her strength, and glad to be alive. 'Oh, very easily. You guessed the truth about me – I am of the Twice Born, the Ramas. I hold the secret of the Sending-on of Minds, which this great ox Kynon pretended to have. I can give you life now – and forever. Remember, wild man – forever!'

He bent his dark face to hers, so that their lips touched, and murmured, 'Would I have you forever, Berild?'

'Until you tire of me – or I of you.' She kissed him, and then added mockingly, 'Delgaun has had me for a thousand years, and I am weary of him. So very weary!'

'A thousand years is a long time,' said Stark, 'and I am not Delgaun.'

'No. You're a beast, a savage, a most magnificent cold-eyed animal, and that is why I love you.' She touched the muscle of his breast, and then his throat, and added, 'It's a pity there will never be another body like this one. We must keep it as long as we can.'

'What is your plan?' Stark asked her.

'Simply this. I will place your mind in Kynon's body. You will *be* Kynon, with all his power. You will be able then to keep Delgaun in check – later, you can destroy him, but not until after the battle is won, for we need the men of Valkis and Jekkara. You can keep your own body safe from him, and at the worst, if by some chance he should succeed in slaying the man he believes to be you, *you* will still be alive.'

'And after the battle,' said Stark softly. 'What then, Berild?'

'We will rule together.' She held his palms against hers. 'You have strong hands, wild man. Would you not like to hold a world between them – and me?'

She looked up at him, her eyes suddenly shrewd and probing. 'Or do you still believe the nonsense you talked to Kynon, about the tribes?'

Stark smiled. 'It's easy to have principles when there's no gain involved. No. I am as my name says – a man without a tribe. I have no loyalties. And if I had, would I remember them now?'

He held her, as she had said, between his hands, and they were very strong.

But even then, Berild could warn him.

'Keep faith with me, then! My wisdom is greater than yours, and I have powers you don't dream of. What I give, I can take away.'

For answer, Stark silenced her mouth with his own.

When she drew away, she said rather breathlessly, 'Let us hurry. The tribes are gathered, and Kynon was to have given the signal for war at dawn. There is much I must teach you between now and then.'

She paused with her hand on the lid of the golden coffer. 'This is a secret place,' she said quietly. 'Since before the ocean died, it has been secret. Not even Kynon knew of it. I think only Delgaun and I, the last of the Twice-Born, knew – and now you.'

'What about Fianna?'

Berild shrugged. 'She is only my servant. To her, this is only a little cavern where I keep my private wealth.'

She pressed a series of patterned bosses in intricate sequence, and there was the sharp click of an opening lock. A shiver ran up along Stark's spine. The beast in him longed to run, to be away from this whole business that smelled of evil. But the man in him knelt at Berild's wish, and waited, and did not flinch when the blank-eyed Kynon came like a moving corpse beside him.

Berild raised the golden lid. And there was a great silence.

On the slave block of Valkis, Kynon had brought forth two

crowns of shining crystal and a rod of flame. As glass is to diamond, as the pallid moon to the light of the sun, were those things to the reality.

In her two hands Berild held the ancient crowns of the Ramas, the givers of life. Twin circlets of glorious fire, dimming the shallow glare of the torches, putting a nimbus of light around the white-clad woman so that she was like a goddess walking in a cloud of stars. Stark's whole being contracted to a point of icy pain at the beauty and the wonder and the terror of them.

She set one crown on Kynon's head, and even the drugged automaton shivered and sighed at its touch.

Stark's mind veered away from the incredible thing that was about to happen. It spoke words to him, hurried desperate words of sanity, about the electrical patterns of the mind, and the sensitivity of crystals, and conductors, and electro-magnetic impulses. But that was only the top of his brain. At base it was still the brain of N'Chaka that believed in gods and demons and all the sorceries of darkness. Only pride kept him from cowering abjectly at Berild's feet.

She stood above him, a creature of dreams in the unearthly light. She smiled and whispered, 'Do not fear,' – and she placed the second crown upon his head.

A strange, shuddering fire swept through him. It was as though some chip of the primal heart of all creation had been set by an unguessed magic into the cells of the crystal. The force that shaped the universe and scattered forth the stars, and set the great suns to spinning. There was something awesome about it, something almost holy.

And yet he was afraid. Most shockingly afraid.

His brain was set free, in some strange fashion. The walls of his skull vanished. His mind floated in a dim vastness. It was like a tiny sun, glowing, spinning, swelling ...

Berild lifted a crystal rod from the coffer, a wand of sorcerous fire. And now Stark's thoughts had lost all track of science. A cloud of misty darkness flowed around him, thickened ...

A great leaping flare of light, a distant echo of a cry that he did not recognise as his own, and then ...

Nothing.

11

He was lying on his face, his cheek pressed against the cool coral. He opened his eyes, his mind groping for the shreds of some remembered terror. He saw, vaguely at first and then with terrible clarity as his vision became clear, a man lying close beside him.

A tall man, very strongly built, with skin burned almost to blackness by exposure. A man who looked at him with eyes that were startlingly light in his dark face ...

His own eyes. His own face.

He cried out and struggled to his feet, trembling, staggering, and his body felt strange to him. He looked down upon the strangeness of another man's limbs, the alien shaping of flesh and sinew upon alien bones.

The face of the dark giant who lay upon the coral mocked him. It watched, but did not see. The eyes were blank, empty, without soul or intelligence.

The mind of Eric John Stark fought, in its alien prison, for sanity.

Berild's voice spoke to him. Her hand was on his shoulder – Kynon's shoulder ...

'All is well, wild man. Do not fear. Kynon's mind is in your body, still sleeping at my command. And you are Kynon now.'

It was not an easy thing to accept, but he knew that it was so, and he knew that he had wished it to be so. It was easier to be calm after he turned his back on *the other*.

Berild took him in her arms and held him until he had stopped shuddering, oddly like a mother with a frightened child. Then she kissed him, smiling, and said,

'The first time is hard. I can remember – and that was very long ago.' She shook him gently. 'Now come. We'll take your body to a place of safety. And then I must tell you all of Kynon's plans for those outside.'

She spoke to the thing that lay upon the coral, saying, 'Get up,' and it rose obediently and followed where Berild led, to a tiny barred niche in a side passage. It made no protest when it was left, locked safely in.

'Only I can give it back to you,' said Berild softly. 'Remember that.'

Stark said, 'I will remember.'

He went with Berild to Kynon's quarters in the palace. He sat among Kynon's possessions, clothed in Kynon's flesh, and learned how Kynon's mind had planned to loose a red tide upon the peaceful cities of the Border.

Only a small part of his mind was attentive to this. The rest of it was concerned with the redness of Berild's hair and the warmth of her lips, and with the heady knowledge that it was possible to be alive and young forever.

Never to lose the pride of strength, never to know the dimming sight and failing mind of age. To go on, like a child in an endless playground, with no fear of tomorrow.

It was nearly dawn.

Berild rose. She had told him much, but not the things Fianna had told him, of the secret treachery she had planned with Delgaun. She helped Stark to clothe Kynon's body in the harness of war, with the longsword and the shield and the shining spear. Then she set her lips to his so that his borrowed heart threatened to choke him with its pounding, and her eyes were wondrously bright and beautiful.

'It is time,' she whispered.

She walked beside him, as he had seen her beside Kynon in Valkis, stepping like a queen.

They came out of the palace, onto the steps where Luhar had died. There were beasts waiting, trapped for war, and an escort of tall chiefs, with pipers and drummers and link-boys to light the way.

Stark mounted Kynon's beast. It sensed the wrongness in him, hissing and rearing, but he held it down, and imperiously raised his hand.

Throbbing drums and skirling pipes, tossing flames where the link-boys ran with the torches, a clash of metal and a cheer, and Kynon of Shun rode down through the streets of Sinharat to the coral cliffs, with the red-haired woman at his side.

They were waiting.

The men of Kesh and the men of Shun were gathered below the cliffs, waiting. Stark led the way, as Berild had told him to, onto a ledge of coral above them. Delgaun was there, with the outlanders and a handful of Valkisians. He looked tired and ill-tempered. Stark knew that he had been busy for hours with last-minute preparations.

The first pale rays of dawn broke across the desert. A vast ringing cry went up from the gathered armies. After that there was silence, a taunt expectant hush.

There was no fear in Stark now. He was past that. Fear was too small an emotion for what was about to be.

He saw Delgaun's golden eyes, hot with a cruel excitement. He saw Berild's secret triumph in her smile. He looked down upon the warriors, and let the magnificent voice of Kynon ring out across the soundless air.

'There will be no war,' he said. 'You have been betrayed.'

In the moment that was left to him, he confessed the lie of the Rama crowns. And then Berild, who was behind him now, had moved like a red-haired fury to drive her dagger into his heart.

In his own body, Stark might have escaped the blow. But the reflexes of Kynon were not as his. They were swift enough to postpone death – the blade bit deep, but not where Berild had wished it. He turned and caught her by the wrists, and said to Delgaun,

'She has betrayed you, too. Freka lies in a coral pit – and I am not Kynon.'

Berild tore away from him. She spurred her beast toward the Valkisian. She would have broken past him, through the escort, and up the cliffs to safety in the tunnels under Sinharat. But Delgaun was too quick.

One hand caught in the masses of her hair. She was dragged screaming from the saddle, and even then her screams were not of fear, but of fury. She clawed at Delgaun, and he fell with her to the ground.

The tall chieftains of the escort came forward, but they were dazed, and confused by the anger that was rising in them.

Delgaun's wiry body arched. He flung the woman over the ledge, and what happened to her after that Stark did not see, nor wish to see.

He was shouting again to the barbarians, the tale of Delgaun's treachery.

Behind him on the ledge there was turmoil where Delgaun ran on foot between the beasts, and the outlanders made their try for safety. Below him in the desert, where there had been silence, a great deep muttering was growing, like the first growling of a storm, and the ranks of spears rippled like wheat before the wind.

And Stark felt the slow running out of Kynon's blood inside him, where Berild's dagger stood out from his back.

They had headed Delgaun away from the path up the cliff. The two loose mounts had been caught and held. They had tried to catch Delgaun, but he was light and fast and slipped away from them. Now he broke back, toward Kynon's great beast.

Knock the dying man from the saddle, charge through the milling chieftains, who were hampered by their own numbers in that narrow space ...

He leaped. And the arms of Kynon, driven by the will of Eric John Stark, encircled him and held him and would not let him go.

The two men crashed to the ledge. Stark let out one harsh cry of agony, and then was still, his hands locked around the Valkisian's throat, his eyes intent and strange.

Men came up, and he gasped, 'He is mine,' and they let him be.

Delgaun did not die easily. He managed to get his dagger out, and gashed the other's side until the naked ribs showed through. But once again Stark's mind was free in some dark immensity of its own. He was living again the dream he had in Valkis, and this was the end of the dream. N'Chaka had a grip at last on the demon with yellow eyes that hungered for his life, and he would not let go.

The yellow eyes widened. They blazed, and then they slowly dimmed until the last flicker of life was gone. The strength went out of N'Chaka's hands. He fell forward, over his prey.

Below, on the sand, Berild lay, and her outspread hair was as red as blood in the fiery dawn.

The men of Kesh and the men of Shun flowed, in a resistless tide up over the coral cliffs. The chieftains and the pipers and the link-boys joined them, hunting the outlanders and the wolves of Valkis through the streets of Sinharat.

Unnoticed, a dark-haired girl ran down the path to the ledge. She bent over the body of Kynon, pressing her hand to its heart. Tears ran down and mingled with the blood.

A low, faint moan came from the man's lips. Weeping like a child, Fianna drew a tiny vial from her girdle and poured three drops of pale liquid on the unresponsive tongue.

12

He had come a long way. He had been down in the deep black valleys of the Place of Darkness, and the iron frost was in his bones. He had climbed the bitter mountains where no creature of the Twilight Belt might go and live.

There was light, now. He had been lost and wandering, but he had won back to the light. His tribe, his people would be waiting for him. But he knew that he would never see them.

He remembered, then, with the old terrible loneliness, that they were not truly his people. They had raised him, but they were not of his blood.

And he remembered also that they were dead, slain by the miners who had needed all the water of the valley for themselves. Slain by the miners who had taken N'Chaka and put him in a cage.

With a start of terror, he thought he was again in that cage, with the leering bearded faces peering in at him. But in the blinding dazzle of light he could see no bars.

There was only one face. The anxious, pitying face of a girl.

Fianna.

His brain began to clear. Memory returned bit by bit, the fragments fitting themselves gradually into place.

Kynon. Delgaun. Berild. Sinharat, the Ever-Living.

He remembered now with perfect clarity that he was dying, and it seemed a terrible thing to die in the body of another man. For the first time, fully, he felt the separation from his own flesh. It seemed a blasphemous thing, more terrible than death.

Fianna was weeping. She stroked his hair, and whispered, 'I am so glad. I was afraid – afraid you would never wake.'

He was touched, because he knew that she loved him and would be sad. He lifted his hand to touch her face, to comfort her.

He saw the fingers of that hand, dark against her cheek. Dark...

His own fingers. His own hand.

He was not on the ledge. He was back in the coral crypt beneath the palace. The light that had dazzled his eyes was not the sun, but only the flare of torches.

He sat up, his heart pounding wildly.

Kynon of Shun lay beside him on the coral. He was quite dead, his head encircled by a crown of fire, his side open to the white bone where Delgaun's blade had struck.

The wound that Kynon himself had never felt.

The golden coffer was open. The second crown lay near Fianna, with the rod beside it.

Stark looked at her, deep into her eyes. Very softly he said, 'I would not have dreamed it.'

'You will understand, now – many things,' she said. 'And I was glad of my power today, because I could truly give you life!'

She rose, and he saw that she was very tired. Her voice was dull, as though it counted over old things that no longer mattered.

'You see why I was afraid. If *they* had ever suspected that I, too, was of the Twice-Born ... Berild or Delgaun, each alone, I might have destroyed, but I could not destroy both of them. And if I had, there was still Kynon. You did what I could not, Eric John Stark.'

'Why were you against them, Fianna? How were you proof against the poison that made them what they were?'

She answered angrily, 'Because I am weary of evil, of scheming for power and shedding the blood of men as though they were sheep! I am not better than Berild was. I, too, have lived a long time, and my hands are not clean. But perhaps, by what you helped me do, I have made up a little for my sins.'

She paused, her thoughts turned darkly inward, and it was strange to see the shadow of age touching her sweet young face. Then she said, very slowly, like an old, old woman speaking,

'I am weary of living. No matter where I go, I am a stranger. You can understand that, though not so well as I. There is an end to pleasure, and after that only loneliness is left.

'I have remembered that I was human once. That is why I set myself against their plan of empire. After all these ages I have come round full circle to the starting point, and things seem to me now as they seemed then, before I was tempted by the Sending-on of Minds.

'It is a wicked thing!' she cried suddenly. 'Against nature and the gods, and it has never brought anything but evil!'

She caught up the rod and held it in her hands.

'This is the last,' she said. 'Cities die, and nations perish, and material things, even such as these, are destroyed. One by one the Twice-Born have perished also, through accident or swift disease or murder, as Berild would have slain Delgaun. Now only this, and I, are left.'

Quite suddenly, she flung the rod against the coral, and it broke in a cloudy flame and a tinkling of crystal shards. Then, one by one, she broke the crowns.

She stood still for a long moment. Then she whispered, 'Now only I am left.'

Again there was silence, and Stark was shaken by the magnitude of the thing that she had done. Her slim girl's body somehow took on the stature of a goddess.

After a while he went to her and said awkwardly, 'I have not thanked you, Fianna. You brought me here, you saved me ...'

'Kiss me once, then,' she answered, and raised her lips to his.

'For I love you, Eric John Stark – and that is the pity of it. Because I am not for you, nor for any man.'

He kissed her, very tenderly, and there was the bitter taste of tears on her soft lips.

'Now come,' she whispered, and took his hand.

She led him back through the labyrinth, into the palace, and then out again into the streets of Sinharat. Stark saw that it was sunset, and that the city was deserted. The tribes of Kesh and Shun had broken camp and gone.

There was a beast ready for him, supplied with food and water. Fianna asked him where he wished to go, and pointed the way to Tarak.

'And you?' he asked. 'Where will you go, little one?'

'I have not thought.' She lifted her head, and the wind played with her dark hair. She did not smile, and yet suddenly Stark knew that she was happy.

'I am free of a great burden,' she whispered. 'I shall stay here for a while, and think, and after that I shall know what to do. But whatever it is there will be no evil in it, and in the end I shall rest.'

He mounted, and she looked up at him, with a look that wrung his heart although it was not sad.

'Go now,' she said, 'and the gods go with you.'

'And with you.' He bent and kissed her once again, and then rode away, down to the coral cliffs.

Far out on the desert he turned and looked back, once, at the white towers of Sinharat rising against the larger moon.

ENCHANTRESS OF VENUS

1

The ship moved slowly across the Red Sea, through the shrouding veils of mist, her sail barely filled by the languid thrust of the wind. Her hull, of a thin light metal, floated without sound, the surface of the strange ocean parting before her prow in silent rippling streamers of flame.

Night deepened toward the ship, a river of indigo flowing out of the west. The man known as Stark stood alone by the after rail and watched its coming. He was full of impatience and a gathering sense of danger, so that it seemed to him that even the hot wind smelled of it.

The steersman lay drowsily over his sweep. He was a big man, with skin and hair the colour of milk. He did not speak, but Stark felt that now and again the man's eyes turned toward him, pale and calculating under half-closed lids, with a secret avarice.

The captain and the two other members of the little coasting vessel's crew were forward, at their evening meal. Once or twice Stark heard a burst of laughter, half-whispered and furtive. It was as though all four shared in some private joke, from which he was rigidly excluded.

The heat was oppressive. Sweat gathered on Stark's dark face. His shirt stuck to his back. The air was heavy with moisture, tainted with the muddy fecundity of the land that brooded westward behind the eternal fog.

There was something ominous about the sea itself. Even on its own world, the Red Sea is hardly more than legend. It lies behind the Mountains of White Cloud, the great barrier wall that hides away half a planet. Few men have gone beyond that barrier, into the vast mystery of Inner Venus. Fewer still have come back.

Stark was one of that handful. Three times before he had crossed the mountains, and once he had stayed for nearly a year. But he had never quite grown used to the Red Sea.

It was not water. It was gaseous, dense enough to float the buoyant hulls of the metal ships, and it burned perpetually with its deep inner fires. The mists that clouded it were stained with the bloody glow. Beneath the surface Stark could see the drifts of flame where the lazy currents ran, and the little coiling bursts of sparks that came upward and spread and melted into other bursts, so that the face of the sea was like a cosmos of crimson stars.

It was very beautiful, glowing against the blue, luminous darkness of the night. Beautiful, and strange.

There was a padding of bare feet, and the captain, Malthor, came up to Stark, his outline dim and ghostly in the gloom.

'We will reach Shuruun,' he said, 'before the second glass is run.'

Stark nodded. 'Good.'

The voyage had seemed endless, and the close confinement of the narrow deck had got badly on his nerves.

'You will like Shuruun,' said the captain jovially. 'Our wine, our food, our women – all superb. We don't have many visitors. We keep to ourselves, as you will see. But those who do come...'

He laughed, and clapped Stark on the shoulder. 'Ah, yes. You will be happy in Shuruun!'

It seemed to Stark that he caught an echo of laughter from the unseen crew, as though they listened and found a hidden jest in Malthor's words.

Stark said, 'That's fine.'

'Perhaps,' said Malthor, 'you would like to lodge with me. I could make you a good price.'

He had made a good price for Stark's passage from up the coast. An exorbitantly good one.

Stark said, 'No.'

'You don't have to be afraid,' said the Venusian, in a confidential tone. 'The strangers who come to Shuruun all have the same reaction. It's a good place to hide. We're out of everybody's reach.'

He paused, but Stark did not rise to his bait. Presently he chuckled and went on, 'In fact, it's such a safe place that most of the strangers decide to stay on. Now, at my house, I could give you …'

Stark said again, flatly, 'No.'

The captain shrugged. 'Very well. Think it over, anyway.' He peered ahead into the red, coiling mists. 'Ah! See there?' He pointed, and Stark made out the shadowy loom of cliffs. 'We are coming into the strait now.'

Malthor turned and took the steering sweep himself, the helmsman going forward to join the others. The ship began to pick up speed. Stark saw that she had come into the grip of a current that swept toward the cliffs, a river of fire racing ever more swiftly in the depths of the sea.

The dark wall seemed to plunge toward them. At first Stark could see no passage. Then, suddenly, a narrow crimson streak appeared, widened, and became a gut of boiling flame, rushing silently around broken rocks. Red fog rose like smoke. The ship quivered, sprang ahead, and tore like a mad thing into the heart of the inferno.

In spite of himself, Stark's hands tightened on the rail. Tattered veils of mist swirled past them. The sea, the air, the ship itself, seemed drenched in blood. There was no sound, in all that wild sweep of current through the strait. Only the sullen fires burst and flowed.

The reflected glare showed Stark that the Straits of Shuruun were defended. Squat fortresses brooded on the cliffs. There were ballistas, and great windlasses for the drawing of nets across the narrow throat. The men of Shuruun could enforce their law, that barred all foreign shipping from their gulf.

They had reason for such a law, and such a defence. The legitimate trade of Shuruun, such as it was, was in wine and the delicate laces woven from spider-silk. Actually, however, the city lived and throve on piracy, the arts of wrecking, and a contraband trade in the distilled juice of the *vela* poppy.

Looking at the rocks and the fortresses, Stark could

understand how it was that Shuruun had been able for more centuries than anyone could tell to victimise the shipping of the Red Sea, and offer a refuge to the outlaw, the wolf's-head, the breaker of taboo.

With startling abruptness, they were through the gut and drifting on the still surface of this all but landlocked arm of the Red Sea.

Because of the shrouding fog, Stark could see nothing of the land. But the smell of it was stronger, warm damp soil and the heavy, faintly rotten perfume of vegetation half jungle, half swamp. Once, through a rift in the wreathing vapour, he thought he glimpsed the shadowy bulk of an island, but it was gone at once.

After the terrifying rush of the strait, it seemed to Stark that the ship barely moved. His impatience and the subtle sense of danger deepened. He began to pace the deck, with the nervous, velvet motion of a prowling cat. The moist, steamy air seemed all but unbreathable after the clean dryness of Mars, from whence he had come so recently. It was oppressively still.

Suddenly he stopped, his head thrown back, listening.

The sound was borne faintly on the slow wind. It came from everywhere and nowhere, a vague dim thing without source or direction. It almost seemed that the night itself had spoken – the hot blue night of Venus, crying out of the mists with a tongue of infinite woe.

It faded and died away, only half heard, leaving behind it a sense of aching sadness, as though all the misery and longing of a world had found voice in that desolate wail.

Stark shivered. For a time there was silence, and then he heard the sound again, now on a deeper note. Still faint and far away, it was sustained longer by the vagaries of the heavy air, and it became a chant, rising and falling. There were no words. It was not the sort of thing that would have need of words. Then it was gone again.

Stark turned to Malthor. 'What was that?'

The man looked at him curiously. He seemed not to have heard.

'That wailing sound,' said Stark impatiently.

'Oh, that.' The Venusian shrugged. 'A trick of the wind. It sighs in the hollow rocks around the strait.'

He yawned, giving place again to the steersman, and came to stand beside Stark. The Earthman ignored him. For some reason, that sound half heard through the mists had brought his uneasiness to a sharp pitch.

Civilisation had brushed over Stark with a light hand. Raised from infancy by half-human aboriginals, his perceptions were still those of a savage. His ear was good.

Malthor lied. That cry of pain was not made by any wind.

'I have known several Earthmen,' said Malthor, changing the subject, but not too swiftly. 'None of them were like you.'

Intuition warned Stark to play along. 'I don't come from Earth,' he said. 'I come from Mercury.'

Malthor puzzled over that. Venus is a cloudy world, where no man has ever seen the Sun, let alone a star. The captain had heard vaguely of these things. Earth and Mars he knew of. But Mercury was an unknown word.

Stark explained. 'The planet nearest the Sun. It's very hot there. The Sun blazes like a huge fire, and there are no clouds to shield it.'

'Ah. That is why your skin is so dark.' He held his own pale forearm close to Stark's and shook his head. 'I have never seen such skin,' he said admiringly. 'Nor such great muscles.'

Looking up, he went on in a tone of complete friendliness, 'I wish you would stay with me. You'll find no better lodgings in Shuruun. And I warn you, there are people in the town who will take advantage of strangers – rob them, even slay them. Now, I am known by all as a man of honour. You could sleep soundly under my roof.'

He paused, then added with a smile, 'Also, I have a daughter. An excellent cook – and very beautiful.'

The woeful chanting came again, dim and distant on the wind, an echo of warning against some unimagined fate.

Stark said for the third time, 'No.'

He needed no intuition to tell him to walk wide of the captain. The man was a rogue, and not a very subtle one.

A flint-hard, angry look came briefly into Malthor's eyes.

'You're a stubborn man. You'll find that Shuruun is no place for stubbornness.'

He turned and went away. Stark remained where he was. The ship drifted on through a slow eternity of time. And all down that long still gulf of the Red Sea, through the heat and the wreathing fog, the ghostly chanting haunted him, like the keening of lost souls in some forgotten hell.

Presently the course of the ship was altered. Malthor came again to the afterdeck, giving a few quiet commands. Stark saw land ahead, a darker blur on the night, and then the shrouded outlines of a city.

Torched blazed on the quays and in the streets, and the low buildings caught a ruddy glow from the burning sea itself. A squat and ugly town, Shuruun, crouching witch-like on the rocky shore, her ragged skirts dipped in blood.

The ship drifted in toward the quays.

Stark heard a whisper of movement behind him, the hushed and purposeful padding of naked feet. He turned, with the astonishing swiftness of an animal that feels itself threatened, his hand dropping to his gun.

A belaying pin, thrown by the steersman, struck the side of his head with stunning force. Reeling, half blinded, he saw the distorted shapes of men closing in upon him. Malthor's voice sounded, low and hard. A second belaying pin whizzed through the air and cracked against Stark's shoulder.

Hands were laid upon him. Bodies, heavy and strong, bore him down. Malthor laughed.

Stark's teeth glinted bare and white. Someone's cheek brushed past, and he sank them into the flesh. He began to growl, a sound that should never have come from a human throat. It seemed to the startled Venusians that the man they had attacked had by some wizardly become a beast, at the first touch of violence.

The man with the torn cheek screamed. There was a voiceless scuffling on the deck, a terrible intensity of motion, and then the great dark body rose and shook itself free of the tangle, and was gone, over the rail, leaving Malthor with nothing but the silken rags of a shirt in his hands.

The surface of the Red Sea closed without a ripple over Stark.

There was a burst of crimson sparks, a momentary trail of flame going down like a drowned comet, and then – nothing.

2

Stark dropped slowly downward through a strange world. There was no difficulty about breathing, as in a sea of water. The gases of the Red Sea support life quite well, and the creatures that dwell in it have almost normal lungs.

Stark did not pay much attention at first, except to keep his balance automatically. He was still dazed from the blow, and he was raging with anger and pain.

The primitive in him, whose name was not Stark but N'Chaka, and who had fought and starved and hunted in the blazing valleys of Mercury's Twilight Belt, learning lessons he never forgot, wished to return and slay Malthor and his men. He regretted that he had not torn out their throats, for now his trail would never be safe from them.

But the man Stark, who had learned some more bitter lessons in the name of civilisation, knew the unwisdom of that. He snarled over his aching head, and cursed the Venusians in the harsh, crude dialect that was his mother tongue, but he did not turn back. There would be time enough for Malthor.

It struck him that the gulf was very deep.

Fighting down his rage, he began to swim in the direction of the shore. There was no sign of pursuit, and he judged that Malthor had decided to let him go. He puzzled over the reason for the attack. It could hardly be robbery, since he carried nothing but the clothes he stood in, and very little money.

No. There was some deeper reason. A reason connected with Malthor's insistence that he lodge with him. Stark smiled. It was not a pleasant smile. He was thinking of Shuruun, and the things men said about it, around the shores of the Red Sea.

He had not been alone then. Helvi had gone with him – the tall son of a barbarian kinglet up-coast by Yarell. They had hunted strange beasts through the crystal forests of the sea-bottom and bathed in the welling flames that pulse from the very heart of Venus to feed the ocean. They had been brothers.

Now Helvi was gone, into Shuruun. He had never returned.

Stark swam on. And presently he saw below him in the red gloom something that made him drop lower, frowning with surprise.

There were trees beneath him. Great forest giants towering up into an eerie sky, their branches swaying gently to the slow wash of the currents.

Stark was puzzled. The forests where he and Helvi had hunted were truly crystalline, without even the memory of life. The 'trees' were no more trees in actuality than the branching corals of Terra's southern oceans.

But these were real, or had been. He thought at first that they still lived, for their leaves were green, and here and there creepers had starred them with great nodding blossoms of gold and purple and waxy white. But when he floated down close enough to touch them, he realised that they were dead – trees, creepers, blossoms, all.

They had not mummified, nor turned to stone. They were pliable, and their colours were very bright. Simply, they had ceased to live, and the gases of the sea had preserved them by some chemical magic, so perfectly that barely a leaf had fallen.

Stark did not venture into the shadowy denseness below the topmost branches. A strange fear came over him, at the sight of that vast forest dreaming in the depths of the gulf, drowned and forgotten, as though wondering why the birds had gone, taking with them the warm rains and the light of day.

He thrust his way upward, himself like a huge dark bird above the branches. An overwhelming impulse to get away from that unearthly place drove him on, his half-wild sense shuddering with an impression of evil so great that it took all his acquired common sense to assure him that he was not pursued by demons.

He broke the surface at last, to find that he had lost his direction in the red deep and made a long circle around, so that he was far below Shuruun. He made his way back, not hurrying now, and presently clambered out over the black rocks.

He stood at the end of a muddy lane that wandered in toward the town. He followed it, moving neither fast nor slow, but with a wary alertness.

Huts of wattle-and-daub took shape out of the fog, increased in numbers, became a street of dwellings. Here and there rush-lights glimmered through the slitted windows. A man and a woman clung together in a low doorway. They saw him and sprang apart, and the woman gave a little cry. Stark went on. He did not look back, but he knew that they were following him quietly, at a little distance.

The lane twisted snakelike upon itself, crawling now through a crowded jumble of houses. There were more lights, and more people, tall white-skinned folk of the swamp-edges, with pale eyes and long hair the colour of new flax, and the faces of wolves.

Stark passed among them, alien and strange with his black hair and sun-darkened skin. They did not speak, nor try to stop him. Only they looked at him out of the red fog, with a curious blend of amusement and fear, and some of them followed him, keeping well behind. A gang of small naked children came from somewhere among the houses and ran shouting beside him, out of reach, until one boy threw a stone and screamed something unintelligible except for one word – *Lhari*. Then they all stopped, horrified, and fled.

Stark went on, through the quarter of the lacemakers, heading by instinct toward the wharves. The glow of the Red Sea pervaded all the air, so that it seemed as though the mist was full of tiny drops of blood. There was a smell about the place he did not like, a damp miasma of mud and crowding bodies and wine, and the breath of the *vela* poppy. Shuruun was an unclean town, and it stank of evil.

There was something else about it, a subtle thing that touched Stark's nerves with a chill finger. Fear. He could see the shadow of it in the eyes of the people, hear its undertone in their voices. The wolves of Shuruun did not feel safe in their own kennel.

Unconsciously, as this feeling grew upon him, Stark's step grew more and more wary, his eyes more cold and hard.

He came out into a broad square by the harbour front. He could see the ghostly ships moored along the quays, the piled casks of wine, the tangle of masts and cordage dim against the background of the burning gulf. There were many torches here. Large low buildings stood around the square. There was laughter and the sound of voices from the dark verandas, and somewhere a woman sang to the melancholy lilting of a reed pipe.

A suffused glow of light in the distance ahead caught Stark's eye. That way the streets sloped to a higher ground, and straining his vision against the fog, he made out very dimly the tall bulk of a castle crouched on the low cliffs, looking with bright eyes upon the night, and the streets of Shuruun.

Stark hesitated briefly. Then he started across the square toward the largest of the taverns.

There were a number of people in the open space, mostly sailors and their women. They were loose and foolish with wine, but even so they stopped where they were and stared at the dark stranger, and then drew back from him, still staring.

Those who had followed Stark came into the square after him and then paused, spreading out in an aimless sort of way to join with other groups, whispering among themselves.

The woman stopped singing in the middle of a phrase.

A curious silence fell on the square. A nervous sibilance ran round and round under the silence, and men came slowly out from the verandas and the doors of the wine shops. Suddenly a woman with dishevelled hair pointed her arm at Stark and laughed, the shrieking laugh of a harpy.

Stark found his way barred by three tall young men with hard mouths and crafty eyes, who smiled at him as hounds smile before the kill.

'Stranger,' they said. 'Earthman.'

'Outlaw,' answered Stark, and it was only half a lie.

One of the young men took a step forward. 'Did you fly like a dragon over the Mountains of White Cloud? Did you drop from the sky?'

'I came on Malthor's ship.'

A kind of sigh went round the square, and with it the name of Malthor. The eager faces of the young men grew heavy with disappointment. But the leader said sharply, 'I was on the quay when Malthor docked. You were not on board.'

It was Stark's turn to smile. In the light of the torches, his eyes blazed cold and bright as ice against the sun.

'Ask Malthor the reason for that,' he said. 'Ask the man with the torn cheek. Or perhaps,' he added softly, 'you would like to learn for yourselves.'

The young men looked at him, scowling, in an odd mood of indecision. Stark settled himself, every muscle loose and ready. And the woman who had laughed crept closer and peered at Stark through her tangled hair, breathing heavily of the poppy wine.

All at once she said loudly, 'He came out of the sea. That's where he came from. He's ...'

One of the young men struck her across the mouth and she fell down in the mud. A burly seaman ran out and caught her by the hair, dragging her to her feet again. His face was frightened and very angry. He hauled the woman away, cursing her for a fool and beating her as he went. She spat out blood, and said no more.

'Well,' said Stark to the young men. 'Have you made up your minds?'

'Minds!' said a voice behind them – a harsh-timbred, rasping voice that handled the liquid vocables of the Venusian speech very clumsily indeed. 'They have no minds, these whelps! If they had, they'd be off about their business, instead of standing here badgering a stranger.'

The young men turned, and now between them Stark could see the man who had spoken. He stood on the steps of the tavern. He was an Earthman, and at first Stark thought he was old, because his hair was white and his face deeply lined. His body was wasted with fever, the muscles all gone to knotty strings twisted over bone. He leaned heavily on a stick, and one leg was crooked and terribly scarred.

He grinned at Stark and said, in colloquial English, 'Watch me get rid of 'em!'

He began to tongue-lash the young men, telling them that they were idiots, the misbegotten offspring of swamp-toads, utterly without manners, and that if they did not believe the stranger's story they should go and ask Malthor, as he suggested. Finally he shook his stick at them, fairly screeching.

'Go on, now. Go away! Leave us alone – my brother of Earth and I!'

The young men gave one hesitant glance at Stark's feral eyes. Then they looked at each other and shrugged, and went away across the square half sheepishly, like great loutish boys caught in some misdemeanour.

The white-haired Earthman beckoned to Stark. And, as Stark came up to him on the steps he said under his breath, almost angrily, 'You're in a trap.'

Stark glanced back over his shoulder. At the edge of the square the three young men had met a fourth, who had his face bound up in a rag. They vanished almost at once into a side street, but not before Stark had recognised the fourth man as Malthor.

It was the captain he had branded.

With loud cheerfulness, the lame man said in Venusian, 'Come in and drink with me, brother, and we will talk of Earth.'

3

The tavern was of the standard low-class Venusian pattern – a single huge room under bare thatch, the wall half open with the reed shutters rolled up, the floor of split logs propped up on piling out of the mud. A long low bar, little tables, mangy skins and heaps of dubious cushions on the floor around them, and at one end the entertainers – two old men with a drum and a reed pipe, and a couple of sulky, tired-looking girls.

The lame man led Stark to a table in the corner and sank down calling for wine. His eyes, which were dark and haunted by long pain, burned with excitement. His hands shook. Before Stark had sat down he had begun to talk, his words stumbling over themselves as though he could not get them out fast enough.

'How is it there now? Has it changed any? Tell me how it is – the cities, the lights, the paved street, the women, the Sun. Oh Lord, what I wouldn't give to see the Sun again, and women with dark hair and their clothes on!' He leaned forward, staring hungrily into Stark's face, as though he could see those things mirrored there. 'For God's sake, talk to me – talk to me in English, and tell me about Earth!'

'How long have you been here?' asked Stark.

'I don't know. How do you reckon time on a world without a Sun, without one damned little star to look at? Ten years, a hundred years, how should I know? Forever. Tell me about Earth.'

Stark smiled wryly. 'I haven't been there for a long time. The police were too ready with a welcoming committee. But the last time I saw it, it was just the same.'

The lame man shivered. He was not looking at Stark now, but at some place far beyond him.

'Autumn woods,' he said. 'Red and gold on the brown hills. Snow. I can remember how it felt to be cold. The air bit you when you breathed it. And the women wore high-heeled slippers. No big bare feet tromping in the mud, but little sharp heels tapping on clean pavement.'

Suddenly he glared at Stark, his eyes furious and bright with tears.

'Why the hell did you have to come here and start me remembering? I'm Larrabee. I live in Shuruun. I've been here forever, and I'll be here till I die. There isn't any Earth. It's gone. Just look up into the sky, and you'll know it's gone. There's nothing anywhere but clouds, and Venus, and mud.'

He sat still, shaking, turning his head from side to side. A man came with wine, put it down, and went away again. The tavern was very quiet. There was a wide space empty around the two Earthmen. Beyond that people lay on the cushions, sipping the poppy wine and watching with a sort of furtive expectancy.

Abruptly, Larrabee laughed, a harsh sound that held a certain honest mirth.

'I don't know why I should get sentimental about Earth at this late date. Never thought much about it when I was there.'

Nevertheless, he kept his gaze averted, and when he picked up his cup his hand trembled so that he spilled some of the wine.

Stark was staring at him in unbelief. 'Larrabee,' he said. 'You're Mike Larrabee. You're the man who got half a million credits out of the strong room of the *Royal Venus*.'

Larrabee nodded. 'And got away with it, right over the Mountains of White Cloud, that they said couldn't be flown. And do you know where that half a million is now? At the bottom of the Red Sea, along with my ship and my crew, out there in the gulf. Lord knows why I lived.' He shrugged. 'Well, anyway, I was heading for Shuruun when I crashed, and I got here. So why complain?'

He drank again, deeply, and Stark shook his head.

'You've been here nine years, then, by Earth time,' he said. He had never met Larrabee, but he remembered the pictures of him that had flashed across space on police bands. Larrabee had been a young man then, dark and proud and handsome.

Larrabee guessed his thought. 'I've changed, haven't I?'

Stark said lamely, 'Everybody thought you were dead.'

Larrabee laughed. After that, for a moment, there was silence. Stark's ears were straining for any sound outside. There was none.

He said abruptly, 'What about this trap I'm in?'

'I'll tell you one thing about it,' said Larrabee. 'There's no way out. I can't help you. I wouldn't if I could, get that straight. But I can't, anyway.'

'Thanks,' Stark said sourly. 'You can at least tell me what goes on.'

'Listen,' said Larrabee. 'I'm a cripple, and an old man, and Shuruun isn't the sweetest place in the solar system to live. But I do live. I have a wife, a slatternly wench I'll admit, but good enough in her way. You'll notice some little dark-haired brats rolling in the mud. They're mine, too. I have some skill at setting bones and such, and so I can get drunk for nothing as often as I will – which is often. Also, because of this bum leg,

I'm perfectly safe. So don't ask me what goes on. I take great pains not to know.'

Stark said, 'Who are the Lhari?'

'Would you like to meet them?' Larrabee seemed to find something very amusing in that thought. 'Just go on up to the castle. They live there. They're the Lords of Shuruun, and they're always glad to meet strangers.'

He leaned forward suddenly. 'Who are you anyway? What's your name, and why the devil did you come here?'

'My name is Stark. And I came here for the same reason you did.'

'Stark,' repeated Larrabee slowly, his eyes intent. 'That rings a faint bell. Seems to me I saw a *Wanted* flash once, some idiot that had led a native revolt somewhere in the Jovian Colonies – a big cold-eyed brute they referred to colourfully as the wild man from Mercury.'

He nodded, pleased with himself. 'Wild man, eh? Well, Shuruun will tame you down!'

'Perhaps,' said Stark. His eyes shifted constantly, watching Larrabee, watching the doorway and the dark veranda and the people who drank but did not talk among themselves. 'Speaking of strangers, one came here at the time of the last rains. He was Venusian, from up-coast. A big young man. I used to know him. Perhaps he could help me.'

Larrabee snorted. By now, he had drunk his own wine and Stark's too. 'Nobody can help you. As for your friend, I never saw him. I'm beginning to think I should never have seen you.' Quite suddenly he caught up his stick and got with some difficulty to his feet. He did not look at Stark, but said harshly, 'You better get out of here.' Then he turned and limped unsteadily to the bar.

Stark rose. He glanced after Larrabee, and again his nostrils twitched to the smell of fear. Then he went out of the tavern the way he had come in, through the front door. No one moved to stop him. Outside, the square was empty. It had begun to rain.

Stark stood for a moment on the steps. He was angry, and filled with a dangerous unease, the hair-trigger nervousness of a tiger that senses the beaters creeping toward him up the wind.

He would almost have welcomed the sight of Malthor and the three young men. But there was nothing to fight but the silence and the rain.

He stepped out into the mud, wet and warm around his ankles. An idea came to him, and he smiled, beginning now to move with a definite purpose, along the side of the square.

The sharp downpour strengthened. Rain smoked from Stark's naked shoulders, beat against thatch and mud with a hissing rattle. The harbour had disappeared behind boiling clouds of fog, where water struck the surface of the Red Sea and was turned again instantly by chemical action into vapour. The quays and the neighbouring street were being swallowed up in the impenetrable mist. Lightning came with an eerie bluish flare, and thunder came rolling after it.

Stark turned up the narrow way that led toward the castle.

Its lights were winking out now, one by one, blotted by the creeping fog. Lightning etched its shadowy bulk against the night, and then was gone. And through the noise of the thunder that followed, Stark thought he heard a voice calling.

He stopped, half crouching, his hand on his gun. The cry came again, a girl's voice, thin as the wail of a seabird through the driving rain. Then he saw her, a small white blur in the street behind him, running, and even in that dim glimpse of her every line of her body was instinct with fright.

Stark set his back against a wall and waited. There did not seem to be anyone with her, though it was hard to tell in the darkness and the storm.

She came up to him, and stopped, just out of his reach, looking at him and away again with a painful irresoluteness. A bright flash showed her to him clearly. She was young, not long out of her childhood, and pretty in a stupid sort of way. Just now her mouth trembled on the edge of weeping, and her eyes were very large and scared. Her skirt clung to her long thighs, and above it her naked body, hardly fleshed into womanhood, glistened like snow in the wet. Her pale hair hung dripping over her shoulders.

Stark said gently, 'What do you want with me?'

She looked at him, so miserably like a wet puppy that he

smiled. And as though that smile had taken what little resolution she had out of her, she dropped to her knees, sobbing.

'I can't do it,' she wailed. 'He'll kill me, but I just can't do it!'

'Do what?' asked Stark.

She stared up at him. 'Run away,' she urged him. 'Run away *now!* You'll die in the swamps, but that's better than being one of the Lost Ones!' She shook her thin arms at him. '*Run away!*'

4

The street was empty. Nothing showed, nothing stirred anywhere. Stark leaned over and pulled the girl to her feet, drawing her in under the shelter of the thatched eaves.

'Now then,' he said. 'Suppose you stop crying and tell me what this is all about.'

Presently, between gulps and hiccoughs, he got the story out of her.

'I am Zareth,' she said. 'Malthor's daughter. He's afraid of you, because of what you did to him on the ship, so he ordered me to watch for you in the square, when you would come out of the tavern. Then I was to follow you, and ...'

She broke off, and Stark patted her shoulder. 'Go on.'

But a new thought had occurred to her. 'If I do, will you promise not to beat me, or ...' She looked at his gun and shivered.

'I promise.'

She studied his face, what she could see of it in the darkness, and then seemed to lose some of her fear.

'I was to stop you. I was to say what I've already said, about being Malthor's daughter and the rest of it, and then I was to say that he wanted me to lead you into an ambush while pretending to help you escape, but that I couldn't do it, and would help you to escape anyhow because I hated Malthor and the whole business about the Lost Ones. So you would believe me, and follow me, and I would lead you into the ambush.'

She shook her head and began to cry again, quietly this time, and there was nothing of the woman about her at all now. She was just a child, very miserable and afraid. Stark was glad he had branded Malthor.

'But I can't lead you into the ambush. I do hate Malthor, even if he is my father, because he beats me. And the Lost Ones ...' She paused. 'Sometimes I hear them at night, chanting way out there beyond the mist. It is a very terrible sound.'

'It is,' said Stark. 'I've heard it. Who are the Lost Ones, Zareth?'

'I can't tell you that,' said Zareth. 'It's forbidden even to speak of them. And anyway,' she finished honestly, 'I don't even know. People disappear, that's all. Not our own people of Shuruun, at least not very often. But strangers like you – and I'm sure my father goes off into the swamps to hunt among the tribes there, and I'm sure he comes back from some of his voyages with nothing in his hold but men from some captured ship Why, or what for, I don't know. Except I've heard the chanting.'

'They live out there in the gulf, do they, the Lost Ones?'

'They must. There are many islands there.'

'And what of the Lhari, the Lords of Shuruun? Don't they know what's going on? Or are they part of it?'

She shuddered, and said, 'It's not for us to question the Lhari, nor even to wonder what they do. Those who have are gone from Shuruun, nobody knows where.'

Stark nodded. He was silent for a moment, thinking. Then Zareth's little hand touched his shoulder.

'Go,' she said. 'Lose yourself in the swamps. You're strong, and there's something about you different from other men. You may live to find your way through.'

'No. I have something to do before I leave Shuruun.' He took Zareth's damp fair head between his hands and kissed her on the forehead. 'You're a sweet child, Zareth, and a brave one. Tell Malthor that you did exactly as he told you, and it was not your fault I wouldn't follow you.'

'He will beat me anyway,' said Zareth philosophically, 'but perhaps not quite so hard.'

'He'll have no reason to beat you at all, if you tell him the truth – that I would not go with you because my mind was set on going to the castle of the Lhari.'

There was a long, long silence, while Zareth's eyes widened slowly in horror, and the rain beat on the thatch, and fog and thunder rolled together across Shuruun.

'To the castle,' she whispered. 'Oh, no! Go into the swamps, or let Malthor take you – but don't go to the castle!' She took hold of his arm, her fingers biting into his flesh with the urgency of her plea. 'You're a stranger, you don't know ... Please, don't go up there!'

'Why not?' asked Stark. 'Are the Lhari demons! Do they devour men?' He loosened her hands gently. 'You'd better go now. Tell your father where I am, if he wishes to come after me.'

Zareth backed away slowly, out into the rain, staring at him as though she looked at someone standing on the brink of hell, not dead, but worse than dead. Wonder showed in her face, and through it a great yearning pity. She tried once to speak, and then shook her head and turned away, breaking into a run as though she could not endure to look upon Stark any longer. In a second she was gone.

Stark looked after her for a moment, strangely touched. Then he stepped out into the rain again, heading upward along the steep path that led to the castle of the Lords of Shuruun.

The mist was blinding. Stark had to feel his way, and as he climbed higher, above the level of the town, he was lost in the sullen redness. A hot wind blew, and each flare of lightning turned the crimson fog to a hellish purple. The night was full of a vast hissing where the rain poured into the gulf. He stopped once to hide his gun in a cleft between the rocks.

At length he stumbled against a carven pillar of black stone and found the gate that hung from it, a massive thing sheathed in metal. It was barred, and the pounding of his fists upon it made little sound.

Then he saw the gong, a huge disc of beaten gold beside the gate. Stark picked up the hammer that lay there, and set the deep voice of the gong rolling out between the thunderbolts.

A barred slit opened and a man's eyes looked out at him. Stark dropped the hammer.

'Open up!' he shouted. 'I would speak with the Lhari!'

From within he heard an echo of laughter. Scraps of voices came to him on the wind, and then more laughter, and then, slowly, the great valves of the gate creaked open, wide enough only to admit him.

He stepped through, and the gateway shut behind him with a ringing clash.

He stood in a huge open court. Enclosed within its walls was a village of thatched huts, with open sheds for cooking, and behind them were pens for the stabling of beasts, the wingless dragons of the swamps that can be caught and broken to the goad.

He saw this only in vague glimpses, because of the fog. The men who had let him in clustered around him, thrusting him forward into the light that streamed from the huts.

'He would speak with the Lhari!' one of them shouted, to the women and children who stood in the doorways watching. The words were picked up and tossed around the court, and a great burst of laughter went up.

Stark eyed them, saying nothing. They were a puzzling breed. The men, obviously, were soldiers and guards to the Lhari, for they wore the harness of fighting men. As obviously, these were their wives and children, all living behind the castle walls and having little to do with Shuruun.

But it was their racial characteristics that surprised him. They had interbred with the pale tribes of the Swamp-Edges that had peopled Shuruun, and there were many with milk-white hair and broad faces. Yet even these bore an alien stamp. Stark was puzzled, for the race he would have named was unknown here behind the Mountains of White Cloud, and almost unknown anywhere on Venus at Sea-level, among the sweltering marshes and the eternal fogs.

They stared at him even more curiously, remarking on his skin and his black hair and the unfamiliar modelling of his face. The women nudged each other and whispered, giggling, and one of them said aloud, 'They'll need a barrel-hoop to collar that neck!'

The guards closed in around him. 'Well, if you wish to see the

Lhari, you shall,' said the leader, 'but first we must make sure of you.'

Spear-points ringed him round. Stark made no resistance while they stripped him of all he had, except for his shorts and sandals. He had expected that, and it amused him, for there was little enough for them to take.

'All right,' said the leader. 'Come on.'

The whole village turned out in the rain to escort Stark to the castle door. There was about them the same ominous interest that the people of Shuruun had had, with one difference. They knew what was supposed to happen to him, knew all about it, and were therefore doubly appreciative of the game.

The great doorway was square and plain, and yet neither crude nor ungraceful. The castle itself was built of the black stone, each block perfectly cut and fitted, and the door itself was sheathed in the same metal as the gate, darkened but not corroded.

The leader of the guard cried out to the warder, 'Here is one who would speak with the Lhari!'

The warder laughed. 'And so he shall! Their night is long, and dull.'

He flung open the heavy door and cried the word down the hallway. Stark could hear it echoing hollowly within, and presently from the shadows came servants clad in silks and wearing jewelled collars, and from the guttural sound of their laughter Stark knew that they had no tongues.

Stark faltered, then. The doorway loomed hollowly before him, and it came to him suddenly that evil lay behind it and that perhaps Zareth was wiser than he when she warned him from the Lhari.

Then he thought of Helvi, and of other things, and lost his fear in anger. Lightning burned the sky. The last cry of the dying storm shook the ground under his feet. He thrust the grinning water aside and strode into the castle, bringing a veil of red fog with him, and did not listen to the closing of the door, which was stealthy and quiet as the footfall of approaching Death.

Torches burned here and there along the walls, and by their smoky glare he could see that the hallway was like the entrance

– square and unadorned, faced with the black rock. It was high, and wide, and there was about the architecture a calm reflective dignity that had its own beauty, in some ways more impressive than the sensuous loveliness of the ruined palaces he had seen on Mars.

There were no carvings here, no paintings nor frescoes. It seemed that the builders had felt that the hall itself was enough, in its massive perfection of line and the sombre gleam of polished stone. The only decoration was in the window embrasures. These were empty now, open to the sky with the red fog wreathing through them, but there were still scraps of jewel-toned panes clinging to the fretwork, to show what they had once been.

A strange feeling swept over Stark. Because of his wild upbringing, he was abnormally sensitive to the sort of impressions that most men receive either dully or not at all.

Walking down the hall, preceded by the tongueless creatures in their bright silks and blazing collars, he was struck by a subtle *difference* in the place. The castle itself was only an extension of the minds of its builders, a dream shaped into reality. Stark felt that that dark, cool, curiously timeless dream had not originated in a mind like his own, nor like that of any man he had ever seen.

Then the end of the hall was reached, the way barred by low broad doors of gold fashioned in the same chaste simplicity.

A soft scurrying of feet, a shapeless tittering from the servants, a glancing of malicious, mocking eyes. The golden doors swung open, and Stark was in the presence of the Lhari.

5

They had the appearance in that first glance, of creatures glimpsed in a fever-dream, very bright and distant, robed in a misty glow that gave them an illusion of unearthly beauty.

The place in which the Earthman now stood was like a

cathedral for breadth and loftiness. Most of it was in darkness, so that it seemed to reach without limit above and on all sides, as though the walls were only shadowy phantasms of the night itself. The polished black stone under his feet held a dim translucent gleam, depthless as water in a black tarn. There was no substance anywhere.

Far away in this shadowy vastness burned a cluster of lamps, a galaxy of little stars to shed a silvery light upon the Lords of Shuruun.

There had been no sound in the place when Stark entered, for the opening of the golden doors had caught the attention of the Lhari and held it in contemplation of the stranger. Stark began to walk toward them in this utter stillness.

Quite suddenly, in the impenetrable gloom somewhere to his right, there came a sharp scuffling and a scratching of reptilian claws, a hissing and a sort of low angry muttering, all magnified and distorted by the echoing vault into a huge demoniac whispering that swept all around him.

Stark whirled around, crouched and ready, his eyes blazing and his body bathed in cold sweat. The noise increased, rushing toward him. From the distant glow of the lamps came a woman's tinkling laughter, thin crystal broken against the vault. The hissing and snarling rose to hollow crescendo, and Stark saw a blurred shape bounding at him.

His hands reached out to receive the rush, but it never came. The strange shape resolved itself into a boy of about ten, who dragged after him on a bit of rope a young dragon, new and toothless from the egg, and protesting with all its strength.

Stark straightened up, feeling let down and furious – and relieved. The boy scowled at him through a forelock of silver curls. Then he called him a very dirty word and rushed away, kicking and hauling at the little beast until it raged like the father of all dragons and sounded like it, too, in that vast echo chamber.

A voice spoke. Slow, harsh, sexless, it rang thinly through the vault. Thin – but a steel blade is thin, too. It speaks inexorably, and its word is final.

The voice said, 'Come here, into the light.'

Stark obeyed the voice. As he approached the lamps, the aspect of the Lhari changed and steadied. Their beauty remained, but it was not the same. They had looked like angels. Now that he could see them clearly, Stark thought that they might have been the children of Lucifer himself.

There were six of them, counting the boy. Two men, about the same age as Stark, with some complicated gambling game forgotten between them. A woman, beautiful, gowned in white silk, sitting with her hands in her lap, doing nothing. A woman, younger, not so beautiful perhaps, but with a look of stormy and bitter vitality. She wore a short tunic of crimson, and a stout leather glove on her left hand, where perched a flying thing of prey with its fierce eyes hooded.

The boy stood beside the two men, his head poised arrogantly. From time to time he cuffed the little dragon, and it snapped at him with its impotent jaws. He was proud of himself for doing that. Stark wondered how he would behave with the beast when it had grown its fangs.

Opposite him, crouched on a heap of cushions, was a third man. He was deformed, with an ungainly body and long spidery arms, and in his lap a sharp knife lay on a block of wood, half formed into the shape of an obese creature half woman, half pure evil. Stark saw with a flash of surprise that the face of the deformed young man, of all the faces there, was truly human, truly beautiful. His eyes were old in his boyish face, wise, and very sad in their wisdom. He smiled upon the stranger, and his smile was more compassionate than tears.

They looked at Stark, all of them, with restless, hungry eyes. They were the pure breed, that had left its stamp of alienage on the pale-haired folk of the swamps, the serfs who dwelt in the huts outside.

They were of the Cloud People, the folk of the High Plateaus, kings of the land on the farther slopes of the Mountains of White Cloud. It was strange to see them here, on the dark side of the barrier wall, but here they were. How they had come, and why, leaving their rich cool plains for the fetor of these foreign swamps, he could not guess. But there was no mistaking them – the proud fine shaping of their bodies, their alabaster skin, their eyes that were all colours and none, like the dawn sky, their hair that was pure warm silver.

They did not speak. They seemed to be waiting for permission to speak, and Stark wondered which one of them had voiced that steely summons.

Then it came again. 'Come here – come closer.' And he looked beyond them, beyond the circle of lamps into the shadows again, and saw the speaker.

She lay upon a low bed, her head propped on silken pillows, her vast, her incredibly gigantic body covered with a silken pall. Only her arms were bare, two shapeless masses of white flesh ending in tiny hands. From time to time she stretched one out and took a morsel of food from the supply laid ready beside her, snuffling and wheezing with the effort, and then gulped the tidbit down with a horrible voracity.

Her features had long ago dissolved into a shaking formlessness, with the exception of her nose, which rose out of the fat curved and cruel and thin, like the bony beak of the creature that sat on the girl's wrist and dreamed its hooded dreams of blood. And her eyes...

Stark looked into her eyes and shuddered. Then he glanced at the carving half formed in the cripple's lap, and knew what thought had guided the knife.

Half woman, half pure evil. And strong. Very strong. Her strength lay naked in her eyes for all to see, and it was an ugly strength. It could tear down mountains, but it could never build.

He saw her looking at him. Her eyes bored into his as though they would search out his very guts and study them, and he knew that she expected him to turn away, unable to bear her gaze. He did not. Presently he smiled and said, 'I have outstared a rock-lizard, to determine which of us should eat the other. And I've outstared the very rock while waiting for him.'

She knew that he spoke the truth. Stark expected her to be angry, but she was not. A vague mountainous rippling shook her and emerged at length as a voiceless laughter.

'You see that?' she demanded, addressing the others. 'You whelps of the Lhari – not one of you dares to face me down, yet here is a great dark creature from the gods know where who can stand and shame you.'

She glanced again at Stark. 'What demon's blood brought you forth, that you have learned neither prudence nor fear?'

Stark answered sombrely, 'I learned them both before I could walk. But I learned another thing also – a thing called anger.'

'And you are angry?'

'Ask Malthor if I am, and why!'

He saw the two men start a little, and a slow smile crossed the girl's face.

'Malthor,' said the hulk upon the bed, and ate a mouthful of roast meat dripping with fat. 'That is interesting. But rage against Malthor did not bring you here. I am curious, Stranger. Speak.'

'I will.'

Stark glanced around. The place was a tomb, a trap. The very air smelled of danger. The younger folk watched him in silence. Not one of them had spoken since he came in, except the boy who had cursed him, and that was unnatural in itself. The girl leaned forward, idly stroking the creature on her wrist so that it stirred and ran its knife-like talons in and out of their bony sheathes with sensuous pleasure. Her gaze on Stark was bold and cool, oddly challenging. Of them all, she alone saw him as a man. To the others he was a problem, a diversion – something less than human.

Stark said, 'A man came to Shuruun at the time of the last rains. His name was Helvi, and he was son of a little king by Yarell. He came seeking his brother, who had broken taboo and fled for his life. Helvi came to tell him that the ban was lifted, and he might return. Neither one came back.'

The small evil eyes were amused, blinking in their tallowy creases. 'And so?'

'And so I have come after Helvi, who is my friend.'

Again there was the heaving of that bulk of flesh, the explosion of laughter that hissed and wheezed in snake-like echoes through the vault.

'Friendship must run deep with you, Stranger. Ah, well. The Lhari are kind of heart. You shall find your friend.'

And as though that were the signal to end their deferential silence, the younger folk burst into laughter also, until the vast hall rang with it, giving back a sound like demons laughing on the edge of Hell.

The cripple only did not laugh, but bent his bright head over his carving, and sighed.

The girl sprang up. 'Not yet, Grandmother! Keep him awhile.'

The cool, cruel eyes shifted to her. 'And what will you do with him, Varra? Haul him about on a string, like Bor with his wretched beast?'

'Perhaps – though I think it would need a stout chain to hold him.' Varra turned and looked at Stark, bold and bright, taking in the breadth and the height of him, the shaping of the great smooth muscles, the iron line of the jaw. She smiled. Her mouth was very lovely, like the red fruit of the swamp tree that bears death in its pungent sweetness.

'Here is a man,' she said. 'The first man I have seen since my father died.'

The two men at the gaming table rose, their faces flushed and angry. One of them strode forward and gripped the girl's arm roughly.

'So I am not a man,' he said, with surprising gentleness. 'A sad thing, for one who is to be your husband. It's best that we settle that now, before we wed.'

Varra nodded. Stark saw that the man's fingers were cutting savagely into the firm muscle of her arm, but she did not wince.

'High time to settle it all, Egil. You have borne enough from me. The day is long overdue for my taming. I must learn now to bend my neck, and acknowledge my lord.'

For a moment Stark thought she meant it, the note of mockery in her voice was so subtle. Then the woman in white, who all this time had not moved nor changed expression, voiced again the thin, tinkling laugh he had heard once before. From that, and the dark suffusion of blood in Egil's face, Stark knew that Varra was only casting the man's own phrases back at him. The boy let out one derisive bark, and was cuffed into silence.

Varra looked straight at Stark. 'Will you fight for me?' she demanded.

Quite suddenly, it was Stark's turn to laugh. 'No!' he said.

Varra shrugged. 'Very well, then. I must fight for myself.'

'Man,' snarled Egil. 'I'll show you who's a man, you scapegrace little vixen!'

He wrenched off his girdle with his free hand, at the same time bending the girl around so he could get a fair shot at her. The creature of prey, a Terran falcon, clung to her wrist, beating its wings and screaming, its hooded head jerking.

With a motion so quick that it was hardly visible, Varra slipped the hood and flew the creature straight for Egil's face.

He let go, flinging up his arms to ward off the talons and the tearing beak. The wide wings beat and hammered. Egil yelled. The boy Bot got out of range and danced up and down shrieking with delight.

Varra stood quietly. The bruises were blackening on her arm, but she did not deign to touch them. Egil blundered against the gaming table and sent the ivory pieces flying. Then he tripped over a cushion and fell flat, and the hungry talons ripped his tunic to ribbons down the back.

Varra whistled, a clear peremptory call. The creature gave a last peck at the back of Egil's head and flopped sullenly back to its perch on her wrist. She held it, turning toward Stark. He knew from the poise of her that she was on the verge of launching her pet at him. But she studied him and then shook her head.

'No,' she said, and slipped the hood back on. 'You would kill it.'

Egil had scrambled up and gone off into the darkness, sucking a cut on his arm. His face was black with rage. The other man looked at Varra.

'If you were pledged to me,' he said, 'I'd have that temper out of you!'

'Come and try it,' answered Varra.

The man shrugged and sat down. 'It's not my place. I keep the peace in my own house.' He glanced at the woman in white, and Stark saw that her face, hitherto blank of any expression, had taken on a look of abject fear.

'You do,' said Varra, 'and, if I were Arel, I would stab you while you slept. But you're safe. She had no spirit to begin with.'

Arel shivered and looked steadfastly at her hands. The man began to gather up the scattered pieces. He said casually, 'Egil will wring your neck some day, Varra, and I shan't weep to see it.'

All this time the old woman had eaten and watched, watched and eaten, her eyes glittering with interest.

'A pretty brood, are they not?' she demanded of Stark. 'Full of spirit, quarrelling like young hawks in the nest. That's why I keep them around me, so – they are such sport to watch. All except Treon there.' She indicated the crippled youth. 'He does nothing. Dull and soft-mouthed, worse than Arel. What a grandson to be cursed with! But his sister has fire enough for two.' She munched a sweet, grunting with pride.

Treon raised his head and spoke, and his voice was like music, echoing with an eerie liveliness in that dark place.

'Dull I may be, Grandmother, and weak in body, and without hope. Yet I shall be the last of the Lhari. Death sits waiting on the towers, and he shall gather you all before me. I know, for the winds have told me.'

He turned his suffering eyes upon Stark and smiled, a smile of such woe and resignation that the Earthman's heart ached with it. Yet there was a thankfulness in it too, as though some long waiting was over at last.

'You,' he said softly. 'Stranger with the fierce eyes. I saw you come, out of the darkness, and where you set foot there was a bloody print. Your arms were red to the elbows, and your breast was splashed with the redness, and on your brow was the symbol of death. Then I knew, and the wind whispered into my ear, "It is so. This man shall pull the castle down, and its stones shall crush Shuruun and set the Lost Ones free".'

He laughed, very quietly. 'Look at him, all of you. For he will be your doom!'

There was a moment's silence, and Stark, with all the superstitions of a wild race thick within him, turned cold to the roots of his hair. Then the old woman said disgustedly, 'Have the winds warned you of this, my idiot?'

And with astonishing force and accuracy she picked up a ripe fruit and flung it at Treon.

'Stop your mouth with that,' she told him. 'I am weary to death of your prophecies.'

Treon looked at the crimson juice trickling slowly down the breast of his tunic, to drip upon the carving in his lap. The half formed head was covered with it. Treon was shaken with silent mirth.

'Well,' said Varra, coming up to Stark, 'what do you think of the Lhari?' The proud Lhari, who would not stoop to mingle their blood with the cattle of the swamps. My half-witted brother, my worthless cousins, that little monster Bor who is the last twig of the tree – do you wonder I flew my falcon at Egil?'

She waited for an answer, her head thrown back, the silver curls framing her face like wisps of storm-cloud. There was a swagger about her that at once irritated and delighted Stark. A hellcat, he thought, but a mighty fetching one, and bold as brass. Bold – and honest. Her lips were parted, midway between anger and a smile.

He caught her to him suddenly and kissed her, holding her slim strong body as though she were a doll. He was in no hurry to set her down. When at last he did, he grinned and said, 'Was that what you wanted?'

'Yes,' answered Varra. 'That was what I wanted.' She spun about, her jaw set dangerously. 'Grandmother ...'

She got no farther. Stark saw that the old woman was attempting to sit upright, her face purpling with effort and the most terrible wrath he had ever seen.

'You,' she gasped at the girl. She choked on her fury and her shortness of breath, and then Egil came soft-footed into the light, bearing in his hand a thing made of black metal and oddly shaped, with a blunt, thick muzzle.

'Lie back, Grandmother,' he said. 'I had a mind to use this on Varra—'

Even as he spoke he pressed a stud, and Stark in the act of leaping for the sheltering darkness, crashed down and lay like a dead man. There had been no sound, no flash, nothing, but a vast hand that smote him suddenly into oblivion.

Egil finished, '—but I see a better target.'

6

Red. Red. Red. The colour of blood. Blood in his eyes. He was remembering now. The quarry had turned on him, and they had fought on the bare, blistering rocks.

Nor had N'Chaka killed. The Lord of the Rocks was very big, a giant among lizards, and N'Chaka was small. The Lord of the Rocks had laid open N'Chaka's head before the wooden spear had more than scratched his flank.

It was strange that N'Chaka still lived. The Lord of the Rocks must have been full fed. Only that had saved him.

N'Chaka groaned, not with pain, but with shame. He had failed. Hoping for a great triumph, he had disobeyed the tribal law that forbids a boy to hunt the quarry of a man, and he had failed. Old One would not reward him with the girdle and the flint spear of manhood. Old One would give him to the women for the punishment of little whips. Tika would laugh at him, and it would be many seasons before Old One would grant him permission to try the Man's Hunt.

Blood in his eyes.

He blinked to clear them. The instinct of survival was prodding him. He must arouse himself and creep away, before the Lord of the Rocks returned to eat him.

The redness would not go away. It swam and flowed, strangely sparkling. He blinked again, and tried to lift his head, and could not, and fear struck down upon him like the iron frost of night upon the rocks of the valley.

It was all wrong. he could see himself clearly, a naked boy dizzy with pain, rising and clambering over the ledges and the shale to the safety of the cave. He could see that, and yet he could not move.

All wrong. Time, space, the universe, darkened and turned.

A voice spoke to him. A girl's voice. Not Tika's and the speech was strange.

Tika was dead. Memories rushed through his mind, the bitter things, the cruel things. Old One was dead, and all the others...

The voice spoke again, calling him by a name that was not his own.

Stark.

Memory shattered into a kaleidoscope of broken pictures, fragments, rushing, spinning. He was adrift among them. He was lost, and the terror of it brought a scream into his throat.

Soft hands touching his face, gentle words, swift and soothing. The redness cleared and steadied, though it did not go away, and quite suddenly he was himself again, with all his memories where they belonged.

He was lying on his back, and Zareth, Malthor's daughter, was looking down at him. He knew now what the redness was. He had seen it too often before not to know. He was somewhere at the bottom of the Red Sea – that weird ocean in which a man can breathe.

And he could not move. That had not changed, nor gone away. His body was dead.

The terror he had felt before was nothing to the agony that filled him now. He lay entombed in his own flesh, staring up at Zareth, wanting an answer to a question he dared not ask.

She understood, from the look in his eyes.

'It's all right,' she said, and smiled. 'It will wear off. You'll be all right. It's only the weapon of the Lhari. Somehow it puts the body to sleep, but it will wake again.'

Stark remembered the black object that Egil had held in his hands. A projector of some sort, then, beaming a current of high-frequency vibration that paralysed the nerve centres. He was amazed. The Cloud People were barbarians themselves, though on a higher scale than the swamp-edge tribes, and certainly had no such scientific proficiency. He wondered where the Lhari had got hold of such a weapon.

It didn't really matter. Not just now. Relief swept over him, bringing him dangerously close to tears. The effect would wear off. At the moment, that was all he cared about.

He looked up at Zareth again. Her pale hair floated with the slow breathing of the sea, a milky cloud against the spark-shot crimson. He saw now that her face was drawn and shadowed, and there was a terrible hopelessness in her eyes. She had been alive when he first saw her – frightened, not too bright, but full of emotion and a certain dogged courage. Now the spark was gone, crushed out.

She wore a collar around her white neck, a ring of dark metal with the ends fused together for all time.

'Where are we?' he asked.

And she answered, her voice carrying deep and hollow in the dense substance of the sea, 'We are in the place of the Lost Ones.'

Stark looked beyond her, as far as he could see, since he was unable to turn his head. And wonder came to him.

Black walls, black vault above, a vast hall filled with the wash of the sea that slipped in streaks of whispering flame through the high embrasures. A hall that was twin to the vault of shadows where he had met the Lhari.

'There is a city,' said Zareth dully. 'You will see it soon. You will see nothing else until you die.'

Stark said, very gently, 'How do you come here, little one?'

'Because of my father. I will tell you all I know, which is little enough. Malthor has been slaver to the Lhari for a long time. There are a number of them among the captains of Shuruun, but that is a thing that is never spoken of – so I, his daughter, could only guess. I was sure of it when he sent me after you.'

She laughed, a bitter sound. 'Now I'm here, with the collar of the Lost Ones on my neck. But Malthor is here, too.' She laughed again, ugly laughter to come from a young mouth. Then she looked at Stark, and her hand reached out timidly to touch his hair in what was almost a caress. Her eyes were wide, and soft, and full of tears.

'Why didn't you go into the swamps when I warned you?'

Stark answered stolidly, 'Too late to worry about that now.' Then, 'You say Malthor is here, a slave?'

'Yes.' Again, that look of wonder and admiration in her eyes. 'I don't know what you said or did to the Lhari, but the Lord Egil came down in a black rage and cursed my father for a bungling fool because he could not hold you. My father whined and made excuses, and all would have been well – only his curiosity got the better of him and he asked the Lord Egil what had happened. You were like a wild beast, Malthor said, and he hoped you had not harmed the Lady Varra, as he could see from Egil's wounds that there had been trouble.

'The Lord Egil turned quite purple. I thought he was going to fall in a fit.'

'Yes,' said Stark. 'That was the wrong thing to say.' The ludicrous side of it struck him, and he was suddenly roaring with laughter. 'Malthor should have kept his mouth shut!'

'Egil called his guard and ordered them to take Malthor. And when he realised what had happened, Malthor turned on me, trying to say that it was all my fault, that I let you escape.'

Stark stopped laughing.

Her voice went on slowly, 'Egil seemed quite mad with fury. I have heard that the Lhari are all mad, and I think it is so. At any rate, he ordered me taken too, for he wanted to stamp Malthor's seed into the mud forever. So we are here.'

There was a long silence. Stark could think of no word of comfort, and as for hope, he had better wait until he was sure he could at least raise his head. Egil might have damaged him permanently, out of spite. In fact, he was surprised he wasn't dead.

He glanced again at the collar on Zareth's neck. Slave. Slave to the Lhari, in the City of the Lost Ones.

What the devil did they do with slaves, at the bottom of the sea?

The heavy gases conducted sound remarkably well, except for an odd property of diffusion which made it seem that a voice came from everywhere at once. Now, all at once, Stark became aware of a dull clamour of voices drifting towards him.

He tried to see, and Zareth turned his head carefully so that he might.

The Lost Ones were returning from whatever work it was they did.

Out of the dim red murk beyond the open door they swam, into the long, long vastness of the hall that was filled with the same red murk, moving slowly, their white bodies trailing wakes of sullen flame. The host of the damned drifting through a strange red-lit hell, weary and without hope.

One by one they sank onto pallets laid in rows on the black stone floor, and lay there, utterly exhausted, their pale hair lifting and floating with the slow eddies of the sea. And each one wore a collar.

One man did not lie down. He came toward Stark, a tall barbarian who drew himself with great strokes of his arms so that he was wrapped in wheeling sparks. Stark knew his face.

'Helvi,' he said, and smiled in welcome.

'Brother!'

Helvi crouched down – a great handsome boy he had been the time Stark saw him, but he was a man now, with all the laughter turned to grim deep lines around his mouth and the bones of his face standing out like granite ridges.

'Brother,' he said again, looking at Stark through a glitter of unashamed tears. 'Fool.' And he cursed Stark savagely because he had come to Shuruun to look for an idiot who had gone the same way, and was already as good as dead.

'Would you have followed me?' asked Stark.

'But I am only an ignorant child of the swamps,' said Helvi. 'You come from space, you know the other worlds, you can read and write – you should have better sense!'

Stark grinned. 'And I'm still an ignorant child of the rocks. So we're two fools together. Where is Tobal?'

Tobal was Helvi's brother, who had broken taboo and looked for refuge in Shuruun. Apparently he had found peace at last, for Helvi shook his head.

'A man cannot live too long under the sea. It is not enough merely to breathe and eat. Tobal overran his time, and I am close to the end of mine.' He held up his hand and then swept it down sharply, watching the broken fires dance along his arms.

'The mind breaks before the body,' said Helvi casually, as though it were a matter of no importance.

Zareth spoke. 'Helvi has guarded you each period while the others slept.'

'And not I alone,' said Helvi. 'The little one stood with me.'

'Guarded me!' said Stark. 'Why?'

For answer, Helvi gestured toward a pallet not far away. Malthor lay there, his eyes half open and full of malice, the fresh scar livid on his cheek.

'He feels,' said Helvi, 'that you should not have fought upon his ship.'

Stark felt an inward chill of horror. To lie here helpless, watching Malthor come toward him with open fingers reaching for his helpless throat ...

He made a passionate effort to move, and gave up, gasping. Helvi grinned.

'Now is the time I should wrestle you, Stark, for I never could throw you before.' He gave Stark's head a shake, very gentle for all its apparent roughness. 'You'll be throwing me again. Sleep now, and don't worry.'

He settled himself to watch, and presently in spite of himself Stark slept, with Zareth curled at his feet like a little dog.

There was no time down there in the heart of the Red Sea. No daylight, no dawn, no space of darkness. No winds blew, no rain nor storm broke the endless silence. Only the lazy currents, whispered by on their way to nowhere, and the red sparks danced, and the great hall waited, remembering the past.

Stark waited, too. How long he never knew, but he was used to waiting. He had learned his patience in the knees of the great mountains whose heads lift proudly into open space to look at the Sun, and he had absorbed their own contempt for time.

Little by little, life returned to his body. A mongrel guard came now and again to examine him, pricking Stark's flesh with his knife to test the reaction, so that Stark should not malinger.

He reckoned without Stark's control. The Earthman bore his prodding without so much as a twitch until his limbs were completely his own again. Then he sprang up and pitched the man half the length of the hall, turning over and over, yelling with startled anger.

At the next period of labour, Stark was driven with the rest out into the City of the Lost Ones.

7

Stark had been in places before that oppressed him with a sense of their strangeness or their wickedness – Sinharat, the lovely ruin of coral and gold lost in the Martian wastes; Jekkara, Valkis – the Low-Canal towns that smell of blood and wine; the cliff-caves of Arianrhod on the edge of the Darkside, the buried tomb-cities of Callisto. But this – this was nightmare to haunt a man's dreams.

He stared about him as he went in the long line of slaves, and felt such a cold shuddering contraction of his belly as he had never known before.

Wide avenues paved with polished blocks of stone, perfect as ebon mirrors. Buildings, tall and stately, pure and plain, with a calm strength that could outlast the ages. Black, all black, with no fripperies of paint or carving to soften them, only here and there a window like a drowned jewel glinting through the red.

Vines like drifts of snow cascading down the stones. Gardens with close-clipped turf and flowers lifting bright on their green stalks, their petals open to a daylight that was gone, their heads bending as though to some forgotten breeze. All neat, all tended, the branches pruned, the fresh soil turned this morning – by whose hand?

Stark remembered the great forest dreaming at the bottom of the gulf, and shivered. He did not like to think how long ago these flowers must have opened their young bloom to the last light they were ever going to see. For they were dead – dead as the forest, dead as the city. Forever bright – and dead.

Stark thought that it must always have been a silent city. It was impossible to imagine noisy throngs flocking to a market square down those immense avenues. The black walls were not made to echo song or laughter. Even the children must have moved quietly along the garden paths, small wise creatures born to an ancient dignity.

He was beginning to understand now the meaning of that weird forest. The Gulf of Shuruun had not always been a gulf. It had been a valley, rich, fertile, with this great city in its arms, and here and there on the upper slopes the retreat of some noble or philosopher – of which the castle of the Lhari was a survivor.

A wall or rock had held back the Red Sea from this valley. And then, somehow, the wall had cracked, and the sullen crimson tide had flowed slowly, slowly into the fertile bottoms, rising higher, lapping the towers and the treetops in swirling flame, drowning the land forever. Stark wondered if the people had known the disaster was coming, if they had gone forth to tend their gardens for the last time so that they might remain perfect in the embalming gases of the sea.

The columns of slaves, herded by overseers armed with small black weapons similar to the one Egil had used, came out into a broad square whose farther edges were veiled in the red murk. And Stark looked on ruin.

A great building had fallen in the centre of the square. The gods only knew what force had burst its walls and tossed the giant blocks like pebbles into a heap. But there it was, the one untidy thing in the city, a mountain of debris.

Nothing else was damaged. It seemed that this had been the place of temples, and they stood unharmed, ranked around the sides of the square, the dim fires rippling through their open porticoes. Deep in their inner shadows Stark thought he could make out images, gigantic things brooding in the spark-shot gloom.

He had no chance to study them. The overseers cursed them on, and now he saw what use the slaves were put to. They were clearing away the wreckage of the fallen building.

Helvi whispered, 'For sixteen years men have slaved and died down here, and the work is not half done. And why do the Lhari want it done at all? I'll tell you why. Because they are mad, mad as swamp-dragons gone *musth* in the spring!'

It seemed madness indeed, to labour at this pile of rocks in a dead city at the bottom of the sea. It was madness. And yet the Lhari, though they might be insane, were not fools. There was a reason for it, and Stark was sure it was a good reason – good for the Lhari, at any rate.

An overseer came up to Stark, thrusting him roughly toward a sledge already partly loaded with broken rocks. Stark hesitated, his eyes turning ugly, and Helvi said,

'Come on, you fool! Do you want to be down flat on your back again?'

Stark glanced at the little weapon, blunt and ready, and turned reluctantly to obey. And there began his servitude.

It was a weird sort of life he led. For a while he tried to reckon time by the periods of work and sleep, but he lost count, and it did not greatly matter anyway.

He laboured with the others, hauling the huge blocks away, clearing out the cellars that were partly bared, shoring up weak walls underground. The slaves clung to their old habit of thought, calling the work-periods 'days' and the sleep-periods 'nights.'

Each 'day' Egil, or his brother Cond, came to see what had been done, and went away black-browed and disappointed, ordering the work speeded up.

Treon was there also much of the time. He would come slowly in his awkward crabwise way and perch like a pale gargoyle on the stones, never speaking, watching with his sad beautiful eyes. He woke a vague foreboding in Stark. There was something awesome in Treon's silent patience, as though he waited the coming of some black doom, long delayed but inevitable. Stark would remember the prophecy, and shiver.

It was obvious to Stark after a while that the Lhari were clearing the building to get at the cellars underneath. The great dark caverns already bared had yielded nothing, but the brothers still hoped. Over and over Cond and Egil sounded the walls and the floors, prying here and there, and chafing at the delay in opening up the underground labyrinth. What they hoped to find, no one knew.

Varra came, too. Alone, and often, she would drift down through the dim mist-fires and watch, smiling a secret smile, her hair like blown silver where the currents played with it. She had nothing but curt words for Egil, but she kept her eyes on the great dark Earthman, and there was a look in them that stirred his blood. Egil was not blind, and it stirred his too, but in a different way.

Zareth saw that look. She kept as close to Stark as possible, asking no favours, but following him around with a sort of quiet devotion, seeming contented only when she was near him. One 'night' in the slave barracks she crouched beside his pallet, her hand on his bare knee. She did not speak, and her face was hidden by the floating masses of her hair.

Stark turned her head so that he could see her, pushing the pale cloud gently away.

'What troubles you, little sister?'

Her eyes were wide and shadowed with some vague fear. But she only said, 'It's not my place to speak.'

'Why not?'

'Because ...' Her mouth trembled, and then suddenly she said, 'Oh, it's foolish, I know. But the woman of the Lhari ...'

'What about her?'

'She watches you. Always she watches you! And the Lord Egil is angry. There is something in her mind, and it will bring you only evil. I know it!'

'It seems to me,' said Stark wryly, 'that the Lhari have already done as much evil as possible to all of us.'

'No,' answered Zareth, with an odd wisdom. 'Our hearts are still clean.'

Stark smiled. He leaned over and kissed her. 'I'll be careful, little sister.'

Quite suddenly she flung her arms around his neck and clung to him tightly, and Stark's face sobered. He patted her, rather awkwardly, and then she had gone, to curl up on her own pallet with her head buried in her arms.

Stark lay down. His heart was sad, and there was a stinging moisture in his eyes.

The red eternities dragged on. Stark learned what Helvi had meant when he said that the mind broke before the body. The sea bottom was no place for creatures of the upper air. He learned also the meaning of the metal collars, and the manner of Tobal's death.

Helvi explained.

'There are boundaries laid down. Within them we may range, if we have the strength and the desire after work. Beyond them we may not go. And there is no chance of escape by breaking through the barrier. How this is done I do not understand, but it is so, and the collars are the key to it.

'When a slave approaches the barrier the collar brightens as though with fire, and the slave falls. I have tried this myself, and I know. Half paralysed, you may crawl back to safety. But if you are mad, as Tobal was, and charge the barrier strongly ...'

He made a cutting motion with his hands.

Stark nodded. He did not attempt to explain electricity or electronic vibrations to Helvi, but it seemed plain enough that the force with which the Lhari kept their slaves in check was something of the sort. The collars acted as conductors, perhaps for the same type of beam that was generated in the hand-weapons. When the metal broke the invisible boundary line it triggered off a force-beam from the central power station, in the manner of the obedient electric eye that opens doors and rings alarm bells. First a warning – then death.

The boundaries were wide enough, extending around the city and enclosing a good bit of forest beyond it. There was no possibility of a slave hiding among the trees, because the collar could be traced by the same type of beam, turned to low power, and the punishment meted out to a retaken man was such that few were foolish enough to try that game.

The surface, of course, was utterly forbidden. The one unguarded spot was the island where the central power station was, and here the slaves were allowed to come sometimes at night. The Lhari had discovered that they lived longer and worked better if they had an occasional breath of air and a look at the sky.

Many times Stark made that pilgrimage with the others. Up from the red depths they would come, through the reeling bands of fire where the currents ran, through the clouds of crimson sparks and the sullen patches of stillness that were like pools of blood, a company of white ghosts shrouded in flame, rising from their tomb for a little taste of the world they had lost.

It didn't matter that they were so weary they had barely the strength to get back to the barracks and sleep. They found the strength. To walk again on the open ground, to be rid of the eternal crimson dusk and the oppressive weight on the chest – to look up into the hot blue night of Venus and smell the fragrance of the *liha*-trees borne on the land wind ... They found the strength.

They sang here, sitting on the island rocks and staring through the mists toward the shore they would never see again. It was their chanting that Stark had heard when he came down the gulf with Malthor, that wordless cry of grief and loss. Now he was here himself, holding Zareth close to comfort her and joining his own deep voice into that primitive reproach to the gods.

While he sat, howling like the savage he was, he studied the power plant, a squat blockhouse of a place. On the nights the slaves came guards were stationed outside to warn them away. The blockhouse was doubly guarded with the shock-beam. To attempt to take it by force would only mean death for all concerned.

Stark gave that idea up for the time being. There was never a second when escape was not in his thoughts, but he was too old in the game to break his neck against a stone wall. Like Malthor, he would wait.

Zareth and Helvi both changed after Stark's coming. Though they never talked of breaking free, both of them lost their air of hopelessness. Stark made neither plans nor promises. But Helvi knew him from of old, and the girl had her own subtle understanding, and they held up their heads again.

Then, one 'day' as the work was ending, Varra came smiling out of the red murk and beckoned to him, and Stark's heart gave a great leap. Without a backward look he left Helvi and Zareth, and went with her, down the wide still avenue that led outward to the forest.

8

They left the stately buildings and the wide spaces behind them, and went in among the trees. Stark hated the forest. The city was bad enough, but it was dead, honestly dead, except for those neat nightmare gardens. There was something terrifying about these great trees, full-leafed and green, rioting with flowering vines and all the rich undergrowth of the jungle, standing like massed corpses made lovely by mortuary art. They swayed and rustled as the coiling fires swept them, branches bending to that silent horrible parody of wind. Stark always felt trapped there, and stifled by the stiff leaves and the vines.

But he went, and Varra slipped like a silver bird between the great trunks, apparently happy.

'I have come here often, ever since I was old enough. It's wonderful. Here I can stoop and fly like one of my own hawks.' She laughed and plucked a golden flower to set in her hair, and then darted away again, her white legs flashing.

Stark followed. He could see what she meant. Here in this strange sea one's motion was as much flying as swimming, since the pressure equalised the weight of the body. There was a queer sort of thrill in plunging headlong from the treetops, to arrow down through a tangle of vines and branches and then sweep upward again.

She was playing with him, and he knew it. The challenge got his blood up. He could have caught her easily but he did not, only now and again he circled her to show his strength. They sped on and on, trailing wakes of flame, a black hawk chasing a silver dove through the forests of a dream.

But the dove had been fledged in an eagle's nest. Stark wearied of the game at last. He caught her and they clung together, drifting still among the trees with the momentum of that wonderful weightless flight.

Her kiss at first was lazy, teasing and curious. Then it changed. All Stark's smouldering anger leaped into a different kind of flame. His handling of her was rough and cruel, and she laughed, a little fierce voiceless laugh, and gave it back to him, and remembered how he had thought her mouth was like a bitter fruit that would give a man pain when he kissed it.

She broke away at last and came to rest on a broad branch, leaning back against the trunk and laughing, her eyes brilliant and cruel as Stark's own. And Stark sat down at her feet.

'What do you want?' he demanded. 'What do you want with me?'

She smiled. There was nothing sidelong or shy about her. She was bold as a new blade.

'I'll tell you, wild man.'

He started. 'Where did you pick up that name?'

'I have been asking the Earthman Larrabee about you. It suits you well.' She leaned forward. 'This is what I want of you. Slay me Egil and his brother Cond. Also Bor, who will grow up worse than either – although that I can do myself, if you're averse to killing children, though Bor is more monster than child. Grandmother can't live forever, and with my cousins out of the way she's no threat. Treon doesn't count.'

'And if I do – what then?'

'Freedom. And me. You'll rule Shuruun at my side.'

Stark's eyes were mocking. 'For how long, Varra?'

'Who knows? And what does it matter? The years take care of themselves.' She shrugged. 'The Lhari blood has run out, and it's time there was a fresh strain. Our children will rule after us, and they'll be men.'

Stark laughed. He roared with it.

'It's not enough that I'm a slave to the Lhari. Now I must be executioner and herd bull as well!' He looked at her keenly. 'Why me, Varra? Why pick on me?'

'Because, as I have said, you are the first man I have seen since my father died. Also, there is something about you ...'

She pushed herself upward to hover lazily, her lips just brushing his.

'Do you think it would be so bad a thing to live with me, wild man?'

She was lovely and maddening, a silver witch shining among

the dim fires of the sea, full of wickedness and laughter. Stark reached out and drew her to him.

'Not bad,' he murmured. 'Dangerous.'

He kissed her, and she whispered, 'I think you're not afraid of danger.'

'On the contrary, I'm a cautious man.' He held her off, where he could look straight into her eyes. 'I owe Egil something of my own, but I will not murder. The fight must be fair, and Cond will have to take care of himself.'

'Fair! Was Egil fair with you – or me?'

He shrugged. 'My way, or not at all.'

She thought it over a while, then nodded. 'All right. As for Cond, you will give him a blood debt, and pride will make him fight. The Lhari are all proud,' she added bitterly. 'That's our curse. But it's bred in the bone, as you'll find out.'

'One more thing. Zareth and Helvi are to go free, and there must be an end to this slavery.'

She stared at him. 'You drive a hard bargain, wild man!'

'Yes or no?'

'Yes *and* no. Zareth and Helvi you may have, if you insist, though the gods know what you see in that pallid child. As to the other ...' She smiled very mockingly. 'I'm no fool, Stark. You're evading me, and two can play that game.'

He laughed. 'Fair enough. And now tell me this, witch with the silver curls – how am I to get at Egil that I may kill him?'

'I'll arrange that.'

She said it with such vicious assurance that he was pretty sure she would arrange it. He was silent for a moment, and then he asked,

'Varra – what are the Lhari searching for at the bottom of the sea?'

She answered slowly, 'I told you that we are a proud clan. We were driven out of the High Plateaus centuries ago because of our pride. Now it's all we have left, but it's a driving thing.'

She paused, and then went on. 'I think we had known about the city for a long time, but it had never meant anything until my father became fascinated by it. He would stay down here days at a time, exploring, and it was he who found the weapons and the machine of power which is on the island. Then he found the chart and the metal book, hidden away in a secret place. The book was written in pictographs – as though it was meant to be deciphered – and the chart showed the square with the ruined building and the temples, with a separate diagram of catacombs underneath the ground.

'The book told of a secret – a thing of wonder and of fear. And my father believed that the building had been wrecked to close the entrance to the catacombs where the secret was kept. He determined to find it.'

Sixteen years of other men's lives. Stark shivered. 'What was the secret, Varra?'

'The manner of controlling life. How it was done I do not know, but with it one might build a race of giants, of monsters, or of gods. You can see what that would mean to us, a proud and dying clan.'

'Yes,' Stark answered slowly. 'I can see.'

The magnitude of the idea shook him. The builders of the city must have been wise indeed in their scientific research to evolve such a terrible power. To mould the living cells of the body to one's will – to create, not life itself but its form and fashion ...

A race of giants, or of gods. The Lhari would like that. To transform their own degenerate flesh into something beyond the race of men, to develop their followers into a corps of fighting men that no one could stand against, to see that their children were given an unholy advantage over all the children of men ... Stark was appalled at the realisation of the evil they could do if they ever found that secret.

Varra said, 'There was a warning in the book. The meaning of it was not quite clear, but it seemed that the ancient ones felt that they had sinned against the gods and been punished, perhaps by some plague. They were a strange race, and not human. At any rate, they destroyed the great building there as a barrier against anyone who should come after them, and then let the Red Sea in to cover their city forever. They must have been superstitious children, for all their knowledge.'

'Then you all ignored the warning, and never worried that a whole city had died to prove it.'

She shrugged. 'Oh, Treon has been muttering prophecies about it for years. Nobody listens to him. As for myself, I don't care whether we find the secret or not. My belief is that it was destroyed along with the building, and besides, I have no faith in such things.'

'Besides,' mocked Stark shrewdly, 'you wouldn't care to see Egil and Cond striding across the heavens of Venus, and you're doubtful just what your own place would be in the new pantheon.'

She showed her teeth at him. 'You're too wise for your own good. And now goodbye.' She gave him a quick, hard kiss and was gone, flashing upward, high above the treetops where he dared not follow.

Stark made his way slowly back to the city, upset and very thoughtful.

As he came back into the great square, heading toward the barracks, he stopped, every nerve taut.

Somewhere, in one of the shadowy temples, the clapper of a votive bell was swinging, sending its deep pulsing note across the silence. Slowly, slowly, like the beating of a dying heart it came, and mingled with it was the faint sound of Zareth's voice, calling his name.

9

He crossed the square, moving very carefully through the red murk, and presently he saw her.

It was not hard to find her. There was one temple larger than all the rest. Stark judged that it must once have faced the entrance of the fallen building, as though the great figure within was set to watch over the scientists and the philosophers who came there to dream their vast and sometimes terrible dreams.

The philosophers were gone, and the scientists had destroyed themselves. But the image still watched over the drowned city, its hand raised both in warning and in benediction.

Now, across its reptilian knees, Zareth lay. The temple was open on all sides, and Stark could see her clearly, a little white scrap of humanity against the black unhuman figure.

Malthor stood beside her. It was he who had been tolling the votive bell. He had stopped now, and Zareth's words came clearly to Stark.

'Go away, go away! They're waiting for you. Don't come in here!'

'I'm waiting for you, Stark,' Malthor called out, smiling. 'Are you afraid to come?' And he took Zareth by the hair and struck her, slowly and deliberately, twice across the face.

All expression left Stark's face, leaving it perfectly blank except for his eyes, which took on a sudden lambent gleam. He began to move toward the temple, not hurrying even then, but moving in such a way that it seemed an army could not have stopped him.

Zareth broke free from her father. Perhaps she was intended to break free.

'Egil!' she screamed. 'It's a trap ...'

Again Malthor caught her and this time he struck her harder, so that she crumpled down again across the image that watched with its jewelled, gentle eyes and saw nothing.

'She's afraid for you,' said Malthor. 'She knows I mean to kill you if I can. Well, perhaps Egil is here also. Perhaps he is not. But certainly Zareth is here. I have beaten her well, and I shall beat her again, as long as she lives to be beaten, for her treachery to me. And if you want to save her from that, you outland dog, you'll have to kill me. Are you afraid?'

Stark was afraid. Malthor and Zareth were alone in the temple. The pillared colonnades were empty except for the dim fires of the sea. Yet Stark was afraid, for an instinct older than speech warned him to be.

It did not matter. Zareth's white skin was mottled with dark bruises, and Malthor was smiling at him, and it did not matter.

Under the shadow of the roof and down the colonnade he

went, swiftly now, leaving a streak of fire behind him. Malthor looked into his eyes, and his smile trembled and was gone.

He crouched. And at the last moment, when the dark body plunged down at him as a shark plunges, he drew a hidden knife from his girdle and struck.

Stark had not counted on that. The slaves were searched for possible weapons every day, and even a sliver of stone was forbidden. Somebody must have given it to him, someone...

The thought flashed through his mind while he was in the very act of trying to avoid that death blow. *Too late, too late, because his own momentum carried him onto the point*...

Reflexes quicker than any man's, the hair-trigger reactions of a wild thing. Muscles straining, the centre of balance shifted with an awful wrenching effort, hands grasping at the fire-shot redness as though to force it to defy its own laws. The blade ripped a long shallow gash across his breast. But it did not go home. By a fraction of an inch, it did not go home.

While Stark was still off balance, Malthor sprang.

They grappled. The knife blade glittered redly, a hungry tongue eager to taste Stark's life. The two men rolled over and over, drifting and tumbling erratically, churning the sea to a froth of sparks, and still the image watched, its calm reptilian features unchanging benign and wise. Threads of a darker red laced heavily across the dancing fires.

Stark got Malthor's arm under his own and held it there with both hands. His back was to the man now. Malthor kicked and clawed with his feet against the backs of Stark's thighs, and his left arm came up and tried to clamp around Stark's throat. Stark buried his chin so that it could not, and then Malthor's hand began to tear at Stark's face, searching for his eyes.

Stark voiced a deep bestial sound in his throat. He moved his head suddenly, catching Malthor's hand between his jaws. He did not let go. Presently his teeth were locked against the thumb-joint, and Malthor was screaming, but Stark could give all his attention to what he was doing with the arm that held the knife. His eyes had changed. They were all beast now, the eyes of a killer blazing cold and beautiful in his dark face.

There was a dull crack, and the arm ceased to strain or fight.

It bent back upon itself, and the knife fell, drifting quietly down. Malthor was beyond screaming now. He made one effort to get away as Stark released him, but it was a futile gesture, and he made no sound as Stark broke his neck.

He thrust the body from him. It drifted away, moving lazily with the suck of the currents through the colonnade, now and again touching a black pillar as though in casual wonder, wandering out at last into the square. Malthor was in no hurry. He had all eternity before him.

Stark moved carefully away from the girl, who was trying feebly now to sit up on the knees of the image. He called out, to some unseen presence hidden in the shadows under the roof.

'Malthor screamed your name, Egil. Why didn't you come?'

There was a flicker of movement in the intense darkness of the ledge at the top of the pillars.

'Why should I?' asked the Lord Egil of the Lhari. 'I offered him his freedom if he could kill you, but it seems he could not – even though I gave him a knife, and drugs to keep your friend Helvi out of the way.'

He came out where Stark could see him, very handsome in a tunic of yellow silk, the blunt black weapon in his hands.

'The important thing was to bait a trap. You would not face me because of this—' He raised the weapon. 'I might have killed you as you worked, of course, but my family would have had hard things to say about that. You're a phenomenally good slave.'

'They'd have said hard words like "coward," Egil,' Stark said softly. 'And Varra would have set her bird at you in earnest.'

Egil nodded. His lip curved cruelly. 'Exactly. That amused you, didn't it? And now my little cousin is training another falcon to swoop at me. She hooded you today, didn't she, Outlander?'

He laughed. 'Ah well. I didn't kill you openly because there's a better way. Do you think I want it gossiped all over the Red Sea that my cousin jilted me for a foreign slave? Do you think I wish it known that I hated you, and why? No. I would have killed Malthor anyway, if you hadn't done it, because he knew. And when I have killed you and the girl I shall take your bodies to the barrier and leave them there together, and it will be obvious to everyone, even Varra, that you were killed trying to escape.'

The weapon's muzzle pointed straight at Stark, and Egil's finger quivered on the trigger stud. Full power, this time. Instead of paralysis, death. Stark measured the distance between himself and Egil. He would be dead before he struck, but the impetus of his leap might carry him on, and give Zareth a chance to escape. The muscles of his thighs stirred and tensed.

A voice said, 'And it will be obvious how and why *I* died, Egil? For if you kill them, you must kill me too.'

Where Treon had come from, or when, Stark did not know. But he was there by the image, and his voice was full of a strong music, and his eyes shone with a fey light.

Egil had started, and now he swore in fury. 'You idiot! You twisted freak! How did you come here?'

'How does the wind come, and the rain? I am not as other men.' He laughed, a sombre sound with no mirth in it. 'I am here, Egil, and that's all that matters. And you will not slay this stranger who is more beast than man, and more man than any of us. The gods have a use for him.'

He had moved as he spoke, until now he stood between Stark and Egil.

'Get out of the way,' said Egil.

Treon shook his head.

'Very well,' said Egil. 'If you wish to die, you may.'

The fey gleam brightened in Treon's eyes. 'This is a day of death,' he said softly, 'but not of his, or mine.'

Egil said a short, ugly word, and raised the weapon up.

Things happened very quickly after that. Stark sprang, arching up and over Treon's head, cleaving the red gases like a burning arrow. Egil started back, and shifted his aim upward, and his finger snapped down on the trigger stud.

Something white came between Stark and Egil, and took the force of the bolt.

Something white. A girl's body, crowned with streaming hair, and a collar of metal glowing bright around the slender neck.

Zareth.

They had forgotten her, the beaten child crouched on the knees of the image. Stark had moved to keep her out of danger, and she was no threat to the mighty Egil, and Treon's thoughts were known only to himself and the winds that taught him. Unnoticed, she had crept to a place where one last plunge would place her between Stark and death.

The rush of Stark's going took him on over her, except that her hair brushed softly against his skin. Then he was on top of Egil, and it had all been done so swiftly that the Lord of the Lhari had not had time to loose another bolt.

Stark tore the weapon from Egil's hand. He was cold, icy cold, and there was a strange blindness on him, so that he could see nothing clearly but Egil's face. And it was Stark who screamed this time, a dreadful sound like the cry of a great cat gone beyond reason or fear.

Treon stood watching. He watched the blood stream darkly into the sea, and he listened to the silence come, and he saw the thing that had been his cousin drift away on the slow tide, and it was as though he had seen it all before and was not surprised.

Stark went to Zareth's body. The girl was still breathing, very faintly, and her eyes turned to Stark, and she smiled.

Stark was blind now with tears. All his rage had run out of him with Egil's blood, leaving nothing but an aching pity and a sadness, and a wondering awe. He took Zareth very tenderly into his arms and held her, dumbly, watching the tears fall on her upturned face. And presently he knew that she was dead.

Sometime later Treon came to him and said softly, 'To this end she was born, and she knew it, and was happy. Even now she smiles. And she should, for she had a better death than most of us.' He laid his hand on Stark's shoulder. 'Come, I'll show you where to put her. She will be safe there, and tomorrow you can bury her where she would wish to be.'

Stark rose and followed him, bearing Zareth in his arms.

Treon went to the pedestal on which the image sat. He pressed in a certain way upon a series of hidden springs, and a section of the paving slid noiselessly back, revealing stone steps leading down.

10

Treon led the way down, into darkness that was lightened only by the dim fires they themselves woke in passing. No current ran here. The red gas lay dull and stagnant, closed within the walls of a square passage built of the same black stone.

'These are the crypts,' he said. 'The labyrinth that is shown on the chart my father found.' And he told about the chart, as Varra had.

He led the way surely, his misshapen body moving without hesitation past the mouths of branching corridors and the doors of chambers whose interiors were lost in shadow.

'The history of the city is here. All the books and the learning, that they had not the heart to destroy. There are no weapons. They were not a warlike people, and I think that the force we of Lhari have used differently was defensive only, protection against the beasts and the raiding primitives of the swamps.'

With a great effort, Stark wrenched his thoughts away from the light burden he carried.

'I thought,' he said dully, 'that the crypts were under the wrecked building.'

'So we all thought. We were intended to think so. That is why the building was wrecked. And for sixteen years we of the Lhari have killed men and women with dragging the stones of it away. But the temple was shown also in the chart. We thought it was there merely as a landmark, an identification for the great building. But I began to wonder ...'

'How long have you known?'

'Not long. Perhaps two rains. It took many seasons to find the secret of this passage. I came here at night, when the others slept.'

'And you didn't tell?'

'No!' said Treon. 'You are thinking that if I had told, there would have been an end to the slavery and the death. But what then? My family, turned loose with the power to destroy a world, as this city was destroyed? No! It was better for the slaves to die.'

He motioned Stark aside, then, between doors of gold that stood ajar, into a vault so great that there was no guessing its size in the red and shrouding gloom.

'This was the burial place of their kings,' said Treon softly. 'Leave the little one here.'

Stark looked around him, still too numb to feel awe, but impressed even so.

They were set in straight lines, the beds of black marble – lines so long that there was no end to them except the limit of vision. And on them slept the old kings, their bodies, marvellously embalmed, covered with silken palls, their hands crossed upon their breasts, their wise unhuman faces stamped with the mark of peace.

Very gently, Stark laid Zareth down on a marble couch, and covered her also with silk, and closed her eyes and folded her hands. And it seemed to him that her face, too, had that look of peace.

He went out with Treon, thinking that none of them had earned a better place in the hall of kings than Zareth.

'Treon,' he said.

'Yes?'

'That prophecy you spoke when I came to the castle – I will bear it out.'

Treon nodded. 'That is the way of prophecies.'

He did not return toward the temple, but led the way deeper into the heart of the catacombs. A great excitement burned within him, a bright and terrible thing that communicated itself to Stark. Treon had suddenly taken on the stature of a figure of destiny, and the Earthman had the feeling that he was in the grip of some current that would plunge on irresistibly until everything in its path was swept away. Stark's flesh quivered.

They reached the end of the corridor at last. And there, in the red gloom, a shape sat waiting before a black, barred door. A shape grotesque and incredibly misshapen, so horribly malformed that by it Treon's crippled body appeared almost beautiful. Yet its face was as the faces of the images and the old kings, and its sunken eyes had once held wisdom, and one of its seven-fingered hands was still slim and sensitive.

Stark recoiled. The thing made him physically sick, and he would have turned away, but Treon urged him on.

'Go closer. It is dead, embalmed, but it has a message for you. It has waited all this time to give that message.'

Reluctantly, Stark went forward.

Quite suddenly, it seemed that the thing spoke.

Behold me. Look upon me, and take counsel before you grasp that power which lies beyond the door!

Stark leapt back, crying out, and Treon smiled.

'It was so with me. But I have listened to it many times since then. It speaks not with a voice, but within the mind, and only when one has passed a certain spot.'

Stark's reasoning mind pondered over that. A thought-record, obviously, triggered off by an electronic beam. The ancients had taken good care that their warning would be heard and understood by anyone who should solve the riddle of the catacombs. Thought-images, speaking directly to the brain, know no barrier of time or language.

He stepped forward again, and once more the telepathic voice spoke to him.

'We tampered with the secrets of the gods. We intended no evil. It was only that we love perfection, and wished to shape all living things as flawless as our buildings and our gardens. We did not know that it was against the Law ...

'I was one of those who found the way to change the living cell. We used the unseen force that comes from the Land of the Gods beyond the sky, and we so harnessed it that we could build from the living flesh as the potter builds from the clay. We healed the halt and the maimed, and made those stand tall and straight who came crooked from the egg, and for a time we were as brothers to the gods themselves. I myself, even I, knew the glory of perfection. And then came the reckoning.

'The cell, once made to change, would not stop changing. The growth was slow, and for a while we did not notice it, but when we did it was too late. We were becoming a city of monsters. And the force we had used was worse than useless, for the more we tried to mould the monstrous flesh to its normal shape, the more the stimulated cells grew and grew, until the bodies we laboured over were like things of wet mud that flow and change even as you look at them.

'One by one the people of the city destroyed themselves. And those of us who were left realised the judgement of the gods, and our duty. We made all things ready, and let the Red Sea hide us forever from our own kind, and those who should come after.

'Yet we did not destroy our knowledge. Perhaps it was our pride only that forbade us, but we could not bring ourselves to do it. Perhaps other gods, other races wiser than we, can take away the evil and keep only the good. For it is good for all creatures to be, if not perfect, at least strong and sound.

'But heed this warning, whoever you may be that listen. If your gods are jealous, if your people have not the wisdom or the knowledge to succeed where we failed in controlling this force, then touch it not! Or you, and all your people, will become as I.'

The voice stopped. Stark moved back again, and said to Treon incredulously, 'And your family would ignore that warning?'

Treon laughed. 'They are fools. They are cruel and greedy and very proud. They would say that this was a lie to frighten away intruders, or that human flesh would not be subject to the laws that govern the flesh of reptiles. They would say anything, because they have dreamed this dream too long to be denied.'

Stark shuddered and looked at the black door. 'The thing ought to be destroyed.'

'Yes,' said Treon softly.

His eyes were shining, looking into some private dream of his own. He started forward, and when Stark would have gone with him he thrust him back, saying, 'No. You have no part in this.' He shook his head.

'I have waited,' he whispered, almost to himself. 'The winds bade me wait, until the day was ripe to fall from the tree of death. I have waited, and at dawn I knew, for the wind said, *Now is the gathering of the fruit at hand.*'

He looked suddenly at Stark, and his eyes had in them a clear sanity, for all their feyness.

'You heard, Stark. "We made those stand tall and straight who came crooked from the egg". I will have my hour. I will stand as a man for the little time that is left.'

He turned, and Stark made no move to follow. He watched Treon's twisted body recede, white against the red dusk, until it passed the monstrous watcher and came to the black door. The long thin arms reached up and pushed the bar away.

The door swung slowly back. Through the opening Stark glimpsed a chamber that held a structure of crystal rods and discs mounted on a frame of metal, the whole thing glowing and glittering with a restless bluish light that dimmed and brightened as though it echoed some vast pulse-beat. There was other apparatus, intricate banks of tubes and condensers, but this was the heart of it, and the heart was still alive.

Treon passed within and closed the door behind him.

Stark drew back some distance from the door and its guardian, crouched down, and set his back against the wall. He thought about the apparatus. Cosmic rays, perhaps – the unseen force that came from beyond the sky. Even yet, all their potentialities were not known. But a few luckless spacemen had found that under certain conditions they could do amazing things to human tissue.

It was a line of thought Stark did not like at all. He tried to keep his mind away from Treon entirely. He tried not to think at all. It was dark there in the corridor, and very still, and the shapeless horror sat quiet in the doorway and waited with him. Stark began to shiver, a shallow animal-twitching of the flesh.

He waited. After a while he thought Treon must be dead, but he did not move. He did not wish to go into that room to see.

He waited.

Suddenly he leaped up, cold sweat bursting out all over him. A crash had echoed down the corridor, a clashing of shattered crystal and a high singing note that trailed off into nothing.

The door opened.

A man came out. A man tall and straight and beautiful as an angel, a strong-limbed man with Treon's face, Treon's tragic eyes. And behind him the chamber was dark. The pulsing heart of power had stopped.

The door was shut and barred again. Treon's voice was saying,

'There are records left, and much of the apparatus, so that the secret is not lost entirely. Only it is out of reach.'

He came to Stark and held out his hand. 'Let us fight together, as men. And do not fear. I shall die, long before this body changes.' He smiled, the remembered smile that was full of pity for all living things. 'I know, for the winds have told me.'

Stark took his hand and held it.

'Good,' said Treon. 'And now lead on, stranger with the fierce eyes. For the prophecy is yours, and the day is yours, and I who have crept about like a snail all my life know little of battles. Lead, and I will follow.'

Stark fingered the collar around his neck. 'Can you rid me of this?'

Treon nodded. 'There are tools and acid in one of the chambers.'

He found them, and worked swiftly, and while he worked Stark thought, smiling – and there was no pity in that smile at all.

They came back at last into the temple, and Treon closed the entrance to the catacombs. It was still night, for the square was empty of slaves. Stark found Egil's weapon where it had fallen, on the ledge where Egil died.

'We must hurry,' said Stark. 'Come on.'

11

The island was shrouded heavily in mist and the blue darkness of the night. Stark and Treon crept silently among the rocks until they could see the glimmer of torchlight through the window-slits of the power station.

There were seven guards, five inside the blockhouse, two outside to patrol.

When they were close enough, Stark slipped away, going like a shadow, and never a pebble turned under his bare foot. Presently he found a spot to his liking and crouched down.

A sentry went by not three feet away, yawning and looking hopefully at the sky for the first signs of dawn.

Treon's voice rang out, the sweet unmistakable voice. 'Ho, there, guards!'

The sentry stopped and whirled around. Off around the curve of the stone wall someone began to run, his sandals thud-thudding on the soft ground, and the second guard came up.

'Who speaks?' one demanded. 'The Lord Treon?'

They peered into the darkness, and Treon answered, 'Yes.' He had come forward far enough so that they could make out the pale blur of his face, keeping his body out of sight among the rocks and the shrubs that sprang up between them.

'Make haste,' he ordered. 'Bid them open the door, there.' He spoke in breathless jerks, as though spent. 'A tragedy – a disaster! Bid them open!'

One of the men leaped to obey, hammering on the massive door that was kept barred from the inside. The other stood goggle-eyed, watching. Then the door opened, spilling a flood of yellow torchlight into the red fog.

'What is it?' cried the men inside. 'What has happened?'

'Come out!' gasped Treon. 'My cousin is dead, the Lord Egil is dead, murdered by a slave.'

He let that sink in. Three or more men came outside into the circle of light, and their faces were frightened, as though somehow they feared they might be held responsible for this thing.

'You know him,' said Treon. 'The great black-haired one from Earth. He has slain the Lord Egil and got away into the forest, and we need all extra guards to go after him, since many must be left to guard the other slaves, who are mutinous. You, and you—' He picked out the four biggest ones. 'Go at once and join the search. I will stay here with the others.'

It nearly worked. The four took a hesitant step or two, and then one paused, and said doubtfully,

'But my lord, it is forbidden that we leave our posts, for any reason. Any reason at all, my lord! The Lord Cond would slay us if we left this place.'

'And you fear the Lord Cond more than you do me,' said Treon philosophically. 'Ah, well. I understand.'

He stepped out, full into the light.

A gasp went up, and then a startled yell. The three men from inside had come out armed only with swords, but the two sentries had their shock-weapons. One of them shrieked,

'It is a demon, who speaks with Treon's voice!'

And the two black weapons started up.

Behind them, Stark fired two silent bolts in quick succession, and the men fell, safely out of the way for hours. Then he leaped for the door.

He collided with two men who were doing the same thing. The third had turned to hold Treon off with his sword until they were safely inside.

Seeing that Treon, who was unarmed, was in danger of being spitted on the man's point, Stark fired between the two lunging bodies as he fell, and brought the guard down. Then he was involved in a thrashing tangle of arms and legs, and a lucky blow jarred the shock-weapon out of his hand.

Treon added himself to the fray. Pleasuring in his new strength, he caught one man by the neck and pulled him off. The guards were big men, and powerful, and they fought desperately. Stark was bruised and bleeding from a cut mouth before he could get in a finishing blow.

Someone rushed past him into the doorway. Treon yelled. Out of the tail of his eyes Stark saw the Lhari sitting dazed on the ground. The door was closing.

Stark hunched up his shoulders and sprang.

He hit the heavy panel with a jar that nearly knocked him breathless. It slammed open, and there was a cry of pain and the sound of someone falling. Stark burst through, to find the last of the guards rolling every which way over the floor. But one rolled over onto his feet again, drawing his sword as he rose. He had not had time before.

Stark continued his rush without stopping. He plunged headlong into the man before the point was clear of the scabbard, bore him over and down, and finished the man off with savage efficiency.

He leaped to his feet, breathing hard, spitting blood out of his mouth, and looked around the control room. But the others had fled, obviously to raise the warning.

The mechanism was simple. It was contained in a large black metal oblong about the size and shape of a coffin, equipped with grids and lenses and dials. It hummed softly to itself, but what its source of power was Stark did not know. Perhaps those same cosmic rays, harnessed to a different use.

He closed what seemed to be a master switch, and the humming stopped, and the flickering light died out of the lenses. He picked up the slain guard's sword and carefully wrecked everything that was breakable. Then he went outside again.

Treon was standing up, shaking his head. He smiled ruefully.

'It seems that strength alone is not enough,' he said. 'One must have skill as well.'

'The barriers are down,' said Stark. 'The way is clear.'

Treon nodded, and went with him back into the sea. This time both carried shock-weapons taken from the guards – six in all, with Egil's. Total armament for war.

As they forged swiftly through the red depths, Stark asked, 'What of the people of Shuruun? How will they fight?'

Treon answered, 'Those of Malthor's breed will stand for the Lhari. They must, for all their hope is there. The others will wait, until they see which side is safest. They would rise against the Lhari if they dared, for we have brought them only fear in their lifetimes. But they will wait, and see.'

Stark nodded. He did not speak again.

They passed over the brooding city, and Stark thought of Egil and of Malthor who were part of that silence now, drifting slowly through the empty streets where the little currents took them, wrapped in their shrouds of dim fire.

He thought of Zareth sleeping in the hall of kings, and his eyes held a cold, cruel light.

They swooped down over the slave barracks. Treon remained on watch outside. Stark went in, taking with him the extra weapons.

The slaves still slept. Some of them dreamed, and moaned in their dreaming, and others might have been dead, with their hollow faces white as skulls.

Slaves. One hundred and four, counting the women.

Stark shouted out to them, and they woke, starting up on their pallets, their eyes full of terror. Then they saw who it was that called them, standing collarless and armed, and there was a great surging and a clamour that stilled as Stark shouted again, demanding silence. This time Helvi's voice echoed his. The tall barbarian had wakened from his drugged sleep.

Stark told them, very briefly, all that happened.

'You are freed from the collar,' he said. 'This day you can survive or die as men, and not slaves.' He paused, then asked, 'Who will go with me into Shuruun?'

They answered with one voice, the voice of the Lost Ones, who saw the red pall of death begin to lift from over them. The Lost Ones, who had found hope again.

Stark laughed. He was happy. He gave the extra weapons to Helvi and three others that he chose, and Helvi looked into his eyes and laughed too.

Treon spoke from the open door. 'They are coming!'

Stark gave Helvi quick instructions and darted out, taking with him one of the other men. With Treon, they hid among the shrubbery of the garden that was outside the hall, patterned and beautiful, swaying its lifeless brilliance in the lazy drifts of fire.

The guards came. Twenty of them, tall armed men, to turn out the slaves for another period of labour, dragging the useless stones.

And the hidden weapons spoke with their silent tongues.

Eight of the guards fell inside the hall. Nine of them went down outside. Ten of the slaves died before the remaining three were overcome.

Now there were twenty swords among ninety-four slaves, counting the women.

They left the city and rose up over the dreaming forest, a flight of white ghosts with flames in their hair, coming back from the red dusk and the silence to find the light again.

Light, and vengeance.

The first pale glimmer of dawn was sifting through the clouds as they came up among the rocks below the castle of the Lhari.

Stark left them and went like a shadow up the tumbled cliffs to where he had hidden his gun on the night he had first come to Shuruun. Nothing stirred. The fog lifted up from the sea like a vapour of blood, and the face of Venus was still dark. Only the high clouds were touched with pearl.

Stark returned to the others. He gave one of his shock-weapons to a swamp-lander with a cold madness in his eyes. Then he spoke a few final words to Helvi and went back with Treon under the surface of the sea.

Treon led the way. He went along the face of the submerged cliff, and presently he touched Stark's arm and pointed to where a round mouth opened in the rock.

'It was made long ago,' said Treon, 'so that the Lhari and their slavers might come and go and not be seen. Come – and be very quiet.'

They swam into the tunnel mouth, and down the dark way that lay beyond, until the lift of the floor brought them out of the sea. Then they felt their way silently along, stopping now and again to listen.

Surprise was their only hope. Treon had said that with the two of them they might succeed. More men would surely be discovered, and meet a swift end at the hands of the guards.

Stark hoped Treon was right.

They came to a blank wall of dressed stone. Treon leaned his weight against one side, and a great block swung slowly around on a central pivot. Guttering torchlight came through the crack. By it Stark could see that the room beyond was empty.

They stepped through, and as they did so a servant in bright silks came yawning into the room with a fresh torch to replace the one that was dying.

He stopped in mid-step, his eyes widening. He dropped the torch. His mouth opened to shape a scream, but no sound came, and Stark remembered that these servants were tongueless – to prevent them from telling what they saw or heard in the castle, Treon said.

The man spun about and fled, down a long dim-lit hall. Stark ran him down without effort. He struck once with the barrel of his gun, and the man fell and was still.

Treon came up. His face had a look almost of exaltation, a queer shining of the eyes that made Stark shiver. He led on, through a series of empty rooms, all sombre black, and they met no one else for a while.

He stopped at last before a small door of burnished gold. He looked at Stark once, and nodded, and thrust the panels open and stepped through.

12

They stood inside the vast echoing hall that stretched away into darkness until it seemed there was no end to it. The cluster of silver lamps burned as before, and within their circle of radiance the Lhari started up from their places and stared at the strangers who had come in through their private door.

Cond, and Arel with her hands idle in her lap. Bor, pummelling the little dragon to make it hiss and snap, laughing at its impotence. Varra, stroking the winged creature on her wrist, testing with her white finger the sharpness of its beak. And the old woman, with a scrap of fat meat halfway to her mouth.

They had stopped, frozen, in the midst of these actions. And Treon walked slowly into the light.

'Do you know me?' he said.

A strange shivering ran through them. Now, as before, the old woman spoke first, her eyes glittering with a look as rapacious as her appetite.

'You are Treon,' she said, and her whole vast body shook.

The name went crying and whispering off around the dark walls, *Treon! Treon! Treon!* Cond leaped forward, touching his cousin's straight strong body with hands that trembled.

'You have found it,' he said. 'The secret.'

'Yes.' Treon lifted his silver head and laughed, a beautiful ringing bell-note that sang from the echoing corners. 'I found it, and it's gone, smashed, beyond your reach forever. Egil is dead, and the day of the Lhari is done.'

There was a long, long silence, and then the old woman whispered, '*You lie!*'

Treon turned to Stark.

'Ask him, the stranger who came bearing doom upon his forehead. Ask him if I lie.'

Cond's face became something less than human. He made a queer crazed sound and flung himself at Treon's throat.

Bor screamed suddenly. He alone was not much concerned with the finding or the losing of the secret, and he alone seemed to realise the significance of Stark's presence. He screamed, looking at the big dark man, and went rushing off down the hall, crying for the guard as he went, and the echoes roared and racketed. He fought open the great doors and ran out, and as he did so the sound of fighting came through the compound.

The slaves, with their swords and clubs, with their stones and shards of rock, had come over the wall from the cliffs.

Stark had moved forward, but Treon did not need his help. He had got his hands around Cond's throat, and he was smiling. Stark did not disturb him.

The old woman was talking, cursing, commanding, choking on her own apoplectic breath. Arel began to laugh. She did not move, and her hands remained limp and open in her lap. She laughed and laughed, and Varra looked at Stark and hated him.

'You're a fool, wild man,' she said. 'You would not take what I offered you, so you shall have nothing – only death.'

She slipped the hood from her creature and set it straight at Stark. Then she drew a knife from her girdle and plunged it into Treon's side.

Treon reeled back. His grip loosened and Cond tore away, half throttled, raging, his mouth flecked with foam. He drew his short sword and staggered in upon Treon.

Furious wings beat and thundered around Stark's head, and talons were clawing for his eyes. He reached up with his left hand and caught the brute by one leg and held it. Not long, but long enough to get one clear shot at Cond that dropped him in his tracks. Then he snapped the falcon's neck.

He flung the creature at Varra's feet, and picked up the gun again. The guards were rushing into the hall now at the lower end, and he began to fire at them.

Treon was sitting on the floor. Blood was coming in a steady trickle from his side, but he had the shock-weapon in his hands, and he was still smiling.

There was a great boiling roar of noise from outside. Men were fighting there, killing, dying, screaming their triumph or their pain. The echoes raged within the hall, and the noise of Stark's gun was like a hissing thunder. The guards, armed only with swords, went down like ripe wheat before the sickle, but there were many of them, too many for Stark and Treon to hold for long.

The old woman shrieked and shrieked, and was suddenly still.

Helvi burst in through the press, with a knot of collared slaves. The fight dissolved into a whirling chaos. Stark threw his gun away. He was afraid now of hitting his own men. He caught up a sword from the fallen guard and began to hew his way to the barbarian.

Suddenly Treon cried his name. He leaped aside, away from the man he was fighting, and saw Varra fall with the dagger still in her hand. She had come up behind him to stab, and Treon had seen and pressed the trigger stud just in time.

For the first time, there were tears in Treon's eyes.

A sort of sickness came over Stark. There was something horrible in this spectacle of a family destroying itself. He was too much the savage to be sentimental over Varra, but all the same he could not bear to look at Treon for a while.

Presently he found himself back to back with Helvi, and as they swung their swords – the shock-weapons had been discarded for the same reason as Stark's gun – Helvi panted,

'It has been a good fight, my brother! We cannot win, but we can have a good death, which is better than slavery!'

It looked as though Helvi was right. The slaves, unfortunately, weakened by their long confinement, worn out by overwork, were being beaten back. The tide turned, and Stark was swept with it out into the compound, fighting stubbornly.

The great gate stood open. Beyond it stood the people of

Shuruun, watching, hanging back – as Treon had said, they would wait and see.

In the forefront, leaning on his stick, stood Larrabee the Earthman.

Stark cut his way free of the press. He leaped up onto the wall and stood there, breathing hard, sweating, bloody, with a dripping sword in his hand. He waved it, shouting down to the men of Shuruun.

'What are you waiting for, you scuts, you women? The Lhari are dead, the Lost Ones are freed – must we of Earth do all your work for you?'

And he looked straight at Larrabee.

Larrabee stared back, his dark suffering eyes full of a bitter mirth. 'Oh, well,' he said in English. 'Why not?'

He threw back his head and laughed, and the bitterness was gone. He voiced a high, shrill rebel yell and lifted his stick like a cudgel, limping toward the gate, and the men of Shuruun gave tongue and followed him.

After that, it was soon over.

They found Bor's body in the stable pens, where he had fled to hide when the fighting started. The dragons, maddened by the smell of blood, had slain him very quickly.

Helvi had come through alive, and Larrabee, who had kept himself carefully out of harm's way after he had started the men of Shuruun on their attack. Nearly half the slaves were dead, and the rest wounded. Of those who had served the Lhari, few were left.

Stark went back into the great hall. He walked slowly, for he was very weary, and where he set his foot there was a bloody print, and his arms were red to the elbows, and his breast was splashed with the redness. Treon watched him come, and smiled, nodding.

'It is as I said. And I have outlived them all.'

Arel had stopped laughing at last. She had made no move to run away, and the tide of battle had rolled over her and drowned her unaware. The old woman lay still, a mountain of inert flesh upon her bed. Her hand still clutched a ripe fruit, clutched convulsively in the moment of death, the red juice dripping through her fingers.

'Now I am going, too,' said Treon, 'and I am well content. With me goes the last of our rotten blood, and Venus will be the cleaner for it. Bury my body deep, stranger with the fierce eyes. I would not have it looked on after this.'

He sighed and fell forward.

Bor's little dragon crept whimpering out from its hiding place under the old woman's bed and scurried away down the hall, trailing its dragging rope.

Stark leaned on the taffrail, watching the dark mass of Shuruun recede into the red mists.

The decks were crowded with the outland slaves, going home. The Lhari were gone, the Lost Ones freed forever, and Shuruun was now only another port on the Red Sea. Its people would still be wolf's-heads and pirates, but that was natural and as it should be. The black evil was gone.

Stark was glad to see the last of it. He would be glad also to see the last of the Red Sea.

The off-shore wind set the ship briskly down the gulf. Stark thought of Larrabee, left behind with his dreams of winter snows and city streets and women with dainty feet. It seemed that he had lived too long in Shuruun, and had lost the courage to leave it.

'Poor Larrabee,' he said to Helvi, who was standing near him. 'He'll die in the mud, still cursing it.'

Someone laughed behind him. He heard a limping step on the deck and turned to see Larrabee coming toward him.

'Changed my mind at the last minute,' Larrabee said. 'I've been below, lest I should see my muddy brats and be tempted to change it again.' He leaned beside Stark, shaking his head. 'Ah, well, they'll do nicely without me. I'm an old man, and I've a right to choose my own place to die. I'm going back to Earth, with you.'

Stark glanced at him. 'I'm not going to Earth.'

Larrabee sighed. 'No. No, I suppose you're not. After all,

you're no Earthman, really, except for an accident of blood. Where are you going?'

'I don't know. Away from Venus, but I don't know yet where.'

Larrabee's dark eyes surveyed him shrewdly. '"A restless, cold-eyed tiger of a man", that's what Varra said. He's lost something, she said. He'll look for it all his life, and never find it.'

After that there was silence. The red fog wrapped them, and the wind rose and sent them scudding before it.

Then, faint and far off, there came a moaning wail, a sound like broken chanting that turned Stark's flesh cold.

All on board heard it. They listened, utterly silent, their eyes wide, and somewhere a woman began to weep.

Stark shook himself. 'It's only the wind,' he said roughly, 'in the rocks by the strait.'

The sound rose and fell, weary, infinitely mournful, and the part of Stark that was N'Chaka said that he lied. It was not the wind that keened so sadly through the mists. It was the voices of the Lost Ones who were forever lost – Zareth, sleeping in the hall of kings, and all the others who would never leave the dreaming city and the forest, never find the light again.

Stark shivered, and turned away, watching the leaping fires of the strait sweep toward them.

BLACK AMAZON OF MARS

1

Through all the long cold hours of the Norland night the Martian had not moved nor spoken. At dusk of the day before Eric John Stark had brought him into the ruined tower and laid him down, wrapped in blankets, on the snow. He had built a fire of dead brush, and since then the two men had waited, alone in the vast wasteland that girdles the polar cap of Mars.

Now, just before dawn, Camar the Martian spoke.

'Stark.'

'Yes?'

'I am dying.'

'Yes.'

'I will not reach Kushat.'

'No.'

Camar nodded. He was silent again.

The wind howled down from the northern ice, and the broken walls rose up against it, brooding, gigantic, roofless now but so huge and sprawling that they seemed less like walls than cliffs of ebon stone. Stark would not have gone near them but for Camar. They were wrong, somehow, with a taint of forgotten evil still about them.

The big Earthman glanced at Camar, and his face was sad. 'A man likes to die in his own place,' he said abruptly. 'I am sorry.'

'The Lord of Silence is a great personage,' Camar answered. 'He does not mind the meeting place. No. It was not for that I came back into the Norlands.'

He was shaken by an agony that was not of the body. 'And I shall not reach Kushat!'

Stark spoke quietly, using the courtly High Martian almost as fluently as Camar.

'I have known that there was a burden heavier than death upon my brother's soul.'

He leaned over, placing one large hand on the Martian's shoulder. 'My brother has given his life for mine. Therefore, I will take his burden upon myself, if I can.'

He did not want Camar's burden, whatever it might be. But the Martian had fought beside him through a long guerilla campaign among the harried tribes of the nearer moon. He was a good man of his hands, and in the end had taken the bullet that was meant for Stark, knowing quite well what he was doing. They were friends.

That was why Stark had brought Camar into the bleak north country, trying to reach the city of his birth. The Martian was driven by some secret demon. He was afraid to die before he reached Kushat.

And now he had no choice.

'I have sinned, Stark. I have stolen a holy thing. You're an outlander, you would not know of Ban Cruach, and the talisman that he left when he went away forever beyond the Gates of Death.'

Camar flung aside the blankets and sat up, his voice gaining a febrile strength.

'I was born and bred in the Thieves' Quarter under the Wall. I was proud of my skill. And the talisman was a challenge. It was a treasured thing – so treasured that hardly a man has touched it since the days of Ban Cruach who made it. And that was in the days when men still had the lustre on them, before they forgot that they were gods.

'"Guard well the Gates of Death," he said, "that is the city's trust. And keep the talisman always, for the day may come when you will need its strength. Who holds Kushat holds Mars – and the talisman will keep the city safe."

'I was a thief, and proud. And I stole the talisman.'

His hands went to his girdle, a belt of worn leather with a boss of battered steel. But his fingers were already numb.

'Take it, Stark. Open the boss – there, on the side, where the beast's head is carved ...'

Stark took the belt from Camar and found the hidden spring.

The rounded top of the boss came free. Inside it was something wrapped in a scrap of silk.

'I had to leave Kushat,' Camar whispered. 'I could never go back. But it was enough – to have taken that.'

He watched, shaken between awe and pride and remorse, as Stark unwrapped the bit of silk.

Stark had discounted most of Camar's talk as superstition, but even so he had expected something more spectacular than the object he held in his palm.

It was a lens, some four inches across – man-made, and made with great skill, but still only a bit of crystal. Turning it about, Stark saw that it was not a simple lens, but an intricate interlocking of many facets. Incredibly complicated, hypnotic if one looked at it too long.

'What is its use?' he asked of Camar.

'We are as children. We have forgotten. But there is a legend, a belief – that Ban Cruach himself made the talisman as a sign that he would not forget us, and would come back when Kushat is threatened. Back through the Dates of Death, to teach us again the power that was his!'

'I do not understand,' said Stark. 'What are the Gates of Death?'

Camar answered, 'It is a pass that opens into the black mountains beyond Kushat. The city stands guard before it – why, no man remembers, except that it is a great trust.'

His gaze feasted on the talisman.

Stark said, 'You wish me to take this to Kushat?'

'Yes. Yes! And yet …' Camar looked at Stark, his eyes filling suddenly with tears. 'No. The North is not used to strangers. With me, you might have been safe. But alone … No, Stark. You have risked too much already. Go back, out of the Norlands, while you can.'

He lay back on the blankets. Stark saw that a bluish pallor had come into the hollows of his cheeks.

'Camar,' he said. And again, 'Camar!'

'Yes?'

'Go in peace, Camar. I will take the talisman to Kushat.'

The Martian sighed, and smiled, and Stark was glad that he had made the promise.

'The riders of Mekh are wolves,' said Camar suddenly. 'They hunt these gorges. Look out for them.'

'I will.'

Stark's knowledge of the geography of this part of Mars was vague indeed, but he knew that the mountain valleys of Mekh lay ahead and to the north, between him and Kushat. Camar had told him of these upland warriors. He was willing to heed the warning.

Camar had done with talking. Stark knew that he had not long to wait. The wind spoke with the voice of a great organ. The moons had set and it was very dark outside the tower, except for the white glimmering of the snow. Stark looked up at the brooding walls, and shivered. There was a smell of death already in the air.

To keep from thinking, he bent closer to the fire, studying the lens. There were scratches on the bezel, as though it had been held sometime in a clamp, or setting, like a jewel. An ornament, probably, worn as a badge of rank. Strange ornament for a barbarian king, in the dawn of Mars. The firelight made tiny dancing sparks in the endless inner facets. Quite suddenly, he had a curious feeling that the thing was alive.

A pang of primitive and unreasoning fear shot through him, and he fought it down. His vision was beginning to blur, and he shut his eyes, and in the darkness it seemed to him that he could see and hear ...

He started up, shaken now with an eerie terror, and raised his hand to hurl the talisman away. But the part of him that had learned with much pain and effort to be civilised made him stop, and think.

He sat down again. An instrument of hypnosis? Possibly. And yet that fleeting touch of sight and sound had not been his own, out of his own memories.

He was tempted now, fascinated, like a child that plays with fire. The talisman had been worn somehow. Where? On the breast? On the brow?

He tried the first, with no result. Then he touched the flat surface of the lens to his forehead.

The great tower of stone rose up monstrous to the sky. It was whole, and there were pallid lights within that stirred and flickered, and it was crowned with a shimmering darkness.

He lay outside the tower, on his belly, and he was filled with fear and a great anger, and a loathing such as turns the bones to water. There was no snow. There was ice everywhere, rising to half the tower's height, sheathing the ground.

Ice. Cold and clear and beautiful – and deadly.

He moved. He glided snakelike, with infinite caution, over the smooth surface. The tower was gone, and far below him was a city. He saw the temples and the palaces, the glittering lovely city beneath him in the ice, blurred and fairylike and strange, a dream half glimpsed through crystal.

He saw the Ones that lived there, moving slowly through the streets. He could not see them clearly, only the vague shining of their bodies, and he was glad.

He hated them, with a hatred that conquered even his fear, which was great indeed.

He was not Eric John Stark. He was Ban Cruach.

The tower and the city vanished, swept away on a reeling tide.

He stood beneath a scarp of black rock, notched with a single pass. The cliffs hung over him, leaning out their vast bulk as though to crush him, and the narrow mouth of the pass was full of evil laughter where the wind went by.

He began to walk forward, into the pass. He was quite alone.

The light was dim and strange at the bottom of that cleft. Little veils of mist crept and clung between the ice and the rock, thickened, became more dense as he went farther and farther into the pass. He could not see, and the wind spoke with many tongues, piping in the crevices of the cliffs.

All at once there was a shadow in the mist before him, a dim gigantic shape that moved toward him, and he knew that he looked at death. He cried out ...

It was Stark who yelled in blind atavistic fear, and the echo of his own cry brought him up, standing, shaking in every limb.

He had dropped the talisman. It lay gleaming in the snow at his feet, and the alien memories were gone – and Camar was dead.

After a time he crouched down, breathing harshly. He did not want to touch the lens again. The part of him that had learned to fear strange gods and evil spirits with every step he took, the primitive aboriginal that lay so close under the surface of his mind, warned him to leave it, to run away, to desert this place of death and ruined stone.

He forced himself to take it up. He did not look at it. He wrapped it in the bit of silk and replaced it inside the iron boss, and clasped the belt around his waist. Then he found the small flask that lay with his gear beside the fire and took a long pull, and tried to think rationally of the thing that had happened.

Memories. Not his own, but the memories of Ban Cruach, a million years ago in the morning of a world. Memories of hate, a secret war against unhuman beings that dwelt in crystal cities cut in the living ice, and used these ruined towers for some dark purpose of their own.

Was that the meaning of the talisman, the power that lay within it? Had Ban Cruach, by some elder and forgotten science, imprisoned the echoes of his own mind in the crystal?

Why? Perhaps as a warning, as a reminder of ageless, alien danger beyond the Gates of Death?

Suddenly one of the beasts tethered outside the ruined tower started up from its sleep with a hissing snarl.

Instantly Stark became motionless.

They came silently on their padded feet, the rangy mountain brutes moving daintily through the sprawling ruin. Their riders too were silent – tall men with fierce eyes and russet hair, wearing leather coats and carrying each a long, straight spear.

There were a score of them around the tower in the windy gloom. Stark did not bother to draw his gun. He had learned very young the difference between courage and idiocy.

He walked out toward them, slowly lest one of them be startled into spearing him, yet not slowly enough to denote fear. And he held up his right hand and gave them greeting.

They did not answer him. They sat their restive mounts and

stared at him, and Stark knew that Camar had spoken the truth. These were the riders of Mekh, and they were wolves.

2

Stark waited, until they should tire of their own silence.

Finally one demanded, 'Of what country are you?'

He answered, 'I am called N'Chaka, the Man-Without-a-Tribe.'

It was the name they had given him, the half-human aboriginals who had raised him the blaze and thunder and bitter frosts of Mercury.

'A stranger,' said the leader, and smiled. He pointed at the dead Camar and asked, 'Did you slay him?'

'He was my friend,' said Stark, 'I was bringing him home to die.'

Two riders dismounted to inspect the body. One called up to the leader, 'He was from Kushat, if I know the breed, Thord! And he has not been robbed.' He proceeded to take care of that detail himself.

'A stranger,' repeated the leader, Thord. 'Bound for Kushat, with a man of Kushat. Well. I think you will come with us, stranger.'

Stark shrugged. And with the long spears pricking him, he did not resist when the tall Thord plundered him of all he owned except his clothes – and Camar's belt, which was not worth the stealing. His gun Thord flung contemptuously away.

One of the men brought Stark's beast and Camar's from where they were tethered, and the Earthman mounted – as usual, over the violent protest of the creature, which did not like the smell of him. They moved out from under the shelter of the walls, into the full fury of the wind.

For the rest of that night, and through the next day and the night that followed it they rode eastward, stopping only to rest the beasts and chew on their rations of jerked meat.

To Stark, riding a prisoner, it came with full force that this was the North country, half a world away from the Mars of spaceships and commerce and visitors from other planets. The future had never touched these wild mountains and barren plains. The past held pride enough.

To the north, the horizon showed a strange and ghostly glimmer where the barrier wall of the polar pack reared up, gigantic against the sky. The wind blew, down from the ice, through the mountain gorges, across the plains, never ceasing. And here and there the cryptic towers rose, broken monoliths of stone. Stark remembered the vision of the talisman, the huge structure crowned with eerie darkness. He looked upon the ruins with loathing and curiosity. The men of Mekh could tell him nothing.

Thord did not tell Stark where they were taking him, and Stark did not ask. It would have been an admission of fear.

In mid-afternoon of the second day they came to a lip of rock where the snow was swept clean, and below it was a sheer drop into a narrow valley. Looking down, Stark saw that on the floor of the valley, up and down as far as he could see, were men and beasts and shelters of hide and brush, and fires burning. By the hundreds, by the several thousand, they camped under the cliffs, and their voices rose up on the thin air in a vast deep murmur that was deafening after the silence of the plains.

A war party, gathered now, before the thaw. Stark smiled. He became curious to meet the leader of this army.

They found their way single file along a winding track that dropped down the cliff face. The wind stopped abruptly, cut off by the valley walls. They came in among the shelters of the camp.

Here the snow was churned and soiled and melted to slush by the fires. There were no women in the camp, no sign of the usual cheerful rabble that follows a barbarian army. There were only men – hillmen and warriors all, tough-handed killers with no thought but battle.

They came out of their holes to shout at Thord and his men, and stare at the stranger. Thord was flushed and jovial with importance.

'I have no time for you,' he shouted back. 'I go to speak with the Lord Ciaran.'

Stark rode impassively, a dark giant with a face of stone. From time to time he made his beast curvet, and laughed at himself inwardly for doing it.

They came at length to a shelter larger than the others, but built exactly the same and no more comfortable. A spear was thrust into the snow beside the entrance, and from it hung a black pennant with a single bar of silver across it, like lightning in a night sky. Beside it was a shield with the same device. There were no guards.

Thord dismounted, bidding Stark to do the same. He hammered on the shield with the hilt of his sword, announcing himself.

'Lord Ciaran! It is Thord – with a captive.'

A voice, toneless and strangely muffled, spoke from within.

'Enter, Thord.'

Thord pushed aside the hide curtain and went in, with Stark at his heels.

The dim daylight did not penetrate the interior. Cressets burned, giving off a flickering brilliance and a smell of strong oil. The floor of packed snow was carpeted with furs, much worn. Otherwise there was no adornment, and no furniture but a chair and a table, both dark with age and use, and a pallet of skins in one shadowy corner with what seemed to be a heap of rags upon it.

In the chair sat a man.

He seemed very tall, in the shaking light of the cressets. From neck to thigh his lean body was cased in black link mail, and under that a tunic of leather, dyed black. Across his knees he held a sable axe, a great thing made for the shearing of skulls, and his hands lay upon it gently, as though it were a toy he loved.

His head and face were covered by a thing that Stark had seen before only in very old paintings – the ancient war-mask of the inland Kings of Mars. Wrought of black and gleaming steel, it presented an unhuman visage of slitted eyeholes and a barred slot for breathing. Behind, it sprang out in a thin, soaring sweep, like a dark wing edge-on in flight.

The intent, expressionless scrutiny of that mask was bent, not upon Thord, but upon Eric John Stark.

The hollow voice spoke again, from behind the mask. 'Well?'

'We were hunting in the gorges to the south,' said Thord. 'We saw a fire ...' He told the story, of how they had found the stranger and the body of the man from Kushat.

'Kushat!' said the Lord Ciaran softly. 'Ah! And why, stranger, were you going to Kushat?'

'My name is Stark. Eric John Stark, Earthman, out of Mercury.' He was tired of being called stranger. Quite suddenly, he was tired of the whole business.

'Why should I not go to Kushat? Is it against some law, that a man may not go over in peace without being hounded all over the Norlands? And why do the men of Mekh make it their business? They have nothing to do with the city.'

Thord held his breath, watching with delighted anticipation.

The hands of the man in armour caressed the axe. They were slender hands, smooth and sinewy – small hands, it seemed, for such a weapon.

'We make what we will our business, Eric John Stark.' He spoke with a peculiar gentleness. 'I have asked you. Why were you going to Kushat?'

'Because,' Stark answered with equal restraint, 'my comrade wanted to go home to die.'

'It seems a long, hard journey, just for dying.' The black helm bent forward, in an attitude of thought. 'Only the condemned or banished leave their cities, or their clans. Why did your comrade flee Kushat?'

A voice spoke suddenly from out of the heap of rags that lay on the pallet in the shadows of the corner. A man's voice, deep and husky, with the harsh quaver of age or madness in it.

'Three men beside myself have fled Kushat, over the years that matter. One died in the spring floods. One was caught in the moving ice of winter. One lived. A thief named Camar, who stole a certain talisman.'

Stark said, 'My comrade was called Greshi.' The leather belt weighed heavy about him, and the iron boss seemed hot against his belly. He was beginning, now, to be afraid.

*

The Lord Ciaran spoke, ignoring Stark. 'It was the sacred talisman of Kushat. Without it, the city is like a man without a soul.'

As the Veil of Tanit was to Carthage, Stark thought, and reflected on the fate of that city after the Veil was stolen.

'The nobles were afraid of their own people,' the man in armour said. 'They did not dare to tell that it was gone. But we know.'

'And,' said Stark, 'you will attack Kushat before the thaw, when they least expect you.'

'You have a sharp mind, stranger. Yes. But the great wall will be hard to carry, even so. If I came, bearing in *my* hands the talisman of Ban Cruach …'

He did not finish, but turned instead to Thord. 'When you plundered the dead man's body, what did you find?'

'Nothing, Lord. A few coins, a knife, hardly worth the taking.'

'And you, Eric John Stark. What did you take from the body?'

With perfect truth he answered, 'Nothing.'

'Thord,' said the Lord Ciaran, 'search him.'

Thord came smiling up to Stark and ripped his jacket open.

With uncanny swiftness, the Earthman moved. The edge of one broad hand took Thord under the ear, and before the man's knees had time to sag Stark had caught his arm. He turned, crouching forward, and pitched Thord through the door flap.

He straightened and turned again. His eyes held a feral glint. 'The man has robbed me once,' he said. 'It is enough.'

He heard Thord's men coming. Three of them tried to jam through the entrance at once, and he sprang at them. He made no sound. His fists did the talking for him, and then his feet, as he kicked the stunned barbarians back upon their leader.

'Now,' he said to the Lord Ciaran, 'will we talk as men?'

The man in armour laughed, a sound of pure enjoyment. It seemed that the gaze behind the mask studied Stark's savage face, and then lifted to greet the sullen Thord who came back into the shelter, his cheeks flushed crimson with rage.

'Go,' said the Lord Ciaran. 'The stranger and I will talk.'

'But Lord,' he protested, glaring at Stark, 'it is not safe ...'

'My dark mistress looks after my safety,' said Ciaran, stroking the axe across his knees. 'Go.'

Thord went.

The man in armour was silent then, the blind mask turned to Stark, who met that eyeless gaze and was silent also. And the bundle of rags in the shadows straightened slowly and became a tall old man with rusty hair and beard, through which peered craggy juts of bone and two bright, small points of fire, as though some wicked flame burned within him.

He shuffled over and crouched at the feet of the Lord Ciaran, watching the Earthman. And the man in armour leaned forward.

'I will tell you something, Eric John Stark. I am a bastard, but I come from the blood of kings. My name and rank I must make with my own hands. But I will set them high, and my name will ring in the Norlands!

'I will take Kushat. Who holds Kushat, holds Mars – and the power and the riches that lie beyond the Gates of Death!'

'I have seen them,' said the old man, and his eyes blazed. 'I have seen the temples and the palaces glitter in the ice. I have seen *Them*, the shining ones. Oh, I have seen them, the beautiful, hideous ones!'

He glanced sidelong at Stark, very cunning. 'That is why Otar is mad, stranger. *He has seen.*'

A chill swept Stark. He too had seen, not with his own eyes but with the mind and memories of Ban Cruach, of a million years ago.

Then it had been no illusion, the fantastic vision opened to him by the talisman now hidden in his belt! If this old madman had seen ...

'What beings lurk beyond the Gates of Death I do not know,' said Ciaran. 'But my dark mistress will test their strength – and I think my red wolves will hunt them down, once they get a smell of plunder.'

'The beautiful, terrible ones,' whispered Otar. 'And oh, the temples and the palaces, and the great towers of stone!'

'Ride with me, Stark,' said the Lord Ciaran abruptly. 'Yield up the talisman, and be the shield at my back. I have offered no other man that honour.'

Stark asked slowly, 'Why do you choose me?'

'We are of one blood, Stark, though we be strangers.'

The Earthman's cold eyes narrowed. 'What would your red wolves say to that? And what would Otar say? Look at him, already stiff with jealousy, and fear lest I answer, "Yes".'

'I do not think you would be afraid of either of them.'

'On the contrary,' said Stark, 'I am a prudent man.' He paused. 'There is one other thing. I will bargain with no man until I have looked into his eyes. Take off your helm, Ciaran – and then perhaps we will talk!'

Otar's breath made a snakelike hissing between his toothless gums, and the hands of the Lord Ciaran tightened on the haft of the axe.

'No!' he whispered. 'That I can never do.'

Otar rose to his feet, and for the first time Stark felt the full strength that lay in this strange old man.

'Would you look upon the face of destruction?' he thundered. 'Do you ask for death? Do you think a thing is hidden behind a mask of steel without a reason, that you demand to see it?'

He turned. 'My Lord,' he said. 'By tomorrow the last of the clans will have joined us. After that, we must march. Give this Earthman to Thord, for the time that remains – and you will have the talisman.'

The blank, blind mask was unmoving, turned toward Stark, and the Earthman thought that from behind it came a faint sound that might have been a sigh.

Then ...

'Thord!' cried the Lord Ciaran, and lifted up the axe.

3

The flames leaped high from the fire in the windless gorge. Men sat around it in a great circle, the wild riders out of the mountain valleys of Mekh. They sat with the curbed and shivering eagerness of wolves around a dying quarry. Now and again their white teeth showed in a kind of silent laughter, and their eyes watched.

'He is strong,' they whispered, one to the other. 'He will live the night out, surely!'

On an outcrop of rock sat the Lord Ciaran, wrapped in a black cloak, holding the great axe in the crook of his arm. Beside him, Otar huddled in the snow.

Close by, the long spears had been driven deep and lashed together to make a scaffolding, and upon this frame was hung a man. A big man, iron-muscled and very lean, the bulk of his shoulders filling the space between the bending shafts. Eric John Stark of Earth, out of Mercury.

He had already been scourged without mercy. He sagged with his own weight between the spears, breathing in harsh sobs, and the trampled snow around him was spotted red.

Thord was wielding the lash. He had stripped off his own coat, and his body glistened with sweat in spite of the cold. He cut his victim with great care, making the long lash sing and crack. He was proud of his skill.

Stark did not cry out.

Presently Thord stepped back, panting, and looked at the Lord Ciaran. And the black helm nodded.

Thord dropped the whip. He went up to the big dark man and lifted his head by the hair.

'Stark,' he said, and shook the head roughly. 'Stranger!'

Eyes opened and stared at him, and Thord could not repress a slight shiver. It seemed that the pain and indignity had wrought some evil magic on this man he had ridden with, and thought he knew. He had seen exactly the same gaze as a big snow-cat caught in a trap, and he felt suddenly that it was not a man he spoke to, but a predatory beast.

'Stark,' he said. 'Where is the talisman of Ban Cruach?'

The Earthman did not answer.

Thord laughed. He glanced up at the sky, where the moons rode low and swift.

'The night is only half gone. Do you think you can last it out?'

The cold, cruel, patient eyes watched Thord. There was no reply.

Some quality of pride in that gaze angered the barbarian. It seemed to mock him, who was so sure of his ability to loosen a reluctant tongue.

'You think I cannot make you talk, don't you? You don't know me, stranger! You don't know Thord, who can make the rocks speak out if he will!'

He reached out with his free hand and struck Stark across the face.

It seemed impossible that anything so still could move so quickly. There was an ugly flash of teeth, and Thord's wrist was caught above the thumb-joint. He bellowed, and the iron jaws closed down, worrying the bone.

Quite suddenly, Thord screamed. Not for pain, but for panic. And the rows of watching men swayed forward, and even the Lord Ciaran rose up, startled.

'*Hark*!' ran the whispering around the fire. 'Hark how he growls!'

Thord had let go of Stark's hair and was beating him about the head with his clenched fist. His face was white.

'Werewolf!' he screamed. 'Let me go, beast-thing! Let me go!'

But the dark man clung to Thord's wrist, snarling, and did not hear. After a bit there came the dull crack of bone.

Stark opened his jaws. Thord ceased to strike him. He backed off slowly, staring at the torn flesh. Stark had sunk down to the length of his arms.

With his left hand, Thord drew his knife. The Lord Ciaran stepped forward. 'Wait, Thord!'

'It is a thing of evil,' whispered the barbarian. 'Warlock. Werewolf. Beast.'

He sprang at Stark.

The man in armour moved, very swiftly, and the great axe went whirling through the air. It caught Thord squarely where the cords of his neck ran into the shoulder – caught, and shore on through.

There was a silence in the valley.

The Lord Ciaran walked slowly across the trampled snow and took up his axe again.

'I will be obeyed,' he said. 'And I will not stand for fear, not of god, man, nor devil.' He gestured toward Stark. 'Cut him down. And see that he does not die.'

He strode away, and Otar began to laugh.

From a vast distance, Stark heard that shrill, wild laughter. His mouth was full of blood, and he was mad with a cold fury.

A cunning that was purely animal guided his movements then. His head fell forward, and his body hung inert against the thongs. He might almost have been dead.

A knot of men came toward him. He listened to them. They were hesitant and afraid. Then, as he did not move, they plucked up courage and came closer, and one prodded him gently with the point of his spear.

'Prick him well,' said another. 'Let us be sure!'

The sharp point bit a little deeper. A few drops of blood welled out and joined the small red streams that ran from the weals of the lash. Stark did not stir.

The spearman grunted. 'He is safe enough now.'

Stark felt the knife blades working at the thongs. He waited. The rawhide snapped, and he was free.

He did not fall. He would not have fallen then if he had taken a death wound. He gathered his legs under him and sprang.

He picked up the spearman in that first rush and flung him into the fire. Then he began to run toward the place where the scaly mounts were herded, leaving a trail of blood behind him on the snow.

A man loomed up in front of him. He saw the shadow of a spear and swerved, and caught the haft in his two hands. He wrenched it free and struck down with the butt of it, and went on. Behind him he heard voices shouting and the beginning of turmoil.

The Lord Ciaran turned and came back, striding fast.

There were men before Stark now, many men, the circle of watchers breaking up because there had been nothing more to watch. He gripped the long spear. It was a good weapon, better than the flint-tipped stick with which the boy N'Chaka had hunted the giant lizard of the rocks.

His body curved into a half crouch. He voiced one cry, the challenging scream of a predatory killer, and went in among the men.

He did slaughter with that spear. They were not expecting attack. They were not expecting anything. Stark had sprung to life too quickly. And they were afraid of him. He could smell the fear on them. Fear not of a man like themselves, but of a creature less and more than man.

He killed, and was happy.

They fell away from him, the wild riders of Mekh. They were sure now that he was a demon. He raged among them with the bright spear, and they heard again that sound that should not have come from a human throat, and their superstitious terror rose and sent them scrambling out of his path, trampling on each other in childish panic.

He broke through, and now there was nothing between him and escape but two mounted men who guarded the herd.

Being mounted, they had more courage. They felt that even a warlock could not stand against their charge. They came at him as he ran, the padded feet of their beasts making a muffled drumming in the snow.

Without breaking stride, Stark hurled his spear.

It drove through one man's body and tumbled him off, so that he fell under his comrade's mount and fouled its legs. It staggered and reared up, hissing, and Stark fled on.

Once he glanced over his shoulder. Through the milling, shouting crowd of men he glimpsed a dark, mailed figure with a winged mask, going through the ruck with a loping stride and bearing a sable axe raised high for the throwing.

Stark was close to the herd now. And they caught his scent.

The Norland brutes had never liked the smell of him, and now the reek of blood upon him was enough in itself to set them wild. They began to hiss and snarl uneasily, rubbing their reptilian flanks together as they wheeled around, staring at him with lambent eyes.

He rushed them, before they could quite decide to break. He was quick enough to catch one by the fleshy comb that served it for a forelock, held it with savage indifference to its squealing, and leaped to its back. Then he let it bolt, and as he rode it he yelled, a shrill brute cry that urged the creatures on to panic.

The herd broke, stampeding outward from its centre like a bursting shell.

Stark was in the forefront. Clinging low to the scaly neck, he saw the men of Mekh scattered and churned and tramped into the snow by the flying pads. In and out of the shelters, kicking the brush walls down, lifting up their harsh reptilian voices, they went racketting through the camp, leaving behind them wreckage as of a storm. And Stark went with them.

He snatched a cloak from off the shoulders of some petty chieftain as he went by, and then, twisting cruelly on the fleshy comb, beating with his fist at the creature's head, he got his mount turned in the way he wanted it to go, down the valley.

He caught one last glimpse of the Lord Ciaran, fighting to hold one of the creatures long enough to mount, and then a dozen striving bodies surged around him, and Stark was gone.

The beast did not slacken pace. It was as though it thought it could outrun the alien, bloody thing that clung to its back. The last fringes of the camp shot by and vanished in the gloom, and the clean snow of the lower valley lay open before it. The creature laid its belly to the ground and went, the white spray spurting from its heels.

Stark hung on. His strength was gone now, run out suddenly with the battle-madness. He became conscious now that he was sick and bleeding, that his body was one cruel pain. In that moment, more than in the hours that had gone before, he hated the black leader of the clans of Mekh.

That flight down the valley became a sort of ugly dream.

Stark was aware of rock walls reeling past, and then they seemed to widen away and the wind came out of nowhere like the stroke of a great hammer, and he was on the open moors again.

The beast began to falter and slow down. Presently it stopped.

Stark scooped up snow to rub on his wounds. He came near to fainting, but the bleeding stopped and after that the pain was numbed to a dull ache. He wrapped the cloak around him and urged the beast to go on, gently this time, patiently, and after it had breathed it obeyed him, settling into the shuffling pace it could keep up for hours.

He was three days on the moors. Part of the time he rode in a sort of stupor, and part of the time he was feverishly alert, watching the skyline. Frequently he took the shapes of thrusting rocks for riders, and found what cover he could until he was sure they did not move. He was afraid to dismount, for the beast had no bridle. When it halted to rest he remained upon its back, shaking, his brow beaded with sweat.

The wind scoured his tracks clean as soon as he made them. Twice, in the distance, he did see riders, and one of those times he burrowed into a tall drift and stayed there for several hours.

The ruined towers marched with him across the bitter land, lonely giants fifty miles apart. He did not go near them.

He knew that he wandered a good bit, but he could not help it, and it was probably his salvation. In those tortured badlands, riven by ages of frost and flood, one might follow a man on a straight track between two points. But to find a single rider lost in that wilderness was a matter of sheer luck, and the odds were with Stark.

One evening at sunset he came out upon a plain that sloped upward to a black and towering scarp, notched with a single pass.

The light was level and blood-red, glittering on the frosty rock so that it seemed the throat of the pass was aflame with evil fires. To Stark's mind, essentially primitive and stripped now of all its acquired reason, that narrow cleft appeared as the doorway to the dwelling place of demons as horrible as the fabled creatures that roamed the Darkside of his native world.

He looked long at the Gates of Death, and a dark memory crept into his brain. Memory of that nightmare experience when the talisman had made him seem to walk into that frightful pass, not as Stark, but as Ban Cruach.

He remembered Otar's words – *I have seen Ban Cruach the mighty*. Was he still there beyond those darkling gates, fighting his unimagined war, alone?

Again, in memory, Stark heard the evil piping of the wind. Again, the shadow of a dim and terrible shape loomed up before him...

He forced remembrance of that vision from his mind, by a great effort. He could not turn back now. There was no place to go.

His weary beast plodded on, and now Stark saw as in a dream that a great walled city stood guard before that awful Gate. He watched the city glide toward him through a crimson haze, and fancied he could see the ages clustered like birds around the towers.

He had reached Kushat, with the talisman of Ban Cruach still strapped in the bloodstained belt around his waist.

4

He stood in a large square, lined about with hucksters' stalls and the booths of wine-sellers. Beyond were buildings, streets, a city. Stark got a blurred impression of a grand and brooding darkness, bulking huge against the mountains, as bleak and proud as they, and quite as ancient, with many ruins and deserted quarters.

He was not sure how he had come there, but he was standing on his own feet, and someone was pouring sour wine into his mouth. He drank it greedily. There were people around him, jostling, chattering, demanding answers to their questions. A girl's voice said sharply, 'Let him be! Can't you see he's hurt?'

Stark looked down. She was slim and ragged, with black hair and large eyes yellow as a cat's. She held a leather bottle in her hands. She smiled at him and said, 'I'm Thanis. Will you drink more wine?'

'I will,' said Stark, and did, and then said, 'Thank you, Thanis.' He put his hand on her shoulder, to steady himself. It was a supple shoulder, surprisingly strong. He liked the feel of it.

The crowd was still churning around him, growing larger, and now he heard the tramp of military feet. A small detachment of men in light armour pushed their way through.

A very young officer whose breastplace hurt the eye with brightness demanded to be told at once who Stark was and why he had come there.

'No one crosses the moors in winter,' he said, as though that in itself were a sign of evil intent.

'The clans of Mekh are crossing them,' Stark answered. 'An army, to take Kushat – one, two days behind me.'

The crowd picked that up. Excited voices tossed it back and forth, and clamoured for more news. Stark spoke to the officer.

'I will see your captain, and at once.'

'You'll see the inside of a prison, more likely!' snapped the young man. 'What's this nonsense about the clans of Mekh?'

Stark regarded him. He looked so long and so curiously that the crowd began to snicker and the officer's beardless face flushed pink to the ears.

'I have fought in many wars,' said Stark gently. 'And long ago I learned to listen, when someone came to warn me of attack.'

'Better take him to the captain, Lugh,' cried Thanis. 'It's our skins too, you know, if there is war.'

The crowd began to shout. They were all poor folk, wrapped in threadbare cloaks or tattered leather. They had no love for the guards. And whether there was war or not, their winter had been long and dull, and they were going to make the most of this excitement.

'Take him, Lugh! Let him warn the nobles. Let them think how they'll defend Kushat and the Gates of Death, now that the talisman is gone!'

'That is a lie!' Lugh shouted. 'And you know the penalty for telling it. Hold your tongues, or I'll have you all whipped.' He gestured angrily at Stark. 'See if he is armed.'

One of the soldiers stepped forward, but Stark was quicker. He slipped the thong and let the cloak fall, baring his upper body.

'The clansmen have already taken everything I owned,' he said. 'But they gave me something in return.'

The crowd stared at the half healed stripes that scarred him, and there was a drawing in of breath.

The soldier picked up the cloak and laid it over the Earthman's shoulders. And Lugh said sullenly, 'Come, then.'

Stark's fingers tightened on Thanis' shoulder. 'Come with me, little one,' he whispered. 'Otherwise, I must crawl.'

She smiled at him and came. The crowd followed.

The captain of the guards was a fleshy man with a smell of wine about him and a face already crumbling apart though his hair was not yet grey. He sat in a squat tower above the square, and he observed Stark with no particular interest.

'You had something to tell,' said Lugh. 'Tell it.'

Stark told them, leaving out all mention of Camar and the talisman. This was neither the time nor the man to hear that story. The captain listened to all he had to say about the gathering clans of Mekh, and then sat studying him with a bleary shrewdness.

'You have proof of all this?'

'These stripes. Their leader Ciaran ordered them laid on himself.'

The captain sighed, and leaned back.

'Any wandering band of hunters could have scourged you,' he said. 'A nameless vagabond from the gods know where, and a lawless one at that, if I'm any judge of men – you probably deserved it.'

He reached for wine, and smiled. 'Look you, stranger. In the Norlands, no one makes war in the winter. And no one ever heard of Ciaran. if you hoped for a reward from the city, you overshot badly.'

'The Lord Ciaran,' said Stark, grimly controlling his anger, 'will be battering at your gates within two days. And you will hear of him then.'

'Perhaps. You can wait for him – in a cell. And you can leave Kushat with the first caravan after the thaw. We have enough rabble here without taking in more.'

Thanis caught Stark by the cloak and held him back.

'*Sir,*' she said, as though it were an unclean word. 'I will vouch for the stranger.'

The captain glanced at her. 'You?'

'Sir, I am a free citizen of Kushat. According to law, I may vouch for him.'

'If you scum of the Thieves' Quarter would practise the law as well as you prate it, we would have less trouble,' growled the captain. 'Very well, take the creature, if you want him. I don't suppose you've anything to lose.'

Lugh laughed.

'Name and dwelling place,' said the captain, and wrote them down. 'Remember, he is not to leave the Quarter.'

Thanis nodded. 'Come,' she said to Stark. He did not move, and she looked up at him. He was staring at the captain. His beard had grown in these last days, and his face was still scarred by Thord's blows and made wolfish with pain and fever. And now, out of this evil mask, his eyes were peering with a chill and terrible intensity at the soft-bellied man who sat and mocked him.

Thanis laid her hand on his rough cheek. 'Come,' she said. 'Come and rest.'

Gently she turned his head. He blinked and swayed, and she took him around the waist and led him unprotesting to the door.

There she paused, looking back.

'Sir,' she said, very meekly, 'news of this attack is being shouted through the Quarter now. If it *should* come, and it were known that you had the warning and did not pass it on …' She made an expressive gesture, and went out.

Lugh glanced uneasily at the captain. 'She's right, sir. If by chance the man did tell the truth …'

The captain swore. 'Rot. A rogue's tale. And yet …' He scowled indecisively, and then reached for parchment. 'After all, it's a simple thing. Write it up, pass it on, and let the nobles do the worrying.'

His pen began to scratch.

Thanis took Stark by steep and narrow ways, darkling now in the afterglow, where the city climbed and fell again over the uneven rock. Stark was aware of the heavy smells of spices and unfamiliar foods, and the musky undertones of a million generations swarmed together to spawn and die in these crowded catacombs of slate and stone.

There was a house, blending into other houses, close under the loom of the great Wall. There was a flight of steps, hollowed deep with use, twisting crazily around outer corners.

There was a low room, and a slender man named Balin, vaguely glimpsed, who said he was Thanis' brother. There was a bed of skins and woven cloths.

Stark slept.

Hands and voices called him back. Strong hands shaking him, urgent voices. He started up growling, like an animal suddenly awaked, still lost in the dark mists of exhaustion. Balin swore and caught his fingers away.

'What is this you have brought home, Thanis? By the gods, it snapped at me!'

Thanis ignored him. 'Stark,' she said. 'Stark! Listen. Men are coming. Soldiers. They will question you. Do you hear me?'

Stark said heavily, 'I hear.'

'*Do not speak of Camar!*'

Stark got to his feet, and Balin said hastily, 'Peace! The thing is safe. I would not steal a death warrant!'

His voice had a ring of truth. Stark sat down again. It was an effort to keep awake. There was clamour in the street below. It was still night.

Balin said carefully, 'Tell them what you told the captain, nothing more. They will kill you if they know.'

A rough hand thundered at the door, and a voice cried, 'Open up!'

Balin sauntered over to lift the bar. Thanis sat beside Stark, her hand touching his. Stark rubbed his face. He had been shaved and washed, his wounds rubbed with salve. The belt was gone, and his bloodstained clothing. He realised only then that he was naked, and drew a cloth around him. Thanis whispered, 'The belt is there on that peg, under your cloak.'

Balin opened the door, and the room was full of men.

Stark recognised the captain. There were others, four of them, young, old, intermediate, annoyed at being hauled away from their beds and their gaming tables at this hour. The sixth man wore the jewelled cuirass of a noble. He had a nice, a kind face. Grey hair, mild eyes, soft cheeks. A fine man, but ludicrous in the trappings of a soldier.

'Is this the man?' he asked, and the captain nodded.

'Yes.' It was his turn to say Sir.

Balin brought a chair. He had a fine flourish about him. He wore a crimson jewel in his left ear, and every line of him was quick and sensitive, instinct with mockery. His eyes were brightly cynical, in a face worn lean with years of merry sinning. Stark liked him.

He was a civilised man. They all were – the noble, the captain, the lot of them. So civilised that the origins of their culture were forgotten half an age before the first clay brick was laid in Babylon.

Too civilised, Stark thought. Peace had drawn their fangs and cut their claws. He thought of the wild clansmen coming fast across the snow, and felt a certain pity for the men of Kushat.

The noble sat down.

'This is a strange tale you bring, wanderer. I would hear it from your own lips.'

Stark told it. He spoke slowly, watching every word, cursing the weariness that fogged his brain.

The noble, who was called Rogain, asked him questions. Where was the camp? How many men? What were the exact words of the Lord Ciaran, and who was he?

Stark answered, with meticulous care.

Rogain sat for some time lost in thought. He seemed worried and upset, one hand playing aimlessly with the hilt of his sword. A scholar's hand, without a callus on it.

'There is one thing more,' said Rogain. 'What business had you on the moors in winter?'

Stark smiled. 'I am a wanderer by profession.'

'Outlaw?' asked the captain, and Stark shrugged.

'Mercenary is a kinder word.'

Rogain studied the pattern of stripes on the Earthman's dark skin. 'Why did the Lord Ciaran, so-called, order you scourged?'

'I had thrashed one of his chieftains.'

Rogain sighed and rose. He stood regarding Stark from under brooding brows, and at length he said, 'It is a wild tale. I can't believe it – and yet, why should you lie?'

He paused, as though hoping that Stark would answer that and relieve him of worry.

Stark yawned. 'The tale is easily proved. Wait a day or two.'

'I will arm the city,' said Rogain. 'I dare not do otherwise. But I will tell you this.' An astonishing unpleasant look came into his eyes. 'If the attack does not come – if you have set a whole city by the ears for nothing – I will have you flayed alive and your body tumbled over the Wall for the carrion birds to feed on.'

He strode out, taking his retinue with him. Balin smiled. 'He will do it, too,' he said, and dropped the bar.

Stark did not answer. He stared at Balin, and then at Thanis, and then at the belt hanging on the peg, in a curiously blank and yet penetrating fashion, like an animal that thinks its own thoughts. He took a deep breath. Then, as though he found the air clean of danger, he rolled over and went instantly to sleep.

Balin lifted his shoulders expressively. He grinned at Thanis. 'Are you positive it's human?'

'He's beautiful,' said Thanis, and tucked the cloths around him. 'Hold your tongue.' She continued to sit there, watching Stark's face as the slow dreams moved across it. Balin laughed.

It was evening again when Stark awoke. He sat up, stretching lazily. Thanis crouched by the hearthstone, stirring something savoury in a blackened pot. She wore a red kirtle and a necklet of beaten gold, and her hair was combed out smooth and shining.

She smiled at him and rose, bringing him his own boots and

trousers, carefully cleaned, and a tunic of leather tanned fine and soft as silk. Stark asked her where she got it.

'Balin stole it – from the baths where the nobles go. He said you might as well have the best.' She laughed. 'He had a devil of a time finding one big enough to fit you.'

She watched with unashamed interest while he dressed. Stark said, 'Don't burn the soup.'

She put her tongue out at him. 'Better be proud of that fine hide while you have it,' she said. 'There's no sign of attack.'

Stark was aware of sounds that had not been there before – the pacing of men on the Wall above the house, the calling of the watch. Kushat was armed and ready – and his time was running out. He hoped that Ciaran had not been delayed on the moors.

Thanis said, 'I should explain about the belt. When Balin undressed you, he saw Camar's name scratched on the inside of the boss. And, he can open a lizard's egg without harming the shell.'

'What about you?' asked Stark.

She flexed her supple fingers. 'I do well enough.'

Balin came in. He had been seeking news, but there was little to be had.

'The soldiers are grumbling about a false alarm,' he said. 'The people are excited, but more as though they were playing a game. Kushat has not fought a war for centuries.' He sighed. 'The pity of it is, Stark, I believe your story. And I'm afraid.'

Thanis handed him a steaming bowl. 'Here – employ your tongue with this. Afraid, indeed! Have you forgotten the Wall? No one has carried it since the city was built. Let them attack!'

Stark was amused. 'For a child, you know much concerning war.'

'I knew enough to save your skin!' she flared, and Balin smiled.

'She has you there, Stark. And speaking of skins ...' He glanced up at the belt. 'Or better, speaking of talismans, which we were not. How did you come by it?'

Stark told him. 'He had a sin on his soul, did Camar. And – he was my friend.'

Balin looked at him with deep respect. 'You were a fool,' he said. 'Look you. The thing is returned to Kushat. Your promise is kept. There is nothing for you here but danger, and were I you I would not wait to be flayed, or slain, or taken in a quarrel that is not yours.'

'Ah,' said Stark softly, 'but it is mine. The Lord Ciaran made it so.' He, too, glanced at the belt. 'What of the talisman?'

'Return it where it came from,' Thanis said. 'My brother is a better thief than Camar. He can certainly do that.'

'No!' said Balin, with surprising force. 'We will keep it, Stark and I. Whether it has power, I do not know. But if it has – I think Kushat will need it, and in strong hands.'

Stark said sombrely, 'It has power, the Talisman. Whether for good or evil, I don't know.

They looked at him, startled. But a touch of awe seemed to repress their curiosity.

He could not tell them. He was, somehow, reluctant to tell anyone of that dark vision of what lay beyond the Gates of Death, which the talisman of Ban Cruach had lent him.

Balin stood up. 'Well, for good or evil, at least the sacred relic of Ban Cruach has come home.' He yawned. 'I am going to bed. Will you come, Thanis, or will you stay and quarrel with our guest?'

'I will stay,' she said, 'and quarrel.'

'Ah, well.' Balin sighed puckishly. 'Good night.' He vanished into an inner room. Stark looked at Thanis. She had a warm mouth, and her eyes were beautiful, and full of light.

He smiled, holding out his hand.

The night wore on, and Stark lay drowsing. Thanis had opened the curtains. Wind and moonlight swept together into the room, and she stood leaning upon the sill, above the slumbering city. The smile that lingered in the corners of her mouth was sad and far-away, and very tender.

Stark stirred uneasily, making small sounds in his throat. His motions grew violent. Thanis crossed the room and touched him.

Instantly he was awake.

'Animal,' she said softly. 'You dream.'

Stark shook his head. His eyes were still clouded, though not with sleep. 'Blood,' he said, 'heavy in the wind.'

'I smell nothing but the dawn,' she said, and laughed.

Stark rose. 'Get Balin. I'm going up on the Wall.'

She did not know him now. 'What is it, Stark? What's wrong?'

'Get Balin.' Suddenly it seemed that the room stifled him. He caught up his cloak and Camar's belt and flung open the door, standing on the narrow steps outside. The moonlight caught in his eyes, pale as frost-fire.

Thanis shivered. Balin joined her without being called. He, too, had slept but lightly. Together they followed Stark up the rough-cut stair that led to the top of the Wall.

He looked southward, where the plain ran down from the mountains and spread away below Kushat. Nothing moved out there. Nothing marred the empty whiteness. But Stark said,

'They will attack at dawn.'

5

They waited. Some distance away a guard leaned against the parapet, huddled in his cloak. He glanced at them incuriously. It was bitterly cold. The wind came whistling down through the Gates of Death, and below in the streets the watchfires shuddered and flared.

They waited, and still there was nothing.

Balin said impatiently, 'How can you know they're coming?'

Stark shivered, a shallow rippling of the flesh that had nothing to do with cold, and every muscle of his body came alive. Phobos plunged downward. The moonlight dimmed and changed, and the plain was very empty, very still.

'They will wait for darkness. They will have an hour or so, between moonset and dawn.'

Thanis muttered, 'Dreams! Besides, I'm cold.' She hesitated, and then crept in under Balin's cloak. Stark had gone away from her. She watched him sulkily where he leaned upon the stone. He might have been part of it, as dark and unstirring.

Deimos sank low toward the west.

Stark turned his head, drawn inevitably to look toward the cliffs above Kushat, soaring upward to blot out half the sky. Here, close under them, they seemed to tower outward in a curving mass, like the last wave of eternity rolling down, crested white with the ash of shattered worlds.

I have stood beneath those cliffs before. I have felt them leaning down to crush me, and I have been afraid.

He was still afraid. The mind that had poured its memories into that crystal lens had been dead a million years, but neither time nor death had dulled the terror that beset Ban Cruach in his journey through that nightmare pass.

He looked into the black and narrow mouth of the Gates of Death, cleaving the scarp like a wound, and the primitive ape-thing within him cringed and moaned, oppressed with a sudden sense of fate.

He had come painfully across half a world, to crouch before the Gates of Death. Some evil magic had let him see forbidden things, had linked his mind in an unholy bond with the long-dead mind of one who had been half a god. These evil miracles had not been for nothing. He would not be allowed to go unscathed.

He drew himself up sharply then, and swore. He had left N'Chaka behind, a naked boy running in a place of rocks and sun on Mercury. He had become Eric John Stark, a man, and civilised. He thrust the senseless premonition from him, and turned his back upon the mountains.

Deimos touched the horizon. A last gleam of reddish light tinged the snow, and then was gone.

Thanis, who was half asleep, said with sudden irritation, 'I do not believe in your barbarians. I'm going home.' She thrust Balin aside and went away, down the steps.

The plain was now in utter darkness, under the faint, far Northern stars.

Stark settled himself against the parapet. There was a sort of timeless patience about him. Balin envied it. He would have liked to go with Thanis. He was cold and doubtful, but he stayed.

Time passed, endless minutes of it, lengthening into what seemed hours.

Stark said, 'Can you hear them?'

'No.'

'They come.' His hearing, far keener than Balin's, picked up the little sounds, the vast inchoate rustling of an army on the move in stealth and darkness. Light-armed men, hunters, used to stalking wild beasts in the show. They could move softly, very softly.

'I hear nothing,' Balin said, and again they waited.

The westering stars moved toward the horizon, and at length in the east a dim pallor crept across the sky.

The plain was still shrouded in night, but now Stark could make out the high towers of the King City of Kushat, ghostly and indistinct – the ancient, proud high towers of the rulers and their nobles, set above the crowded Quarters of merchants and artisans and thieves. He wondered who would be king in Kushat by the time this unrisen sun had set.

'You were wrong,' said Balin, peering. 'There is nothing on the plain.'

Stark said, 'Wait.'

Swiftly now, in the thin air of Mars, the dawn came with a rush and a leap, flooding the world with harsh light. It flashed in cruel brilliance from swordblades, from spearheads, from helmets and beasts, glistened on bare russet heads and coats of leather, set the banners of the clans to burning, crimson and gold and green, bright against the snow.

There was no sound, not a whisper, in all the land.

Somewhere a hunting horn sent forth one deep cry to split the morning. Then burst out the wild skirling of the mountain pipes and the broken thunder of drums, and a wordless scream of exultation that rang back from the Wall of Kushat like the very voice of battle. The men of Mekh began to move.

Raggedly, slowly at first, then more swiftly as the press of warriors broke and flowed, the barbarians swept toward the city as water sweeps over a broken dam.

Knots and clumps of men, tall men running like deer, leaping, shouting, swinging their great brands. Riders, spurring their mounts until they fled belly down. Spears, axes, swordblades tossing, a sea of men and beasts, rushing, trampling, shaking the ground with the thunder of their going.

And ahead of them all came a solitary figure in black mail, riding a raking beast trapped all in black, and bearing a sable axe.

Kushat came to life. There was a swarming and a yelling in the streets, and soldiers began to pour up onto the Wall. A thin company, Stark thought, and shook his head. Mobs of citizens choked the alleys, and every rooftop was full. A troop of nobles went by, brave in their bright mail, to take up their post in the square by the great gate.

Balin said nothing, and Stark did not disturb his thoughts. From the look of him, they were dark indeed.

Soldiers came and ordered them off the Wall. They went back to their own roof, where they were joined by Thanis. She was in a high state of excitement, but unafraid.

'Let them attack!' she said. 'Let them break their spears against the Wall. They will crawl away again.'

Stark began to grow restless. Up in their high emplacements, the big ballistas creaked and thrummed. The muted song of the bows became a wailing hum. Men fell, and were kicked off the ledges by their fellows. The blood-howl of the clans rang unceasing on the frosty air, and Stark heard the rap of scaling ladders against stone.

Thanis said abruptly. 'What is that – that sound like thunder?'

'Rams,' he answered. 'They are battering the gate.'

She listened, and Stark saw in her face the beginning of fear.

It was a long fight. Stark watched it hungrily from the roof all that morning. The soldiers of Kushat did bravely and well, but they were as folded sheep against the tall killers of the mountains. By noon the officers were beating the Quarters for men to replace the slain.

Stark and Balin went up again, onto the Wall.

The clans had suffered. Their dead lay in windrows under the Wall, amid the broken ladders. But Stark knew his barbarians. They had sat restless and chafing in the valley for many days, and now the battle-madness was on them and they were not going to be stopped.

Wave after wave of them rolled up, and was cast back, and came on again relentlessly. The intermittent thunder boomed still from the gates, where sweating giants swung the rams under cover of their own bowmen. And everywhere, up and down through the forefront of the fighting, rode the man in black armour, and wild cheering followed him.

Balin said heavily, 'It is the end of Kushat.'

A ladder banged against the stones a few feet away. Men swarmed up the rungs, fierce-eyed clansmen with laughter in their mouths. Stark was first at the head.

They had given him a spear. He spitted two men through with it and lost it, and a third man came leaping over the parapet. Stark received him into his arms.

Balin watched. He saw the warrior go crashing back, sweeping his fellows off the ladder. He saw Stark's face. He heard the sounds and smelled the blood and sweat of war, and he was sick to the marrow of his bones, and his hatred of the barbarians was a terrible thing.

Stark caught up a dead man's blade, and within ten minutes his arm was as red as a butcher's. And ever he watched the winged helm that went back and forth below, a standard to the clans.

By mid-afternoon the barbarians had gained the Wall in three places. They spread inward along the ledges, pouring up in a resistless tide, and the defenders broke. The rout became a panic.

'It's all over now,' Stark said. 'Find Thanis, and hide her.'

Balin let fall his sword. 'Give me the talisman,' he whispered, and Stark saw that he was weeping. 'Give it me, and I will go beyond the Gates of Death and rouse Ban Cruach from his sleep. And if he has forgotten Kushat, I will take his power into my own hands. I will fling wide the Gates of Death and loose destruction on the men of Mekh – or if the legends are all lies, then I will die.'

He was like a man crazed. 'Give me the talisman!'

Stark slapped him, carefully and without heat, across the face.

'Get your sister, Balin. Hide her, unless you would be uncle to a red-haired brat.'

He went then, like a man who has been stunned. Screaming women with their children clogged the ways that led inward from the Wall, and there was bloody work afoot on the rooftops and in the narrow alleys.

The gate was holding, still.

Stark forced his way toward the square. The booths of the hucksters were overthrown, the wine-jars broken and the red wine spilled. Beasts squealed and stamped, tired of their chafing harness, driven wild by the shouting and the smell of blood. The dead were heaped high where they had fallen from above.

They were all soldiers here, clinging grimly to their last foothold. The deep song of the rams shook the very stones. The iron-sheathed timbers of the gate gave back an answering scream, and toward the end all other sounds grew hushed. The nobles came down slowly from the Wall and mounted, and sat waiting.

There were fewer of them now. Their bright armour was dented and stained, and their faces had a pallor on them.

One last hammer-stroke of the rams.

With a bitter shriek the weakened bolts tore out, and the great gate was broken through.

The nobles of Kushat made their first, and final charge.

As soldiers they went up against the riders of Mekh, and as soldiers they held them until they died. Those that were left were borne back into the square, caught as in the crest of an avalanche. And first through the gates came the winged battle-mask of the Lord Ciaran, and the sable axe that drank men's lives where it hewed.

There was a beast with no rider to claim it, tugging at its headrope. Stark swung onto the saddle pad and cut it free. Where the press was thickest, a welter of struggling brutes and men fighting knee to knee, there was the man in black armour, riding like a god, magnificent, born to war. Stark's eyes shone with a strange, cold light. He struck his heels hard into the scaly flanks. The beast plunged forward.

In and over and through, making the long sword sing. The beast was strong, and frightened beyond fear. It bit and trampled, and Stark cut a path for them, and presently he shouted above the din,

'Ho, there! *Ciaran!*'

The black mask turned toward him, and the remembered voice spoke from behind the barred slot, joyously.

'The wanderer. The wild man!'

Their two mounts shocked together. The axe came down in a whistling curve, and a red swordblade flashed to meet it. Swift, swift, a ringing clash of steel, and the blade was shattered and the axe fallen to the ground.

Stark pressed in.

Ciaran reached for his sword, but his hand was numbed by the force of that blow and he was slow, a split second. The hilt of Stark's weapon, still clutched in his own numbed grip, fetched him a stunning blow on the helm, so that the metal rang like a flawed bell.

The Lord Ciaran reeled back, only for a moment, but long enough. Stark grasped the war-mask and ripped it off, and got his hands around the naked throat.

He did not break that neck, as he had planned. And the Clansmen who had started in to save their leader stopped and did not move.

Stark knew now why the Lord Ciaran had never shown his face.

The throat he held was white and strong, and his hands around it were buried in a mane of red-gold hair that fell down over the shirt of mail. A red mouth passionate with fury, wonderful curving bone under sculptured flesh, eyes fierce and proud and tameless as the eyes of a young eagle, fire-blue, defying him, hating him ...

'By the gods,' said Stark, very softly. 'By the eternal gods!'

6

A woman! And in that moment of amazement, she was quicker than he.

There was nothing to warn him, no least flicker of expression. Her two fists came up together between his outstretched arms and caught him under the jaw with a force that nearly snapped his neck. He went over backward, clean out of the saddle, and lay sprawled on the bloody stones, half stunned, the wind knocked out of him.

The woman wheeled her mount. Bending low, she took up the axe from where it had fallen, and faced her warriors, who were as dazed as Stark.

'I have led you well,' she said. 'I have taken you Kushat. Will any man dispute me?'

They knew the axe, if they did not know her. They looked from side to side uneasily, completely at a loss, and Stark, still gasping on the ground, thought that he had never seen anything as proud and beautiful as she was then in her black mail, with her bright hair blowing and her glance like blue lightning.

The nobles of Kushat chose that moment to charge. This strange unmasking of the Mekhish lord had given them time to rally, and now they thought that the Gods had wrought a miracle to help them. They found hope, where they had lost everything but courage.

'A wench!' they cried. 'A strumpet of the camps. *A woman!*'

They howled it like an epithet, and tore into the barbarians.

She who had been the Lord Ciaran drove the spurs in deep, so that the beast leaped forward screaming. She went, and did not look to see if any had followed, in among the men of Kushat. And the great axe rose and fell, and rose again.

She killed three, and left two others bleeding on the stones, and not once did she look back.

The clansmen found their tongues.

'*Ciaran! Ciaran!*'

The crashing shout drowned out the sound of battle. As one man, they turned and followed her.

Stark, scrambling for his life underfoot, could not forbear smiling. Their childlike minds could see only two alternatives – to slay her out of hand, or to worship her. They had chosen to worship. He thought the bards would be singing of the Lord Ciaran of Mekh as long as there were men to listen.

He managed to take cover behind a wrecked booth, and presently make his way out of the square. They had forgotten him, for the moment. He did not wish to wait, just then, until they – or she – remembered.

She.

He still did not believe it, quite. He touched the bruise under his jaw where she had struck him, and thought of the lithe, swift strength of her, and the way she had ridden alone into battle. He remembered the death of Thord, and how she had kept her red wolves tamed, and he was filled with wonder, and a deep excitement.

He remembered what she had said to him once – *We are of one blood, though we be strangers.*

He laughed, silently, and his eyes were very bright.

The tide of war had rolled on toward the King City, where from the sound of it there was hot fighting around the castle. Eddies of the main struggle swept shrieking through the streets, but the rat-runs under the Wall were clear. Everyone had stampeded inward, the victims with the victors close on their heels. The short northern day was almost gone.

He found a hiding place that offered reasonable safety, and settled himself to wait.

Night came, but he did not move. From the sounds that reached him, the sacking of Kushat was in full swing. They were looting the richer streets first. Their upraised voices were thick with wine, and mingles with the cries of women. The reflection of many fires tinged the sky.

By midnight the sounds began to slacken, and by the second hour after the city slept, drugged with wine and blood and the weariness of battle. Stark went silently out into the streets, toward the King City.

According to the immemorial pattern of Martian city-states, the castles of the king and the noble families were clustered together in solitary grandeur. Many of the towers were fallen now, the great halls open to the sky. Time had crushed the grandeur that had been Kushat more fatally than the boots of an conqueror.

In the house of the king, the flamboys guttered low and the chieftains of Mekh slept with their weary pipers among the benches of the banquet hall. In the niches of the tall, carved portal, the guards nodded over their spears. They, too, had fought that day. Even so, Stark did not go near them.

Shivering slightly in the bitter wind, he followed the bulk of the massive walls until he found a postern door, half open as some kitchen knave had left it in his flight. Stark entered, moving like a shadow.

The passageway was empty, dimly lighted by a single torch. A stairway branched off from it, and he climbed that, picking his way by guess and his memories of similar castles he had seen in the past.

He emerged into a narrow hall, obviously for the use of servants. A tapestry closed the end, stirring in the chill draught that blew along the floor. He peered around it, and saw a massive, vaulted corridor, the stone walls panelled in wood much split and blackened by time, but still showing forth the wonderful carvings of beasts and men, larger than life and overlaid with gold and bright enamel.

From the corridor a single doorway opened – and Otar slept before it, curled on a pallet like a dog.

Stark went back down the narrow hall. He was sure that there must be a back entrance to the king's chambers, and he found the little door he was looking for.

From there on was darkness. He felt his way, stepping with infinite caution, and presently there was a faint gleam of light filtering around the edges of another curtain of heavy tapestry.

He crept toward it, and heard a man's slow breathing on the other side.

He drew the curtain back, a careful inch. The man was

sprawled on a bench athwart the door. He slept the honest sleep of exhaustion, his sword in his hand, the stains of his day's work still upon him. He was alone in the small room. A door in the farther wall was closed.

Stark hit him, and caught the sword before it fell. The man grunted once and became utterly relaxed. Stark bound him with his own harness and shoved a gag in his mouth, and went on, through the door in the opposite wall.

The room beyond was large and high and full of shadows. A fire burned low on the hearth, and the uncertain light showed dimly the hangings and the rich stuffs that carpeted the floor, and the dark, sparse shapes of furniture.

Stark made out the lattice-work of a covered bed, let into the wall after the northern fashion.

She was there, sleeping, her red-gold hair the colour of the flames.

He stood a moment, watching her, and then, as though she sensed his presence, she stirred and opened her eyes.

She did not cry out. He had known that she would not. There was no fear in her. She said, with a kind of wry humour, 'I will have a word with my guards about this.'

She flung aside the covering and rose. She was almost as tall as he, white-skinned and very straight. He noted the long thighs, the narrow loins and magnificent shoulders, the small virginal breasts. She moved as a man moves, without coquetry. A long furred gown, that Stark guessed had lately graced the shoulders of the king, lay over a chair. She put it on.

'Well, wild man?'

'I have come to warn you.' He hesitated over her name, and she said,

'My mother named me Ciara, if that seems better to you.' She gave him her falcon's glance. 'I could have slain you in the square, but now I think you did me a service. The truth would have come out sometime – better then, when they had no time to think about it.' She laughed. 'They will follow me now, over the edge of the world, if I ask them.'

Stark said slowly, 'Even beyond the Gates of Death?'

'Certainly, there. Above all, there!'

She turned to one of the tall windows and looked out at the cliffs and the high notch of the pass, touched with greenish silver by the little moons.

'Ban Cruach was a great king. He came out of nowhere to rule the Norlands with a rod of iron, and men speak of him still as half a god. Where did he get his power, if not from beyond the Gates of Death? Why did he go back there at the end of his days, if not to hide away his secret? Why did he build Kushat to guard the pass forever, if not to hoard that power out of reach of all the other nations of Mars?

'Yes, Stark. My men will follow me. And if they do not, I will go alone.'

'You are not Ban Cruach. Nor am I.' He look her by the shoulders. 'Listen, Ciara. You're already king in the Norlands, and half a legend as you stand. Be content.'

'Content!' Her face was close to his, and he saw the blaze of it, the white intensity of ambition and an iron pride. 'Are you content?' she asked him. 'Have you ever been content?'

He smiled. 'For strangers, we do know each other well. No. But the spurs are not so deep in me.'

'The wind and the fire. One spends its strength in wandering, the other devours. But one can help the other. I made you an offer once, and you said you would not bargain unless you could look into my eyes. Look now!'

He did, and his hands upon her shoulders trembled.

'No,' he said harshly. 'You're a fool, Ciara. Would you be as Otar, mad with what you have seen?'

'Otar is an old man, and likely crazed before he crossed the mountains. Besides – I am not Otar.'

Stark said sombrely, 'Even the bravest may break. Ban Cruach himself...'

She must have seen the shadow of that horror in his eyes, for he felt her body tense.

'What of Ban Cruach? What do you know, Stark? Tell me!'

He was silent, and she went from him angrily.

'You have the talisman,' she said. 'That I am sure of. And if need be, I will flay you alive to get it!' She faced him across the room. 'But whether I get it or not, I will go through the Gates of Death. I must wait, now, until after the thaw. The warm wind will blow soon, and the gorges will be running full. But afterward, I will go, and no talk of fears and demons will stop me.'

She began to pace the room with long strides, and the full skirts of the gown made a subtle whispering about her.

'You do not know,' she said, in a low and bitter voice. 'I was a girl-child, without a name. By the time I could walk, I was a servant in the house of my grandfather. The two things that kept me living were pride and hate. I left my scrubbing of floors to practise arms with the young boys. I was beaten for it every day, but every day I went. I knew even then that only force would free me. And my father was a king's son, a good man of his hands. His blood was strong in me. I learned.'

She held her head very high. She had earned the right to hold it so. She finished quietly.

'I have come a long way. I will not turn back now.'

'Ciara.' Stark came and stood before her. 'I am talking to you as a fighting man, an equal. There may be power behind the Gates of Death, I do not know. But this I have seen – madness, horror, an evil that is beyond our understanding.

'I think you will not accuse me of cowardice. And yet I would not go into that pass for all the power of all the kings of Mars!'

Once started, he could not stop. The full force of that dark vision of the talisman swept over him again in memory. He came closer to her, driven by the need to make her understand.

'Yes, I have the talisman! And I have had a taste of its purpose. I think Ban Cruach left it as a warning, so that none would follow him. I have seen the temples and the palaces glitter in the ice. I have seen the Gates of Death – *not with my own eyes, Ciara, but with his. With the eyes and the memories of Ban Cruach!*'

He had caught her again, his hands strong on her strong arms.

'Will you believe me, or must you see for yourself – the dreadful things that walk those buried streets, the shapes that rise from nowhere in the mists of the pass?'

Her gaze burned into his. Her breath was hot and sweet upon

his lips, and she was like a sword between his hands, shining and unafraid.

'Give me the talisman. Let me see!'

He answered furiously, 'You are mad. As mad as Otar.' And he kissed her, in a rage, in a panic lest all that beauty be destroyed – a kiss as brutal as a blow, that left him shaken.

She backed away slowly, one step, and he thought she would have killed him. He said heavily:

'If you will see, you will. The thing is here.'

He opened the boss and laid the crystal in her outstretched hand. He did not meet her eyes.

'Sit down. Hold the flat side against your brow.'

She sat, in a great chair of carven wood. Stark noticed that her hand was unsteady, her face the colour of white ash. He was glad she did not have the axe where she could reach it. She did not play at anger.

For a long moment she studied the intricate lens, the incredible depository of a man's mind. Then she raised it slowly to her forehead.

He saw her grow rigid in the chair. How long he watched beside her he never knew. Seconds, an eternity. He saw her eyes turn blank and strange, and a shadow came into her face, changing it subtly, altering the lines, so that it seemed almost a stranger was peering through her flesh.

All at once, in a voice that was not her own, she cried out terribly, '*Oh gods of Mars!*'

The talisman dropped rolling to the floor, and Ciara fell forward into Stark's arms.

He thought at first that she was dead. He carried her to the bed, in an agony of fear that surprised him with its violence, and laid her down, and put his hand over her heart.

It was beating strongly. Relief that was almost a sickness swept over him. He turned, searching vaguely for wine, and saw the talisman. He picked it up and put it back inside the boss. A jewelled flagon stood on a table across the room. He took it and started back, and then, abruptly, there was a wild clamour in the hall outside and Otar was shouting Ciara's name, pounding on the door.

It was not barred. In another moment they would burst through, and he knew that they would not stop to enquire what he was doing there.

He dropped the flagon and went out swiftly, the way he had come. The guard was still unconscious. In the narrow hall beyond, Stark hesitated. A woman's voice was rising high above the tumult in the main corridor, and he thought he recognised it.

He went to the tapestry curtain and looked for the second time around its edge.

The lofty space was full of men, newly wakened from their heavy sleep and as nervous as so many bears. Thanis struggled in the grip of two of them. Her scarlet kirtle was torn, her hair flying in wild elf-locks, and her face was the face of a mad thing. The whole story of the doom of Kushat was written large upon it.

She screamed again and again, and would not be silenced.

'Tell her, the witch that leads you! Tell her that she is already doomed to death, with all her army!'

Otar opened up the door of Ciara's room.

Thanis surged forward. She must have fled through all that castle before she was caught, and Stark's heart ached for her.

'You!' she shrieked through the doorway, and poured out all the filth of the quarter upon Ciara's name. 'Balin has gone to bring doom upon you! He will open wide the Gates of Death, and then you will die! – die! – *die!*'

Stark felt the shock of a terrible dread, as he let the curtain fall. Mad with hatred against conquerors, Balin had fulfilled his raging promise and had gone to fling open the Gates of Death.

Remembering his nightmare vision of the shining, evil ones whom Ban Cruach had long ago prisoned beyond those gates, Stark felt a sickness grow within him as he went down the stair and out the postern door.

It was almost dawn. He looked up at the brooding cliffs, and it seemed to him that the wind in the pass had a sound of laughter that mocked his growing dread.

He knew what he must do, if an ancient, mysterious horror was not to be released upon Kushat.

I may still catch Balin before he has gone too far! If I don't—

He dared not think of that. He began to walk very swiftly through the night streets, toward the distant, towering Gates of Death.

7

It was past noon. He had climbed high toward the saddle of the pass. Kushat lay small below him, and he could see now the pattern of the gorges, cut ages deep in the living rock, that carried the spring torrents of the watershed around the mighty ledge on which the city was built.

The pass itself was channelled, but only by its own snows and melting ice. It was too high for a watercourse. Nevertheless, Stark thought, a man might find it hard to stay alive if he were caught there by the thaw.

He had seen nothing of Balin. The gods knew how many hours' start he had. Stark imagined him, scrambling wild-eyed over the rocks, driven by the same madness that had sent Thanis up into the castle to call down destruction on Ciara's head.

The sun was brilliant but without warmth. Stark shivered, and the icy wind blew strong. The cliffs hung over him, vast and sheer and crushing, and the narrow mouth of the pass was before him. He would go no farther. He would turn back, now.

But he did not. He began to walk forward, into the Gates of Death.

The light was dim and strange at the bottom of that cleft. Little veils of mist crept and clung between the ice and the rock, thickened, became more dense as he went farther and farther into the pass. He could not see, and the wind spoke with many tongues, piping in the crevices of the cliffs.

The steps of the Earthman slowed and faltered. He had known

fear in his life before. But now he was carrying the burden of two men's terror – Ban Cruach's, and his own.

He stopped, enveloped in the clinging mist. He tried to reason with himself – that Ban Cruach's fears had died a million years ago, that Otar had come this way and lived, and Balin had come also.

But the thin veneer of civilisation sloughed away and left him with the naked bones of truth. His nostrils twitched to the smell of evil, the subtle unclean taint that only a beast, or one as close to it as he, can sense and know. Every nerve was a point of pain, raw with apprehension. An overpowering recognition of danger, hidden somewhere, mocking at him, made his very body change, draw in upon itself and flatten forward, so that when at last he went on again he was more like a four-footed thing than a man walking upright.

Infinitely wary, silent, moving surely over the ice and the tumbled rock, he followed Balin. He had ceased to think. He was going now on sheer instinct.

The pass led on and on. It grew darker, and in the dim uncanny twilight there were looming shapes that menaced him, and ghostly wings that brushed him, and a terrible stillness that was not broken by the eerie voices of the wind.

Rock and mist and ice. Nothing that moved or lived. And yet the sense of danger deepened, and when he paused the beating of his heart was like thunder in his ears.

Once, far away, he thought he heard the echoes of a man's voice crying, but he had no sight of Balin.

The pass began to drop, and the twilight deepened into a kind of sickly night.

On and down, more slowly now, crouching, slinking, heavily oppressed, tempted to snarl at boulders and tear at wraiths of fog. He had no idea of the miles he had travelled. But the ice was thicker now, the cold intense.

The rock walls broke off sharply. The mist thinned. The pallid darkness lifted to a clear twilight. He came to the end of the Gates of Death.

Stark stopped. Ahead of him, almost blocking the end of

the pass, something dark and high and massive loomed in the thinning mists.

It was a great cairn, and upon it sat a figure, facing outward from the Gates of Death as though it kept watch over whatever country lay beyond.

The figure of a man in antique Martian armour.

After a moment, Stark crept toward the cairn. He was still almost all savage, torn between fear and fascination.

He was forced to scramble over the lower rocks of the cairn itself. Quite suddenly he felt a hard shock, and a flashing sensation of warmth that was somehow inside his own flesh, and not in any tempering of the frozen air. He gave a startled leap forward, and whirled, looking up into the face of the mailed figure with the confused idea that it had reached down and struck him.

It had not moved, of course. And Stark knew, with no need of anyone to tell him, that he looked into the face of Ban Cruach.

It was a face made for battles and for ruling, the bony ridges harsh and strong, the hollows under them worn deep with years. Those eyes, dark shadows under the rusty helm, had dreamed high dreams, and neither age nor death had conquered them.

And even in death, Ban Cruach was not unarmed.

Clad as for battle in his ancient mail, he held upright between his hands a mighty sword. The pommel was a ball of crystal large as a man's fist, that held within it a spark of intense brilliance. The little, blinding flame throbbed with its own force, and the sword-blade blazed with a white, cruel radiance.

Ban Cruach, dead but frozen to eternal changelessness by the bitter cold, sitting here upon his cairn for a million years and warding forever the inner end of the Gates of Death, as his ancient city of Kushat warded the outer.

Stark took two cautious steps closer to Ban Cruach, and felt again the shock and the flaring heat in his blood. He recoiled, satisfied.

The strange force in the blazing sword made an invisible barrier across the mouth of the pass, protected Ban Cruach himself. A barrier of short waves, he thought, of the type used in deep therapy, having no heat in themselves but increasing the heat in body cells by increasing their vibration. But these waves were stronger than any he had known before.

A barrier, a wall of force, closing the inner end of the Gates of Death. A barrier that was not designed against man.

Stark shivered. he turned from the sombre, brooding form of Ban Cruach and his eyes followed the gaze of the dead king, out beyond the cairn.

He looked across this forbidden land within the Gates of Death.

At his back was the mountain barrier. Before him, a handful of miles to the north, the terminus of the polar cap rose like a cliff of bluish crystal soaring up to touch the early stars. Locked in between those two titanic walls was a great valley of ice.

White and glimmering that valley was, and very still, and very beautiful, the ice shaped gracefully into curving domes and hollows. And in the centre of it stood a dark tower of stone, a cyclopean bulk that Stark knew must go down an unguessable distance to its base on the bedrock. It was like the tower in which Camar had died. But this one was not a broken ruin. It loomed with alien arrogance, and within its bulk pallid lights flickered eerily, and it was crowned by a cloud of shimmering darkness.

It was like the tower of his dread vision, the tower that he had seen, not as Eric John Stark, but as Ban Cruach!

Stark's gaze dropped slowly from the evil tower to the curving ice of the valley. And the fear within him grew beyond all bounds.

He had seen that, too, in his vision. The glimmering ice, the domes and hollows of it. He had looked down through it at the city that lay beneath, and he had seen those who came and went in the buried streets.

Stark hunkered down. For a long while he did not stir.

He did not want to go out there. He did not want to go out from the grim, warning figure of Ban Cruach with his blazing sword, into that silent valley. He was afraid, afraid of what he might see if he went there and looked down through the ice, afraid of the final dread fulfilment of his vision.

But he had come after Balin, and Balin must be out there

somewhere. He did not want to go, but he was himself, and he must.

He went, going very softly, out toward the tower of stone. And there was no sound in all that land.

The last of the twilight had faded. The ice gleamed, faintly luminous under the stars, and there was light beneath it, a soft radiance that filled all the valley with the glow of a buried moon.

Stark tried to keep his eyes upon the tower. He did not wish to look down at what lay under his stealthy feet.

Inevitably, he looked.

The temples and the palaces glittering in the ice ...

Level upon level, going down. Wells of soft light spanned with soaring bridges, slender spires rising, an endless variation of streets and crystal walls exquisitely patterned, above and below and overlapping, so that it was like looking down through a thousand giant snowflakes. A metropolis of gossamer and frost, fragile and lovely as a dream, locked in the clear, pure vault of ice.

Stark saw the people of the city passing along the bright streets, their outlines blurred by the icy vault as things are half obscured by water. The creatures of vision, vaguely shining, infinitely evil.

He shut his eyes and waited until the shock and the dizziness left him. Then he set his gaze resolutely on the tower, and crept on, over the glassy sky that covered those buried streets.

Silence. Even the wind was hushed.

He had gone perhaps half the distance when the cry rang out.

It burst upon the valley with a shocking violence. '*Stark! Stark!*' The ice rang with it, curving ridges picked up his name and flung it back and forth with eerie crystal voices, and the echoes fled out whispering. *Stark! Stark!* until it seemed that the very mountains spoke.

Stark whirled about. In the pallid gloom between the ice and the stars there was light enough to see the cairn behind him, and the dim figure atop it with the shining sword.

Light enough to see Ciara, and the dark knot of riders who had followed her through the Gates of Death.

She cried his name again. 'Come back! Come back!'

The ice of the valley answered mockingly, *'Come back! Come back!'* and Stark was gripped with a terror that held him motionless.

She should not have called him. She should not have made a sound in that deathly place.

A man's hoarse scream rose above the flying echoes. The riders turned and fled suddenly, the squealing, hissing beasts crowding each other, floundering wildly on the rocks of the cairn, stampeding back into the pass.

Ciara was left alone. Stark saw her fight the rearing beast she rode and then fling herself out of the saddle and let it go. She came toward him, running, clad all in her black armour, the great axe swinging high.

'Behind you, Stark! Oh, gods of Mars!'

He turned then and saw them, coming out from the tower of stone, the pale, shining creatures that move so swiftly across the ice, so fleet and swift that no man living could outrun them.

He shouted to Ciara to turn back. He drew his sword and over his shoulder he cursed her in a black fury because he could hear her mailed feet coming on behind him.

The gliding creatures, sleek and slender, reedlike, bending, delicate as wraiths, their bodies shaped from northern rainbows of amethyst and rose – if they should touch Ciara, if their loathsome hands should touch her ...

Stark let out one raging catlike scream, and rushed them.

The opalescent bodies slipped away beyond his reach. The creatures watched him.

They had no faces, but they watched. They were eyeless but not blind, earless, but not without hearing. The inquisitive tendrils that formed their sensory organs stirred and shifted like the petals of ungodly flowers, and the colour of them was the white frost-fire that dances on the snow.

'Go back, Ciara!'

But she would not go, and he knew that they would not have

let her. She reached him, and they set their backs together. The shining ones ringed them round, many feet away across the ice, and watched the long sword and the great hungry axe, and there was something in the lissome swaying of their bodies that suggested laughter.

'You fool,' said Stark. 'You bloody fool.'

'And you?' answered Ciara. 'Oh, yes, I know about Balin. That mad girl, screaming in the palace – she told me, and you were seen from the wall, climbing to the Gates of Death. I tried to catch you.'

'Why?'

She did not answer that. 'They won't fight us, Stark. Do you think we could make it back to the cairn?'

'No. But we can try.'

Guarding each others' backs, they began to walk toward Ban Cruach and the pass. If they could once reach the barrier, they would be safe.

Stark knew now what Ban Cruach's wall of force was built against. And he began to guess the riddle of the Gates of Death.

The shining ones glided with them, out of reach. They did not try to bar the way. They formed a circle around the man and woman, moving with them and around them at the same time, an endless weaving chain of many bodies shining with soft jewel tones of colour.

They drew closer and closer to the cairn, to the brooding figure of Ban Cruach and his sword. It crossed Stark's mind that the creatures were playing with him and Ciara. Yet they had no weapons. Almost, he began to hope ...

From the tower where the shimmering cloud of darkness clung came a black crescent of force that swept across the ice-field like a sickle and gathered the two humans in.

Stark felt a shock of numbing cold that turned his nerves to ice. His sword dropped from his hand, and he heard Ciara's axe go down. His body was without strength, without feeling, dead.

He fell, and the shining ones glided in toward him.

8

Twice before in his life Stark had come near to freezing. It had been like this, the numbness and the cold. And yet it seemed that the dark force had struck rather at his nerve centres than at his flesh.

He could not see Ciara, who was behind him, but he heard the metallic clashing of her mail and one small, whispered cry, and he knew that she had fallen, too.

The glowing creatures surrounded him. He saw their bodies bending over him, the frosty tendrils of their faces writhing as though in excitement of delight.

Their hands touched him. Little hands with seven fingers, deft and frail. Even his numbed flesh felt the terrible cold of their touch, freezing as outer space. He yelled, or tried to, but they were not abashed.

They lifted him and bore him toward the tower, a company of them, bearing his heavy weight upon their gleaming shoulders.

He saw the tower loom high and higher still above him. The cloud of dark force that crowned it blotted out the stars. It became too huge and high to see at all, and then there was a low flat arch of stone close above his face, and he was inside.

Straight overhead – a hundred feet, two hundred, he could not tell – was a globe of crystal, fitted into the top of the tower as a jewel is held in a setting.

The air around it was shadowed with the same eerie gloom that hovered outside, but less dense, so that Stark could see the smouldering purple spark that burned within the globe, sending out its dark vibrations.

A globe of crystal, with a heart of sullen flame. Stark remembered the sword of Ban Cruach, and the white fire that burned in its hilt.

Two globes, the bright-cored and the dark. The sword of Ban Cruach touched the blood with heat. The globe of the tower deadened the flesh with cold. It was the same force, but at opposite ends of the spectrum.

Stark saw the cryptic controls of that glooming globe – a bank of them, on a wide stone ledge just inside the tower, close beside him. There were shining ones on that ledge tending those controls, and there were other strange and massive mechanisms there too.

Flying spirals of ice climbed up inside the tower, spanning the great stone well with spidery bridges, joining icy galleries. In some of those galleries, Stark vaguely glimpsed rigid, gleaming figures like statues of ice, but he could not see them clearly as he was carried on.

He was being carried downward. He passed slits in the wall, and knew that the pallid lights he had seen through them were the moving bodies of the creatures as they went up and down these high-flung, icy bridges. He managed to turn his head to look down, and saw what was beneath him.

The well of the tower plunged down a good five hundred feet to bedrock, widening as it went. The web of ice-bridges and the spiral ways went down as well as up, and the creatures that carried him were moving smoothly along a transparent ribbon of ice no more than a yard in width, suspended over that terrible drop.

Stark was glad that he could not move just then. One instinctive start of horror would have thrown him and his bearers to the rock below, and would have carried Ciara with them.

Down and down, gliding in utter silence along the descending spiral ribbon. The great glooming crystal grew remote above him. Ice was solid now in the slots of the walls. He wondered if they had brought Balin this way.

There were other openings, wide arches like the one they had brought their captives through, and these gave Stark brief glimpses of broad avenues and unguessable buildings, shaped from the pellucid ice and flooded with the soft radiance that was like eerie moonlight.

At length, on what Stark took to be the third level of the city, the creatures bore him through one of these archways, into the streets beyond.

Below him now was the translucent thickness of ice that formed the floor of this level and the roof of the level beneath. He could see the blurred tops of delicate minarets, the clustering roofs that shone like chips of diamond.

Above him was an ice roof. Elfin spires rose toward it, delicate as needles. Lacy battlements and little domes, buildings star-shaped, wheel-shaped, the fantastic, lovely shapes of snow-crystals, frosted over with a sparkling foam of light.

The people of the city gathered along the way to watch, a living, shifting rainbow of amethyst and rose and green, against the pure blue-white. And there was no least whisper of sound anywhere.

For some distance they went through a geometric maze of streets. And then there was a cathedral-like building all arched and spired, standing in the centre of a twelve-pointed plaza. Here they turned, and bore their captives in.

Stark saw a vaulted roof, very slim and high, etched with a glittering tracery that might have been carving of an alien sort, delicate as the weavings of spiders. The feet of his bearers were silent on the icy paving.

At the far end of the long vault sat seven of the shining ones in high seats marvellously shaped from the ice. And before them, grey-faced, shuddering with cold and not noticing it, drugged with a sick horror, stood Balin. He looked around once, and did not speak.

Stark was set on his feet, with Ciara beside him. He saw her face, and it was terrible to see the fear in her eyes, that had never shown fear before.

He himself was learning why men went mad beyond the Gates of Death.

Chill dreadful fingers touched him expertly. A flash of pain drove down his spine, and he could stand again.

The seven who sat in the high seats were motionless, their bright tendrils stirring with infinite delicacy as though they studied the three humans who stood before them.

Stark thought he could feel a cold, soft fingering of his brain. It came to him that these creatures were probably telepaths. They lacked organs of speech, and yet they must have some efficient means of communications. Telepathy was not uncommon among the many races of the Solar System, and Stark had had experience with it before.

He forced his mind to relax. The alien impulse was instantly stronger. He sent out his own questing thought and felt it brush the edges of a consciousness so utterly foreign to his own that he knew he could never probe it, even had he had the skill.

He learned one thing – that the shining faceless ones looked upon him with equal horror and loathing. They recoiled from the unnatural human features, and most of all, most strongly, they abhorred the warmth of human flesh. Even the infinitesimal amount of heat radiated by their half-frozen bodies caused the ice-folk discomfort.

Stark marshalled his imperfect abilities and projected a mental question to the seven.

'What do you want of us?'

The answer came back, faint and imperfect, as though the gap between their alien minds was almost too great to bridge. And the answer was one word.

'*Freedom!*'

Balin spoke suddenly. He voiced only a whisper, and yet the sound was shockingly loud in that crystal vault.

'They have asked me already. Tell them no, Stark! Tell them no!'

He looked at Ciara then, a look of murderous hatred. 'If you turn them loose upon Kushat, I will kill you with my own hands, before I die.'

Stark spoke again, silently, to the seven. 'I do not understand.'

Again the struggling, difficult thought. 'We are the old race, the kings of the glacial ice. Once we held all the land beyond the mountains, outside the pass you call the Gates of Death.'

Stark had seen the ruins of the towers out on the moors. He knew how far their kingdom had extended.

'We *controlled* the ice, far outside the polar cap. Our towers blanketed the land with the dark force drawn from Mars itself, from the magnetic field of the planet. That radiation bars out heat, from the Sun, and even from the awful winds that blow warm from the south. So there was never any thaw. Our cities were many, and our race was great.

'Then came Ban Cruach, from the south ...

'He waged a war against us. He learned the secret of the crystal globes, and learned how to reverse their force and use it against us. He, leading his army, destroyed our towers one by one, and drove us back ...

'Mars needed water. The outer ice was melted, our lovely cities crumbled to nothing, so that creatures like Ban Cruach might have water! And our people died.

'We retreated at last, to this our ancient polar citadel behind the Gates of Death. Even here, Ban Cruach followed. He destroyed even this tower once, at the time of the thaw. But this city is founded in polar ice – and only the upper levels were harmed. Even Ban Cruach could not touch the heart of the eternal polar cap of Mars!

'When he saw that he could not destroy us utterly, he set himself in death to guard the Gates of Death with his blazing sword, that we might never again reclaim our ancient domination.

'That is what we mean when we ask for freedom. We ask that you take away the sword of Ban Cruach, so that we may once again go out through the Gates of Death!'

Stark cried aloud, hoarsely, '*No!*'

He knew the barren deserts of the south, the wastes of red dust, the dead sea bottoms – the terrible thirst of Mars, growing greater with every year of the million that had passed since Ban Cruach locked the Gates of Death.

He knew the canals, the pitiful waterways that were all that stood between the people of Mars and extinction. He remembered the yearly release from death when the spring thaw brought the water rushing down from the north.

He thought of these cold creatures going forth, building again their great towers of stone, sheathing half a world in ice that would never melt. he thought of the people of Jekkara and Valkis and Barrakesh, of the countless cities of the south, watching for the flood that did not come, and falling at last to mingle their bodies with the blowing dust.

He said again, 'No. Never.'

The distant thought-voice of the seven spoke, and this time the question was addressed to Ciara.

Stark saw her face. She did not know the Mars he knew, but she had memories of her own – the mountain-valleys of Mekh, the moors, the snowy gorges. She looked at the shining ones in their high seats, and said,

'If I take that sword, it will be to use it against you as Ban Cruach did!'

Stark knew that the seven had understood the thought behind her words. He felt that they were amused.

'The secret of that sword was lost a million years ago, the day Ban Cruach died. Neither you nor anyone now knows how to use it as he did. But the sword's radiations of warmth still lock us here.

'We cannot approach that sword, for its vibrations of heat slay us if we do. But you warm-bodied ones can approach it. And you will do so, and take it from its place. *One of you will take it!*'

They were very sure of that.

'We can see, a little way, into your evil minds. Much we do not understand. But – the mind of the large man is full of the woman's image, and the mind of the woman turns to him. Also, there is a link between the large man and the small man, less strong, but strong enough.'

The thought-voice of the seven finished, 'The large man will take away the sword for us because he must – to save the other two.'

Ciara turned to Stark. 'They cannot force you, Stark. Don't let them. No matter what they do to me, don't let them!'

Balin stared at her with a certain wonder. 'You would die, to protect Kushat?'

'Not Kushat alone, though its people too are human,' she said, almost angrily. 'There are my red wolves – a wild pack, but my own. And others.' She looked at Balin. 'What do *you* say? Your life against the Norlands?'

Balin made an effort to life his head as high as hers, and the red jewel flashed in his ear. He was a man crushed by the falling of his world, and terrified by what his mad passion had led him into, here beyond the Gates of Death. But he was not afraid to die.

He said so, and even Ciara knew that he spoke the truth.

But the seven were not dismayed. Stark knew that when their thought-voice whispered in his mind,

'It is not death alone you humans have to fear, but the manner of your dying. You shall see that, before you choose.'

Swiftly, silently, those of the ice-folk who had borne the captives into the city came up from behind, where they had stood withdrawn and waiting. And one of them bore a crystal rod like a sceptre, with a spark of ugly purple burning in the globed end.

Stark leaped to put himself between them and Ciara. He struck out, raging, and because he was almost as quick as they, he caught one of the slim luminous bodies between his hands.

The utter coldness of that alien flesh burned his hands as frost will burn. Even so, he clung on, snarling, and saw the tendrils writhe and stiffen as though in pain.

Then, from the crystal rod, a thread of darkness spun itself to touch his brain with silence, and the cold that lies between the worlds.

He had no memory of being carried once more through the shimmering streets of that elfin, evil city, back to the stupendous well of the tower, and up along the spiral path of ice that soared those dizzy hundreds of feet from bedrock to the glooming crystal globe. But when he again opened his eyes, he was lying on the wide stone ledge at ice-level.

Beside him was the arch that led outside. Close above his head was the control bank that he had seen before.

Ciara and Balin were there also, on the ledge. They leaned stiffly against the stone wall beside the control bank, and facing them was a squat, round mechanism from which projected a sort of wheel of crystal rods.

Their bodies were strangely rigid, but their eyes and minds were awake. Terribly awake. Stark saw their eyes, and his heart turned within him.

Ciara looked at him. She could not speak, but she had no need to. *No matter what they do to me ...*

She had not feared the swordsmen of Kushat. She had not feared her red wolves, when he unmasked her in the square. She was afraid now. But she warned him, ordered him not to save her.

They cannot force you, Stark! Don't let them.

And Balin, too, pleaded with him for Kushat.

They were not alone on the ledge. The ice-folk clustered there, and out upon the flying spiral pathway, on the narrow bridges and the spans of fragile ice, they stood in hundreds watching, eyeless, faceless, their bodies drawn in rainbow lines across the dimness of the shaft.

Stark's mind could hear the silent edges of their laughter. Secret, knowing laughter, full of evil, full of triumph, and Stark was filled with a corroding terror.

He tried to move, to crawl toward Ciara standing like a carven image in her black mail. He could not.

Again her fierce, proud glance met his. And the silent laughter of the ice-folk echoed in his mind, and he thought it very strange that in this moment, now, he should realise that there had never been another woman like her on all of the worlds of the Sun.

The fear she felt was not for herself. It was for him.

Apart from the multitudes of the ice-folk, the group of seven stood upon the ledge. And now their thought-voice spoke to Stark, saying,

'Look about you. Behold the men who have come before you through the Gates of Death!'

Stark raised his eyes to where their slender fingers pointed, and saw the icy galleries around the tower, saw more clearly the icy statues in them that he had only glimpsed before.

Men, set like images in the galleries. Men whose bodies were sheathed in a glittering mail of ice, sealing them forever. Warriors, nobles, fanatics and thieves – the wanderers of a million years who had dared to enter this forbidden valley, and had remained forever.

He saw their faces, their tortured eyes wide open, their features frozen in the agony of a slow and awful death.

'They refused us,' the seven whispered. 'They would not take away the sword. And so they died, as this woman and this man will die, unless you choose to save them.

'We will show you, human, how they died!'

One of the ice-folk bent and touched the squat, round mechanism that faced Balin and Ciara. Another shifted the pattern of control on the master-bank.

The wheel of crystal rods on that squat mechanism began to turn. The rods blurred, became a disc that spun faster and faster.

High above in the top of the tower the great globe brooded, shrouded in its cloud of shimmering darkness. The disc became a whirling blur. The glooming shadow of the globe deepened, coalesced. It began to lengthen and descend, stretching itself down toward the spinning disc.

The crystal rods of the mechanism drank the shadow in. And out of that spinning blur there came a subtle weaving of threads of darkness, a gossamer curtain winding around Ciara and Balin so that their outlines grew ghostly and the pallor of their flesh was as the pallor of snow at night.

And still Stark could not move.

The veil of darkness began to sparkle faintly. Stark watched it, watched the chill motes brighten, watched the tracery of frost whiten over Ciara's mail, touched Balin's dark hair with silver.

Frost. Bright, sparkling, beautiful, a halo of frost around their bodies. A dust of splintered diamond across their faces, an aureole of brittle light to crown their heads.

Frost. Flesh slowly hardening in marbly whiteness, as the cold slowly increased. And yet their eyes still lived, and saw, and understood.

The thought-voice of the seven spoke again.

'You have only minutes now to decide! Their bodies cannot endure too much, and live again. Behold their eyes, and how they suffer!

'Only minutes, human! Take away the sword of Ban Cruach! Open for us the Gates of Death, and we will release these two, alive.'

Stark felt again the flashing stab of pain along his nerves, as one of the shining creatures moved behind him. Life and feeling came back into his limbs.

He struggled to his feet. The hundreds of the ice-folk on the bridges and galleries watched him in eager silence.

He did not look at them. His eyes were on Ciara's. And now, her eyes pleaded.

'Don't, Stark! Don't barter the life of the Norlands for me!'

The thought-voice beat at Stark, cutting into his mind with cruel urgency.

'Hurry, human! They are already beginning to die. Take away the sword, and let them live!'

Stark turned. He cried out, in a voice that made the icy bridges tremble:

'I will take the sword!'

He staggered out, then. Out through the archway, across the ice, toward the distant cairn that blocked the Gates of Death.

9

Across the glowing ice of the valley Stark went at a stumbling run that grew swifter and more sure as his cold-numbed body began to regain its functions. And behind him, pouring out of the tower to watch, came the shining ones.

They followed after him, gliding lightly. He could sense their excitement, the cold, strange ecstasy of triumph. He knew that already they were thinking of the great towers of stone rising again above the Norlands, the crystal cities still and beautiful under the ice, all vestige of the ugly citadels of man gone and forgotten.

The seven spoke once more, a warning.

'If you turn toward us with the sword, the woman and the man will die. And you will die as well. For neither you nor any other can now use the sword as a weapon of offence.'

Stark ran on. He was thinking then only of Ciara, with the

frost-crystals gleaming on her marble flesh and her eyes full of mute torment.

The cairn loomed up ahead, dark and high. It seemed to Stark that the brooding figure of Ban Cruach watched him coming with those shadowed eyes beneath the rusty helm. The great sword blazed between those dead, frozen hands.

The ice-folk had slowed their forward rush. They stopped and waited, well back from the cairn.

Stark reached the edge of tumbled rock. He felt the first warm flare of the force-waves in his blood, and slowly the chill began to creep out from his bones. He climbed, scrambling upward over the rough stones of the cairn.

Abruptly, then, at Ban Cruach's feet, he slipped and fell. For a second it seemed that he could not move.

His back was turned toward the ice-folk. His body was bent forward, and shielded so, his hands worked with feverish speed.

From his cloak he tore a strip of cloth. From the iron boss he took the glittering lens, the talisman of Ban Cruach. Stark laid the lens against his brow, and bound it on.

The remembered shock, the flood and sweep of memories that were not his own. The mind of Ban Cruach thundering its warning, its hard-won knowledge of an ancient, epic war ...

He opened his own mind wide to receive those memories. Before he had fought against them. Now he knew that they were his one small chance in his swift gamble with death. Two things only of his own he kept firm in that staggering tide of another man's memories. Two names – Ciara and Balin.

He rose up again. And now his face had a strange look, a curious duality. The features had not changed, but somehow the lines of the flesh had altered subtly, so that it was almost as though the old unconquerable king himself had risen again in battle.

He mounted the last step or two and stood before Ban Cruach. A shudder ran through him, a sort of gathering and settling of the flesh, as though Stark's being had accepted the stranger within it. His eyes, cold and pale as the very ice that sheathed the valley, burned with a cruel light.

He reached and took the sword, out of the frozen hands of Ban Cruach.

As though it were his own, he knew the secret of the metal rings that bound its hilt, below the ball of crystal. The savage throb of the invisible radiation beat in his quickening flesh. He was warm again, his blood running swiftly, his muscles sure and strong. He touched the rings and turned them.

The fan-shaped aura of force that had closed the Gates of Death narrowed in, and as it narrowed it leaped up from the blade of the sword in a tongue of pale fire, faintly shimmering, made visible now by the full focus of its strength.

Stark felt the wave of horror bursting from the minds of the ice-folk as they perceived what he had done. And he laughed.

His bitter laughter rang harsh across the valley as he turned to face them, and he heard in his brain the shuddering, silent shriek that went up from all that gathered company...

'*Ban Cruach! Ban Cruach has returned!*'

They had touched his mind. They knew.

He laughed again, and swept the sword in a flashing arc, and watched the long bright blade of force strike out more terrible than steel, against the rainbow bodies of the shining ones.

They fell. Like flowers under a scythe they fell, and all across the ice the ones who were yet untouched turned about in their hundreds and fled back toward the tower.

Stark came leaping down the cairn, the talisman of Ban Cruach bound upon his brow, the sword of Ban Cruach blazing in his hand.

He swung that awful blade as he ran. The force-beam that sprang from it cut through the press of creatures fleeing before him, hampered by their own numbers as they crowded back through the archway.

He had only a few short seconds to do what he had to do.

Rushing with great strides across the ice, spurning the withered bodies of the dead ... And then, from the glooming darkness that hovered around the tower of stone, the black cold beam struck down.

Like a coiling whip it lashed him. The deadly numbness

invaded the cells of his flesh, ached in the marrow of his bones. The bright force of the sword battled the chill invaders, and a corrosive agony tore at Stark's inner body where the antipathetic radiations waged war.

His steps faltered. He gave one hoarse cry of pain, and then his limbs failed and he went heavily to his knees.

Instinct only made him cling to the sword. Waves of blinding anguish racked him. The coiling lash of darkness encircled him, and its touch was the abysmal cold of outer space, striking deep into his heart.

Hold the sword close, hold it closer, like a shield. The pain is great, but I will not die unless I drop the sword.

Ban Cruach the mighty had fought this fight before.

Stark raised the sword again, close against his body. The fierce pulse of its brightness drove back the cold. Not far, for the freezing touch was very strong. But far enough so that he could rise again and stagger on.

The dark force of the tower writhed and licked about him. He could not escape it. He slashed it in a blind fury with the blazing sword, and where the forces met a flicker of lightning leaped in the air, but it would not be beaten back.

He screamed at it, a raging cat-cry that was all Stark, all primitive fury at the necessity of pain. And he forced himself to run, to drag his tortured body faster across the ice. *Because Ciara is dying, because the dark cold wants me to stop* ...

The ice-folk jammed and surged against the archway, in a panic hurry to take refuge far below in their many-levelled city. He raged at them, too. They were part of the cold, part of the pain. Because of them Ciara and Balin were dying. He sent the blade of force lancing among them, his hatred rising full tide to join the hatred of Ban Cruach that lodged in his mind.

Stab and cut and slash with the long terrible beam of brightness. They fell and fell, the hideous shining folk, and Stark sent the light of Ban Cruach's weapon sweeping through the tower itself, through the openings that were like windows in the stone.

Again and again, stabbing through those open slits as he ran. And suddenly the dark beam of force ceased to move. He tore out of it, and it did not follow him, remaining stationary as though fastened to the ice.

The battle of forces left his flesh. The pain was gone. He sped on to the tower.

He was close now. The withered bodies lay in heaps before the arch. The last of the ice-folk had forced their way inside.

Holding the sword level like a lance, Stark leaped in through the arch, into the tower.

The shining ones were dead where the destroying warmth had touched them. The flying spiral ribbons of ice were swept clean of them, the arching bridges and the galleries of that upper part of the tower.

They were dead along the ledge, under the control bank. They were dead across the mechanism that spun the frosty doom around Ciara and Balin. The whirling disc still hummed.

Below, in that stupendous well, the crowding ice-folk made a seething pattern of colour on the narrow ways. But Stark turned his back on them and ran along the ledge, and in him was the heavy knowledge that he had come too late.

The frost had thickened around Ciara and Balin. It encrusted them like stiffened lace, and now their flesh was overlaid with a diamond shell of ice.

Surely they could not live!

He raised the sword to smite down at the whirring disc, to smash it, but there was no need. When the full force of that concentrated beam struck it, meeting the focus of shadow that it held, there was a violent flare of light and a shattering of crystal. The mechanism was silent.

The glooming veil was gone from around the ice-shelled man and woman. Stark forgot the creatures in the shaft below him. He turned the blazing sword full upon Ciara and Balin.

It would not affect the thin covering of ice. If the woman and the man were dead, it would not affect their flesh, any more than it had Ban Cruach's. But if they lived, if there was still a spark, a flicker beneath that frozen mail, the radiation would touch their blood with warmth, start again the pulse of life in their bodies.

He waited, watching Ciara's face. It was still as marble, and as white.

Something – instinct, or the warning mind of Ban Cruach that had learned a million years ago to beware the creatures of the ice – made him glance behind him.

Stealthy, swift and silent, up the winding ways they came. They had guessed that he had forgotten them in his anxiety. The sword was turned away from them now, and if they could take him from behind, stun him with the chill force of the sceptre-like rods they carried...

He slashed them with the sword. He saw the flickering beam go down and down the shaft, saw the bodies fall like drops of rain, rebounding here and there from the flying spans and carrying the living with them.

He thought of the many levels of the city. He thought of all the countless thousands that must inhabit them. He could hold them off in the shaft as long as he wished if he had no other need for the sword. But he knew that as soon as he turned his back they would be upon him again, and if he should once fall...

He could not spare a moment, or a chance.

He looked at Ciara, not knowing what to do, and it seemed to him that the sheathing frost had melted, just a little, around her face.

Desperately, he struck down again at the creatures in the shaft, and then the answer came to him.

He dropped the sword. The squat, round mechanism was beside him, with its broken crystal wheel. He picked it up.

It was heavy. It would have been heavy for two men to lift, but Stark was a driven man. Grunting, swaying with the effort, he lifted it and let it fall, out and down.

Like a thunderbolt it struck among those slender bridges, the spiderweb of icy strands that spanned the shaft. Stark watched it go, and listened to the brittle snapping of the ice, the final crashing of a million shards at the bottom far below.

He smiled, and turned again to Ciara, picking up the sword.

It was hours later. Stark walked across the glowing ice of the valley, toward the cairn. The sword of Ban Cruach hung at his side. He had taken the talisman and replaced it in the boss, and he was himself again.

Ciara and Balin walked beside him. The colour had come back into their faces, but faintly, and they were still weak enough to be glad of Stark's hands to steady them.

At the foot of the cairn they stopped, and Stark mounted it alone.

He looked for a long moment into the face of Ban Cruach. Then he took the sword, and carefully turned the rings upon it so that the radiation spread out as it had before, to close the Gates of Death.

Almost reverently, he replaced the sword in Ban Cruach's hands. Then he turned and went down over the tumbled stones.

The shimmering darkness brooded still over the distant tower. Underneath the ice, the elfin city still spread downward. The shining ones would rebuild their bridges in the shaft, and go on as they had before, dreaming their cold dreams of ancient power.

But they would not go out through the Gates of Death. Ban Cruach in his rusty mail was still lord of the pass, the warder of the Norlands.

Stark said to the others, 'Tell the story in Kushat. Tell it through the Norlands, the story of Ban Cruach and why he guards the Gates of Death. Men have forgotten. And they should not forget.'

They went out of the valley then, the two men and the woman. They did not speak again, and the way out through the pass seemed endless.

Some of Ciara's chieftains met them at the mouth of the pass above Kushat. They had waited there, ashamed to return to the city without her, but not daring to go back into the pass again. They had seen the creatures of the valley, and they were still afraid.

They gave mounts to the three. They themselves walked behind Ciara, and their heads were low with shame.

They came into Kushat through the riven gate, and Stark

went with Ciara to the King City, where she made Balin follow too.

'Your sister is there,' she said. 'I have had her cared for.'

The city was quiet, with the sullen apathy that follows after battle. The men of Mekh cheered Ciara in the streets. She rode proudly, but Stark saw that her face was gaunt and strained.

He, too, was marked deep by what he had seen and done, beyond the Gates of Death.

They went up into the castle.

Thanis took Balin into her arms, and wept. She had lost her first wild fury, and she could look at Ciara now with a restrained hatred that had a tinge almost of admiration.

'You fought for Kushat,' she said, unwillingly, when she had heard the story. 'For that, at least, I can thank you.'

She went to Stark then, and looked up at him. 'Kushat, and my brother's life ...' She kissed him, and there were tears on her lips. But she turned to Ciara with a bitter smile.

'No one can hold him, any more than the wind can be held. You will learn that.'

She went out then with Balin, and left Stark and Ciara alone, in the chambers of the king.

Ciara said, 'The little one is very shrewd.' She unbuckled the hauberk and let it fall, standing slim in her tunic of black leather, and walked to the tall windows that looked out upon the mountains. She leaned her head wearily against the stone.

'An evil day, an evil deed. And now I have Kushat to govern, with no reward of power from beyond the Gates of Death. How man can be misled!'

Stark poured wine from the flagon and brought it to her. She looked at him over the rim of the cup, with a certain wry amusement.

'The little one is shrewd, and she is right. I don't know that I can be as wise as she ... Will you stay with me, Stark, or will you go?'

He did not answer at once, and she asked him, 'What hunger drives you, Stark? It is not conquest, as it was with me. What are you looking for that you cannot find?'

He thought back across the years, back to the beginning – to the boy N'Chaka who had once been happy with Old One and little Tika, in the blaze and thunder and bitter frosts of a valley in the Twilight Belt of Mercury. He remembered how all that had ended, under the guns of the miners – the men who were his own kind.

He shook his head. 'I don't know. It doesn't matter.' He took her between his two hands, feeling the strength and the splendour of her, and it was oddly difficult to find words.

'I want to stay, Ciara. Now, this minute, I could promise that I would stay forever. But I know myself. You belong here, you will make Kushat your own. I don't. Someday I will go.'

Ciara nodded. 'My neck, also, was not made for chains, and one country was too little to hold me. Very well, Stark. Let it be so.'

She smiled, and let the wine-cup fall.

THE LAST DAYS OF SHANDAKOR

1

He came alone into the wineshop, wrapped in a dark red cloak, with the cowl drawn over his head. He stood for a moment by the doorway and one of the slim dark predatory women who live in those places went to him, with a silvery chiming from the little bells that were almost all she wore.

I saw her smile up at him. And then, suddenly, the smile became fixed and something happened to her eyes. She was no longer looking at the cloaked man but through him. In the oddest fashion – it was as though he had become invisible.

She went by him. Whether she passed some word along or not I couldn't tell but an empty space widened around the stranger. And no one looked at him. They did not avoid looking at him. They simply refused to see him.

He began to walk slowly across the crowded room. He was very tall and he moved with a fluid, powerful grace that was beautiful to watch. People drifted out of his way, not seeming to, but doing it. The air was thick with nameless smells, shrill with the laughter of women.

Two tall barbarians, far gone in wine, were carrying on some intertribal feud and the yelling crowd had made room for them to fight. There was a silver pipe and a drum and a double-banked harp making old wild music. Lithe brown bodies leaped and whirled through the laughter and the shouting and the smoke.

The stranger walked through all this, alone, untouched, unseen. He passed close to where I sat. Perhaps because I, of all the people in that place, not only saw him but stared at him, he gave me a glance of black eyes from under the shadow of his cowl – eyes like blown coals, bright with suffering and rage.

I caught only a glimpse of his muffled face. The merest glimpse – but that was enough. *Why did he have to show his face to me in that wineshop in Barrakesh?*

He passed on. There was no space in the shadowy corner where he went but space was made, a circle of it, a moat between the stranger and the crowd. He sat down. I saw him lay a coin on the outer edge of the table. Presently a serving wench came up, picked up the coin and set down a cup of wine. But it was as if she waited on an empty table.

I turned to Kardak, my head drover, a Shunni with massive shoulders and uncut hair braided in an intricate tribal knot. 'What's all that about?' I asked.

Kardak shrugged. 'Who knows?' He started to rise. 'Come, JonRoss. It is time we got back to the serai.'

'We're not leaving for hours yet. And don't lie to me, I've been on Mars a long time. What is that man? Where does he come from?'

Barrakesh is the gateway between north and south. Long ago, when there were oceans in equatorial and southern Mars, when Valkis and Jekkara were proud seats of empire and not thieves' dens, here on the edge of the northern Drylands the great caravans had come and gone to Barrakesh for a thousand thousand years. It is a place of strangers.

In the time-eaten streets of rock you see tall Keshi hillmen, nomads from the high plains of Upper Shun, lean dark men from the south who barter away the loot of forgotten tombs and temples, cosmopolitan sophisticates up from Kahora and the trade cities, where there are spaceports and all the appurtenances of modern civilisation.

The red-cloaked stranger was none of these.

A glimpse of a face – I am a planetary anthropologist. I was supposed to be charting Martian ethnology and I was doing it on a fellowship grant I had wangled from a Terran university too ignorant to know that the vastness of Martian history makes such a project hopeless.

I was in Barrakesh, gathering an outfit preparatory to a year's study of the tribes of Upper Shun. And suddenly there had passed close by me a man with golden skin and un-Martian black eyes and a facial structure that belonged to no race I knew. I have seen the carven faces of fauns that were a little like it.

Kardak said again, 'It is time to go, Jon Ross!'

I looked at the stranger, drinking his wine in silence and alone. 'Very well, *I'll* ask him.'

Kardak sighed. 'Earthmen,' he said, 'are not given much to wisdom.' He turned and left me.

I crossed the room and stood beside the stranger. In the old courteous High Martian they speak in all the Low-Canal towns I asked permission to sit.

Those raging, suffering eyes met mine. There was hatred in them, and scorn, and shame. 'What breed of human are you?'

'I am an Earthman.'

He said the name over as though he had heart it before and was trying to remember. 'Earthman. Then it is as the winds have said, blowing across the desert – that Mars is dead and men from other worlds defile her dust.' He looked out over the wineshop and all the people who would not admit his presence. 'Change,' he whispered. 'Death and change and the passing away of things.'

The muscles of his face drew tight. He drank and I could see now that he had been drinking for a long time, for days, perhaps for weeks. There was a quiet madness on him.

'Why do the people shun you?'

'Only a man of Earth would need to ask,' he said and made a sound of laughter, very dry and bitter.

I was thinking. *A new race, an unknown race!* I was thinking of the fame that sometimes comes to men who discover a new thing, and of a Chair I might sit in at the University if I added one bright unheard-of piece of the shadowy mosaic of Martian history. I had had my share of wine and a bit more. That Chair looked a mile high and made of gold.

The stranger said softly, 'I go from place to place in this wallow of Barrakesh and everywhere it is the same. I have ceased to be.' His white teeth glittered for an instant in the shadow of the cowl. 'They were wiser than I, my people. When Shandakor is dead, we are dead also, whether our bodies live or not.'

'Shandakor?' I said. It had a sound of distant bells.

'How should an Earthman know? Yes, Shandakor! Ask of the men of Kesh and the men of Shun! Ask the kings of Mekh, who are half around the world! Ask of all the men of Mars – they have not forgotten Shandakor! But they will not tell you. It is a bitter shame to them, the memory and the name.'

He stared out across the turbulent throng that filled the room and flowed over to the noisy street outside. 'And I am here among them – lost.'

'Shandakor is dead?'

'Dying. There were three of us who did not want to die. We came south across the desert – one turned back, one perished in the sand, I am here in Barrakesh.' The metal of the wine-cup bent between his hands.

I said, 'And you regret your coming.'

'I should have stayed and died with Shandakor. I know that now. But I cannot go back.'

'Why not?' I was thinking how the name John Ross would look, inscribed in golden letters on the scroll of the discoverers.

'The desert is wide, Earthman. Too wide for one alone.'

And I said, 'I have a caravan. I am going north tonight.'

A light came into his eyes, so strange and deadly that I was afraid. 'No,' he whispered. '*No!*'

I sat in silence, looking out across the crowd that had forgotten me as well, because I sat with the stranger. *A new race, an unknown city. And I was drunk.*

After a long while the stranger asked me, 'What does an Earthman want in Shandakor?'

I told him. He laughed. 'You study men,' he said and laughed again, so that the red cloak rippled.

'If you want to go back I'll take you. If you don't, tell me where the city lies and I'll find it. Your race, your city, should have their place in history.'

He said nothing but the wine had made me very shrewd and I could guess at what was going on in the stranger's mind. I got up.

'Consider it,' I told him. 'You can find me at the serai by the northern gate until the lesser moon is up. Then I'll be gone.'

'Wait.' His fingers fastened on my wrist. They hurt. I looked into his face and I did not like what I saw there. But, as Kardak had mentioned, I was not given much to wisdom.

The stranger said, 'Your men will not go beyond the Wells of Karthedon.'

'Then we'll go without them.'

A long long silence. Then he said, 'So be it.'

I knew what he was thinking as plainly as though he had spoken the words. He was thinking that I was only an Earthman and that he would kill me when we came in sight of Shandakor.

2

The caravan tracks branch off at the Wells of Karthedon. One goes westward into Shun and one goes north through the passes of Outer Kesh. But there is a third one, more ancient than the others. It goes toward the east and it is never used. The deep rock wells are dry and the stone-built shelters have vanished under the rolling dunes. It is not until the track begins to climb the mountains that there are even memories.

Kardak refused politely to go beyond the Wells. He would wait for me, he said, a certain length of time, and if I came back we would go on into Shun. If I didn't – well, his full pay was left in charge of the local headman. He would collect it and go home. He had not liked having the stranger with us. He had doubled his price.

In all that long march up from Barrakesh I had not been able to get a word out of Kardak or the men concerning Shandakor. The stranger had not spoken either. He had told me his name – Corin – and nothing more. Cloaked and cowled he rode alone and brooded. His private devils were still with him and he had a new one now – impatience. He would have ridden us all to death if I had let him.

So Corin and I went east alone from Karthedon, with two led animals and all the water we could carry. And now I could not hold him back.

'There is no time to stop,' he said. 'The days are running out. There is no time!'

When we reached the mountains we had only three animals left and when we crossed the first ridge we were afoot and leading the one remaining beast which carried the dwindling water skins.

We were following a road now. Partly hewn and partly worn it led up and over the mountains, those naked leaning mountains that were full of silence and peopled only with the shapes of red rock that the wind had carved.

'Armies used to come this way,' said Corin. 'Kings and caravans and beggars and human slaves, singers and dancing girls, and the embassies of princes. This was the road to Shandakor.'

And we went along it at a madman's pace.

The beast fell in a slide of rock and broke its neck and we carried the last water skin between us. It was not a heavy burden. It grew lighter and lighter and then was almost gone.

One afternoon, long before sunset, Corin said abruptly, 'We will stop here.'

The road went steeply up before us. There was nothing to be seen or heard. Corin sat down in the drifted dust. I crouched down too, a little distance from him. I watched him. His face was hidden and he did not speak.

The shadows thickened in that deep and narrow way. Overhead the strip of sky flared saffron and then red – and then the bright cruel stars came out. The wind worked at its cutting and polishing of stone, muttering to itself, an old and senile wind full of dissatisfaction and complaint. There was the dry faint click of falling pebbles.

The gun felt cold in my hand, covered with my cloak. I did not want to use it. But I did not want to die here on this silent pathway of vanished armies and caravans and kings.

A shaft of greenish moonlight crept down between the walls. Corin stood up.

'Twice now I have followed lies. Here I am met at last by truth.'

I said, 'I don't understand you.'

'I thought I could escape the destruction. That was a lie. Then

I thought I could return to share it. That too was a lie. Now I see the truth. Shandakor is dying. I fled from that dying, which is the end of the city and the end of my race. The shame of flight is on me and I can never go back.'

'What will you do?'

'I will die here.'

'And I?'

'Did you think,' asked Corin softly, 'that I would bring an alien creature in to watch the end of Shandakor?'

I moved first. I didn't know what weapons he might have, hidden under that dark red cloak. I threw myself over on the dusty rock. Something went past my head with a hiss and a rattle and a flame of light and then I cut the legs from under him and he fell down forward and I got on top of him, very fast.

He had vitality. I had to hit his head twice against the rock before I could take out of his hands the vicious little instrument of metal rods. I threw it far away. I could not feel any other weapons on him except a knife and I took that, too. Then I got up.

I said, 'I will carry you to Shandakor.'

He lay still, draped in the tumbled folds of his cloak. His breath made a harsh sighing in his throat. 'So be it.' And then he asked for water.

I went to where the skin lay and picked it up, thinking that there was perhaps a cupful left. I didn't hear him move. What he did was done very silently with a sharp-edged ornament. I brought him the water and it was already over. I tried to lift him up. His eyes looked at me with a curiously brilliant look. Then he whispered three words, in a language I didn't know, and died. I let him down again.

His blood had poured out across the dust. And even in the moonlight I could see that it was not the colour of human blood.

I crouched there for a long while, overcome with a strange sickness. Then I reached out and pushed that red cowl back to bare his head. It was a beautiful head. I had never seen it. If I had, I would not have gone alone with Corin into the mountains. I would have understood many things if I had seen it and not for fame nor money would I have gone to Shandakor.

His skull was narrow and arched and the shaping of the bones was very fine. On that skull was a covering of short curling fibres that had an almost metallic lustre in the moonlight, silvery and bright. They stirred under my hand, soft silken wires responding of themselves to an alien touch. And even as I took my hand away the lustre faded from them and the texture changed.

When I touched them again they did not stir. Corin's ears were pointed and there were silvery tufts on the tips of them. On them and on his forearms and his breast were the faint, faint memories of scales, a powdering of shining dust across the golden skin. I looked at his teeth and they were not human either.

I knew now why Corin had laughed when I told him that I studied men.

It was very still. I could hear the falling of pebbles and the little stones that rolled all lonely down the cliffs and the shift and whisper of dust in the settling cracks. The Wells of Karthedon were far away. Too far by several lifetimes for one man on foot with a cup of water.

I looked at the road that went steep and narrow on ahead. I looked at Corin. The wind was cold and the shaft of moonlight was growing thin. I did not want to stay alone in the dark with Corin.

I rose and went on along the road that led to Shandakor.

It was a long climb but not a long way. The road came out between two pinnacles of rock. Below that gateway, far below on the light of the little low moons that pass so swiftly over Mars, there was a mountain valley.

Once around that valley there were great peaks crowned with snow and crags of black and crimson where the flying lizards nested, the hawk-lizards with the red eyes. Below the crags there were forests, purple and green and gold, and a black tarn deep on the valley floor. But when I saw it it was dead. The peaks had fallen away and the forests were gone and the tarn was only a pit in the naked rock.

In the midst of that desolation stood a fortress city.

There were lights in it, soft lights of many colours. The outer walls stood up, black and massive, a barrier against the creeping dust, and within them was an island of life. The high towers were not ruined. The lights burned among them and there was movement in the streets.

A living city – and Corin had said that Shandakor was almost dead.

A rich and living city. I did not understand. But I knew one thing. Those who moved along the distant streets of Shandakor were not human.

I stood shivering in that windy pass. The bright towers of the city beckoned and there was something unnatural about all light-life in the deathly valley. And then I thought that human or not the people of Shandakor might sell me water and a beast to carry it and I could get away out of these mountains, back to the Wells.

The road broadened, winding down the slope. I walked in the middle of it, not expecting anything. And suddenly two men came out of nowhere and barred the way.

I yelled. I jumped backward with my heart pounding and the sweat pouring off me. I saw their broadswords glitter in the moonlight. And they laughed.

They were human. One was a tall red barbarian from Mekh, which lay to the east half around Mars. The other was a leaner browner man from Tarak, which was further still. I was scared and angry and astonished and I asked a foolish question.

'What are you doing *here?*'

'We wait,' said the man of Tarak. He made a circle with his arm to take in all the darkling slopes around the valley. 'From Kesh and Shun, from all the countries of the Norlands and the Marches men have come, to wait. And you?'

'I'm lost,' I said. 'I'm an Earthman and I have no quarrel with anyone.' I was still shaking but now it was with relief. I would not have to go to Shandakor. If there was a barbarian army gathered here it must have supplies and I could deal with them.

I told them what I needed. 'I can pay for them, pay well.'

They looked at each other.

'Very well. Come and you can bargain with the chief.'

They fell in on either side of me. We walked three paces and then I was on my face in the dirt and they were all over me like two great wildcats. When they were finished they had everything I owned except the few articles of clothing for which they had no use. I got up again, wiping the blood from my mouth.

'For an outlander,' said the man of Mekh, 'you fight well.' He chinked my money-bag up and down in his palm, feeling the weight of it, and then he handed me the leather bottle that hung at his side. 'Drink,' he told me. 'That much I can't deny you. But our water must be carried a long way across these mountains and we have none to waste on Earthmen.'

I was not proud. I emptied his bottle for him. And the man of Tarak said, smiling, 'Go on to Shandakor. Perhaps they will give you water.'

'But you've taken all my money!'

'They are rich in Shandakor. They don't need money. Go ask them for water.'

They stood there, laughing at some secret joke of their own, and I did not like the sound of it. I could have killed them both and danced on their bodies but they had left me nothing but my bare hands to fight with. So presently I turned and went on and left them grinning in the dark behind me.

The road led down and out across the plain. I could feel eyes watching me, the eyes of the sentinels on the rounding slopes, piercing the dim moonlight. The walls of the city began to rise higher and higher. They hid everything but the top of one tall tower that had a queer squat globe on top of it. Rods of crystal projected from the globe. It revolved slowly and the rods sparkled with a sort of white fire that was just on the edge of seeing.

A causeway lifted toward the Western Gate. I mounted it, going very slowly, not wanting to go at all. And now I could see that the gate was open. *Open* – and this was a city under siege!

I stood still for some time, trying to puzzle out what meaning this might have – an army that did not attack and a city with open gates. I could not find a meaning. There were soldiers on the walls but they were lounging at their ease under the bright banners. Beyond the gate many people moved about but they were intent on their own affairs. I could not hear their voices.

I crept closer, closer still. Nothing happened. The sentries did not challenge me and no one spoke.

You know how necessity can force a man against his judgement and against his will?

I entered Shandakor.

3

There was an open space beyond the gate, a square large enough to hold an army. Around its edges were the stalls of merchants. Their canopies were of rich woven stuffs and the wares they sold were such things as have not been seen on Mars for more centuries than men can remember.

There were fruits and rare furs, the long-lost dyes that never fade, furnishings carved from vanished woods. There were spices and wines and exquisite cloths. In one place a merchant from the far south offered a ceremonial rug woven from the long bright hair of virgins. And it was new.

These merchants were all human. The nationalities of some of them I knew. Others I could guess at from traditional accounts. Some were utterly unknown.

Of the throngs that moved about among the stalls, quite a number were human also. There were merchant princes come to barter and there were companies of slaves on their way to the auction block. But the others ...

I stayed where I was, pressed into a shadowy corner by the gate, and the chill that was on me was not all from the night wind.

The golden-skinned silver-crested lords of Shandakor I knew well enough from Corin. I say lords because that is how they bore themselves, walking proudly in their own place, attended by human slaves. And the humans who were not slaves made way for them and were most deferential as though they knew that they were greatly favoured to be allowed inside the city at all. The women of Shandakor were very beautiful, slim golden sprites with their bright eyes and pointed ears.

And there were others. Slender creatures with great wings, some who were lithe and furred, some who were hairless and ugly and moved with a sinuous gliding, some so strangely shaped and coloured that I could not even guess at their possible evolution.

The lost races of Mars. The ancient races, of whose pride and power nothing was left but the half-forgotten tales of old men in the farthest corners of the planet. Even I, who had made the anthropological history of Mars my business, had never heard of them except as the distorted shapes of legend, as satyrs and giants used to be known on Earth.

Yet here they were in gorgeous trappings, served by naked humans whose fetters were made of precious metals. And before them too the merchants drew aside and bowed.

The lights burned, many-coloured – not the torches and cressets of the Mars I knew but cool radiances that fell from crystal globes. The walls of the buildings that rose around the market-place were faced with rare veined marbles and the fluted towers that crowned them were inlaid with turquoise and cinnabar, with amber and jade and the wonderful corals of the southern oceans.

The splendid robes and the naked bodies moved in a swirling pattern about the square. There was buying and selling and I could see the mouths of the people open and shut. The mouths of the women laughed. But in all that crowded place there was no sound. No voice, no scuff of sandal, no chink of mail. There was only silence, the utter stillness of deserted places.

I began to understand why there was no need to shut the gates. No superstitious barbarian would venture himself into a city peopled by living phantoms.

And I – I was civilised. I was, in my non-mechanical way, a scientist. And had I not been trapped by my need for water and supplies I would have run away right out of the valley. But I had no place to run to and so I stayed and sweated and gagged on the acrid taste of fear.

What were these creatures that made no sound? Ghosts –

images – dreams? The human and the non-human, the ancient, the proud, the lost and forgotten who were so insanely present – did they have some subtle form of life I knew nothing about? Could they see me as I saw them? Did they have thought and volition of their own?

It was the solidity of them, the intense and perfectly prosaic business in which they were engaged. Ghosts do not barter. They do not hang jewelled necklets upon their women nor argue about the price of a studded harness.

The solidity and the silence – that was the worst of it. If there had been one small living sound ...

A dying city, Corin had said. *The days are running out.* What if they had run out? What if I were here in this massive pile of stone with all its countless rooms and streets and galleries and hidden ways, alone with the lights and the soundless phantoms?

Pure terror is a nasty thing. I had it then.

I began to move, very cautiously, along the wall. I wanted to get away from that market-place. One of the hairless gliding non-humans was bartering for a female slave. The girl was shrieking. I could see every drawn muscle in her face, the spasmodic working of her throat. Not the faintest sound came out.

I found a street that paralleled the wall. I went along it, catching glimpses of people – human people – inside the lighted buildings. Now and then men passed me and I hid from them. There was still no sound. I was careful how I set my feet. Somehow I had the idea that if I made a noise something terrible would happen.

A group of merchants came toward me. I stepped back into an archway and suddenly from behind me there came three spangled women of the serais. I was caught.

I did not want those silent laughing women to touch me. I leaped back toward the street and the merchants paused, turning their heads. I thought that they had seen me. I hesitated and the women came on. Their painted eyes shone and their red lips glistened. The ornaments on their bodies flashed. They walked straight into me.

I made noise then, all I had in my lungs. And the women passed through me. They spoke to the merchants and the merchants laughed. They went off together down the street. They hadn't seen me. They hadn't heard me. And when I got in their way I was no more than a shadow. They passed through me.

I sat down on the stones of the street and tried to think. I sat for a long time. Men and women walked through me as through the empty air. I sought to remember any sudden pain, as of an arrow in the back that might have killed me between two seconds, so that I hadn't known about it. It seemed more likely that I should be the ghost than the other way around.

I couldn't remember. My body felt solid to my hands as did the stones I sat on. They were cold and finally the cold got me up and sent me on again. There was no reason to hide any more. I walked down the middle of the street and I got used to not turning aside.

I came to another wall, running at right angles back into the city. I followed that and it curved around gradually until I found myself back at the market-place, at the inner end of it. There was a gateway, with the main part of the city beyond it, and the wall continued. The non-humans passed back and forth through the gate but no human did except the slaves. I realised then that all this section was a ghetto for the humans who came to Shandakor with the caravans.

I remembered how Corin had felt about me. And I wondered – granted that I were still alive and that some of the people of Shandakor were still on the same plane as myself – how they would feel about me if I trespassed in their city.

There was a fountain in the market-place. The water sprang up sparkling in the coloured light and filled a wide basin of carved stone. Men and women were drinking from it. I went to the fountain but when I put my hands in it all I felt was a dry basin filled with dust. I lifted my hands and let the dust trickle from them. I could see it clearly. But I saw the water too. A child leaned over and splashed it and it wetted the garments of the people. They struck the child and he cried and there was no sound.

I went on through the gate that was forbidden to the human race.

The avenues were wide. There were trees and flowers, wide

parks and garden villas, great buildings as graceful as they were tall. A wise proud city, ancient in culture but not decayed, as beautiful as Athens but rich and strange, with a touch of the alien in every line of it. Can you think what it was like to walk in that city, among the silent throngs that were not human – to see the glory of it, that was not human either?

The towers of jade and cinnabar, the golden minarets, the lights and the coloured silks, the enjoyment and the strength. And the people of Shandakor! No matter how far their souls have gone they will never forgive me.

How long I wandered I don't know. I had almost lost my fear in wonder at what I saw. And then, all at once in that deathly stillness, I heard a sound – the quick, soft scuffing of sandalled feet.

4

I stopped where I was, in the middle of a plaza. The tall silver-crested ones drank wine under canopies of dusky blooms and in the centre a score of winged girls as lovely as swans danced a slow strange measure that was more like flight than dancing. I looked all around. There were many people. How could you tell which one had made a noise?

Silence.

I turned and ran across the marble paving. I ran hard and then suddenly I stopped again, listening. *Scuff-scuff* – no more than a whisper, very light and swift. I spun around but it was gone. The soundless people walked and the dancers wove and shifted, spreading their white wings.

Someone was watching me. Some one of those indifferent shadows was not a shadow.

I went on. Wide streets led off from the plaza. I took one of them. I tried the trick of shifting pace and two or three times I caught the echo of other steps than mine. Once I knew it was deliberate. Whoever followed me slipped silently among the noiseless crowd, blending with them, protected by them, only making a show of footsteps now and then to goad me.

I spoke to that mocking presence. I talked to it and listened to my own voice ringing hollow from the walls. The groups of people ebbed and flowed around me and there was no answer.

I tried making sudden leaps here and there among the passersby with my arms outspread. But all I caught was empty air. I wanted a place to hide and there was none.

The street was long. I went its length and the someone followed me. There were many buildings, all lighted and populous and deathly still. I thought of trying to hide in the buildings but I could not bear to be closed in between walls with those people who were not people.

I came into a great circle, where a number of avenues met around the very tall tower I had seen with the revolving globe on top of it. I hesitated, not knowing which way to go. Someone was sobbing and I realized that it was myself, labouring to breathe. Sweat ran into the corners of my mouth and it was cold, and bitter.

A pebble dropped at my feet with a brittle *click*.

I bolted out across the square. Four or five times, without reason, like a rabbit caught in the open, I changed course and fetched up with my back against an ornamental pillar. From somewhere there came a sound of laughter.

I began to yell. I don't know what I said. Finally I stopped and there was only the silence and the passing throngs, who did not see nor hear me. And now it seemed to me that the silence was full of whispers just below the threshold of hearing.

A second pebble clattered off the pillar above my head. Another stung my body. I sprang away from the pillar. There was laughter and I ran.

There were infinities of streets, all glowing with colour. There were many faces, strange faces, and robes blown out on a night wind, litters with scarlet curtains and beautiful cars like chariots drawn by beasts. They flowed past me like smoke, without sound, without substance, and the laughter pursued me, and I ran.

Four men of Shandakor came toward me. I plunged through

them *but their bodies opposed mine, their hands caught me and I could see their eyes, their black shining eyes, looking at me ....*

I struggled briefly and them it was suddenly very dark.

The darkness caught me up and took me somewhere. Voices talked far away. One of them was a light young shiny sort of voice. It matched the laughter that had haunted me down the streets. I hated it.

I hated it so much that I fought to get free of the black river that was carrying me. There was a vertiginous whirling of light and sound and stubborn shadow and then things steadied down and I was ashamed of myself for having passed out.

I was in a room. It was fairly large, very beautiful, very old, the first place I had seen in Shandakor that showed real age – Martian age, that runs back before history had begun on Earth. The floor, of some magnificent sombre stone the colour of a moonless night, and the pale slim pillars that upheld the arching roof all showed the hollowings and smoothnesses of centuries. The wall paintings had dimmed and softened and the rugs that burned in pools of colour on that dusky floor were worn as thin as silk.

There were men and women in that room, the alien folk of Shandakor. But these breathed and spoke and were alive. One of them, a girl-child with slender thighs and little pointed breasts, leaned against a pillar close beside me. Her black eyes watched me, full of dancing lights. When she saw that I was awake again she smiled and flicked a pebble at my feet.

I got up. I wanted to get that golden body between my hands and make it scream. And she said in High Martian, 'Are you a human? I have never seen one before close to.'

A man in a dark robe said, 'Be still, Duani.' He came and stood before me. He did not seem to be armed but others were and I remembered Corin's little weapon. I got hold of myself and did none of the things I wanted to do.

'What are you doing here?' asked the man in the dark robe.

I told him about myself and Corin, omitting only the fight that he and I had had before he died, and I told him how the hillmen had robbed me.

'They sent me here,' I finished, 'to ask for water.'

Someone made a harsh humourless sound. The man before me said, 'They were in a jesting mood.'

'Surely you can spare some water and a beast!'

'Our beasts were slaughtered long ago. And as for water ...' He paused, then asked bitterly, 'Don't you understand? We are dying here of thirst!'

I looked at him and at the she-imp called Duani and the others. 'You don't show any signs of it,' I said.

'You saw how the human tribes have gathered like wolves upon the hills. What do you think they wait for? A year ago they found and cut the buried aqueduct that brought water into Shandakor from the polar cap. All they needed then was patience. And their time is very near. The store we had in the cisterns is almost gone.'

A certain anger at their submissiveness made me say, 'Why do you stay here and die like mice bottled up in a jar? You could have fought your way out. I've seen your weapons.'

'Our weapons are old and we are very few. And suppose that some of us did survive – tell me again, Earthman, how did Corin fare in the world of men?' He shook his head. 'Once we were great and Shandakor was mighty. The human tribes of half a world paid tribute to us. We are only the last poor shadow of our race but we will not beg from men!'

'Besides,' said Duani softly, 'where else could we live but in Shandakor?'

'What about the others?' I asked. 'The silent ones.'

'They are the past,' said the dark-robed man and his voice rang like a distant flare of trumpets.

Still I did not understand. I did not understand at all. But before I could ask more questions a man came up and said, 'Rhul, he will have to die.'

The tufted tips of Duani's ears quivered and her crest of silver curls came almost erect.

'No, Rhul!' she cried. 'At least not right away.'

There was a clamour from the others, chiefly in a rapid angular speech that must have predated all the syllables of men. And the one who had spoken before to Rhul repeated, 'He will have to die! He has no place here. And we can't spare water.'

'I'll share mine with him,' said Dunai, 'for a while.'

I didn't want any favours from her and said so. 'I came here after supplies. You haven't any, so I'll go away again. It's as simple as that.' I couldn't buy from the barbarians, but I might make shift to steal.

Rhul shook his head. 'I'm afraid not. We are only a handful. For years our single defence has been the living ghosts of our past who walk the streets, the shadows who man the walls. The barbarians believe in enchantments. If you were to enter Shandakor and leave it again alive the barbarians would know that the enchantment cannot kill. They would not wait any longer.'

Angrily, because I was afraid, I said, 'I can't see what difference that would make. You're going to die in a short while anyway.'

'But in our own way, Earthman, and in our own time. Perhaps, being human, you can't understand that. It is a question of pride. The oldest race of Mars will end well, as it began.'

He turned away with a small nod of the head that said *kill him* – as easily as that. And I saw the ugly little weapons rise.

5

There was a split second then that seemed like a year. I thought of many things but none of them were any good. It was a devil of a place to die without even a human hand to help me under. And then Duani flung her arms around me.

'You're all so full of dying and big thoughts!' she yelled at them. 'And you're all paired off or so old you can't do anything but think! What about *me?* I don't have anyone to talk to and I'm sick of wandering alone, thinking how I'm going to die! Let me have him just for a little while? I told you I'd share my water.'

On Earth a child might talk that way about a stray dog. And it is written in an old Book that a live dog is better than a dead lion. I hoped they would let her keep me.

They did. Rhul looked at Duani with a sort of weary compassion and lifted his hand. 'Wait,' he said to the men with the weapons. 'I have thought how this human may be useful to us. We have so little time left now that it is a pity to waste any of it, yet much of it must be used up in tending the machine. He could do that labour – and a man can keep alive on very little water.'

The others thought that over. Some of them dissented violently, not so much on the grounds of water as that it was unthinkable that a human should intrude on the last days of Shandakor. Corin had said the same thing. But Rhul was an old man. The tufts of his pointed ears were colourless as glass and his face was graven deep with years and wisdom had distilled in him its bitter brew.

'A human of our own world, yes. But this man is of Earth and the men of Earth will come to be the new rulers of Mars as we were the old. And Mars will love them no better than she did us because they are as alien as we. So it is not unfitting that he should see us out.'

They had to be content with that. I think they were already so close to the end that they did not really care. By ones and twos they left as though already they had wasted too much time away from the wonders that there were in the streets outside. Some of the men still held the weapons on me and others went and brought precious chains such as the human slaves had worn – shackles, so that I should not escape. They put them on me and Duani laughed.

'Come,' said Rhul, 'and I will show you the machine.'

He led me from the room and up a winding stair. There were tall embrasures and looking through them I discovered that we were in the base of the very high tower with the globe. They must have carried me back to it after Duani had chased me with her laughter and her pebbles. I looked out over the glowing streets, so full of splendour and of silence, and asked Rhul why there were no ghosts inside the tower.

'You have seen the globe with the crystal rods?'

'Yes.'

'We are under the shadow of its core. There had to be some retreat for us into reality. Otherwise we would lose the meaning of the dream.'

The winding stair went up and up. The chain between my

ankles clattered musically. Several times I tripped on it and fell.

'Never mind,' Duani said. 'You'll grow used to it.'

We came at last into a circular room high in the tower. And I stopped and stared.

Most of the space in that room was occupied by a web of metal girders that supported a great gleaming shaft. The shaft disappeared upward through the roof. It was not tall but very massive, revolving slowly and quietly. There were traps, presumably for access to the offset shaft and the cogs that turned it. A ladder led to a trap in the roof.

All the visible metal was sound with only a little surface corrosion. What the alloy was I don't know and when I asked Rhul he only smiled rather sadly. 'Knowledge is found,' he said, 'only to be lost again. Even we of Shandakor forget.'

Every bit of that enormous structure had been shaped and polished and fitted into place by hand. Nearly all the Martian peoples work in metal. They seem to have a genius for it and while they are not and apparently never have been mechanical, as some of our races are on Earth, they find many uses for metal that we have never thought of.

But this before me was certainly the highest point of the metal-workers' craft. When I saw what was down below, the beautifully simple power plant and the rotary drive set-up with fewer moving parts than I would have thought possible, I was even more respectful. 'How old is it?' I asked and again Rhul shook his head.

'Several thousand years ago there is a record of the yearly Hosting of the Shadows and it was not the first.' He motioned me to follow him up the ladder, bidding Duani sternly to remain where she was. She came anyway.

There was a railed platform open to the universe and directly above it swung the mighty globe with its crystal rods that gleamed so strangely. Shandakor lay beneath us, a tapestry of many colours, bright and still, and out along the dark sides of the valley the tribesmen waited for the light to die.

'When there is no one left to tend the machine it will stop in time and then the men who have hated us so long will take what they want of Shandakor. Only fear has kept them out this long. The riches of half a world flowed through these streets and much of it remained.'

He looked up at the globe. 'Yes,' he said, 'we had knowledge. More, I think, than any other race of Mars.'

'But you wouldn't share it with the humans.'

Rhul smiled. 'Would you give little children weapons to destroy you? We gave men better ploughshares and brighter ornaments and if they invented a machine we did not take it from them. But we did not tempt and burden them with knowledge that was not their own. They were content to make war with sword and spear and so they had more pleasure and less killing and the world was not torn apart.'

'And you – how did you make war?'

'We defended our city. The human tribes had nothing that we coveted, so there was no reason to fight them except in self-defence. When we did we won.' He paused. 'The other non-human races were more stupid or less fortunate. They perished long ago.'

He turned again to his explanations of the machine. 'It draws its power directly from the sun. Some of the solar energy is converted and stored within the globe to serve as a light-source. Some is sent down to turn the shaft.'

'What if it should stop,' Duani said, 'while we're still alive?' She shivered, looking out over the beautiful streets.

'It won't – not if the Earthman wishes to live.'

'What would I have to gain by stopping it?' I demanded.

'Nothing. And that,' said Rhul, 'is why I trust you. As long as the globe turns you are safe from the barbarians. After we are gone you will have the pick of the loot of Shandakor.

How I was going to get away with it afterward he did not tell me.

He motioned me down the ladder again but I asked him, 'What *is* the globe, Rhul? How does it make the – the Shadows?'

He frowned. 'I can only tell you what has become, I'm afraid, more traditional knowledge. Our wise men studied deeply into the properties of light. They learned that light has a definite effect upon solid matter and they believed, because of that effect, that stone and metal and crystalline things retain a "memory" of all that they have "seen." Why this should be I do not know.'

I didn't try to explain to him the quantum theory and the photo-electric effect nor the various experiments of Einstein and Millikan and the men who followed them. I didn't know them well enough myself and the old High Martian is deficient in such terminology.

I only said, 'The wise men of my world also know that the impact of light tears away tiny particles from the substance it strikes.'

I was beginning to get a glimmering of the truth. Light-patterns 'cut' in the electrons of metal and stone – sound-patterns cut in unlikely looking mediums of plastic, each needing only the proper 'needle' to recreate the recorded melody or the recorded picture.

'They constructed the globe,' said Rhul. 'I do not know how many generations that required nor how many failures they must have had. But they found at last the invisible light that makes the stones give up their memories.'

In other words they had found their needle. What wave-length or combination of wave-lengths in the electromagnetic spectrum flowed out from those crystal rods, there was no way for me to know. But where they probed the walls and the paving blocks of Shandakor they scanned the hidden patterns that were buried in them and brought them forth again in form and colour – as the electron needle brings forth whole symphonies from a little ridged disc.

How they had achieved sequence and selectivity was another matter. Rhul said something about the 'memories' having different lengths. Perhaps he meant depth of penetration. The stones of Shandakor were ages old and the outer surfaces would have worn away. The earliest impressions would be gone altogether or at least have become fragmentary and extremely shallow.

Perhaps the scanning beams could differentiate between the overlapping layers of impressions by that fraction of a micron difference in depth. Photons only penetrate so far into any given substance but if that substance is constantly growing less in thickness the photons would have the effect of going deeper.

I imagine the globe was accurate in centuries or numbers of centuries, not in years.

However it was, the Shadows of a golden past walked the streets of Shandakor and the last men of the race waited quietly for death, remembering their glory.

Rhul took me below again and showed me what my tasks would be, chiefly involving a queer sort of lubricant and a careful watch over the power leads. I would have to spend most of my time there but not all of it. During the free periods, Duani might take me where she would.

The old man went away. Duani leaned herself against a girder and studied me with intense interest. 'How are you called?' she asked.

'John Ross.'

'JonRoss,' she repeated and smiled. She began to walk around me, touching my hair, inspecting my arms and chest, taking a child's delight in discovering all the differences there were between herself and what we call a human. And that was the beginning of my captivity.

6

There were days and nights, scant food and scanter water. There was Duani. And there was Shandakor. I lost my fear. And whether I lived to occupy the Chair or not, this was something to have seen.

Duani was my guide. I was tender of my duties because my neck depended on them but there was time to wander in the streets, to watch the crowded pageant that was not and sense the stillness and the desolation that were so cruelly real.

I began to get the feel of what this alien culture had been like and how it had dominated half a world without the need of conquest.

In a Hall of Government, built of white marble and decorated with wall friezes of austere magnificence, I watched the careful choosing and the crowning of a king. I saw the places of learning. I saw the young men trained for war as fully as they were instructed in the arts of peace. I saw the pleasure gardens, the theatres, the forums, the sporting fields – and I saw the places of work, where the men and women of Shandakor coaxed beauty from their looms and forges to trade for the things they wanted from the human world.

The human slaves were brought by their own kind to be sold, and they seemed to be well treated, as one treats a useful animal in which one has invested money. They had their work to do but it was only a small part of the work of the city.

The things that could be had nowhere else on Mars – the tools, the textiles, the fine work in metal and precious stones, the glass and porcelain – were fashioned by the people of Shandakor and they were proud of their skill. Their scientific knowledge they kept entirely to themselves, except what concerned agriculture or medicine or better ways of building drains and houses.

They were the lawgivers, the teachers. And the humans took all they would give and hated them for it. How long it had taken these people to attain such a degree of civilisation Duani could not tell me. Neither could old Rhul.

'It is certain that we lived in communities, had a form of civil government, a system of numbers and written speech, before the human tribes. There are traditions of an earlier race than ours, from whom we learned these things. Whether or not this is true I do not know.'

In its prime Shandakor had been a vast and flourishing city with countless thousands of inhabitants. Yet I could see no signs of poverty or crime. I couldn't even find a prison.

'Murder was punishable by death,' said Rhul, 'but it was most infrequent. Theft was for slaves. We did not stoop to it.' He watched my face, smiling a little acid smile. 'That startles you – a great city without suffering or crime or places of punishment.'

I had to admit that it did. 'Elder race or not, how did you manage to do it? I'm a student of cultures, both here and on my own world. I know all the usual patterns of development and I've read all the theories about them – but Shandakor doesn't fit any of them.'

Rhul's smile deepened. 'You are human,' he said. 'Do you wish the truth?'

'Of course.'

'Then I will tell you. We developed the faculty of reason.'

For a moment I thought he was joking. 'Come,' I said, 'man is a reasoning being – on Earth the only reasoning being.'

'I do not know of Earth,' he answered courteously. 'But on Mars man has always said, 'I reason, I am above the beasts because I reason.' And he has been very proud of himself because he could reason. It is the mark of his humanity. Being convinced that reason operates automatically within him he orders his life and his government upon emotion and superstition.

'He hates and fears and believes, not with reason but because he is told to by other men or by tradition. He does one thing and says another and his reason teaches him no difference between fact and falsehood. His bloodiest wars are fought for the merest whim – and that is why we did not give him weapons. His greatest follies appear to him the highest wisdom, his basest betrayals become noble acts – and that is why we could not teach him justice. We learned to reason. Man only learned to talk.'

I understood then why the human tribes had hated the men of Shandakor. I said angrily, 'Perhaps that is so on Mars. But only reasoning minds can develop great technologies and we humans of Earth have outstripped yours a million times. All right, you know or knew some things we haven't learned yet, in optics and some branches of electronics and perhaps in metallurgy. But...'

I went on to tell him all the things we had that Shandakor did not. 'You never went beyond the beast of burden and the simple wheel. We achieved flight long ago. We have conquered space and the planets. We'll go on to conquer the stars!'

Rhul nodded. 'Perhaps we were wrong. We remained here and conquered ourselves.' He looked out toward the slopes where the barbarian army waited and he sighed. 'In the end it is all the same.'

Days and nights and Duani, bringing me food, sharing her water, asking questions, taking me through the city. The only thing she would not show me was something they called the Place of Sleep. 'I shall be there soon enough,' she said and shivered.

'How long?' I asked. It was an ugly thing to say.

'We are not told. Rhul watches the level in the cisterns and when it's time ...' She made a gesture with her hands. 'Let us go up on the wall.'

We went up among the ghostly soldiery and the phantom banners. Outside there were darkness and death and the coming of death. Inside there were light and beauty, the last proud blaze of Shandakor under the shadow of its doom. There was an eerie magic in it that had begun to tell on me. I watched Duani. She leaned against the parapet, looking outward. The wind ruffled her silver crest, pressed her garments close against her body. Her eyes were full of moonlight and I could not read them. Then I saw that there were tears.

I put my arm around her shoulders. She was only a child, an alien child, not of my race or breed ...

'JonRoss.'

'Yes?'

'There are so many things I will never know.'

It was the first time I had touched her. Those curious curls stirred under my fingers, warm and alive. The tips of her pointed ears were soft as a kitten's.

'Duani.'

'What?'

'I don't know ...'

I kissed her. She drew back and gave me a startled look from those black brilliant eyes and suddenly I stopped thinking that she was a child and I forgot that she was not human and – I didn't care.

'Duani, listen. You don't have to go to the Place of Sleep.'

She looked at me, her cloak spread out upon the night wind, her hands against my chest.

'There's a whole world out there to live in. And if you aren't happy there I'll take you to my world, to Earth. There isn't any reason why you have to die!'

Still she looked at me and did not speak. In the streets below the silent throngs went by and the towers glowed with many colours. Duani's gaze moved slowly to the darkness beyond the wall, to the barren valley and the hostile rocks.

'No.'

'Why not? Because of Rhul, because of all this talk of pride and race?'

'Because of truth. Corin learned it.'

I didn't want to think about Corin. 'He was alone. You're not. You'd never be alone.'

She brought her hands up and laid them on my cheeks very gently. 'That green star, that is your world. Suppose it were to vanish and you were the last of all the men of Earth. Suppose you lived with me in Shandakor forever – would you not be alone?'

'It wouldn't matter if I had you.'

She shook her head. 'It would matter. And our two races are as far apart as the stars. We would have nothing to share between us.'

Remembering what Rhul had told me I flared up and said some angry things. She let me say them and then she smiled. 'It is none of that, JonRoss.' She turned to look out over the city. 'This is my place and no other. When it is gone I must be gone too.'

Quite suddenly I hated Shandakor.

I didn't sleep much after that. Every time Duani left me I was afraid she might never come back. Rhul would tell me nothing and I didn't dare to question him too much. The hours rushed by like seconds and Duani was happy and I was not. My shackles had magnetic locks. I couldn't break them and I couldn't cut the chains.

One evening Duani came to me with something in her face and in the way she moved that told me the truth long before I could make her put it into words. She clung to me, not wanting to talk, but at last she said, 'Today there was a casting of lots and the first hundred have gone to the Place of Sleep.'

'It is the beginning, then.'

She nodded. 'Every day there will be another hundred until all are gone.'

I couldn't stand it any longer. I thrust her away and stood up. 'You know where the "keys" are. Get these chains off me!'

She shook her head. 'Let us not quarrel now, JonRoss. Come. I want to walk in the city.'

We had quarrelled more than once, and fiercely. She would not leave Shandakor and I couldn't take her out by force as long as I was chained. And I was not to be released until everyone but Rhul had entered the Place of Sleep and the last page of that long history had been written.

I walked with her among the dancers and the slaves and the bright-cloaked princes. There were no temples in Shandakor. If they worshipped anything it was beauty and to that their whole city was a shrine. Duani's eyes were rapt and there was a remoteness on her now.

I held her hand and looked at the towers of turquoise and cinabar, the pavings of rose quartz and marble, the walls of pink and white and deep red coral, and to me they were hideous. The ghostly crowds, the mockery of life, the phantom splendours of the past were hideous, a drug, a snare.

'The faculty of reason!' I thought and saw no reason in any of it.

I looked up to where the great globe turned and turned against the sky, keeping these mockeries alive. 'Have you ever seen the city as it is – without the Shadows?'

'No. I think only Rhul, who is the oldest, remembers it that way. I think it must have been very lonely. Even then there were less than three thousand of us left.'

It must indeed have been lonely. They must have wanted the Shadows as much to people the empty streets as to fend off the enemies who believed in magic.

I kept looking at the globe. We walked for a long time. And then I said, 'I must go back to the tower.'

She smiled at me very tenderly. 'Soon you will be free of the tower – and of these.' She touched the chains. 'No, don't be sad, JonRoss. You will remember me and Shandakor as one remembers a dream.' She held up her face, that was so lovely and so unlike the meaty faces of human women, and her eyes were full of sombre lights. I kissed her and then I caught her up in my arms and carried her back to the tower.

In that room, where the great shaft turned, I told her, 'I have to tend the things below. Go up onto the platform, Duani, where you can see all Shandakor. I'll be with you soon.'

I don't know whether she had some hint of what was in my mind or whether it was only the imminence of parting that made her look at me as she did. I thought she was going to speak but she did not, climbing the ladder obediently. I watched her slender golden body vanish upward. Then I went into the chamber below.

There was a heavy metal bar there that was part of a manual control for regulating the rate of turn. I took it off its pin. Then I closed the simple switches on the power plant. I tore out all the leads and smashed the connections with the bar. I did what damage I could to the cogs and the offset shaft. I worked very fast. Then I went up into the main chamber again. The great shaft was still turning but slowly, ever more slowly.

There was a cry from above me and I saw Duani. I sprang up the ladder, thrusting her back onto the platform. The globe moved heavily of its own momentum. Soon it would stop but the white fires still flickered in the crystal rods. I climbed up onto the railing, clinging to a strut. The chains on my wrists and ankles made it hard but I could reach. Duani tried to pull me down. I think she was screaming. I hung on and smashed the crystal rods with the bar, as many as I could.

There was no more motion, no more light. I got down on the platform again and dropped the bar. Duani had forgotten me. She was looking at the city.

The lights of many colours that had burned there were burning still but they were old and dim, cold embers without radiance. The towers of jade and turquoise rose up against the little moons and they were broken and cracked with time and there was no glory in them. They were desolate and very sad. The night lay clotted around their feet. The streets, the plazas and the market-squares were empty, their marble paving blank and bare. The soldiers had gone from the walls of Shandakor, with their banners and their bright mail, and there was no longer any movement anywhere within the gates.

Duani let out one small voiceless cry. And as though in answer to it, suddenly from the darkness of the valley and the slopes beyond there rose a thin fierce howling as of wolves.

'Why?' she whispered. '*Why?*' She turned to me. Her face was pitiful. I caught her to me.

'I couldn't let you die! Not for dreams and visions, nothing. Look, Duani. Look at Shandakor.' I wanted to force her to understand. 'Shandakor is broken and ugly and forlorn. It is a dead city – but you're alive. There are many cities but only one life for you.'

Still she looked at me and it was hard to meet her eyes. She said, 'We knew all that, JonRoss.'

'Duani, you're a child, you've only a child's way of thought. Forget the past and think of tomorrow. We can get through the barbarians. Corin did. And after that ...'

'And after that you would still be human – and I would not.'

From below us in the dim and empty street there came a sound of lamentation. I tried to hold her but she slipped out from between my hands. 'And I am glad that you are human,' she whispered. 'You will never understand what you have done.'

And she was gone before I could stop her, down into the tower.

I went after her. Down the endless winding stairs with my chains clattering between my feet, out into the streets, the dark and broken and deserted streets of Shandakor. I called her name and her golden body went before me, fleet and slender, distant and more distant. The chains dragged upon my feet and the night took her away from me.

I stopped. The whelming silence rushed smoothly over me and I was bitterly afraid of this dark dead Shandakor that I did not know. I called again to Duani and then I began to search for her in the shattered shadowed streets. I know now how long it must have been before I found her.

For when I found her, she was with the others. The last people of Shandakor, the men and the women, the women first, were walking silently in a long line toward a low flat-roofed building that I knew without telling was the Place of Sleep.

They were going to die and there was no pride in their faces now. There was a sickness in them, a sickness and a hurt in their eyes as they moved heavily forward, not looking, not wanting to look at the sordid ancient streets that I had stripped of glory.

'*Duani!*' I called, and ran forward but she did not turn in her place in the line. And I saw that she was weeping.

Rhul turned toward me, and his look had a weary contempt that was bitterer than a curse. 'Of what use, after all, to kill you now?'

'But I did this thing! *I* did it!'

'You are only human.'

The long line shuffled on and Duani's little feet were closer to that final doorway. Rhul looked upward at the sky. 'There is still time before the sunrise. The women at least will be spared the indignity of spears.'

'Let me go with her!'

I tried to follow her, to take my place in line. And the weapon in Rhul's hand moved and there was the pain and I lay as Corin had lain while they went silently on into the Place of Sleep.

The barbarians found me when they came, still half doubtful, into the city after dawn. I think they were afraid of me. I think they feared me as a wizard who had somehow destroyed all the folk of Shandakor.

For they broke my chains and healed my wounds and later they even gave me out of the loot of Shandakor the only thing I wanted – a bit of porcelain, shaped like the head of a young girl.

I sit in the Chair that I craved at the University and my name is written on the roll of the discoverers. I am eminent, I am respectable – I, who murdered the glory of a race.

Why didn't I go after Duani into the Place of Sleep? I could have crawled! I could have dragged myself across those stones. And I wish to God I had. I wish that I had died with Shandakor!

THE TWEENER

A taxicab turned the corner and came slowly down the street.

'Here he is!' shrieked the children, tearing open the white gate. 'Mother! Dad! He's here, Uncle Fred's here!'

Matt Winslow came out onto the porch, and in a minute Lucille came too, flushed from the purgatory of a kitchen on a July day. The cab stopped in front of the house. Josh and Barbie pounced on it like two small tigers, howling, and from up and down the street the neighbours' young came drifting, not making any noise, recognising that this was the Winslows' moment and not intruding on it, but wanting to be close to it, to breathe and see and hear the magic.

'Look at them,' said Matt, half laughing. 'You'd think Fred was Tarzan, Santa Claus, and Superman, all rolled into one.'

'Well,' said Lucille proudly, 'not many people have been where he has.'

She went running down the path. Matt followed her. Inside, he was jealous. It was nothing personal, he liked Lucille's brother and respected him. It was only that Josh and Barbie had never had that look in their eyes for him. This was a secret jealousy, that Matt hid carefully, frighteningly, even from himself.

Fred got out of the cab, trim and soldierly in his uniform with the caduceus on the collar tabs, but forgetting all about dignity as he tried to hug the kids and kiss his sister and shake Matt's hand all at once. 'I'll get your bags,' said Matt, and the neighbours' children stared with enormous eyes and sent the name of Mars whispering back and forth between them.

'Be careful,' Fred said. 'That one there, with the handle on it – let me.' He lifted it out, a smallish box made from pieces of packing case that still showed Army serial numbers. It had little round holes bored in its top and sides. Fred waved the children back. 'Don't joggle it, it's a rare Martian vase I brought back for your mother, and I don't want it broken. Presents for you? Now what do you think of that – I clean forgot! Oh well, there wasn't much out there you'd have wanted, anyway.'

'Not even a *rock?*' cried Josh, and Fred shook his head solemnly. 'Not a pebble.' Barbie was staring at the holes in the box. Matt picked up Fred's suitcase. 'He hasn't changed,' he thought. 'Lost some weight, and got some new lines in his face, but with the kids he hasn't changed. He still acts like one himself.' He, too, looked at the holes in the box, but with apprehension. 'This is going to be good,' he thought. 'Something special.'

'God, it's hot,' said Fred, screwing up his eyes as though the sunlight hurt them. 'Ten months on Mars is no way to train up for an eastern summer. Barbie, don't hang on your old uncle, he's having trouble enough.' He glanced at Matt and Lucille, grinning ruefully, and made a pantomime of giving at the knees. 'I feel as though I'm wading in glue.'

'Sit down on the porch,' Lucille said. 'There's a little breeze—'

'In a minute,' Fred said. 'But first, don't you want to see your present?' He set the box down, in a shady spot under the big maple at the corner of the house.

'Now Fred, what are you up to?' she demanded suspiciously. 'Martian vases, indeed!'

'Well, it's not exactly a vase. It's more of a— *I'll* open it, Josh, you just stand back. This doesn't concern you.'

'Oh, Uncle Fred!' wailed Barbie, dancing up and down like a doll on strings. 'Open it up, *please* open it up.'

Matt had put the suitcase inside the door. Now he came and joined the others under the tree.

Fred opened the lid of the box. Then he sat back on his heels, watching the children's faces, and Matt thought, 'He's been waiting for this for nearly a year, dreaming it up ... he should have married and had kids of his own.'

Josh and Barbie let out one mingled cry, and then were still. For a moment.

'Is it really alive?'
'Can we touch it?'
'Will it bite?'

'Oh, Uncle Fred – oh, *look* – it does belong to us, doesn't it?'

Along the fence small boys and girls impaled their meagre bellies on the pickets in an effort to see. Matt and Lucille peered down into the box. On a mat of red sand and dry lichens a thing was crouching, a neat furry thing about the size of a big rabbit and not unlike one in outline, except that its ears were cup-shaped, and except that its coat was mottled in the exact rust red and greenish grey of the native sand and lichens. It looked up at the unfamiliar faces with a sort of mild incuriosity, its eyes half shut against the glare, but otherwise it did not move.

'What on earth is it?' asked Lucille.

'Nothing,' said Fred 'on Earth. On Mars, he's the dominant form of life – or was, until we came. In fact, he's the sole surviving mammal, and almost the sole surviving invertebrate. He doesn't have an official name yet. It'll be years before the zoologists can decide on their classifications. But the boys out there call him tweener.'

'What?' said Lucille.

'Tweener. Because he's sort of between things. You know – if anyone asked you what he was like, you'd say he was something between a rabbit and a ground-hog, or maybe between a monkey and a squirrel. Go ahead, Barbie, pick him up.'

'Now wait a minute,' said Matt. He pushed Barbie back. 'Wait just a minute, Fred, are you sure about this thing? Is he safe? I don't want the kids bitten, or catching anything.'

'Beside him,' said Fred, 'a rabbit is dangerous. The tweeners have had no enemies for so long they've forgotten how to fight, and they haven't yet acquired any fear of man. I've pulled 'em out of their burrows with my bare hands.'

He reached into the box and lifted the creature gently, clucking to it. 'Anyway, this one has been a pet all his life. I picked him especially because of that. He's acclimated to warmer temperatures and approximately Earth-normal atmosphere, from living in a Base hut, and I thought he'd stand the shock of transplanting better.' He held the tweener out. 'Here, you take him, Matt. You and Lucille. Set your minds at rest.'

Matt hesitated, and then received the tweener into his hands.

It felt like – well, like an animal. Like any small animal you might pick up. Warm, very thick-furred, perhaps more slight in the bone and light in the muscle than he had expected. It had no tail. Its hind legs were not at all rabbit-like, and its forelegs were longer than he had thought. It placed a paw on his arm, a curious paw with three strong fingers and a thumb, and lifted its head, sniffing. The sunlight was brighter here, falling in a shaft between the branches, and the tweener's eyes were almost shut, giving it a look of sleepy imbecility. Matt stroked it awkwardly, once or twice, and it rubbed its head against his arm. Matt shivered. 'That soft fur,' he said. 'It tickles, sort of. Want him, Lucille?'

She looked sternly at Fred. 'No germs?'

'No germs.'

'All right.' She took the tweener the way she would have taken a cat, holding him up under the forelegs and looking him over while he dangled, limp and patient. Finally she smiled. 'He's cute. I think I'm going to like him.' She set him carefully on his feet in the green grass. 'All right, you kids. And be careful you don't hurt him.'

Once more Josh and Barbie were speechless, if not silent. They lay on the ground and touched and patted and peered and took turns holding, and the ragged fringe of small bodies on the fence dripped and flowed inward until the yard was full of children and the stranger from Mars was hidden out of sight.

'Kids,' said Fred, and laughed. 'It's nice to see them again. And normal people.'

'What do you mean, normal?'

Fred said wryly, 'I had to be doctor *and* psychiatrist. I've had xenophobes crawling all over me for ten long months.'

'Xeno— what?' asked Lucille.

'A two-dollar word for men who fear the unknown. When chaps got to worrying too much about what was over the horizon, they were dumped on me. But the heck with that. Take me somewhere cool and drown me in beer.'

It was a long hot afternoon, and a long hot evening, and they belonged mostly to Fred. To the children he seemed ten feet high and shining with the hero-light. To the neighbours who dropped in to say hello, he was a man who had actually visited a place they still did not quite believe in.

The children, the whole gaggle of them, hunkered in a circle around the chairs that had been dragged to the coolest spot in the yard.

'Is it like in the books, Uncle Fred? Is it?'

Fred groaned, and pointed to the tweener in Barbie's arms. 'Get him to tell you. He knows better than I do.'

'Of course he does,' said Barbie; 'John Carter knows everything. But—'

'Who?' asked Fred.

'John Carter. John Carter of Mars.'

Fred laughed. 'Good. That's a good name. You get it, don't you, Matt? Remember all those wonderful Edgar Rice Burroughs stories about the Warlord of Mars, and the Swordsman of Mars, and the Gods of Mars?'

'Sure,' said Matt, rather sourly. 'The kids read 'em all the time. John Carter is the hero, the kind with a capital H.' He turned to the children. 'But John Carter was an Earthman, who went to Mars.'

'Well,' said Josh, scornfully impatient of adult illogic, '*he's* a Martian who came to Earth. It's the same thing. Isn't it, Uncle Fred?'

'You might say that, like the other John Carter, he's a citizen of two worlds.'

'Yes,' said Barbie. 'But anyway, we can't understand his language yet, so you'll have to tell us about Mars.'

'Oh, all right,' said Fred, and he told them about Mars, about the dark canals and the ruined cities, about the ancient towers standing white and lonely under the twin moons, about beautiful princesses and wicked kings and mighty swordsmen. And after they had gone away again to play with John Carter, Matt shook his head and said, 'You ought to be ashamed, filling their heads up with that stuff.'

Fred grinned. 'Time enough for reality when they grow up.'

It got later, and the night closed in. Neighbours came and went. The extra children disappeared. It grew quiet, and finally there was no one left but the Winslows and Fred. Matt went inside to the kitchen for more beer.

From somewhere in the remote darkness beyond the open windows, Barbie screamed.

The can he was opening fell out of Matt's hand, making a geyser of foam where it hit the floor. 'If that little—' he said, and did not stop to finish the sentence. He ran out the kitchen door.

Fred and Lucille had jumped up. Barbie's shrieks were coming from the foot of the lot, where the garage was, and now Matt could hear Josh yelling. He ran across the lawn and onto the drive. Lucille was behind him, calling, 'Barbie! Josh! What is it?'

In the dim reflection of light from the house, Matt could make out the small figure of Josh bent over and tugging frantically at the handle of the overhead door, which was closed tight. 'Help!' he panted. 'It's stuck, or something.'

Matt brushed him aside. Beyond the door, in the dark garage, Barbie was still screaming. Matt took hold of the handle and heaved.

It was jammed, but not so badly that his greater strength could not force it up. It slid, clicking and grumbling, into place, and Matt rushed into the opening.

Barbie was standing just inside, her mouth stretched over another scream, her cheeks running streams of tears. John Carter was beside her. He was standing on his hind legs, almost erect, and the fingers of one forepaw were gripped tightly around Barbie's thumb. His eyes were wide open. In the kindly night there was no hot glare to bother them, and they looked out, green-gold and very, very bright. Something rose up into Matt's throat and closed it. He reached out, and Barbie shook off John Carter's grip and flung herself into Matt's arms.

'Oh, Daddy, it was so dark and Josh couldn't get the door open—'

Josh came in and picked up John Carter. 'Aw, girls,' he said, quite scornful now that the emergency was over. 'Just because she gets stuck in the garage for a few minutes, she has to have hysterics.'

'What in the world were you doing?' Lucille demanded weakly, feeling Barbie all over.

'Just playing,' said Josh, sulking. 'How should I know the old door wouldn't work?'

'She's okay,' Fred said. 'Just scared.'

Lucille groaned deeply. 'And they wonder why mothers turn grey at an early age. All right, you two, off to bed. Scoot!'

Josh started toward the house with Barbie, still clutching John Carter.

'Oh, no,' said Matt. 'You're not taking that thing to bed with you.' He caught John Carter by the loose skin of his shoulders and pulled him out of the boy's arms. Josh spun around, all ready to make trouble about it, and Fred said smoothly, 'I'll take him.'

He did, holding him more gently than Matt. 'Your father's right, Josh. No pets in the bedroom. And anyway, John Carter wouldn't be comfortable there. He likes a nice cool place where he can dig his own house and make the rooms just to suit him.'

'Like a catacomb?' asked Barbie, in a voice still damp and tremulous.

'Or a cave?' asked Josh.

'Exactly. Now you run along, and your father and I will fix him up.'

'Well,' said Josh. 'Okay.' He held out a finger and John Carter wrapped a paw around it. Josh shook hands solemnly. 'Good night.' Then he looked up. 'Uncle Fred, if he digs like a woodchuck, how come his front feet are like a monkey's?'

'Because,' said Fred, 'he didn't start out to be a digger. And he is much more like an ape than a woodchuck. But there haven't been any trees in his country for a long time, and he had to take to the ground anyway to keep warm. That's what we call adaptation.' He turned to Matt. 'How about the old root cellar? It'd be ideal for him, if you're still not using it for anything.'

'No,' said Matt slowly. 'I'm not using it.' He looked at John Carter in the dim light from the house, and John Carter looked back at him with those bright unearthly eyes.

Matt put a hand up to his head, aware that it had begun to

ache. 'My sinus is kicking up – probably going to rain tomorrow. I think I'll turn in myself, if you don't mind.'

'Go ahead, honey,' Lucille said. 'I'll help Fred with the tweener.'

Matt took two aspirin on top of his beer, which made him feel no better, and retired into a heavy sleep, through which stalked dark and unfamiliar dreams that would not show their faces.

The next day was Sunday. It did not rain, but Matt's head went on aching.

'Are you sure it's your sinus?' Lucille asked.

'Oh, yes. All in the right side, frontal and maxillary. Even my teeth hurt.'

'Hm,' said Fred. 'Don't ever go to Mars. Sinusitis is an occupational hazard there, in spite of oxygen masks. Something about the difference in pressure that raises hob with terrestrial insides. Why, do you know—'

'No,' said Matt sourly, 'and I don't want to know. Save your gruesome stories for your medical conference.'

Fred winced. 'I wish you hadn't mentioned that. I hate the thought of New York in this kind of weather. Damn it, it's cruelty to animals. And speaking of which—' he turned to Josh and Barbie— 'keep John Carter in the cellar until this heat wave breaks. At least it's fairly cool down there. Remember he wasn't built for this climate, nor for this world. Give him a break.'

'Oh, we will,' said Barbie earnestly. 'Besides, he's busy, building his castle. You ought to see the wall he's making around it.'

Working slowly, resting often, John Carter had begun the construction of an elaborate burrow in the soft floor of the old root cellar. They went down and watched him from time to time, bringing up earth and then patting and shaping it with his clever paws into a neat rampart to protect his front door. 'To deflect wind and sand,' Fred said, and Barbie, watching with fascinated eyes, murmured, 'I'll bet he could build anything he wanted to, if he was big enough.'

'Maybe. Matter of fact, he probably was a good bit bigger once, a long time ago when things weren't so tough. But—'

'As big as me?' asked Josh.

'Possibly. But if he built anything then we haven't been able to find it. Or anything at all that *anybody* built. Except, of course,' he added hastily, 'those cities I was telling you about.'

The heat wave broke that night in a burst of savage line-squalls. 'That's what my head was complaining about,' thought Matt, rousing up to blink at the lightning. And then he slept again, and dreamed, dim sad dreams of loss and yearning. In the morning his head still ached.

Fred went down to New York for his conference. Matt went to the office and stewed, finding it hard to keep his mind on his work with the nagging pain in the side of his skull. He began to worry. He had never had a bout go on this long. He fidgeted more and more as the day wore on, and then hurried home oppressed by a vague unease that he could find no foundation for.

'All right?' Lucille echoed. 'Of course everything's all right. Why?'

'I don't know. Nothing. The kids—?'

'They've been playing Martian all day. Matt, I've never seen them so tickled with anything in their lives as they are with that little beastie. And he's so cute and patient with them. Come here a minute.'

She led him to the door of the children's room, and pointed in. Josh and Barbie arrayed in striped beach towels and some of Lucille's junkier costume jewellery, were engaged in a complicated ritual that involved much posturing and waving of wooden swords. In the centre of the room enthroned on a chair, John Carter sat. He had a length of bright cloth wrapped around him and a gold bracelet on his neck. He sat perfectly still, watching the children with his usual half-lidded stare, and Matt said harshly, 'It isn't right.'

'What isn't?'

'Any ordinary animal wouldn't stand for it. Look at him, just squatting there like a—' He hunted for a word and couldn't find it.

'The gravity,' Lucille reminded him. 'He hardly moves at all, poor little thing. And it seems quite hard for him to breathe.'

Josh and Barbie knelt side by side in front of the throne, holding their swords high in the air. '*Kaor!*' they cried to John Carter, and then Josh stood up again and began to talk in gibberish, but respectfully, as though addressing a king.'

That's Martian,' said Lucille, and winked at Matt. 'Sometimes you'd swear they were actually speaking a language. Come on and stretch out on the couch a while, honey, why don't you? You look tired.'

'I am tired,' he said. 'And I—' He stopped.

'What?'

'Nothing.' No, nothing at all. He lay down on the couch. Lucille went into the kitchen. He could hear her moving about, making the usual noises. Faintly, far off, he heard the children's voices. Sometimes you'd swear they were actually speaking a language. Sometimes you'd swear—

No. No you wouldn't. You know what is, and what isn't. Even the kids know.

He dozed, and the children's voices crept into his dream. They spoke in the thin and icy wind and murmured in the dust that blew beneath it, and there was no doubt at all now that they were speaking a tongue they knew and understood. He called to them, but they did not answer, and he knew that they did not want to answer, that they were hiding from him somewhere among the ridges of red sand that flowed and shifted so that there was never a trail or a landmark. He ran among the dunes, shouting their names, and then there was a tumble of ancient rock where a mountain had died, and a hollow place below it with a tinge of green around a meagre pool. He knew that they were there in that hollow place. He raced toward it, racing the night that deepened out of a sky already dark and flecked with stars, and in the dusk a shape rose up and blocked his way. It bore in its right hand a blade of grass – no, a sword. A sword, and its face was shadowed, but its eyes looked out at him, green-gold and bright and not of the Earth—

'For heaven's sake, Matt – wake up!' Lucille was shaking him. He sprang up, still in the grip of his dream, and saw Josh and Barbie standing on the other side of the room. They had their ordinary clothes on, and they were grinning, and Barbie said,

'How can you have a nightmare when it's still daytime?'

'I don't know,' said Lucille, 'but it must have been a dandy. Come on Matt, and get your dinner, before the neighbours decide I'm beating you.'

'Other people's nightmares,' Matt snarled, 'are always so funny. Where's John Carter?'

'Oh, we put him back down the cellar,' Josh said, quite unconcerned. 'Mom, will you get him some more lettuce tomorrow? He sure goes for it.'

Feeling shamefaced and a little sick, Matt sat down and ate his dinner. He did not enjoy it. Nor did he sleep well that night, starting up more than once from the verge of an ugly dream. Next day Gulf Tropical had come in again worse than before, and his head had not stopped aching.

He went to his doctor, who could find no sign of infection but gave him a shot on general principles. He went to his office, but it was only a gesture. He returned home at noon on a two-day sick leave. The temperature had crashed up to ninety and humidity dripped out of the air in sharp crashing showers.

'I'll bet Fred's suffering in New York,' Lucille said. 'And poor John Carter! I haven't let the kids take him out of the cellar at all.'

'Do you know what he did, Daddy?' Barbie said. 'Josh found it this morning after you left.'

'What?' asked Matt, with an edge in his voice.

'A hole,' said Josh. 'He must've tunnelled right under the foundation. It was in the lawn, just outside where the root cellar is. I guess he's used to having a back door to his castle, but I filled it in. I filled it real good and put a great big stone on top.'

Matt relaxed. 'He'll only dig another.'

Barbie shook her head. 'He better not. I told him what would happen if he did, how a big dog might kill him, or he might get lost and never find his way home again.'

'Poor little tyke,' Lucille said. 'He'll never find *his* home again.'

'Oh, the hell with him,' Matt said angrily. 'Couldn't you waste a little sympathy on me? I feel lousy.'

He went upstairs away from them and tried to lie down, but

the room was a sweat-box. He tossed and groaned and came down again, and Lucille fixed him iced lemonade. He sat in the shade on the back porch and drank it. It hit his stomach cold and sour-sweet and it tied him in knots, and he got up to pace the lawn. The heat weighed and dragged at him. His head throbbed and his knees felt weak. He passed the place where Josh had filled in the new tunnel, and from the cellar window he heard the children's voices. He turned around and stamped back into the house.

'What are you doing down there?' he shouted, through the open cellar door.

Barbie's answer came muffled and hollow from the gloom below. 'We brought John Carter some ice to lick on, but he won't come out.' She began to talk in a different tone, softly, crooning, calling. Matt said, 'Come up out of there before you catch cold!'

'In a minute,' Josh said.

Matt went down the steps, his shoes thumping on the wooden treads. They had not turned on the lights, and what came through the small dusty windows was only enough to show the dim outlines of things. He banged his head on a heating duct and swore, and Barbie said rather impatiently, 'We said we'd be up in a minute.'

'What's the matter?' Matt demanded, blundering around the furnace. 'Am I not supposed to come down here any more?'

'Sh-h!' Josh told him. 'There, he's just coming out. Don't scare him back in again!'

The door of the root cellar was open. The children were crouched inside it, by the earthen rampart John Carter had constructed with such labour. In the circle of the rampart was a dark hole, and from it John Carter was emerging, very slowly, his eyes luminescent in the gloom. Barbie put two ice cubes on the ground before him, and he set his muzzle against them and lay panting, his flanks pulsing in a shallow, uneven rhythm.

'You'll be all right,' Josh told him, and stroked his head. To Matt he said, 'You don't understand how important he is. There isn't another kid anywhere around who has a real genuine Martian for a pet.'

'Come on,' said Matt harshly. 'Upstairs.' The clammy air was making him shiver. Reluctantly the children rose and went past him. John Carter did not stir. He looked at Matt, and Matt drew back, slamming the door shut. He followed the children out of the cellar, but in his mind's eye he could still see John Carter crouched behind his wall in the dark, tortured by a world that was not his, a world too big, too hot, too heavy.

Crouched behind his wall in the dark, and thinking.

No. Animals do not think. They feel. They can be lost, or frightened, or suffering, or a lot of things, but they're all feelings, not thoughts. Only humans think.

On Earth.

Matt went out in the yard again. He went clear to the back of it where the fence ran along the alley, and took hold of the pickets in his two hands. He stood there staring at the neighbours' back fences, at their garages and garbage cans, not seeing them, feeling the vague conviction that had been in the back of his mind grow and take shape and advance to a point where he could no longer pretend he didn't see it.

'No,' he said to himself. 'Fred would have known. The scientists would know. It couldn't be, and not be known.'

Or couldn't it? How did you measure possibility on another world?

The only mammal, Fred had said, and almost the only vertebrate. Why should one sole species survive when all the others were gone, unless it had an edge to begin with, an advantage?

Suppose a race. Suppose intelligence. Intelligence, perhaps, of a sort that human men, Earthly men, would not understand.

Suppose a race and a world. A dying world. Suppose that race being forced to change with its dying, to dwindle and adapt, to lose its cities and its writings and inventions, or whatever had taken the place of them, but not its mind. Never its mind, because mind would be the only barrier against destruction.

Suppose that race, physically altered, environmentally destitute, driven inward on its own thoughts. Wouldn't it evolve all kinds of mental compensations, powers no Earthman would suspect or look for because he would be thinking in terms of what he knew, of Earthly life-forms? And wouldn't such a race go to any lengths to hide its intelligence, its one last weapon, from the strangers who had come trampling in to take its world away?

Matt trembled. He looked up at the sky, and he knew what was different about it. It was no longer a solid shell that covered him. It was wide open, ripped and torn by the greedy ships, carrying the greedy men who had not been content with what they had. And through those rents the Outside had slipped in, and it would never be the same again. Never more the safe familiar Earth containing only what belonged to it, only what men could understand.

He stood there while a shower of rain crashed down and drenched him, and he did not feel it.

Then again, fiercely, Matt said, 'No. I won't believe that, it's too – it's like the kids believing their games while they play them.'

But were they only games?

He started at the sound of Lucille's voice calling him in. He knew by the sound of it she was worried. He went back toward the house. She came part way to meet him, demanding to know what he was doing out in the rain. He let her chivvy him into the house and into dry clothes, and he kept telling her there was nothing wrong, but she was alarmed now and would not listen. 'You lie down,' she said and covered him with a quilt, and then he heard her go downstairs and get on the telephone. He lay quiet for a few minutes, trying to get himself in hand, frightened and half ashamed of the state of his nerves. Sweat began to roll off him. He kicked the quilt away. The air inside the room was thick with moisture, heavy, stale. He found himself panting like—

Hell, it was no different from any summer heat wave, the bedroom was always hot and suffocating. It was always hard to breathe.

He left it and went downstairs.

Lucille was just getting up from the phone. 'Who were you calling?' he asked.

'Fred,' she said, giving him that non-nonsense look she got when she decided that something had to be done. 'He said he'd be here in the morning. I'm going to find out what's the matter with you.'

Matt said irritably, 'But my doctor—'

'Your doctor doesn't know you like Fred does, and he doesn't care as much about you, either.'

Matt grumbled, but it was too late to do anything about it now. Then he began to think that maybe Fred was the answer. Maybe if he told him—

What?

All right, drag it out, put it into words. I think John Carter is more than a harmless little beast. I think he's intelligent. I think that he hates me, that he hates this Earth where he's been brought so casually as a pet. I think he's doing something to my children.

Could he say that to Fred?

Lucille was calling the children for supper. 'Oh lord, they're down in that damp cellar again. Josh, Barbie, come up here this minute!'

Matt put his head between his hands. It hurt.

He slept downstairs that night, on the living-room couch. He had done that before during heat waves. It gave the illusion of being cooler. He dosed himself heavily with aspirin, and for a time he lapsed into a drugged slumber full of dark shapes that pursued him over a landscape he could not quite see but which he knew was alien and hateful. Then in the silent hours between midnight and dawn he started up in panic. He could not breathe. The air was as thick as water, and a weight as of mountain ranges lay along his chest, his thighs, his shoulders.

He turned on a lamp and began to move up and down, his chest heaving, his hands never still, a glassy terror spreading over him, sheathing him as a sleet storm sheathes a tree.

The living room looked strange, the familiar things overlaid with a gloss of fear, traces everywhere of Josh and Barbie, of Lucille and himself, suddenly significant, suddenly sharp and poignantly symbolic as items in a Dali painting. Lucille's lending-library novel with the brown paper cover, Lucille's stiff Staffordshire figures on the mantel staring with their stiff white faces. An empty pop bottle, no, two empty pop bottles shoved guiltily behind the couch. Small blue jacket with a pocket torn, a drift of comic books under the lamp, his own chair with the cushion worn hollow by his own sitting. Patterns. Wall-paper, slipcovers, rug. Colours, harsh and queer. He was aware of the floor beneath his feet. It was thin. It was a skim of ice over a black pool, ready to crack and let him fall, into the place where the stranger lay, and thought, and waited.

All over Mars they lie and wait, he thought, in their places under the ground. Thinking back and forth in the bitter nights, hating the men, human men who pull them out of their burrows and kill them and dissect them and pry at their brains and bones and nerves and organs. The men who tie little strings around their necks and put them in cages, and never think to look behind their eyes and see what lurks there.

Hating, and wanting their world back. Hating, and quietly driving men insane.

Just as this one is doing to me, he thought. He's suffering. He's crushed in this gravity, and strangling in this air, and he's going to make me suffer too. He knows he can never go home. He knows he's dying. How far can he push it? Can he only make me feel what he's feeling, or can he ... ?

Suppose he can. Suppose he knows I'm going to tell Fred. Suppose he stops me.

After that, what? Josh? Barbie? Lucille?

Matt stood still in the middle of the floor. 'He's killing me,' he thought. 'He knows.'

He began to shake. The room turned dark in front of him. He wanted to vomit, but there was a strange paralysis creeping over him, tightening his muscles, knotting them into ropes to bind him. He felt cold, as though he were already dead.

He turned. He did not run, he was past running, but he walked faster with every step, stiffly, like a mechanical thing wound up and accelerating toward a magnetic goal. He opened the cellar door, and the steps took him down. He remembered to switch on the light.

It was only a short distance to the north corner, and the half-open door.

John Carter made a sound, the only one Matt had ever heard him make. A small thin shriek, purely animal and quite, quite brainless.

It was the next morning, and Fred had come on the early train. They were standing, all of them, grouped together on the lawn near the back fence, looking down. The children were crying.

'A dog must have got him,' Matt said. He had said that before, but his voice still lacked the solid conviction of a statement known and believed. He wanted to look up and away from what lay on the ground by his feet, but he did not. Fred was facing him.

'Poor little thing,' said Lucille. 'I suppose it must have been a dog. Can you tell, Fred?'

Fred bent over. Matt stared at his own shoes. Inside his pockets, his hands were curled tightly into fists. He wanted to talk. The temptation, the longing, the lust to talk was almost more than he could endure. He put the edges of his tongue between his teeth and bit it.

After a minute Fred said, 'It was a dog.'

Matt glanced at him, and now it was Fred who scowled at his shoes.

'I hope it didn't hurt him,' Lucille said.

Fred said, 'I don't think it did.'

Miserably between his sobs, Josh wailed, 'I used the biggest stone I could find. I never thought he could have moved it.'

'There, now,' said Lucille, putting her arms around the children. She led them away toward the house, talking briskly, the usual mixture of nonsense and sound truth that parents administer at such times. Matt wanted to go away too, but Fred made no move, and somehow he knew that it was no use going. He stood with his head down, feeling the sun beat on the back of it like a hammer on a flinching anvil.

He wished Fred would say something. Fred remained silent.

Finally Matt said, 'Thanks.'

'I didn't see any reason to tell them. They'd find it hard to understand.'

'Do *you* understand?' Matt cried out. 'I don't. Why did I do such a thing? How could I have done such a thing?'

'Fear. I think I mentioned that once. Xenophobia.'

'But that's not – I mean, I don't see how it applies.'

'It's not just a fear of unknown places, but of unknown *things*. Anything at all that's strange and unfamiliar.' He shook his head. 'I'll admit I didn't expect to find that at home, but I should have thought of the possibility. It's something to remember.'

'I was so sure,' Matt said. 'It all fitted together, everything.'

'The human imagination is a wonderful thing. I know, I've just put in ten months nursing it. I suppose you had symptoms?'

'God, yes.' Matt enumerated them. 'Last night it got so bad I thought—' He glanced at the small body by his feet. 'As soon as I did that it all went away. Even the headache. What's the word? Psycho-something?'

'Psychosomatic. Yes. The guys out there developed everything from corns to angina, scared of where they were and wanting to leave it.'

'I'm ashamed,' Matt said. 'I feel ...' He moved his hands.

'Well,' said Fred, 'it was only an animal. Probably it wouldn't have lived long anyway. I shouldn't have brought it.'

'Oh for Chrissake,' Matt said, and turned away. Josh and Barbie were coming out of the house again. Josh carried a box, and Barbie had a bunch of flowers and a spade. They passed by the place on the lawn where the big stone had been moved and the hole opened up again – only part way, and from the outside, but Matt hoped they would not know that. He hoped they would not ever know that.

He went to meet them.

He kneeled down and put an arm around each of them. 'Don't feel bad,' he said desperately. 'Look I'll tell you what we'll do. We'll go and find the best place in the country to buy a pup. Wouldn't you like that, a fine new puppy, all your own?'

THE ROAD TO SINHARAT

1

The door was low, deep-sunk into the thickness of the wall. Carey knocked and then he waited, stooped a bit under the lintelstone, fitting his body to the meagre shadow as though he could really hide it there. A few yards away, beyond cracked and tilted paving-blocks, the Jekkara Low Canal showed its still black water to the still black sky, and both were full of stars.

Nothing moved along the canal site. The town was closed tight, and this in itself was so unnatural that it made Carey shiver. He had been here before and he knew how it ought to be. The chief industry of the Low Canal towns is sinning of one sort or another, and they work at it right around the clock. One might have thought that all the people had gone away, but Carey knew they hadn't. He knew that he had not taken a single step unwatched. He had not really believed that they would let him come this far, and he wondered why they had not killed him. Perhaps they remembered him.

There was a sound on the other side of the door.

Carey in the antique High Martian, 'Here is one who claims the guest-right.' In Low Martian, the vernacular that fitted more easily on his tongue, he said, 'Let me in, Derech. You owe me blood.'

The door opened narrowly and Carey slid through it, into lamplight and relative warmth. Derech closed the door and barred it, saying, 'Damn you, Carey. I knew you were going to turn up here babbling about blood-debts. I swore I wouldn't let you in.'

He was a Low Canaller, lean and small and dark and predatory. He wore a red jewel in his left earlobe and a totally incongruous but comfortable suit of Terran synthetics, insulated against heat and cold. Carey smiled.

'Sixteen years ago,' he said, 'you'd have perished before you'd have worn that.'

'Corruption. Nothing corrupts like comfort, unless it's kindness.' Derech sighed. 'I knew it was a mistake to let you save my neck that time. Sooner or later you'd claim payment. Well now that I have let you in, you might as well sit down.' He poured wine into a cup of alabaster worn thin as an eggshell and handed it to Carey. They drank, sombrely, in silence. The flickering lamplight showed the shadows and the deep lines in Carey's face.

Derech said, 'How long since you've slept?'

'I can sleep on the way,' said Carey, and Derech looked at him with amber eyes as coldly speculative as a cat's.

Carey did not press him. The room was large, richly furnished with the bare, spare, faded richness of a world that had very little left to give in the way of luxury. Some of the things were fairly new, made in the traditional manner by Martian craftsmen. They were almost indistinguishable from the things that had been old when the Reed Kings and the Bee Kings were little boys along the Nile-bank.

'What will happen,' Derech asked, 'if they catch you?'

'Oh,' said Carey, 'they'll deport me first. Then the United Worlds Court will try me, and they can't do anything but find me guilty. They'll hand me over to Earth for punishment, and there will be further investigations and penalties and fines and I'll be a thoroughly broken man when they've finished, and sorry enough for it. Though I think they'll be sorrier in the long run.'

'That won't help matters any,' said Derech.

'No.'

'Why,' asked Derech, 'why is it that they will not listen?'

'Because they know that they are right.'

Derech said an evil word.

'But they do. I've sabotaged the Rehabilitation Project as much as I possibly could. I've rechannelled funds and misdirected orders so they're almost two years behind schedule. These are the things they'll try me for. But my real crime is that I have questioned Goodness and the works thereof. Murder they might forgive me, but not that.'

He added wearily, 'You'll have to decide quickly. The UW boys are working closely with the Council of City-States, and Jekkara is no longer untouchable. It's also the first place they'll look for me.'

'I wondered if that had occurred to you.' Derech frowned. 'That doesn't bother me. What does bother me is that I know where you want to go. We tried it once, remember? We ran for our lives across that damned desert. Four solid days and nights.' He shivered.

'Send me as far as Barrakesh. I can disappear there, join a southbound caravan. I intend to go alone.'

'If you intend to kill yourself, why not do it here in comfort and among friends? Let me think,' Derech said. 'Let me count my years and my treasure and weigh them against a probable yard of sand.'

Flames hissed softly around the coals in the brazier. Outside, the wind got up and started its ancient work, rubbing the house walls with tiny grains of dust, rounding off the corners, hollowing the window-places. All over Mars the wind did this, to huts and palaces, to mountains and the small burrow-heaps of animals, labouring patiently toward a day when the whole face of the planet should be one smooth level sea of dust. Only lately new structures of metal and plastic had appeared beside some of the old stone cities. They resisted the wearing sand. They seemed prepared to stay forever. And Carey fancied that he could hear the old wind laughing as it went.

There was a scratching against the closed shutter in the back wall, followed by a rapid drumming of fingertips. Derech rose, his face suddenly alert. He rapped twice on the shutter to say that he understood and then turned to Carey. 'Finish your wine.'

He took the cup and went into another room with it. Carey stood up. Mingling with the sound of the wind outside, the gentle throb of motors became audible, low in the sky and very near.

Derech returned and gave Carey a shove toward an inner wall. Carey remembered the pivoted stone that was there, and the space behind it. He crawled through the opening. 'Don't sneeze or thrash about,' said Derech. 'The stonework is loose, and they'd hear you.'

He swung the stone shut. Carey huddled as comfortably as possible in the uneven hole, worn smooth with the hiding of illegal things for countless generations. Air and a few faint gleams of light seeped through between the stone blocks, which were set without mortar as in most Martian construction. He could even see a thin vertical segment of the room.

When the sharp knock came at the door, he discovered that he could hear quite clearly.

Derech moved across his field of vision. The door opened. A man's voice demanded entrance in the name of the United Worlds and the Council of Martian City-States.

'Please enter,' said Derech.

Carey saw, more or less fragmentarily, four men. Three were Martians in the undistinguished cosmopolitan garb of the City-States. They were the equivalent of the FBI. The fourth was an Earthman, and Carey smiled to see the measure of his own importance. The spare, blond, good-looking man with the sunburn and the friendly blue eyes might have been an actor, a tennis player, or a junior executive on holiday. He was Howard Wales, Earth's best man in Interpol.

Wales let the Martians do the talking, and while they did it he drifted unobtrusively about, peering through doorways, listening, touching, *feeling*. Carey became fascinated by him, in an unpleasant sort of way. Once he came and stood directly in front of Carey's crevice in the wall. Carey was afraid to breathe, and he had a dreadful notion that Wales would suddenly turn about and look straight in at him through the crack.

The senior Martian, a middle-aged man with an able look about him, was giving Derech a briefing on the penalties that awaited him if he harboured a fugitive or withheld information. Carey thought that he was being too heavy about it. Even five years ago he would not have dared to show his face in Jekkara.

He could picture Derech listening amiably, lounging against something and playing with the jewel in his ear. Finally Derech got bored with it, and said without heat, 'Because of our geographical position, we have been exposed to the New Culture.'

The capitals were his. 'We have made adjustments to it. But this is still Jekkara and you're here on sufferance, no more. Please don't forget it.'

Wales spoke, deftly forestalling any comment from the City-Stater. 'You've been Carey's friend for many years, haven't you?'

'We robbed tombs together in the old days.'

'"Archaeological research" is a nicer term, I should think.'

'My very ancient and perfectly honourable guild never used it. But I'm an honest trader now, and Carey doesn't come here.'

He might have added a qualifying 'often,' but he did not.

The City-Stater said derisively, 'He has or will come here now.'

'Why?' asked Derech.

'He needs help. Where else could he go for it?'

'Anywhere. He has many friends. And he knows Mars better than most Martians, probably a damn sight better than you do.'

'But,' said Wales quietly, 'outside of the City-states all Earthmen are being hunted down like rabbits, if they're foolish enough to stay. For Carey's sake, if you know where he is, tell us. Otherwise he is almost certain to die.'

'He's a grown man,' Derech said. 'He must carry his own load.'

'He's carrying too much ...' Wales said, and then broke off. There was a sudden gabble of talk, both in the room and outside. Everybody moved toward the door, out of Carey's vision, except Derech, who moved into it, relaxed and languid and infuriatingly self-assured. Carey could not hear the sound that had drawn the others but he judged that another flier was landing. In a few minutes Wales and the others came back, and now there were some new people with them. Carey squirmed and craned, getting closer to the crack, and he saw Alan Woodthorpe, his superior, Administrator of the Rehabilitation Project for Mars, and probably the most influential man on the planet. Carey knew that he must have rushed across a thousand miles of desert from his headquarters at Kahora, just to be here at this moment.

Carey was flattered and deeply moved.

Woodthorpe introduced himself to Derech. He was disarmingly simple and friendly in his approach, a man driven and wearied by many vital matters but never forgetting to be warm, gracious, and human. And the devil of it was that he was exactly what he appeared to be. That was what made dealing with him so impossibly difficult.

Derech said, smiling a little, 'Don't stray away from your guards.'

'Why is it?' Woodthorpe asked. 'Why this hostility? If only your people would understand that we're trying to help them.'

'They understand that perfectly,' Derech said. 'What they can't understand is why, when they have thanked you politely and explained that they neither need nor want your help, you still refuse to leave them alone.'

Because we know what we can do for them! They're destitute now. We can make them rich, in water, in arable land, in power — we can change their whole way of life. Primitive people are notoriously resistant to change, but in time they'll realise...'

'Primitive?' said Derech.

'Oh, not the Low Canallers,' said Woodthorpe quickly. 'Your civilisation was flourishing, I know, when Proconsul was still wondering whether or not to climb down out of his tree. For that very reason I cannot understand why you side with the Drylanders.'

Derech said, 'Mars is an old, cranky, dried-up world, but we understand her. We've made a bargain with her. We don't ask too much of her, and she gives us sufficient for our needs. We can depend on her. We do not want to be made dependent on other men.'

'But this is a new age,' said Woodthorpe. 'Advanced technology makes anything possible. The old prejudices, the parochial viewpoints are no longer...'

'You were saying something about primitives.'

'I was thinking of the Dryland tribes. We had counted on Dr Carey, because of his unique knowledge, to help them understand us. Instead, he seems bent on stirring them up to war. Our survey parties have been set upon with the most shocking violence. If Carey succeeds in reaching the Drylands there's no telling what he may do. Surely you don't want …'

'Primitive,' Derech said, with a ring of cruel impatience in his voice. 'Parochial. The gods send me a wicked man before a well-meaning fool. Mr Woodthorpe, the Drylanders do not need Dr Carey to stir them up to war. Neither do we. We do not want our wells and our water courses rearranged. We do not want our population expanded. We do not want the resources that will last us for thousands of years yet, if they're not tampered with, pumped out and used up in a few centuries. We are in balance with our environment; we want to stay that way. And we will fight, Mr Woodthorpe. You're not dealing with theories now. You're dealing with our lives. We are not going to place them in your hands.'

He turned to Wales and the Martians. 'Search the house. If you want to search the town, that's up to you. But I wouldn't be too long about any of it.'

Looking pained and hurt, Woodthorpe stood for a moment and then went out, shaking his head. The Martians began to go through the house. Carey heard Derech's voice say, 'Why don't you join them, Mr Wales?'

Wales answered pleasantly, 'I don't like wasting my time.' He bade Derech good night and left, and Carey was thankful.

After a while the Martians left too. Derech bolted the door and sat down again to drink his interrupted glass of wine. He made no move to let Carey out, and Carey conquered a very strong desire to yell at him. He was getting just a touch claustrophobic now. Derech sipped his wine slowly, emptied the cup and filled it again. When it was half empty for the second time a girl came in from the back.

She wore the traditional dress of the Low Canals, which Carey was glad to see because some of the women were changing it for the cosmopolitan and featureless styles that made all women look alike, and he thought the old style was charming. Her skirt was a length of heavy orange silk caught at the waist with a broad girdle. Above that she wore nothing but a necklace and her body was slim and graceful as a bending reed. Twisted around her ankles and braided in her dark hair were strings of tiny bells, so that she chimed as she walked with a faint elfin music, very sweet and wicked.

'They're all gone now,' she told Derech, and Derech rose and came quickly toward Carey's hiding place.

'Someone was watching through the chinks in the shutters,' he said as he helped Carey out. 'Hoping I'd betray myself when I thought they were gone.' He asked the girl, 'It wasn't the Earthman, was it?'

'No.' She had poured herself some wine and curled up with it in the silks and warm furs that covered the guest-bench on the west wall. Carey saw that her eyes were green as emerald, slightly tilted, bright, curious and without mercy. He became suddenly very conscious of his unshaven chin and the grey that was beginning to be noticeable at his temples, and his general soiled and weary condition.

'I don't like that man Wales,' Derech was saying. 'He's almost as good as I am. We'll have him to reckon with yet.'

'We,' said Carey. 'You've weighed your yard of sand?'

Derech shrugged ruefully. 'You must have heard me talking myself into it. Well, I've been getting a little bored with the peaceful life.' He smiled, the smile Carey remembered from the times they had gone robbing tombs together in places where murder would have been a safer occupation. 'And it's always irked me that we were stopped that time. I'd like to try again. By the way, this is Arrin. She'll be going with us as far as Barrakesh.'

'Oh.' Carey bowed, and she smiled at him from her nest in the soft furs. Then she looked at Derech. 'What is there beyond Barrakesh?'

'Kesh,' said Derech. 'And Shun.'

'But you don't trade in the Drylands,' she said impatiently. 'And if you did, why should I be left behind?'

'We're going to Sinharat,' Derech said. 'The Ever-living.'

''Sinharat?' Arrin whispered. There was a long silence, and then she turned her gaze on Carey. 'If I had known that, I would have told them where you were. I would have let them take you.' She shivered and bent her head.

'That would have been foolish,' Derech said, fondling her.

'You'd have thrown away your chance to be the lady of one of the two saviours of Mars.'

'If you live,' she said.

'But my dear child,' said Derech, 'can you, sitting there, guarantee to me that you will be alive tomorrow?'

'You will have to admit,' said Carey slowly, 'that her odds are somewhat better than ours.'

2

The barge was long and narrow, buoyed on pontoon-like floats so that it rode high even with a full cargo. Pontoons, hull, and deck were metal. There had not been any trees for shipbuilding for a very long time. In the centre of the deck was a low cabin where several people might sleep, and forward toward the blunt bow was a fire-pit where the cooking was done. The motive power was animal, four of the scaly-hided, bad-tempered, hissing beasts of Martian burden plodding along the canal bank with a tow cable.

The pace was slow. Carey had wanted to go across country direct to Barrakesh, but Derech had forbidden it.

'I can't take a caravan. All my business goes by the canal, and everyone knows it. So you and I would have to go alone, riding by night and hiding by day, and saving no time at all.' He jabbed his thumb at the sky. 'Wales will come when you least expect him and least want him. On the barge you'll have a place to hide, and I'll have enough men to discourage him if he should be rash enough to interfere with a trader going about his normal and lawful business.'

'He wouldn't be above it,' Carey said gloomily.

'But only when he's desperate. That will be later.'

So the barge went gliding gently on its way southward along the thread of dark water that was the last open artery of what had once been an ocean. It ran snow-water now, melted from the polar cap. There were villages beside the canal, and areas of cultivation where long fields showed a startling green against the reddish-yellow desolation. Again there were places where the sand had moved like an army, overwhelming the fields and occupying the houses, so that only mounded heaps would show where a village had been. There were bridges, some of them sound and serving the living, others springing out of nowhere and standing like broken rainbows against the sky. By day there was the stinging sunlight that hid nothing, and by night the two moons laid a shifting loveliness on the land. And if Carey had not been goaded by a terrible impatience he would have been happy.

But all this, if Woodthorpe and the Rehabilitation Project had their way, would go. The waters of the canals would be impounded behind great dams far to the north, and the sparse populations would be moved and settled on new land. Deep-pumping operations, tapping the underground sources that fed the wells, would make up the winter deficit when the cap was frozen. The desert would be transformed, for a space anyway, into a flowering garden. Who would not prefer it to this bitter marginal existence? Who could deny that this was Bad and the Rehabilitation Project Good? No one but the people and Dr Matthew Carey. And no one would listen to them.

At Sinharat lay the only possible hope of making them listen.

The sky remained empty. Arrin spent most of her time on deck, sitting among the heaped-up bales. Carey knew that she watched him a great deal but he was not flattered. He thought that she hated him because he was putting Derech in danger of his life. He wished that Derech had left her behind.

On the fourth day at dawn the wind dropped to a flat calm. The sun burned hot, setting sand and rock to shimmering. The water of the canal showed a surface like polished glass, and in the east the sharp line of the horizon thickened and blurred and was lost in a yellow haze. Derech stood sniffing like a hound at the still air, and around noon he gave the order to tie up. The crew, ten of them, ceased to lounge on the bales and got to work, driving steel anchor pins for the cables, rigging a shelter for the beasts, checking the lashings of the deck cargo.

Carey and Derech worked beside them, and when he looked up briefly from his labours Carey saw Arrin crouched over the fire-pit cooking furiously. The eastern sky became a wall, a wave curling toward the zenith, sooty ochre below, a blazing brass-colour at its crest. It rushed across the land, roared, and broke upon them.

They helped each other to the cabin and crouched knee to knee in the tight space, the twelve men and Arrin, while the barge kicked and rolled, sank down deep and shot upward, struggling like a live thing under the blows of the wind. Dust and sand sifted through every vent-hole, tainting the air with a bitter taste. There was a sulphurous darkness, and the ear was deafened. Carey had been through sandstorms before, and he wished that he was out in the open where he was used to it, and where he did not have to worry about the barge turning turtle and drowning him idiotically on the driest world in the System. And while all this was going on, Arrin was grimly guarding her pot.

The wind stopped its wild gusting and settled to a steady gale. When it appeared that the barge was going to remain upright after all, the men ate from Arrin's pot and were glad of the food. After that most of them went down into the hold to sleep because there was more room there.

Arrin put the lid back on the pot and weighted it to keep the sand out, and then she said quietly to Derech, 'Why is it that you have to go – where you're going?'

'Because Dr Carey believes that there are records there that may convince the Rehabilitation people that our "primitives" know what they are talking about.'

Carey could not see her face clearly in the gloom, but he thought she was frowning, thinking hard.

'You believe,' she said to Carey. 'Do you know?'

'I know that there were records, once. They're referred to in other records. Whether they still exist or not is another matter. But because of the peculiar nature of the place, and of the people who made them, I think it is possible.'

He could feel her shiver. 'But the Ramas were so long ago.'

She barely whispered the name. It meant Immortal, and it

had been a word of terror for so long that no amount of time could erase the memory. The Ramas had achieved their immortality by a system of induction that might have been liked to the pouring of old wine into new bottles, and though the principle behind the transplanting of a consciousness from one host to another was purely scientific, the reactions of the people from among whom they requisitioned their supply of hosts was one of simple emotional horror. The Ramas were regarded as vampires. Their ancient island city of Sinharat lay far and forgotten now in the remotest desolation of Shun, and the Drylanders held it holy, and forbidden. They had broken their own taboo just once, when Kynon of Shun raised his banner, claiming to have rediscovered the lost secret of the Ramas and promising the tribesmen and the Low Canallers both eternal life and all the plunder they could carry. He had given them only death and since then the taboo was more fanatically enforced than ever.

'Their city had not been looted,' Carey said. 'That is why I have hope.'

'But,' said Arrin, 'they weren't human. They were only evil.'

'On the contrary. They were completely human. And at one time they made a very great effort to atone.'

She turned again to Derech. 'The Shunni will kill you.'

'That is perfectly possible.'

'But you must go.' She added shrewdly, 'If only to see whether you can.'

Derech laughed. 'Yes.'

'Then I'll go with you. I'd rather see what happens to you than wait and wait and never know.' As though that settled it, she curled up in her bunk and went to sleep.

Carey slept too, uneasily, dreaming shadowed dreams of Sinharat and waking from them in the dusty claustrophobic dark to feel hopelessly that he would never see it.

By mid-morning the storm had blown itself out, but now there was a sandbar forty feet long blocking the channel. The beasts were hitched to scoops brought up from the hold and put to dredging, and every man aboard stripped and went in with a shovel.

Carey dug in the wet sand, his taller stature and lighter skin perfectly separating him from the smaller, darker Low Canallers. He felt obvious and naked, and he kept a wary eye cocked toward the heavens. Once he got among the Drylanders, Wales would have to look very hard indeed to spot him. At Valkis, where there was some trade with the desert men, Derech would be able to get him the proper clothing and Carey would arrive at the Gateway, Barrakesh, already in the guise of a wandering tribesman. Until then he would have to be careful, both of Wales and the local canal-dwellers, who had very little to choose between Earthmen and the Drylanders who occasionally raided this far north, stripping their fields and stealing their women.

In spite of Carey's watchfulness, it was Derech who gave the alarm. About the middle of the afternoon he suddenly shouted Carey's name. Carey, labouring now in a haze of sweat and weariness, looked up and saw Derech pointing at the sky. Carey dropped his shovel and dived for the water.

The barge was close by, but the flier came so fast that by the time he had reached the ladder he knew he could not possibly climb aboard without being seen.

Arrin's voice said calmly from overhead, 'Dive under. There's room.'

Carey caught a breath and dived. The water was cold, and the sunlight slanting through it showed it thick and roiled from the storm. The shadow of the barge made a total darkness into which Carey plunged. When he thought he was clear of the broad pontoons he surfaced, hoping Arrin had told the truth. She had. There was space to breathe, and between the pontoons he could watch the flier come in low and hover on its rotors above the canal, watching. Then it landed. There were several men in it, but only Howard Wales got out.

Derech went to talk to him. The rest of the men kept on working, and Carey saw that the extra shovel had vanished into the water. Wales kept looking at the barge. Derech was playing with him, and Carey cursed. The icy chill of the water was biting him to the bone. Finally, to Wales' evident surprise, Derech invited him aboard. Carey swam carefully back and forth in the dark space under the hull, trying to keep his blood moving. After a long long time, a year or two, he saw Wales walking back to the flier. It seemed another year before the flier took off. Carey fought his way out from under the barge and into the sunlight again, but he was too stiff and numb to climb the ladder. Arrin and Derech had to pull him up.

'Anyone else,' said Derech, 'would be convinced. But this one – he gives his opponent credit for all the brains and deceitfulness he needs.'

He poured liquor between Carey's chattering teeth and wrapped him in thick blankets and put him in a bunk. Then he said, 'Could Wales have any way of guessing where we're going?'

Carey frowned. 'I suppose he could, if he bothered to go through all my monographs and papers.'

'I'm sure he's bothered.'

'It's all there,' Carey said dismally. 'How we tried it once and failed – and what I hoped to find, though the Rehabilitation Act hadn't come along then, and it was pure archaeological interest. And I have, I know, mentioned the Ramas to Woodthorpe when I was arguing with him about the advisability of all these Earth-shattering – Mars-shattering – changes. Why? Did Wales say something?'

'He said, "Barrakesh will tell the story."'

'He did, did he?' said Carey viciously. 'Give me the bottle.' He took a long pull and the liquor went into him like fire into glacial ice. 'I wish to heaven I'd been able to steal a flier.'

Derech shook his head. 'You're lucky you didn't. They'd have had you out of the sky in an hour.'

'Of course you're right. It's just that I'm in a hurry.' He drank again and then he smiled, a very unscholarly smile. 'If the gods are good to me, someday I'll have Mr Wales between my hands.'

The local men came along that evening, about a hundred of them with teams and implements. They had already worked all day clearing other blocks, but they worked without question all that night and into the next day, each man choosing his own time to fall out and sleep when he could no longer stand up. The canal was their life, and their law said that the canal came first, before wife, child, brother, parent, or self, and it was a hanging matter. Carey stayed out of sight in the cabin, feeling guilty about not helping, but not too guilty. It was backbreaking work. They had the channel clear by the middle of the morning, and the barge moved on southward.

Three days later a line of cliffs appeared in the east, far away at first but closing gradually until they marched beside the canal. They were high and steep, coloured softly in shades of red and gold. The faces of the rock were fantastically eroded by a million years of water and ten millennia of wind. These were the rim of the sea basin, and presently Carey saw in the distance ahead a shimmering line of mist on the desert where another canal cut through it. They were approaching Valkis.

It was sunset when they reached it. The low light struck in level shafts against the cliffs. Where the angle was right, it shone through the empty doors and window holes of the five cities that sprawled downward over the ledges of red-gold rock. It seemed as though hearthfires burned there, and warm lamplight to welcome home men weary from the sea. But in the streets and squares and on the long flights of rock-cut steps only slow shadows moved with the sinking sun. The ancient quays stood stark as tombstones, marking the levels where new harbours had been built and then abandoned as the water left them, and the high towers that had flown the banners of the Sea-Kings were bare and broken.

Only the lowest city lived, and only a part of that, but it lived fiercely, defiant of the cold centuries towering over it. From the barge deck Carey watched the torches flare out like yellow stars in the twilight, and he heard voices, and the wild and lovely music of the double-banked harps. The dry wind had a smell in it of dusty spices and strange exotic things. The New Culture had not penetrated here, and Carey was glad, though he did think that Valkis could stand being cleaned up just a little without hurting it any. They had two or three vices for sale there that were quite unbelievable.

'Stay out of sight,' Derech told him, 'til I get back.'

It was full dark when they reached their mooring, at an ancient stone dock beside a broad square with worn old buildings on three sides of it. Derech went into the town and so did the crew, but for different reasons. Arrin stayed on deck, lying on the bales with her chin on her wrists, staring at the lights and listening to the noises like a sulky child forbidden to play some dangerous but fascinating game. Derech did not allow her in the streets alone.

Out of sheer boredom, Carey went to sleep.

He did not know how long he had slept, a few minutes or a few hours, when he was wakened sharply by Arrin's wildcat scream.

3

There were men on the deck outside. Carey could hear them scrambling around and cursing the woman, and someone was saying something about an Earthman. He rolled out of his bunk. He was still wearing the Earth-made coverall that was all the clothing he had until Derech came back. He stripped it off in a wild panic and shoved it far down under the tumbled furs. Arrin did not scream again but he thought he could hear muffled sounds as though she were trying to. He shivered, naked in the chill dark.

Footsteps came light and swift across the deck. Carey reached out and lifted from its place on the cabin wall a long-handled axe that was used to cut loose the deck cargo lashings in case of emergency. And as though the axe had spoken to him, Carey knew what he was going to do.

The shapes of men appeared in the doorway, dark and huddled against the glow of the deck lights.

Carey gave a Dryland war-cry that split the night. He leaped forward, swinging the axe.

The men disappeared out of the doorway as though they had been jerked on strings. Carey emerged from the cabin onto the deck, where the torchlight showed him clearly, and he whirled the axe around his head as he had learned to do years ago when he first understood both the possibility and the immense value of being able to go Martian. Inevitably he had got himself embroiled in unscholarly, unarchaeological matters like tribal wars and raiding, and he had acquired some odd skills. Now he drove the dark, small, startled men ahead of the axe-blade. Yelling, he drove them in the torchlight while they stared at him, five astonished men with silver rings in their ears and very sharp knives in their belts.

Carey quoted some Dryland sayings about Low Canallers that brought the blood flushing into their cheeks. Then he asked them what their business was.

One of them, who wore a kilt of vivid yellow, said, 'We were told there was an Earthman hiding.'

And who told you? Carey wondered. Mr Wales, through some Martian spy? Of course, Mr Wales – who else? He was beginning to hate Mr Wales. But he laughed and said, 'Do I look like an Earthman?'

He made the axe-blade flicker in the light. He let his hair grow long and ragged, and it was a good desert colour, tawny brown. His naked body was lean and long-muscled like a desert man's, and he had kept it hard. Arrin came up to him, rubbing her bruised mouth and staring at him as surprised as the Valkisians.

The man in the yellow kilt said again, 'We were told ...'

Other people had begun to gather in the dockside square, both men and women, idle, curious, and cruel.

'My name is Marah,' Carey said. 'I left the Wells of Tamboina with a price on my head for murder.' The Wells were far enough away that he need not fear a fellow-tribesman rising to dispute his story. 'Does anybody here want to collect it?'

The people watched him. The torch flames blew in the dry wind, scattering the light across their upturned faces. Carey began to be afraid.

Close beside him Arrin whispered, 'Will you be recognised?'

'No.' He had been here three times with Dryland bands but it was hardly likely that anyone would remember one specific tribesman out of the numbers that floated through.

'Then stand steady,' Arrin said.

He stood. The people watched him, whispering and smiling

among themselves. Then the man in the yellow kilt said, 'Earthman or Drylander, I don't like your face.'

The crowd laughed, and a forward movement began. Carey could hear the sweet small chiming of the bells the women wore. He gripped the axe and told Arrin to get away from him. 'If you know where Derech's gone, go after him. I'll hold them as long as I can.'

He did not know whether she left him or not. He was watching the crowd, seeing the sharp blades flash. It seemed ridiculous, in this age of space flight and atomic power, to be fighting with axe and knife. But Mars had had nothing better for a long time, and the UW Peace and Disarmament people hoped to take even those away from them someday. On Earth, Carey remembered, there were still peoples who hardened their wooden spears in the fire and ate their enemies. The knives, in any case, could kill efficiently enough. He stepped back a little from the rail to give the axe free play, and he was not cold any longer, but warm with a heat that stung his nerve-ends.

Derech's voice shouted across the square.

The crowd paused. Carey could see over their heads to where Derech, with about half his crew around him, was forcing his way through. He looked and sounded furious.

'I'll kill the first man that touches him!' he yelled.

The man in the yellow kilt asked politely, 'What is he to you?'

'He's money, you fool! Passage money that I won't collect till I reach Barrakesh, and not then unless he's alive and able to get it for me. And if he doesn't, I'll see to him myself.' Derech sprang up onto the barge deck. 'Now clear off. Or you'll have more killing to do than you'll take pleasure in.'

His men were lined up with him now along the rail, and the rest of the crew were coming. Twelve tough armed men did not look like much fun. The crowd began to drift away, and the original five went reluctantly with them. Derech posted a watch and took Carey into the cabin.

'Get into these,' he said, throwing down a bundle he had taken from one of the men. Carey laid aside his axe. He was shaking now with relief and his fingers stumbled over the knots. The outer wrappings was a thick desert cloak. Inside was a leather kilt, well worn and adorned with clanking bronze bosses, a wide bronze collar for the neck and a leather harness for weapons that was black with use.

'They came off a dead man,' Derech said. 'There are sandals underneath.' He took a long desert knife from his girdle and tossed it to Carey. 'And this. And now, my friend, we are in trouble.'

'I thought I did rather well,' Carey said, buckling kilt and harness. They felt good. Perhaps someday, if he lived, he would settle down to being a good grey Dr Carey, archaeologist emeritus, but the day was not yet. 'Someone told them there was an Earthman here.'

Derech nodded. 'I have friends here, men who trust me, men I trust. They warned me. That's why I routed my crew out of the brothels, and unhappy they were about it, too.'

Carey laughed. 'I'm grateful to them.' Arrin had come in and was sitting on the edge of her bunk, watching Carey. He swung the cloak around him and hooked the bronze catch at the throat. The rough warmth of the cloth was welcome. 'Wales will know now that I'm with you. This was his way of finding out for sure.'

'You might have been killed,' Arrin said.

Carey shrugged. 'It wouldn't be a calamity. They'd rather have me dead than lose me, though of course none of them would dream of saying so. Point is, he won't be fooled by the masquerade, and he won't wait for Barrakesh. He'll be on board as soon as you're well clear of Valkis and he'll have enough force with him to make it good.'

'All true,' said Derech. 'So. Let him have the barge.' He turned to Arrin. 'If you're still hell-bent to come with us, get ready. And remember, you'll be riding for a long time.'

To Carey he said, 'Better keep clear of the town. I'll have mounts and supplies by the time Phobos rises. Where shall we meet?'

'By the lighthouse,' Carey said. Derech nodded and went out. Carey went out too and waited on the deck while Arrin changed her clothes. A few minutes later she joined him, wrapped in a long cloak. She had taken the bells from her hair and around her ankles, and she moved quietly now, light and lithe as a boy. She grinned at him. 'Come, desert man. What did you say your name was?'

'Marah.'

'Don't forget your axe.'

They left the barge. Only one torch burned now on the deck. Some of the lights had died around the square. This was deserted, but there was still sound and movement in plenty along the streets that led into it. Carey guided Arrin to the left along the canal bank. He did not see anyone watching them, or following them. The sounds and the lights grew fainter. The buildings they passed now were empty, their doors and windows open to the wind. Deimos was in the sky, and some of the roofs showed moonlight through them, shafts of pale silver touching the drifted dust that covered the floors. Carey stopped several times to listen, but he heard nothing except the wind. He began to feel better. He hurried Arrin with long strides, and now they moved away from the canal and up a broken street that led toward the cliffs.

The street became a flight of steps cut in the rock. There were roofless stone houses on either side, clinging to the cliffs row on ragged row like the abandoned nests of sea-birds. Carey's imagination, as always, peopled them, hung them with nets and gear, livened them with lights and voices and appropriate smells. At the top of the steps he paused to let Arrin get her breath, and he looked down across the centuries at the torches of Valkis burning by the canal.

'What are you thinking?' Arrin asked.

'I'm thinking that nothing, not people nor oceans, should ever die.'

'The Ramas lived forever.'

'Too long, anyway. And that wasn't good, I know. But still it makes me sad to think of men building these houses and working and raising their families, looking forward to the future.'

'You're an odd one,' Arrin said. 'When I first met you I couldn't understand what it was that made Derech love you. You were so – quiet. Tonight I could see. But now you've gone all broody and soft again. Why do you care so much about dust and old bones?'

'Curiosity. I'll never know the end of the story, but I can at least know the beginning.'

They moved on again, and now they were walking across the basin of a harbour, with the great stone quays towering above them, gnawed and rounded by the wind. Ahead on a crumbling promontory the shaft of a broken tower pointed skyward. They came beneath it, where ships had used to come, and presently Carey heard the jingling and padding of animals coming toward them. Before the rise of Phobos they were mounted and on their way.

'This is your territory,' said Derech. 'I will merely ride.'

'Then you and Arrin can handle the pack animals.' Carey took the lead. They left the city behind, climbing to the top of the cliffs. The canal showed like a ribbon of steel in the moonlight far below, and then was gone. A range of mountains had come down here to the sea, forming a long curving peninsula. Only their bare bones were left, and through that skeletal mass of rock Carey took his little band by a trail he had followed once and hoped that he remembered.

They travelled all that way by night, lying in the shelter of rocks by day, and three times a flier passed over them like a wheeling hawk, searching. Carey thought more than once that he had lost the way, though he never said so, and he was pleasantly surprised when they found the sea bottom again just where it should be on the other side of the range, with the ford he remembered across the canal. They crossed it by moonlight, stopping only to fill up their water bags. At dawn they were on a ridge above Barrakesh.

They looked down, and Derech said, 'I think we can forget about our southbound caravan.'

Trade was for times of peace, and now the men of Kesh and Shun were gathering for war, even as Derech had said, without need of any Dr Carey to stir them to it.

They filled the streets. They filled the *serais*. They camped in masses by the gates and along the banks of the canal and around the swampy lake that was its terminus. The vast herds of animals broke down the dikes, trampled the irrigation ditches and devoured the fields. And across the desert more riders were coming, long files of them with pennons waving and lances glinting in the morning light. Wild and far away, Carey heard the skirling of the desert pipes.

'The minute we go down there,' he said, 'we are part of the army. Any man that turned his back on Barrakesh now will get a spear through it for cowardice.'

His face became hard and cruel with a great rage. Presently this horde would roll northward, sweeping up more men from the Low Canal towns as it passed, joining ultimately with other hordes pouring in through the easterly gates of the Drylands. The people of the City-States would fall like butchered sheep, and perhaps even the dome of Kahora would come shattering down. But sooner or later the guns would be brought up, and then the Drylanders would do the falling, all because of good men like Woodthorpe who only wanted to help.

Carey said, 'I am going to Sinharat. But you know how much chance a small party has, away from the caravan track and the wells.'

'I know,' said Derech.

'You know how much chance we have of evading Wales, without the protection of a caravan.'

'You tell me how I can go quietly home, and I'll do it.'

'You can wait for your barge and go back to Valkis.'

'I couldn't do that,' Derech said seriously. 'My men would laugh at me. I suggest we stop wasting time. Here in the desert, time is water.'

'Speaking of water,' Arrin said, 'how about when we get there? And how about getting back?'

Derech said, 'Dr Carey has heard that there is a splendid well at Sinharat.'

'He's heard,' said Arrin, 'but he doesn't know. Same as the records.' She gave Carey a look, only half scornful.

Carey smiled briefly. 'The well I have on pretty good authority. It's in the coral deep under the city, so it can be used without actually breaking the taboo. The Shunni don't go near it unless they're desperate, but I talked to a man who had.'

He led them down off the ridge and away from Barrakesh. And Derech cast an uneasy glance at the sky.

'I hope Wales did set a trap for us there. And I hope he'll sit a while waiting for us to spring it.'

There was a strict law against the use of fliers over tribal lands without special permission, which would be unprocurable now. But they both knew that Wales would not let that stop him.

'The time could come,' Carey said grimly, 'that we'd be glad to see him.'

He led them a long circle northward to avoid the war parties coming into Barrakesh. Then he struck out across the deadly waste of the sea bottom, straight for Sinharat.

He lost track of time very quickly. The days blurred together into one endless hell wherein they three and the staggering animals toiled across vast slopes of rock up-tilted to the sun, or crept under reefs of rotten coral with sand around them as smooth and bright as a burning-glass. At night there was moonlight and bitter cold, but the cold did nothing to alleviate their thirst. There was only one good thing about the journey, and that was the thing that worried Carey the most. In all that cruel and empty sky, no flier ever appeared.

'The desert is a big place,' Arrin said, looking at it with loathing. 'Perhaps he couldn't find us. Perhaps he's given up.'

'Not him,' said Carey.

Derech said, 'Maybe he thinks we're dead anyway, and why bother.'

Maybe, Carey thought. *Maybe*. But sometimes as he rode or walked he would curse at Wales out loud and glare at the sky, demanding to know what he was up to. There was never any answer.

The last carefully-hoarded drop of water went. And Carey forgot about Wales and thought only of the well of Sinharat, cold and clear in the coral.

He was thinking of it as he plodded along, leading the beast that was now almost as weak as he. The vision of the well so occupied him that it was some little time before the message from his bleared and sun-struck eyes got through it and registered on his brain. Then he halted in sudden wild alarm.

He was walking, not on smooth sand, but in the trampled marks of many riders.

4

The others came out of their stupor as he pointed, warning them to silence. The broad track curved ahead and vanished out of sight beyond a great reef of white coral. The wind had not had time to do more than blur the edges of the individual prints.

Mounting and whipping their beasts unmercifully, Carey and the others fled the track. The reef stood high above them like a wall. Along its base were cavernous holes, and they found one big enough to hold them all. Carey went on alone and on foot to the shoulder of the reef, where the riders had turned it, and the wind went with him, piping and crying in the vast honeycomb of the coral.

He crept around the shoulder and then he saw where he was.

On the other side of the reef was a dry lagoon, stretching perhaps half a mile to a coral island that stood up tall in the hard clear sunlight, its naked cliffs beautifully striated with deep rose and white and delicate pink. A noble stairway went up from the desert to a city of walls and towers so perfectly built from many-shaded marble and so softly sculptured by time that it was difficult to tell where the work of men began and ended. Carey saw it through a shimmering haze of exhaustion and wonder, and knew that he looked at Sinharat, the Ever-Living.

The trampled track of the Shunni warriors went out across the lagoon. It swept furiously around what had been a parked flier, and then passed on, leaving behind it battered wreckage and two dark sprawled shapes. It ended at the foot of the cliffs, where Carey could see a sort of orderly turmoil of men and animals. There were between twenty-five and thirty warriors, as nearly as he could guess. They were making camp.

Carey knew what that meant. There was someone in the city.

Carey did not move for some time. He stared at the

beautiful marble city shimmering on its lovely pedestal of coral. He wanted to weep, but there was not enough moisture left in him to make tears, and his despair was gradually replaced by a feeble anger. *All right, you bastards*, he thought. *All right!*

He went back to Derech and Arrin and told them what he had seen.

'Wales just came ahead of us and waited. Why bother to search a whole desert when he knew where we were going? This time he'd have us for sure. Water. We couldn't run away.' Carey grinned horribly with his cracked lips and swollen tongue. 'Only the Shunni found him first. War party. They must have seen the flier go over – came to check if it landed here. Caught two men in it. But the rest are in Sinharat.'

'How do you know?' asked Derech.

'The Shunni won't go into the city except as a last resort. If they catch a trespasser there they just hold the well and wait. Sooner or later he comes down.'

Arrin said. 'How long can we wait? We've had no water for two days.'

'Wait, hell,' said Carey. 'We can't wait. I'm going in.'

Now, while they still had a shred of strength. Another day would be too late.

Derech said, 'I suppose a quick spear is easier than thirst.'

'We may escape both,' said Carey, 'if we're very careful. And very lucky.'

He told them what to do.

An hour or so later Carey followed the warriors' track out across the dry lagoon. He walked, or rather staggered, leading the animals. Arrin rode on one, her cloak pulled over her head and her face covered in sign of mourning. Between two of the beasts, on an improvised litter made of blankets and pack lashings, Derech lay wrapped from head to foot in his cloak, a too-convincing imitation of a corpse. Carey heard the shouts and saw the distant riders start toward them, and he was frightened. The smallest slip, the most minor mistake, could give them away, and then he did not think that anything on Mars could save them. But thirst was more imperative than fear.

There was something more. Carey passed the two bodies in

the sand beside the wrecked flier. He saw that they were both dark-haired Martians, and he looked at the towers of Sinharat with wolfish eyes. Wales was up there, still alive, still between him and what he wanted. Carey's hand tightened on the axe. He was no longer entirely sane on the subject of Howard Wales and the records of the Ramas.

When the riders were within spear range he halted and rested the axehead in the sand, as a token. He waited, saying softly, 'For God's sake now, be careful.'

The riders reined in, sending the sand flying. Carey said to them, 'I claim the death right.'

He stood swaying over his axe while they looked at him, and at the muffled woman, and at the dusty corpse. They were six, tall, hard fierce-eyed men with their long spears held ready. Finally one of them said, 'How did you come here?'

'My sister's husband,' said Carey, indicating Derech, 'died on the march to Barrakesh. Our tribal law says he must rest in his own place. But there are no caravans now. We had to come alone, and in a great sandstorm we lost the track. We wandered for many days until we crossed your trail.'

'Do you know where you are?' asked the Drylander.

Carey averted his eyes from the city. 'I know now. But if a man is dying it is permitted to use the well. We are dying.'

'Use it, then,' said the Drylander. 'But keep your ill omen away from our camp. We are going to the war as soon as we finish our business here. We want no corpse-shadow on us.'

'Outlanders?' Carey asked, a rhetorical question in view of the flier and the un-Dryland bodies.

'Outlanders. Who else is foolish enough to wake the ghosts in the Forbidden City?'

Carey shook his head. 'Not I. I do not wish even to see it.'

The riders left them, returning to the camp. Carey moved on slowly toward the cliffs. It became apparent where the well must be. A great arching cave-mouth showed in the rose-pink coral and men were coming and going there, watering their animals. Carey approached it and began the monotonous chant that etiquette required, asking that way be made for the dead, so that warriors and pregnant women and persons undergoing ritual purifications would be warned to go aside. The warriors made way. Carey pressed out of the cruel sunlight into the shadow of an irregular vaulted passage, quite high and wide, with a floor that sloped upward, at first gently and then steeply, until suddenly the passage ended in an echoing cathedral room dim-lit by torches that picked out here and there the shape of a fantastic flying buttress of coral. In the centre of the room, in a kind of broad basin, was the well.

Now for the first time Arrin broke her silence with a soft anguished cry. There were seven or eight warriors guarding the well, as Carey had known there would be, but they drew away and let Carey's party severely alone. Several men were in the act of watering their mounts, and as though in deference to taboo Carey circled around to get as far away from them as possible. In the gloom he made out the foot of an age-worn stairway leading upward through the coral. Here he stopped.

He helped Arrin down and made her sit, and then dragged Derech from the litter and laid him on the hard coral. The animals bolted for the well and he made no effort to hold them. He filled one of the bags for Arrin and then he flung himself alongside the beasts and drank and soaked himself in the beautiful cold clear water. After that he crouched still for a few moments, in a kind of daze, until he remembered that Derech too needed water.

He filled two more bags and took them to Arrin, kneeling beside her as though in tender concern as she sat beside her dead. His spread cloak covered what she was doing, holding the water bag to Derech's mouth so that he could drink. Carey spoke softly and quickly. Then he went back to the animals. He began to fight them away from the water so that they should not founder themselves. The activity covered what was going on in the shadows behind them. Carey led them, hissing and stamping, to where Arrin and Derech had been, still using them as a shield in case the guards were watching. He snatched up his axe and the remaining water bag and let the animals go and ran fast as he could up the stairway. It spiralled, and he was stumbling in pitch-darkness around the second curve before the guards below let out a great angry cry.

He did not know whether they would follow or not. Somebody fumbled for him in the blackness and Derech's voice muttered something urgent. He could hear Arrin panting like a spent hound. His own knees shook with weakness and he thought what a fine militant crew they were to be taking on Wales and his men and thirty angry Shunni. Torchlight flickered against the turn of the wall below and there was a confusion of voices. They fled upward, pulling each other along, and it seemed that the Shunni reached a point beyond which they did not care to go. The torchlight and the voices vanished. Carey and the others climbed a little farther and then dropped exhausted on the worn treads.

Arrin asked, 'Why didn't they follow us?'

'Why should they? Our water won't last long. They can wait.'

'Yes,' said Arrin. And then, 'How *are* we going to get away?'

Carey answered, 'That depends on Wales.'

'I don't understand.'

'On whether, and how soon, somebody sends a flier out here to see what happened to him.' He patted the water bags. 'That's why these are so important. They give us time.'

They started up the stair again, treading in the worn hollows made by other feet. The Ramas must have come this way for water for a very long time. Presently a weak daylight filtered down to them. And then a man's voice, tight with panic, cried out somewhere above them, 'I hear them! They're coming …'

The voice of Howard Wales answered sharply. 'Wait!' Then in English it called down, 'Carey. Dr Carey. Is that you?'

'It is,' Carey shouted back.

'Thank Heaven' said Wales. 'I saw you, but I wasn't sure … Come up, man, come up, and welcome. We're all in the same trap now.'

5

Sinharat was a city without people, but it was not dead. It had a memory and a voice. The wind gave it breath, and it sang, from the countless tiny organ-pipes of the coral, from the hollow mouths of marble doorways and the narrow throats of streets. The slender towers were like tall flutes, and the wind was never still. Sometimes the voice of Sinharat was soft and gentle, murmuring about everlasting youth and the pleasures thereof. Again it was strong and fierce with pride, crying, *You die, but I do not!* Sometimes it was mad, laughing and hateful. But always the song was evil.

Carey could understand now why Sinharat was taboo. It was not only because of an ancient dread. It was the city itself, now, in the sharp sunlight or under the gliding moons. It was a small city. There had never been more than perhaps three thousand Ramas, and this remote little island had given them safety and room enough. But they had built close, and high. The streets ran like topless tunnels between the walls and the towers reached impossibly thin and tall into the sky. Some of them had lost their upper storeys and some had fallen entirely, but in the main they were still beautiful. The colours of the marble were still lovely. Many of the buildings were perfect and sound, except that wind and time had erased the carvings on their walls so that only in certain angles of light did a shadowy face leap suddenly into being, prideful and mocking with smiling lips, or a procession pass solemnly toward some obliterated worship.

Perhaps it was only the wind and the half-seen watchers that gave Sinharat its feeling of eerie wickedness. Carey did not think so. The Ramas had built something of themselves into their city, and it was rather, he imagined, as one of the Rama women might have been had one met her, graceful and lovely but with something wrong about the eyes. Even the matter-of-fact Howard Wales was uncomfortable in the city, and the three surviving City-State men who were with him went about like dogs with their tails tight to their bellies. Even Derech lost some of his cheerful arrogance, and Arrin never left his side.

The feeling was worse inside the buildings. Here were the halls and chambers where the Ramas had lived. Here were the possessions they had handled, the carvings and faded frescoes they had looked at. The ever-young, the ever-living immortals, the stealers of others' lives, had walked these corridors and seen themselves reflected in the surfaces of polished marble, and Carey's nerves quivered with the nearness of them after all this long time.

There were traces of a day when Sinharat had had an advanced technology equal to, if not greater, than any Carey had yet seen on Mars. The inevitable reversion to the primitive had come with the exhaustion of resources. There was one rather small room where much wrecked equipment lay in crystal shards and dust, and Carey knew that this was the place where the Ramas had exchanged their old bodies for new. From some of the frescoes, done with brilliantly sadistic humour, he knew that the victims were generally killed soon, but not too soon, after the exchange was completed.

Still he could not find the place where the archives had been kept. Outside, Wales and his men, generally with Derech's help and Arrin as a lookout, were sweating to clear away rubble from the one square that was barely large enough for a flier to land in. Wales had been in contact with Kahora before the unexpected attack. They knew where he was, and when there had been too long a time without a report from him they would certainly come looking. If they had a landing place cleared by them, and the scanty water supply, severely rationed, kept them alive, and the Shunni did not become impatient, they would be all right.

'Only,' Carey told them, 'if that flier does come, be ready to jump quick. Because the Shunni will attack then.'

He had not had any trouble with Howard Wales. He had expected it. He had come up the last of the stairway with his axe ready. Wales shook his head. 'I have a heavy-duty shocker,' he said. 'Even so, I wouldn't care to take you on. You can put down the axe, Dr Carey.'

The Martians were armed too. Carey knew they could have

taken him easily. Perhaps they were saving their charges against the Shunni, who played the game of war for keeps.

Carey said, 'I will do what I came here to do.'

Wales shrugged. 'My assignment was to bring you in. I take it there won't be any more trouble about that now – if any of us get out of here. Incidentally, I saw what was happening at Barrakesh, and I can testify that you could not possibly have had any part in it. I'm positive that some of my superiors are thundering asses, but that's nothing new, either. So go ahead. I won't hinder you.'

Carey had gone ahead, on a minimum of water, sleep, and the dry desert rations he had in his belt-pouch. Two and a half days were gone, and the taste of defeat was getting stronger in his mouth by the hour. Time was getting short, no one could say how short. And then almost casually he crawled over a great fallen block of marble into a long room with rows of vault doors on either side, and a hot wave of excitement burned away his weariness. The bars of beautiful rustless alloy slid easily under his hands. And he was dazed at the treasure of knowledge that he had found, tortured by the realisation that he could only take a fraction of it with him and might well never see the rest of it again.

The Ramas had arranged their massive archives according to a simple and orderly dating system. It did not take him long to find the records he wanted, but even that little time was almost too much.

Derech came shouting after him. Carey closed the vault he was in and scrambled back over the fallen block, clutching the precious spools. 'Flier!' Derech kept saying. 'Hurry!' Carey could hear the distant cries of the Shunni.

He ran with Derech and the cries came closer. The warriors had seen the flier too and now they knew that they must come into the city. Carey raced through the narrow twisting street that led to the square. When he came into it he could see the flier hanging on its rotors about thirty feet overhead, very ginger about coming down in that cramped space. Wales and the Martians were frantically waving. The Shunni came in two waves, one from the well-stair and one up the cliffs. Carey picked up his axe. The shockers began to crackle.

He hoped they would hold the Drylanders off because he did not want to have to kill anyone, and he particularly did not want to get killed, not right now. 'Get to the flier!' Wales yelled at him, and he saw that it was just settling down, making a great wind and dust. The warriors in the forefront of the attack were dropping or staggering as the stunning charges hit them, sparking off their metal ornaments and the tips of their spears. The first charge was broken up, but no one wanted to stay for the second. Derech had Arrin and was lifting her bodily into the flier. Hands reached out and voices shouted unnecessary pleas for haste. Carey threw away his axe and jumped for the hatch. The Martians crowded in on top of him and then Wales, and the pilot took off so abruptly that Wales' legs were left dangling outside. Carey caught him and pulled him in. Wales laughed, in an odd wild way, and the flier rose up among the towers of Sinharat in a rattle of flung spears.

The technicians had had trouble regearing their equipment to the Rama microtapes. The results were still far from perfect, but the United Worlds Planetary Assistance Committee, hastily assembled at Kahora, were not interested in perfection. They were Alan Woodthorpe's superiors, and they had a decision to make, and little time in which to make it. The great tide was beginning to roll north out of the Drylands, moving at the steady marching pace of the desert beasts. And Woodthorpe could no longer blame this all on Carey.

Looking subdued and rather frightened, Woodthorpe sat beside Carey in the chamber where the hearing was being held. Derech was there, and Wales, and some high brass from the City-States who were getting afraid for their borders, and two Dryland chiefs who knew Carey as Carey, not as a tribesman, and trusted him enough to come in. Carey thought bitterly that this hearing should have been held long ago. Only the Committee had not understood the potential seriousness of the situation. They had been told, plainly and often. But they had preferred to believe experts like Woodthorpe rather than men like Carey, who had some specialised knowledge but were not trained to evaluate the undertaking as a whole.

Now in a more chastened mood they watched as Carey's tapes went whispering through the projectors.

They saw an island city in a blue sea. People moved in its streets. There were ships in its harbours and the sounds of life. Only the sea had shrunk down from the tops of the coral cliffs. The lagoon was a shallow lake wide-rimmed with beaches, and the outer reef stood bare above a feeble surf. A man's voice spoke in the ancient High Martian, somewhat distorted by the reproduction and blurred by the voice of a translator speaking Esperanto. Carey shut his ears to everything but the voice, the man, who spoke across the years.

'Nature grins at us these days, reminding us that even planets die. We who have loved life so much that we have taken the lives of countless others in order to retain it, can now see the beginning of our inevitable end. Even though this may yet be thousands of years in the future, the thought of it has had strange effects. For the first time some of our people are voluntarily choosing death. Others demand younger and younger hosts, and change them constantly. Most of us have come to have some feeling of remorse, not for our immortality but for the method by which we achieved it.

'One murder can be remembered and regretted. Ten thousand murders become as meaningless as ten thousand love affairs or ten thousand games of chess. Time and repetition grind them all to the same dust. Yet now we do regret, and a naïve passion has come to us, a passion to be forgiven, if not by our victims then perhaps by ourselves.

'Thus our great project is undertaken. The people of Kharif, because their coasts are accessible and their young people exceptionally handsome and sturdy, have suffered more from us than any other single nation. We will try to make some restitution.'

The scene shifted from Sinharat to a desolated stretch of desert coastline beside the shrunken sea. The land had once been populous. There were the remains of cities and towns, connected by paved roads. There had been factories and power stations, all the appurtenances of an advanced technology. These were now rusting away, and the wind blew ochre dust to bury them.

'For a hundred years,' said the Rama voice, 'it has not rained.'

There was an oasis, with wells of good water. Tall brown-haired men and women worked the well-sweeps, irrigating fields of considerable extent. There was a village of neat huts, housing perhaps a thousand people.

'Mother Mars has killed far more of her children than we. The fortunate survivors live in "cities" like these. The less fortunate ...'

A long line of beasts and hooded human shapes moved across a bitter wasteland. And the Dryland chiefs cried out, 'Our people!'

'We will give them water again,' said the Rama voice.

The spool ended. In the brief interval before the next one began, Woodthorpe coughed uneasily and muttered, 'This was all long ago, Carey. The winds of change ...'

'Are blowing up a real storm, Woodthorpe. You'll see why.'

The tapes began again. A huge plant now stood at the edge of the sea, distilling fresh water from the salt. A settlement had sprung up beside it, with fields and plantations of young trees.

'It has gone well,' said the Rama voice. 'It will go better with time, for their short generations move quickly.'

The settlement became a city. The population grew, spread, built more cities, planted more crops. The land flourished.

'Many thousands live,' the Rama said, 'who would otherwise not have been born. We have repaid our murders.'

The spool ended.

Woodthorpe said, 'But we're not trying to atone for anything. We ...'

'If my house burns down,' said Carey, 'I do not greatly care whether it was by a stroke of lightning, deliberate arson, or a child playing with matches. The end result is the same.'

The third spool began.

A different voice spoke now. Carey wondered if the owner of the first had chosen death himself, or simply lacked the heart to go on with the record. The distilling plant was wearing out and metals for repair were poor and difficult to find. The solar batteries could not be replaced. The stream of water dwindled. Crops died. There was famine and panic, and then the pumps stopped altogether and the cities were stranded like the hulks of ships in dry harbours.

The Rama voice said, 'These are the consequences of the one kind act we have ever done. Now these thousands that we called into life must die as their forebears did. The cruel laws of survival that we caused them to forget are all to be learned again. They had suffered once, and mastered it, and were content. Now there is nothing we can do to help. We can only stand and watch.'

'Shut it off,' said Woodthorpe.

'No,' said Carey, 'see it out.'

They saw it out.

'Now,' said Carey, 'I will remind you that Kharif was the homeland from which most of the Drylands were settled.' He was speaking to the Committee more than to Woodthorpe. 'These so-called primitives have been through all this before, and they have long memories. Their tribal legends are explicit about what happened to them the last time they put their trust in the transitory works of men. Now can you understand why they're so determined to fight?'

Woodthorpe looked at the disturbed and frowning faces of the Committee. 'But,' he said, 'it wouldn't be like that now. Our resources ...'

'Are millions of miles away on other planets. How long can you guarantee to keep *your* pumps working? And the Ramas at least had left the natural water sources for the survivors to go back to. You want to destroy those so they would have nothing.' Carey glanced at the men from the City-States. 'The City-States would pay the price for that. They have the best of what there is, and with a large population about to die of famine and thirst ...' He shrugged, and then went on, 'There are other ways to help. Food and medicines. Education, to enable the young people to look for greener pastures in other places, if they wish to. In the meantime, there is an army on the move. You have the power to stop it. You've heard all there is to be said. Now the chiefs are waiting to hear what you will say.'

The Chairman of the Committee conferred with the members. The conference was quite brief.

'Tell the chiefs,' the Chairman said, 'that it is not our intent to create wars. Tell them to go in peace. Tell them the Rehabilitation Project for Mars is cancelled.'

The great tide rolled slowly back into the Drylands and dispersed. Carey went through a perfunctory hearing on his activities, took his reprimand and dismissal with a light heart, shook hands with Howard Wales, and went back to Jekkara, to drink with Derech and walk beside the Low Canal that would be there now for whatever ages were left to it in the slow course of a planet's dying.

And this was good. But at the end of the canal was Barrakesh, and the southward-moving caravans, and the long road to Sinharat. Carey thought of the vaults beyond the fallen block of marble, and he knew that someday he would walk that road again.

AFTERWORD

Enchantress of Worlds
by Stephen Jones

Take the swashbuckling interplanetary heroes of Edgar Rice Burroughs and Otis Adelbert Kline; add the sword and sorcery of Robert E. Howard, the cosmic horrors of H.P. Lovecraft and the lost civilisations of Abraham Merritt; mix together with the rich and decadent language of Clark Ashton Smith, and introduce a pinch of tough feminism that is entirely the author's own, and what you have is the work of Leigh Brackett.

Leigh Douglass Brackett was born on 7 December 1915, in Southern California. As a child she was something of a tomboy, and would often play at being a pirate in front of her grandfather's old beach house.

'The beach where we lived was a wonderful place to grow up in,' she recalled. 'In those days there was a handful of little houses, an overarching sky, wind and sun and seagulls, and I loved it. There were winter gales that never seem to blow anymore, and beautiful fogs so thick you could bite them and taste the salt. It was a place where I could be alone. I used to walk out to the end of a long jetty and sit on the stringer with my feet in the ocean, feeling it breathe, looking out to where the Pacific ran over the edge of the world and dreaming great dreams ...'

Brackett began to write fiction at an early age, as she revealed: 'I became a writer because, I suppose, I couldn't help myself. From earliest childhood I had a compulsive desire to fill up blank pages in copybooks. When I was seven or eight, I wrote a sequel to a Douglas Fairbanks film because I wanted more and there wasn't any. Infantile scribbling on odd bits of paper, but still, a beginning. At thirteen, I made a mature, reasoned decision to be a professional writer. Ten years later I sold my first story.'

After graduation, she moved to another school where she taught swimming and drama until a copy of Edgar Rice Burroughs' *The Gods of Mars* (1918), given to her as a gift, provided an inspiration. Stimulated by the alien exploits of adventurer John Carter, she soon began weaving her own exotic tales of Mars and, later, Venus and Mercury.

'In the beginning of my writing career, I tried my hand at nearly everything and failed miserably,' Brackett admitted. 'I hadn't enough experience of writing or anything else to compete in the adventure field, for instance. I had been advised to try this market or that market but not science fiction, because there wasn't much money there. Finally, I decided I was going to do what I wanted to do, which was to write fantasy and science fiction, where I could really let my imagination go ... even if I starved to death.'

Self-deprecatingly, she recalled some early advice from established SF author Henry Kuttner that helped her writing, '... part of which was a gentle insistence on buying more purple pencils to cope with my purple prose.'

But Kuttner's guidance paid off and, in late 1939, her first two stories were bought in one week by legendary pulp magazine editor John W. Campbell, Jr. 'Martian Quest' appeared in the February 1940 issue of Campbell's influence *Astounding Science Fiction*. It was quickly followed by 'The Teasure of Ptakuth' in the April edition.

There were not that many women writing science fiction or fantasy in the 1940s (Catherine Moore was a rare exception, and even she hid her femininity behind the asexual byline 'C.L. Moore'), but it helped that Brackett wrote like a man, with tough though flawed no-nonsense heroes who, more often than not, ended up with neither the girl nor the prize.

Anthony Boucher (real name, William A.P. White), the renowned writer and founding editor of *The Magazine of Fantasy and Science Fiction*, called Brackett 'The acknowledged mistress of the flamboyant interplanetary adventure'. However, not everyone appreciated the author's particular brand of 'space opera', as she explained: 'Space opera, as every reader doubtless knows, is a prejorative term often applied to a story that has an element of adventure. Over the decades, brilliant and talented new writers appear, receiving great acclaim, and each and every one of them can be expected to write at least one article stating flatly that the day of space opera is over and done, thank goodness, and that henceforth these crude tales of interplanetary nonsense will be replaced by whatever type of story that writer happens to favour – closet dramas, psychological dramas, sex dramas, etc, but by God *important* dramas, containing nothing but Big Thinks.

'Ten years later, the writer in question may or may not still be around, but space opera can be found right where it always was, sturdily driving its dark trade in heroes.'

Although she only sold one further tale to Campbell's *Astounding* ('The Sorcerer of Rhiannon') and a single horror story to *Strange Stories* ('The Tapestry Gate'), Brackett's action-packed planetary romances soon began appearing regularly in such SF adventure pulps as *Thrilling Wonder Stories*, *Astonishing Stories*, *Super Science Stories*, *Startling Stories* and, most notably, *Planet Stories*.

'For fifteen years, from 1940 to 1955, when the magazine ceased publication, I had the happiest relationship possible for a writer with the editors of *Planet Stories*,' the author remembered.

'They gave me, in the beginning, a proving-ground where I could gain strength and confidence in the exercise of my fledgling skills, a thing of incalculable value for a young writer. They sent me cheques, which enabled me to keep on eating. In latter years, they provided a steady market for the kind of stories I liked best to write. In short, I owe them much.'

Brackett also wrote a number of crime stories for such magazines as *Flynn's Detective Fiction*, *New Detective*, *Thrilling Detective* and *Mammoth Detective*, and her first novel was a mystery, *No Good from a Corpse* (1944), which led directly to another career as a screenwriter.

That same year, Brackett had finished half a novella when she received a call to work in Hollywood. She gave the story to her friend and fellow Los Angeles Science Fantasy Society member, Ray Bradbury, to finish.

'Leigh called and asked me to finish a novella which she had just begun for *Planet*,' Bradbury recalled. 'In ten days I wrote the last half.'

'Lorelei of the Red Mist' appeared under both authors' bylines in the Summer of 1946 issue of *Planet Stories*.

'Years later,' said Bradbury, 'I hand a copy to friends and dare them to find the paragraph in the middle of the story where Brackett stops being Brackett and becomes Bradbury. Can't be done. Even I have problems finding that exact place.'

'He had nothing to go on but what I had down on paper,' admitted Brackett, who used to meet Bradbury every Sunday afternoon at the beach, where they would read each other's manuscripts. 'I never worked from an outline in those days (and often regretted it) and I had no idea where the story was going. Ray took the story and finished it, completely on his own.

'I never read a word of it until he handed me the manuscript, and I never changed a word after that. I'm convinced to this day that he did a better job with the second half than I would have done.'

She also later revealed that she regretted using the Celtic name 'Conan' for their traitorous protagonist as it had become so strongly identified with the very different character created by Robert E. Howard.

Having first been introduced in 1940 by their mutual agent Julius Schwartz and mutual editor Mort Weisinger, six years later she married fellow SF writer Edmond Hamilton, who was eleven years older than Brackett and had been writing professionally a dozen years longer. Ray Bradbury was best man at their wedding.

The newly married couple lived in Venice, California, in a beach house amongst the oil wells and sand dunes.

Despite his extensive experience as a prolific pulp author, Hamilton was among those who credited his wife for improving his own writing skills.

'It might seem that for two full-time professional writers to marry and set up housekeeping together would create problems,' recalled Hamilton. 'But it never did. As we both knew how hard it is to write a story, we respected each other's work-habits from the first. When one of us goes into a workroom and to a typewriter, everything else is ignored and we don't interrupt one another.'

In 1964, Brackett and Hamilton were co-Guests of Honour at the World Science Fiction Convention in Oakland, California.

As well as publishing two novels set on an ancient Mars, *Shadow Over Mars* (aka *The Nemsis from Terra*, 1951) and *The Sword of Rhiannon* (1953), Brackett moved into hard-boiled space operas during the 1950s and '60s with *The Starmen* (aka *The Galactic Breed* and *The Starmen of Llyrdis*, 1952), *The Big Jump* (1955) and *Alpha Centauri – or Die!* (1963). Widely considered her best work, *The Long Tomorrow* (1955) was set in a post-Apocalyptic United States.

Although she only wrote around sixty short stories in all genres, some of Brackett's best work is collected in *The Coming of the Terrans* (1967), *The Halfling and Other Stories* (1973) and *Martian Quest: The Early Brackett* (2002), while *No Good for a Corpse* (1999) was a collection of her crime and mystery stories introduced by Ray Bradbury. She also paid tribute to her roots by editing the 1975 anthology *The Best Planet Stories # 1*. Unfortunately, it did not sell well enough to warrant further volumes in the series.

Shortly before his death in 1977, Edmond Hamilton edited *The Best of Leigh Brackett* in a hardcover for the Nelson Doubleday book club, and his wife returned the favour by editing *The Best of Edmond Hamilton* the same year.

As Hamilton explained in his Introduction, 'When Leigh was working on a story and I asked her, "Where is your plot?" she answered, "There isn't any ... I just start writing the first page and let it grow." I exclaimed, "That's a devil of a way to write a story!" But for her, it seemed to work fine.'

'Ed always knew the last line of a story before he wrote the first one,' explained Brackett, 'and every line he wrote aimed straight at that target. I used the opposite method – write an opening and let it grow. Outlining a plot seemed to kill it for me.'

Brackett and Hamilton officially collaborated on only one story, 'Stark and the Star Kings', which revolved around a meeting between their respective favourite heroes. It was written in the mid-1970s for Harlan Ellison's long-overdue anthology *Last Dangerous Visions*, and was finally published as the title story of a 2004 collection containing the work of both authors.

Two of Brackett's stories, 'Queen of the Martian Catacombs' (*Planet Stories*, 1949) and 'Black Amazon of Mars' (*Planet Stories*, 1951), both featuring her wild and brooding hero, Eric John Stark, were reputedly expanded by Hamilton into the book-length novels *The Secret of Sinharat* and *People of the Talisman*, both published in 1964. They were later reissued as the 1982 omnibus *Eric John Stark: Outlaw of Mars*.

As science fact began to overtake science fiction when it came to knowledge of our solar system, Brackett gamely maintained that 'Mars is still fun. So is Venus – not, perhaps, as the actual and factual worlds so named, but simply as creations of a writer's imagination, full of wonders that may perfectly well exist on *some* world, somewhere.'

With Mars and Venus no longer the romantic locations they had once been thanks to NASA's probes, in the mid-1970s Brackett revived her most popular character, Eric John Stark, as an interstellar buccaneer in a trio of new novels: *The Ginger Star* (1974), *The Hound of Skaith* (1974) and *The Reavers of Skaith* (1976). These were collected in the book club omnibus *The Book of Skaith* (1976).

Never content to be restricted as a genre writer, Brackett also ghosted the mystery *Stranger at Home* (1946) credited to the actor George Sanders, and wrote a couple of Westerns: *Rio Bravo* (1959), based on the Howard Hawks film she co-scripted, and *Follow the Free Wind* (1963). She also published a series of crime novels: *An Eye for an Eye* (1957), *The Tiger Among Us* (aka *Fear No Evil* and *13 West Street*, 1957; filmed as an Alan Ladd movie in 1962) and *Silent Partner* (1969, the basis for the CBS-TV series *Markham*).

'I never had any trouble at all constructing or plotting mystery stories,' Brackett revealed. 'But it's more like working out an equation; given a certain event, other events will inevitably follow, and variables are limited by the space-time framework in which these events occur. In science fiction, the space-time framework has to be invented and the variables are what you make them. Which is of course why it's more fun to write science fiction, though the discipline of the murder mystery has its own special joys.'

During the 1940s, Leigh Brackett enjoyed a second career as a Hollywood scriptwriter. A friend of Brackett's, who worked in a Beverly Hills bookstore, ensured that a copy of her crime novel *No Good from a Corpse* was in a stack of thrillers he sold to legendary film director Howard Hawks.

Hawks, who once said: 'For me, the best drama is one that deals with a man in danger,' obviously recognised a kindred spirit in Brackett's work and he quickly summoned the thirty-year-old writer to Hollywood.

After some uncredited work on Hawks' *To Have and Have Not* (1944), Brackett soon found herself collaborating with the distinguished American novelist William Faulkner on the screenplay for the now-classic murder mystery *The Big Sleep* (1946, but actually made two years earlier), also starring Humphrey Bogart and Lauren Bacall, and based on Raymond Chandler's first novel.

'I was overawed to be working with William Faulkner,' revealed Brackett, 'although, despite American Lit. professors and critics, I had always found him quite unreadable.

'In the event, we had very little contact in working, since we did alternate sections of the book with a minimum of conferring. He was punctilious, polite, unfailingly courteous, and as remote as the moon. A closed-in, closed-up, lonely man, driven by some dark inner devil.

'I suppose it is no secret to anyone that he would vanish sometimes for days while his loyal friends – and he had them – would front for him at the studio, seek him out, take care of him, and get him back on his feet again. Everybody pretended not to notice. Apart from these absences, he worked hard, worked long hours and proved to be remarkably good on construction.

'As to his dialogue, he was famous as the writer who had never had one line of dialogue actually spoken by an actor. It was, quite simply, unreadable, and it was all changed on the set – not by me, by Mr Hawks and Bogey, both of whom were pretty good at it.'

On arriving in Hollywood, Brackett had signed a seven-year contract, but it was cancelled after two-and-a-half years when the independent production company who had hired her was dissolved for tax purposes.

She moved to Republic Pictures, where she co-scripted the low budget 'B' movie *The Vampire's Ghost* (1945), starring John Abbott. Based on her original story, it was in fact a reinterpretation of John Polidori's 1819 tale 'The Vampyre', relocated to the west coast of Africa.

Following her script for the Columbia programmer *Crime Doctor's Manhunt* (1946), she was let go by the studio. 'I don't think it was a bad script,' she later recalled. 'But it was an off-beat story, and off-beat stories they did not want. So I had to go back to work, as it were.'

With Hollywood's movie industry shut down by a craft union strike in 1946, Brackett returned for a while to writing science fiction but, by the mid-1950s onwards, she began to concentrate her efforts into writing for films and such television series as *Alfred Hitchcock Hour*, *The Rockford Files* and *Archer*.

'The bad thing about film or TV work is that you have to wait for someone to ask you to do it,' cautioned Brackett, 'whereas you can sit down and write a novel when and as you wish; and if you have a reasonable degree of competence you can be fairly sure of selling it somewhere.'

She co-scripted the low budget Western *Gold of the Seven Saints* (1961), and worked uncredited on *Man's Favorite Sport?* (1964), Howard Hawks' remake of his own 1938 screwball comedy *Bringing Up Baby*.

More importantly, Brackett co-wrote another classic movie, the Western *Rio Bravo* (1959), for Hawks and his star John Wayne, and collaborated with them again on *Hatari!* (1962), *El Dorado* (1967) and *Rio Lobo* (1970), which was Hawks' last film. In 1973 she adapted another Raymond Chandler novel, *The Long Goodbye*, starring a laconic Elliott Gould as a contemporary Philip Marlowe, for director Robert Altman.

In later years, Brackett and Hamilton divided their time

between a renovated nineteenth century farmhouse in Ohio and their home in the California desert. Her final screen credit was for the first draft of *Star Wars: The Empire Strikes Back* (1980), for which she won a posthumous Hugo Award. The film was dedicated to her memory.

In 1978, Brackett saw in the new year with Ray Bradbury and his wife at their home in Los Angeles. 'A wonderful time,' Bradbury remembered, 'but I sensed she was in her final year.

'A few months later she called me from a hospital in the high desert in grand laughing humour. The doctor, bless him, had injected a huge overdose of pain-killing drugs so that she could die joyfully. She did just that, the next day, before I could make it to the desert to give her a final embrace. Her laughter still sounds. My love remains.'

Leigh Brackett died of cancer on 18 March 1978, aged 62. She left behind her a legacy of stories that are as fresh and exciting today as they were when they were first published in the pulp magazines more than half-a-century ago.

'The tale of adventure – of great courage and daring, of battle against the forces of darkness and the unknown – has been with the human race since it first learned to talk,' explained the author. 'It began as part of the primitive survival technique, interwoven with magic and ritual, to explain and propitiate the vast forces of nature with which man could not cope in any other fashion. The tales grew into religions. They became myth and legend. They became the Mabinogion and the Ulster Cycle and the Voluspa. They became Arthur and Robin Hood, and Tarzan of the Apes.

'The so-called space opera is a folk-tale, a hero-tale, of our particular niche in history. If you want accurate up-to-date science, buy a book and be prepared to buy a new one every week or so as the state of knowledge continues to move ahead in quantum jumps. Furthermore, if you are looking for the delights of cannibalism, incest, *outré* sex, or a general feeling of dismal gloom, you will not find them here. These stories, shameful as it may seem, were written to be entertaining, to be exciting, to impart to the reader some of the pleasure we had in writing them.'

With her masterful stories of lost races and other worlds, there is no doubt that Leigh Brackett accomplished exactly what she set out to do as a writer. And for that, we fans of her romantic interplanetary adventures should be forever grateful.

Stephen Jones
London, England
October 2004